He realized with a start that she still didn't understand the finality of this. Curbing the pang of unease, he kissed her to expunge some of his guilt. 'I'm not sure . . . but you know I'll always be with you in thought.' He spent a moment wondering why God had taken all the hundreds of Boer children with measles, scarlet fever, dysentery and chosen to let this little Kaffir flourish. It seemed wrong somehow, when he'd been a mistake in the first place. Baby fingers worked at his tunic buttons.

The woman raised her head. 'We must say goodbye now?'

'There's no rush,' he soothed. 'We'll have one more night.'

'I shall wait for you.' Detaching the child's hand from the buttons, she pulled away, stared him full in his eyes for long seconds . . . then she was gone.

69

Also in Arrow by Sheelagh Kelly

A LONG WAY FROM HEAVEN
FOR MY BROTHER'S SINS
ERIN'S CHILD

MY FATHER, MY SON

Sheelagh Kelly

ARROW BOOKS

Arrow Books Limited
62-65 Chandos Place, London WC2N 4NW

An imprint of Century Hutchinson Limited

London Melbourne Sydney Auckland
Johannesburg and agencies throughout
the world

First published in Great Britain by Century 1988
Arrow edition 1989

Printed and bound in Great Britain by
Courier International Ltd, Tiptree, Essex

ISBN 0 09 960570 8

For Cecilia and Cyril Webster

Author's Note

Though there was a similar incident at the Guildhall in 1913 to the one described in this book, the characters are in no way meant to represent real life persons – this being a novel and not a history book. For this same reason I had no wish to recreate every blow of the Great War, hence I have mustered a fictitious regiment – the King's Own Yorkshire North Riding. This said, even a novel requires an authentic background and I have tried to be as accurate as possible when portraying specific battles and the lives of our soldiers in the trenches.

CHAPTER ONE

Had he guessed she was going to bring such catastrophe he would never have touched her. He had just been through a war – catastrophic enough, without fretting over hypotheses. Besides, how could he foresee repercussions that lay eleven years hence? At this moment he was not even thinking about her. His prime concern was how to escape this oppressive South African climate.

The sun was a crucible, tipping its molten metal down onto his shoulders. He and two other soldiers lounged in the meagre shade of a bell tent, trying to glean a little respite from its skin-sizzling heat. Beads of sweat evaporated at the moment of birth, leaving scales of salt to tighten and chafe the brow. Such temperature discouraged exertion. Only one of the men showed signs of movement; he was cleaning a rifle. His companions, eyes slitted against the glare of sun on the ranks of white canvas tents, were content to observe the Boer women and children who roamed the camp. So intense were the sun's rays that they distorted the men's vision; to their eyes, the more distant figures moved in a weird, gyrating fashion – like drunken bellydancers.

Corporal Russ Hazelwood took off his pith helmet to rake his fingernails over an itching scalp. As often in times of war, his brown hair had been allowed to grow almost to collar length. When at his military best – even on civvy street – Russ was a strikingly dapper young man, always neatly-pressed, hair trimmed regularly, moustache waxed to precision. He fingered the limp effort under his nose and gave a mental sigh. Trying to wax one's moustache here was like trying to butter coals. This dusty bloody hole denied even the most elementary toilet. To one as fastidious as Russ it was purgatory. He licked the dust from his lips,

1

keen blue eyes attending one particular figure who headed for the school building. 'Ever fancied a nibble at one o' them vrouws then, Pinner?' The precursor to this remark had been an exchange on the private's state of virginity and how on earth he was going to lose it when he was stuck out here in this annex of Hades.

Private Pinner gave a bark, as much to show his distaste of this suggestion as to dislodge the coating of South African dust from his throat. 'I'd rather stay pure, thank you very much for the kind proposition, Corp.'

The corporal's voice was coaxing. 'It'd be a magnificent initiation though, wouldn't it?'

'Aye – like joining the bloody Freemasons,' muttered the private, gnawing on a pencil which a moment ago had been scribbling a letter home. 'Talk about "on pain of death".'

'Oh, look at that one, Pinner!' crooned Hazelwood, wearing the impish grin that was a regular visitor. 'She's all woman. Can't you just feel them muscly thighs squeezing you?' It was said that the stuff they put in your tea was meant to stop you feeling the urge. It didn't, Russ could vouch for that.

The young private issued another bark and, begging the corporal to desist with this subject, addressed himself to the third man. 'Christ, doesn't this fella think of anything but his nuts, Sarg? He must've been on about it for the past half-hour.'

'Why d'you think we call him Filbert?' The rag in Sergeant Jack Daw's hand caressed the barrel of the rifle. Twenty-eight years ago he had been christened Stanley but no one ever called him that. The reply was given without looking up. There was little room in the sergeant's vocabulary for small-talk; this was only the second contribution he had made in fifteen minutes.

Pinner, who had hitherto linked the pseudonym with the corporal's surname, now grinned his understanding. Reaching a thumb and two fingers into his flap pocket he withdrew a deformed stub of cigarette and lit it.

'You're a fine one to hang labels on folk,' grumbled Hazelwood, then turned back to the private. 'Look at the way he's fondling that rifle – you'd think he was making love to it.'

He and Sergeant Daw had known each other most of their lives, came from the same city, the same street. 'He's pretendin' it's a nice plump Boer maiden.' He gave Daw a nudge. 'Come on, Sarg, admit it – you really fancy one.'

Sergeant Daw glanced up briefly to survey the inmates under his protection. The lids which veiled his pale-grey eyes had a permanent droop to them, lending him a look of arrogance. His mousy hair sheared by his own razor to a point well above his ears, was invisible beneath his hat at the moment. The tip of his nose was of squashed appearance – as if in childhood it had been so used to pressing against toyshop windows that now it had become a permanent feature – and the mouth under the moustache often emitted bad odours, for Daw had never visited a dentist after being terrified by one as a youngster. His voice was gruff and, like the others, held a Yorkshire accent. 'You don't imagine I've come through a bleedin' war just to commit suicide, do you, Corporal?' A sideways glance of near-contempt for his questioner. 'The blink of an eyelash from one o' them would disembowel you.'

The corporal replaced his hat at a rakish tilt, rested his chin on one of his knees and, with fingers laced round a putteed shin, mused, 'Oh, I don't know . . . I like a big woman – something to get your teeth into.'

'Big?' exploded the private. 'I'll say so! One of 'em hung her drawers out to dry the other day, when she went back to unpeg 'em she found three hundred squatters'd moved in.'

'Oh! Fancy a music-hall career, do we, Pinner?' Corporal Hazelwood's chin came up from his knee, face mocking. 'Well, let's see how bleedin' funny you can be when you're mucking them latrines out.'

'Aw, have a heart, Corp! I was only tryin' to give you good advice.'

'Hah! Did you catch that, Sar'nt Daw?' spluttered Hazelwood. 'Him just out o' babby's frocks giving me advice . . .'

'What I meant was, I don't want to see my dear Corporal

3

gettin' himself badly mauled by one o' them girls. It isn't worth it, is it, Sarg? Another three or four weeks an' you'll be back to your wife an' getting all the hows-yer-father you want.'

The sergeant's dour face cracked then. 'Not from his missus he won't, Pinner. Why d'you think he's always talking about it? Them as can – do, them as can't – talk about it. Poor Filbert'll be lucky if she even lets him out to the pub – now that's what I really miss,' he announced before Hazelwood could object to this slander. 'My mind is set on a much higher plain than the corporal's. The minute these size elevens land on English soil they're off to take me to the nearest Sam Smith's house – none o' that southern piss, I'm straight onto a northbound train. By, I can just feel that pint slitherin' down me throat like melted velvet.' Only now did he pause in the cleaning of the rifle to savour the proposed experience, shuddering with delight.

His two companions made noises of attunement, then the corporal issued a warning grunt, 'CO's coming.'

The sergeant shoved the Mauser behind him into the tent, the private plunged his cigarette into the dust and all clambered to attention as the officer strolled towards them between the neat rows of bell tents, his boots hidden behind a cloud of dust.

There was minimal recognition of the salute. After he had passed, the three were about to assume their previous roles when the officer spun, 'Sar'nt!' snapped his fingers and jabbed another at a group of internees amongst whom a squabble had broken out.

'No bloody peace for the wicked . . . is there, Pinner lad?' The sergeant flicked his head at the spot the officer had indicated. The sour-faced private seized a Lee Enfield and tramped off to sort out the disturbance, whilst Sergeant Daw and Corporal Hazelwood resettled their lean rears on the ground.

Daw retrieved the Mauser and, snapping its barrel into place, studied the assembled effect with pride. After picking it off a dead Boer he had secreted it amongst his kit, itching but not daring to use the superior weapon for fear of

4

having his prize confiscated. But he would use it when he got home, if only for bagging pigeons in Knavesmire Wood. Daw was fascinated by guns and weaponry. To him there was something much more stimulating about stroking a trigger than feeling a woman – but try explaining that to Russ – women were all the same, guns were unique. His fingers travelled the warm steel as he pondered on the craftsmanship, then raising it to his cheek squinted along the barrel, setting his sights on the distant figure of the camp superintendent.

Hazelwood's pleasantly-pitched voice broke in on his thoughts. 'How're you going to get that home without havin' it whipped, then?'

Sergeant Daw lowered the weapon and bound it reverently in a scarf which his wife had sent him a few weeks ago – by her reckoning if it was Christmas then he must need a scarf. 'If you're hoping to smuggle your little trophy out the same way, forget it. I doubt that'd fit in my pack even if I'd want it there.'

'What little trophy would that be, Sarg?' It was said with carefree lilt and the expression barely flinched, but Hazelwood had become wary.

The sergeant, finished with his labour of love, turned to lock knowing eyes with the narrowed ones of his subordinate. Little pink rivers dissected his caked cheeks where the act of squinting had produced moisture. 'Come on, Filbert, don't sell me rubber pokers, we both know what I'm talking about. Going to apply to have her put on the strength, are we?' This was the first reference he had ever made to Hazelwood's indiscretion. He did so now mainly because he didn't want the corporal to think he had got away with it.

I might have known your big ears would be flapping, thought Russ, but merely gazed into the middle distance and pulled a face. 'Christ, don't them latrines hum? They could set up their own choir – Comical Kruger and the Cape Colony Crappers.'

'Rachel'll hang you up by your moustaches if she finds out.'

The corporal's stomach performed a tippletail. 'An' how is she gonna find out?'

'Oh, given up pleading the innocent, have we? Well, stand easy, there's only me that knows . . . though personally speaking and confidentially between ourselves, Russell lad, I think you're a bit of a cheating bastard.'

Russ tossed a pebble at a lizard that basked on one of the rocks which were dotted about, using it as a scapegoat for Daw. It peeved him that this creature could sit there quite calmly without bursting into flames; he had damaged his own rear by doing likewise before gaining experience of the terrain. Employing one of these rocks as a seat was akin to perching one's buttocks on a hot griddle. At his silence, Daw said, 'All right, suit your bloody self. I was only giving you chance to cleanse yourself of your sins before we go home.'

An unrepentant laugh from Hazelwood. 'Now who's doing the kidding? You just want to hear all my exploits 'cause you'd like to be doing them yourself but haven't the nerve.'

'Cobblers,' replied the sergeant and rose abruptly, stirring up the parched ground.

'Deary me, I've upset him,' said the corporal rashly.

'Don't overestimate our friendship, Filbert!' warned the other.

Realizing his stupidity, Russ made an overdue attempt at mitigation. 'Ah, it's all right for you – you don't have the same needs . . .' He heaved a sigh. 'Anyway, what does it matter? It's all over now. In a few weeks we'll be back in old Eboracum an' this'll be forgotten.'

'Obviously it will by you,' retorted Daw coldly. Sometimes he found Hazelwood's preoccupation with women nauseating.

'How long have you known about it?'

'It?' Daw looked at the sky as if thinking. 'That depends on which "it" we're referring to. It number one, or it number two.'

Russ' heart sank. 'So, you know about . . . as well?'

'Yes, I know about . . .' Daw rolled his hand in exaggerated fashion, 'as well. How long? Oh, since the sound of lustful boots woke me from my slumber. Two years or so.'

Right from the beginning. Russ felt queasy. 'Have you told . . .'

'Don't worry,' said the sergeant testily. 'I won't be reporting you.' Scornful eyes looked down at the other. 'Anyway, what exactly are you supposed to be doing, Corporal?'

Relief caused the other to stretch and grin. 'I thought I might be permitted a short breather, Sarg, after being so industrious this morning.'

'As industrious as a dead sloth – well, Corporal, you seem to have formed such an affection for the Kaffirs you can go help 'em clean out the bog.' When Hazelwood grimaced but did not stir he bent forward and thrust his face into the other. 'I said *mooove*, Corporal!'

The tremendous heat and the difference in rank superceded the friendship. Corporal Hazelwood swore to himself and hauled his bottom from the flap of canvas that had shielded it from the red-hot dust. Standing, he was four inches shorter than the other man – though Daw was exceptionally tall. Even so, it often made Russ feel infantile in the sergeant's presence. He was the same age as Jack, but looked younger – felt younger, the way Daw treated him.

He lingered as the sergeant ambled away, cursing Daw and the whole caboodle. Oh! to feel the wind ripping across Knavesmire, forcing itself into his lungs and making his eyes water. Even on a hot day it never seemed robbed of breath. Not so here: any breeze was quickly suffocated at birth for having the gall to oppose the omnipotent sun. The mere effort of inhaling produced a steel band around his ribs. An absent hand touched his side – his brain still faraway. For that moment his mind burst with the greenness of his hometown, the brilliant reds, pinks and blues of an Ebor meeting, the flurry of breeze through the jockeys' silks . . . then once more it dissolved into the dusty reality of Orange River. Everything here was one colour – khaki. Faces washed this morning had, by midday, taken on the sickly pall. One could not move without stirring up clouds of choking dust, coating everything – uniform, eyebrows, lungs. Walking slowly helped to avoid this, but sometimes a brisk march was needed to relieve the stifling tedium of camp life. Such irony, to escape the Boer bullet and to face two new potential killers in peacetime – to be stifled by dust or stifled by boredom. Russ straightened his helmet. It deterred sunstroke but tended to compress the skull into one's shoulders, feeling, in this heat, like a half-barrel under the khaki linen. Reaching a hand over his shoulder he tugged at the collar of his tunic trying to induce a draught between the sweat-drenched garment and his skin. But all this did was to fan his own stench at his nostrils and once released the tunic clung again at spine and armpit.

He was about to move off, when his narrowed eyes settled on a figure by the perimeter of the camp. Slowly, he came to attention as the black woman beckoned to him. When she moved elegantly down a road mapped out by gleaming white stones, he followed. As ever, the roll of the prominent buttocks beneath the shift stirred him. Be damned to the sergeant's opinion, he must press his hands to that one more time . . .

She had disappeared behind a group of acacias. The shade of the helmet's peak hid his furtive glance to right and left before he, too, slipped around the sun-scorched bushes. Her face was sombre as, downing weapon, his dusty arms encircled her. 'I am told you leave tomorrow.' She spoke in the broken English learnt from the Women's Relief Committee who had come here to alleviate the Boers' distress.

Russ hesitated, then nodded and tried to pull her body into his, but she resisted, moving her face away. 'Why you not tell me?'

He did not press his suit, but continued to hold her arms. 'I didn't want to upset you.'

It was obvious he had – her lips formed a petulant thrust. 'Why must you go?'

'The war's over.' In actuality it had been over for many months, only the camps lingered on. 'I have to go home.'

'You have won the war. You could take a piece of the land your leaders give away and make your home here.'

He performed his attractive smile, blue eyes fond. 'A nice

thought, me lass.' Normally he would see her face light up whenever he called her his lass; today it remained unmoved. 'But I'm a regular soldier, I have to go where the Army sends me.' Only half the truth: with his stint almost at an end Russ didn't intend signing on for a further term. He and Rachel had decided – or rather, his wife had decided – that by the end of this spell they should have enough saved to invest in a small business. Naturally, the money had not all come from his Army pay – Rachel had been left a nice amount in her mother's will.

'So . . . you go away and forget me,' accused the woman.

'Forget you?' It was delivered in amazed tone. He held her at arms' length, bending at the knee in order to see into her lowered face. 'How could I forget someone as dear to me as you are?' At least part of that was honest; he would never forget her. This thing they had was the most – the only – daring exploit he had known in all his twenty-eight years, including his armed service. Russ had always been the kind who played it safe, who did as he was told, who followed the rules – how could he forget the one time he had dared to sling his leg over the imaginary barbed-wire fence marked '*Forbidden*'?

She permitted him to hug her. He took advantage, sliding his hands down her back to cup her large bottom. Still, she did not return his embrace. 'I'll never forget you, lass, never,' he told her earnestly, rotating his palms around the warm flesh. 'But you know this is the way it has to be. I couldn't settle in your country, just as you couldn't settle in mine, we've different ways of doing things. That's why I'm wiser than to offer to take you with me, you'd never fit in – you'd hate it. But just because we'll be apart doesn't mean to say I'll forget you or you'll forget me.'

'I will not forget.' Moist eyes searched his. 'I will never take another man.'

He acknowledged her remark with gratitude. The heat of her skin burnt through the thin material, making it cling damply to his palms. He rubbed them over her, pulling her against his crumpled uniform.

'Oh, my husband!' She held him then, pressed herself at

his hard soldier's body and wept into his chest. The knot of fuzzy hair at her crown tickled his face. 'If you go there will be darkness always.'

'Nay . . . I'd hate for you to brood,' coaxed Russell, tearing one moist palm away to cup her face. 'Just you think of all the happy times we've spent together and the sun'll shine again. I'll miss you terribly as well, you know.'

They stood embracing thus for some time, until the black woman heaved a shuddering sigh and said, 'You would see your son?'

'Oh, I would that!' Russ donned a cheerful smile as the photograph in his breast pocket materialised before his eyes: the bald little fellow propped in the photographer's chair, eyes and mouth round with the shock of the flash. Fifteen months ago – during a year of upset in which his wife had lost her own father and mother, the first from old age, the latter from illness – Russ' parents had been killed in a dreadful traffic accident, for which he had been given compassionate leave. During his emotionally trying seven days at home, Russ and his wife achieved that which they had been trying for in all their five year marriage: they had conceived a child – his son. The smile was still on Russ' face . . . until he realized she was not speaking of this child. Straightening, he said kindly, 'Aye, I'd like to see him before I go.'

His manufactured pleasure folded as she left him, displaced by guilt. She knew nothing of his wife at home, saw herself in that role – though of course there had been no ceremony. The liaison had begun two years ago soon after she had arrived in the camp with the Boer family to whom she was servant. Theirs had been one of the first groups to be brought in; thousands followed. Most of the men in Corporal Hazelwood's battalion had complained about having to play nursemaid to women and children and being taken away from the fighting, but not Russ. A lover of female company, he had welcomed the new job – at least until he discovered the hostility it brought. He supposed it was understandable when the British were burning these people's homes and killing their stock – but Russ had tried to impress upon the women that he wasn't of that persuasion, had tried to be kind and sympathetic to their plight. At their rejection he had turned to her, the only one who recognised his charm . . . and things had just sort of happened. Henceforth, whenever he had returned from a foray with another batch of refugees she would be waiting to greet him as a wife.

He had welcomed the intermittent stays in this camp. Despite his claims of being a regular soldier and his sociability with the men, Russ preferred to shoot at targets and not people – though he had managed to get through this war without actually killing anybody. He had joined the Army in peacetime. The draper's shop where he had worked as an assistant had been forced into liquidation and, there being a lot of unemployment around at that time, he had seen the armed forces as a means to a steady income. Then, he had been unmarried, but his immaculate turn-out had soon captured a young woman's eye – as, indeed, her own neat and fresh presentation had attracted his. Russ saw, too, somebody who wanted to get on in life like himself. Abandoning all other flirtations he had married her.

It had worked well. With his young wife's natural thrift and her small inheritance they would soon be able to set up in business. Unfortunately, before his term was up, this blessed skirmish had started and Russ' record of not having fired a shot in anger was drastically changed. Belligerence had never been one of his traits. It was commonsense as opposed to bravado that had achieved his rank of corporal. This affair had frightened him badly at first. Even the old regulars declared that here was a different enemy to the ones they had faced before. The Boojer was invisible and with the new smokeless powder he used there was no way to pinpoint him even when he fired at you. There was a *phut* in the sand beside his boot. Answering the call for self-preservation Russ ducked to his haunches, before realizing it was not a bullet, just a bird dropping its waste. God! He ran a hand over his slippery brow and emerged from his crouch, he was getting to be a nervous wreck. Often was the time he came out of his sleep with the boom of *Long Tom* rebounding in his eardrums. Thank the Lord it was all over now.

His smile reinstated itself as the woman returned bearing a chubby brown infant in the crook of her arm. He chucked the baby's cheek with a finger. 'Now then, young Charlie! What mischief have you been up to today?' The brown eyes danced and the lips turned up to emit a noise of pleasure. He certainly is a canny little chap, thought the corporal regretfully. I really have grown quite attached to him . . . but only inasmuch as he was fond of any child. When Russ thought of his son it was the one who had been born to his wife Rachel six months ago. He could never equate that term with this one year old, fine as he was.

It had been the woman's idea to name him Charles. She had wanted to call him after his soldier father but Russ, envisioning a court martial at this blatant sign of paternity, had forbidden it. However, at her hurt face he had grudgingly proffered his second name and she had accepted that. They had managed to keep it quiet so far – from the authorities, if not Daw – but once the child was able to talk it might be a little harder. He could just imagine his commanding officer's face if a little piccaninny was running around calling one of the NCO's daddy.

Russ looked down at the woman's moon face, recalling the excitement of that first night: sidling past the sentry, creeping back hours later and trying not to waken his tentmates. Just looking at her could inspire the same illicit tingle. It conjured, too, his mother's voice the time he had sneaked down before time one Christmas morning and opened all the presents round the tree including those that weren't his: 'Oh, Russell, you naughty boy!'

'God, I wish I wasn't going!' The words were expelled as a warm rush into her ear, and for that brief second he meant them – not that she was in any way pretty or even good-looking . . . apart from her antelope eyes and inviting bottom. But she had provided him with the comfort he had needed and for that he owed her some affection, and Russ, whilst irresponsible and disloyal, was a very affectionate sort.

'What is to become of your son?'

Again the little bald fellow was the first to manifest himself. Russ looked at the pair before him. He didn't love them, it would be too deceitful to state that, but he did owe them something. In fact, what he was about to offer was not a spontaneous gesture; ever since being informed that the battalion was going home Russ had been wondering how he could provide for them. 'You know Father Guillaume who calls to bring relief to the vrouws?' She nodded gravely. 'I've spoken with him, told him about you and the boy.' Not who had fathered him naturally, but it hadn't been too difficult for the priest to guess – why else would a British Tommy offer to pay for a child's upkeep and education? But there had been no vocal condemnation, only a brief spark of disapproval in the blue eye. 'He's agreed for you to live at the mission. You'll work as his servant. It'll be no different to what you're used to – well I expect it might, 'cause you weren't very well treated by this lot, were you?' He jerked his head in the direction of the Boer women. 'I've told him I'll send some money every month to pay for Charlie's schooling.' Just how he would do that without Rachel noticing he hadn't worked out yet but he would keep his promise. 'He'll get a good education there and you'll be well looked after too.' He put his head to one side. 'Well, what have you to say to that?'

'I will do as you wish,' came the obedient response.

How could he have expected enthusiasm? 'Good – and see that Charlie here doesn't skip his lessons. Tell him I expect him to make more of himself than his father did.'

She gripped his arm and answered earnestly, 'I will tell him what a fine soldier his father is and teach him to be proud of you.' The baby between them, she leaned her woolly head on his shoulder to be hugged comfortingly. 'How many years before the Army allows you to return to us?'

He realized with a start that she still didn't understand the finality of this. Curbing the pang of unease, he kissed her to expunge some of his guilt. 'I'm not sure . . . but you know I'll always be with you in thought.' He spent a

13

moment wondering why God had taken all the hundreds of Boer children with measles, scarlet fever, dysentry and chosen to let this little Kaffir flourish. It seemed wrong somehow, when he'd been a mistake in the first place. Baby fingers worked at his tunic buttons.

The woman raised her head. 'We must say goodbye now?'

'There's no rush,' he soothed. 'We'll have one more night.'

'I shall wait for you.' Detaching the child's hand from the buttons, she pulled away, stared him full in his eyes for long seconds . . . then she was gone.

CHAPTER TWO

When the ship carrying the 1st battalion, the King's Own Yorkshire North Riding regiment – or KOYNeRs as they were known in the ranks – docked at Portsmouth, there was no flag-waving for the homecoming heroes, no brass band playing Rule Britannia, no pretty girls handing out roses. Eight months earlier the quay would have been thronged with people all cheering and weeping jingoistic tears, today only a handful of shivering relatives mingled with the dockworkers as the troopship edged into harbour.

The sergeant replied to this acerbic observation from his corporal as both relaxed over the rail of the ship, watching the quay move nearer. 'I'm bloody glad. I couldn't stomach all that palaver.'

Russ shifted his weight to his other leg and shrugged himself further into his tunic against the cold. 'Oh, I don't know . . . a bit of celebration wouldn't've gone amiss – helped me to feel that this lot really is over.' It was going to be difficult to adapt to home service again.

Daw agreed. 'Aye, it's a funny thing, war. One minute you're working your trigger finger into a palsy and the next some bugger says, "Right, chaps, cease fire, war's over". It's a bit hard tapping the old juices in midstream. I see something move out o' the corner o' my eye and I tend to want to blow its head off.'

Russ formed an irreverent grin. 'To be hoped our Rachel hasn't set a trend in Boer headgear, then.' His wife, an expert and innovatory milliner, made hats for the whole neighbourhood.

'Will she be here?' asked Daw. Mooring lines were snaking through the air to the quay where they were caught and attached to thicker ropes.

'Shouldn't think so. I did scribble a few lines when we got our marching orders but even if my letter's arrived she'll be too busy getting the house clean and tidy for my home-coming. What about Ella?' Arabella, Jack's wife.

The sergeant shook his closely-cropped head. His ears were bright red with the drop in temperature. 'She'll probably be round at her mother's – doesn't know I'm coming.'

Daw was wrong in part. When he and Hazelwood turned into the York street in which they lived, both women were outside their respective houses. It was Arabella who spotted them first, being no more occupied than chatting to her neighbour. The men saw her lips move, at which, the slim person in the brown, fur-trimmed coat looked up from pruning her roses and by the time they had taken three more strides was running up the terrace to fling herself into Russell's arms.

'I wasn't expecting you so soon! I only got your letter this morning – ooh, let me look at you!' She laughed de-lightedly, planted a smacking kiss on his cheek and unhooked herself from his neck to accept the flowers he had bought on the way home. 'Oh, how lovely – but you shouldn't have!' She thrust her face into the bouquet, then straightaway began to tug his uniform into place, patting and dusting. 'Look at you! What've you been doing to get in this state?' Yet more tugging.

'Well, they tell me I've been fighting a war.' Russ grinned and repositioned the hat that had been knocked lopsided with her onslaught. He was as pleased to see her as she was to see him. Using his hands to belt her waist, he commented on how she had managed to keep her slender proportions. The only indication that she had been through pregnancy was the softening of her face. His hands moved up to cradle her cheeks. 'Even bonnier than I left you. You're a bit pale though, lass.'

'Bound to be after what you've been used to,' offered Jack, making the other's skin prickle – then added innocently at the taut expression, 'I mean anyone would seem pale alongside those sunbronzed mitts, wouldn't they?'

16

Russ looked at his hands against his wife's fair skin and exclaimed, 'Oh . . . oh, aye!' Yet felt a twitch of ire, knowing very well that this was not what Daw had meant at all.

Arabella had arrived to greet her own husband, though in less boisterous fashion. There was no bouquet here; she knew Jack too well to expect one. After a fond hug and a kiss she linked her arm through his and tossed an amused expression at Russ who was being pulled towards his house with a hasty, 'So long!' over his shoulder.

'By, it's grand to be home!' Russ paused at the gate to run his eyes from roof to foundation. Though the upper storey had only a sash window, the ground floor was set off by a large bay. Picked out in grey brick against the red, it looked very elegant; the reason his wife had selected it. The front door was painted dark blue and had a letterbox and knob of brass which sparkled even on this overcast day. Between door and gate was a small strip of garden. The row of houses formed part of a longer crescent which, bisected by another road seemed more like two separate streets. There were no houses opposite, though the splendid view this might have given them was marred by an ugly sleeper fence. Looking over his shoulder, Russ snatched a final glimpse of Knavesmire before going inside.

Rachel preceded him over the threshold. Shrugging off her coat she revealed a grey ankle length skirt and a blue knitted jacket. The blouse underneath was crisp and white with a mourning brooch at the throat, worn in memory of her parents. 'Wipe your feet, love! I don't want half of South Africa in my hall, we've just cleaned it.' That which she grandly termed the hall was no more than a passage. She called for the maid whilst divesting Russ of his cap and tutted again at his appearance. 'Oh dear, we'll have to find a place for this.' She studied the dusty kitbag as if it were a problem of world importance then said decisively, 'It can go in the coalhole until you go – ah, Nancy!' A maid had appeared by the door of the back room. 'This is Mr Hazelwood. He's had a long journey and I'm sure he'd welcome a cup of tea.'

17

'Aye, I would that.' Russ' face had lit up, though not entirely at the thought of tea; the maid was a comely sort, bonnier than the one who had been here on his previous leave. He questioned the latter's absence as Nancy retreated, taking the flowers with her.

'Oh, I had to dismiss her, Russ,' Rachel informed him seriously. 'She was much too lax – ooh, come on it's chilly stood here! Let's go where it's warm.' She moved off. 'We'll take our tea in the kitchen I think, we can't have you dusting up all my best upholstery. Then afterwards Nancy'll draw you a bath.'

Same old Rachel, Russ smiled as he followed her to where Nancy busied herself with the brewing of tea, it wouldn't do to go untidying the best sofa by putting bodies on it. Funny, how he had said same *old* Rachel, for she was only twenty-eight, the same as himself. It was just the way she bustled about organizing – or rather disorganizing – folk with her old-fashioned attitude that made him think of her that way. Before taking his kitbag into the yard he had reached into it for the present he had brought her. Rachel held the carved wooden bust of an African woman this way and that, remarking on its oddity, then placed it on the mantel. After which, she clapped both delicately-boned hands to his face and pressed her lips to his, just to emphasize her gladness at his return.

When he came in from the backyard he seated himself at the table and tried to insert his request, which was difficult as she kept chattering away excitedly. One could liken Rachel to a flea – though she herself would have found this a most distasteful analogy – one minute she was sitting in a chair, the next she was in a totally different part of the room, putting some ornament into position or straightening a picture that to anyone else would seem straight already. There she was at the mirror, patting her chignoned, honey-brown hair into place, though not one strand had escaped from the pins inserted this morning. After a final pluck of the curls on her brow she began to fuss over something else. She was extremely thin – no wonder; her fuel intake was expended on nervous energy before it ever had the chance

18

to manufacture flesh. Her chocolate-drop eyes were always darting about in the way of nervous folk. She had piquant features and a pretty mouth that was forever spilling words, but the sentences had little depth for Rachel, though pleasant and friendly, was an empty-headed creature.

'Rachel, Rachel!' begged her husband as she flitted about the spotlessly clean room getting nowhere. 'If you let me get a word in edgeways there's something I fancy much more than tea.'

Her frenetic movement ended abruptly and she donned a look of reproach, seeking innuendo – which was one of Russell's faults. Then she understood and slapped her hands to her cheeks. 'Oh, aren't I a dope! You must be dying to see him and here I am going on about nothing – I'll fetch him this minute!' She set off a brisk pace.

'He isn't asleep is he?' called Russ anxiously. 'Don't wake him on my account.'

'Nonsense!' came her shrill rejoinder as she hared up the staircase. 'He'll wake up to see his father, I'm sure.'

Russ smiled his contentment and leaned back in the chair to accustom himself once more to his surroundings. The house had barely been up for three years and to Russ who had only been here on two previous leaves it still held the air of newness – but it was cosier by far than the barracks. The kitchen was of the size that one might expect from a modest terraced dwelling, with a scullery attached. Despite the installation of gas, Rachel preferred to use the built-in range for her cooking. This was decorated with shiny green tiles which never *ever* bore traces of ash, a brass fender and an oak surround. The table at which Russ was seated took up most of the space in the centre of the room and was covered with a brown chenille cloth edged with tassels. Around it were grouped two carver and four spindle-backed chairs, the former with added cushions, and a baby's high-chair. If extra seating were needed there were two stools tucked away in a corner. The floor was covered in linoleum with a predominantly blue flowered carpet over the top.

On the innermost wall was a brown velvet sofa, the arm of which let down to convert the sofa to a bed. Above this hung a pendulum clock. In one fireside alcove was a built-in cupboard housing linen and crockery, in the other was a small oak dresser. There was a further, understairs, cupboard by the scullery door. His eyes swept over each of Rachel's personal additions – brass candlesticks, brass coal-scuttle and companion set, all gleaming, a commemorative mug for the new King's Coronation, an oval mahogany-framed mirror . . . through which Nancy's reflection was studying him. Lacing his hands over his belt, Russ smiled and said, for want of a better conversation-opener, 'So . . . you're Nancy, are you?'

'Yes, sir.' She tossed a smile into the glass then moved past him at a more leisurely pace than his wife, to fetch the teapot from the scullery. It was entirely due to Rachel's millinery feats that they could afford the domestic help. Russ had protested to his wife that corporals didn't hire maids, to which Rachel had replied rather loftily that he may be only a corporal, but *she* enjoyed important status in this neighbourhood and it was ungracious of him to deny her this token of gentility. More truthfully, it was that the scatterbrained woman could never have coped alone – giving orders made her feel as though she were in command.

'And how long have you been here, Nancy?' Russ craned his neck to spy into the scullery, eyes on the woollen-clad hips. Telling him a couple of months, she made her return to the kettle. This time as she passed he slapped her bottom, the audacity of which pulled her up sharply. He responded with his mischievous twinkle. 'You don't mind, d'you, Nance? S'only my bit o' fun. Sally never used to mind.' Nancy's predecessor had accepted it as part of the job, coming to understand that Mr Hazelwood didn't intend anything further to spring from his cheek, he was simply unable to keep his hands off what he regarded as the most delectable portion of a woman's anatomy.

Then Nancy smiled – no, something more salacious than a smile, thought Russ and was almost relieved when his wife chose this point to return. Her re-entry to the kitchen was somewhat less bouncy, due to her sleepy burden – who had obviously been woken up for the honour. Russ shoved his chair back, stood and said, 'Aw . . . w!' and held out his arms to his son. The child let out a squawk which, as Russ continued to press his attentions, soon grew to hysteria. The disappointed corporal stepped back and lowered his arms. 'I suppose he's frightened 'cause he doesn't know who I am.'

'He's just genny because his naughty mother woke him up.' Rachel cooed to the baby and jiggled him in an attempt to stem the flood of tears. 'Aw, now now! Poor Father's come all this way to see his little Robert.' Rachel had decided it would be nice to choose a name with the same initial as the baby's parents. 'Aren't you just going to let him have a tiny cuddle?' The child continued to howl and bury his mottled face in her shoulder.

'Don't force him, Rache.' Russ contented himself with admiring his son from afar. 'He'll get used to me after I've been home a few days.'

'He'd better,' she warned the baby, then turned loving eyes back to the man. 'How long will you be home, then?' He told her seven days. 'Oh, is that all?' Her smile turned to disappointment. 'And what foreign devils have they got lined up for you to fight this time?'

'None, we're on home base at Limerick . . . on second thoughts that could be more dangerous than Africa.' A laugh. 'Never mind, love, only a couple of months and I'll be out for good.'

'And aren't I grateful!' Rachel had never cared for his profession – apart from the smart uniform, and with this substituted by the unflattering khaki there seemed little reason for him to stay in the Army. She used a handkerchief to dab at the sobbing child's face. 'So what do you think to your son, then?'

'He's grand. I've thought of nowt but seeing that little fella while I was away. He kept me from going crackers with all that heat.'

'Oh, did you hear that, Robert?' the mother enquired airily. 'Not a mention of the wife who's stuck here holding the home together.' At Russ' scolding, her feigned disapproval melted into a smile. 'Aw, I missed you as well – he's stopped crying now – would you like another try?'

'No . . . better not. We don't want to start him off again.' Russ was a bit piqued at this inauspicious start to the relationship. It was to have been a wonderful moment, holding his son for the first time. 'Maybe when he's got used to my ugly mug.' He sat back on his chair, not bothering to pull it right under the table.

'Right, I'll put Robert back then,' said Rachel brightly, not noticing his disillusionment. 'Pull your chair in, Russ, before you start tucking in. I know what you're like for crumbs.' She left him to Nancy's care.

'Would you like a biscuit, sir?' Nancy shoved a plate at him.

Russ had ignored his wife's dictate and was balancing on the rear legs of the chair. 'I'll tell you what I would like,' he grinned again, 'to get my hands round that lovely bustle o' yours. It's a right smasher.'

Nancy decided to curtail this at once. He was probably quite harmless apart from having itchy fingers – his sort usually were – but she wasn't going to risk it going further. Slinking round the table she deposited herself brazenly on his lap.

His hands which had been laced idly round the back of his neck, came unloose at the surprise of it, hanging in mid-air and making no move to keep her there. 'Eh, Nancy . . .'

'You don't mind, d'you, sir? Only you seemed to fancy me so I didn't see the point of wastin' chat.' One of her arms encircled his neck, her free hand toying provocatively with his collar. 'I like a man in uniform. There's something . . . exciting about him.'

'Nancy,' he gave a nervous chuckle and made weak play of tapping her bottom. 'I think you'd best get to yon side of the table before your mistress gets back.'

'Is she a jealous person, the mistress, sir?' purred the maid, fingers trailing his tunic buttons.

'Nancy,' he tried to sound stern, 'I didn't mean to give the impression . . . it was just a joke I used to share with our other maid . . .'

22

'Oh, come on!' Her hand was massaging his chest now. 'A man doesn't fondle a girl's bottom unless he's keen on her – and I'm certainly not the type who'd allow the liberty unless I was keen on a chap . . . like I'm keen on you.' She was enjoying this.

'Will you take your hands off please?'

'What're you worried about, sir? She won't come in.'

'Look . . .'

'Nancy!'

At Rachel's yelp of horror the maid shot from Russell's lap and pretended to be pouring the tea, head tucked into her chest.

Russ chanced his escape. 'Well, I think I'll just go . . .'

'Stay where you are, Russell!' commanded his wife, then pressed ungenerous lips together.

'Rachel, it wasn't what you think . . .'

'I know what I saw! And that slut isn't stopping here one moment longer.'

'I was only teasing, Mrs Hazelwood,' protested Nancy.

'I could see that perfectly well!'

'No, I didn't mean . . . I was just showing Mr Hazelwood how far he could go . . .' Nancy shrivelled as the ill-formed sentence emerged.

'Miss Brown, I think you had better collect your coat before you incriminate yourself further!' was Rachel's tart advice.

'I can't go having you thinking I'm . . . forward,' began Nancy.

'Forward! My goodness I could have chosen a much better word!'

'Look! Mr Hazelwood smacked my bottom! I don't allow liberties like that and thought to put him in his place.'

'My husband knows his place well enough without your assistance, Miss Brown,' snapped Rachel. 'And resorting to slander isn't likely to procure a good reference. He is far too much of a gentleman to enact such familiarity even with his own wife. Now will you please leave my house at once.' She bustled forward and, taking some money from a cashbox on the mantel, thrust it at Nancy. 'Here you are! That's what you've earned and I'll have no complaints of unfairness.' The maid saw it was pointless to deny what her mistress had thought she had seen. After a fruitless attempt to gain a reference she glanced helplessly at Russ, pocketed the money and left the kitchen to collect her things.

Rachel began to pile all the crockery in the sink.

'Eh, I haven't started that yet!' objected her husband as she snatched his cup. 'And what are you doing now?' She was taking all the crockery from the shelves, transporting it to the scullery ready for washing.

'What does it look like?' Cupboards were flung open.

'It looks like you're washing clean cups.'

'They are not clean! Not when that woman's had her hands on them. The sly, dirty . . .'

'Rachel, it wasn't what you're thinking . . .'

With the crockery soaking in hot water, she squeezed out a cloth, applied disinfectant and began to rub down every surface with a vigorous back and forth movement, muttering endlessly about, 'That woman's dirty hands on everything . . . nowhere fit to eat off.'

'It's not a very good start to my leave, is it?' Russ proffered quietly. 'I'm sorry, lass.'

'Oh, don't think I hold you to blame, Russell!' She ceased her rigorous task to look up at him. 'You can't help your bonny face – I must admit if you weren't my husband I'd be after you myself. No, it's that floozy! I always thought she was brazen, I should never have employed her, but there you are, that's the sort of soft article I am. I felt sorry for her because she spun me some tale about having to support her invalid mother – and this is where a soft heart gets you! This is how she repays my charity, by trying to steal my husband – and in my own kitchen!' The cloth began to rub back and forth again. All the ornaments were collected from the mantelshelf and placed alongside the pots to be washed.

Russ sighed. 'Will the water be heated enough for a bath?'

'Yes, I'll come and do it.' She flung the cloth down but his upraised palms warded her off.

'No, no you carry on with that, I can see to myself.' He went upstairs to get some clean clothes.

Before going to his and Rachel's room, however, he responded to impulse by opening the door of the room he knew – by way of his wife's letters – to have been assigned as a nursery, and peeped in. The child was seated in his cot, gnawing on a wooden toy and making noises. His chavelling stopped when the man's moustachioed face appeared. The toy was dropped and the lower lip jutted out and downwards. 'All right, all right!' muttered Russ hastily, staving off the fresh outpouring. 'You miserable little sod, I'm not stopping.' He closed the door quickly and moved on to get his civvies, taking some consolation in their clean smell.

By the time he returned to the kitchen the pots were already on their way back to the shelves. His wife said nothing as he passed into the scullery and closed the door. Putting his clothes on a chair he lifted a board and drew back a curtain to reveal a bath – which had been one of his wife's requirements and not a standard fitment of the house; his neighbours relied on the old zinc variety. While the water ran he stripped off, then stood scratching until the bath was full enough. A twist of the taps and he was stepping in to take a welcome soak.

CHAPTER THREE

'I thought I might go for a stroll later.' Russ, spruced and curried, was tucking into a meal of bacon and egg.

'In this weather?' was his wife's astonished comment. But she smiled fondly at him across the table. Most of the upset had been worked from her system now that the kitchen had been purged. Her husband looked more like his old self too, moustache waxed into two sharp spikes, damp brown hair slicked neatly from a side parting, freshly-laundered shirt and pressed trousers. Warm thoughts stirred her breast. Had the table not been between them she would have wrapped her arms round him.

'I'll be all right with my coat on.' He savoured every mouthful. Even though he had had plenty of bacon in South Africa, done in a billycan it tasted nothing like bacon done at home. 'I'd like a wander round the old place after seeing nothing but dust for months, and a nipped nose won't come amiss after being subjected to ninety degrees in the shade.'

'Oh, you poor hard-done-by soul,' teased his wife, placing her own knife and fork together on the plate. 'You'll be wanting some company, I suppose?'

'I'd hate to drag you from the fire.' He tried to sound concerned. 'Anyway, what about the lad?' His wife answered that Robert could come with them. 'Are you sure? He might catch a chill.'

'Maybe you're right,' mused Rachel, then leapt into action again. 'I'll ask Ella if she'll mind him for an hour or so. He's been fed and changed so there's nothing to get her into a flap.'

Russ reminded her that Ella's husband had just come home too. 'Happen she and Jack might want to go out themselves.'

Rachel was undeterred. 'There's still Mrs Parker. It's probably more sensible to ask her anyway, Ella not having any children of her own. I wonder how much I should offer her?'

'She won't want paying, surely.'

'I daresay she won't, but I'm not about to feel beholden to any of these people. If you accept a favour there's always that degree of familiarity and I don't want them to think I regard them as equals.'

'Are you sure you ought to leave him? I mean he's only little, what if something should happen to him and Mrs Parker doesn't know what to do?'

She studied him peevishly. 'Russell, don't you want me to come with you?'

'Course I do! It's just . . .'

'Then I'm certain Mrs Parker's capable of looking after Robert for an hour.' She came up behind him and crossed her arms over his chest, inhaling the smell of clean shirt. 'Don't be so old womanish, nothing will happen to him.' Donating a final kiss, she began moving again. 'Where shall we go?'

He vacillated. 'By the river?' It was a different sort of liquid to that which he had planned for his first night home but he dare not say more, she had been upset enough already.

'Yes all right, we can get the ferry over to Fulford and visit the cemetery while we're there, take some flowers to Mother and Father.'

Nodding, Russ left the table to wander in the direction of the sofa. 'Jacket, dear.' He had left his jacket over the back of the dining chair. Obediently, he went back to put it on. When he made for the sofa again Rachel followed. 'Oh, wouldn't you know it! There's Robert crying.' She cocked her pert head at the ceiling as Russ took advantage of the fire. 'That boy is forever hungry. I shall have to go and see to him – he's determined his mother's not going to be alone with the strange man.'

'I wonder what he'll say when he sees me in your bed?' His eyes crinkled at the corners.

She gave him an admonishing smile then brought him a cup of tea before leaving. Russ grabbed this chance to relax which he could never totally do in his wife's fidgety presence. Whilst she was away someone called, not knocking but coming straight in through the back entrance.

'Now then, Filbert.' Jack Daw's humourless face preceded his body round the door. 'Managed to persuade your jailer to let you out for a pint?' His khaki had been swapped for an ill-fitting drab suit which looked as if it had spent the time since its last airing crumpled on the bedroom floor. Once away from the Army, Jack didn't give a toss for the way he looked.

'I thought I said we'd meet down the pub?' Russ' tranquil pose vanished as the man sat down; Rachel wasn't keen on her husband's friend – on any of his friends for that matter, but particularly Daw – she said he made the place look untidy. He stood as if to advertise his unwillingness for Jack to tarry. It didn't work. 'I don't think I'll be able to make it,' he whispered urgently. 'I told her I was going for a walk and she wants to come with me.'

Jack's droopy eyes projected impatience. 'Why didn't you just tell her you'd arranged to go out with me?'

'That'd look nice, first night home after fifteen months apart, wouldn't it? Telling her I'd rather be in the company of the bloke who's never been out of my pocket for three years. Plus . . . I'm not exactly on the Honours List.' He told Daw about the incident with the maid. 'Christ! I do believe if Rachel hadn't been in the house I'd've been made.'

Jack sniffed and said with fake despondency. 'Ah well, it looks like I'll have to sup all that ale on my own.'

Before he could make a start on this proposal, a knock came at the front door. Russ, averse to leaving Jack sitting here in case Rachel came down and found him, dithered on the threshold. The knocker sounded again.

Daw made an exaggerated oath. 'I won't pinch anything, you know!'

'I never said you would.' Yet Russ made it obvious he was none too happy on leaving Jack unattended.

But when he returned he was smiling broadly.

'Good value was it?' enquired Jack. At the other's quizzing look he added, 'Well, you went out looking like a professional mourner and came back grinning like a Cheshire cat. I thought Half-price Hilda must've done a quick turn on the doormat.'

'Mrs Haines' mother's dead.' Russ twanged on a brace.

'I'm sure that'll make the whole street smile.'

'Rachel's millinery services are required urgently.'

'What – for the corpse?'

'Dozy bugger, shut up and go wait at the end o' the street. I won't be long.' Russ, in lighter mood now, succeeded in shoving the other from the room.

The latch of the gate had just settled when Rachel came back. One step inside the room, she stopped dead. 'You've had somebody in here!'

'Sorry, love?' Russ glanced up nonchalantly from the paper he had snatched before her entry.

She marched up to the sofa, pointed at the crumpled cushion and shook it briskly, replacing it in orderly fashion, at the same time touching her palm to the upholstery. 'This seat's still warm! Come on, who was it? I hope you haven't had that Jackie Daw in my kitchen? Honestly, I could slave for a year and it would only take one blink from that ragamuffin to make the entire place look like a tip.' Not satisfied with the cushion, she shook it and plumped it again.

'Somebody called with a message from Mrs Haines,' said Russ hurriedly. 'Something about you making her a hat for her mother's funeral. It's the day after tomorrow so apparently there's not much time.'

Rachel planted her hands on her hips. 'Oh, the inconvenient times people choose to die! You'd think Mrs Haines would have a black hat somewhere, wouldn't you? Everyone has a black hat. But no, she expects me to put myself out . . .'

'I did say we were going out tonight,' said Russ apprehensively, then breathed an inward sigh of relief as his wife replied:

'Aw, Russ, I'm sorry to disappoint you! But I'll have to go.' She came to him, stroking his arm in sympathy. 'That's the trouble with being an expert at something, people are forever calling on your talents as if you don't deserve a life of your own.' After a tut she added, 'Still, it's all money in the bank, isn't it? We'll pretty soon have that shop of ours. Well . . . what will you do now?'

He shrugged plaintively. 'There's not much point in going out on my own.'

'Now I don't want you moping at home on my account. Besides, if Robert cries you wouldn't know which end is which. I'll pop into Mrs Parker's and ask her to step in for an hour while you go for your walk. Then when we both get back we'll have a chat and a cuddle and you can tell me all about what you've been doing while you've been away.'

The image of his illicit affair made his skin creep, but he managed not to display the guilt on his face. 'Aye well . . . I might just have a short wander, then.' He tried not to sound eager, and waited for the door to slam before donning a wide grin and a coat.

Daw, lounging against the wall in the back lane, saw Rachel's silhouette bob past the entrance and wandered out to watch her bounce smartly down the street. She moved just like Russ – shoulders back, left, right, left, right, face ever smiling. Ella always had a chuckle whenever she saw the married couple out together and would say, 'There they are on parade again'. He wondered what would happen to that permanent smile of Rachel's if she knew what her husband had been doing in Africa. Russ crept round the corner then, interrupting his thoughts. Fifteen minutes later the two were entering *The Trafalgar Bay*.

Few words were exchanged while the pints were being pulled, both men's eyes fixed to the landlord's hand at the pump. It was not until a good half had been consumed that Russ said, 'Eh, I haven't told you about my lad, have I? By, he's a right cracker – screamed the place down when he saw me, mindst, but eh! he's really grand. Big as well.'

'Aye?' Jack had guessed from the way Russ perched forward on the edge of his stool that this was going to be a long homily if anyone showed the slightest interest. Well, that wasn't going to be him. He wiped the froth from his moustache and lit a cigarette.

'Aye! You'll have to come and see him – when she's out of the way o'course.' Russell's face brimmed with paternity.

Daw nodded, but seemed more interested in a game of darts that was being played. Russ felt a pang of affront, then recognizing his own tactlessness, settled back to his seat and was thoughtful. It hadn't been very diplomatic of him to waffle on about his son when Jack and Ella were having the same problem that he and his own wife had once had. He sought to appease. 'You never know, Jack, you might have your own lad to brag about next year.' Daw shook his head dismissively and took another drink. 'It's never too late, you know. Look at me and Rachel, we'd almost given up after five years. I think it was the shock of both our mams and dads dying within such a short time of one another that altered things – must've jolted Rachel's works or something.'

'I should send your findings to *The Lancet*,' was Jack's dry utterance. 'I'm sure the medical profession would be impressed with your novel solution to sterility.'

Russ clicked his tongue. 'I'm just sayin' that's what seemed to sort out our problem, that's all.'

'Some people take powdered rhino horn, some take minced-up bats, Filbert advocates disposing of one's respected elders. I'm sure my mother'll be delighted when I tell her she's going to be a granny . . . before plunging the knife in her ribs.'

Russ sighed. 'I was only trying to offer my assistance.'

'Father of two and he thinks he qualifies as a stud.'

'Father of one, Jack,' growled an alarmed Russ. 'Father of one.'

Daw turned to look him in the eye, but said nothing.

Neither did Russ for a while. He called Daw his friend and knew that Jack would address him likewise, but a friend was someone you liked, someone in whom you could confide – neither was pertinent to this relationship. Why, then, did it continue? Russ couldn't say. It was possibly because the two had grown so used to being together as boys that the partnership had just automatically extended to adulthood. Everyone else regarded the pair as close friends, but it was more a case of them enduring each other than actual liking. In fact, Russ found Jack's holier than thou attitude very irksome – though in the present clime it could well be advantageous; sanctimony would forbid Jack to break his secret . . . or so Russ could only hope. One never quite knew with Jack. He might just drop one of his sarcastic hints and spawn mayhem. With Jack there was never that safe feeling one experienced with true friends. Both sat watching the darts thud into the board until, after a space of three minutes, Jack announced, 'Anyway, I'm buying her a dog.' This drew a blank look from Russ. 'You know, a dog.' Jack stuck his tongue out and panted. 'One o' them things that barks and pisses up the rhubarb.'

'Oh . . . very nice,' answered Russ, then reached for a cigarette to cover the smell of Jack's breath.

'It'll be company for her while I'm away.'

'Aye . . . it will be.' Russ ignited the cigarette and took a long drag. 'You'll be signing on for another spell will you, Jack?' Daw, too, was nearing the end of his present term.

A nod. 'You?'

'No, a bit keen for my liking. I wasn't expecting that little lot we've just been in.'

'Funny, I always thought that's what armies were meant to do – fight. So what're you going to do instead, then?'

Russ was a time in answering. Whenever he had spoken to Jack of his intentions in the past his so-called friend had always beaten him to it, then made out it had been his idea and that Russ was the one who was copying. Whatever it was, however trivial it might seem to others it never ceased to infuriate Russ. Right from their school days it had been the same: Jack would say, 'What're you going to draw?' and Russ would answer, 'An elephant fighting with a giraffe' or something equally unusual, and the instant he said it Jack would start scribbling away and sure enough the picture he presented for the teacher's inspection – seconds before Russ – was of an elephant fighting with a giraffe. The teacher would say, 'Most original, Daw' and give him a star and pin his picture on the wall for all to envy, whilst Russ would receive only a look of rebuke for his lack of imagination.

If he had refused to divulge what he was going to draw or crouched over his paper with his arm curled round like a protective fence, then Jack would go into a sulk for days and Russ would be at the mercy of the playground bully from whom the tougher Daw normally protected him. When Jack had asked, 'What're you going to be when you leave school?' and Russ had answered rashly, 'I'm going to be apprenticed to Mr Sanderson the joiner', sure enough, Jack was there before him and Russ had been forced to make do with the job at the drapery.

When Russ had married, so had Jack. Russ doubted that his pal had ever done anything of his own volition. It had been more or less the same in the Army: Russ had told his friend he was thinking of joining up and had found himself on parade with Daw. It seemed that Jack had got himself dismissed from his trade – accidentally or on purpose, Russ never knew, only that here he was stuck with Jack again. On a par with all their other undertakings it was Daw who gained first promotion. At least in this instance it had been well deserved, for Daw was the better soldier – but that hadn't made it any less annoying. And then when Rachel decided that she wasn't going to live in the barracks among all those rough soldiers' wives and had hankered after one of the modern houses being built on South Bank, who should he find as a neighbour? It was unbelievable, the lengths to which Daw would go to emulate.

Now, in response to Jack's question as to what he would do when discharged from the Army, he hedged. 'I haven't really decided.'

Jack was not to be duped. 'You always know exactly what you're going to do, have it all mapped out before you make your move. That's what I admire about you.'

This was obviously a revelation to the other. 'Do you?'

'Aye . . . it's the only bloody thing, mind.' Jack took a drag of the newly-lit cigarette and tossed the match on the floor. There was no doubting his gist.

Russ felt compelled to say, 'Look Jack, I know you regard what I did over there as cheating . . .'

'Is there any other word for it?'

'No . . . no, you're right . . . but I'd like to think I'm going to be allowed to make amends without . . .'

'Without living in fear of me shopping you,' finished Jack.

'Will you?' Russ tried not to make it sound as if he were begging.

'If, by some improbable chance, I'd been the one to go astray, would you rat on me?'

'No, of cour . . .'

'Then what're you worrying about?' This was all the reassurance Russ was going to get. 'Now come on, about leaving the Army, what've you got tucked under your wig?'

'Well, it's nothing really definite . . .' At Daw's expression the reluctant corporal disclosed his plan. 'Me and Rachel are going to buy ourselves a business.'

'Be a shopkeeper?' Jack sounded slightly amazed.

'What's wrong with that? Better than being shot up the arse.'

'I suppose so.' Daw was thoughtful. 'Rachel's idea, was it?'

'Eh, I can make my own decisions, you know,' retorted the other acidly.

'Getaway! She's always been after you leaving the Army.'

Russ performed a gesture of acceptance. 'So, how long will you be staying with the Colours, then?'

A shrug. 'Till I make General.'

'General shit-shoveller.' Russ took Daw's glass and his own to be refilled, asking on his return, 'When you do pack it in, what might you do for a living?'

'I haven't given that much thought.'

No, you want to pinch my bloody ideas, thought Russ, angry at himself for being talked into divulging his own scheme. He fully expected Jack to be out of uniform by the end of the year, despite the man's statement to the contrary.

The barmaid came round to empty the ashtrays and wipe the tables. 'Eh, we don't put these here for ornament, you know.' She flourished one of the ignored beermats, lifted Russ' glass and wiped the wet ring from the wood.

'Sorry, my darling.' Russ, as was his penchant, gently cupped her bottom.

'I'll give you my darling! And get your hand off my bum.'

'It's clean,' he told her. 'Feel.'

She swiped at him. 'Save your sauce for your chops.' And to Daw, 'Can't you keep him under control?'

Jack tossed his partner a disdainful glance. 'It's with being out in Africa – he's like a wild animal.'

'Well, you know what they do to animals,' riposted the girl.

When he arrived home Rachel was cutting out a pattern in the front parlour. Hearing the door, she called, 'Is that you, Russ?'

'No, it's Nimble Nip and his elephant.' He hung up his hat and wandered grinning to the doorway, not wanting to go too close for fear of betraying where he had been. 'What're you doing?' This room reeked of lavender polish. Choose any piece of furniture – oval mahogany table, elaborate sideboard with marquetry flowers on the doors, piano – one could see one's face in it. Around the dining table were grouped eight Hepplewhite reproduction chairs with red moquette seats. These matched the two armchairs, one on either side of the fireplace. There was a sofa in here too, and in the bay of the window stood Rachel's sewing machine. Over the fireplace was a large mirror. The other walls held family photographs, two landscapes and Russ and Rachel's wedding portrait.

Rachel's speech was handicapped by a mouthful of pins. 'I thought I'd get Mrs Haines' hat cut out before bedtime. Did you have a pleasant walk?'

'Aye, very bracing.'

'But I doubt very straight,' she said wryly, and at his frown, 'You shouldn't've bothered with the peppermints, Russell, they don't cover it you know. Scoundrel! No wonder you didn't want me to come with you. You've been with that Jackie Daw.'

'Never had a whiff of him,' came the firm reply.

Her brown eyes upbraided him. 'I've just had Ella round – seems we were both deserted. You ought to be ashamed of yourselves!'

He hung there like a chastened infant, until she grinned forgivingly and, sticking in her final pin, said, 'Oh I'm only kidding! It is your first night home, I wouldn't begrudge you a bit of relief – but don't think you're sloping off every night. I've been without you for fifteen months, I expect some attention you know.' She took the completed effort and laid it on top of her sewing basket, along with scissors and pins, then picked up a lamp. 'Come on, I'll make us some cocoa before we go up.'

Once this was made, Rachel joined him on the sofa in the kitchen. 'Oh, it is nice to have you back, Russ.' She cuddled up to him.

He returned the fond gesture, rubbing his head to hers. 'It's lovely to be back. An' I'm sorry again about . . . you know, Nancy and that.'

'Oh, please! Don't mention that woman's name to me.' Rachel snatched a sip of her cocoa. 'She's left me everything to see to on my own.'

'You'll have to hire someone else.' He raised his own cup.

She was dubious. 'I don't know about that. If you're going to be home a lot more often . . . the girls of today can't be trusted.'

'Not all of them can find me fatally attractive – I mean, I know I'm gorgeous but there must be one who . . .' He ducked his head laughingly as she tapped him.

She told him they would see. 'Now less about that! I want to hear what you've been doing since last I saw you.'

'Well, only what I told you in my letters.' Russ hid his face in the cup.

'You're not exactly the world's greatest letter writer are you? I mean, what were these Boer people like?' She ceased leaning on him and tugged the creases from her skirt, sitting primly.

He rested his cup on a knee. 'Oh, you know, they had two eyes, a nose . . .' He laughed again. 'Well, they were a tough lot, I can tell you, Rache.' Russ soon found himself slipping back into the dust of the veld. 'Half the time you couldn't see what you were firing at and their weapons were a lot more advanced than ours, massacred a lot of our brave lads . . .' The heat of the cup seeped through his trousers and he shifted its location. 'And it wasn't all done on a gentlemanly basis either. I saw some dreadful injuries from dum-dum bullets.' Rachel interrupted to ask what these were. He demonstrated with his fingers on the cup. 'You make a couple of cuts on the nose of the bullet like this, so's when it hits somebody it spreads out inside them and causes massive internal damage. I saw one poor chap hit in the side of the head, it took the best part of his face off.'

'Oh, that's dreadful – Russ, d'you think those curtains would match better if they were beige?'

Puzzlement drew him from his trance. 'What?'

She was staring intently at the window. 'Those curtains, d'you think they'd go better with this sofa if they were beige? I bought the material thinking it was a bargain but I'm not sure that shade of green goes well with brown. What d'you think?'

'I think . . . they look fine to me.' That was obviously the end of their meaningful tête-à-tête. He loved Rachel but oh, he did sometimes wish she had more inclination towards serious debate.

'Good . . . still, I'm not convinced.' She was probing her lip. 'I'd like another woman's opinion.'

'You've just had Ella in here, haven't you?'

'Russ!' His wife dealt him a scolding laugh. 'You've seen the Daws' parlour – Ella couldn't be trusted to furnish a dosshouse. Hmm . . . I suppose I could ask her and if she says the curtains look all right I'd know to take them down – sorry, love, you were telling me about South Africa.'

'Oh, it's all a bit dreary really. I haven't been in the fighting much since I went back.' His cup was hoisted to his mouth.

'Then I don't see why they had to keep you out there while we at home had to suffer all manner of atrocities. I didn't write and tell you because I thought you were having a hard time of it . . .'

The vision of the naked African woman dissolved and his face adopted a look of concern as he asked what had happened.

'I had my window broken, that's what happened! And all because I spoke my mind in the shop. Of course we all know it's fatal to do that; Mrs Phillips is such a gossip.' Russ asked what she had said. 'I said, I thought it was a disgrace what the Army was doing to those wretched women and children in South Africa and how I was sometimes ashamed to be British.'

Russ groaned and, finishing the last dregs of cocoa, leaned forward to put the cup on the table.

'It's getting to something, Russ, when a person can't speak her mind without inciting violence against her personal property. Five shillings it cost me! Five shillings for saying what a lot of other people are thinking but aren't brave enough to come out with. The Army's made this country look the villain to the eyes of the world – of course, I blame half of it on this new King, he's undermining the whole nation's morals.' She bobbed up to place her cup next to his, then fell back on the sofa.

Russ had always liked Edward – thought him a 'bit of a lad', a man after his own persuasion – but he said nothing in defence.

'You only have to look at the quality of general help to see that! None of them are willing to do a proper day's work – d'you know I still can't settle to those curtains, they're making me feel quite ill.' She jumped up and, pulling a chair up to the window, began to unhook the offending articles.

'What the . . . Rachel, you can't start faffing around with them at this time of night!' He came round the table to coax her from the task. 'Leave it till morning, then tomorrow we'll go out and buy some more.'

'Oh yes, and where's the money going to come from?' She placed her palms to the sides of his head as he grasped her waist and lifted her down. His ears were cool to the touch.

'Getaway! You make it sound like we're destitute.' He

watched amusedly as she put the chair back into place, sliding its feet into the exact hollows they had made in the carpet.

'As well we might be if we had to rely on the Army – oh, and that reminds me!' Grinning, she turned and held out her hand, palm upwards. Russ didn't bother feigning ignorance. Ruefully, he handed over his accumulated pay, out of which she returned half a crown before putting the rest in the cashbox. She then washed and dried the cocoa cups and afterwards said, 'Right then, Russ, bedtime.' She tried to make it sound casual. Rachel had always felt guilty for enjoying their lovemaking. To show eagerness would seem indecent . . . but she couldn't suppress the thrill which his expression induced, knowing how much he wanted her. Lamp in hand she led the way, tiptoeing past the nursery. Her hair, loosed of its pins, tumbled to her waist, drawing a sigh. Soon they were abed. 'Oh, you don't know how much I've been aching for this!' Russ wasted no time in reaching for her.

But hardly had his fingers settled then she mouthed softly, 'Picture, love,' putting a brake on his romance.

After a moment of incomprehension, he gave a smiling sigh, 'Shows how long I've been away,' and climbed out of bed. Approaching the portrait of Rachel's mother he turned it to face the wall. Only when this ritual was done did his pretty wife allow him to claim her body. His fingers sought her in the darkness and, 'Oh, I do love you, Russ,' she murmured in his ear.

And with these words the vision of the plump black thighs vanished. He cupped his wife's slim buttocks and cleaved her to him.

CHAPTER FOUR

The translation to civilian life was always difficult. Last night Russ had promised himself a lie in, but even without the intrusion of the bugler he found himself awake at first light. He turned his head to look at the sleeping woman beside him, smiled, then rose quietly so as not to wake her and went for a stroll across Knavesmire. There was the smell of cocoa on the air from the factory at Clementhorpe. The dew on the greenbelt spangled his boots and the air was chill, but he found it pleasantly refreshing and continued right across to the far side where he spent a short time in the woods. Here, he sat on a log, lit a cigarette and listened to the sounds from the trees. His ears picked up a scuffling sound. Looking about him he spotted a red squirrel rifling one of its winter hoards. Armed with a nut, the creature bounded up the trunk of a fir. Russell's eyes followed it to an untidy bundle of twigs way up amid the branches. After a second, the animal came back down the tree and the act was repeated several times. He watched it until his cigarette burnt down to his fingertips. Taking a final puff he crushed it on the ground.

The squirrel was on its way up again. Russ decided to make his way back. He rose. There was a *bang*! The squirrel, halfway up the trunk, lost its grip and plummeted to the ground. Mouth open, Russ stared at it.

Daw came past him and bent to retrieve the furry corpse, holding it aloft to inspect where his bullet had landed. 'Mm, not bad.'

Russ was still staring at the dead creature. 'What d'you want to go and do a thing like that for?' Daw beheld him quizzically. 'It could have had young 'ns up there!' Russ gestured at the drey. 'How're they going to survive without a mother?'

Jack examined the corpse. 'Father,' he corrected. 'And fathers often do desert their offspring, don't they?' Then he laughed and clapped his friend on the shoulder. 'Sorry, only joking. Away!' He balanced the Mauser on his shoulder. 'Come and have a shot with this, it's . . .'

Russ had turned away. 'I have to get back for breakfast.'

Jack gave a derogatory laugh and shouted after him, 'Ah, you're too soft, Russ! I don't know what you're bothered about, they're only bloody vermin.'

Russ tightened his jaw, but made no answer and headed for home. He heard the Mauser's bark several times before he got there. On his return he found his wife had risen. But his complaints about Daw's behaviour went almost unheard for Rachel was in far too much of a flap cooking breakfast and seeing to Robert whilst heartily bemoaning the lack of a maid. When he had eaten he went to the yard and gave his kitbag a good brushing, then took it upstairs to unpack. Shortly, Rachel followed him up to make their bed.

'Russell, what do you think you're up to?' Horrified eyes took in the contents of the wardrobe which were now strewn about the room. His reply was muffled, his head amongst the hanging garments, telling her that he was seeking his cigarette card albums. 'Well, do you have to make so much mess about it?' She tugged at the waistband of his trousers. 'Come out! They aren't in there anyway.'

He emerged, the hair on his crown sticking up like a duck's tail. He smoothed it. 'They were in there when I left.' She told him well, they weren't in there now and pushed him out of the way in order to stack everything in its place. Russ sighed heavily. 'Do you think I might be privy to their whereabouts or do I have to start snapping arms and legs?' He was asked what he wanted them for. 'I want to light a bonfire, what d'you think I want them for?' He waved a fistful of the cigarette cards. 'These are what I've saved while I've been away.' Everything replaced in the wardrobe, she clicked the door shut and went to a chest of drawers. From here she withdrew an album.

'Thank you!' He whipped it from her hand and made to open the drawer. 'Are they all in there?'

The sheets were being hauled into place. 'No, that's all there is.' Grasping the corners of the red counterpane she gave a flourish to send it floating down on the bed. He asked where the rest were. 'Gone.' She moved onto the landing.

'Gone!' His pursuance was swift. 'Oy! Come back – gone where?'

'Russ, don't shout so!' On turning she spied a crumpled fold in the bedroom curtain and marched back in to tug it straight.

Russ charged after her. 'Rachel, what've you done with all my albums – eh, you haven't burnt them, have you?'

'Don't be daft!' She spoke as if he were mad. 'I've sold them.'

'What!'

'Ogdens were paying ten shillings each for them, they were going to send them to hospitals or something – though Heaven knows what for. I thought it was an excellent offer, don't you?'

'But . . .' he could barely speak. 'I've been collecting them for years!'

'Yes, I had noticed.' A duster whisked from surface to surface.

'I was saving them for the lad!'

She laughed lightly. 'You daft 'aporth, what does Robert want with them? He's only a baby, they're only bits of paper.'

'They were full collections! I had every single card.'

'Not in that one, you didn't, it only had sixty-seven photographs in.'

'Oh! I wondered why you'd been so kind as to leave me this'n! Would you like to stand there while I stick these in?' He waved the loose cards. 'Then you can get another ten bob.'

'No, I can't, the offer finished last January.'

'Oh, Rachel, sometimes I could . . .' his voice tailed off helplessly. 'You know how I like saving them.'

'It's all very well for you to have the luxury of saving them out there in Africa with nothing better to do, but we at home have to make ends meet.'

He had a sudden chilling thought and rushed up the short flight to the attic – which had been another of Rachel's specifications to the builder. When she caught up with him he was gazing at the cabinet that housed his birds' egg collection. 'Well, you didn't think I'd sell those, did you?' she demanded in a hurt tone as, summoning the courage, he opened the drawers to find his collection intact.

Russ offered a prayer of thankfulness and studied the magnificent array of blue, buff and speckled eggs. The cigarette cards had been a hobby, this was a lifetime's study. His cabinet housed every British bird's egg from the wren's pea-sized effort to the great Golden Eagle, each tray meticulously numbered and cross-sectioned. It was his joy to come up here and just look at them – sometimes for hours. He eyed his wife tellingly, then carefully slid the drawer back in. A faint knocking saved further altercation. Rachel went down a storey to peer from a window. On seeing the fruit and vegetable cart in the road she duly rushed off to make her purchases. Russ sighed and turned back to the cabinet. Soon, though, a commotion brought him down a flight to the window that overlooked the street where he leaned, palms on sill, and watched the exchange between the two women.

Rachel stood on the pavement, flourishing a shovel at her neighbour. The object of the disagreement appeared to be a pile of horse-droppings which steamed in the road. 'Ella, I tell you it's mine! Anyway, what do you need if for?' She indicated the bare plot under Ella's front window.

Ella, one hand holding her own shovel, the other on her hip retorted mildly, 'I need it for my rhubarb.' She was a woman of gaunt appearance, though the manner she had of drawing in her chin – which she was doing now – gave a false impression of fleshiness. Her eyes and hair were very dark, her skin verging on the sallow, but there was a humourous twist to her mouth as she stood opposing Rachel. She enjoyed nothing more than getting her neighbour rattled.

'Rhubarb doesn't grow in March!' parried Rachel, eyes sweeping Ella's unflattering brown dress.

The impatient vegetable seller tried to intervene. 'I've got some nice big onions . . .'

'Stop bragging,' mocked Ella, then to Rachel, 'Roses don't grow in March neither.'

'They need the manure while they're dormant!' The calmer Ella was, the angrier it made Rachel.

'Well, when there's a pile on your front they'll be able to have it, won't they?'

'Ella, the cart *is* on my front!'

'Well, if I'm not mistaken this didn't drop off the cart,' Ella responded breezily, 'it dropped out of the horse – and the horse is on my front.' With this she scooped up the droppings and, holding the shovel proudly before her, went into her house.

'That . . . woman!' Rachel, now in the spare bedroom where she had stormed in defeat, watched Ella deposit her prize on the small square of earth in her back yard – then sprang from the window as Ella looked up with a grin. 'She's insufferable! Oh, we'll have to move, Russ, it's no good.'

Russ had donned his jacket and was examining his smart presentation in the wardrobe mirror. He shook his head amusedly and called, 'What, over a pile of hossmuck?'

'It's not just that!' Rachel changed rooms like a whirlwind. 'It's everything: that self-satisfied smirk when she thinks she's got the better of me . . . I'd hoped to get away from that when we moved here but no! your friend has to copy your idea and come here and ruin it all. I just can't live with her, Russell, I've tried my best to be sociable but that woman is so . . . ooh!' Injustice provoked another display of fist-clenching and she sped back to the spare bedroom. Russ finished preening and followed her to the window. 'She's not a bad lass at heart – and she was entitled to it really, the horse was on her front.'

'I might have known you'd side with her!'

'I'm siding with nobody. I just think it's daft to fall out over something as trivial as a pile o' manure . . . what was second prize by the way?'

His wife gasped her disgust and stormed out; Rachel had no sense of humour. Russ was about to turn from the window when Jack Daw stepped into his yard. The Mauser was wrapped up now, but the bundle of corpses that dangled from the man's hand showed it had been busy. Russ' nostrils flared with disgust – not simply at Daw, but at himself for not being more strident in his condemnation. He turned his back on the sight.

Downstairs, he tried to make amends to his wife for his tactless wit. 'Would you like me to put an advertisement in the press for another servant? I've nothing much to do this morning, I thought I might have a wander into town.'

'If you like.' She had taken out the material for Mrs Haines' hat and was stabbing pins into it.

'You really need one, don't you? All this hat-making . . . you won't have time for housework and such.'

Her brown eyes came up like arrows. 'Are you insinuating I neglect my duties?'

'No, no! I'm saying nothing of the sort, I'm just trying to help.'

'Trying to get back into favour, you mean – and don't go spending all your money in town.'

He averted his face, muttering under his breath, 'No love, I'll just have the odd gallon o' beer and three whores and put the rest in the bank.'

'Sorry, Russell, I didn't catch that.'

He swept across the room and squeezed a pacific arm round her. 'I said would it be possible to have the money for the advertisement?'

She tuttered at his ingratiating posture, 'What about the half-crown I gave you last night?' then butted him lightly with her brow, 'Oh, go on then!' and took the money from the cashbox. 'But make sure you get the wording correct.'

'Respectable young woman required for the post of general maid, wages by arrangement – how's that?'

'I didn't mean it that way, I meant be succinct; I don't want charging for a line that only has one word on it.'

The advertisement which Russ placed in the *Evening Press* was answered before his leave was up by four young women in turn. The first two were much too attractive to be trusted with Rachel's husband and were dismissed without interview. The third, a plain woman of thirty, was entertained quite hopefully until Rachel had the awful thought that, being two years older than her employer the woman might try to usurp command – she did seem a very confident sort – Rachel could not have that. The fourth, an Irish girl of fifteen called Biddy Kelly was ugly of feature and totally subservient – ideal for Rachel's requirements.

The two faced each other across the table this chilly morning. Biddy wore an ancient plaid dress which was patched in several places and stained on the bodice, and a green woollen shawl which was milled and motheaten. She wore no hat; Rachel was quick to comment on this. Biddy replied apologetically that she didn't have one.

'Goodness me! Biddy, a young woman's outfit is incomplete without a hat. I must make you one.'

'Thank ye very much, ma'am, I'm sure.' The girl nodded.

'It'll come out of your first week's wages, naturally,' said Rachel.

'Does that mean I've got the job, ma'am?' ventured Biddy.

Rachel pondered for a moment, then said, 'Let's see you make a pot of tea, then we'll decide.'

Biddy delivered a vacuous nod, stood and looked around. Rachel pointed out the teapot and caddy. With elephantine movements Biddy transferred two spoonfuls of the tea from the caddy to the pot and was about to add a third when Rachel stopped her.

'Two is sufficient – and you forgot to warm the pot.' The big ugly face turned to stare at her. 'You're meant to pour a little water from the kettle into the teapot.'

'But, I'm about to do that now, ma'am.' Rachel said she was meant to do it before she put in the leaves. 'So . . . I put the water in first, then the tea?'

'No, you . . . oh, never mind! Just do it and I'll show you what I mean another time – and you didn't wash your hands, did you?'

'They're clean already, ma'am.' Biddy displayed two huge red hands that would have done credit to a prize-fighter. 'I washed 'em before I came out.'

Rachel examined them closely. 'Yes, they do look clean, I must say, but I would prefer it when you come to work for me if you wash them immediately before handling food.' At Biddy's apology she gave a kind smile. 'That's all right. Now, the cups you will find in that cupboard.' She pointed – then felt her heart lurch as the big mitts clamped on two pieces of china. But Biddy got the cups to the table without mishap and shortly poured tea into them. 'Not a bad effort, Biddy.' She gave a commending nod then, over tea, went on to ask where Biddy lived.

'Bedern, ma'am.' The cup had totally disappeared as the great hands lifted it to her face.

Rachel pictured it: an impoverished area with over-crowded accommodation. 'And have you a mother and father, brothers, sisters?'

'I got a mother, a father, three brothers an' one sister, ma'am.' She was asked if she was the eldest. 'No, ma'am, my brother Paddy – well he's really called Seamus but we know him as Paddy 'cause me father's called Seamus an' we'd get mixed up, d'ye see – he's the eldest. Then there's me brother Peter who's known as Sean 'cause Peter is me grandad's name but he's dead now o' course, then Mary who we call Molly 'cause me mammy's name is Mary, then me, then me brother Thomas.'

'And what is Thomas called?' asked Rachel politely.

There was a puzzled frown. 'He's called Thomas, ma'am.'

Rachel said, 'Oh,' and took another drink. Then she enquired as to Biddy's previous employment.

Biddy looked down at the table. 'Rowntrees' factory, ma'am.'

Rachel showed surprise. 'And you left?'

'Not exactly, ma'am.' The minute blue eyes were lost beneath a Neanderthal brow.

Rachel downed the cup. 'You were dismissed!'

'I didn't do anything really wrong! 'Twas just . . . well, 'tis me hands ye see, ma'am, they weren't fitted to handling chocolate.'

'Ah,' Rachel nodded understandingly at the great paws, 'they kept melting it, I suppose?'

'No, ma'am . . . they kept putting it in me mouth.'

'In other words you were sacked for stealing!'

'Oh, ma'am, please gimme a chance!' Biddy's face beseeched her. 'I promise I ain't never done anything like that before, it were just that I'd never tasted chocolate an' I kinda got the cravin' for it – couldn't stop. I swear by the Holy Virgin I won't ever lick so much as the smell o' cookin' in your house.'

After a stern examination Rachel asked how much the girl had earned and on being provided with the answer said, 'Well, you won't earn anything like that here. I don't suppose there would be many willing to employ you at all with those credentials. Still . . . you've been open with me and I do have some sympathy for your social background. I was never one for shirking my responsibility to those worse off than myself. I'll take you on a month's trial.'

Biddy was overwhelmed. 'Oh, God bless ye, ma'am! You're a saint!'

'But I'm warning you I will not countenance any form of dishonesty.'

'I swear I'll be on immaculate behaviour, ma'am.'

'Your wage will be three shillings a week.'

Biddy nodded, though less exuberantly. However, she could hardly complain after the lady had displayed such compassion. This was the sixth interview she had been to and she had almost resigned herself to joining the queue at the soup kitchen, for her mother swore she would get nothing under her roof if she didn't bring a wage in. When Rachel asked when she could start she gave the eager reply of, 'Right away, ma'am!'

Rachel agreed, then passed a short spell in thought before asking, 'How do you feel about living in?' None of her other maids had been resident, but Rachel was now seized with the idea of how welcome it would be to have someone to cook breakfast instead of arriving halfway through the morning. She wouldn't have to waste the spare bedroom, that would be needed for future children. The girl could have the attic once a space had been cleared among the junk for a bed. This she told Biddy. The Irish girl was delighted at the prospect of having a room to herself after sharing with her brothers and sister.

'Naturally I shall have to deduct a sum from your wage for your board,' Rachel told her.

'Oh . . . naturally, ma'am.'

'Then if you're agreeable you can start by helping me with lunch. There's only myself; Mr Hazelwood has gone out for the day. He's on leave from the Army at present. Oh, one more thing, Biddy. I really feel that your outfit is unsuitable for a respectable household. This afternoon we'll go to the Stuff Warehouse and buy a dresslength.'

'Er, that'd come out of me first week's wages, ma'am?' surmised Biddy.

'Oh, gracious no,' replied Rachel, then doused Biddy's relief by adding, 'I should imagine we'll have to break into your second week's money – but never mind, I'm sure you'll appreciate the improvement in your appearance.'

Russ, having been on a bird-spotting expedition for the best part of the day, did not meet his new servant until shortly before teatime.

'I'm back!' he called the minute he was through the front door and unhooking his haversack laid it to one side and shouted, 'Which room are we in?'

'The front – but don't . . .' Rachel's warning came too late.

'Oh bl . . . I'm sorry!' Russ stared aghast at the strapping Irish girl who was trying vainly to cover her private portions with her hands – vainly, because her private portions were even more impressive than her hands. She tugged the hem of her grubby chemise over her drawers, then pulled the neckline up under her chin, not knowing which bit to pull where.

'Russell, get out!' Rachel came at him and slapped him from the room. 'I told you not to come in!'

'Sorry, I never heard you,' he bumbled, craning his neck to catch another glimpse of the disrobed figure who was now crouching over to defend her modesty and weeping openly. 'Who is she, anyway?'

'She's our new maid – now will you kindly give her some privacy?' She slammed the door on him and went back to comfort the distraught girl. 'There, there don't be silly it's only Mr Hazelwood.'

'Oh, ma'am!' keened Biddy. 'What's the mammy going to say? An' worse still what's Father Boyle going to say? He'll throw me out o' the church!' Rachel asked why on earth this should happen. 'I've committed a deadly sin! I'm going to have a baby!'

Rachel blenched, then demanded, 'Why didn't you tell me that this morning?'

'I wasn't having one this morning!'

'Then how . . . do you know who the father is?'

''Tis himself!' Biddy pointed at the door . . . Rachel almost collapsed. 'Ma'am ye saw it wasn't my fault!' Biddy tugged at her arm. 'Maybe if you should tell the mammy I never meant for it to happen . . .'

'Biddy! I demand to know what substance there is to your allegation. When did you meet my husband?'

'Why . . . just now, ma'am,' sniffed the girl.

'Then how can you possibly claim that he is the perpetrator of this disgusting mess?' Biddy didn't understand the long words. 'How can you say he's the father of your child?' shouted Rachel.

''Cause he's seen me knickers!' wailed Biddy. 'Didn't me mammy say I must never let a man see me knickers or I'd fall for a baby.'

Rachel heaved an exasperated sigh and flopped into a chair. 'You addlebrained idiot!' She stood up again. 'Just put your dress on! I've taken all your measurements. I'll cut the pattern out now and you can put it together in your spare time.'

'But . . .' Biddy clutched her abdomen.

'Biddy Kelly, you are not having a child! And if I hear you telling anyone – and more importantly that my husband is the father, then you will be in very serious trouble. Do you understand?'

Biddy ran an arm over her eyes. 'Yes'm.'

'Good! Now get dressed we've the tea to attend to. By the

way I forgot to ask, can you read and write?' Rachel supposed it was too much to expect for an outlay of three shillings per week, but was surprised when Biddy said she could in a fashion. 'What sort of fashion?'

'I can read little words – an' me name o' course.'

'Well, we're not likely to find your name in a receipt book which is what I'm proposing as your reading matter. But it's written in simple sentences so you should be able to comprehend. How is your cooking?'

'Oh, 'tis fine, ma'am,' vouched Biddy as the other buttoned her up the back. 'Haven't I cooked enough chitterlings to go round the globe an' tie in a bow.'

'Chitterlings are not something we eat in this house, Biddy.' Rachel patted the row of buttons and took the girl to the kitchen. Opening the recipe book at the relevant page she said, 'As I've been good enough to spend time on your dress you can bake me some bread. I thought I'd done enough to last but I forgot my husband was home. While you're waiting for the dough to rise there's a pile of ironing needs doing. Now, will you be all right with that while I finish cutting out your dress?' At Biddy's confident nod she returned to the front parlour.

Some time later after fitting in her son's feeding time Rachel went back to the kitchen to see how the new maid was coping. Her husband was just on his way down and paused on the stair to survey her sheepishly. 'Is it safe to come down? I thought it might be about teatime.'

The skin around her brown eyes creased. 'It is, unless Biddy's got herself into a tangle with the dough. Honestly, that silly girl, you'll never guess what she thought when . . .' She changed her mind. 'Anyway, it doesn't matter! I can't see her being any worse than the last one once I get her trained.' She opened the door of the kitchen but got no further, her face clothed in wonderment. Russ peered over her shoulder.

The maid was standing in the hearth – right inside the fender, holding a bowl of dough, a look of intense boredom on her face. Rachel descended on her and seeing the pile of ironing still waiting for attention became even angrier.

51

'What're you idling there for? I expected to see all this done and put away – it won't do itself!'

'Sure, how can I do the ironing, ma'am, when the table's over there an' I'm over here?'

'Biddy,' said Rachel tiredly, 'for what reason are you standing in the hearth?'

'Didn't that receipt book have it written down?' At her mistress's questioning face Biddy stepped out of the fireplace, still cradling the bowl of dough and pointed to the words, 'Cover with a cloth and stand on hearth or in a warm place for one hour until dough rises . . .'

Russ sniggered as his wife snatched the bowl from the perfectly serious maid and planted it on the hearth in an exaggerated manner. 'There! That's what it means, girl. It doesn't need to be nursed for heaven's sake.'

'Sure now, why doesn't it say that in the book?' said a scornful Biddy. 'Ye'd think the person that writ it could tell it in proper English, wouldn't ye? Will I do that ironin' now, ma'am?'

Rachel was about to say yes, when a thin grizzling wail percolated from the nursery. 'Oh Heaven help us! He's so colicky today. I seem to have done nothing but rub his back – Biddy, you go see to him. It's tiring me out, all this running about after people.' She prepared to do the ironing herself.

Biddy shambled off in the direction of the noise, then turned back. 'Oh, what about the bread, ma'am?'

'I'll see to it!' The gas iron was already in operation. 'Here! Take this spoon with you. There's some Croskell's in the medicine chest; give Robert a spoonful of that and throw him over your shoulder – I mean,' she elucidated, foreseeing disaster from this apparently harmless command, 'put his chin on your shoulder and pat his back – gently.'

'Sure, I know how to do it, ma'am. Haven't I squeezed out great trumps of wind.' Biddy went off to the nursery, telling the screaming babe, 'I'll not be a minute, Your Highness. I'll just get the stuff to soothe your wee belly.' There were several bottles in the chest. Biddy ran her thick digit along the shelf, squinting and muttering, 'Iodine, quinine and iron tonic, cal . . . can't read that bugger, ah, that's it! Croskell's Yellow Mixture.' Turning the key in the cabinet she took the bottle over to the cot and sniffed the contents before pouring a little onto a spoon. 'I'd just better taste it to make sure 'tis not poison or the missus'll kill me.' The baby waved clenched fists, his face mottled with rage and discomfort. 'God, that's not a bad drop o' stuff,' she told him, wrapping a long tongue almost down to her chin and pouring another measure. 'Too good for the likes o' you, ye raucous wee son of a lobster.' She extended the spoonful towards the gaping orifice and tipped it in. He was forced to close his mouth or choke.

'Good, is it not? Now you sit on Biddy's lap an' get rid o' that there bellyache.' She settled back into a rocking chair and, with the aid of one expansive palm, managed to support the baby and pat his back at the same time, whilst her other hand transferred the contents of the bottle to her mouth. She rocked contentedly back and forth. 'Oh, God that's great – 'tis Heaven.' She continued to praise the liquid and sip happily until ten minutes later she found, with a guilty start, that she had consumed half the bottle. 'Oh Jesus, your mammy'll rip the skin off me back!' she told the baby who had now grown sleepy from the rocking. 'What am I to do?'

With a spark of inspiration she topped the bottle up from the water jug . . . after taking 'Just one last sip'.

When she got downstairs the bread had been put into the oven and the ironing was nearly done. Her mistress told her to take over, asking if she had given Robert any Croskell's. 'Oh yes, ma'am – he seemed to like it.'

'He does. He'd drink the whole bottle if you let him. But don't be tempted by his angelic charm; one teaspoon only, it's very potent stuff.'

Biddy hoped the mistress would not notice that the mixture was a slightly paler yellow than before. Keeping her guilty face hidden, she smoothed the iron over a pillowslip.

'Well, Biddy,' said Russ in a friendly tone, trying to

make up for the earlier embarrassment he had caused her, 'Are you going to like working for Mrs Hazelwood?'

'Oh, she's a wonderful lady, sir! I'll give her my utmost ability.'

Rachel smiled at her husband. The Irish girl, though more than a little dilatory, had a very accommodating nature and would soon learn. 'We'll be very pleased to have you, Biddy, though we'll have to make you a bed in the nursery until the attic is cleared. Still, you'll be able to hear Robert more clearly if he should cry in the night – oh, did I forget to say? He does sometimes wake up for a cuddle, but I'm sure you won't mind getting up with him, will you?'

CHAPTER FIVE

After his leave expired, Russ set sail for Limerick to spend his last few months with the Army. His first act was to pen a hasty letter to the priest in South Africa apologizing for being unable to send any money to pay for Charlie's upkeep at the moment, but promising that as soon as he set up in business this would be rectified. He had decided it was impossible to put any aside from his Army pay, for Rachel would spot the discrepancy at once. At first, he continued to feel unease over his adultery – especially when Sergeant Daw brought it flashing back with a well-timed jibe – but as, in time, Daw grew bored with the subject, the fear began to recede and was completely forgotten by the month of May when a letter arrived from his wife to say she was pregnant again.

In July he was discharged from the Colours and entered the Reserve which would last for a period of six years. God willing, no one would pick a fight with the British Empire in that period. Russ had his future neatly planned. By the year following his discharge Russell Hazelwood and Wife had acquired a small property in Nunnery Lane. With his previous experience in drapery this was the chosen commodity, enjoined with Rachel's millinery skills.

It transpired that Russ had more flair for business than he had previously dared to hope. Examination of the accounts showed that each week's takings always exceeded those of the previous week, a fact which Russ took great delight in pointing out to his wife. There was, however, one item of book-keeping about which he was not so ready to brag, and it was as well that Rachel was totally inept at figurework. A name appeared in the accounts, that of a Mr Cranley, a wholesaler who supplied various items of haberdashery. Mr

55

Cranley did not exist. Russ had seen this fictitious client as the ideal way to cover his former sins – the money paid to Mr Cranley was in fact sent to a Father Albert Guillaume in South Africa for the upkeep of an illegitimate son. Unless Rachel had reason to get in touch with Mr Cranley – highly improbable unless Russ expired suddenly overnight – the boy was assured a decent life and Russ could forget all about him.

By 1906 the combined business was doing well enough for the Hazelwoods to move to a more commercial position in Micklegate and for Russ to take on a young male assistant. Naturally Rachel continued to churn out her creations at home; with four infants to bring up now she had no time for the shop. Her body seemed to be making up for all the time it had wasted in their early years of marriage, dealing her a child almost every year. However, the children were not allowed to impinge too frequently on her time and Biddy attended to most of their needs.

At this moment, Biddy was attempting to get the children ready for their constitutional. The youngest, Rebecca, was spread face down on the maid's lap, having her arms thrust into her flannel. Two rough red hands turned the child over and pinned the ends of the flannel up over Rebecca's kicking legs. The baby roared her protest at Biddy's harsh ministrations. 'Away with your noise,' scolded Biddy, reaching for a petticoat to put over the flannel. 'Didn't I sample enough o' that last night.' Her eyes were heavy from lack of sleep, her mouth drooping at the corners. 'Miss Rosalyn, I'd ask ye not to do that!' The two year old had tripped her elder sister Rowena as she had trotted past. Poor Rowena was now in tears. 'God! Haven't I enough to listen to with this skinful o' bad humours?' An embroidered dress was tugged over the crimson face. 'Master Bertie, would ye be so kind as to pass me that there cardigan?'

'No,' said four year old Robert bluntly and continued to float his battleship in the baby's bath.

'I'll box your ears, Bertie,' warned the maid.

'And I'll tell,' replied an unconcerned Robert, being aware that Biddy held his mother in awe.

The maid issued a gasp of frustration and, with the child still draped across her lap, rose and half-shuffled, half-jumped to reach the cardigan. This was getting to be nearly as bad as being at home and having her own family to fetch and carry for – and even now she only got three shillings per week. Oh, she had asked for a rise, but the mistress had looked so offended, and pointed out that she had been kind enough to relent over deducting a sum for the maid's board, that Biddy, feeling ungrateful, had not dared to ask again. The promise of a room had never come to fruition. The mistress answered her complaints with, 'You can make a space in the attic when you've a spare minute,' but as Biddy never had a spare *second* the attic was still crammed with junk and she was still in here with the squawling brats. The two older children had been given the last unoccupied bedroom but the two whom Biddy was left with were not the most amenable of room-mates.

'I'll give you a pasting one o' these days,' she muttered darkly at Robert.

Having dressed the baby she dumped it in the crib. With a wipe of her flustered brow she took a covert glance at her charges, went to the cupboard and stepped right inside, squeezing the door as near shut as possible. From her pocket came a bottle of Croskell's which was uncorked and applied to her lips. She had tried to give this up for Lent but her craving had got the better of her.

The nursery door flew open and Rachel burst upon the room, her face becoming even more annoyed at seeing the children unattended. 'Where's that Biddy Kelly?' she demanded above the din.

'In the cupboard,' replied her son in between making boat noises.

'Doing what? Oh, Robert, look at your ribbons!' Rachel fussed over the child's long hair, retying the bows. The boy's father had suggested it was time his hair was cut, but Robert had such lovely blond waves that his mother couldn't bear to see them hacked off. 'And look at your dress! It's drenched – Biddy Kelly, come out here at once!'

Biddy, responding to the angry voice, had just time to

slap the cork back into place and be reaching her hands up to a shelf when the door was flung open. 'Biddy Kelly, can one ask what you're doing in here? Can't you hear Rebecca screaming the place down? And Robert is absolutely soaking wet.'

'Sure, I'm just getting Miss Becky a . . .'

'Rebecca!' snapped the child's irascible mother. 'Not Becky. Rebecca, Rebecca, Rebecca! How many times do I have to tell you?'

'Sorry, ma'am. Well, I was just getting herself a clean shawl ready for her outing.' Biddy's great paws seized the article. She stepped past her mistress and went to pluck the roaring child from the crib, swaddling her in the shawl.

Rachel said that the baby shouldn't be allowed to cry like that. The maid replied that she had done everything she could to stop her. 'But I think she's teething, ma'am – look can ye just see that little tooth busting out o' the gum?'

'Ooh yes!' Rachel's face brightened as she peered into the noisesome maw. 'Poor mite, she wants a little bone to chew on.'

'Sure, it'd have to be an elephant bone to fit that gob,' sulked Biddy in a private aside. Rachel, overhearing the remark, reminded Biddy of her station. The maid apologized. 'But she kept me awake all last night with her fratchin', ma'am. I never got a wink o' sleep.'

'There *are* others living here, Biddy. While you're carping just think of your mistress hard at work all day then having to put up with that all night. I had to stuff cottonwool in my ears and even that didn't drown it completely.'

Sure, wouldn't I like to drown it, thought a malevolent Biddy, jiggling the screaming culprit up and down.

'And think of Mr Hazelwood too! He works hard, he doesn't want to be kept awake all night. Get something from the chemist when you go out.'

Don't you mean the ironmonger's, thought Biddy, but said she would. 'Oh, an' I'll need some money for another bottle o' jollop, ma'am.' An argument took place about when Biddy had bought the last bottle. 'No, I'm positive 'twas last month, ma'am – an' there isn't just the baby takes it – I mean, there *are* the four o' them an' Master Robert gets the upset belly quite reg'lar.' She was censured for the language and Rachel demanded to see the bottle. 'Oh, er, 'twas completely empty, so I threw it out, ma'am – with the dustmen last week.' With a gesture of surrender Rachel said she could have the money when she came down.

Later, when Biddy manoeuvred the large perambulator bearing the two youngest through the front door, her mistress was performing a hectic motion with a sweeping brush. 'Biddy, do watch the paintwork! There's a good two inches clearance on either side of those wheels without demolishing the jambs.' Rachel's eyes flitted to next door where Ella was just emerging with her little dog. She bestowed a neighbourly smile. 'Good morning, Ella! Late for work?' Ella was employed at Terry's factory. It wasn't the usual procedure for a woman to continue after she was married but, Ella being childless, allowances had been made.

'Oh hello, Rache.' Ella locked the door then shoved the string holding the key through the letterbox. 'Aye, I'll be locked out now so I'm just popping into town. Is there anything you want?'

Rachel answered that Biddy had her list. 'Go on, Biddy! You needn't think I'm spending all morning on your jobs.' She turned to smile at another neighbour who paused to chat. Ella broke into a trot to catch up with Biddy. 'Bye, Ella! Have a nice time.'

Rachel brushed haphazardly at the pavement whilst murmuring to the other woman, 'If I were a betting person I'd lay odds she's off on one of her sprees.' Ella had become very involved with the Suffrage Movement lately. 'As if she hasn't anything better to do – just look at the colour of those curtains.' The other remarked that Ella was expecting her front brushing as well, judging by the litter that was about. 'Oh yes! That's what I'm here for, didn't you know?' Rachel threw up her eyes. 'And if I don't do it it'll all blow onto my front. It makes me wonder what she does with no family to look after – though she makes as much fuss over that blessed dog. You'd think it was a baby the way she goes on.'

Ella and Biddy were now in Albemarle Road, both forced to walk slowly being handicapped by the children and the dog who kept stopping to sniff the wall. 'Young Becky was working overtime last night, wasn't she?' said Ella, tugging on the lead.

'Oh dear, did she keep you awake too, Mrs Daw?' said Biddy.

'Do you think I always have these matchsticks propping my eyelids up? What's matter with her, is she ill?' Ella peered into the pram where the screams were only just being lulled into sobs by the motion. Biddy explained it was the child's teeth. 'Tell her false ones aren't half so much trouble,' replied Ella, who had had all her own removed at the age of twenty-three, thinking the artificial ones much nicer and more fashionable.

'Mrs Hazelwood's angry at me for the noise. I don't see as how it's my fault.'

'You want to stand up for yourself a bit more,' instructed Ella. 'She works you far too hard.' Biddy said she would get the sack if she complained. 'I doubt it. She wouldn't get anyone else to work for a wage as small as the one she gives you. You want to tell her you won't be exploited anymore.'

'Oh, I wouldn't like . . .'

'Listen, Biddy,' Ella stopped her and spoke fervently, leaning on the hood of the pram, 'it's no good moaning to me all the time, you've got to do something about it. The time has come for us women to throw aside all our old-fashioned ideas, we have to have a say in the way our lives are run. The men've been getting too much of their own way – and so have women like Rachel. It's up to you and me to change Society, to get ourselves the right to vote. If we don't act now we'll be stuck in these subservient roles forever.'

'So what're ye going to do, ma'am?' asked Biddy, walking again.

'Biddy, you don't have to call me ma'am.' Ella moved with her. 'Unlike your mistress I know my class. We're going to do all sorts of things . . . smash windows, throw rotten eggs . . .'

Biddy stopped again. 'Smash windows! Won't they lock y'up?'

'That's the idea, Biddy!' Ella linked arms with the maid and spoke zealously. 'If they send us to prison people'll start taking us seriously. It'll be reported in all the newspapers. Listen, why don't you join us?'

Biddy looked agog. 'Sure, the mammy'd kill me if I got me name in the papers.' Ella said Biddy's mother should thank her for helping to change her life. 'An' what use would I be?'

'It's women like you that we're desperate to get through to,' persisted Ella. 'To show you that you *can* have a say in how much work you do and what kind of work – I mean, you might want to be something higher than a maid-of-all-work, like a carpenter, say, or a bricklayer.'

'Or a chemist,' mused Biddy, gathering interest.

'Anything you like! Once we get that vote we can do as we damn well please. Listen, I'm off to a meeting of the WSPU, d'you want to come?'

Knowing how her mistress held Mrs Daw in contempt, Biddy said that she couldn't, because of the children. But Ella was very good at manipulating, especially pliable bodies like the Irish girl, and said that the children could come too. 'You can leave the pram in the lobby with my Kim, he'll look after it. Young Bertie and Wena won't be any trouble, will you loveys?' She bent to address the children who were hanging onto the handle of the pram. 'An' we'll buy you some sweeties.' Biddy said the mistress didn't allow them to eat between meals. 'Tosh! She's so prissy – anyway, she won't know will she?'

And Biddy found herself carried along to the meeting in the city centre, though she understood little of what was said. However, what was proposed on the way home she understood only too well. 'Oh God, I daresn't get mixed up in anything like that, Mrs Daw!'

'You're committed now, Biddy. Come on, let's have a practice.' Ella looked around for a target and spotted a shop selling menswear. 'That one'll do perfectly.'

'Oh, I couldn't!' Biddy twittered nervously. 'Oh, no!'

'Eh, you are weak-livered for a big lump of a lass, Biddy. Don't tell me I've gone to all that trouble of getting you into the movement and you're too cowardly even to sling a brick.' Still evasive, Biddy said she hadn't got a brick. Ella soon provided one. 'Go on – be brave.' She raised her voice. 'Votes for women! Go on, chuck it, Biddy. Votes for women!'

Biddy stared at the cobble on her big palm. She stared at the people going about their business. She stared at her charges. Robert gazed back with interest.

'Biddy!' prompted Ella sternly.

Accompanied by a moan, the Irish girl's arm came up in a sudden movement and – like a mangonel – propelled the cobble at the large pane of glass. Faces that had previously been directed at the contents of other shop windows now turned at the abrupt shattering. Biddy poised there, hand over mouth, 'Oh, Jesus!' staring at the jagged remnant of window, then looked at Ella who beamed her triumph and shouted again, 'Votes for women!'

The noise had woken the baby who started to scream again. It jerked Biddy from her stupor. She set off at a swift pace, children in tow and Ella hurrying after her. 'Biddy, don't run away! We want them to see who did it.'

'I don't!' Biddy continued her escape, her too-large boots slopping on-off-on-off. 'The mistress'll take my blood for her roses.' She chanced a backwards look. An angry shopkeeper had now emerged and fingers were being pointed. 'Oh, sweet Virgin!' Biddy's pace increased, nearly dragging the children off their feet. When the pram almost knocked the breath from a policeman who had just turned the corner she screamed out loud, 'I didn't do it, yer honour!'

Placing a delaying hand on the hood of the pram, the officer foiled her escape, allowing a breathless shopkeeper to catch up. When the constable had ascertained the reason for Biddy's rush he turned to her. 'Can you offer an explanation for breaking this gentleman's window?'

'Oh no, sir!' Biddy sobbed piteously. 'Please, I never meant to do it.'

'The cobblestone just sort of found its way into your hand, did it?'

Ella pitched in. 'There's no call to be patronizing!' The officer asked who she was. 'I am Mrs Arabella Daw and I demand . . .'

'I'm not here to answer demands. I'm here to investigate a case of criminal damage. Now . . .'

'If there's anything criminal around here it's your attitude! Speaking to us as if we're idiots . . .' The officer interrupted to scribble her name in his notebook, asking also for her address. Ella told him.

He turned to Biddy. 'And you are?'

'Biddy Kelly,' provided Ella. 'And her address . . .'

'Ventriloquist, is she?' asked the constable mildly.

'Tell him, Biddy!' Ella delivered a forceful nudge. 'Go on! Give him your name and address, we're not ashamed.' She encompassed the crowd in this statement; it was amazing how fast one could gather.

'Well you should be!' shouted a woman, to loud agreement. 'You want horse-whipping – what's her husband thinking of?'

'Votes for women!' rallied Ella.

'Oh please, can't I just pay for the window?' Biddy entreated the officer. The latter consulted the shopkeeper whom Biddy also beseeched tearfully. 'Please, please! 'Twas an accident. I didn't mean no mischief.'

'Biddy!' chastised Ella. 'You coward.'

'You keep your neb out,' ordered the constable and awaited the shopkeeper's decision.

Just as a lenient response was about to be granted, Ella, forseeing failure, lashed out and knocked the notepad from the policeman's hands. She glared her defiance at the crowd which rumbled condemnations and at the policeman who was brandishing a broken pencil. 'Up the Suffragettes!'

'Oh, Mrs Daw!' Biddy chewed on a work-hardened finger as the two of them, pram, children and dog were hauled away to the police station.

'What'll we do? What'll we do?'

*

'That woman!' Rachel was in the act of stabbing a pin into her hat when Russ entered for his lunch. When he asked what woman she cried, 'That Ella Daw! Subverting my staff – it's no good looking for any dinner, there is none!' She hared about collecting hat and jacket and to her husband's enquiry as to where she was going said, 'Down to the police station, that's where I'm going! Yes! That woman has had my children locked up like common criminals!'

'Oh, blimey . . . eh, hold on.' Russ grabbed her as she brushed past. 'Just stand still and tell me what's happened.'

'I've just had a policeman on my doorstep, that's what's happened! That woman waylaid my servant on her way to the shops and instead of the children receiving their fresh air they've been stifled in a filthy prison cell. Breaking windows! That's what they've been learning to do this morning.'

Russ groaned. 'Ella's been up to her Suffragette tricks, has she?'

'Tricks? I'll give her tricks! She knows I'm much too intelligent to get mixed up in her criminal activities so she picks on my dim-witted servant – I'll bet it was her who broke my window when you were in South Africa. Well, the first thing I shall be doing after freeing my children is to demand compensation. Five shillings it cost me, Russ!'

'I'd better go with you,' Russ sighed and reached for his hat.

At the police station they were met by a remorseful Biddy who wrung her great mitts pleadingly. 'Oh, ma'am, I'm ever so sorry to drag ye here! I never meant . . .'

'Shut up, Biddy!' rasped her mistress, then to the police sergeant on the desk, 'Where are my children? I demand that they be freed.' The sergeant commanded a constable to bring forth the young detainees. He would be glad to see the back of them; the baby had been screeching something awful. Rachel was duly reunited with her brood and after fussing and clucking over them to make sure there were no ill-effects she turned on Biddy. 'This is absolutely disgraceful! Heaven knows, it's bad enough having one's servant bringing one's house into disrepute, but to drag respectable and impressionable children into this abominable place – I should dismiss you!'

'Oh please, ma'am!' Biddy beseeched her, then genuflected to Russ. 'Sir, I'm beggin' ye! 'Twasn't my idea.'

'I'm well aware whose idea it was!' Rachel interjected before her husband could speak. 'And consider yourself lucky that I know you too well, know how easily you allow yourself to be led. But!' she added as Biddy almost wept with relief, 'if I ever catch you talking to Mrs Daw again I shall not hesitate to cast you out.'

'Oh, God bless ye, ma'am! May every one o' your fingers be a candle to light your path to Heaven.'

'Now officer,' Rachel spun on the sergeant, 'if you've finished with my servant we shall take her and the children home.'

'I'm sorry, madam, Kelly faces a charge of criminal damage, she'll have to stay here while we get particulars.'

Rachel made a noise of irritation. 'So! I shall have to cook dinner myself?' She glowered as a tearful Biddy was led away. 'What's going to happen to her?' When told it would probably be a fine her eyes dilated in horror. 'Russ, do you realize this could get into the papers?' At his shrug she squeaked, 'Don't you care that the address they print will be ours – I don't suppose we could forbid them to print it?' This to the policeman.

'Be a bit difficult, it's a topical story . . . but then they might not print the whole address. I could arrange for you to have a word with Mrs Daw while you're here if that would help?'

'What! You'd need to hold me for murder if I got my hands on her – oh yes and I'd like to make a complaint against her myself.' She applied her elbows to the counter and laced her fingers in businesslike manner.

'Rachel, leave go, lass,' coaxed Russ as the sergeant positioned his pencil.

She ignored him. 'Someone broke my window and I believe it was her.'

'Did anyone witness this incident?'

'No, but it doesn't require the brain of a mathematician

65

to work it out, does it? I mean, here she is incarcerated for a similar crime.'

'That's not technically correct, madam. Mrs Daw is being held on a charge of assaulting a police officer. But,' he reached for a piece of paper, 'if you'd like to tell me the details . . .' He went through all the particulars with her, asking finally, 'And what date did this take place?'

'The first of May 1902,' declared Rachel.

The pencil stopped writing and its holder looked up. 'That's over four years ago, madam.'

'Your arithmetic impresses me!'

The form was crumpled slowly in the sergeant's fist, his patience flagging. 'A bit late to be making a complaint, isn't it?'

'I didn't know who did it then, did I?' An agitated Rachel started to rock the perambulator; the baby had been working up to this crescendo since being brought in.

'You don't really know that it was Mrs Daw now, do you?'

'She's . . .'

'And even if you did it'd be a bit late to do anything – I'm sorry, madam.' He glanced at the pram. 'Looks like it's past his dinnertime.'

'*He's* a *she*!' The ruffled woman made ready to leave, eyes brimming with tears of injustice. 'Come on, Russ, it's clear we're not going to get any recompense for our ordeal. Honestly! They're all the same, these policemen – and that Ella Daw! For once I'll be glad when that scruffy friend of yours gets some leave. She needs a man to sort her out does that one!'

CHAPTER SIX

Rachel's hopes that Jack Daw would knock some sense into his wife were dashed when next he came home on leave. She was incensed to find that he actually supported his wife's activities! It was so embarrassing, she declared, being associated with them. But if she believed that things could get no worse she found out otherwise when Jack decided not to sign on again with the Colours. His first act – harmless enough – was to find employment at the Carriage Works. However, freed from the restrictions imposed on him by the Army, his second move was to join the Labour Party, and just to compound the sin he became deeply involved in the struggle to bring trade unionism to the railways. Russ, now a thriving businessman, had also become interested in politics during the last few years, though his allegiance lay with the Tories. He had been a shade surprised that his friend had not followed him into commerce and was rather cynical of Jack's support for the WSPU – he had always regarded Jack as something of a misogynist – but at least his friend was beginning to think for himself and this pleased Russ. So even if, politically speaking, they were at opposing corners, they remained on equable terms. After all, it was the aim of both men to improve the community. Despite Russ' commercial attachments he had always seen himself as having a social conscience. He was well aware of the terrible slums in this otherwise beautiful city and felt that something should be done about them – and he was doing his bit, wasn't he, by employing Biddy and thereby taking her out of her atrocious living conditions.

To Russ it seemed that all successive councils wanted to do was to pretend that these places didn't exist and use the city's budget for banquets and festivals. But how could anyone fail to be aware of their existence? They had been slums for Russ' lifetime – and probably long before. 'It's high time these blokes on the Council did something,' it became his habit to complain to Rachel, virtually every time he picked up the *Evening Press*. 'Knock the whole lot down and start again. All they ever seem to do at these meetings is discuss the evils of Sunday trading. If I was on the Council I'd have that sorted out straightaway. If folk want to trade on a Sunday good luck to 'em, I say. We could do a nice bit o' business ourselves . . . mindst, I have to admit I enjoy my day's rest with you and the sprites – but, Lord, these council gadgers . . .' A shake of the head at the paper. 'I could do better myself.'

'Why don't you, love?' Rachel decided to enquire this evening whilst busy on one of her creations.

'Eh?' he turned the page absently.

'Don't say eh in front of the children, Russ.' Their expanding brood was passing an hour with the grown-ups before bedtime. 'The word is pardon – I said, why don't you go on the Council?' At his look of astonishment she asked, 'Well what's wrong with that? You've been a member of the Conservative Party for quite a time now, all you need is someone to propose and second you.' Russ never pushed himself forward enough in her view.

'And a good few to vote for me.'

'That's not impossible. You're a very clever man – look how well the business is doing.'

'Ah well, there's the thing – would I have time?'

'I swear I don't know, Russ! You moan about the Council not getting things done but when I suggest the obvious you go all coy – make your mind up. You could do something about getting that horrible fence out there replaced.' She grew more ambitious. 'And perhaps get some trees planted all along that Knavesmire road. It'd make a lovely avenue.'

'You know . . . you've got me interested, Rache.' He put down the newspaper and crossed his legs. 'I have been to enough meetings to know what it's all about. I mean, they're only ordinary fellows like me, there's no reason why I shouldn't have a bash.'

'None whatsoever, and I wouldn't say they were like you at all, Russ. You've a great deal more up top than some of them.'

'He-hey! D'you think your dad's got more up top?' Assuming a paternal grin Russ grabbed his son and swung him onto his knee. Robert, though seven, had not outgrown the occasional cuddle and returned his father's gesture, answering the question with a firm nod. The unease of their first encounter had long since vanished. He and Russ were very close and Bertie, being the only son, felt himself in a special position. His blond locks were gone now. His hair was cut into a pudding basin style by Rachel and had deepened to her own honey colour. He had her brown eyes too which sparkled with hero worship whenever his father asked his opinion.

'So our Bertie thinks I could teach these Council chaps how to run a city, does he?'

Bertie's smile widened. 'You'd beat them all.'

'Oh, fighting talk! Like to see your father Lord Mayor, would you?'

'I'd rather have you be a general,' admitted Bertie. 'But Lord Mayor would be quite good too, I suppose.'

Russ laughed. That was his own fault for telling the boy so many tales about his days in the Army. He was duly asked for another. 'Oh, I'm sure your sisters are bored with hearing about soldiers,' he answered, taking Rowena on his other knee while the younger ones clustered about him. 'Aren't you, me bonny lasses?'

'I don't mind – whatever the others choose.' Rowena was a placid girl, always eager to please. She, too, had her mother's colouring, though to much softer effect. There was an overall gentleness about Rowena.

'Summat wi' plenty o' blood in it,' demanded Rosalyn eagerly. This child was fair-haired – not quite blonde, not quite brown – with the mischievous blue eyes of her father and a wide mouth that was capable of a formidable sulk. She was also a tomboy. Like her sisters, her locks had been bound into rags for the night, but instead of ringlets hers would emerge like sparse bunches of catkins.

69

'Rosalyn, that is not the sort of thing to go to bed on,' scolded her mother. 'And do speak properly!'

'And guns goin' bang!' put in three year old Becky as if her mother had not spoken. The red hair must have been a throwback to some distant ancestor. Her eyes were brown, but had little green flecks in them.

'Right, well there I was all on me own and the bullets were whizzing like wasps . . .'

'War, war, war!' complained Rachel. 'Whatever happened to the nice bedtime stories we used to hear as children?'

'You're quite right, Mother.' Russ nodded contritely. 'Away now, stop dancing on my feet, Spindleshanks,' this to Lyn. 'Once upon a time, there was this very peculiar woman. Oh, she was quite ordinary enough while she was sitting there stitching her hats, but should anybody say a wrong word and – glump! – she'd leap up and bite their heads right off . . .'

Bertie saw the sly glance from his father to his mother, the twinkle in Russ' eye. He giggled, looking at his sisters to see if they had picked up the joke – they hadn't of course. This pleased him, as though only he were privileged to share his father's humour. He laid a fond head on Russ' chest, feeling a rush of warmth for the bond they shared. If there was any scrap of insecurity in young Robert's life it occurred but once a year when the new baby was coming. From the moment the nurse knocked on the door Bertie would begin to worry: would the bag which she carried hold another girl or was he going to have a rival? His father seemed to guess the torment he went through, for Bertie was always the first to be informed of the new child's sex. When Father came down from visiting Mother he would say, 'Well, Bertie, it looks like there's still just the two of us poor fellows to be nagged by all these women', and for another year Bertie could feel safe. Thinking of this, he snuggled even closer to his father whilst Russ adopted his nightly role of raconteur until the maid entered twenty minutes later to take them up to bed.

At the children's departure, Russ said casually, 'I think

I'll just pop and see how Jack's foot is. I promised I'd look in tonight.' Daw had miscalculated when handling a railway sleeper and had broken two toes, earning himself a spell off work.

'Tut! I really don't know why you have to keep being so pally with him – and don't think you're sneaking off to the pub either.'

'Jack isn't likely to be able to afford beer is he? Him being off work.'

'Good thing too,' nodded Rachel as he left.

Russ found Jack with his foot on a stool, a rifle on his lap and cleaning implements in his hand. Even having left the Regulars he still enjoyed his periodical training with the Territorials. A glass of beer stood at his right elbow. Ella, also enjoying a drink, nodded and gave her half-smile as Russ came straight in – one didn't have to knock at the Daws' house. 'I don't know why you haven't thought of getting a job in the police force, Russ.'

He responded with a smiling frown. 'My feet are too dainty.'

'I mean as a bloodhound. Marvellous sense of smell you've got.'

'You've stumped me, Ella.' Russ collapsed into a chair, eyeing the untidy parlour. Rachel very rarely came here: to a woman so fastidious it was torture to look upon such a mess and be unable to rectify it.

Ella raised her glass. 'I was just saying to our Jack, the minute I pour this out you'd get a whiff through them walls.'

Russ understood now. 'Ah, you were right then, weren't you?' He looked hopefully at the beer. 'And you've made a liar of me. I told Rachel you wouldn't be able to afford ale, him being off work.'

'He can't,' supplied Ella, rising. 'A pal brought it round. I'm just helping him get rid of it. He can't bear to see the stuff lying about the house, you know.' Russ said that was how he felt. 'I know it'll be sheer hell, but could you find it in yourself to help us dispose of it? I wouldn't ask but . . .'

'Eh, I don't know if I could, Ella,' came the doubtful

reply. 'It might make me sick.' Russ grinned as she passed him the glass of dark ale. 'Still, I'll try and force it down for a friend.'

The three sat and chatted for a while, the main contributors being Russ and Ella; Jack, as usual, interspersed the dialogue with his rare but relevant comments whilst polishing the rifle. Then Russ happened to mention his thoughts about standing for the Council. 'I sit and read these reports and wonder what the hell they do at those meetings apart from sup tea and have a good binge at the ratepayers' expense. They do nowt for people like Biddy, you know.'

'And you would?' questioned Daw, motioning for his wife to pass his cigarettes.

'That'd be the first thing on my list – get rid of all the slums. Bloody eyesores – oh, 'scuse my language, Ella.' He often forgot he was in female company with Ella; she had a slightly masculine edge to her.

Jack lit up and tossed the packet at Russ who withdrew a cigarette. 'Are you sure you'll be doing it for the poor folk's benefit?'

'Oh, not just for theirs of course,' granted Russ on an exhalation of smoke. 'Everybody'd benefit.'

'Specially you,' observed Jack with an imperceptible wink at his wife. At Russ' demand for an explanation he went on, 'You never could stand mess, could you, Russ? You're not so much concerned with the inmates of those slums as with the slums themselves – they offend your sense of neatness.'

'Well that's blinking good isn't it! Here I am trying to do something for people less well off than me and you pour scorn on it. I thought your lot were meant to be all for that kind of thing.'

'I'm all for helping folk worse off,' replied Jack evenly. 'And I'll agree that razing those places would go a long way towards that aim, but have you considered the people who're renting them? Where will they go?' Catching Russ' look of unpreparedness he said, 'No, all you're bothered about is getting rid of the houses and be jiggered the folk that live in 'em.'

'Aw well, if you're going to be clever about it . . .' Russ started to rise, putting aside his glass. 'I thought you'd be interested in my idea but I can see you're not. Time I was off, Rachel will wonder where I've got to. Thanks for the beer.' On this short note he left.

It was not until he found his friend alongside him at a Council meeting that he realized how his idea *had* interested Daw. After a period of strenuous involvement both men stood for election and both found popularity with the voters – Daw because of his sincere connections with the trade unions and his proposals to obtain better treatment for the working man in his own city; Russ because of his charming smile, approachable manner and his plausible speeches.

1910 was one of those years that seemed crammed with unusual events from start to finish. Between the two General Elections, one in January the other in December – each seeing the return of a Liberal Government, much to the disgust of both Jack and Russ – there was a great deal of change in the two men's attitudes to each other. They were still on speaking terms, but no longer did Russ fraternize so much with Daw, finding it terribly hard to separate the man in the Guildhall from the one in *The Trafalgar Bay*. To Russ the insults which Jack flung at him across Council chambers were personal. He could not, as others did, turn off when the meeting ended and consequently saw little of his neighbour on a social basis. This suited Rachel nicely; it was what she had been wanting for years. Since Russ had become a councillor her reluctance to mix with his socially inferior friends had become more staunch. That Daw was a councillor too did not seem to matter – he was a Labour councillor, not the same breed at all.

Unfortunately, there were times when she could not help but socialize. Tonight, both parties found themselves in their respective yards at the same time and were forced to communicate.

'Evening, Rachel.' Ella, cradling a dog wrapped in a shawl, nodded to the other woman and her husband over the wall. 'Come to see the Comet?'

Rachel lifted her eyes to the black sky, searching. It was a

73

chilly night and there were many stars. 'We're allowing the children to stay up a bit later than usual, they may not see it again in their lifetime.'

Ella clutched her terrier to her bosom and stood on the balls of her feet to peer over the wall. Four pairs of eyewhites shone up at her through the darkness – Bertie's were fixed to a telescope which was scanning the heavens. 'A fair few now, haven't you?'

Rachel, taking this to be a compliment, preened and replied, 'Yes, my Russ only has to look at me and I fall.'

Ella's glance hovered on the swelling that protruded from her neighbour's open coat. 'He's been looking at you again, judging by the cut of your dress.' She stroked the dog's ears. 'Haven't you ever considered birth control?'

Rachel could scarcely believe what she had heard. In front of the children too! 'I most certainly have not! Children are God's blessing on a marriage. Naturally you couldn't be expected to understand that.' She was about to move away when a shout from her son brought her eyes skywards. 'Where?' She squinted. 'Oh . . . are you sure that's it, Robert?'

'Of course! I've checked my compass.'

'But it isn't moving.' Rachel had expected the Comet to be hurtling across the sky.

'It's still a rare sight though, isn't it?' contributed Russ. 'Just think it won't be here for another seventy-odd years.'

'By then you should've got around to carrying out all these grand plans you've been regaling us with, Filbert.' Jack used the nickname as a form of retaliation – he couldn't stand it when Rachel thrust Ella's childlessness in her face. One of these days he would tell her just how fruitful her husband's loins really were.

'If my Russ says he's going to do a thing then he'll do it!' volleyed Rachel. 'He got that ugly fence at the front taken down, didn't he? And the nice low one put up.'

Daw pretended to be thoughtful. 'Aye, I'll admit that us being able to have a proper view over Knavesmire is a great benefit to t'community . . . pity we had to fork out half the cost ourselves.'

'We'd have had to pay more if you'd had your way!'

'I don't agree with spending Council money on tarting up our own property. T'other one was perfectly adequate.'

'Only to someone with no taste,' replied Rachel, then winced and put a hand to her side. 'Oh, come on I'll have to go in, this stitch is getting worse. I hope it's nothing to do with the baby.'

'It'd be a good thing if it was,' muttered Ella thoughtlessly within hearing range. 'She's had far too many.'

'Did you hear what that jealous cat said?' Rachel demanded of her husband when they were inside. 'She'd actually be happy if something happened to our baby.' She clutched him. 'Oh Russ, I don't feel at all well. I'm off to bed.'

In the morning it became clear that this was no mere stitch and the doctor was sent for. ''Tis that there Comet what's done it, ma'am,' swore Biddy, tending her stricken mistress. 'Ye must've breathed in all that poisonous gas. I knew we shouldn't ought to have watched it. 'Tis a bad influence on all the world it's brought with it, mark my words. This is just the start.' Russ told her not to talk so daft, she was upsetting the mistress. 'Oh 'tis right I am, sir! You watch, there'll be worse things happen than the mistress losing the baby.'

'Ssh!' He waved her to silence. 'She is not going to lose the baby and I don't want to hear you say it again.'

But Rachel did lose the baby, and to add even more truth to Biddy's prediction within days the King was dead. Strangely, this was to aid Rachel's convalescence. The Monarch's demise brought a stream of orders for black hats and drapery of a similar hue. Russ, having had the foresight to visit the wholesaler's within an hour of hearing about the King's passing, was now well-stocked and able to deal with the heavy demand. With her husband supplying all her requirements and the young assistant shuttling between shop and home, Rachel was soon sitting up working contentedly away and almost forgetting her own sad loss. Then of course came the Coronation and another spate of orders – this time for brighter coloured headwear. So, if

Halley's comet had brought disaster, with 1911 seeing railstrikes and disputes from sailors, firemen, miners and dockers, it had in turn granted great prosperity to the Hazelwoods, the high point of which appeared in the street in 1912.

Biddy was cursing the children's table manners and scrubbing for all she was worth at an area of once-white cloth with a bar of naphtha soap. 'Ah Jesus, will ye look at that!' she instructed the culprit. ''Twon't shift at all. If the mistress sees it she'll turn me into a stain on me own clothes. Bertie, you're a devil for makin' work for folk – an' put that thing away else I'll chop it off!' The dirty little devil was always showing himself to his sisters. 'Oh, what the hell is that row?' A persistent honking could be heard from the street. Biddy wiped her hands and, children in tow, plodded from the kitchen to open the front door. The towel she held flew up to cover her mouth. 'Holy Saints deliver us!'

'I thought you'd all gone deaf in there!' shouted the driver of the vehicle parked outside. 'Where's your mistress, Bid?' Not waiting for an answer, Russ flung open the door and climbed out.

'Is it ours?' asked an amazed Bertie, eyes shining.

'Well you don't think anybody'd let your father loose in a car as posh as this if it wasn't, do you?'

Bertie leapt onto the runningboard and leaned over the spare wheel to pump at the horn before asking what sort of car it was. 'A Fiat,' said his father. 'Hop in and try it for size.' Bertie spent a moment circling the green vehicle with its brass trimmings, then bounced into the driving seat and gripped the large steering wheel, taking lungfuls of the scent of new leather. Russ broke off from telling his son what all the instruments were for to herald his wife. 'Ah, here's the lady herself!'

Rachel, as taken aback as the others, had appeared behind Biddy whom she now elbowed out of the way in order to approach the motor car. 'A car?' she managed to breathe.

'Aye well somebody pinched me bikeclips so I had to . . .'

'Russ what have you *done*?' She strode forth, encompassing the car with agitated eyes. 'Where did you get the money?'

'Soft article! It's proceeds from the business. I reckoned it was time an important man like me got his due.' This was not the only thought Russ had had recently. Whilst undertaking routine accounts his eyes had settled upon the fictitious Mr Cranley. For nine years he had been paying out good money to someone who, for all he knew, might well be dead – after all, he had heard nothing from South Africa. That money could be better spent on his own family, to pay for a car perhaps. Why should he have to fork out for the rest of his life for someone who meant nothing to him? Surely after this many years he had done sufficient penance? Hadn't he been fairer than a lot of men in his position? Considering this to be so, he had decided that he would continue the payments up until the end of the year, just to round off the account, so to speak, and then all dealings with Mr Cranley would cease.

After a further period of twittering inspection Rachel gave a cursory nod of her head, announcing, 'You're quite right!' making him grin at his children. She took a step back to examine the shiny green vehicle as a whole, then clapped gleeful hands to her white-muslined bosom. 'Oh, won't the Daws' noses be put out of joint! Ella will be greener than that car.'

'Eh, now I don't want you to go taunting them with this,' Russ warned. 'They'll be scratching my bodywork. Anyway, am I going to hear what you think to this here car? Is it befitting of an esteemed Councillor?' Both he and Jack had been re-elected for a further term.

'I think it was very sneaky of you to take money from the business without consulting me,' she scolded, but without conviction for she smiled almost instantly. 'But as it's such a splendid car I'll let you off this time – only don't think I'm condoning such extravagance. How much will it take to run per week?' When he told her she was horrified. 'That would keep us in jam for a month!'

'Aye well, I'm sorry I can't make it run on jam – forget about the cost for once, lass! Come for a ride with us.'

She didn't take much coaxing, squeezing into the back beside the girls. 'Away, Biddy, you an' all!' shouted Russ to the forlorn-looking specimen on the doorstep. 'We might as well ruin t'springs completely.'

Biddy seized the nearest girl and swung into her place, child on lap. The car was only intended to seat four but somehow they all managed to pack themselves in. Rachel begged her husband to fold down the canvas hood so that everyone could see them. With a laugh he unclipped the leather straps that secured the hood and wound it back. After a few sharp twists of the starting handle the car began to chug. To cries of delight Russ took his seat at the wheel and performed a three point turn. Biddy and some of the girls screamed as it appeared to be rolling back into the iron railings but Russ just laughed and sent it flying down the street. Lyn sounded the horn incessantly until her brother knocked her hand away to take over. The odd net curtain was hoisted and neighbours' heads revolved to watch its passage. Rachel waved to all delightedly. But for her, the best moment came when the car turned the corner and who should she see coming up Queen Victoria Street but Jack Daw and Wife.

'Looks like they've been campaigning again,' murmured Russ. On drawing nearer they could read the placards carried by the couple: What Price Your Coal? and Support The Miners.

'Give them a honk, Robert,' cued the boy's mother as the car neared the couple. 'Oh go on, let him!' she urged Russ at his look of smiling reproach.

Bertie hooted long and loud as the car sailed past the astonished pair. Rachel craned her smiling face back over the folded hood, instructing the children, 'Wave, wave!' and felt the glee bubble up inside her at the look on her neighbours' faces.

CHAPTER SEVEN

The fact that Russ was in possession of the automobile did nothing for his lapsed friendship with the Daws. Over the next year the ferocity of his neighbours' antics burgeoned. Jack's endeavours saw the formation of the NUR, whilst Ella's earned her a term of imprisonment. This followed a demonstration in London shortly after the terrible Derby Day occurrence when Emily Davidson had thrown herself under the King's horse.

'Of course,' opined Rachel sapiently, 'it's all because she's got no children – too much time on her hands,' she elaborated for a confused Russ as they breakfasted this crisp October morning. 'And I mean, that husband of hers actually encourages her! You'd think he'd be embarrassed at having a jailbird for a wife but no he laps it up. It's a wonder he hasn't been thrown off the council after this last episode.' Russ said that no one on the council was aware of Ella's imprisonment as far as he knew. 'Well, at least it hasn't got into the local papers. I'd never live it down, having folk know I've got a criminal for a neighbour. It'd bring the price of our house down, you know.'

'Eh, I hope she behaves herself in the future,' sighed Russ, turning a page of his newspaper. 'I've read they do all sorts of unpleasant things to these lasses in prison, shoving tubes down their throats and whatnot when they go on hunger strike. She didn't look too well to me when she came home.'

'It's no more than she deserves, the silly woman.'

He laid the paper to one side. 'Eh, that's a bit catty, isn't it, Rache? I mean, she's doing it for you.'

'Doing it for me?' She was astounded enough to stop spreading marmalade on her toast. 'And did I ask her to?

Did the sane and rational women of this country ask that stupid hussy to throw herself under the King's horse? That poor animal – and they have the audacity to claim that they're doing it in the name of the women of Britain! Well, if this is an example of the sort of people who'd be in power if women had the vote then I for one would sooner be without it. The system has worked perfectly well up to now. In any case, Russ, politics isn't a fitting occupation for a woman. They're better suited doing what they were meant for, which is having children and keeping house for their husbands. And that of course is where the trouble stems from; most of them are unmarried or childless – no man would have them . . . Anyway,' she brought her incisors together in a delicate crunch, and brushed the crumbs from her fingers, 'let's not pursue this dreary topic when we've more important things to discuss.' An intoxicated grin. 'Only a couple of weeks now, Russ!'

'Eh, I wish you wouldn't go on as if it's all in the bag,' he chivvied. 'There's no guarantee.' The election for the post of Lord Mayor was looming. As in other years the vote would merely be a formality; the candidate had already been selected. This year's Lord Mayor Elect, Councillor James Ridsdale, had confided to Russ that the latter was the prime runner for Sheriff. Alderman Anthony Carr was to move that Russ be appointed and the motion would be seconded by Councillor John Spring. Rachel had gone wild at the news and to mark her husband's promotion had taken to employing the best dining table in the front parlour for her meals and generally acting the lady even more than was usual. 'It's always the same, you convince yourself that there's no hurdle then when one comes up – bang! down you go for days.'

She tossed her long hair over her shoulder. 'Tsk! What could happen?'

'Anything . . . Carr could change his mind about putting me forward, the Council might not carry the motion, I could have an accident or something . . .'

She exclaimed at his pessimism. 'I could kill you!'

'There you are, you see – anything could happen.' Russ

grinned and reached over to grip her arm. 'I just don't want to see you disappointed, that's all, lass.'

'I won't be, because you're going to be the next Sheriff of York and that is that!'

For reply he offered a smiling shake of his head and shortly went off to work, while Rachel summoned Biddy to clear the pots. She herself brushed and pinned up her hair then set about forming the hat of the next Lady Mayoress whose custom she had just managed to acquire. Though she had many other councillor's wives on her books this was the most important of them . . . until next year's elections of course. She worked until ten when she took an interval for a cup of tea. At the same time Ella Daw paid an unexpected visit. 'Biddy, fetch another cup for Mrs Daw,' she instructed as her neighbour limped to a chair, and to the latter, 'Ella, what have you been doing with your foot?'

'I haven't been doing anything,' grumbled Ella. 'Some silly little devil left a toy on the pavement and I went flying over it. I've wrenched my ankle – just on my way to work an' all. I could hardly put my foot to the ground, it was agony. So . . . I had to hop back home. I'd best have it seen to, it might be broken – look how it's swelled up.' Rachel expressed concern at the ballooning ankle. 'That's why I came round; I thought Russ might run me down to the hospital when he comes in for his dinner. I wouldn't ask but I couldn't even make it to the tram stop. It's taken me all my time to hobble round here – ooh, you're an angel, Biddy!' She accepted the cup from the maid.

'I'm sure Russ won't mind,' said Rachel, then thought to add a little taunt for her neighbour's previous disdain of the car. 'You see – these fancy automobiles can come in useful after all.'

Ella took the rebuke with dignity. 'Aye, I have to admit you're right, Rache. We'll probably have to have one ourselves shortly.'

'They're very expensive, you know, Ella.' Then Rachel's ears pricked in alarm and she rested the cup and saucer on her brown tweed skirt. 'What would you be needing one for?' She knew as soon as she said it, knew by Ella's casual air, that a bomb was about to explode.

'Well, if our Jack's in line for Mayor he can hardly perform all his civic duties on a bike – eh, this blasted foot!' She screwed up her face in discomfort.

'Lord Mayor?' responded the other loudly, almost knocking the cup over in her lap.

'Didn't you know?' Ella eased her ankle into a more comfortable position, still grimacing. 'I thought Russ would've mentioned it.'

'But James Ridsdale is going to be Mayor!'

'Is he now? I think there's a little matter of an election to be disposed of first.'

Slight relief – it wasn't definite then. Rachel's voice was a little calmer. 'But, Ella, I think you'll agree that Mr Ridsdale is the obvious candidate.'

'I wouldn't agree at all. I'd say it's about time this city had a Labour Lord Mayor.'

Good Grief! That would mean Ella would be Lady Mayoress – no, don't think about it! Rachel urged herself. 'But how would you cope?'

'There'd still be one of us working. I get plenty of overtime. I think it's worth the sacrifice for one year . . . oh, I see! You weren't referring to the job not carrying a salary – you mean, how will two peasants like us fit into all that splendour.'

'I didn't mean that at all.' Rachel buried her acute dismay in her teacup.

'Oh well, you needn't worry yourself on that score, Rachel. I doubt we'll be spending much time in the Mansion House. Jack doesn't believe in that sort of thing. He won't be wearing any fancy necklace neither.' The cup was lowered, Rachel's chocolate-drop eyes questioning. 'Being the Lord Mayor isn't just an opportunity to dress up and give parties, you know, Rachel. It's chance to put this city's priorities in order, which in Jack's case would be the citizens – the working citizens.'

Rachel could not countenance such a viewpoint. To act so disparagingly in the face of so noble an office verged on infamy. She was unable to speak for fear of losing her temper.

'I know what you're worried about,' Ella's voice roused her. 'Jack told me that Russ was banking on being made Sheriff. Well, don't concern yourself any more, love. I'm sure Jack wouldn't disappoint an old friend, he thinks very highly of Russ' administrative capabilities however he might scorn his politics. I'm certain his Sheriff's job'll be safe.' She shuffled her buttocks onto the edge of the chair.

With a lame mutter of thanks, Rachel put her empty cup aside and rose to take Ella's. 'I'll call Biddy to see you home.'

Ella hoisted herself and stood with her weight on one leg whilst Biddy was summoned. 'So shall I come round later then?'

'Pardon?' came Rachel's vague answer. 'Oh . . . no, I'll send Russ the minute he gets in.'

Ella said to let him have his dinner first and draped an arm round the solicitous Biddy. 'Eh, I'll look good like this at the investiture won't I? Cockling along Coney Street with a big plaster on me foot and a Biddy under me arm!'

Rachel managed a weak response. 'I'm sure it'll be sorted out by then.' It will if I get my way, she thought darkly.

There was no more work to be done that morning. Nothing would go right. She kept pricking her finger or sewing the wrong decoration on the wrong hat. Until Russ came home, Biddy was the main recipient of her wrath. Even so, when he finally did arrive the frustration was in no way dissipated.

'I know! I know what you're going to tell me!' He raised his hands to ward off the outburst before it became fully fledged. The set of his features showed that he too was aware that the Mayoral position was to be contested.

'If you knew you might have spared me the humiliation!'

'I didn't know until an hour ago,' was his helpless protest. 'Till Ridsdale came into the shop and brandished the press report under my nose.' He waved a morning paper at his wife, a different publication to the one they took. 'He's mad as hell that it's been leaked.'

'*He's* mad!'

'Aye . . . it must've been upsetting for you – but there you are, this is just what I was warning you about. I'm disappointed as well, you know, I was looking forward to being Sheriff.'

'Oh, there's no call for you to disappoint yourself on that score!' she dealt cuttingly. 'Ella has very kindly said that her husband never forgets his old pals, the job's yours if you want it.'

His expression turned to one of interest. 'She said that, did she?'

Rachel erupted. 'And you'd take it, wouldn't you? You'd be quite happy to play second fiddle to that wastrel just as you've always done. For Heaven's sake assert yourself for once and do something!'

'What d'you expect me to do? I've no power to say who'll be elected apart for my personal vote.'

'Well, I'm going to do something!' She banged her chest.

'What?'

An indecisive hiatus. 'I don't know yet . . . but I'm not going to stand by and let him snatch this one from under your nose!'

'But you didn't seem to mind the idea of me being second-in-command to Ridsdale,' he pointed out.

'That's entirely different! Ridsdale is a gentleman. Ridsdale hasn't done what your so-called friend has done to you over the years, aping your every move – anyway, the main item isn't about whether you'll be Jack Daw's Sheriff, it's that Jack Daw shouldn't be Lord Mayor at all!' And Rachel swore to herself that nor was he going to be. To her, Russell's post of Sheriff was to have been the pinnacle of all she had ever worked for: recognition of her true status. She wasn't going to be robbed. She hadn't decided how, but by heavens he wasn't going to filch her husband's glory this time. 'Oh, by the way, she wants you to take her down to the hospital in the car. She thinks she's broken her ankle – a pity it's not her neck!'

'Hello, Mrs Danby, do come in!' Rachel greeted her client with a charming smile and directed her to the front parlour. 'I shan't keep you a second, I must just pack this hat away before it comes to any harm. It's for the new Lady Mayoress to wear at her husband's inauguration.'

Mrs Danby took the offered seat. 'Mrs Daw is a neighbour of yours, I believe?'

Rachel laughed gaily. 'Oh, I wasn't referring to Ella! Her tastes are far less stylish than this, poor dear.' She put the hat in a box and pressed the lid on. 'In any case, I don't think for one moment the Council will be unwise enough to invest her husband as Mayor.'

'And why's that?' Mrs Danby's genuine interest stemmed from the fact that her husband was a councillor too.

Rachel's tapered fingers flew to her lips. 'Oh dear, I didn't mean to say that, it just slipped out . . . I wouldn't want to prejudice his chances, him being an acquaintance of my husband. But well, for me he's much too radical, too much for what he calls "the working man" – as if someone who doesn't hold a shovel doesn't know what work is.'

'Yes, I must admit I find that most galling as well,' agreed the other. 'My husband's worked tremendously hard in his post as Treasurer but people never seem to appreciate how difficult a job it is.'

'Oh, some do, Mrs Danby,' corrected Rachel. 'Russ speaks very highly of Mr Danby. In fact he was singing his praises only the other night. It made me quite cross to tell the truth.' Mrs Danby frowned. 'Oh, not that I don't agree with him,' added Rachel swiftly, 'but I do think we women are never given the credit for our men's success, don't you? I'm very much aware how loyally you have supported Mr Danby.'

'It's most kind of you to say so,' responded the other with a gracious inclination of her head.

'Merely your due – no, I'm only sad that there won't be many such compliments for poor Ella should her husband be elected.'

'You think she's unsuitable for Lady Mayoress?' Mrs Danby removed her gloves a finger at a time.

'Oh, I didn't intend to imply that at all! Ella is a great friend of mine . . . no, it's just that . . . well one can't help comparing her to the present holder of the office – such a placid creature. Ella is much more outgoing, a quality some people – not me, naturally – but some people find overpowering in a woman. But I hope they won't judge her too harshly, she's got some fine qualities – a most courageous woman, Mrs Danby. There's not many would spend weeks in prison in support of one's beliefs.'

'Prison?' breathed Mrs Danby.

A grave nod from Rachel. 'A tragedy that no one in her home town is aware of her pioneering. Our local press didn't seem to regard it as important enough to warrant news space – and of course, Ella is much too modest to tell anyone of her bravery. She was arrested in the Capital whilst marching in support of the Suffragettes – had a really dreadful time of it in prison.'

Mrs Danby was thoughtful. 'And what was Mr Daw's attitude to this?'

Rachel drove home her spear. 'Oh, he was far too busy with his "working men" to help his wife out of her predicament. It's not hard to see why she's fighting for women's rights . . . disgraceful, the way he neglects her. I'm so lucky in that area, you won't catch me having to carry banners, I'm perfectly happy with my husband and children – but that's all by the by, I'm supposed to be attending to your millinery requirements, not gossiping.' She feigned involvement with her measuring tape and Mrs Danby's head.

'I wouldn't say that defending your friend is gossiping, Mrs Hazelwood. It seems most annoying to me, a man like that putting himself forward as a spokesman for the downtrodden when his own wife comes into that category.'

'How I agree – though of course what I've said must go no further than these walls, Mrs Danby. I wouldn't have Ella's hurt made public for all the world.'

The following day, Mrs Danby held an at-home gathering for her female circle. Rachel was invited, but refused apologetically with the excuse that she had too many orders to complete. Whilst coffee was being served Mrs Danby happened to mention the matter of the Labour candidate who was in opposition against Mr Ridsdale, repeating all that Rachel had told her the day before. 'But of course it was relayed to me in confidence and must go no further than these four walls.'

Relying on this transmission, Rachel sat stitching her creations and smiling to herself. It would have been unwise to attend the gathering – if she had raised the subject it would have looked to those who knew about the situation as sour grapes. But with luck Mrs Danby would have done the job for her. Soon they would all be telling their husbands 'in confidence of course' what a brute Labour's man was and influencing the final vote.

Surely someone had tampered with the clock. Rachel was positive it had said that time several minutes ago. She leapt up, went to the window, peered anxiously through the lace curtain then strode back to her seat. It was the day of the Quarterly General Meeting of the Council – election day. She was alone in the front parlour, waiting for her husband to come home with the news. The younger children – not yet at school – had driven her insane in the kitchen, but in here the silence was just as maddening. Her hands were poised on a section of felt that she was meant to be turning into a hat, but her thoughts drifted elsewhere.

A terrible picture kept jarring her mind – that of the Mansion House under Ella Daw's tenancy. There would be all manner of roughs cluttering up its gracious rooms – and beerbottles on the priceless tables! This appalling vision caused her eyes to land on her own table. A finger of sunlight banded the highly-polished mahogany, luring dust particles. The felt in her hand became magnetized towards the surface, launching her from the chair yet again. But however vigorously her elbow moved the dust simply resettled on the strip of sunlit wood. Aggravated, she tugged at the curtain to barricade the offensive glare – then realizing that she had used Mrs Danby's hat as a duster gave the felt a hearty brush and forced herself to get on with her work.

After what seemed an interminable period of stitching she finally heard the sound of the car as it turned the corner.

Throwing down the hat, she dashed from the house to meet him . . . but was arrested by the expression Russ dealt her as the car stopped; his face was grim. She clasped her hands to her bosom in dismay as he emerged from the driver's seat. 'We lost,' she lamented.

'Lost? Lost what – d'you know some little . . . tearaway put broken glass right across the road down there! If I hadn't seen it glinting I'd have gone right over it and cut these tyres to bits.' He stooped to check the rubber.

'Blow the tyres!' she volcanoed.

'Aye, I dare say they would've done.'

'Russell, how can you accept this so calmly?' She hugged her brown cardigan about her to ward off the November chill.

'I'm not calm, I'm blazing mad. Anyway, I know who the culprit is. I shall give him a clipped ear'ole the next time I see him.' He used his cuff to polish an imaginary smear on the wing.

'Russell!' She was about to flounce back into the house when he grabbed her by the waist and swung her around. 'Now is that any way for the Sheriff's Lady to behave?'

She stopped ranting, but was cautious. 'Whose Sheriff are you?'

'Well, that's a nice response to my good news, I don't think! A-a-ah!' He laughed and hoisted her off her feet again. 'Our new Lord Mayor is . . . J-J-James Ridsdale!'

She squealed and locked her arms round his neck, whence he swung her round, equally thrilled. 'Oh, come on we'll have to go tell the children, Biddy – anybody!' Her face glowed.

'Hadn't we better keep it secret until Bertie gets home?' quizzed Russ. 'I'd like him to know first.' His son was going to be so proud! Though bursting to impart the tidings, Rachel agreed. 'Oh, he'll be absolutely chuffed to death!'

There was no such greeting for Jack Daw, only Ella's condolences. 'Never mind, lad, we'll have our Labour Lord Mayor yet – maybe next year.'

The glasses that had been intended for festivity were now

employed in consolation. After his announcement Jack had simply picked up a newspaper which he was now perusing with that familiar unreadable expression on his face. 'Aye, maybe . . .' He knew that the leaked report over his bid for the Mayorship had come from a member of his own party. It had been done with the best of intentions; the person responsible had assumed that the publicity could only help to fight the Conservatives' claim to the post. He had been wrong. In fact, the press had been the main contributors to his downfall, their leader columns damning his involvement with the unions and also raising the issue of his wife's imprisonment.

Ella went over to perch on the arm of his chair, holding a glass of beer for him. It had turned out that her ankle was not broken, but badly sprained. 'D'you think it was because of me that you didn't get it?'

He took the beer from her and gave a rare smile. 'No – I rather thought my face wouldn't fit. The Council got a letter from the York Traders' Association objecting to my election because I'm too biased towards the working class.'

She hugged him. 'Aw, poor lad. I felt sure you'd win. So sure that I couldn't help doing a bit of swanking in front of Rachel. I suppose we'll suffer for that as well.' She frowned thoughtfully. 'Or maybe we already have.' An enquiring eye rolled up at her. 'Could Russ have had anything to do with you not getting it?'

'He wouldn't do that to a mate.'

'You wouldn't, but I'm not so sure that Russ would put friendship before ambition – and I'm damned certain Rachel wouldn't.'

'And what could our resident aristocrat do to influence the vote?'

'I don't know . . . but I am aware she wasn't over fond of the thought of you being Mayor. If she could've done something to stop it then I know she would.'

'Aye, well, don't be turning supposition into reprisal. It's possible that Ridsdale would've won despite the smears from the press.'

'Maybe. But if I thought . . .' For the moment her face

darkened with intent. Then it resumed its natural mien. 'Well, it looks like we'd better go round and offer congratulations.'

'You can go on your own,' said Jack. 'I'm buggered if I'm off there to have her gloat. I'll get round to shaking Russ' hand some time.' When the result of the vote had been announced he and the rest of the Labour councillors had walked out in protest. With a regretful look at each other, he and Ella took solace in their drinks.

Excitement had kept Rachel awake for most of the night. Even now the thrill was still active. Her eyes gleamed as she buttered her breakfast toast and jabbered on about robes and ceremonies and luncheon at the Mansion House – and what would she ever find to wear?

'I thought it was kind of Ella to come round and congratulate us, didn't you?' contributed Russ during a pause in her babble. Jack hadn't accompanied her, but he had shaken hands over the yard wall when their journeys to the privy had coincided.

'I don't know about kind – she looked as though she was going to choke with jealousy.' It had come as a bonus to find that Jack hadn't even been offered the post of Deputy Lord Mayor.

'Oh now be fair, Rachel. The lass must've been disappointed, and upset about some of the things that were printed in the press. She didn't have to come round, but she did.' He donned a look of puzzlement. 'Though I didn't quite get that funny remark about having a stabbing pain between her shoulders when you asked how her ankle was.'

Rachel had understood it all right. More puzzling was whether someone had told Ella of the remarks Rachel had made to Mrs Danby or whether the inference on back-stabbing had been a feeler. Far from experiencing guilt over it Rachel felt a surge of pride at having got the better of Ella at last. The only bad thing about it was that now everyone knew that Rachel lived next door to a convict – still, one had to make sacrifices. 'Oh, I don't care what Ella throws at us! I'm so happy!'

Russ was euphoric too. Life had grown so very comfortable over these last few years and now it was going to be even more splendid. The only worrying aspect was whether his assistant could be trusted to cope while Russ took time off to perform his civic duties – and if you can say that's your only worry, thought Russ, then you're a very lucky man indeed.

'Who will you be choosing as Under-Sheriff?' asked Rachel, then studied him sharply. 'You wouldn't . . . ?'

Russ shook his head. 'I haven't decided yet, but I doubt Jack would take it even if I offered.'

'But you won't, will you?' she pleaded. And when he was slow in answering pressed him. 'For me, Russ – please.'

'Aye . . . all right, if it'll make you happy.' He nodded reluctantly, making her smile again.

'Very happy. It's bad enough living next door to him.'

'Well, maybe you won't have to for much longer.' He smiled again. 'I thought we might make a short move.' She asked what he meant by short. 'Oh, just around the corner.'

'To one of the big houses? Oh, Russ – when?'

'Well, not this afternoon – but as soon as one comes up for sale, we're getting a bit cramped here and the business is doing well.'

Rachel was still exclaiming her delight when Biddy came in bearing the latest screaming arrival and a fistful of letters. Her mistress unclasped ecstatic hands and returned to her breakfast. 'Are the children ready for school?' She always made certain that Robert and his sisters broke their fast at an earlier hour and a different table, giving the dilatory Biddy ample time to prepare them for school. Besides which, they were not the most perfect of tablemates on a morning – though she did permit them to take tea with her in this room.

'Yes'b,' said Biddy nasally and gave a rattling sniff, for which she was rebuked. 'Sorry, ba'ab, I've caughd a code.'

Russ quoted the words of a Yorkshire folksong as he took the mail from her. 'Tha's been a-courtin', Mary Jane.'

Biddy rumpled her brow and tucked the noisome baby under her other arm. 'Oh no, sir!'

'A joke, Biddy.' Russ tossed a weary look at his wife as the maid departed. 'Anybody who courted her would need his bumps feeling. I'll just open these then I'll be off to work.' Downing the last drop of tea he fetched an ivory dagger from the mantelshelf and began to slit the envelopes.

The first three contained bills and after a slight murmur of acknowledgement Russ placed them to one side, reaching for another. This one was a letter. He did not recognize the handwriting and glanced at the sender's address at the top of the page. What he saw produced a sudden, guilt-ridden flush and with as much equilibrium as he could muster he tucked the letter into an inside pocket.

'That must be a large one,' commented Rachel, glancing up briefly from her task of piling the plates.

'Sorry, dear?' He hadn't realized she had been watching. His hands had started to tremble.

She smiled knowingly. 'You put all the others to one side but that one went in your pocket. You can't hide your sins from me, Russ – I assume it *was* a bill?'

Only slightly reassured he managed to utter, 'Er . . . aye, it is a bit of a steep one.'

She threw up her eyes. 'What's it for?'

Speaking as casually as he could he began to slit another envelope to disguise his alarm. 'It's for the car. It broke down last week and I had to take it to the garage for repair. They charge the earth.' His eyes were still adhered to the paper in his hand, but his mind would not leave the one in his pocket.

Her brow quizzed him. 'You never told me – how much?'

Still faking involvement with the document in his hand he tried to bring his mental powers to order. 'Er . . . sorry what did you say, love? Oh, five pounds it cost me.'

She gave an exclamation of disbelief. '*Five pounds*? For a tiny fault?'

He hoped she could not hear the tremor in his voice. 'Who said it was tiny?'

'Well you haven't been without the car, have you? There can't have been much wrong with it.'

'It wasn't so much that the fault was small – it was rather

big actually – but the fact that they did it there and then, so that I wouldn't have to be without it. Good service always costs, doesn't it? Anyway,' in slightly more collected fashion he opened the final envelope and bundled the lot of them behind the clock on the mantel. 'I'd better be off. I'll just go upstairs and get my coat out of mothballs, it's white over out there.'

Once upstairs he whisked the offending letter from his pocket and pored over it anxiously, innards quivering.

St Bridget's Mission
Orange River

Dear Mr Hazelwood

    I hesitated a long time before contacting you, not wishing to visit any embarrassment upon your family. However, I am compelled to inform you that up to the time of writing I have received no money from you since January. As you may be aware the mission relies on charity and without it we should be unable to enact our commitment of educating the poor and ministering to their needs. The young person whom you placed with us many years ago has no other benefactor – sadly, his mother died only six months ago and the Sisters and myself have taken over his guardianship. But without your donations we find it increasingly difficult to do so. Perhaps the payments had slipped your mind? It is, after all, almost eleven years since you left Charlie in our keeping. Even so, I beg you not to discontinue your generous contributions.

Your humble servant
Father Albert Guillaume.

How naive of him to expect no response to his lapsed payments! If he had shown any scrap of intelligence he would have realized that a Catholic priest wasn't going to sit by and see his income docked – that lot were renowned for their acquisition of wealth. He had sent no word of his intention to end the payments, merely stopped sending them, hoping in some foolish way that the priest would simply think he had died or something. He cursed the abject stupidity that had allowed him to disclose his address to the priest. He had never contemplated danger from this quarter, only from the woman. Not once had he bothered to write to her – why should he? – simply sending the money by way of the priest with a covering note.

Damn and blast! He ripped the letter to shreds, made sure that every last scrap was crammed into his fist and tossed the deadly missive onto the fire.

CHAPTER EIGHT

Should he pay up? What if the priest wrote again and
Rachel got hold of the letter? No, he told himself, don't
weaken now or he'll be on your back for the rest of your life
– besides, what can he do from that distance? Just ignore it
and see what happens.

That was easy enough to say, but each morning the sound
of the letterbox brought his breakfast to his throat.
Sometimes he was unable to stomach anything at all until
after the postman's visit – and if the postman hadn't been
before it was time for him to open the shop then he grew
almost demented.

But when a month of such torture had brought no further
demands his innards began to uncoil. When another month
passed and then another, he knew that his approach had
been the right one. Thank God he had had the strength to
sit it out. It was over.

The day of the ceremony came. Jack and Ella Daw
spectated from behind their curtains as the new Sheriff
climbed into his polished vehicle accompanied by his proud
lady and their five eldest children. 'Just look at her with her
chest puffed out,' declared Ella. 'You'd think she was off to a
coronation. Blasted capitalists, the pair of 'em and I still say
it was Rachel who put the spoke in for your Mayorship.'

Jack was now aware that this was so – at least, he knew
that Rachel had spoken of his wife's prison record to others;
whether that had been the reason he hadn't been elected, he
couldn't be sure. Even if he had been sure he wouldn't tell
his wife; that would only cause more bother. But he was
angry at Rachel and angrier at his friend for allowing it to
happen.

Rachel, unable to see them but sensing their observation,

delivered a queenly wave as the car rolled away. She enjoyed every second of the ensuing ceremony, especially the part in which she figured, when the Lady Mayoress' staff was handed over to her. According to tradition the ebony staff was presented to the Sheriff's Lady and used as a threat to keep the Sheriff in order, remaining in her possession until her husband promised to be good. There would be another ceremony later in the year when the staff would be handed back, enabling the Lady Mayoress to keep her husband on the right path.

But the biggest delight was the procession through the streets to and from the Mansion House. 'Look at your father, children!' Rachel exclaimed proudly as he appeared in all his regalia. 'Isn't he grand?' And Bertie's was the loudest acclamation. He could barely wait to get back to school and boast to his friends.

Russ enjoyed the occasion too. The tension of the previous months had finally been dissipated. For once, the smile he gave his wife and children did not have to be forced. He felt happy and proud and glad for them all.

The morning after the ceremony still found them discussing the event. Achievement such as this was difficult to put aside – indeed, they had been talking about it long into the night. Russ ate heartily and without fear of indigestion. The sound of the letterbox had ceased to be an omen of terror for him – in fact he did not even hear it today. The first indication of a delivery of mail was when Biddy brought it in.

So relaxed was he, so utterly confident that his worry was over, that when, unsuspectingly, he lifted the topmost envelope the one beneath drew an audible gasp.

Rachel squinted at him over the breakfast table. 'What's the matter, Russ, have you got a pain?' His face was drained.

'No, no,' he stammered and rubbed frenziedly at his chest. 'Just heartburn. I'll have to stop having a fried breakfast.' He shuffled the letters together and rose, looking at the clock. 'I haven't time to open these now. I'm at court in an hour and I want to give Jimmy instructions before I go. I'll open them on the way.'

'Not while you're driving, I trust?' she quipped as he left the room in a hurry. 'Bye, love!'

Outside in the driving seat he applied fevered digits to the envelope which bore a South African postmark. Once extricated, he couldn't bring himself to unfold it . . . but eventually had to do so.

Dear Mr Hazelwood,

Since I have had no response to my previous letter I must assume that it has gone astray. It is, after all, a long way from South Africa to England and I dare say many letters never reach their destination. So, I am obliged to repeat that letter's contents . . .

Russell's eyes took in the duplicated plea for him not to end his payments. But lower down the page his heart almost leapt right out of his mouth.

Mr Hazelwood, forgive me for putting this in writing and God forbid that if you have a wife she should come to hear of it through my intrusion, but I am aware that you did not make these contributions out of mere benevolence. I fear that Charlie's mother was quite open about his paternity – indeed, before she died she instructed me to continue to speak of you in a good light in front of the boy. She always believed that one day you would return for your son, Mr Hazelwood. Charlie does not know that the money has stopped coming. He speaks frequently of his father in England and is always asking when the two of you will meet. I had no way of answering him until recent events brought a tinge of reality to Charlie's pipe-dream. It is of some coincidence that I have been summoned to England to teach at a college not far from York. Now, I am very fond of Charlie and without your generous donations to his upkeep I am greatly concerned as to his welfare while I am absent. The Sisters will take care of him as much as they are able of course, but frankly, Mr Hazelwood, Charlie needs firm guidance which I fear he will not receive in my absence. I have therefore this question to put to you . . .

Oh, Christ! He guessed what was coming.

What would your reaction be if Charlie travelled to England with me? I should of course make no demands on you to meet him, though I do feel that this would not be a bad idea for then we could all discuss his future more clearly . . .

'Christ!' It was almost a scream – he looked round swiftly to see if anyone had heard before hunching over the letter again. The blackmailing sod!

. . . I have not mentioned this to him, nor have I said that I shall be coming to England in August, so if you decide that you are unable to comply, then Charlie will have no cause to be upset. But I do beseech you to think very deeply about your son's welfare . . .

The last few words were a blur. Russ, body rippled by panic, shoved the letter into his pocket, leapt out of the car, lashed furiously at the starting handle, then jumped back into the vibrating vehicle to tear off down the street. He hardly saw where he was going, the priest's words etched on the windscreen, blinding him. *Your son, your son, your son.* Oh, God! what was he going to do? The blood gushed through the veins in his neck, pounded at his eardrums. Think! *Think!* But he was incapable of any rational thinking, his one preoccupation being – what the hell would Rachel say?

The engine whirred on, reached the main junction. He turned into The Mount without a look to right nor left. Visions flashed past. Russ stared straight ahead, knuckles white on the steering-wheel – then suddenly there was a loud honking, a scream, curses, and a nerve-jarring bump. His head hit the windscreen with a bang and the rim of the steering-wheel dug into his ribs – though he felt no pain as he bounced back into his seat.

Angry faces surrounded the car. 'You stupid dolt! What the devil were you playing at? Somebody call a copper!'

But Russ just sat there paralysed with shock and saw Rachel in the front parlour confronted by the black boy who was his son.

'Oh, Russell, how could you do this to me?' Rachel brandished the newspaper at her husband, face disfigured by anguish. 'I knew, I just knew you were hiding something! For weeks you've been furtive . . . how *could* you?' She threw the paper at him and he caught it in a crumpled mess, seeing again the headline that had provoked this display: *City Sheriff Fined For Speeding.*

'Why on earth didn't you tell me before it got into print? Prepared me . . . you've made me look such a fool! And the expense! Five shillings plus costs – not to mention the embarrassment! I mean, what were you thinking about?'

'I must've been daydreaming,' he mumbled vaguely. The bruises on his chest had turned yellow and the nick on his forehead was healed, but the mental injury was as acute as ever.

'Yes, you must! Well, you'll have plenty of time for daydreaming when you lose your position – you were lucky not to have been imprisoned. The shame of it!' She plucked at the bunch of white lace on her blouse.

'Rachel, I've told you it was an accident,' he offered dispassionately. The only emotion Russ ever shared was happiness. Sadness, shame . . . fear, he kept tighly chained in his breast.

Not so Rachel, who flung herself about the room in humiliation. 'You were speeding! Twenty miles an hour the paper says.'

'They're exaggerating.' He wished she would shut up. If she knew what really caused the crash . . . oh, my!

But Rachel went on and on – then perversely refused to speak to him any further, cutting off any attempt at reunion with a cold flick of her hand.

For the next couple of days every hour spent at home was passed in similar mood, the only ones to hold a conversation with Russ being his elder children. Breakfast became a test of resilience for which he could never raise the stamina and so found it simpler to eat quickly then escape to the shop, where he was at this moment.

'The customer's waiting, Mr Hazelwood!'

The urgent tone penetrated Russ' abstraction and he started. 'What? Oh, sorry!' He counted out the change to his assistant who relayed it to the customer and opened the door for her, coming back to ask,

'Shall I put the kettle on now, Mr H?'

Russ was in a brown study again. 'Aye . . . aye,' he nodded, not really hearing, eyes vacant – then suddenly he came to life. 'Aye, you do that, Jimmy! But if you hear the bell go, will you see to it? I've something important to attend to.' He was permitting this to become more vital than it actually was. He could and would put a stop to it right this minute. With purposeful movements he seated himself behind the cash desk and, selecting a piece of paper from the drawer, dipped his pen into an inkwell and wrote:

Dear Father Guillaume,

I must apologize for falling behind with my payments and herewith enclose the full arrears with this letter. To compensate for any inconvenience I also send an extra five pounds to spend on Charlie as you see fit. In answer to your query, I must tell you that on no account must you allow him to accompany you to England. I accept that he is the result of a mistake on my part and as such will adopt all responsibility of a financial nature . . . after a pause he underlined the word financial before continuing, *for his upbringing, but I must consider my wife and children and in doing so am sure that if Mrs Hazelwood ever finds out about the boy the shock would surely kill her. You must understand that I do not wish to shirk my duties and forthwith I shall endeavour to send regular payments . . . .* It looked as though Mr Cranley would have to be resurrected, *. . . but I insist,* Again he underlined the word insist, *that you make it clear to Charlie that he must relinquish any hope of us meeting in the near future or indeed at any time. I do not wish to see him ever and do not consider him as my son. Do not let him be in any doubt about this. I wish you to be entirely honest. Your cooperation will be greatly appreciated.*

Yours . . .

After a flourishing signature he read and re-read the letter then, with a determined pinch of his fingers, folded it and slipped it into an envelope. Taking a stamp from the petty cash tin he pressed it into place and gave it a final bang with his fist. It was no good mincing about, one had to be resolute in such matters. It was annoying, that he had had to back down over the money, but better that than Rachel finding out.

'D'you want that posting, Mr H?' Jimmy had appeared with two cups of tea as Russ addressed the envelope.

'No . . . I'll do it, lad. I might as well go early if you're sure you'll be all right.' He had a civic engagement in an hour. At the young man's confirmation he made for the door. 'Right, I'll be back as soon as I can. Don't accept any chocolate sovereigns.'

Once the letter had disappeared into the oblong yawn of the pillarbox, he felt able to breathe a little easier and, as the days grew warmer and there was no answering envelope, he was lent the belief that his problem had been solved. He threw himself into his civic and commercial duties, putting Charlie into the file labelled *Things I would rather forget*.

Would that his wife could forget so easily. It had been weeks since the accident yet whenever he made a small digression it was still thrown at him – like this morning when they had had a tiff over breakfast. He wondered as he closed the shop this evening, what he could do to regain her alliance. Maybe his news that there was to be a banquet at the Mansion House would make her sweeter tempered. She loved any excuse to dress up and flash herself off to the neighbours. Oh, that was it! He could take her a dress-length from the shop – that lavender-coloured silk she had so admired when it had arrived from the manufacturer's last week. Aye, that should solve it – and some flowers! Smiling, he postponed his exit to measure a length of the fabric, breaking into song as he did so. After this, he locked up and went to purchase a bouquet.

Rachel was sitting with her children in the front parlour. Bertie, now very much the young man at almost twelve, was seated next to her. He was still the only son. This being so there had perforce been alterations in the sleeping arrangements: the parents had moved into the second largest room at the back of the house and Bertie had taken sole occupancy of the former nursery – much to the complaint of his sisters who had to squeeze into half of the front bedroom which had been partitioned; the other half was the new nursery. The girls' ages ranged from nine months to ten and a half years, there being six of them. The five eldest children were receiving education, leaving only two for Biddy to care for during the day which made her life fractionally easier.

Biddy balanced the tray on one knee before entering the parlour, took a bottle from her apron pocket and enjoyed a long tipple. The Lord grant the mistress a new baby soon or Biddy would be forced to buy the stuff herself and her meagre wage was hardly likely to sustain her addiction.

She finished swigging and, gasping with relief, tucked the bottle back in her pinny, then rattled in with the tray. Bertie was trying to convey the Pythagoras Theorem to his mother, whilst the girls chirruped about who had done what to whom at school. Rachel merely smiled and nodded as she worked on her hat, saying, 'Yes, dear,' and, 'Oh, how interesting!' whilst hearing only a collective prattle.

'Tea, ma'am.' Biddy waited with the tray containing milk and biscuits for the children, tea for Rachel and a plate of bread and butter for all, until Rachel scooped the pieces of material from the table and instructed Biddy to spread the cloth.

Once seated, Bertie clamped his teeth on a piece of bread, using his free hand to reach for another. 'Robert, you can only eat one piece at a time,' reproved his mother.

Deliberately, he left the imprint of his teeth on it before returning it to the main plate and warned his sisters, 'That's mine.'

'Don't worry,' hissed Rosalyn. 'No one wants it when you've spit on it,' and was vociferously rebuked by her mother who sometimes found it very hard to control them.

'And Robina, I hope you don't intend to leave those crusts? There are starving people in the world who'd be most glad of them. Eat up now.'

'But how can eating my crusts help the starving people, Mother?' Robina, or Beany, was the only plain child among them, mousy of hair and muddy of eye – though her family knew that the bland exterior concealed a tempestuous and sensitive nature. All the children had fresh complexions and neat features . . . all except poor Beany whose transluscent skin bore not one smudge of colour save the marbling of blue veins at her temple. 'I mean, if I eat them they'll still be starving, won't they? It would be much better if we parcelled them up and sent them off to the poor people, don't you think?'

'No it wouldn't,' corrected her mother firmly. 'Because by the time they arrived they'd be stale. Now eat them up, they'll make your hair curl.'

'They don't make Lyn's hair curl,' argued Beany, indicating her sister's straggly locks.

'Maybe you're applying them the wrong way,' suggested Bertie. 'Maybe you're meant to wrap the hair round them and not eat them.'

After Rebecca had finished laughing at her brother's joke she said, 'You know that Mrs Wilson down the street? She's off to prison for not paying her rent.'

'Rebecca,' said her mother patiently, 'gentlefolk do not discuss others at the tea-table . . . how do you know this anyway?'

Pretty little dark-haired Rhona was whingeing, as was her habit, 'Lyn's stolen me bread, Mother. Mother-r-r! She's got me bre-ad!' when her tone changed and she pointed at the window. 'Who's that funny lady looking in our house?'

All faces turned to the stooped figure who peered in at them, her head draped with a silk shawl and a very elaborate earring in one ear. Then Becky burst into giggles and jumped from her seat to the window. The others too, gave noise to their amusement and, ignoring their mother's complaint about the din, rushed to the front door to haul the 'woman' into the parlour.

They clamoured round their father as, with grinning face, he unhooked the bunch of keys from his ear, telling him how funny he was. Russ chuckled with them, handing the bunch of flowers to his wife before divesting himself of the silk and spreading it over a chair for Rachel to see. Next, he hung the bunch of keys on Rowena's ear and finally he grabbed three year old Rhona, swinging her up, round and down again whilst sneaking a look at his wife to see if she had found his act amusing too. His spirits were bolstered by a rather reluctant twitch of her lips as she sampled the flowers' perfume – enough to chance curling his arm round her and pressing a sincere kiss to her cheek. 'D'you think your mother's forgiven me, kiddlywinks?' The children, who had been well aware of their father's fall from grace, waited alertly as Rachel picked up the dress-length and held it against herself . . . Then she reached up and gave her husband a soft bang on the face with the bunch of flowers and said by way of absolution, 'Doesn't your father know how to get round me?' And everything was fine again.

On Sunday afternoon Rachel organized a picnic on Knavesmire, which illustrated to Russ that he had been completely forgiven. He was therefore in jovial mood as he and his wife, arms linked, strolled behind their brood across the expansive greenbelt in the direction of the woods. It was very hot and the habitual breeze was most welcome today. It rippled the woman's straight gold skirt and the man's cream-coloured trousers. Russ had already taken off his striped blazer; it was slung over his arm. Now, he lifted his boater to seek yet more relief, delighting in the feel of the breeze on his forehead.

Oh! but it was great walking here – cleansing somehow. All his troubles were swept away. He looked across to his left, to the empty grandstand clearly defined against a blue sky, then let his eyes run along the white fence marking the racetrack, which encircled him and his family in a huge green triangle of meadowland. Someone had been cutting grass; it smelt lovely.

'Rosalyn, try not to be so boisterous, dear!' Rachel's voice cracked the balmy silence as her nine-year-old daughter performed a cartwheel. 'Remember what day it is.'

The tomboy righted herself and untucked her embroidered, kimono-style dress from her knickers, stooping to pull up her stockings.

From under the wide brim of her hat, Rachel smiled fondly at her husband to show how she, too, was enjoying this and how proud she was of them all. Seven healthy children – no wonder the Daws were green-eyed. She felt a wave of sympathy for the couple, then turned to check on the position of the maid. 'Come along, Biddy, do! We don't want to wait half an hour for you to catch up before we can eat.'

Russ glanced back too, also experiencing a rush of compassion, only his was for the red-faced maid struggling with the picnic basket. He acted upon it. 'Shall we rest here? If we get too near the woods there'll be flies.'

Rachel concurred and hailed the children. After pointing excitedly and waving at an aeroplane, they came scampering back to fling themselves on the grass around the cloth their mother had just spread. Rowena, in charge of the perambulator, arrived last and adjusted the baby's bonnet against the sun before sitting her with the others.

'You'd better go help Biddy, Robert,' muttered Rachel. 'Or the silly girl won't get here till Monday.'

Bertie sprang up and pelted towards Biddy. 'Away, Bid!' He tugged at the handle of the wicker basket. 'Everyone's waiting for grub.'

'Sure, your mother made me pack enough to feed the whole o' the British Empire,' grumbled Biddy, allowing him to take it and pushing away the wisps of hair that clung to her streaming brow. ''Tis heavier than the sky before a storm.'

'Oh come on, let a man take charge!' He hoisted the hamper onto his shoulder and strode ahead of her. Though the wicker and its heavy contents cut into him he pretended the task was effortless. A perspiring Biddy still dawdled behind him. When she finally arrived the sandwiches were under attack.

'Oh, this is lovely!' Rowena narrowed her eyes against the dazzling sun and presented her arms to the sky – then lowered them quickly to discourage the baby from eating grass. 'I wish it could be like this every day with no school.'

Her father showed surprise. 'I thought you liked school, Wena?' She had always displayed such studious characteristics, searching out an unoccupied corner of the house to be alone with her books. He didn't realize that it was to escape the others. In truth, Rowena would have been more fitted to being an only child. But then her father wouldn't realize, for she showed her siblings such devotion; she had that kind of nature.

Rowena gave a wan smile and shook her beribboned

head. Russ asked why. 'Because . . . oh, I don't know. I just wish I could stay at home like Mother. I can't wait to grow up and be married.'

Both her parents laughed – then were diverted as Becky gave a scream of pain. The finger she produced for their inspection was red and swollen. A bee lay dying in the grass. 'She kept prodding it,' announced Robina over her sister's sobs. 'I told her not to.'

'Oh, Rebecca!' chided her mother, tugging at the finger to locate the sting. 'Don't you know better than to antagonize a wasp?'

'It isn't a wasp it's a bee.' Bertie was studying the corpse. His mother, rooting in her bag for a pair of tweezers, told him not to contradict. 'But . . .'

'Robert! If I say it's a wasp then I think we can assume it is one.' Bertie turned to his father. 'Father, have a look at it . . .' Russ said diplomatically that he didn't know the difference. 'It *was* a bee,' muttered the boy with a defiant look at his mother. 'Bees always die when they sting. Wasps can sting you as many times as they like.' Russ suddenly noted to his great amusement that the bodice worn by his wife had gold and black stripes. He made signals at Bertie to draw attention to it. His son frowned . . . then, interpreting the message was forced to laugh. It was some minutes before either male felt able to speak without spluttering his mirth.

The finger was dealt with and the picnic resumed. After most of the food had been devoured Russ suggested a walk in the woods. Bertie and three of his sisters accepted eagerly but little Rhona complained that she was too hot and wanted to go home.

'Oh, we don't have to go because of her, do we?' begged Robina. Then to her sister, 'Mona, Mona, you're always moaning!' The smaller child denied this. 'Are! You spoil everything!' A buttoned shoe was stamped in temper – it took very little to throw Robina into a rage.

'Stop that at once!' commanded Rachel, then erected her lace parasol and handed it to the complainant. 'Here, take this.'

'But do we have to take *her*?' Robina entreated her mother, but was glared into silence.

Rachel decided she would sit here until the party came back. 'Rosalyn, come here and let me tie your hair ribbon, you look like a gypsy's child.' Rowena excused herself too, saying she would be bitten to death by flies in the wood.

Russ left his jacket in the care of his wife and with five of his children made the expedition to the woods. It was cooler here and quite dark. The ground was spongy and carpeted with parings from the various trees, which clung to their shoes as they walked. There was the smell of greenery, and the occasional whiff of fox. Bertie, walking side by side with his father, asked why his mother had said the bee was a wasp. 'It *was* a bee, I know it.'

His father laid an arm across his shoulders. 'You shouldn't argue with women, Bertie. You see, they're not the same as us . . . it's best just to humour 'em.' Bertie agreed and said this outing would have been better spent with just the two of them. Russ smiled. 'Ah well, we'll have a few days out together in the school holidays – just you and me. Maybe we could take the tent and camp out – be grand that, wouldn't it?' Bertie said it certainly would. Then his father was detoured as an argument developed between Robina and Rhona. He grabbed the youngest and hoisted her onto his shoulders. Her frilly petticoat caught on his head, changing bad temper to hilarity. 'Oh, do you like my new bonnet? Best pull it from over me eyes though else we'll be falling down a rabbit 'oile'.

'Ooh, d'you think we'll see a rabbit, Father?' Lyn ambled at his heels, stockings sagging once more and the ribbon slipping from its bow.

Russ said yes, they might catch one for tomorrow's dinner. As they walked, Becky tried to take hold of Bertie's hand but he shook her off. She was always trying to tag on to him. Undeterred, she continued to prance alongside her brother, though he took big strides to evade her. Secretly, though, he was proud of this hero worship. Within the family he might scorn them, but outside he guarded his sisters with the possessiveness of one who owns a harem –

107

and his duties as only son did not go unrecognized. If ever one of the girls was being tormented by an outsider Bertie was always the defender. And although he may not be generous with his compliments, he always remembered each sister's birthday – even the ones he most detested – saving all his pocket money to buy a gift. It was Robina's birthday soon. He had almost accrued a shilling. As yet, he hadn't decided what to get her, but was waiting for her to mention something she liked so that he could surprise her with it.

However, Robina was about to spoil her chances. As they sauntered, cracking twigs underfoot, she set up a recitation. 'The owl and the pussycat . . .'

Bertie stiffened. 'Don't you dare!'

'Went to sea . . .'

'Father, make her shut up!'

'In a beautiful pean green boat.'

'Aargh!' Bertie's hands flew to his ears and he bellowed his rage.

'Goodness, what's to do?' Russ looked about in bewilderment as his son grimaced and gnashed his teeth.

Lyn explained, jumping off the fallen log. 'He doesn't like it when she says them words.'

'What words?'

'You dare!' yelled Bertie.

'*Peeean greeen*!' emphasized Robina in delight.

Russ shook his head and marched on. 'You're a queer bunch to have as children and no mistake – and it's not pean green,' his son winced, 'it's pea green.'

Robina delivered a happy retort, 'Well I like pean green,' making Bertie squirm again.

'She just does it to annoy him,' said Lyn, who was not averse to doing this herself. '*And* she bites her velvet dress.'

Bertie yelled his outrage at the very thought of his sister's teeth on velvet. 'Stop tormenting, you two,' said Becky and touched her brother's arm. 'Take no notice, Bertie.'

'Oh get off, you!' The last thing he wanted was to be pitied for his weakness by a girl. To Robina he snapped, 'That's your birthday present up the spout, Beany!'

At her wail Russ sighed, 'Eh, I don't know! You're always scrapping. I wonder if there's any vacancies at the Marmalade Home.'

'Send them two,' sulked the boy.

'The owl and the pussycat . . .'

'Now stop that! Else we'll be sending the lot o' you.' Russ attempted to divert them. 'Eh, look here I think we've found a nest.' Bertie came immediately to his side, edging Rebecca out of the way. Russ stretched his arm into the bush. 'Oh sorry, nothing in this one . . . just a minute, what's that clucking noise?' He put on a quizzical expression. 'I think it's coming from our Becky. Why . . . look at this!' He reached behind her ear and produced a blue-speckled egg. 'Would you believe it?'

'Ooh, can I have it, Father?' asked Bertie, having inherited his father's passion.

'Oh why does he always have to have everything?' wailed Lyn as the egg was placed on her brother's palm.

'Because I'm the boy,' replied Bertie pompously and was aided by Rebecca who said that as the egg had come from her ear she wanted him to have it. 'Anyway, what d'you want with an egg? You haven't got a collection.' Lyn said that she would start one, lower lip thrust out like a shelf.

'We'll see if we can find another,' soothed her father.

Unfortunately, Bertie's was the only egg to be found, which intensified his pleasure but drove Lyn to sulks. However, her good humour was restored when accident-prone Becky tripped and fell, reaching out for support as she did so and smashing the egg in her brother's pocket.

'Oh, bloomin' Nora,' muttered Russ, dashing up to extricate the mess from his son's clothes. 'Let's get that sorted out before your mother sees it else she'll make scrambled egg of the lot of us.' Using his handkerchief he scraped the none too fresh yolk from Bertie's jacket.

'You bloody dummy!' the boy reprimanded his guilty sister who sobbed, as much at his words as at her sore ankle.

'Eh! Now that's swearing, Bertie, and I won't have it! A gentleman doesn't swear in front of ladies.' Bertie apologized to his father, but still glowered threateningly at Becky when Russ wasn't looking.

'I know how disappointing it is,' his father's fingers dripped albumen, 'but never mind, I'll let you have a nice long look at my collection before bedtime – how's that?'

To Bertie this was the biggest treat imaginable, other than actually owning the eggs, and he soon revived his spirits. With order restored, Russ said they should return to the others. Something always happened when he tried to give his children a good time – but then, it could have been partly his fault for favouring Bertie so much. He watched as Lyn set off at full pelt, 'Race you!' and the others hared after her, all except Bertie who, seeing his sister's ten yard start decided not to enter the race. 'I'm not running it's too hot!' and walked beside his father.

'I won!' bawled Lyn as the girls burst upon their mother's reverie and earned a telling off. Robina stated that it was a draw but, '*I* won,' declared an obstinate Lyn. 'Bertie, I beat you!' she announced proudly as her brother came up in an affected saunter.

'I told you I wasn't taking part.' He assumed a lazy, uncaring stance.

'Huh! You're just saying that because you lost!'

'Will you kindly all stop arguing!' ordered their mother, grabbing Lyn to retie her bow. 'Now, would anyone care to finish the food so we don't have to carry it back?'

We carry it back, thought Biddy acidly and fanned her face with her hat.

Becky studied the plate. 'Oh, look, the sandwiches are smiling at us!'

Russ laughed at his daughter's observation and helped himself to one of the curled-up sandwiches as the children satiated their renewed appetite. After spending a while longer enjoying the glorious sunshine the family made for home. Biddy, in addition to the hamper, was now left to push the cumbersome pram and so fell further and further behind while the children, still brimming with energy, gave each other piggybacks and skipped and danced.

Russ took his wife's arm, threaded it through his and looked into her face as they retraced their tracks across the grassland. 'Have you enjoyed yourself then?'

'It was absolutely lovely.' She put up a hand to pat the one that held her other. 'Such a happy day – such a happy year. What a shame it is only a year. I've quite enjoyed playing the lady up to now.'

'You always will be a lady,' came the kind compliment.

'Flatterer . . . it would be nice for it to last forever though.'

'Well, I expect we'll get invited to a few parties even after I've handed in my Sheriff's hat.'

She smiled up at him. His eyes were bright blue and shining in the sun-tanned face, making him even more attractive than usual. A burst of love caused her to reveal, 'I was so proud of you that day, you know. I watched you march majestically along and thought, that's my husband! It was a wonderful feeling. I don't think I'll ever forget it.'

He gave voice to his fondness of her. 'I hope I can give you a lot more days like that, Rachel love.' And their faces met in a kiss.

On their return home, Rachel ordered the children upstairs to wash hands and faces, telling them they could sit and read for the remainder of the time before bed. Instantly, Bertie complained that his father had promised to let him see the egg collection.

'Later,' countered his mother firmly. 'I think your father and I deserve a cup of tea and a little solitude after tolerating your antics all afternoon. Biddy, go put the kettle on then see that these children wash properly – and fetch the baby in.' The pram had been left by the front door. 'She'll want changing.' Poor, overworked Biddy put the hamper down. 'For goodness sake don't leave that there! One of us will fall over it and break our neck.' The maid returned to lug the hamper into the kitchen where she quickly revived herself from a bottle hidden among the lumps of coal in the scuttle – just one of many hiding places.

Rachel emitted a groan of exhaustion. 'Oh, my poor feet! I must sit down.'

'You sound like an old woman,' teased her husband. 'Not the sylph-like girl I know.' He made her giggle by seizing her and transporting her bodily to the front parlour.

A sullen Bertie trailed after them. 'Father, you promised.'

Russ looked round, then silenced another outcry from his wife by dumping her on the sofa and holding up his hands. 'I did, I did! And a promise is a promise, isn't it, Bertie?' And with a manly slap of his son's back he and Bertie went upstairs to the attic.

The first question was always the same. 'Which one d'you like best?' Bertie's covetous eyes brooded over the collection – he always made a different choice. Today it was a turquoise-coloured one. 'That'n.' His voice turned wheedling. 'Can I have it, Father?' Sometimes if the egg was duplicated his father would allow him to have it. But this one was unique.

'Nay, we don't want to split them up.' Russ tousled his son's hair lovingly. 'They'll all belong to you one day, you know.'

Bertie asked when.

'Oh, I think they'd make a splendid coming of age gift, don't you?'

Bertie wasn't too keen on waiting that long. 'Wouldn't it be better for me to have them while I'm young enough to enjoy them?'

His father laughed aloud. 'Eh, Bertie, you make me feel decrepit!'

After a pause, Bertie asked, 'Father . . . have you made a will?'

Russ' laughter was even more uproarious. 'Don't worry, lad, I won't pop off before I've made definite provision for my son and heir.' He slid the drawer back in the cabinet. 'Anyway I'd best go down now, I'm gasping for a cup o' tea. Hadn't you better wash the spuds from your lugs like your mother told you?'

'Aw, can't I just stay and have another little look?' pleaded his son.

Russ did not normally allow unsupervized viewing, but after such an enjoyable day he felt charitable enough to say with a soft cuff, 'Go on then, you young varmint – but try not to touch them, you know how fragile they are. I'll tell your mother you're harvesting the King Edwards.' He left an effusively grateful Bertie drooling over the eggs and went down.

As he reached the bottom stair there was a knock at the door. 'Don't move, Biddy, I'll get it!' He headed down the passage and swung the door open.

The young fellow on the doorstep said only one word, but it was sufficient to plunge Russ from his gay mood into a vortex of unbelievable terror.

'Father?'

CHAPTER NINE

Petrified, Russ stared into the brown face with its apprehensive smile for three full seconds – then slammed the
door! It couldn't be. It couldn't! Make it go away, came the
futile plea – then with gritted teeth and eyes screwed shut,
*for Christ's sake I don't pray much but I'm praying now: I'll do
anything, anything, but please make it all be a bloody
apparition.*

The knock came again. Rachel shouted, 'Is someone
going to answer that door?'

'Yes, dear!' Detesting himself and the person on the
other side of the door, he pulled it open a crack. 'Go away!'
he hissed before the boy had time to make further
utterance. 'You're at the wrong house. For God's sake clear
off!' Every dreg of mental effort was directed at the boy,
willing him to move . . . but the boy did not.

The face continued to smile at him, if a little bemusedly
now, and the voice was polite. 'You are Mr Hazelwood?'

'No! You've got the wrong person. Now . . .'

'Russ, who is it?'

The proximity of his wife's voice made his scalp crawl
with fear. He dared not turn – dared not move one inch.
Rachel, lured from her comfortable position by his tardy
return, came to peer over his shoulder and immediately
assumed that the visitor had knocked to ask for directions.
'Can I help you?' she mouthed in the way that one speaks to
foreigners and idiots. 'Where do you want to be?'

'I was just telling him how to get to Curzon Terrace,'
Russ heard his own voice say, then used his eyes to beseech
the boy: please, please don't ask for Mr Hazelwood.

But Rachel's prompt answer saved him. 'Oh, you turned
right instead of left. Go back to the end and it's up that road
there.' She pointed and smiled. 'You can't miss it.'

'Thank you . . .' said the boy confusedly. And found the door shut in his face.

'That's a bit of a novelty,' said Rachel brightly as she moved back to the parlour.

'What?' Russ lingered, still in turmoil. The way that boy had looked at him . . .

'You don't see too many of his kind round here. It'll give Mrs Phillips something to gossip about – Russ, come on don't dawdle.' She had tarried at the door of the parlour and was regarding him strangely. 'That sun hasn't made you ill, has it?'

'Wh . . . oh, no! No.' He struggled with his migrant senses – how the hell had he got here? Christ, what was he going to do? – then went none too willingly to join his wife.

Charlie picked up his holdall and took a backward step from the Hazelwoods' front door. The reception had bewildered him and he needed a few moments in which to decide upon his action. All of a sudden, he felt very cold and hungry. Though the sun shone it was a different kind of sun to the one at home. His discomfort was augmented by the chill that had begun to spread from within. He had never seen his father, yet he knew for sure that he was the man who had just turned him away – even if the woman had not verified this by the use of his Christian name – his mother had talked about him so often, so descriptively that even without the uniform and the added years Charlie would know him anywhere. But why had he turned Charlie away? Why had he looked so afraid? Perhaps it was because of the woman. Father Guillaume had told him that his father had another wife who knew nothing of Charlie. Yes, that would be it. He had better wait for a while to see if the woman went out, then he would knock again . . . for he had nowhere else to go.

The manliness he felt on making his decision to come here was suddenly stripped away. He felt very young and vulnerable. Wandering across the narrow road, he leaned his back against the iron railings to wait.

'I still say you pushed her into me on purpose!' Bertie,

having rejoined his sisters in their cramped room, was now accusing one of them. 'Just because you wanted my egg.'

'I couldn't give a snot for your stinking old egg,' retorted Lyn. 'I've changed my mind about starting an egg collection anyway.'

'No, she's going to collect the nests instead,' announced Robina importantly.

'Oh, you stupid idiot, Beany!' Lyn collapsed. 'I told you that wasn't for human consumption. Now he'll pinch all the nests before I get to 'em.'

'Don't you call me an idiot!'

'Well, you are!' Lyn slapped her sister who slapped her back and was promptly punched in the chest. Beany threw herself on the floor, screeching in fury.

Rowena, always the peacemaker, was searching for something to distract her sisters when a glance from the window brought an observation, 'Oh, come and look at the darkie, everyone!' and the rage miraculously dispersed as all clustered round the window. Biddy, here to supervise washing, stood flannel in hand, craning her sun-reddened neck over a row of different-coloured heads. 'Jaze, I've never seen the like . . .' she breathed.

'What's he staring at our house for?' demanded Lyn of her elder sister.

'How should I know?' Rowena was fascinated by the boy. 'Why don't we go and ask him?'

'Ooh aye, let's!' Becky clapped her hands. 'I'd love to talk to him.'

'How d'you know he speaks English?' put forward Bertie. 'Anyhow, I don't know that I want to talk to him, he's got a bloomin' cheek staring at our house like that.'

At this juncture, Charlie's disconsolate eyes caught the movement at the window. His misery was displaced by a charming smile. This further captured Becky. 'Ooh, look! He's smiling at us – aw, go on, Bid let us go an' speak to him.'

'Well, I don't know as how . . .'

'Aw, go on, Bid!' chorused the girls.

'Why should you need to ask her?' said an arrogant Bertie. 'Just go if you really want to.'

'Your mother might not be very pleased at your talking to savages, Bertie,' warned the maid. 'Anyway, she said you were to get washed.'

'*Master* Bertie to you,' came the retort, and making a sudden, laughing jump he draped a towel over Biddy's head and ran to the door, urging the others to be quiet as they stepped onto the landing.

Very stealthily, so as not to alert their mother, they descended the stairs. But once in the street they burst forth in a mad helter-skelter to encircle their discovery. Russ chanced a peep from the parlour window and almost died.

'What's going on out there?' asked Rachel, making as if to get up.

'Oh, it's only kids,' he said casually, but was swift in pressing her back into her seat. 'Just relax and enjoy the peace.' He seated himself away from the window in order to draw her eyes from it . . . but his own kept creeping back.

'Who're you?' demanded Bertie squaring up to the stranger. 'And what d'you think you're staring at?'

'I think I'm your brother,' replied the stranger in a foreign but well-spoken accent, bringing gasps of incredulity from the girls.

'How can you be our brother?' scoffed Bertie. 'You're a darkie.' He looked the boy up and down; his clothes were exceedingly crumpled and shabby, in great contrast to their own.

Charlie's smile remained intact. Father Guillaume had explained that his father had other children who would be unaware of Charlie's existence. Likely it was a shock to them. 'Mr Hazelwood is your father?' he asked them and received a stiff nod from Bertie. He *had* got it right then. 'Then I'm your brother – he's my father too.'

'He never mentioned you,' returned Bertie distrustfully, starting to be worried. 'And neither did Mother.'

'Oh, your mother isn't my mother.' Charlie's teeth disappeared. 'My mother is dead. My father met her while he was a soldier in my country.'

'What country?' came the immediate enquiry. Bertie knew that his father had only ever been on foreign service in

117

Africa so if the boy said otherwise it was obviously some sort of trick.

'South Africa,' said Charlie, inserting another sliver of torment under Bertie's skin.

'How can you have the same father but not the same mother?' Bertie hung on doggedly to the interrogation, while the girls simply admired, searching for a likeness to their father. Despite the boy's complexion Rowena noticed a definite similarity, especially round the nose; his eyes, albeit brown and not blue, had the same mischievous twinkle when he smiled. His dark kinky hair, however, was clearly inherited from his mother – though his uneven teeth were once again Father's.

In response to Bertie's query, Charlie performed a shrug; he found it puzzling too. From his Catholic instruction he knew that a man must only have one wife – yet only a few miles up the road from the mission there was a man who had ten wives! Adulthood was full of contradictions.

Becky jumped in to ask the attractive boy his name. When he told her she seemed disillusioned that it was not more exotic. 'Have you killed a lion?'

Charlie, by his hearty guffaw, showed he considered this a strange question. 'No, have you?'

She clutched two handfuls of pinafore and gave a bubbling laugh, infecting the others. 'We don't have lions round here!' Then she thought to introduce her brother and sisters. 'This is Bertie, Wena, Lyn, Beany, Mona – oh, all right!' she stilled the last child's objection. 'I mean *Rhona*, and I'm Becky.' Charlie liked this girl who had inherited her mother's sunny smile. He liked the gentle-looking one as well, but he wasn't sure about the others.

Rhona started to ask a question but Lyn interjected. 'How far can you spit?'

'Lyn! You know Mother'd be cross if she caught you doing that,' said Rowena as her sister demonstrated her prowess.

'I don't suppose I could do it as far as that,' replied Charlie. 'And my mouth's too dry.'

'We'll give you a drink, won't we?' piped up Rhona.

'If you can beat me at arm-wrestling,' said Lyn and presented her arm. 'Bend over, Becky, an' let's use your back.' Her sister formed a platform for the contest. 'You won't win, though. I can beat anybody.'

'Apart from me,' corrected Bertie.

'What're you talking about! I beat you the other day easy.'

'That was a fluke!'

But Lyn ignored her brother's objections to grapple with Charlie. He overpowered her easily, but on noticing that the loser's face had darkened to a sulk, said, 'Best of three?' It was allies he needed here, not enemies.

'Ow, stop diggin' your elbows in!' complained Becky as they struggled over her back.

After being allowed to win the two following bouts Lyn said magnanimously. 'You've got more muscle than Bertie.'

'I told you that was a fluke! I wasn't ready.'

'Challenge him, then,' goaded Lyn. Bertie muttered that he didn't see why he should. 'No, you're afraid you'll lose.'

Once more it was left to Rowena to mediate. 'As he's our brother we should really invite him in for a drink of lemonade.'

Though Bertie abhorred the idea of having his position of only son usurped, his father might be annoyed if they left a relative standing on the pavement. 'I suppose so,' came his cautious drawl.

And with this permission the crowd of giggling females gave Charlie only enough time to seize his holdall before bearing him across the road and into the house. After the slightest hesitation Bertie dashed after them, trying to overtake before they reached the front parlour. If there were any announcements to be made then he would be the one to make them . . . but he had already decided that Charlie wouldn't be staying.

The parlour door burst open, drawing a tiny shriek of alarm from Rachel who berated the children. 'How many times have I told you not to . . . oh, have you got lost again?' The last comment was directed at Charlie who smiled uncertainly, then looked to his father for support.

119

Russ had risen and was coming towards the boy, his face stark. But little bodies got in the way, little bodies that swelled to great immovable proportions . . . before he could spirit Charlie to the safety of the street, the guillotine began its rumbling descent.

'You don't know this boy, Mother,' said Rowena, forestalling Bertie's explanation as she and the others pushed the stranger forward. 'But Father does, don't you, Father?'

'No! At least . . . we did meet a few minutes ago.'

'There you are! I knew he was lying.' Bertie had a smug twist to his mouth.

'Robert!' protested his mother. 'You do not use such words in this house.'

'Sorry, Mother – but I was only trying to save you from entertaining an impostor.' Bertie was asked for explanation. 'He said he was our brother, but I said a darkie couldn't possibly . . .'

'Brother?' Rachel gave a titter of ridicule . . . then her brow became furrowed.

'Father knew this boy's mother in Africa, didn't you, Father?'

At Rowena's innocent divulgence Rachel's head snapped round to meet her husband's drained face, read the awful truth in his expression – and promptly swooned.

Horror immobolized him. He couldn't think straight, couldn't think what to do – his wife was lying in a heap on the carpet, one of his daughters had begun to weep in alarm, and he could *not* think what to do. Somehow, he overcame the paralysis sufficiently to ring the handbell for Biddy, not noticing that the maid had been there all along. She stepped forward, big red hands playing out her uncertainty on her apron. Her agitation captured his staring eye. 'Biddy, take the children into the kitchen and give them tea.'

'Sure, they've just had their picnic tea, sir.'

'Well . . . give them some more.'

'Yes, sir . . . what about the young gentleman, sir?' He looked at her dazedly, the fingers of one hand gouging white hollows in his cheeks. 'What'll I do with him, sir?' She cocked her head at Charlie. Russ closed his eyes then, blotting out the cause of this disaster.

'Better take him too.'

'What're ye going to do about the mistress, sir?'

He unveiled his eyes to stare at the supine form. His wife was just coming round. 'I'll see to her. You just take the children out.'

As the last child was being hustled from the room, Russ went to his wife, supporting her head, then lifting her gently to a dining chair. Neither offered a word as Russ poured out two glasses of sherry, knocking his own back straightaway and refilling his glass before handing one to his wife. Rachel accepted it dumbly, staring right through him. 'Drink it up,' he ordered.

Vague eyes drifted up to his and Rachel lifted the glass. But instead of tipping it into her mouth she flung the sherry directly at his face. He did not move. A glob of the sweet liquid had dribbled over his lips and was licked away by his tongue-tip before he pulled out a handkerchief to dab at the rest.

'Are you going to tell me?' She searched his face. 'Are you just going to stand there as if nothing had happened?'

Shoving the handkerchief back in his pocket he moved away slowly and trained his eyes on the window, downing his second glass of sherry. How did he tell her?

She slammed her glass on the table, uncaring of the wood. 'That *was* your son, wasn't it? Your . . . wild oat!' At his shame-faced nod she expelled a noisy breath. 'My God! What sort of woman must she be to do such a thing – to steal another's husband . . .'

It was time he offered some excuse. 'It wasn't like that! She thought I was *her* husband. We had a sort of marriage.'

'How could you have a *sort* of marriage when you were already married to me?' She drummed her chest. 'I presume it was during the African War?' He moved his head again, making her shriek, 'Well, am I to be forced to keep making these presumptions or are you going to have the decency to tell me why you found the need to . . . when you had me!'

'I didn't think of her as I think of you!' he told her earnestly. 'I was just lonely, being away from home. She just happened along.'

Rachel clutched handfuls of hair and screamed, 'That only makes it worse! Treating the wretched creature like . . .' She couldn't say the word.

'Rache . . .' He put his empty glass on the sideboard and approached her, hands imploring.

'Don't!' Her shrill voice forbade him. 'Don't you dare!' She saw those same hands pawing the African woman.

'You asked me to tell you . . .'

'But I don't want to hear!'

'Let me explain . . . about the boy. I didn't want him to come here.'

'Oh, you *do* surprise me!'

'I told the priest I didn't want anything to do . . .'

'Priest?' She pushed the fringe of curls upwards, revealing a corrugated brow.

Russ stumbled over the explanation of his arrangements for Charlie's upbringing, the recent letters. At his conclusion she enquired acidly as to the whereabouts of this priest. 'I've no idea. Maybe we ought to ask the boy.'

'He's still here?' It came on a gasp.

A short pause. 'He's in the kitchen.'

'Get him out! Don't you dare bring him in here! I refuse to have your . . . in my best parlour! It's bad enough he's under my roof at all.' Her mind reeled with the sudden transition of the beautiful day. Nausea made her grasp at her mouth.

He gestured at the door. 'Shall I go . . .'

'You'd better!'

Then Rachel's eyes fell on the gift he had brought back from Africa. Seizing the wooden bust she shook it at him furiously. She did not have to say anything, he knew well enough what she was thinking. 'Rachel, that wasn't meant as . . .'

'Just go!' She flung the African woman's head on the fire.

Biddy was mopping at Robina's wet face with a teatowel.

122

'There, there, Miss Beany, turn the tap off else we'll all be needin' waders. The mistress'll be fine enough in a while.'

'She isn't dead?' Beany's voice caught with emotion.

'Sure, won't she be comin' in here in two seconds an' chewin' all our ears off, large as Lazarus.' She put the child from her knee and began to lumber about the kitchen, collecting knives and plates.

'But why did she fall down?' sniffed Beany, shuffling onto a stool.

'Hah! Wouldn't the Minster fall down with a shock like himself has just given her?' The maid directed a knife at Charlie who thought her face was rather like Sister Bernadette's donkey with her big furry eyebrows.

'Yes, who gave you the right to go scaring our mother like that with your lies, Fuzzball?' demanded Bertie. 'Making her faint.' He too had been most concerned at the impact on Rachel – though the effect this was going to have on his own life far surpassed anything else.

'I don't lie,' answered Charlie dangerously, 'and *don't* call me Fuzzball.'

'Well I say you do – *Fuzzball*!' Bertie rounded on his sisters. 'Let's take a vote on it: who believes this impostor?'

'I do.' Becky raised her hand to a grateful smile from the good-looking boy.

Bertie was nettled that it should be the one who always professed to think the most of him. 'You'd believe it if somebody told you birdmuck was ice-cream! What about you, Wena? You don't believe he's our brother, do you?'

The eldest girl looked troubled. Whatever the truth, Charlie's appearance had undoubtedly distressed both her parents. 'I'm not sure . . .' She turned to the maid. 'Biddy, is it possible for us to have a brother who's brown like Charlie?'

Biddy, well into her twenties now, was more correctly acquainted with the facts of life than when she had entered this household as a girl. 'Sure an' 'tis possible.'

'Don't take any notice of that peabrain,' snapped Bertie. 'How could Father be this boy's father and ours at the same time?'

'Well, I 'spect it was while he was doin' that fighting in Africa that he met the boy's mammy,' was Biddy's solution.

Bertie had been doing some working out. He knew that he himself had been born while his father had been fighting the Boers. 'But he was married to our mother then! It's bigamy.'

'I thought pygmies were tiny,' said Beany, looking up at Charlie.

'Bigamy! Bigamy! It's against the law to be married to two people at the same time,' rasped her brother tetchily. 'And if he wasn't married to this boy's mother then how can he possibly be his father?'

'Ye don't need to be married to someone to make a baby, Master Bertie,' came the indiscreet snippet from Biddy.

'That just shows how ignorant she is,' sneered Bertie to Rowena. 'You can't possibly have a baby if you're not married.'

'Ye won't be told anything, will ye?' Biddy slammed the plates down.

'You're stupid,' sulked Bertie.

Charlie, standing by the fire, looked around at the uncertain collection of faces. Doubt began to invade him. He fought it off, planted himself on a dining chair and said definitely, 'He *is* my father.'

Bertie gave a howl of disgust, crossed his arms and retreated to the window from where he watched the others set upon the pile of scones that Biddy had just buttered. 'Well you're obviously not a gentleman,' he observed as the ravenous Charlie crammed his mouth with food. 'Gentlemen don't bolt their food.'

'Take no notice,' said Rowena kindly. 'He's only repeating what Mother usually says to him.' She felt sorry for the visitor. If he was their brother it was no sort of welcome he'd received.

Charlie asked them to forgive him. 'But I've been stuck on the train most of the day and there was nowhere to buy food. I haven't eaten since this morning.'

'Lord! 'Tis a wonder your backbone ain't playin' The Funeral March on your ribs,' cried Biddy. 'D'ye want I should make ye a fry-up?'

'Maybe he'd prefer a plate of grubs,' sniped Bertie, watching the scones disappear. 'That's what fuzzballs usually eat, isn't it?'

Charlie chose not to rise to the bait, but simply pondered, 'What day is it?' Becky told him it was Sunday. 'Oh well, that's all right then – I don't eat grubs on a Sunday.' He flashed his teeth at Biddy and said he'd love a fry-up.

'Did you come all the way from Africa on your own?' asked Rowena and when he said he had, 'Oh, aren't you brave!'

'I can't see anything brave about it,' grumbled Bertie. There was one scone left. Saliva flooded his mouth, but if he were to get the scone he would have to go near Fuzzball and he refused to do that.

'Mother won't even allow Bertie to go to school on his own,' said Lyn, inviting further detestation, especially as she took the final scone.

'That's a lie!'

'No it isn't, she says you're not to come home without us.'

'That's for your benefit, not because Mother's worried about me!'

Lyn said, 'Huh!' and turned back to Charlie. 'How old are you?' He told her twelve and a half. 'Heck, I thought you were miles older.' She glanced at his long fawn trousers. With these, his man's jacket and his height, he looked far more mature than her brother. 'Mother won't allow Bertie to have any longs till he's fourteen.'

The newcomer tossed a conciliatory smile at Bertie. 'I've only been wearing them myself since I got to England.' But this did nothing to ease his half-brother's envy.

'And you thought you'd just come here and show them off,' mouthed Bertie, adding angrily to his sister, 'Anyroad, I'm nearly twelve!' He caught Charlie's amusement and demanded to know what was so funny.

'Oh, I wasn't laughing at what you said.' The lively brown eyes turned repentant. 'It's just . . . well, you've all got such funny voices.' He could not prevent the laughter from creeping back to his eyes.

'I don't like people who talk posh,' muttered Bertie.

'I didn't mean it as an insult . . .' Charlie took another bite of the scone.

'You're a lovely colour,' said Becky, stroking his hand with admiration.

Charlie scooped the crumbs from his grinning lips as the little girl turned his hand over to remark on how pink his palm was and responded to her compliment by flattering her hair. She transferred her hand to her red curls. 'Oh, do you like it? No one else does.' Some children at school called her Carrots. She had always felt inferior, being different from the rest of her family. Charlie said he thought it was a glorious colour and very unusual.

'Well it would be to you, wouldn't it?' salvoed Bertie.

'I don't know why you're being so mean to him,' defended Becky. 'He hasn't done anything to you, has he?'

'He's upset Mother, hasn't he?' growled Bertie, then looked to the door where his father had entered and bounced off the stool. If Fuzzball was going to stay for any length of time then he had better be sure of one thing. 'Father, about your birds' eggs . . .'

'Oh, Bertie lad, don't bother me with that now.' His father was unusually dismissive of what he had to say. 'I need to talk to Charlie.'

Bertie was visibly wounded by this curt rebuff. 'But he's telling all sorts of lies!'

'Robert, please go to your room,' commanded Russ, quietly but firmly, then addressed the girls. 'You can come down again later.'

'Is Mother feeling all right now?' enquired Rowena.

'Yes, yes, she's just had a bit of a shock, that's all. Now will you just let me talk to Charlie alone.'

A smarting Bertie left, followed by the girls, but not before Becky had made an incriminating observation to the others. 'You see! Father knew Charlie's name without being told – he *must* be our brother.'

'Biddy, if you wouldn't mind . . .' Russ indicated the door.

She looked up from the pan. 'I was just cooking the lad a meal, sir. He's not eaten since . . .'

'For God's sake! Will somebody just do as they're told for once?'

Biddy was contrite, 'Yes, sir,' and began to exit. 'But if ye should smell the bacon burning would ye just . . .'

'If I smell anything burning it'll probably be me,' he muttered. Then, 'What I have to say won't take long. I'll call you when I've done.'

When she had left he sat down at the table opposite the boy, regarding him silently for a time. The bacon sizzled and spat in the pan, its smell wavering under his nose. His innards still quivered from the shock he had received. Taking a deep breath he said bluntly, 'Right then, where do I find this priest?'

Discountenance shaded Charlie's features. He had not anticipated such a brusque opening to his father's first dialogue. 'He's still in Africa.'

Russ pulled upright in disbelief. 'He sent you all this way on your own?'

Charlie shook his woolly head, looking guilty now. 'He doesn't know I'm here.' At his father's questioning face he lowered his eyes and began to scratch at the chenille cloth with a fingernail.

This action and the boy's reticence scoured Russ' nerves and he gave Charlie's hand a curt tap. 'Stop that! Come on, I'm waiting!'

'I . . . the money you sent with your letter, Father Guillaume put it in the cashbox. I broke it open and took it – it wasn't really stealing!' he added hastily. 'It belonged to me, didn't it? You sent it for me.'

But the rejoinder was bitter. 'I didn't send it so's you could come here and ruin my life! Didn't you see what the shock of meeting you did to Mrs Hazelwood?'

Charlie understood his father's anger now, and showed remorse for his insensitive action. 'I'm sorry . . . I was going to wait outside till you were on your own but the children saw me . . . is she very upset?'

Russ gave a strangled laugh and buried his head in his hands. His eyes emerged slowly over the fingertips, their lower lids being dragged down to expose bloody rims. He examined the face before him, missing its attractiveness, seeing only his own misfortune. 'So . . . you came all the way from Africa on your own?'

An affirmative nod. 'I came on a cargo boat.'

'Why?'

'It was cheaper that way.'

'No – I mean why did you come here at all? If the priest received the money then he must've received my letter – didn't he tell you what was in it?'

Uncertainty flickered in Charlie's eyes. 'He said it was difficult for you to take me to live with you at the moment.'

Russ cursed the priest's diplomacy. 'So why did you choose to ignore that?'

Charlie hesitated, then said, 'My mother's dead.'

'Aye, I heard . . . I'm sorry, but I don't see why that should make you come here.'

'She used to tell me that one day you'd come back for me. When she died, I waited . . . but you didn't come. Father Guillaume said you had another wife who knew nothing about me, said she would be unhappy if she knew, but I thought maybe it was just because he didn't want to take me to England with him that he told me this.'

'Well as you can see,' said Russ candidly, 'Father Guillaume was right – Mrs Hazelwood is unhappy, she's *very* unhappy, but there's not much I can do about it now, is there?'

Charlie's head sagged. All at once the smell of bacon was no longer appetizing.

Through his own despair Russ saw the look and, giving a long exhalation, rose. 'Oh don't worry, I won't chuck you out to fend for yourself . . . there's not much point now, is there?'

'He can't stay here!' Rachel was seized by panic at the information from her husband, envisioning the storm if this should leak out.

Russ spoke deflatedly. He had told her everything now. 'If he's here and the priest's still in Africa I don't see as we've any option.'

'We've every option!'

'Throw him out, you mean?'

'Why not?' she rasped. 'Isn't that what you did eleven years ago? Tossed him aside like some piece of rubbish.'

His eyelids performed a gesture of despair. 'I made provision . . .'

'Well you can make provision again! Put him straight back on the train to . . . wherever it was he landed!' Russ pointed out that the boy had no return passage. 'Buy him one! Take the money – take as much as you need but just get him out!' She dashed about the room in her fury. 'Damn you, Russell!' Her nervous fingers travelled the sideboard, pushing and pulling at the crocheted runner.

The pearl droplets she wore in her ears held him fascinated. With each angry word they would dangle feverishly. Any moment now he fully expected to see them fly across the room. 'I'm truly sorry for . . .'

'Sorry? Sorry!' she shrieked, then flew at him, banging her clenched fists at his chest while he stood and took every blow. 'You're filthy, you . . .' She hurled herself from him to plop lethargically into a chair. Yet in a moment she was up and pacing the room once again.' And how many more have there been? How many more of these children can I expect to come creeping out of your sordid Army career?'

'There's no one else,' he replied quietly. 'Only him.'

'*Only*? Hah!' The earrings oscillated. 'Well I'm not putting up with him – get rid!'

'I'll have to contact the priest,' said Russ lamely.

She pulled open a drawer of the sideboard, screwed a pile of writing paper into her fist and flung that and a pen at him. 'Now! Do it right this minute!' He caught some of the crumpled paper against his chest, the remainder floated to the carpet while she continued to badger. 'How soon will he be here?'

'I think it takes a letter about three wee . . .'

'Weeks! I can't have that boy in my house for weeks! For God's sake!' At his torpor she flew into fresh attack, slapping and lashing out at him. 'Say something! Do something, instead of standing there like a . . . dolt! Oh, what are we going to do?' She broke down sobbing.

Russ stayed motionless, wishing for all the world that he could shed his fear and anger as easily as his wife. But he had never been one to parade his emotions. He groped for a remedy. 'We'll have to try and keep him hidden.' It was meant to ease her sobs but induced only derision.

'How do you hide somebody like him?' she gurgled tearfully. 'Besides I shouldn't wonder if half the street saw him come in here with the children.'

'If they ask we'll say he only came in for directions.'

'But I have to invite people in for fittings! Oh, if the Daws knew about him they'd . . .' She caught the twitch near his eye and was filled with new dread. 'Oh, my God!'

'It's only Jack,' he was quick to tell her. 'And he doesn't know the boy's here. Just about . . . you know.'

'If he knows then his wife does! She must've known for years and been laughing behind my back. How many more has she told? How could you ever do this to me – to your children?' This alerted fresh problems. 'The children! What're we going to say to them?' Distraught hands clamped her temples, dragging the hair back from her tortured face.

'They'll have to be sworn to secrecy.'

'I mean about your betrayal! They don't even know how babies come about, how can we possibly explain that you . . . with a native woman?' It came again, the vision of them together, made her writhe. Russ looked away in shame. 'Don't think that hiding your face is going to excuse you from your responsibilities! It's you who's going to tell them. I refuse to be burdened with this.' All the time her mind screamed its helplessness.

He nodded grimly. 'I'll tell them, best I can.'

She wandered about the parlour, hands squashing her cheeks. 'Well . . . if I'm to suffer his presence for that long I'd better know what to call him.' He informed her. 'Oh, for Heaven's sake! What possessed you to pick a name like that?'

He thought it expedient to stay quiet on that point. Any mention of the boy's mother would only restir emotions.

There was a knock at the front door. Rachel's brown

irises became islands on a sea of white. 'Oh no, that's Mrs Taylor! I forgot all about her. I told her to call this evening and pick the material for her hat. If she sees him – Biddy, stay where you are!' She hurtled down the passage, grabbing her hat and jacket and struggling into them before opening the door. 'Oh, Mrs Taylor, I'm dreadfully sorry!' She came out onto the step, pulling the door shut behind her. 'I'm going to have to cancel our appointment – yes, I know it's short notice and I'm ever so sorry,' she nodded apologetically to the woman, all the time forcing her away from the door and towards the gate, 'but this is an emergency. A friend of mine's been taken ill and I really do have to go to her. I'm so sorry to inconvenience you. Look, tell you what,' she succeeded in edging the perplexed caller onto the pavement and shut the gate, 'I'll call round at your house tomorrow morning with all the samples. How will that be? You'll get a better idea if you can match them up against your outfit, won't you?' Not giving the woman time to get her answer out she began to rush away down the street. 'Sorry again for putting you out but I'll have to dash!'

The woman stared after the hurrying figure for a second, then wandered up the street after her. Luckily, the distance that Rachel had put between them meant that the woman did not see where Rachel went after turning the corner . . . which was straight into the back lane and through the rear entrance of her own house.

Panting, she leaned on the door of the scullery for a second to catch her breath. Then, opening her eyes, she moved into the kitchen. The boy stood as she entered, halting her passage. 'I'm very sorry if I gave you a shock.' He came from behind the table.

'You keep away from me!' She ripped off her hat, her alien glare stifling his overtures. She marched on, but found her way blocked by the children and Biddy who had come down to see if it were safe to re-enter. 'Come out of the way!' She tried to push past them.

'Are you feeling well again now, Mother?' asked Beany.

'Yes, yes, I'm fine!'

'Will himself be stayin'?' enquired Biddy.

Rachel's nostrils flared. 'That's what it looks like – will you please let me through!'

Biddy was slow in unblocking the doorway. 'I was just wonderin' where we're goin' to put him, like.'

Rachel sighed heavily. 'Use your initiative!'

The heavy brow descended. 'I don't think I've got one o' them, ma'am. Should I put him in Master Bertie's room?'

'No!' The word slipped out involuntarily and Bertie sought to be more polite. 'Please, Mother, I'd rather he didn't.'

'Oh, Robert, don't be so difficult!' Rachel tutted. 'All right, he can go in with you, Biddy.'

The maid's hands flew to her face. 'Oh, ma'am! That wouldn't be fittin'.'

Rachel felt about to erupt. 'I don't know what all the fuss is about, he probably sleeps on the floor in Africa!'

'No, I said that to him before, ma'am,' came the sage reply, 'but he says he sleeps in a bed.'

'For Heaven's sake put him where you like!' Rachel was still trying to break through the mass. Biddy said he could have the sofa. 'All right, all right!' Rachel finally succeeded in pushing her way past them. 'Just don't bother me with trivia now – oh, and Biddy!' She spun. 'If anyone should call this evening, do not in any circumstances let them in – particularly Mrs Daw.'

'What if it's somebody important, ma'am?'

'I don't care if it's the King! Don't let him in!' Rachel was about to go into the front parlour, then remembered her husband was in there. She didn't want to see him. Pivoting, she bounded up the stairs and shut herself in her room where she burst into fresh tears of rage and humiliation. Everything she had worked for, gone – and all because of a soldier's lust.

'Ah well,' sighed the maid. 'I'd better get your milk an' biscuits for supper. That suit you too?' She was looking at Charlie. 'Oh, Lord! what happened to the frying pan?' She had turned to the range and was looking for the vessel. 'I forgot all about it!'

'I ate the bacon,' Charlie informed her. 'I hope you don't mind, but it was burnt so I thought no one else would want it.'

'Ye weren't so hungry that ye ate the pan an' all?' responded Biddy, looking in the cupboard where the frying pan was normally kept. Charlie said that he had wiped it out with a piece of bread and put it in the bottom of the oven. 'It doesn't belong here!' reproved Biddy, lifting it out and transferring it to the correct place.

Charlie said he was sorry. 'But that's where we keep it at home.' This was all very bewildering.

While Biddy was pouring the glasses of milk, Rowena said, 'Father tells us a story while we're having supper – usually about what he did in the Army.'

Biddy grinned to herself and took a sly peep at Charlie. We know well enough what he really did now, don't we?

'I'm going to be a soldier when I grow up,' revealed Charlie.

'Oh, so is Bertie, aren't you?' An interested Rowena turned to her brother who merely scowled.

'I want to be in the same regiment as Father,' added Charlie.

'They don't take fuzzballs.'

Anger stirred in Charlie's breast. He looked at his shoes so that Bertie wouldn't see how the insult had wounded, for if he started fighting here they would throw him out. It's just a word, he told himself, just a word. It doesn't mean anything. He attempted to divert Bertie's hostility. 'Maybe we could have a game of football tomorrow.'

'Fuzzball, you mean.' Bertie leered nastily.

'Bertie, stop calling him that.' Rowena turned to Charlie. 'You'll have to excuse him, he's just at that age.'

Biddy finished pouring the milk. 'Oh, if you're sleeping down here I'd best bring some sheets down – an' I'll unpack your bag.' She grasped the holdall and took out his few possessions to lay them on the sofa. The sight of a string of rosary beads provoked rude laughter from Bertie. 'Hah, look at that, he wears a necklace. Big sissy!'

Charlie was beaten to a retort by the maid. 'Master

Bertie!' Biddy put her big hands on her hips. 'I'll thank ye to keep your ignorant remarks to yourself! They're not to wear, they're to pray with.'

Bertie had known this – having shared a room with Biddy when he was small he was used to seeing her kneeling and whispering over her beads at bedtime – he had simply wanted to ridicule. 'That shows he can't be related to us,' he told the girls. 'We don't use them at our church.'

'My mother was a Catholic,' said Charlie.

'I'll bet Father didn't like her as much as he likes our mother,' replied Bertie.

'He must have done!' shot Charlie. 'Because he married her first – I'm older than you.'

Bertie didn't have an answer for this, but mumbled something about his father having probably fought Charlie's relatives in the Zulu War, and was made to look extremely foolish when Charlie replied that Father could hardly have been old enough to be at school then, 'And anyway, I'm not a Zulu!'

Bertie tried to cover his humiliation by using more insults. 'Fuzz-z-z.'

'The owl and the pussycat . . .' Beany positioned her hands as though conducting an orchestra and the others followed her lead, all chanting, 'Went to sea in a beautiful . . . *peeean greeen* boat!'

Bertie stamped from the room to uproarious laughter. Lyn explained to the new boy about the magic words. 'So if he calls you that again just say pean green. Or if you like,' she lowered her voice, 'I can tell you some good swear words. D'you know any? Can you teach me to say shit in African so's I can say it to Bertie and not get into trouble?'

'Shit's the same in any language,' muttered Biddy, eyeing the row of napkins on the line above the fire. 'Lord knows I've seen enough of it in this house.'

Charlie pulled his earlobe and looked at Rowena who told him not to encourage her sister. Despite the girls' affiliation he felt very isolated.

'Have you got a grandma and grandad?' asked Becky. At Charlie's shake of head she said forlornly, 'Neither have we.' How she had always longed for grandparents – everyone she knew had them. Still, it was a comfort to find someone else who hadn't. 'How many aunties and uncles have you got?' Charlie looked blank and said he didn't know. 'We've got . . .' She counted on her fingers. 'Three aunties and . . . two uncles, and four cousins. We don't see them much though 'cause they live a long way away – one of our aunties lives in America – but we usually go to Aunty May's for our holidays in the summer. She lives near a farm. It's really good. If you're still here then I expect you'll be coming with us.'

'Come on now.' Biddy distributed the milk. 'One of yese run to the parlour an' fetch your father.'

Beany volunteered, but was disappointed to find the parlour empty. This she told the maid. Biddy went to the foot of the stairs and hollered, 'Mr Hazelwood! The children're waiting on their story!' But it was unlikely that Mr Hazelwood would hear – he was a mile away in the pub. 'Looks like he's gone out,' Biddy told the dismayed gathering.

'He said he was going to explain about Charlie,' sulked Lyn. 'What're we going to do now until bedtime?'

Becky nudged her craftily, then with innocent face said, 'Biddy, will you dance for us?'

The maid placed a collection of biscuits on the table. 'Sure, 'tis a bit hot for dancin' – but I could sing ye a song.'

'Aw no, a dance!' pressed Beany, then to the African boy, 'She's a remarkable dancer is Biddy.'

'Oh . . . all right then – but just a short one!' Biddy lumbered to the entrance where there was more space and positioned her great feet.

'Hang on while I fetch Bertie!' Becky pushed past the maid's bulk and scrambled up the stairs to tap urgently at her brother's door. 'Bertie, away! Biddy's going to do a dance!' It wasn't actually the maid's dancing prowess that inspired such excitement but that Biddy had a habit of kicking her legs high into the air and revealing her drawers – and that wasn't all, for the drawers had gaping holes in them. There was such laughter afterwards. 'Bertie, hurry up!'

But Bertie stated that he wasn't interested and lay there on his bed of self-pity, while down below the maid entertained the new boy, hurling herself about the room like a playful hippopotamus.

Russ chose not to return until long after the children's bedtime. In fact everyone was in bed barring himself. He sneaked down the passage, intending to make himself a snack before going up. The longer he postponed that moment the more chance of his wife being asleep. On opening the door he was startled by a movement from the sofa and the glint of eyes peered at him over a tartan blanket.

'Oh . . .' he said foolishly. 'Sorry, I was just . . . goodnight!' He closed the door rapidly, hovered in the passage for a while then, with a look of grim resignation, took to the stairs.

He knew the moment he entered that she wasn't asleep – her breathing was too manufactured – but it relieved him to know that she obviously didn't want to start haranguing him. Undressing as quietly as he could, he slipped into bed. The horsehair mattress was worn into a hollow in the centre, so that normally their bodies would roll towards each other. But this evening tensed muscles and repugnance kept Rachel balanced on the outer edge. The pillow beneath her face was soaked, making her cheek sore, but she clung there, limpet-like, for any movement might have him rolling over to offer beer-stinking penance. She couldn't bear that.

Russ pressed his belly into the slope of mattress and hooked a hand over the side as anchorage. Lying thus, he stared into the shadows, trying to think what to do about his problem. But the shadows produced no answer . . . only more shadows.

CHAPTER TEN

With abominable timing a letter arrived the following day informing Russ of the boy's abscondment. 'I fear he may be heading for England,' wrote the priest, bringing a mirthless twist to Russell's lips. The brief letter was seized by his wife's nervous fingers whilst he, looking at the clock, said, 'I'd better go and open the shop.'

She placed her trim body in his path. 'Oh no! You wriggled out of it last night, sneaking off to the pub, but you're not leaving this house until you've done your duty and spoken to the children.' She was facing him, but her eyes avoided his, settling on his hair, nose, mouth – anywhere but his eyes.

'I've been thinking about that.' Russ didn't meet her gaze either. 'It might be better if they didn't know the whole story . . .'

Rachel's unbounded hair twirled like a matador's cape. 'Oh, better for you!' Her head was splitting, her body tense through lack of sleep.

'Better for all – I mean, he'll be gone in a few weeks. Why upset them unnecessarily?'

She stared at him incredulously. 'Of all the . . . haven't they been upset already! What d'you think it's done to them, finding out they have a half-brother whom they knew nothing about?'

'They didn't seem too concerned . . .'

'If that's true then it's only because they don't fully realize what a blackguard you are! No, if they're to be sworn to secrecy then they'll want to know why – have a right to know, before someone else tells them . . . and then he can go.'

'Go?' he repeated stupidly.

She closed her eyes in exasperation. 'For the love of God! Think what this will do to us if it gets out! I wasn't in my right mind last night but I am now – he goes immediately.'

'But I don't see how . . .'

'You're the Sheriff of York, show some spirit!'

The way she goes on, thought Russ, you'd think being the Sheriff of York gave me some sort of magic bloody powers. But he did not oppose her verbally and rubbed his face in a pathetic manner. 'I suppose I could take him back meself . . .'

'Walk down the street with him? You will not! He came on his own, I'm quite sure he's capable of going back in the same mode.'

'He's not much older than Bertie,' Russ pointed out.

She wished he hadn't said that; it brought the picture of him and that woman flashing back, committing their adulterous act while she herself writhed in labour. The disgust showed on her pinched face. 'Same age or no, he's obviously inherited his mother's worldliness. He'll come to no harm. He can wait until it's dark, then go.'

After great prevarication he stuttered, 'I can't just chuck him out like that, Rache.'

She stiffened. 'I thought you said he meant nothing to you?'

'He doesn't . . . but I couldn't do it to any child. It's too cruel.'

She gave a hysterical laugh, presenting her face to the ceiling, then squared her shoulders. 'So, we all have to live with the result of your filthy indiscretion until that wretched priest decides to collect him?' She locked her jaws and a heavy silence ensued while she patrolled the carpet. 'Well! If he's staying he'd better have a proper sleeping place, hadn't he? We can't have our guest dossing down on the sofa for weeks on end. He'd best go in the attic.'

Russ nodded gratefully. 'It'll need cleaning out.'

'It's wanted doing for years. Biddy can do it this afternoon, then he can stay up there. I'm not having him under my nose every second of the day – have you written to that priest by the way?'

138

'I'm going to send a cablegram instead. I'll do it on the way to work.'

'Right! Well now you can go into that kitchen and tell those children how they come to have a brother who is black!' She turned her back on him.

In the kitchen the children were waiting for the moment to leave for school. 'Hello, scalliwags,' was his awkward offering. He cupped Becky's bright head before turning reluctantly to Charlie. 'Did you sleep all right on that sofa?'

Charlie smiled, 'Yes, thank you,' though it wasn't true. He had slept only after crying out his loneliness and disappointment for hours – yet now he was heartened by the fact that his father didn't seem to be as angry this morning.

Russ groped for support, then spotted the coalscuttle was half empty. 'Er, I wonder if you'd mind fetching some more coal in, lad? The children will be off to school in a minute and it'll give Biddy a chance to side away if you help her.'

For some reason Biddy seemed alarmed. 'Oh no, that's my job, sir!'

'Charlie will do it, lass,' came the firm reply. Russ cultured a tight smile as the boy, eager to do right, swung the coalscuttle out to the yard.

Waiting for the noisy scraping of the shovel to begin, Russ bade the maidservant to be about her chores then positioned himself in a falsely confident manner on a dining chair. 'Now then, I'm sorry I had to nip out last night. I expect you're all waiting for an explanation about Charlie.'

'Is it true he's our brother?' demanded Bertie without preamble. He too had been denied proper sleep through worrying about it.

Russ studied the desperate expression, glanced at Biddy who appeared to be immersed in her work, then nodded. 'At least, your half-brother.'

'Ooh, lovely!' Becky hugged her arms around her body.

Her father tore his eyes away from Bertie's sickly face to show surprise. Before he could comment, the questions started popping.

'Why haven't we seen him before, Father?' asked Rowena with no apparent concern.

Russ neutralized his voice. 'Because he lives in Africa.'

'Was Charlie's mother brown?' This was Beany. Russ nodded. 'So, he's half white and half brown?' Another nod.

Rhona viewed the newcomer with curiosity – all the bits she could see were brown – it must be the half under his long trousers that was white.

'But, Father, I don't understand.' Lyn puckered her brow. 'Bertie says you can't be married to two people at once.'

There was a tortured pause, then Russ said, 'I wasn't actually married to Charlie's mother.' He hoped he would not have to explain in more detail.

Bertie was obviously pleased he had got part of it right. 'Then if you weren't married he can't be our proper brother?' Please, *please* say he's not, his mind begged.

The man felt impotent at having to dispel his son's hopes and said awkwardly, 'Folk don't have to be married to have children, Bertie.'

'Didn't I tell him that but he called me a liar!' Biddy had allowed her tongue to get the better of her discretion and flushed instantly. 'Sorry, sir . . . I didn't mean . . .' At Russ' stare she stooped well down over her chore and set-to rubbing and scrubbing.

'Mother isn't very pleased to see Charlie, is she?' proffered Rowena carefully.

'No, I'm afraid she isn't, love.' Russ picked at a piece of loose skin by his thumbnail. This constant action since last night had rendered the area bright red and sore-looking. But still he picked.

'Why?' she persisted quietly.

'Is it 'cause he's brown?' contributed Lyn.

'Half brown,' corrected Rhona, still wondering over the white half.

'Did you love Charlie's mother more than ours?' demanded Beany.

'Look, all of you!' Russ gave a heartfelt sigh. 'Just try to be satisfied with what I'm going to tell you. A long time ago I did a very foolish thing. I didn't do it purposefully to hurt your mother or because I didn't love her – you must never think that – but because I was lonely. You'll understand that, Bertie, when you get to be a man. Anyway . . . because of what I did Charlie was born. He wasn't meant to be, like all of you were, he just happened. That means he's your half-brother. I didn't bring him home with me, well because there was no need to, he had his mother there in Africa. So he stayed there. I never expected to see him again, but he is here and he's got nowhere else so we must let him live with us, for a couple of weeks at least.'

Becky, having formed instant affection for Charlie, gave a moan. 'Aw, can't we keep him?'

'No,' came the blunt response. 'He doesn't belong here, Becky. I'm going to get in touch with Father Guillaume – he's the priest who Charlie normally lives with – and tell him to come and collect the boy.' He paused for so long they thought he had finished, but then he added, 'Now, I want you all to do something for me.' He studied each child's face – Bertie's resentful one, Becky's eager one. 'I want you to promise that you won't tell anyone about Charlie.'

Again, complaint from Becky. 'But I was going to write all about him in my diary at school! I never have anything really interesting to put. My teacher would be ever so . . .'

'No!' Russ tried to disguise the fright but it was evident in his tone. 'Becky, you must swear here and now – you too, Biddy!' he remembered her presence, 'that not one word of what I've said will go among strangers.'

The children looked at each other, unable to decipher the riddle, but nevertheless granted their promise – Biddy too: 'May every bottle in the house be smashed should I ever breathe a word, sir,' was her bizarre oath.

'I'd no intention of telling people anyway,' snapped Bertie, all hope vanquished. 'The sooner he goes the better.'

'Bertie, you're still my only son as far as I'm concerned,' said Russ swiftly and tried to put a hand over the one on the table but it was snatched away. 'I'll make this up to you in the holidays, you and me'll go . . .'

'Please may I leave the table?' Bertie wasn't looking at him.

Russ withdrew his hand, wishing desperately that he could find some word to take that look off his son's face, but he simply nodded. 'Aye . . . you'd all better leave else you'll be late for school.' He rose, accepting each daughter's kiss, but over their heads he watched Bertie depart without a word. After this, all except Biddy left the kitchen.

Charlie leaned against the cool wall, eyes dull. Last night's assumption had been wrong; it wasn't simply because of Mrs Hazelwood that his father had been angry. *He doesn't belong with us*, he had said . . . He was snatched from his daze by Biddy who took rough possession of the coalbucket and began to hurl the uppermost lumps of coal at the floor. After a dozen or so had been cast aside she let out a wail. 'Oh, you clumsy creature! Look what ye've gone an' done – oh!' She moaned and crossed her hands over her breast, clasped her stomach as if in great pain . . . then she recalled her oath to Mr Hazelwood – God had seen the insincerity of it and had shattered this bottle as warning. Well to be sure she wouldn't tell anyone about Charlie after this. Though that decision did not stop her giving him a belt round the head.

Charlie stared into the bucket at the wet coal and fragments of broken glass, accepted Biddy's insulting lamentations dumbly. He had come all this way, waited all these years to see his father . . . and his father didn't want him.

Rachel made claws of her fingers, kneading the bumps of her skull as though this might coax her brain into working more efficiently. What had she told Mrs Taylor last night? Had she said she would go round to the woman's house or was the woman calling here? Was anyone else due for a fitting? Concentrate! She pressed harder, grinding her temples till it hurt. What day was it? Then she exclaimed out loud, 'Oh no! Mrs Banks is coming!' and started to pace around like some creature that has a maggot lodged in its ear, pacing round in circles, heading nowhere while the worm gnawed away at her brain, consuming her sanity. She heard the front door close and the car engine start. Soon after this the children came in to say their goodbyes, which she attended with only half an ear. But as they exited she said sharply, 'Your father did warn you not to speak about the boy outside?'

'Yes, Mother.' Her eldest daughter turned at the door, then frowned. 'But I didn't really under . . .'

'Then run along to school.' Rachel dismissed them expeditiously.

On their departure she strode to the kitchen, halting abruptly when she saw that Biddy was alone. 'Where's that boy?'

A dull-eyed Biddy shoved her hair from her face then continued to pummel the dough. 'He's up in the nursery with the little ones.'

'What's he doing up there with the babies? Go and fetch him and be quick about it – oh, just a minute! If anyone calls while I'm out at Mrs Taylor's you're not to let them in, understand? I've got Mrs Banks coming but there shouldn't be anyone after her. After you've made the bread you can do what you've been promising to do for years, which is clear a space in the attic.' Biddy's face came alive, but was soon altered as her mistress continued, 'We can't have the boy sleeping down here, he's interfering with your duties. You can get him to help you if you're too idle.'

'But that's my room, ma'am!'

Rachel's expression was rife with bad temper. 'Are you paying rent for it?'

'No, ma'am.' Biddy's shoulders drooped. 'But ye promised if I sorted it out . . .'

'You have had eleven years in which to sort it out and chose not to put yourself to the trouble, so how can it be your room?'

'Wouldn't himself be better off sleepin' in the nursery an' me have . . .'

'Most certainly not! I am not having my children influenced by his savage ways.'

'Oh, he's not a savage, ma'am! He's a good Catholic – he told me so.'

'All the more reason why he shouldn't go in the nursery!

143

Anyway, you'd never hear the baby crying if you were in the attic. Now go fetch him!' Rachel's impatient feet zoomed her back to the parlour. Biddy heaved a sigh, ''T ain't bloody fair,' and plodded upstairs to do her mistress's bidding, leaving a faint trail of flour on each step.

Charlie was reading a story to Rhona and the baby. Depositing the book on his lap with a thump he stared at Rhona who seemed more interested in his feet than the fairytale. 'Are you listening?' She stopped craning her neck, saying of course she was, but as soon as he restarted the tale her inquisitive eyes wandered. She began to pull off her socks.

'Now what're you doing?' demanded Charlie.

'Me feet're sweaty – it's very warm, isn't it? Wouldn't you like to take your socks off an' all?' Her enquiring eyes were like bright blue marbles.

Charlie gazed at her, then gave an exasperated tug at his socks. 'There!'

Dissatisfied, Rhona said, 'Maybe you'd like to roll your trousers up too?'

'Lord above,' sighed Charlie. 'I don't see how that will improve your listening powers, but very well!' As he rolled his trouser legs up he was flummoxed to see disenchantment spread across her features – but the reason was denied him as Biddy's glaring face thrust itself into the room.

''Tis not enough for ye to smash me medicine, ye have to rob me of my room an' all!'

He laid the book aside and started towards Biddy, 'I'm . . .'

'Never mind! Just get ye gone. Herself wants to see ye in the parlour.' She gave him a bossy thump as he passed.

Rhona cupped her hand and bent close to the baby's face. 'Did you see, Squawk? He's not really half white – his legs were brown an' all.'

When his anxious face peeped round the parlour door, Rachel's back was to him. She heard his polite cough but did not turn. 'I don't want to hear any information about why you came here, nor excuses.' The prickly words hopped over her shoulder. 'I don't even wish to look at you.

Just listen. I don't want you here, but it appears I'm going to have to put up with you until the priest comes. You'll be given a bed in the attic. You are to remain up there until you are granted leave to come down and on no account are you ever, *ever*, to come into this room, nor at any time will you show your face at the window. Do you understand?'

Charlie stared at the rigid shoulders, then said quietly, 'Yes.'

'Then go and wait for the maid to come and clear it out.' She listened for the door's click before allowing her pose to crumple.

When Russ came home that evening and inspected Charlie's new quarters he found there were two put-up beds in it, but did not comment upon this. Only after dark was he to discover who the second bed was for.

He had tried to make the evening as normal as possible for the children's sake, reading them a story as he usually did – though with Charlie's presence he had not felt able to inject his narrative with the customary verve. When the children went to bed he did not, as he would have liked, escape to the pub, but remained in the cool company of his wife for the entire evening – though conversation was virtually non-existent.

Now it was bedtime. The cocoa was consumed, the lights doused, both went upstairs. But Rachel turned and applied a discouraging palm to his chest as he made to follow her into their room. 'I've decided that I'm getting too old for bearing children. Much as I can't stand Ella Daw I have to agree with her that seven is enough for anybody . . . so there'll be no need for us to sleep in the same room any more, will there?'

He was dumbfounded. 'But, Rachel . . . I mean, all right if you don't want any more babies I'll be all too happy to go along with that . . . but surely that's no reason why you should throw me out of our marriage bed.'

'I don't consider us to have a marriage bed,' Rachel informed him coolly. 'Presumably neither did you when you committed your treachery with that woman.'

'Aw, love . . .'

145

'Do you know – do you truly know how I feel about this?' Her eyes bespoke her torture. 'I feel as though I was never really married to you. I feel as if my children are . . .' She shook her head woefully, unable to say the word illegitimate of her own lovely brood.

'But that's just being daft! Of course we're married. I told you it was just . . .'

'Just! Just! You keep saying *just* this and *only* that – you don't appear to attach any importance whatsoever to what you've done!' He tried to tell her she was wrong but she interrupted again. 'Whether we had a legal marriage or not is immaterial now. It's the way I feel that counts and I don't feel married to you. Whatever sort of marriage we may have had is over in everything but name. However,' she added as his face crumpled, 'I've considered things very carefully and have reached the decision that one of us must think of the children. So . . . I'm going to stay with you. We've got to present ourselves to the world as if everything is normal for their sakes. I shall try my best not to show you any unpleasantness in front of them or anyone else, to all intents and purposes I shall have forgiven you. But of course,' her voice caught, 'I have not. I could never forgive you for the pain and humiliation you've brought us. I despise you. That's all I have to say.' She saw that he was not going to move and added, 'I hope you don't object to sleeping in the same room as your son? I thought the nearness of him might bring back happy memories for you. Goodnight.' She shut him from her room, then pressed her back to the door, holding her breath to listen as he creaked his dispirited way to the attic.

Alone in the cold expanse of bed she lay sleepless for hours. Inexplicably, her most prevalent thought was of the baby she had lost four years ago. What sort of Deity had let her innocent baby perish in the womb and yet allowed this one to live so that he could come here and destroy nine lives? She lay there reciting: Russ, Rachel, Robert, Rowena, Rosalyn, Rebecca, Robina, Rhona, Regina . . . Charlie. Damn him! Damn him for ruining her nice ordered life.

Only seconds before she fell asleep did it occur to her that the names so carefully selected for their initial had been adulterated for years by the children themselves.

CHAPTER ELEVEN

Light streamed in through the window in the roof and woke him. Battling with confusion, he lay there for a moment then, remembering where he was, felt the walls of his mind press in on him with overwhelming depression. What time was it? Reaching a hand from the bed he scraped his watch from the bare floorboards. Five-thirty. Another two and a half hours to suffer before he could escape to the shop. He laid the watch down and crossed his hands over his naked chest. Involuntary eyes were drawn to the other bed. The contrast of the white linen made the boy's skin appear darker than it had been yesterday. He was still asleep, lying on his back, lips slightly apart – a bonny sight to the objective eye, but for Russ it provoked a facsimile of the child's mother and he turned away in self-disgust. How was he ever going to cope until the priest came? *And what makes you think the priest's coming will end it,* came the sudden poser. The boy might be gone but you'll still have to live with the guilt, with those looks . . . Fingers scrabbled under his pillow, withdrawing a box of matches and a pack of cigarettes.

The grating of the matchhead on emery roused Charlie. His nostrils twitched and smarted at the invasive reek of sulphur. He blinked. His thick eyebrows remained puckered for some seconds before he came fully awake, then he rolled on his back to look at his room-mate. 'Good morning.'

Russ inhaled long and fierce on the cigarette, didn't look at him.

Charlie glanced at the patch of blue through the skylight. 'Another nice day.' Still no response. 'Might I be allowed out today, d'you think?'

'No. You're to stay up here out of sight.'

'Why?'

Russ thought he detected a truculent edge to the word and replied stridently, 'Because I say so,' before taking another long drag.

The small attic grew oppressive with smoke. There was an inch of ash balanced precariously on the end of the cigarette. Charlie had not brought any pyjamas with him and his legs were sticking together beneath the weight of the covers; they smarted as he pulled them apart. Pushing aside the sheets he rolled into a sitting position and put his feet to the wood. Beneath the other bed there was a tin lid, containing several spent butts – his father had obviously continued smoking long after he himself had fallen asleep. Reaching over, Charlie took hold of the lid and handed it to his father.

'Thanks.' Russ allowed the ash to fall into it.

'Can you blow smoke rings?' Charlie's bright query was ignored. 'Father Guillaume can. Sometimes . . . sometimes I sneak one of his fags out and have a go, but I'm no good.' His impish smile fizzled out. After a while he reached for his trousers which were folded over a chair, took an object from the pocket and held it out to his father. 'Look.'

Russ' eyes flickered briefly. On the boy's palm was a button from a military tunic.

'It's got the initials of your regiment on it.'

'How do you know anything about my regiment?' The question was surly.

'My mother told me everything about you.'

He had never credited her with that much interest – he himself not being very interested in her background – obviously he had been wrong. Charlie's voice was proud as he referred to the button again. 'I found it sticking in the river bank when I was five. I thought it might be yours.' In this tenuous assumption he had carried it with him wherever he went – regarded it as his talisman.

It didn't bring him much luck here. 'I never had a button loose . . . now if it had been a slate I could've laid claim to it.'

This was too subtle for Charlie, but the tone of voice was enough to transmit its adverse content. At his father's dismissal of the button he paid it thoughtful study himself, rotating it between thumb and forefinger. 'It cleaned up very nicely; it was black when I found it.'

When nothing was forthcoming he replaced the treasured button in his pocket, draped his arms over his bare knees and began to drum his feet on the floorboards while he thought of something else to say. The rhythmic slap of his feet seemed to annoy his father. At Russ' forbidding glower he stilled them and after a second asked, 'Is there anything I can do for you?'

No subtlety this time. 'You could get the boat home.'

A wounded interval, then another query, but softer this time. 'Why don't you want me here, Father?'

Annoyed at his own cruelty as much as the boy's presence, Russ scissored his legs viciously out of the bed and ground the cigarette into the lid. 'Why, bloody why! Can't I have any peace in this house?'

Charlie averted his eyes as his father stripped off his pyjama trousers; he had always been brought up to display modesty. He merely listened to the sound of limbs being rammed into trousers, shirt being tugged over head. When Russ left him alone he lay back and squeezed his eyes shut – not against the lingering smoke, but to stop himself crying. It seemed ages before Biddy slouched in to say, 'Ye can come down now. Ye may as well help me with the breakfast seein' as how ye've given me all this extra work to do.'

Charlie had been dressed for some time before her summons. He followed her down to the kitchen and set to obeying each of her instructions, ducking whenever he did something wrong and she took a swipe at his head. Soon the table was laid for breakfast.

'Right! Now you see to this here pan an' make sure it doesn't boil over while I go get the children up.' Despite her grousing Biddy welcomed somebody to boss about.

While she was absent, a heavy-eyed Rachel wandered in. On seeing the boy she simply about-turned without so much as a 'good morning' and went off to the parlour.

When the children seated themselves round the table Biddy told Charlie to hand out the bowls of cereal. 'I'm not having anything he's touched,' said Bertie.

'So ye'll get nothing,' replied the maid uncaringly. Then, as he shot from his seat, 'Where're y'off?'

'I'm going to tell Mother you're not doing your job right!'

Biddy reacted with haste. 'Oh sit down an' I'll make ye something!'

Pushing Charlie out of the way she set about providing a substitute meal for the mulish boy.

'What'll you be doing today, Charlie?' asked Rowena.

'There's a ropeswing down by the river,' announced Lyn before he could answer. 'You can play on that if you like.'

'It isn't yours to say who goes on it,' vetoed Bertie.

'It isn't yours either, pig-face!'

'I know the lad who put it up,' said Bertie, 'and he wouldn't want Fuzzball swinging on it.'

Charlie's hand tightened on his spoon . . . then he remembered, and said, 'What was it now? The owl and the pussycat . . .'

Bertie left the room.

'Good for you, Charlie,' said Lyn, then used her spoon as a mirror to pull faces in.

But Charlie didn't feel particularly good. The last thing he wanted was to rattle his newfound brother. He couldn't understand it, he himself had been thrilled to find out he had a brother almost the same age, but Bertie seemed so resentful. His spoon was poised at his bowl. He did not plunge it in as the others had done, but turned to Rowena who sat next to him. 'Why doesn't he like me?'

She swallowed and scooped a trickle of milk from her chin. 'I don't really know, you never know anything with Bertie – but the rest of us do, don't we?' Her sisters nodded automatically, though most were indifferent to the newcomer.

'We wish you could stay,' added Becky.

'Your mother doesn't.' Charlie poked the spoon round the bowl but did not eat. He couldn't bring himself to say, 'And neither does Father', because he felt it would make him cry.

'Father'll get round her,' vouched Becky. 'He always does.'

'Father's in bother an' all,' said Lyn.

'As well,' corrected Rowena.

'Oh, shurrup! You're as bad as Mother.' Lyn returned to her theme. 'She's always mitherin' and carryin' on at Father – you'll get used to it. None of us takes any notice.'

Rowena considered this disloyal. 'She's had a very big shock, Lyn. Father himself said it was something he'd done.' She looked at Charlie's serious face, trying to comfort. 'I reckon Bertie's upset at you coming here because he's been used to being the only boy for so long, and the eldest, and always sort of being in charge.'

'*Thinks* he is,' rectified Lyn, scraping the residue from her bowl then sitting spoon in mouth until Biddy snatched it from her.

'Maybe he's jealous,' supplied Beany.

'But I don't want to make him jealous, I want him to like me,' Charlie protested and looked at Rowena for further explanation.

Rowena moved her shoulders in confusion. Bertie was always moaning about his sisters – one would think he'd be glad of male support. But then the whole affair was baffling. Charlie had brought some sort of trouble with him but nobody would be specific. Mother didn't want to speak about him at all, neither did Father really. Her sisters didn't appear to think anything much was amiss, their mother had apparently recovered from her shock, everything seemed to go on as normal . . . yet it wasn't normal.

'Don't take any notice of what Bertie says.' Becky clattered her spoon into her bowl and carried it to the sink. 'You can go on the swing if you want to.'

'I'm not allowed out,' Charlie divulged now. 'Father says I have to stay out of sight in the attic again.'

The girls sympathized. Then Lyn suggested, 'You want to ask Father if you can look at his collection, then. That'll stop you being bored.' When asked what collection, she enlightened, 'Birds' eggs, hundreds of 'em in that cabinet in the attic.'

'Do you mean the one near Father's bed?' asked Charlie.

Several mouths fell open. 'Is Father sleeping in the attic now?' enquired Lyn with a frown. Charlie told her yes. 'Well no wonder our Bertie's mad!' She grinned, then turned thoughtfully to Rowena. 'I've never known Mother chuck him out of bed before, have you?'

Rowena gave a worried no – this was beginning to look very serious. Then she returned to the subject of the eggs, advising hastily, 'Do ask first if you can look at them. Father thinks a lot about them. None of us is allowed to touch them, only Bertie.'

'Is any of ye going to use your jaws for anything other than talkin'?' demanded Biddy then. 'Can ye not see the time? Get your breakfasts finished, them as hasn't, or ye'll be off to school on empty bellies.' When the girls had finished and gone off to fetch their schoolbags, Charlie asked the maid, 'Will Father have gone to work yet?'

'The Lord knows.' Biddy's hands dredged another plate from the sink and put it to drain. 'He went out just as I was gettin' up an' I haven't seen a whisker of him since.' Mr Hazelwood had in fact been getting washed in the scullery. At Biddy's entrance he had run a quick comb through his hair, paid minimum attention to his moustache and, saying he wouldn't require breakfast, had gone out.

'Oh . . . well do you think I should ask Mrs Hazelwood's permission to look at the eggs?'

'Yes, if ye want a few slung at ye.'

Charlie sunk into despondency. He wasn't particularly interested in the eggs but could not bear to spend another entire day in the attic with nothing to do. There was little to lose by asking her. 'I think I will just see what she says.' He left Biddy and went to the door of the front parlour. It was slightly ajar. Hearing Bertie's voice, he did not reveal his presence, but listened.

'Oh, *please* let me have some, Mother!'

'Robert, for the last time you are not going into long trousers! Now go to school!'

Charlie ducked back into the kitchen as the other boy sped down the passage and out of the house. 'I don't think

I'd better ask after all,' he told Biddy and levered himself into a sitting position on the table, legs dangling.

Some time elapsed before he spoke again. 'Biddy . . . will you be going anywhere near a shop that sells trousers this morning?'

'I might.' She seized the youngest child's hands, applying a cloth. 'Why what's up with the ones ye've got on?' The cloth mauled the infant's mouth. Regina, nine months old, tried to twist away as the hand encompassed her face.

His foot swung back and forth. 'Nothing . . . I don't want them for me I want them for Bertie.'

'Oh! An' who's meant to be poppying for them, might I ask?' The cloth was aimed at the sink in the scullery but fell short. Biddy sent Rhona to pick it up.

Charlie withdrew some money from his pocket. The maid towelled her hands and came over to look. 'Will there be enough? It's all I've got.' Biddy counted, then nodded, but pointed out that the mistress would not let Bertie wear them.

'Perhaps not – but he could put them on when he's in his room.'

'He'll not be able to impress many folk up there, will he?' The money found a place in Biddy's apron pocket. 'Anyways, what d'ye want to go spendin' your money on him for when he's treated ye like he has?'

'I know how much he wants them. I think Mrs Hazel-wood's being mean, don't you? And I don't need the money if I'm not allowed out.'

'I doubt ye'll buy him this way.' Biddy donned a look of sympathy, appearing to Charlie more like Sister Bernadette's donkey than ever. 'But, sure I'll get them if that's what ye want – though I could think of a lot better things to spend my money on . . . if I had any o' course.'

'If there's any change you're welcome to it,' said Charlie generously. At her smile of thanks he asked if he should go upstairs now.

Biddy looked at the clock. 'Herself won't have anyone coming for an hour or so; time for you to help me with this washin' up before ye hide your face. 'Twill give ye less time

154

to be bored, will it not?' And she smiled again as though doing him a favour.

Bertie found the trousers on his bed when he came in from school and went up to change out of his school clothes. With a surge of delight he tugged off his shorts and was trying the new ones on when Charlie sneaked down from the attic to tap at his door. Bertie shouted, 'Come in!' and was admiring himself in the wardrobe mirror, until he saw Charlie smiling from the reflection. 'Oh, it's you – what d'you want, Fuzzball?' He continued to turn this way and that, examining the cut of the trousers.

'I just came to see if you like those.'

'Why wouldn't I like them? They're much better than yours'. He marched towards Charlie. 'Gerrout! I'm going to show Mother what they look like.'

Charlie stepped into the doorway. 'Oh, I don't think you'd better!'

The reaction was bellicose. 'Who're you to give me orders?'

'I don't want you to get into trouble, that's all.'

'What're you on about?' growled Bertie. 'She wouldn't've bought me them if she . . .'

'She didn't buy them,' interrupted Charlie.

Bertie faltered. So . . . his father had bought the trousers to make it up to him. Bertie was still annoyed – but it would be childish to say he didn't want the trousers just because of that.

'I bought them,' said Charlie.

Bertie gaped in disbelief – then with all his might shoved Charlie backwards. 'Get out!'

Charlie stumbled. 'I thought you liked . . .'

'Get out, you bloody swine!' He struck out at Charlie, hitting him on the nose.

Charlie cried out in pain and immediately struck back in retaliation. Bertie fell, glared up at the other boy and spat, 'Right! I'm going to tell Father you thumped me – you'll get sent away!'

Charlie stepped forward and stooped to help his brother

up, 'I'm sorry, Bertie, please don't . . .' But he didn't get chance to finish. Bertie grabbed hold of him and kicked his shins, weakening his defence and pushing him out of the door.

On its slamming, Bertie fought with the buttons of the offending trousers, kicking his way out of them and pouncing on them to rive at the legs. They were quite well-made and would not yield. Standing on one of the legs he applied both hands to the other and hauled with every ounce of savagery he had. The seam finally gave, but refused to part at the waistband. Giving up, a tearful Bertie rammed up the sash and hurled the ruined article as far as he could.

'Bertie, away it's teatime!' At his non-appearance at the table Beany had been sent to look for him.

'Bugger off,' came the grumpy command.

'Right, I'm off to tell on you!'

Bertie leapt from his hunched position and flew onto the stairs to intercept his sister. 'Hang on, Bean! I want to talk to you. Come in a minute.'

It was rare for any of the girls to be admitted to Bertie's inner sanctum. Beany forgot all about telling on him and eagerly accepted his invitation. He closed the door and returned to his seat on the bed. Beany came to jump up beside him and shuffled until her back was supported by the wall. 'Mother wants to know why you weren't outside.' Unless it was raining the children weren't allowed to be in their rooms. Bertie didn't answer and she sat looking around at the walls which bore several pennant flags, two pictures of soldiers and lots of other military souvenirs donated by his father.

'Do you like whatsisname?' asked Bertie finally.

'Charlie? He's all right.' Beany kneeled on the bed to take a closer look at a picture while she had the chance.

'He makes me sick,' replied Bertie. 'Trying to buy his way into this family – d'you know he's bought me a pair of longs?'

'Ooh, let's have a look at 'em!' Beany flopped into a sitting posture causing her brother to bounce up and down.

'You don't think I kept them, dummy?' sneered Bertie.

Beany's grey eyebrows met. 'But I thought you wanted a pair?'

'Not until I'm old enough! I can't stand these people who pretend to be older than they are. Anyway, I said this morning I don't want anything he's touched.'

Beany mused, finger to chin. 'I wonder if he'll buy me anything for my birthday.'

Bertie grew impatient. 'Beany, you don't want to upset Mother, d'you? Can't you see how his coming here has made her unhappy?'

She frowned in recognition of this. 'Yes . . . and Father.'

'Father's only got himself to blame! It's his fault.' His sister wanted to know why. 'I don't know! It just is . . . He should've told us about the African.' Bertie moved his body round to face her, brown eyes instructing. 'I say we ought not to have anything to do with Fuzzball. Mother'll think we're all against her if we talk to him. You don't want to make her sad, do you?' Tears sprang into the muddy eyes at the very thought of it and she shook her head solemnly. 'So it's agreed we don't talk to him?' Bertie was cheering up.

Beany used her left hand to cup her right elbow. Her other hand clutched a pasty cheek. 'But what about Father? I can still talk to him, can't I?'

Bertie's eyes reproached. 'I thought you said you didn't want to upset Mother – she will be if she thinks you're on his side.'

'But if I don't talk to him I'll get into bother!' She blinked to clear her vision and smoothed her mousy hair from her brow.

Bertie thought about this, deciding, 'You can answer him when he speaks to you, but just don't talk to him first, all right?' With this compromise, the two went downstairs, Bertie adding that he would buy her a good birthday present if she kept her word.

Their father smiled at their entry. 'Ah come on, you two – we thought you'd got lost, Bertie.' When his son did not answer he picked up a plate and held it out. 'Here, I've stopped your sisters from grabbing all these teacakes. Get a couple while they're still buttery.'

Bertie totally ignored him and turned to the sister seated next to him. 'Pass me one o' those, please.' He took a scone from the plate that was passed. Russ, still holding the teacakes, looked at his wife but she seemed to be ignoring him too. He deposited the plate in front of Lyn who took advantage. Bertie happened to catch Charlie's eye and was delighted to see apprehension – he was terrified that Bertie was going to tell Father about the fight! Had Bertie been speaking to his father at all he would have undoubtedly told on the boy, but as he wasn't . . . it was rather difficult. Instead he narrowed his eyes threateningly and bit into his scone as if he were biting Charlie's head off.

Tea continued in this hostile fashion. Russ, looking round the table as he chewed on a teacake, noted that the cool air was not just blowing from his son and wife, but from Beany too. When he asked what she had been doing at school, she simply murmured, 'Nothing much', and gave similar replies to all his other queries.

'It's somebody's birthday soon, isn't it?' Russ asked his wife who nodded wordlessly. 'I just can't think whose it is.' He made much of scratching his head. 'I can recall seeing this lovely doll in a shop window and thinking, "That'll just do for our so and so's birthday", but I can't for the life of me think who I was going to buy it for. Ah well, never mind, if nobody can tell me . . .'

Beany looked at her brother and bit her lip. It was very difficult to take such a position when one was seven years old. After an agonized hesitation she blurted, 'It's mine.'

'What? Your birthday, is it?' said Russ in mock surprise, then went on eating.

'Are you going to buy it for me?' Beany's eyes were pleading.

'Oh, I thought maybe you weren't interested . . .'

'I am!'

Russ grinned. 'Aye, all right then, we'll see what we can do.'

Beany let out a sigh of relief and pleasure . . . and Bertie had lost his ally.

Just then, there was the sound of the back gate being

opened. Rachel jumped from her seat and looked out of the window. 'It's Jack Daw! Upstairs!' Grabbing Charlie by the collar she hauled him from the room and pushed him up the stairs – just as Daw came into the kitchen. 'Oh hello, Jack, what can we do for you?' Rachel shut the door to the stairway and smoothed imaginary wrinkles from her clothes.

'Sorry to disturb your tea.' Jack's hooded eyes toured the company. 'I just came to see if you've got a small pair of pliers, Russ – no, don't get up now! Finish your tea, I can wait.'

Russ looked uneasily at his wife who was retaking her seat . . . then both noticed the abandoned place setting that had been Charlie's. Rachel's face glowed bright red. 'You're not disturbing anything, Jack!' Quickly, she snatched the plate with its half-eaten teacake and piled it on top of hers. 'We've finished now – Russ, go get your friend what he wants.'

Russ licked his lips and rose. 'Away, Jack, my toolbox is out in the shed.'

With the exit of both men, Rachel slumped in her chair.

'What d'you want them for?' Russ was rummaging in his toolbox.

'Oh . . . it's just one o' them fiddly jobs,' replied Jack. 'Smallest you've got – aye, those'll do.' He took the pliers that Russ offered and, much to the other's relief, didn't linger. 'I'll bring 'em back soon as I've finished.'

'Oh, no!' That had sounded too urgent, and Russ tried to cover it. 'I'll call round for them later.' He lowered his voice. 'It'll give me an excuse to get out for a pint.' Jack nodded and left.

'D'you think he saw?' asked Rachel nervously when her husband returned.

'He never said anything,' answered Russ . . . but of course, that meant nothing. They could only wait and see.

Daw closed his back gate and went straight into the water closet. He pondered briefly on Rachel's state of agitation and the extra place setting, but the thought didn't stay long, driven away by the pain that kept hammering under his cheekbone. He sat on the lavatory, prodding about in his mouth, then applied the borrowed pliers, twisting and wrenching at the source of his pain. But the instrument would not grip. The tooth, however decayed, remained firm.

'D'you mind if I go out for a while?' Russ asked his wife as she and Biddy cleared the table.

'With Jack Daw?' At his explanation that he was going to fetch the pliers so as to keep Jack from their house, she said, 'Well, I suppose it would give you the opportunity to find out if he did notice anything.'

So it was with his wife's rare consent that he met up with Jack later in the pub. Each bought his own liquor. Russ noticed that Daw seemed to be consuming more than usual, and whisky at that. Though never loquacious, his friend seemed even more surly tonight – more than that, he seemed on edge all the time. This made Russ nervous too. Daw was waiting to say something, he could tell.

This was confirmed three whiskies later when Daw motioned for his partner to bring his head closer. 'Look . . . I know we don't see eye to eye about politics, Russ, and that's sort of put us apart . . . but we're still friends, aren't we?'

Russ was immediately on guard and gave a non-committal nod.

'And friends keep each other's secrets, don't they? What I mean is, I've kept secrets of yours, haven't I?'

So, he *had* seen the extra place setting. Russ opened his mouth – but before he could ask what Daw was going to do about Charlie, the other went on, 'I'd like to think that if I asked you to do something for me and keep it secret, you'd honour that.'

Russ was confused now. 'Course I would.' Whatever could it be?

For a moment there was only the collective mumble from the other patrons, then Daw whispered, 'I've got this bloody terrible toothache.' He lifted his tot of whisky. 'That's what this stuff's meant to be in aid of but it isn't

160

working . . . will you pull it out for me, Russ? I can't get a grip on it myself and I can't see what I'm doing.'

Russ was dumbfounded, but managed to say, 'Aye . . . I'll do it o' course I will, Jack,' then excused himself, saying he was visiting the lavatory and hoping Daw wouldn't follow.

Outside in the dim, cobwebby closet, he gave way to furtive but hearty laughter, bending double and chuckling until the tears came to his eyes. He had to stand for a long time before feeling composed enough to face his friend.

'D'you want me to have a go at it now?' He stood looking down at Jack who was nursing another whisky, his eyes bloodshot and heavy with pain. At the reluctant tone of Jack's reply, he added, 'Look, why don't you have it done properly?'

'Oh, no! I'm not off to one o' them butchers.' Daw gave a definite shake of head, downed the last of the whisky and stood with resolution. 'Carry on.'

Around the back of the building the pliers were produced. Russ squinted into Daw's gaping mouth. 'Bend your knees, I can't see owt. Here, you'll have to come under this lamp . . .'

Jack grabbed his arm. 'Somebody might see us – just do your best.'

After several unsuccessful attempts, Russ could stand no more of the man's agonized gurgles as he wrestled with the molar. He pocketed the pliers. 'I'm sorry, Jack, I just can't do it! You're going to have to go to a dentist. I'll come with you if you like.'

But Jack's refusal was adamant. Straightening, he cupped his aching face. 'I'll just have to go back in there and pick a fight with somebody – get it knocked out . . . thanks for trying, anyway. Are you coming back in for one?'

Russ said no, he had better go home. Again, he was requested not to say anything about this. He placed a secretive finger over his lips, watched Daw go back inside then went on his way, chuckling freely now. He had gone to the pub on foot. It took him about fifteen minutes to get home.

'Did he say anything?' Rachel had been waiting to ask the question all evening, flinging it at him before he had chance to even close the door.

'No, you can rest easy.' Charlie was still up and drinking cocoa by the fireside. Russ ignored him, taking off his jacket and putting it round a chair back.

'I don't see how I can rest easy when any minute Jack Daw could walk in and blow this wide open!'

'He won't, take my word for it.' Russ found an ashtray then sat at the table with his back to Charlie.

'Your word counts for nothing – and how can you be so sure?'

'I just am.' He lit a cigarette.

'Oh, I see!' Rachel nodded theatrically. 'A question of honour is it? You don't tell on his secrets and he won't tell on yours!'

'Something like that.' The match was extinguished and put in the ashtray.

'Men! You make me sick – I'm going to bed!' She grabbed Charlie's cup out of his hand, charged to the scullery and rinsed it, then swept off to bed.

After she had gone, Russ leaned on the points of his elbows, holding the cigarette with both clasped hands. How was he ever going to keep this up for three weeks? There was a tap on his shoulder. Charlie was holding out his slippers. He took out his frustration on the boy. 'If I'd wanted a bloody dog I would've bought one!' Snatching the slippers, he hurled them at the wall – and immediately felt cruel and petty and childish as the boy turned quietly and went up to his room.

CHAPTER TWELVE

Dear Mr Hazelwood,
The cablegram informing me of your unfortunate predicament
arrived today . . .

Unfortunate predicament indeed, thought Russ acidly as
his eyes consumed the letter he had been awaiting for more
than three weeks. Three weeks of secrecy, mistrust, fear of
being found out. The strain had taken pounds off him. He
was saying and doing all sorts of inane things in his office of
Sheriff; more than one person had enquired after his health.
Not his wife though. Oh no, she had barely spoken to him at
all, except in official capacity. Neither had his son – at least,
not the son who mattered. The other one was talkative
enough, keeping him awake half the night with questions
about his Army life until Russ told him to shut up – and talk
about trying to be helpful! The minute he got through the
door there would be Charlie hovering to light his cigarette
or fetch a cup of tea . . . God, it made him so furious!

But he managed to control his temper for the girls' sake.
He wondered if they really understood any of this. He had
tried to keep life as normal as possible, continuing the
routine of a story each night, but how could things be
normal when Rachel kept dashing to the window every five
minutes thinking she'd heard the sound of the gate? Jack
had not visited since the evening he had asked Russ to pull
his tooth – probably due to embarrassment. Whatever the
reason, Russ was grateful. Thank goodness no one in the
area appeared to have noticed Charlie's arrival, not even
Mrs Phillips. Russ was sure of that, otherwise the news
would have been all over South Bank. Anyway . . . the boy
should soon be gone. Russ continued with the priest's letter.

I was immensely relieved to hear that Charlie is safe, however unwelcome his presence may be. Though I feel sorrow both for the shock Mrs Hazelwood suffered and for Charlie, I must say that I am pleased that he is now acquainted with the true situation. Charlie has always professed a keen ambition to be a soldier like his father, a wish that I have always discouraged. Perhaps now that he has discovered – forgive me – that his idol has feet of clay he may change his outlook. I certainly hope so, for I should hate to see one so close to my heart destroyed on a battlefield. I realize that I must also take a share of the blame, for keeping Charlie's mother's love for you alive by passing on imaginary messages from your letters. I felt it was cruel of you not to make any inquiry as to her health even, nor of your son's progress. Of course I realize now that I was the cruel one for keeping up the pretence and for transmitting that pretence to Charlie. With your permission, I shall endeavour to steer him on the path befitting his character. If, during the time you are waiting for me to come for him, you could persuade Charlie that a soldier's life is not for him, it would make my task easier. With reference to the former, as I told you in previous correspondence I shall be coming to England at the end of August. This being so, it seems silly to embark on such a long trip to collect the boy, only to have to make it yet again within a matter of weeks. I therefore deem it wiser . . .

'Oh, give me strength!' Just when he had glimpsed the end of this nightmare . . . Russ crushed the letter into a ball and threw it on the table. It bounced off and fell to the carpet. With wooden movements, his wife bent to pick it up. 'I can save you the bother,' Russ told her. 'He isn't coming . . . not for two months, anyway.'

She came to life, fingers scrabbling to unfold the letter. 'He has to!'

'You tell him that. He obviously thinks I'm not worth listening to.' Russ felt trapped.

Rachel gripped the letter not believing its words. Another two months! How would she ever cope? The last three weeks had been torment enough, having to behave as if everything were normal in front of her customers and with Ella. The latter had called once, but had not managed to get beyond the scullery door. Luckily, Charlie had been

164

in the attic. Lucky too, that Ella went out to work and was not the kind who was forever popping in and out – but still Rachel was permanently on edge, especially when she had to accompany her husband to a social function and leave Biddy in charge. What if someone called while they were out and Biddy let them in? What if the boy were to show himself at the window? She worried so much about it that it had affected her appetite. She was thinner than ever, and twice as nervous – and now there were to be two more months of it!

She finished reading and threw her arms up in futility, then gestured at the note in Russ' hand. 'What's in that one?'

He stared down at it. 'It's for Charlie.' The boy's name was written on the outside. It had come in the same envelope as the other.

Rachel snatched it from him and after reading it gave another exclamation of disgust. 'He's only telling the boy he has to go to church every Sunday, that's all! Over my dead body. He doesn't leave this house unless it's for good!' She was about to toss the note onto the fire but Russ stopped her.

'You mustn't do that, lass.'

She compressed her mouth, but after a second said, 'All right – but he isn't showing his face for church or anything else! You realize of course that this letter puts paid to our holiday plans?' They always went away during the first fortnight of the children's school holidays.

Russ groaned and stroked at his mouth. His wife was right, how could he visit his sister with Charlie tagging on behind? 'I'll have to write to our May.'

'I don't suppose you'll be mentioning him in your letter! Although I suppose your May and the others will blame *me* for all this. As if he hasn't caused us enough inconvenience. Thank God my sister lives in America!' This was Rachel's nearest kin; though she did have a second cousin who lived in York they hardly ever saw each other. 'Well! If he's staying that long he'll have to have more to wear. You can fetch something from town, pants, socks, stuff like that.'

Following this, she regressed into her current non-communicative state, mumbling, 'Isn't it about time you went?'

He didn't look at the clock. 'Aye . . . you'll give him the letter?'

Receiving a terse nod, he brought his hands together weakly and turned to the door. 'Right . . . I'll go and open up.'

'Oh, before you do!' Her interjection brought his hopeful face round to look at her. 'There's a spider in the sink.'

The hope died. Was this all he was good for now? Going to the scullery he curled gentle fingers round the spider and carried it in the tunnel of his palm to the backyard. Rachel was terrified of the creatures, but she wouldn't see them killed – wouldn't even let Biddy wash them down the plughole as the maid would have done with this one had she not been sent out on an errand. Russ doubted if this chap would have gone down anyway, he was too big for that. He would have hooked his legs round the outlet and every time the dousing ceased would pop out again. Russ wished he had a spider's tenacity. He watched it scuttle away, then went to work.

After he and the children had left the house, Rachel sought out Charlie and thrust the letter at him. 'That's from your priest – no, don't read it here!' She stayed his enthusiastic fingers. 'I've someone coming in a few minutes and I'm sure neither of us wants to be in your company. Take it upstairs to read – and don't you dare come down before you're invited, understand?'

Charlie delivered a grave nod – as if he didn't understand by now. He was about to go, when Rachel frowned, sniffed and said, 'Just a minute . . . what's that I can smell?' Charlie felt a hot rush to his face as Mrs Hazelwood came closer. 'What on earth have you been doing with your hair?' His thatch had suddenly acquired an odd lustre.

Then she recognized the smell. 'My God – you've put lard on your hair! You stupid child, you'll get it all over the furniture – go wash it off this instant. Idiotic boy!'

And Charlie rushed off clutching his letter. On the

landing he stopped and smoothed a hand over his hair, examining the grease it picked up. Maybe he had overdone it. He had wanted to use his father's haircream, but as there had only been a tiny amount left he had not dared, so had chosen lard instead. Obviously the wrong choice – but then Mrs Hazelwood didn't have to put up with the insults he did. Before going to wash it off he sat on the top step to read his letter.

My dear Charlie,

Or my wicked, wilful Charlie is what I should really be saying. Didn't you realize what trouble you were going to bring on all our heads by your impulsive flight? But no, you get these ideas into your brain and any commonsense you may possess is completely discarded. Mr Hazelwood is greatly annoyed. But then I suppose I have no need to tell you that. I hope, my silly young friend, that you are not too greatly distressed by what you have found there and that your father is not treating you too harshly. You must remember that he has suffered as big a shock as yourself. Try to put yourself in his place and any hurtful words he may have uttered will at least be explained. I did try to be diplomatic about this before, but I see no further point in couching my words. Mr Hazelwood does not want you there. Doubtless he will have made this quite apparent to you. So I shall be coming to collect you some time in late August when I take up my appointment at the college in Yorkshire. The latter being so, we shall not of course be returning to South Africa immediately. You will have to lodge at the college with me. This may be a blessing in disguise as you will be able to take advantage of the fine education there. Until we meet I would ask you to go to Mass every Sunday and not be as big a nuisance to the Hazelwoods as you often are to me. You alone are responsible for your situation and must suffer it with dignity until it can be resolved.

With kind regards,

your loving friend, Father Albert Guillaume.

Charlie was annoyed at the tone of the letter. Like his father, his first impulse was to screw it into his hand, squeezing it tightly. It's your fault! he told the priest, you should've warned me . . . anyway, what d'you know about it? Meditation followed the anger: he was to stay here for another two months – that would give him time to kindle affection in his father. Thus far, his attempts had gone unrewarded, but Charlie's optimism told him that nobody could remain insensitive to such devotion forever. Then, when Father Guillaume came he would be presented with a united family with Charlie at its nucleus. I'll show you, thought the boy . . then felt rather sorry for the priest, envisioning him travelling back to Africa all alone, and decided to reply to his letter – after all there wasn't much else to do. He smoothed out the crumpled note and was about to go and ask Mrs Hazelwood if he might have pen and paper, but on hearing the doorknocker and recalling Rachel's warning, crept stealthily to the girls' room to seek out his requisites. Rowena wouldn't mind. Going to the drawer he knew to be allocated to the eldest girl, he withdrew an exercise book and removed a page. Armed with a pencil, he sat on one of the girls' beds to write:

Dear Father,

I'm sorry for being a nuisance to everyone . . . A brief period of thought. Charlie knew that even if the priest had not mentioned the money, he himself should . . . *And for taking the money sent by my father. It was wrong of me, but I wanted to see him so badly and I could not think of anywhere else to get the fare. When I get home* . . . spotting his slip, he scribbled the last two words out. This was his home now. He changed them to, *see you, I promise to repay you in any way you wish.*

Things here are not so bad as you imagine. My sisters are very friendly. There are six of them. Rowena is the eldest and is very kind. I like Becky too. She has ginger hair and is always following me about. This makes Bertie angry. I don't know why because I've tried to be polite and friendly. I even bought him a pair of long trousers because he envied mine . . . He remembered that he had been wearing shorts the last time the Father had seen him and explained, *which I had to buy when I arrived here because it was so cold. Anyway, Bertie went mad when he found out I'd bought them and ripped them up. They are still on top of a neighbour's shed. He is the only one who*

168

doesn't like me and is always calling me names. I know you are forever saying I should turn the other cheek and not fight with people but I have only two cheeks, Father, and sometimes I would love to bash him. I am telling you this because I cannot go to proper confession. Mrs Hazelwood has even forbidden me to go to Mass. Do you think my not going will be counted as a sin? It's not my fault, is it? It's not just church where I'm not allowed to go, I'm not permitted to go out at all. Of course, it's only Mrs Hazelwood who says this, not my father. She's a bit funny and it isn't only me who she's mean to, but Biddy as well. Biddy is the maid. She lets me help with the housework sometimes. She's very bossy but she is a good Catholic . . .'

The letter then did a backwards leapfrog to give more information about the girls and also mentioned Charlie's opinion that everyone would have got used to him by the time Father Guillaume came. *So don't worry if you can't come for me at the end of August, I quite like it here.* He finished by saying that he was looking forward to seeing the Father and signed himself, *Your obedient servant.* Then as a mischievous afterthought added the prefix 'dis' to obedient before folding the letter.

He had a tiny amount of change left in his pocket so he would not have to beg a stamp. He would, however, have to find an envelope and get someone to post it. But that would have to wait until the house was cleared of visitors. With a sigh, Charlie crossed his arms to stare at the wall. That could be ages. Oh, how monotonous it all was. Feeling in his pocket he took out one of the butts he had salvaged from the ashtray and lit up. The strength of it burnt his tongue, but he didn't care. It was something to do.

The children were on their way home from school. In actuality, the younger ones had already been home but had gone back to the end of the street to await their brother and elder sister who had been to music lessons.

Bertie felt a twitch of anger as he turned a corner to be greeted by Becky's wave. He did not reciprocate, considering her to be a two-faced cat. She had barely looked in his direction since the African had arrived; too busy crawling round Fuzzball, laughing at his jokes. He grimaced again as a breathless Rowena scampered up behind him to pounce on his shoulder.

'Bertie! Didn't you hear me shouting you?' She matched her step with his.

'No.' He continued to look straight ahead.

'You must be deaf. I've been calling you for ages. Why didn't you wait for me?' It was customary for them to meet after their music lessons and travel home together. When her brother didn't answer, she flourished a hand at the fiery-headed child who galloped to meet them. 'Hello, Beck!'

'Charlie's waiting to see you,' Becky informed her brother after responding to Rowena's greeting. 'He wants to know if he can borrow . . .'

'No he can't!'

Becky stuck out her chin. Her brother had been behaving in this stupid fashion for weeks. 'I haven't even said what it is yet!'

'Whatever it is he can't have it!' Bertie widened his step and left them.

Becky pulled a face at her brother's back, then nodded at Rowena who had said, 'Maybe I have what Charlie wants.' The elder girl waved at Rhona, Lyn and Beany who waved back but did not jump from the wall as their sister had done. Beany wasn't speaking to her brother who – as he had sworn on the day she had broken her promise by talking to her father – had not bought her a birthday present. Lyn, never a great fan of her brother, had lent her support. Rhona stayed with them simply because she was not allowed to cross the road on her own.

Bertie marched on, head down like a charging bull. It seemed to him that they were all falling over one another in an attempt to please the cuckoo. He wondered how much longer he would have to put up with the African's presence. The worry was making his school work suffer. Twice today he had had his knuckles rapped for inattentiveness. It was fortunate that he had taken his scholarship exam before the Fuzzball had arrived or he would never have passed. He couldn't decide which was the worst place to be, school or home. In either situation he could not rid himself of his half-brother – and still he couldn't grasp the crux of it: how could Father be father to two boys at the same time in different countries? As yet there had been no proper explanation – not that he would have listened to it if there had been. He was still unforgiving of Russ for letting him believe he was the only son for all these years. There was tiny consolation to be had from the fact that Father didn't seem to welcome Charlie either – yet even here there was paradox, for why was Father sleeping beside the boy he professed not to want? No, Russ had plummeted in his son's estimation. Even when Charlie went things could never be the same.

His thoughts ended with the arrival in the street of an ice-cream vendor who pedalled along shouting encouragement. Only now did Lyn and Beany come running. Children began to swarm from their houses and stampede after the vendor. One of them, returning with an ice, brandished it gleefully at Lyn, knowing that the Hazelwoods were not permitted this treat.

'Hokey pokey, penny a lump, makes you cough and makes you trump!' retorted Lyn, sticking her tongue out. Then said excitedly to the others, 'Aunt Ella's home from work – come on!' and with Bertie leading the way they headed for the back lane and along to the Daws' house where they burst in upon the woman.

'Oh, blimey it's you lot!' After the initial charade of heart failure, Ella turned to scuffle about on a battered dresser. 'Come for your brimstone and treacle, have you?' She too had heard the ice-cream seller's cry and was well prepared. When she faced them she had a bottle and spoon in her hands. 'Right, line up, who's first?' At the row of baggy-mouthed faces she gave a wry smile and, putting down the bottle tendered a florin instead. 'Here you are! I must be daft.' Rowena asked what it was for. 'Eh, you want to go on the stage, you do. What's it for, she says! Ice-cream, that's what you came for, isn't it?'

'We're not allowed ice-cream,' supplied Bertie. 'Mother says it'll give us tuberculosis.'

Ella folded her arms across her off-white blouse. 'I know very well what your mother says, as I know very well you didn't come here just to enquire after my health. Get one for Kim an' all – away! before he goes.'

'Don't worry, I'll catch him at the corner!' Temporarily brightened, Bertie snatched the coin and, with Rowena as helper, charged down the back lane to intercept the man at the corner. When the two returned with dripping cones the children sat in Ella's kitchen to consume them. They came here quite often, though in secret for their mother would not have approved, regarding Ella as a bad influence.

'What a shame Charlie's not allowed out,' sighed Becky, wrapping her tongue round the treat. 'I'm sure he'd love ice-cream. I don't suppose they have it where he comes from. It'd melt, wouldn't it?'

'Oh, and who's Charlie then?' Ella sat down and held out the cone for the dog to lick. She quite enjoyed the children's company. With them not being her own she could send them away when they got too argumentative – as Bertie was wont to do. He was a clever little devil sometimes. But she had to smile at the way, whenever she offered a forbidden treat, he would always put on a disapproving face as though he had no intention of accepting it and that Ella was trying to lead him astray. Ella supposed there was an element of the latter in it – Rachel had no idea how to bring children up. No ice-cream indeed! She opened her mouth in surprise at Becky's yell, saying to the normally placid Rowena, 'Eh, I saw that!' The guilty person apologized. 'Nay, it wasn't my ankle you kicked.' She allowed the dog to take the cone which it ate with much heavy breathing and gyrating of head as the cold ice-cream hit the roof of its mouth. Rowena was forced to explain. 'We're not meant to talk about him, you see.' Another grimace at Becky.

'Oh, I see!' Ella performed an understanding nod and watched as Kim littered the floor with shards of wafer and blobs of ice-cream.

'But when Mother said that, she meant strangers!' complained Becky. 'Not Aunt Ella.' She fetched her knee under her chin to rub at her ankle, daubing herself with ice-cream in the process and having to lick it off.

'Well yes, I suppose so . . . but Becky, you must be more careful with your tongue! What if anyone else had heard?' Rowena took a hesitant lick of her ice, suddenly remembering poor Charlie who had been waiting to see her all day and here she was guzzling ice-cream. In her selfish gluttony she had forgotten all about him. 'Sorry, Aunt Ella . . . I'd like to tell you but . . .'

'If your mother said you're not to speak about him then you'd best not,' advised Ella, scooping the terrier onto her lap where it continued to wrap its tongue round its jowls for some time.

This vow of silence was excruciating. Becky was absolutely bursting to show off her new brother. Now, she said thoughtfully, 'But Mother didn't say anything about *showing* him to anybody, did she?'

'Why do they keep him locked away then, dummy?' Bertie rubbed a drip from the arm of his chair and looked to see if Ella objected. She obviously didn't – didn't even seem to notice. His mother would have heard it drop if she had been over the other side of Knavesmire. The abrasive tone and the question itself prodded Ella's curiosity though she said nothing; it was the best way if you wanted to know anything: let them do the talking. Who the dickens could this Charlie be? Did Rachel have a secret lover? The thought produced an inward grin.

Rowena bit her lip. 'I do feel sorry for him. Look at us sat here scoffing while poor Charlie's stuck in the house . . . if we sneaked him out, Aunt Ella, would you tell?'

'Who me? No, cross my heart and take me for dogmeat.' She fondled the ageing dog who groaned his ecstasy and licked her face.

'There's no ice-cream for him,' said a cross Bertie.

Becky showed more generosity. 'He can share mine.' She had found her new brother much more receptive to her adulation than Bertie.

'Maybe he won't like it.' Bertie was determined that the boy shouldn't come.

But Rowena had made her decision. Rising, she entrusted her half-eaten cone to one of her sisters and ignoring her brother's pettish obstacles, dashed off.

Entering by the back door she silenced Biddy with a finger across her lips, crept on up the stairs to the attic. The door wasn't locked; her parents hadn't actually gone that far. When she peeped in Charlie was not there. Alarmed, she rushed first to the nursery, then to the other rooms, finding him in Bertie's. 'Oh, Charlie, you shouldn't be in here!' Her voice jerked him from the window. 'Bertie'll kill you if he finds out.'

'I haven't touched anything.' He was glad to see Rowena, having made no intelligent contact all day. 'I was only waiting to see . . .'

'And Mother said you weren't to show your face at the window,' she interrupted in a tone that scolded. At his further apology she softened at once. 'I'm not angry, Charlie, I'm just trying to save you from Mother's tongue.'

'She's been madder than ever today,' he confessed. 'Father Guillaume isn't coming until the end of August.'

'Oh . . .' Rowena liked Charlie, but his presence had created an awful atmosphere between her parents. She wasn't sure if she wanted him to remain for another two and a half months. 'Will you have to stay up here for all that time?'

'I hope not!' His eyes widened. 'I think I'd go loony.' He had read every book in the house apart from Bertie's. That was why he was here now, hoping the latter might be swayed.

'Oh, I nearly forgot why I came!' Rowena told him about sneaking into Ella's and the ice-cream. 'Mother doesn't allow us to have it but sometimes Aunt Ella makes us have some. Anyway, Becky let slip about you, but I don't think Aunt Ella will tell so if you like you can come and have some too, but don't clomp.'

Charlie's expression was one of disbelief, but he didn't waste time by putting voice to it. Instead, he dashed as light-footedly as he could after Rowena and, within minutes, was being instructed on how to demolish the fast-melting cone that Becky had been trying her best to save.

Ella's heart had bumped against her stomach at the entry of the dark-skinned youth. But sufficiently recovered now, she smiled and said, 'So, you're Charlie, are you?'

'Oh, aren't we rude!' Rowena, ice-cream dribbling from her lips, swallowed with difficulty and apologized. 'Charlie, this is Mrs Daw or Aunt Ella as we call her, who's kindly bought the ice-cream you're eating.' The introductory hand was turned on the boy. 'Aunt Ella this is Charlie – our brother.'

CHAPTER THIRTEEN

'Black as a collier's horse!' crowed a delighted Ella to her husband, having pounced on him the minute he came in from work. 'Well, no . . . I tell a lie, a sort of light-brown really – well he would be, wouldn't he? I could scarcely believe my ears! Got him locked up in the attic they have, least that's where he was meant to be. Eh, what a going on!' She chortled again.

Jack peeled off his overalls, slung them in a corner and went to wash his grimy hands. His only answer was the elevation of one eyebrow.

'I can't tell you anything, can I?' She slammed his meal onto the table and stood, hands on hips as he emerged from the scullery. 'How long have you known about him?'

He seated himself, picked up his knife and fork and began to eat, confining his chewing to one side – the decayed tooth was still troubling him, though not quite so painful today. 'Oh, I didn't know he was here.'

'But you know how he came into being, don't you?' She narrowed her eyes and received but a nod. 'Well, thank you for keeping it to yourself all these years!' She dragged a chair away from the table and sat opposite him to begin her own meal.

'It's hardly the sort of tale you go spreading about a pal.'

'Eh, what about this pal here?' She thumped her chest, then snatched a mouthful of stew.

'Now what would you have done if I'd told you?'

'Well . . . nowt, I suppose, but . . .'

'Give over! You'd have thrown it at Rachel the first chance you got.' He used his fork as a shovel, crouching over his plate like one who is famished.

'Jackie Daw, fancy accusing me of a thing like that!' Ella dropped her hands to the table.

'Aye well, I know you.' He sprinkled more salt on his meal.

'Stuck-up cow, serve her right if somebody told her.' She resumed eating.

'Well, she knows now well enough, doesn't she?'

A gravy-edged grin from Ella. 'Aye! My God, won't this alter her chest measurement – well come on then! Give us the whole dirty story.' Over the rest of the meal he told her what he knew of the liaison. At his conclusion she used the back of her hand to mop her lips, then made a barbed comment. 'I hope this doesn't mean I can expect a long-lost piccaninny on my doorstep, Stanley Daw.'

For the first time he gave her his entire attention, cutlery poised in mid-passage. 'I'd never do anything like that to you. You believe me, don't you?'

Her hand shot out to grasp one of his. 'Aye . . . otherwise that knife and fork'd be sticking out of your face.' After exchanging dry looks, they scraped up the last of the stew.

'Even if she is a snooty bitch,' said Jack, wiping his mouth and patting his stomach. 'I feel sorry for her. It's no thing for a wife to find out. He's not a bad lad, isn't Russ, but he's weak. I wonder how the kids've taken it?'

'They didn't appear to see anything odd about it,' replied Ella, swapping the empty plates for bowls of sponge pudding and sitting down again. 'Though Bertie was a bit sulkier than normal. I don't suppose I would've known anything about all this if it hadn't been for them.' Another accusing look for her husband. 'Eh, but Rachel can't keep him locked up forever, can she? Apart from anything else it's inhuman.'

Jack downed a huge spoonful of pudding. 'How did he get here d'you know?'

'Could I have that interpreted please?' After her husband had swallowed the mouthful and repeated the question more clearly, she said, 'From what I gather he's been here quite a few weeks, turned up on the doorstep and blithely announced himself. They've done well to keep it quiet for this long, haven't they?'

'I wondered why they were scuttling about the last time I was in there.'

. 'Oh yes, and when was this? You never tell me anything.'

'It didn't seem worth telling . . .' He pondered on his friend's behaviour on their last meeting, feeling rather peeved that Russ hadn't felt able to confide in him. 'This'll finish Russ as far as the council goes if it gets out, you know.'

'Won't it just?' Her eyes were cunning over the spoon.

He pointed his own spoon at her. 'Eh now, Ella . . .'

'I never said a word,' came her light rejoinder.

'Ah, Russ! Come in.' The Lord Mayor rose to greet his Sheriff. 'Will you take a drink with me or is it a bit early?'

'Aye, it is a bit, I won't just now.' Russ looked tense. 'About your letter . . .'

The Lord Mayor ignored his visitor's last comment. 'Early or not, I think I'll have one.'

Russ took the letter from his pocket, the one he had received this morning summoning him to this lavish apartment of the Mansion House. He felt like a schoolboy in the headmaster's study, standing here on the carpet, feeling the plush pile shift under his nervous feet. 'You said you had something to . . .'

'Thank you, Gerald!' The Lord Mayor interjected brightly, accepting his drink and dismissing the butler. 'My goodness! I could do with this.' He tossed the whisky into his mouth and made exaggerated noises of appreciation. Only when they were alone did he become serious. 'Now, my letter . . . I don't want to mess about, Russ – oh, sit down!' He paused while Russ took a seat. 'An allegation has been made which . . .'

After the word allegation, Russ barely heard the rest. A cold feeling began to inch its way over him . . . like being stroked by a corpse. The Mayor finished. 'Can you offer any explanation?'

Russ was toying with the ends of his moustache. At the Mayor's words he started. 'Er . . .'

'Are you feeling all right?' The Lord Mayor frowned, bending forward. 'Here, let me get you that drink.' He did so, handing the glass to Russ who looked at it carefully before disposing of its contents. The Lord Mayor did not appear to notice the trembling hand. 'Now, do you feel able to shed any light on this, Russ? I mean, it's a pretty serious accusation.'

'Could I ask who made it?' mumbled Russ, playing with the empty glass, eyes flitting about the decorous plaster-work so that he wouldn't have to look at the Mayor's face.

'I hardly think that matters. Suffice to say . . .'

'It bloody matters to me!' Russ found the courage to look at the man now. 'I want to know who's been slinging the mud.'

The Lord Mayor came over, decanter in hand, touching it to the other's glass. 'There's no substance . . .?'

'None, none!'

The decanter was put aside. 'As I said, Russ, it's a serious accusation. What the letter is saying is that you commit-ted . . .' he stirred the air with his hand, searching for euphemism, 'an indiscretion in South Africa and that . . . indiscretion, is now locked away in your house.'

'It's all lies!' Russ gulped a drink, then frowned in mid-action. 'Letter, you said?'

'Yes, the allegation came in the form of an anonymous letter . . . so you see, I'm not able to tell you who made it. Luckily for you it was sent to me personally and not the Council.'

'Can I read it?'

The Lord Mayor studied the man carefully, then said, 'I can read it to you.'

Hazelwood's response was derisive. 'Scared I'll rip it up? Destroy the evidence?' The rest of the drink was consumed at one gulp, the glass planted firmly on a table.

The Mayor understood his anger. 'I'm sure I'd feel like doing the same.'

'But you want the proof when it comes to defrocking me!'

This invoked annoyance. 'I'd hardly have worked along-side you if I was that way inclined!'

'No, no, I'm sorry, Jim . . .' Russ looked tired. 'Just read me the letter, will you?'

'We are on the same side, you know.' The Lord Mayor

179

took the letter from his pocket and began to read: 'I feel it is my duty to inform you that the man who holds the honourable position of Sheriff is sadly inadequate for the role. I am sure you cannot be aware – or you would never have dishonoured the post with his name – that Russell Hazelwood is the father of an illegitimate son, conceived while he was married to his present wife, conceived upon a native woman of Africa, conceived whilst on the pretext of fighting for the British Army. Do you not think this disgraceful and hypocritical conduct for a man who professes to be so conscientious about the less-fortunate citizens of York and yet has his own son cruelly locked away in an attic room for fear that the world may learn of his adulterous practices . . .'

Russ, looking sick, held up his hand. 'That's enough.' It was obvious who had written it. So, Daw had known all along about Charlie being here – but why had he waited until now?

The Lord Mayor folded the letter. 'I have to ask you again if it's true?'

'No it's bloody well not!'

A nod. 'As I thought, a cowardly libel. A pity it's not signed, if it was you'd be able to sue.'

Russ dismissed this rapidly. 'Ah, it's best left alone – just rip it up.'

The Lord Mayor hesitated for a long time. Russ turned his back, pretending he wasn't concerned, but remained fearful until Ridsdale finally threw the letter on the fire. But even now he wasn't fully relieved.

'Naturally I didn't believe a word of it . . . but I had to let you know.' The Lord Mayor watched the paper scorch and blacken.

Russ gave a gesture of acquiescence. 'I'm glad you did.' Christ, what was he going to do? The timebomb had been primed. 'Look . . . if you want me to resign . . .'

Incomprehension from the Mayor. 'But why on earth would I want that? You've just shown it's from a crank.'

'But if it should get out? I mean, even the inference . . .'

'I don't think that's likely. Only you and I know about the letter.'

'And the person who wrote it. What if he should write to the press?' Russ condemned his tongue: for God's sake, what are you trying to do to yourself?

The Mayor sighed and puffed out his cheeks. 'It'd cause some fun and games, no doubt. But then if it's not true I think we can weather it, Russ.'

'But how can we prove it's not true?' came the defeatist query. 'Once a thing like this has been said . . . you know the press.'

'The only comfort I can give you is that we must hope it never comes to that – and if it does you have my total support, Russ. By the way, how's Rachel? Marjory suggested we have dinner together next week sometime. I know we see a lot of each other in an official capacity, but we never seem to get a quiet moment to chat about our families and such. Can you make it on Wednesday?' At Russ' vague nod, Ridsdale detached himself. 'Good! I'll have to be off now, I've a lot of bumf to see to before the meeting this afternoon. I'll see you there, will I?'

With a departing nod and still in a daze, Russ left the Mansion House. He lingered at the bottom of the steps, indecisive with shock. Traffic and people milled around Saint Helen's Square. Someone bumped his shoulder, almost knocking him off-balance. He grabbed a railing for support . . . then made for the nearest pub.

Here, he drank more heavily than was usual for him and was forced to sponge up his over-indulgence with a meal of bread and cheese, though he was far from hungry. With nothing more pressing to listen to in the afternoon than the City Engineer's proposal to erect a new convenience at the corner of Kent Street, and discussion of the new road from Pavement to Piccadilly, Russ was able to sit and consider his embroilment with little distraction. However, the final subject on the agenda – the deteriorating state of the slums in the Walmgate sector of the city – lured him from his self-contemplation. Jack Daw was demanding to know why there was still no proposal to lessen the concentration of poor in that area. Russ listened intently, smouldering with frustration. He knew it could only have been Jack who had sent that letter – the bloody traitor!

Daw was stabbing a finger in the direction of the Conservative councillors. 'I've even heard the appalling suggestion from one councillor that these people are used to their environment and it would be a downright cruelty to take them away from the area, split them up from their friends who they've known for years . . .' Judas! seethed Russ. '. . . and there are some among us who claim to be so conscientious about our less-fortunate citizens . . .'

The exact words of the letter! An incensed Hazelwood shot to his feet . . . then realized he could say nothing here and, to a few surprised looks, sat down again to nurse his fury.

After the meeting was over, though, and the council chamber was almost vacated, he approached Daw to prevent his departure. 'We have things to say.'

Jack gathered his papers, responding with brevity as was his style. Russ sought to jolt him from his relaxed manner. 'How's your toothache, Jack? Plucked up enough guts to visit the dentist?'

It had the desired effect. Daw looked around him swiftly. 'Eh, keep your voice down, Russ!' He eyed the door where the last few people were leaving. 'I thought we weren't going to say . . .'

'So did I! It was *you*, wasn't it?'

Jack went back to shuffling his papers, regaining his calm. 'It still is me, as far as I know . . . least it was when I got up this morning.'

'You know bloody-well what I mean!' Suppressed fury and the liquor had tinged Hazelwood's eyes with red. 'How did you know he was here?'

'Do I detect from this frantic tone that your sinful past has caught up with you, Filbert?'

'You bastard!' Russ clenched his fists at his sides.

Daw shoved his papers into a case. 'Not a word to fling about these echoing chambers.'

'I should've known Hawk-eyes would've seen him – you miss nothing! All these weeks I'll bet you've been laughing fit to bust, couldn't wait to pass on the knowledge. You've always been jealous of me, haven't you?'

Jack stopped then, to donate a pitying smile. 'Jealous?'

'Aye, bloody jealous! Jealous of my success, jealous of my brass, jealous of my family – aye and that most of all! What really galls you is that I have so many kids and you're not even man enough to father one!'

There was no raised eyebrow this time, only a raised fist. It was in the act of being aimed at Russell's face when a shout from the Lord Mayor delayed it.

'What the devil is going on here?' An angry Ridsdale strode back into the room. 'Brawling in council chambers – Daw, put your fist down, you damned fool and tell me what's going on – Councillor Hazelwood?'

'He doesn't like the truth!' spat Russ breathlessly as Daw shrugged his jacket into place, both glaring at each other.

'Truth isn't something you're good at either,' returned his opponent. 'I may not have a child as proof of my virility but by Christ if I had to resort to your methods to prove it . . . at least I'm man enough to shoulder my responsibilities.'

'But not man enough to put your name to a letter!' yelled Russ.

Jack's face screwed up in exasperation. 'What're you bloody wittering on about, man?'

The Lord Mayor stiffened. 'Just a minute, Russ, are you inferring that Councillor Daw wrote that letter?'

Russ realized to his horror that he was on dangerous ground. Unsure of the best answer, he said nothing.

'Look, I don't know what either of you are on about,' said Jack tightly. Then, when the Mayor explained, 'I'm not in the habit of writing anonymous letters – you should know that, Russ. If I have anything to say I'll come right out and say it.'

'Oh, don't come that with me!' snapped Russ. 'You were the only one who knew about the la . . .' he broke off, but too late.

'Russ . . . you said there was no substance to the allegation,' Ridsdale pointed out slowly.

'There isn't! I . . .' Russ spun away with an exclamation of surrender. Oh, you bloody imbecile!

'So, it was all true about your liaison? The child?' The Mayor was answered with a defenceless nod. 'Even the piece about you keeping the boy a prisoner?'

'I'm not an animal! I haven't locked him up . . . We were just keeping him safe while . . . somebody comes to collect him and take him back to Africa.'

The Lord Mayor recouped his authority and looked about him, ill at ease. 'We'd better discuss this more privately – come on.' He started to exit. 'You as well, Jack.'

'I want none of him!' shouted Russ. 'He's ruined me with his poison pen.'

Daw came up close then and spoke right into his face. The anger was almost gone, replaced by a kind of amusement. 'Do you want to know something really funny, Russ? You want to know who's responsible for getting you into this mess – your own big mouth. Because though I couldn't tell you who wrote that letter . . . I do know that it certainly wasn't me.'

The first Russ was aware that his confession had received a wider audience than the two people in council chambers, was the following morning when a woman spat in his face. That she was a particularly common woman made it no less shocking. He had emerged through the front door, raised his hat to her as she passed and had been about to climb into his car when she had pursed her lips and aimed the stream of spittle that now wound its way down the side of his nose. Staggered, he did nothing, made no move to wipe it away, simply held her with speechless mien.

Then, 'Adulterer!' she had snarled at him, flung her shoulders round and stalked away.

Still mesmerized, Russ stared after her until the effects of her scorn began to tickle his cheek. Pulling out a handkerchief, he dashed it away. Then, instead of getting into his car, he redirected his feet towards the house.

Rachel took scant notice of his re-entry. She had dealt him few words since Charlie's arrival – at least not civil ones. But when he just stood there, made no excuse for his impromptu return, it sparked a listless question, 'Did you forget something?'

He turned his eyes in the direction of her voice, but gave no answer. He had told her nothing of the anonymous letter, nor the shame induced by his own foolish tongue, nor of the Mayor's advice that he should resign. He opened his mouth but still remained mute, moving his head from side to side.

Rachel scowled – then the doorknocker sounded to divert her focus. 'Answer that: Biddy's gone on an errand.' She reverted to her hat-making, distancing herself once again.

Russ devoted only half an ear to the man on the doorstep, missed his identity. When the caller asked if he could come in and speak to Russ he dazedly agreed.

The young man thanked him, took off his hat and laid it on the hallstand, then reached into an inside pocket. 'I shan't keep you long. I'd just like to know if there's any truth in the rumour that you're about to resign.'

Russ became alert then. 'Who did you say you were?'

The hand came out of the jacket bearing a notepad. 'Brian Green, reporter for the . . .'

'Out!' Russ swung the door open and gestured into the street.

The reporter did not leave; he was finding a clean page in his notepad. 'These imputations . . .' They were the only words he was allowed to utter. Russ cupped his elbow and shoved him forcefully into the street, slamming the door.

He leaned against the wall, chest tight, mind numb. There was no further option. He would have to go in and tell her . . . then he would have to compose a letter of resignation.

CHAPTER FOURTEEN

Sensation At Guildhall! Sheriff Resigns. Illegitimate Son Revealed.

Rachel allotted him the most rancorous, the most despising glare, then closed the evening paper, flung it at him and stormed out of the back door. He did not try to stop her. With jellied legs he moved to where the paper had fallen and picked it up, rustling its pages back to their former neatness then folding it and laying it aside. He hovered, not thinking, just standing. His mind and body seemed in two different places. With their coalition he reached slowly for the paper, bypassing the advertisements on the front to read the impeachment yet again. It was fast work. He could almost admire them for their efficiency. Only a matter of hours had passed since he had given formal notice, but already it was receiving full circulation.

He was still ignorant over the authorship of the damning letter – not that it mattered very much now – but he would like to know who had waged such underhand war on him. Naturally, Rachel thought she knew already, hadn't believed Jack's denial. 'If it wasn't him who wrote it,' she had snapped, 'then it must've been his wife. No one else knew of the boy's existence, did they?'

He looked up sharply as the door was shoved open and his children poured in accompanied by Charlie. Bloody Charlie. How he had come to hate that name. Seeing the boy flinch he realized he had been scowling at him and turned away, feeling guilty. But he couldn't help it, it maddened him the way the boy continued to fetch and carry for him despite the constant rebuttals, smiling that inane smile of his.

'What d'you want?' he asked, uncharacteristically short with them.

'We've come for our story.' It was said as if to an idiot. Rhona was pawing at his trousered leg. He looked at the clock and gave an audible groan before slapping the pages of the newspaper together – then, remembering its startling content, shoved it under the seat of the chair out of their sight.

'Where's Mother gone?' enquired Rowena, having just heard the door slam and knowing it meant Mother and Father had been arguing again.

'I don't know.' Russ went to the sofa as Biddy came out of the scullery with the customary tray of milk and biscuits.

'We've been talking about our holidays,' said Becky. 'Will Charlie be coming to Aunt May's with us?'

'I'm afraid we won't be going to Aunt May's this summer,' replied Russ softly. At their cries of disappointment he added, 'I'm sorry, but she's written to say she and Uncle Bill'll be going away themselves during the fortnight we usually stay with them.' Lies, all lies. There had been communication between Russ and his sister but it was Russ who had made the excuse of going somewhere else this summer. 'Anyway, she says we might be able to spend a week there at spud-picking time so don't be too downhearted.'

This cheered Lyn up if not the others. 'Ooh, I'll enjoy pickin' taties.'

Rhona attempted to climb on her father's lap. He kissed her but dissuaded the motion. 'Listen, Father's got things he needs to do. You'll have to do without a story tonight.'

'Oh why?' moaned the little girl – the others showed surprise too. 'Why, Father, why . . . why?'

He tried to curb his impatience at the whining voice. It wasn't the child's fault. 'Because I'm not very good company tonight. It's better you go up now.'

'What at six-thirty?' bawled an astounded Bertie from reflex.

The man's resolution collapsed. 'I don't care what blasted time it is just do as you're told!' Immediately, he felt brutish at the looks of alarm and tried to repair the damage. 'I didn't mean go straight to bed . . . Biddy might tell you a story if you treat her kindly, won't you, Bid?'

'I will indeed, sir. Off ye go, children an' we'll take our milk upstairs.' A story would give her a chance to sit down.

'Biddy's useless at stories,' objected Bertie.

Russ dithered, groping for something that would make the boy happy again. 'Tell you what, Bertie! You can spend an hour or so with the birds' eggs, how's that?'

Partly mollified, Bertie was about to do this, when Charlie spoke. 'Can I see your eggs, Father?' He had asked before and when his father had refused he had not considered it too important – they were only a load of empty shells, after all. But when he had mentioned the collection once to Bertie and his half-brother had threatened to stab him in his sleep if he ever so much as touched the cabinet, it had become imperative that he be permitted to see inside it.

Russ had sunk back into thoughtfulness. 'What? . . . Oh no, I've told you before, they're very delicate and Bertie's used to handling them.'

'I swear I won't touch them,' Charlie persisted. 'I'll let Bertie open the drawers and just look at them.'

Russ felt weary. It would have been so easy to say, 'Oh, suit your bloody self!' . . . but then he looked at Rachel's son. No, he couldn't heap this indignity on Bertie too. 'No! I've said no, now will you please do as you're bidden and go for a story!'

With only a slight delay from Charlie and a look of triumph from his half-brother, the children trouped after Biddy. However, Rowena tiptoed back to stand before her father's seat, her expression transmitting her worry. 'Is it because of what Becky did that you're angry with us?'

He smiled as convincingly as he could and reached up to stroke her cheek. 'I'm not angry, lass, just a bit tired that's all. Why, what's our walking accident been doing this time? I didn't notice too many arms and legs missing.'

'She didn't mean it. She's just so fond of Charlie that she finds it hard to keep him secret . . . you're not too mad, are you?'

The indulgent smile wavered as the realization hit him between the eyes. Oh God, his own child! He had blamed Jack Daw and it had been one of his own . . . Somehow he managed to resuscitate his smile, though it was a lack-lustred effort. 'No, I'm not mad . . . who did she tell?'

'Well, first it was Aunt Ella . . . and after she'd told her, I took him round – I felt sorry for him not being able to go out and meet anybody and I knew Aunt Ella would keep the secret. We sneaked him out the back way, no one saw him . . . but then Becky went and told Mrs Phillips too.'

She couldn't have chosen a better distributor, thought Russ dully.

'But I told her off and she's promised not to tell anyone else . . . Father, why don't you want anybody to know about Charlie?'

'I told you, he's not meant to be here.'

'Oh well, don't worry,' comforted Rowena before she left. 'Mrs Phillips wasn't very interested.'

Whilst her daughter was uttering this opinion, Rachel was mouthing one of her own. 'I've just one thing to say to you, Ella Daw!' Her slight figure trembled with passion as she faced Ella over her neighbour's threshold. 'I think you're despicable, devious and downright vindictive!'

'That's three things,' replied Ella calmly, further infuriating Rachel.

'Oh, you think you're so witty! Well, I know it was you who wrote that letter to the Mayor and don't think I don't know why!'

Ella relaxed against the jamb. 'If you know what reason I might have to be so spiteful then I'd be grateful if you'd let me in on it.'

Rachel opened her mouth, then shut it again, conscious of her slip.

'It wouldn't be because you think this might be my way of getting revenge?' hazarded Ella. 'For robbing my Jack of his Mayorship.'

'I don't know what you're insinuating! Your husband lost the vote because he was unsuitable for the job. I don't see how it could have been any of my concern.'

'Oh, I'll agree it wasn't any of your concern.' Ella nodded with a mild expression and crossed her arms. 'But that didn't deter you, did it, Rachel?'

'Don't imagine you can wriggle out of this by slandering me!' blustered Rachel, wagging a finger. 'I know you wrote that letter and I just want to say that I'm never going to forgive you.'

'That's it then, is it?' said the unflappable Ella.

Rachel projected astonishment. 'You're not even bothering to deny it, are you?'

'Why should I? You say you know it was me, well fair enough. Was there anything else, Rachel?'

'Yes! From now on I forbid you to enter my house or speak to my children. I've put up with you for so long because I believe in being neighbourly, but I can't forgive this. I want nothing more to do with you!' With this, she marched out of the backyard.

On closing the door, Ella turned to face her husband who was sprawled in an arm chair. 'Did you catch all that?'

'I'd want my ears syringing if I hadn't. Why didn't you just tell her it wasn't you instead of putting up with all that slaver?'

She sashayed across the room. 'Ah, but how d'you know it wasn't?'

He snatched her arm as she passed and pulled her onto his knee. 'Was it?'

She gave an inscrutable smile and prodded the tip of his nose. 'You'll both just have to keep guessing, won't you?'

Rachel's return to her own domain was heralded by another slam of the door. She was about to flounce past her husband when he enquired what she had been doing. 'I've been telling the culprit just what I think of someone who stoops so low!' She was still furious at Ella's calm acceptance.

He groaned. 'Not Ella?'

'Who else?'

'We don't know for sure it was her.'

'I do! She didn't even bother to deny it.'

'Oh . . .' He wiped a thoughtful hand over his mouth.

'I don't know why you should be so surprised! She and that husband of hers were the only ones with a motive.' Her eyes still smarted over the encounter. It was maddening how that woman always made her lose control.

'I don't take your meaning.' Russ looked puzzled.

'She knew I sabotaged her Jack's chances of becoming Mayor – oh, don't look at me like that!' She gave a gesture of irritation. 'Somebody had to do it. We couldn't have him demeaning the title.'

'But you never mentioned anything at the time . . . what did you do?'

She sighed emphatically. 'Nothing really! I just happened to mention Ella's prison sentence to Mrs Danby – it was her who did all the damage.' She reacted fiercely to her husband's look of condemnation. 'Whatever part I played did it warrant this kind of reprisal? She's totally ruined us!'

'I'm not convinced it was Ella,' said Russ worriedly, and told his wife what their daughter had said about Mrs Phillips.

A moment of doubt coloured Rachel's cheeks. Then she shook her head. 'No, if that were the case then why didn't Ella just deny it? I'm positive it was her – the cat! I've told her not to come here again and mind you stay away from that husband of hers, he's just as much to blame – put her up to it, most likely.' She departed, leaving her husband in more of a quandary than ever over who the culprit was . . . but then, did it really matter?

Russ had set a precedent: there was nothing in recent civic records to suggest anything of this nature happening before. But the stripping of his office was not the end, only the beginning of an even worse period of stress. For a start, when Russ had handed in his resignation and the accoutrements that went with the post, he had overlooked the Lady Mayoress' staff that had hitherto taken pride of place in the best parlour. In the normal sequence of things it was to have been handed back to the Lady Mayoress next month, but now the only ceremonial handover that took place was when Rachel threw the ebony rod at her husband the next morning. 'A lot of good this did me!' It came at him like a lance as, finding no table set in the front room, he entered the kitchen. 'I don't suppose the Lady Mayoress will have the problems I've had to contend with but you might as well take it back to her!'

His gut shrivelled at the thought of having to knock at the door of the Mansion House. Stooping, he curled his fingers round the staff and propped it in a corner, saying he would drop it in on his way to work. As to the latter, it was going to take some courage even to open his door after that press report. Please God, nobody would reveal that to his children. They had not come down yet, didn't know their father's shame. He asked his wife now what they should be told.

'I dare say you can make some story up, you usually do.' And this was the extent of her advice.

He did not eat, but waited for the children to come down, which in his wife's presence seemed aeons. When all were finally grouped round the table, he cleared his throat. 'Erm, just in case anybody says anything to you at school, I'll tell you now that I've stopped being Sheriff – there's nothing wrong, it's just that with having a business to see to I haven't got sufficient time.' Some of the children looked at him, though without undue interest, the rest carried on eating. He waited for them to ask for further information, but none showed particular concern. It was quite a relief.

'I've a further thing to add,' announced their mother, drawing his fearful eyes round. 'None of you are to talk to Mr and Mrs Daw. I don't mean that you can't answer if they say hello, that would be impolite, but I don't want you talking to them or going into their house – and don't tell me you don't go in because I know you do!'

'Have they done something naughty?' asked Rhona.

'Yes, but that's between grown-ups.' As she said it, Rachel noticed the morning paper lying within easy access. Fearing it might contain another derogatory headline, she slipped it off the table and out of sight. 'The only thing that should concern you is to remember what I said.' She looked at each of them, lingering over Becky whom she had rebuked last night for telling Mrs Phillips.

'Yes, Mother,' they chorused.

Russ decided to set off for work now, hoping there would be fewer folk about. There were, but the few he did encounter made it seem as if he were facing thousands. His exit came simultaneously with Ella's and Mr Parker's who lived on the other side of Russ. They emerged rather comically like soldiers out of sentry boxes. Russ raised his hat and gave a weak smile, 'Morning.'

Ella muttered a 'Morning' of her own whilst Mr Parker did not answer. Both took their time in coming out of their gates, apparently hanging back while Russ, head down, made a hasty escape to his car, knowing they were about to gossip about him. They had the courtesy to wait until he had wrenched at the starting handle several times and set off, before turning to each other.

'Have you seen him?' an eager Mr Parker asked Ella.

'Who, the boy? Aye I met him t'other day.'

'And is it right about him being black?' When Ella nodded Mr Parker looked shocked. 'Eh, what's the man thinking of, bringing him here.'

Ella laughed. 'Russ didn't bring him, he came on his own – he's been here a few weeks.'

'Has he really?' The elderly man's eyebrows rose. 'I never heard a sound, did you?'

Ella wondered if Mr Parker had expected to hear jungle drums but merely shook her head. 'They've kept him well hidden.'

A disapproving laugh from the other. 'I'm not surprised! Mrs Parker's disgusted. She says she won't speak to Russ again and I'm inclined to agree with her – morning, Mrs Dixon!' Another neighbour was just leaving her house. Guessing their topic of discussion she came scurrying up eagerly, hoping to learn a bit more than the press had told her.

Russ didn't have to look back to know they were watching his journey down the street, a journey that attracted more accusatory looks and pointed fingers, noises which sounded rather like boos. No, you're imagining it, he told himself, hands gripping the steering wheel. As if you haven't enough to worry about you're inventing things – it's the car engine making those noises. Yet he was very glad of this armour-plating.

When he arrived at the shop there was concrete evidence

of the public's ill-feeling towards him: every window was smashed, and not content with daubing 'Rat' on the woodwork, the culprit had tossed the remainder of the paint, pot and all, through a shattered window, ruining every article on display. Determined not to be driven from the only position he had left, Russ despatched his assistant to fetch a glazier while he himself cleaned up the mess of paint. At least tomorrow's business could progress as normal.

When he went home that evening there was another shock in store. He had parked the car, shouted a pleasantry to a couple of neighbours and been ignored – that wasn't a shock after the reception he had had this morning. The shock came shortly after he and his family had eaten. A rap at the front door caused his wife's hands to stop what they were doing.

Rachel's eyes flew at him and she began to usher Charlie from the room. Russ sent Biddy down the passage, telling her, 'If it's more reporters say I'm not in.'

But when the maid returned she was accompanied by another woman. The latter, seeing the look of indignation which Rachel gave the maid, said, 'Excuse me for intruding on your meal, Mr and Mrs Hazelwood, but I should like to speak to you if you can spare a moment.'

Rachel assumed a false smile. 'Of course – do sit down . . .'

'Mrs Ingram,' supplied the middle-aged woman, a kindly individual dressed in mauve, with plump breast and greying hair. She took a seat on the sofa.

Rachel excused herself for the moment and assisted Biddy in clearing the table. When the two were in the scullery she whispered, 'I thought I told you not to let anyone in except those people I'm expecting!'

Biddy mouthed an apology. 'I couldn't stop her, ma'am. She just sorta wangled her way in.'

'Who is she anyway?' Rachel shook her head rapidly. 'No, no! I don't mean her name – I mean what does she want?' When Biddy said she didn't know Rachel sighed loudly and returned to confront the woman who by now had set up a conversation with the children.

'And how old are you my dear?' She had turned to Lyn who said she was nine and a half. 'You are very thin.' Mrs Ingram slanted her head to take in Lyn's overall appearance. 'Don't you eat your meals up?'

Lyn replied, 'Sometimes, if I like what we're having.' She looked the woman up and down. 'My mother says if we eat too much we'll get fat.'

Mrs Ingram's eyes twinkled and she looked around at the group of faces as if searching for someone else. 'I believe you have another young man staying with you?'

Rachel's smile became fixed and she looked at her husband as Mrs Ingram added, 'I should very much like to meet him.'

'He's not available at the moment,' said Rachel immediately.

'Mrs Hazelwood, I'm not here to pry but to help – I do realize that you will have had plenty of interference to suffer already. I really do sympathize with your plight.'

So kindly did she say this, that Rachel began to warm to her. She sighed and offered tea, which Mrs Ingram accepted. Then she sat down. 'I hope you don't think I've been overly rude. It's been a most dreadful time.'

Mrs Ingram sipped her tea. 'I quite understand, my dear, and as I said I'm here to help.'

'Yours is the first such offer we've received,' confessed Rachel. 'People are quick to point the finger but slow to offer assistance.'

A gloved finger was directed at the ceiling. 'Is the child upstairs?'

Rachel closed her eyes and nodded. 'Could we call him down?' At Rachel's obvious reluctance, Mrs Ingram said firmly, 'Mrs Hazelwood, the last thing I want to do is intrude, but if we are to discuss his welfare and education then it is better that I meet him.'

'Ah, so that's it,' said Russ, tapping a cigarette on its pack and lighting it. 'You're from the Education Department.' Not giving her time to confirm this he added, 'Well there's no need to be concerned, the boy'll be going back to Africa at the end of August.'

'We'll see, shall we?' Mrs Ingram smiled and, cup in hand, looked at Rachel who went to the foot of the stairs and shouted for Charlie. While they awaited him she rubbed her arms nervously and passed a timorous smile to the woman.

Mrs Ingram turned her face to the doorway as the foreign voice enquired what was wanted of him. 'Oh, come in, my dear! How do you do? I am Mrs Ingram.' She held out her hand and Charlie engaged it in a limp handshake, looking bemusedly from his father to Rachel and back to the furry-cheeked woman. Mrs Ingram continued to make polite conversation with him, asking him all about his journey here, had anyone questioned him when he had got off the boat? Did he like being here? What meal was his favourite?

Rachel found it hard to grasp the reasoning behind these queries – the woman had said she was here to help but as yet there had been little indication of this. She looked at the clock. 'I don't want to appear rude but . . .'

Mrs Ingram inclined her head. 'Of course, my dear . . . do you think I might have a private word with you and Mr Hazelwood before I leave?' Slightly puzzled, Rachel sent the children upstairs and shut the scullery door on Biddy's prying ears.

'Firstly,' said Mrs Ingram, 'let me say that the boy looks perfectly healthy . . .'

Rachel gave a tight laugh. 'He should be, the amount he eats.'

'But I have to tell you that to keep a child confined to one room is not only bad for his mental state but also against the law.'

Russ frowned. 'Look, I've told you, I can't see the point in going to the trouble of getting him into school when he'll be gone in a few . . .'

'Mr Hazelwood, it isn't simply Charlie's education I'm worried about but his whole welfare, I . . .'

Rachel guessed at last, her face turning pale. 'My God . . . you're from the cruelty people!'

'The NSPCC, yes.' Mrs Ingram stood and placed what was meant to be a reassuring hand on the younger woman's arm. 'Please forgive me for not informing you of my intended visit, but after those press reports I had to come and see the situation for myself.' Neither Rachel nor her husband could speak, allowing Mrs Ingram the platform. 'However, I find little to concern me. He seems clean and well-nourished – but I must insist that he be allowed outside for fresh air and a change of scenery. Will you do that for me?' Rachel could only nod mechanically. 'Good.' Mrs Ingram made to exit. 'You say he will be leaving at the end of August? Well, I'm aware that the schools will be breaking up for the summer holidays in a fortnight but I really feel that he should be enrolled for temporary education – when the schools reassemble there'll still be three weeks until the end of August, that's five weeks in which he could be doing something useful. A child needs mental stimulation. I can arrange it for you. I know how embarrassing all this must . . .'

'No thank you!' Russ found his voice. 'I think I can manage to find the Education Department.' As a councillor, Russ had sat on the Education Committee.

'As you wish. I'll call again before Charlie goes back to Africa, just to make certain you're not experiencing any more problems. Could we make an appointment for a month today?' At Rachel's weak affirmation Mrs Ingram said goodbye and went down the passage.

Still shaken, Rachel saw her out, then came back to gape at her husband. Her voice was disbelieving. 'Did you see? She wasn't just looking at him – she was examining our children!' Her voice rose. 'Looking for bruises, asking if they got enough to eat – she thought we'd been neglecting our own children!'

Equally shocked, Russ could not answer.

'See what you've done!' Her tone grew shrill. 'Are you satisfied? Oh, my God! I can't bear this!' Sobbing, she ran upstairs.

Russ looked at the clock – another twelve hours before he could escape to work.

The following day his takings were eleven and three ha'pence. The day after, he arrived to find every window

197

smashed again. This time he simply boarded up the jagged vents, gave his assistant two weeks' wages and sent him home, then went to the pub.

Luckily, no one in *The Falcon* put a name to his face for almost two hours. He was able to get well and truly saturated before the hiss came: 'Oy, isn't that the bloody Sheriff what . . . ?' When the whispers began, he tottered out on to the highway and fell into his car. He drove as though participating in a race. How desperately he wanted somebody to pull out of a side road as they had done before and send him into oblivion. But when the car stopped somewhere in the countryside he was still in one piece.

The liquor made him sleep for the best part of the afternoon. When he awoke he had sobered up . . . and immediately set about remedying this before going home. Once there, he parked three feet from the kerb and staggered towards the house – at the same moment that Jack Daw chose to enter his own abode. Russ had not noticed him coming down the street. Now, both men stepped through their respective gates almost simultaneously. Jack was eyeing him. Russ knew that he should apologize for the nasty things he had said, but while it was still possible that Daw's wife had written that letter he felt unwilling to humble himself and so continued his unsteady course, saying nothing.

Inside, he made straight for the kitchen, until he heard voices in the front parlour. He didn't know what made his feet carry him there, he didn't want to talk to anyone – least of all the policeman who was keeping his wife company. His first thought was: Christ have I had an accident and didn't know it? He frowned at the assembly. Rowena was there too, and a man he wasn't familiar with.

Rachel bounded to her feet, not bothering to shield her distaste from the visitors. 'We've been looking for you everywhere!'

'Well now you've found me. What d'you want?' His expression was cagey.

'Why weren't you at the shop?'

'Some bugger smashed it up again.'

198

'Do you mind not using such language! I demand to know where you've been – oh, don't bother to lie! I can smell you've been drinking.'

This belittlement in front of strangers annoyed him and he replied perversely. 'Well you see, it was one o' them big magnets that John Smith's insists on hanging over their pubs – got attached to the nails in me boots and dragged me feet inside before I knew where I was. So if you've any complaints direct 'em at the brewery.'

'I'm not interested in your stupid explanations – Robert's gone missing!'

He gaped. 'What d'you mean, gone missing?'

She squealed her intolerance. 'Pull your stupid self together!'

Rowena looked at the carpet, tracing round each blob of colour with her toe. The man whom Russ did not know rose and introduced himself as Bertie's form teacher. 'We think he may have been abducted, Mr Hazelwood.'

Russ recognized him then. 'Oh yes, we've met before, haven't we?' Then he squinted at the policeman and ran a hand over his tousled hair. 'Well what . . . how . . . ?'

'Robert hasn't come home from school!' snapped his wife. 'Rowena was out earlier than normal so she knew she hadn't missed him. She waited and waited but he didn't come, so she went to his classroom to look for him. Mr Wooler,' she indicated the teacher, 'says he didn't come back in the afternoon. He assumed Robert was ill and marked him absent. Rowena says,' she drew a shuddering breath, 'Rowena says a tramp has been loitering in the area and she saw Robert talking to him just before she left him this morning.'

'I told him not to,' supplied a grave Rowena. 'But you know what he is.'

'Well why isn't anyone out looking for him?' Russ demanded of the policeman.

'Half the police force is looking for him!' screeched Rachel. 'While you drink yourself silly. Oh, my God, if anything else happens . . .' She gnawed at a knuckle.

Then all they could do was wait.

It was nearly ten o'clock and still there was no news. With the departure of the teacher and policeman, the family had moved into the kitchen where it was a little more cosy. The children had been made ready for bed and sat drinking milk. Becky had begged her mother to let them stay up until their brother had been found and Rachel had allowed it, simply because she had no more strength to oppose anyone.

Russ had employed a book for the bedtime story, his mind too befogged to concoct a tale this evening. But there was no inflection to his words and the children grouped around him were beginning to fidget. Occasionally, between pages, his eyes would drift up to catch a fleeting look at the woman who sat at the table. With each piteous sighting he wanted to fold her in his arms and press his cheek to her little face . . . then she would catch his inspection and all sentimental notions were dissuaded. Charlie sat on the rug, chin pressed into his knees, arms locked round shins. His brown eyes flitted from one worried face to the other.

There came a knock at the door. Everyone sat to attention and looked at each other, but none seemed keen to answer it. Russ dropped the book to his lap, but continued to stare at his wife. In the end Biddy was sent. She reappeared with a policeman.

'We've found him,' said the latter, and by his tone they knew that Bertie was in one piece. The tension dispersed. 'Seems he fancied an afternoon in the woods and forgot the time – well, it doesn't get dark till late does it . . .'

'I'll bloody kill him,' swore Russ, throwing the book aside as he rose.

The runaway, sullen and dishevelled, was brought in, deposited among his chattering siblings and plied with milk and biscuits by his mother. 'Robert, how could you have been so naughty? We were dreadfully worried.' His failure to answer and his refusal of sustenance concerned her even more. 'Why did you do it?' she entreated, pulling at his clothes and smoothing his hair. 'It's so thoughtless – not like you at all.' Still Bertie said nothing, just stared morosely into the fire. Rachel gave a mew of exasperation, then turned to thank the policeman who, now that the lad was safe, duly departed.

'Girls, it's time you were in bed,' decided Rachel. 'And you!' This was directed at Charlie. She gathered her daughters round and began to kiss them. 'Goodness, look at the hour! You'll all be sleeping in tomorrow. Off you go, your brother's safe now, he'll be up shortly.'

'Not before he's given us some explanation for his behaviour, he won't,' said his annoyed father, in more sober state now.

For the first time, Bertie's eyes looked at him – they burned with contempt. The boy rose in a half crouch, like some badger tormented by baiters. He wanted to fling at his father what he had had flung at him today, make him squirm and bleed and suffer. Fornicator! Walker had called his father. What's one of them? Bertie had foolishly demanded. It's somebody who fucks women, the elder boy had sneered. No he doesn't! retorted Bertie, though not fully understanding the word he knew it was swearing. You don't even know what it means, Walker had smirked and had proceeded to convey all the revolting details before adding, that's what your father does – he does it with black women too, it's been in the papers. Then Bertie had tried to thump him, but Walker being two years older had dragged him into the lavatory and shoved his head down the bowl and called him more names while his cronies had cackled their mirth.

So, instead of going back into school with the others when the bell clanged he had hidden in the cubicle, sneaking out later to spend the rest of the day crying in Knavesmire Wood – until the policeman had found him. Yes, he wanted to hurl all this at his father . . . but he couldn't say such things in front of his mother.

Russ flinched under his son's deprecation, but said again, 'Come on, Robert, we're waiting for your explanation.'

'You've never given me one, why should I give you one?'

'Robert!' exclaimed his mother at the vehement disrespect. 'That's no way to speak to your father.'

201

The fevered eyes took her in. 'I don't know how you can bear to be in the same house with him, Mother, after he's done such a despicable thing.'

'What thing?' asked the inquisitive Beany.

'Go to bed!' ordered Russ, sensing total disaster. Oh God, he knew, *he knew*! 'It's very late. I'll come up and kiss you in a minute.'

Biddy, keen not to miss the show, was tardy in removing her charges, hence they caught Bertie's forceful indictment. 'I hate you! I wish you were dead!' He seized a vase from the mantel and threw it at his father. The latter was spared a cut head by a fraction of an inch as it shattered on the door that had just closed on the others. Rachel gave a little cry – it had been her favourite vase. 'And I wish that bloody Fuzzball was dead an' all!' shrieked Bertie. 'Trying to shove me out!'

The yell caused Charlie to falter on the stair. Bertie had run away because of him! He turned back to the door, wanting to go in and say, 'I'm not trying to shove you out. I want you to be my brother.' But his father's words stopped him.

Hardly recovered from the unexpected attack, Russ said, 'Bertie, you know I'd never allow tha . . .'

'Then why do you sleep in the same room as him?' yelled his son, eyes swimming.

Russ looked helplessly at his wife who offered no support. 'It's not that I want to!' Charlie's eyes dulled and his fingers dropped from the knob. 'Listen, you can come and sleep in the attic with me and Charlie can have . . .'

'I don't want to! You can't make it right now! Everybody's laughing at me . . . everybody knows.' He began to sob with such heartbreak that for a moment both parents were too stunned to react.

But finally Rachel intervened, putting her arms around the wretched child and bidding her husband, 'Get out!' Charlie pelted up the stairs before his father complied. 'Get out! Can't you see it's you who's causing this? Get out!'

Once beyond the barrier of the door Russ closed his eyes, feeling sick.

'Has our Bertie gone mad?'

He glanced up to see Rhona's quizzical face at the top of the stair. Beside her Beany was weeping as she always did at the first sign of raised voices. 'Ssh!' Biddy coralled the mavericks. 'Away now to your beds and leave that lot to the Marquess o' Queensbury.'

'Is he coming to live with us an' all?' came Beany's faint question as the door of their room closed behind them.

Russ placed one foot on the staircase, not wanting to go up to the attic but knowing he must. On the landing he faltered . . . then opened the door of the girls' room. Biddy was tucking them in. She now hopped from foot to foot in embarrassment. Russ looked at each bed with its row of expectant little faces . . . but he couldn't answer their queries, he just couldn't.

Instead, he bent and kissed each child, cupping soft cheeks in his hands, and said simply, 'Don't worry, things'll be all right in the morning.'

But once in the attic he sank his buttocks onto the bed and rested arms on knees in a position of utter dejection. Feeling eyes on him he wondered if Charlie could read the thought that was going through his mind: God knew how he was going to do it, but it would be better for all of them . . .

By a weird quirk, Charlie's next words made it appear as though he *had* read his father's mind, but in truth it was just innocent comment on Bertie's display. 'I don't wish you were dead, Father.'

Russ gave a little gasp of a laugh, then sighed with feeling. 'Oh I do, lad . . . by God, I do.'

He keeled over onto his back, not bothering to undress. But weary as he was, with this thought to plague his brain he remained sleepless even longer than usual. By morning he still hadn't decided how or even *if* he could do it. By evening he knew that he was much too cowardly– yet was equally sure that it would be impossible to live with this shame. He just could not see any escape.

However, in a virtually unheard of place called Sarajevo, someone else's son was committing an act that was to alter everything.

CHAPTER FIFTEEN

BRITAIN WILL DO HER DUTY. WAR DECLARED ON GERMANY.
What a change to read a headline that excluded the word Sheriff, thought Russ whose grave eyes toured the columns of newsprint. At least the mob had something else to sink its teeth into now. Was it too much to hope that the same spirit would prevail in his home? Of course, this announcement had come as no surprise to the country – indeed, Russ felt he had been living in a war zone for the past two months. Even the fact that Bertie had been excused school for his last few weeks there hadn't made him any sweeter to his father. Only the girls had remained pleasant to him – simply because they don't know what a bastard I am, thought Russ. Oh, and Charlie of course . . . bloody Charlie. He shouldn't say that really, he was a nice enough lad. If he had been someone else's son Russ would have taken to that impish smile at once. As it was, it simply irked and irritated.

He thought of a naked Rachel. He had been having many such thoughts lately – had to make do with them, for thinking about it was as near as he got. Two months without her! He tried to drive away the ache by concentrating on something else. The woman from the NSPCC had kept her appointment – seemed to be the only person who was talking to them. She had not been too pleased to discover that they still hadn't arranged any schooling for Charlie but fortunately had not taken the matter any further as Charlie himself had stated that everything was fine and that he was now allowed out regularly. This was a downright lie – Charlie had been told to say these things by his father, prior to Mrs Ingram's visit. 'You'll make it harder for yourself if

204

you tell her we keep you indoors,' Russ had said. 'They'll take you away and put you in a home until Father Guillaume comes.' Russ could not have given a cuss if this had happened, his only reason for saying it was to keep the interfering woman from his house and upsetting Rachel. Charlie, wanting to do the right thing for a change and fearing being sent away, had agreed to do this. Mrs Ingram, convinced that the boy was in no danger, had said that perhaps it was a bit futile to arrange education for him now. Telling them she saw no need to call again she asked them to contact her when Charlie finally left and, 'If you experience any difficulty in your situation please don't hesitate to contact me.' This they had promised to do.

Russ' other bugbear, Jack Daw, had gone – called up from the Reserve late last night. Had he wanted he could probably have claimed exemption on the grounds of his council status but the thought of a good scrap on the battlefield pushed the tussles of local government into a poor second. There had been doorknockers going thirteen to the dozen throughout the district. Oh, that Russ could be summoned from this nightmare so easily!

'Well at least this puts paid to his aspirations of being next year's Lord Mayor.'

Russ frowned and looked up from the newsprint. 'Sorry?'

'Him next door!' Rachel got up to straighten a picture that was slightly crooked. 'Let's hope this lot lasts till November. He'll miss the elections and we'll be spared the ordeal of having him sneer at us every time we leave the house.'

He returned his depressed gaze to the evening paper. 'That isn't very often in your case, is it?'

An acid laugh as she sat down again. 'Do you blame me?' In the six weeks since Bertie's upset she had rarely been out. The fact that her neighbours may know of the NSPCC's visit did not help. Rachel feared another call at any day, despite being told by Mrs Ingram that all was fine – it *wasn't* fine, it was hell! The children, at home all day, were driving her mad, especially Rebecca with her 'Charlie this' and

'Charlie that'. That was the only reason Rachel was sitting in the front parlour with her husband; at least he didn't giggle and fawn around the boy.

Russ left the account of the German war which wasn't half as vicious as his own private battle, and began to peruse the local information. 'You can't stay in forever.' He himself had only reached this conclusion a fortnight ago and had decided to reopen the shop. For one thing he couldn't keep drawing the housekeeping money from the bank and for another, being in the house with a wife and a son who could not hide their repugnance did nothing for his mental health. Also, there was his assistant to consider; Russ couldn't keep paying him to do nothing. The Germans had done him a favour – people would be too concerned with rallying to the war cry to bother smashing his windows now.

'I am not having folk tittle-tattling about me every time I show my face!'

'They're not tittle-tattling about you, they're tittle-tattling about me.'

'And that's meant to make me feel better? Knowing that everyone in the city knows what my husband is?'

He gave a curt shuffle of the pages and mumbled, 'Well, at least you still have your custom.'

She thrust her face at him. 'Yes! And do you know why? They come here to gloat! To see if they can get a glimpse of your Charlie!' After the prolonged glare, she adopted a false pose of relaxation. 'But I suppose I must be grateful they're still buying my hats or we'd have used up all the money in the bank with the way you're performing – and this war's not going to make things any better, is it? Why, no sooner has it started than the prices are shooting up . . .'

'Aye well , now I've reopened the shop we should be back to normal soon.'

'Normal?'

His breast heaved. 'I meant as far as housekeeping is concerned.'

'Yes, well while we're on the subject I'll need some extra cash for tomorrow morning. Biddy went to the shop and there wasn't a piece of bacon to be had, so it looks like I'm going to have to send her into town for it. And we'll need plenty of tinned stuff in, we don't know how long this war's going to last, it could be months.'

He lifted a buttock to dig into his pocket, examining the change in his hand. 'Will twenty-three bob be all right?'

'Good gracious no! Flour's already up to half a crown a stone and I'll need a full side of bacon, not to mention anything else.'

'Sorry, it's all I have.' He extended his palm.

'There was hardly any point in asking if it was enough, then, was there?' Every word she formed was used as a knife.

Replacing the money in his pocket, Russ abandoned any attempt at reading the paper and rose, intending to leave the parlour. 'I'll fetch some home from the shop tomorrow evening.' He did not come home for his lunch these days.

'Oh, it'll be no use then! You may as well not bother. Everything will have been snapped up.'

He kept his patience. 'All right, I'll go to the bank first thing . . . and I'll hire Pickfords while I'm at it – well, I can't see Biddy being able to carry all the stuff you're proposing to buy.'

'It's all very well for you to be flippant! We're all aware that you couldn't give a fig about this family's welfare. Oh, never mind!' She waved airily. 'I'm sure I'm not going to beg for it.'

'Rachel, lass,' he came forward, hands beseeching her, 'nobody's asking you to beg. I'll get some cash from the bank – oh, hell! I forgot, they don't open again till Friday.' He rubbed at his forehead and sighed. 'Look, I'll take Biddy into town first thing and get everything you need and pay by cheque, they're telling us to use our cheque books as much as we can anyway. How's that?'

Only slightly placated, she delivered a terse nod.

He lingered. 'About what you said . . . we can't go on hiding forever, you know. I say we should brazen it out.'

'You might be brazen, I am not!'

He persevered. 'There isn't just us to consider. We can't keep Charlie penned up indefinitely or we'll be having the

207

cruelty woman back. Everybody knows he's here anyhow.'
Charlie had still not been beyond the door of the backyard.

She couldn't believe this. 'Are you suggesting we disport him?'

'I'm suggesting that a day out as a family would do us all . . .'

'He is *not* family!'

His expression grew pained. 'I know, I know . . . but if we show them we don't care what they say . . .'

'I care!' Time heals all wounds – what an idiotic adage that was! Far from healing the wound of his betrayal, the days had brought putrefaction.

His head lolled in defeat. 'Oh, Rache . . .' and he sought for some form of inducement. 'Look, how would you like a new dress?'

She donned a look of utter disbelief. 'You really think you can wipe this away with a new dress?'

'Of course I don't! I'm not trying to . . . what I meant was, well, you're always saying you feel nice in something new.'

'I'll never feel nice again – and I am not going out and there's an end to it!'

He backed off and stood with hands in pockets. 'So how long d'you intend to keep this up?' His enquiry was ignored. 'Till Father whatsisname comes? Then will you show your face?'

'I may do. Then again I may not. I fail to see that it should concern you.'

'They'll still talk. Just because Charlie mightn't be with us doesn't mean he'll be forgotten.'

She slammed her work onto her knee. 'How very reassuring!'

'Rachel.' He sank onto the sofa beside her. 'I know, I know I did wrong, but for pity's sake . . .'

'Pity?' she snarled, rearing away from his touch. 'Pity me and your poor children who have to put up with the gossip! Pity poor Robert who'll probably have to face more bullies at his new school – you've ruined him! Ruined him! He thought the world of you!' *And so did I*, she wanted to sob.

'I know he did.' Russ hung his head. 'I've tried my best to make things right between us, but he doesn't seem to want anything to do with me. I'm desperately sorry for the hurt I've caused you, but acting like hermits isn't going to make it any easier. We must try to get back into some sort of routine . . . even if, as you say, it'll never be normal.'

After a look of pure contempt, she picked up her sewing and replied, 'I'll consider your proposal,' and from then until suppertime, when she asked if he wanted tea or cocoa, never said another word.

It wasn't until the following morning that he received an answer. 'I've decided,' she told him before he left for the shop. 'We shall go out as a family. I don't see why we should all suffer because of you. The children are back at school on Monday and they've been nowhere in these holidays. There's a show on at the Empire tonight. The first performance starts at seven.'

Taken aback, he waited for her to say more, but with the long silence that ensued it became clear that this was to be the limit of her breakfast conversation. He could not conjure a suitable response. The one he gave sounded totally false. 'Well, that'll be very nice I'm sure.' A thoughtful nod. 'The children'll like that.' He looked at her again. 'Rachel . . .'

She turned her face away, indicating that she did not intend to chat. He turned his gaze down at his plate, fingered a knife, put it down again. His hand reached for a slice of toast from the rack . . . then laid that down too. 'I'll go then . . .'

After a short delay he swivelled his knees from under the table and left, taking Biddy shopping as he had promised. This took longer than he had anticipated for not only was the city centre jammed with traffic but there were long queues outside every foodstore. By the time Biddy got to the counter there was little to be had in the way of tinned produce.

'I'm sorry, ma'am,' wailed Biddy on presenting her paltry haul to the mistress. 'That's all there was left. We shoulda been there yesterday.'

Rachel made scathing examination of the purchases, then tossed a similar expression at her husband who hung in the doorway. 'It was hardly worth writing a cheque for, was it? You're useless, the pair of you!'

Russ gave way to his depression and trudged out.

The children, told about the concert at teatime, were thrilled, for up until this point in the school holidays they had been forced to make their own amusement. Rowena was the first to ask what sort of show it was.

'A variety,' said her mother and gestured at the paper rack – there was no longer the need to conceal every journal; the wayward Sheriff was yesterday's news. 'There's a list of the cast in the press. You can have a look after you've finished eating – Robert, take some more bread, dear.' She spoke coaxingly. The boy had become very subdued in his father's presence, although when Russell was absent his unhappiness seemed not to be so acute.

There was only the mumbled reply, 'I'm not hungry.'

'Now you don't want to end up falling down the cracks in the pavement, do you?' attempted Russ with a smile.

Bertie acted as if he hadn't even heard. All the boy's father got for his pains was a show of compressed lips from Rachel.

Rowena nibbled her bread and watched the play of feature. She had tried asking Bertie why he was so unhappy and why he had run away, but he had refused to tell her, saying only what she knew already, that it was because of Charlie. Her sisters assumed it was mere jealousy, but she regarded this as an inadequate explanation for it wasn't just Charlie who was receiving hostile treatment but Father too. It must be really serious. He had never been out of favour for this long.

She finished eating and, gaining permission to leave the table, picked up the press to read aloud, 'The Great Garenzos – they're acrobats, Marvellous Marco the Magician, Robinson's Nigger Minstrels . . .'

'Ooh, Charlie!' Becky clapped her hands chirpily. 'You might see someone you know among them.'

210

But Charlie's reply was cut short by Rachel who said coolly, 'He won't be coming.'

All eyes turned to her, including her husband's. 'I thought you said we'd all be going out together.'

'I said as a *family*,' came her stiff reply. 'It could hardly be an enjoyable evening if everybody was staring at us.'

'Aw that's not fair!' objected Becky.

'Don't you dare speak to me like that, young lady,' warned Rachel. 'When you're older you'll learn that nothing is fair.'

Becky said she was very sorry. 'Oh, but please can't Charlie come?'

'I'm not coming if he's coming,' contributed Bertie.

'Don't come then!' retorted Becky. 'I'd rather have Charlie.' This sparked another burst of squabbling.

Oh God, make it end, prayed Russ, listening to the arguments for and against Charlie. Please just let me die or something.

'I don't like going to the theatre,' Charlie announced above the row.

'Well there you are,' said Rachel. 'All that fuss was for nothing. Now if you've all finished eating you can go and get washed and change into your Sunday clothes. We set off in half an hour.' She rose from the table and went off to change herself.

'I am sorry, Charlie.' Becky hooked a sisterly arm through his and patted his hand.

He formed an unconvincing smile. 'I told you, I don't want to go.'

'I think you're just saying that. You would've enjoyed it, especially the nigger minstrels.'

'They're not *real* niggers like him, stupid,' spat Bertie, kicking his chair back. 'They're only white men with stuff on their faces.' He left them. They heard his feet thud on every stair until he reached his room.

'They're not are they, Father?' Becky turned to Russ for confirmation. At his nod she said deflatedly, 'Oh well, I'm sure Charlie would enjoy the magician anyway . . . that's if Mother wasn't so mean and allowed him to come.'

'You shouldn't say that about Mother,' accused Rowena. The fact that she liked Charlie made her feel disloyal to her mother. Someone should support her. Beany thought so too and added her alliance.

Becky stood firm. 'Well *I* think she's mean, don't you, Lyn?'

'Yes, she's been really nasty to Father as well, hasn't she?' came the reply. Despite Rachel's attempts to be civil to her husband in front of the children they could not fail to detect the coldness in her voice nor hear the arguments that went on in the front parlour.

Russ came out of his nightmare. 'No, no.' He shook his head wearily, not caring for the way this was going. There was the danger that his family would be split down the middle, some of the children on Rachel's side, some on his, he didn't want that. 'You don't understand. Your mother, well . . . she isn't herself lately.'

'Can't you buy her some flowers and get round her?' pleaded Becky.

'I'm afraid they don't sell the blooms of Utopia round here, lass.' He rose, saying tiredly, 'Sorry, Charlie, but it'll only make things worse for you if I were to argue with her. Come on now, girls, you'd best get ready else your mother'll be cross.' Some evening out this was going to be. He wished he had never suggested it.

Shepherding his daughters from the room he went to prepare himself for his ordeal. Half an hour later as he stood aside for his wife to leave the kitchen he glanced at the scullery where the door was ajar. Charlie was standing by the sink, helping Biddy with the washing up. Hearing the children's goodbyes, he turned, caught his father's eye and gave a tentative smile. To the beleaguered Russ it punished as effectively as his wife's rejection.

He couldn't stand this. He couldn't stand it one moment longer. He might as well be dead for all the quality of his life now. The heat in here was terrible, squashed as he was into this inadequate theatre seat between a portly gent and Rachel. A sweat had broken out all over his body and his starched collar was like a garrotte. His temples throbbed. On the stage a pack of idiots yelped and cavorted in time to a concertina. His mind kept drifting away, but their noise denied its total absence and brought him crashing back to reality every five seconds, when his palms would move in edgy fashion up and down his trousered knees in an effort to calm himself. He must get out.

The decision was made. Leaning to one side he whispered in his wife's ear. She eyed him testily as his rising frame blocked the stage from the view of the people behind. He struggled to the end of the row, standing on toes, excusing himself. Outside, he took three deeply grateful breaths of sultry air, then set off with intent in his step.

After the final curtain, a very annoyed Rachel led the exit from the concert hall, bent on another flailing when she caught up with her husband. By coming here she had laid herself bare to the gossips, had put herself out for the sake of presenting the family as 'normal' – all at his suggestion – and what did he do? He sneaked away and left her to face the ordeal alone. He had forfeited the right of respect in front of the children; they would have to be made aware just how fickle their father was.

But he wasn't outside and neither was the motor car. Disconcerted, she gathered her family around her and looked up and down Clifford Street. 'Wherever can your father have got to? It's disgraceful of him to leave us alone like this.' She struck out a brisk march. 'Come along, it looks as if we'll have to make our own way home. It's a good thing it's not dark. This is typical of your father.'

Because the town centre was still crawling with military traffic and soldiers, Rachel decided to make the journey home on foot by way of Skeldergate Bridge and Bishopthorpe Road. All the while she berated the absent Russ, seeing him in her mind's eye back there drinking himself silly. When the family turned into the last stretch she was still debasing him. The children tried to divert her by discussing the show.

'I loved those little dogs, didn't you, Mother?' attempted Rowena.

213

Rachel performed her darting smile. 'Yes, they were excellent.'

'It's a pity Father missed them,' said Beany, earning disgruntled grimaces from her sisters.

'Yes, well your father obviously had more pressing things to do,' was Rachel's starchy response.

'Which act did you like best, Mother?' Rowena tried again.

'Oh, I don't know . . . the magician. Though your father does a pretty good disappearing act himself.'

Here and there along the way a man in uniform would emerge from his house and, after a clinging kiss, march off along the street. The pavement began to incline. There were two soldiers marching some thirty yards in front of the family. One was only half a soldier – khaki tunic and cap, but civilian trousers. The other was clearly proud to be fully kitted out for he carried his civvies in a rolled up bundle under his arm. Bertie, the variety show having produced a temporary lightening of mood, let his own feet walk in unison with the men's brisk step. The ringing of the soldiers' boots lured the girls into following suit. Talk of the show was forgotten with the rhythmic swinging of arms and striding legs. Rachel barely noticed anything, dominated by her own furious thoughts.

At the junction in the road, the soldiers parted company. The children continued to ape the one with the bundle under his arm who was going in their direction. Shortly after the soldier turned the corner, so did they. The soldier came to a halt further down the street and opened a blue gate.

Rachel stopped dead – it was her gate. He couldn't . . . He couldn't have done that to her, not on top of everything else. The soldier caught the marching children from the corner of his eye and, turning full face, lingered on the threshold to wait for them. All but the boy gave a squeal of recognition and scampered up to jostle him. His wife came more slowly, face rosy and glistening with the heat. She looks so pretty, agonized Russ as he removed his peak cap, fingering the brim. On her way she caught Bertie's elbow and piloted him forward. Wordlessly, he performed a detour round his father, back glued to the passage wall in order not to be contaminated by his touch. Once past, he went straight up to his room.

The rest remained downstairs, packed into the narrow space twixt front door and kitchen, the girls uttering noises of admiration for their father's uniform. On hearing the excited voices, Charlie came out of his lonely attic to crane his head round the corner. But he could see only legs and was forced to move onto the staircase . . . and there was his father as his mother had always described him in all his military glory. He perched on a step and gazed on him.

Rachel seemed oblivious of the audience, forgoing the last shreds of dignity she had promised her husband. 'You coward,' she breathed. 'You cringing coward!'

'They're asking for soldiers,' he answered lamely.

'Soldiers! Not weak-kneed cheats who're running away from their responsibilities. You're a married man unless you'd forgotten. There's no need for you to join up. You've a business to run and a family to support. How're we to live if you go? I can't manage the shop I have my own work to see to.'

The children had become silent, calcified by the desperate accusations from their mother. Upstairs with the baby, Biddy listened eagerly.

In his chronic melancholia he had genuinely forgotten about the shop. 'Jimmy's a good lad, he'll do most of the work . . .'

'He'll have to! And you're too old! I thought they only wanted men up to thirty?'

'That's for the New Army.' He explained falteringly how it was possible for exNCOs to rejoin their old regiment, then said plaintively, 'It's best for all of us if I go, Rachel. . . I just can't take any more.' The alacrity of it all had amazed him. In the space of a few hours he had been signed up, given instructions to report at a local church hall tomorrow morning for medical inspection and fitted with one of the few uniforms available. He had kept it on: it would save on explanations to his wife.

'*You* can't take any more? So you creep off leaving me your black son as evidence of your betrayal and cowardice!'

'Oh, Rachel . . . only a few weeks more and the priest'll be here to take him back and it'll all be over. Don't be hard on him, he's only a lad.' He failed to perceive his own hypocrisy.

Scornful eyes swept him from head to toe. 'Taking my husband's by-blow off the streets, housing him, feeding him, that's being hard on him?'

'You see! You see!' he cried in desperation, falling back against the wall. 'It's going to be like this all the time if I stay. You'll never let me forget.'

'So you think you'll just crawl away and join the big boys? Well, go on then! I don't care. Because you're right, I won't let you forget and I'll never forgive you, never. I hope you catch a bullet – I do! I'm only sorry you're not taking that one upstairs so's he can catch one as well. I'm sick of looking at him, sick of being told only another few weeks and he'll be gone – he'll never go! Because he'll always be up here.' She beat a vicious tattoo on her head. 'Staring out at me, reminding me of how little you thought of our marriage and my children. Go on, clear off! You can go right away. We don't want you. Go to your precious Army!'

Russ was acutely embarrassed and stole a look at his daughters. 'Rachel, you're upsetting the lasses . . .'

'It's a pity you never thought of them when you brought your strumpet's son into their home!' With a last exasperated sound she launched herself at the staircase, braking as she came upon Charlie, then pounding past him.

Beany's mouth trembled, 'What's a strumpet?' but Rowena nudged her into silence and gestured for her sisters to go into the kitchen.

Russ stood alone in the dim passageway. Oh God, what was he doing to them all? Their little faces . . . He would have to speak to them before he left. Pushing himself from the wall he wandered into the kitchen and looked at each concerned child. There was another missing besides Bertie. 'Where's Lyn?' Rowena whispered that she was in the backyard. Her father stepped out into the sunlit yard and

216

spoke at the door of the water closet. 'When you've done, Lyn, I've something to say to you all.' He was about to go, when he heard a juddering intake of breath that bespoke tears. Opening the closet door he looked in, but it was empty.

Taking a few more steps he found his daughter round the back of the building, crouched in an attitude of sheer misery. Squatting beside her he pulled her into his side and tried to see her face, but she kept her arms wrapped tightly round it. No one was allowed to witness Lyn crying. 'Your mam's all right,' he soothed gently. 'Don't worry, lass.'

She gave a great sniff and lifted her head, though keeping her face averted. 'I'm not bothered about Mother.'

'Ah . . . well, if it's me, then don't . . .'

'I've swallowed a tooth!' she squeaked and the tears streamed down her face.

Russ tried his best not to laugh. He hugged her. 'I don't know! Here's me thinking it's because I'm off to war . . . you soft aporth. Was it loose?'

She nodded and dashed her arm over her eyes. 'I've kept jiggling it all week and when Mother shouted she made me jump an' I went and swallowed it. I won't get me money off the tooth fairy now!'

'Come here!' Her smiling father reached into his pocket for a handkerchief. 'Let's see this face – come on, you can't go in looking like that. There.' He dabbed away the tears. 'Now, I'll have a word with the tooth fairy and tell him what happened.'

Red eyes beheld him hopefully over the linen square. 'Will I get me money, then?' When told that it would be there when she woke up, Lyn blew her nose, sniffed and examined him. 'You look nice as a soldier.'

'Aye, not bad am I?'

'But what'll happen to the tooth?'

'Oh, don't worry about that, it'll go all the way through . . . mindst, it might give you a nasty nip on the way out – no, no, I'm only kidding!' He cuffed her lightly, took the handkerchief from her and pushed himself up. 'You won't feel a thing. Away now, 'cause I want to talk to you all.'

In the scullery, she left him to splash cold water on her face. When Russ re-entered the kitchen Charlie had joined the gathering. It was this that prompted Russ to go upstairs and speak to Bertie first. It was only fitting. His son's door was closed. After a couple of soft taps went unheeded, Russ went in. Bertie looked up from the pillow, then flung himself onto his side to face the wall. Russ stood there for a second then, closing the door, came to sit on the bed. At the contact of his father's thigh against his body, Bertie shuffled away from it.

'I just want to say goodbye, Robert . . . I'll miss you, son.' Russ reached out a hand and placed it on the warm head, but it was rebuffed. After a moment he got up from the bed, said, 'Bye, lad,' and went out.

Passing his wife's room he had a sudden thought and tapped softly. 'Rachel, I thought you might wonder where the car is – I'm sorry, it's been requisitioned. Somebody copped me when I went into the recruiting office . . . anyway, I've told them to send the money here, so you won't be short.' Rachel, tear-stained and blotchy-faced, covered her ears. *Damn the car! Damn the Army! Damn you!* Receiving no answer, Russ went down to the kitchen where the girls waited. Taking a dining chair from the table he sat on it and held out his arms for them to gather round him. Charlie moved up too. Russ felt the urge to scream, I bloody hate you! You've killed me! but he didn't. He took a daughter's hand in each of his and said evenly, 'Now then, I want you all to promise you'll be good lasses while I'm away. No squabbling. D'you think you can manage that?' They all murmured that they could. Rhona wanted to climb on his knee. He took his hand out of Rowena's to hitch the smallest child up. 'Good, and when I come back from France I'll bring you all a present.'

They brightened. 'A French doll?' asked Beany.

'That's what you want is it?' He bent his face down to her level. 'Then that's what you shall have.'

If the others seemed to have forgotten Mother's shrieks then Rowena had not. 'You won't really get killed will you, Father?' she asked in a small voice.

He put on a show of vivacity. 'Me, get killed? No! By gum, I'll have them Germans whipped before you can say tickle-me-fancy.' His hand shot out to tickle her ribs and she gave a relieved giggle, doubling over. But looking at Charlie who stood behind the row of pretty faces, he pictured his wife and son and thought bitterly, oh, dear Christ I hope Fritz does it for me . . . because my life will be worth nothing if I have to come home to this.

CHAPTER SIXTEEN

After passing a while longer reassuring his daughters, he made himself scarce for the rest of the evening, spending most of it in a public house. When he came in they were all asleep. Unwilling to see Charlie again, he prepared a bed on the sofa. Sleep was impossible of course – even without the annoying tick of the pendulum clock. He lay there, staring into the embers for ages. When he did close his eyes the warmth of the fire on his face became South African sunshine and he opened them quickly, not wanting to be there. But the vision had been formed . . . he felt her hot skin beneath his palms, her legs drawing him into her . . . and Charlie being squirted from his body to her womb.

The door opened then. He turned to see the subject of his nightmare, then turned away again. Charlie pressed the door shut, and came over to stand by the fire, hands in pockets. The glow of the coals burnished his face. He wanted to ask if his father was leaving because of him . . . but did not want to hear his father's yes. 'Aren't you coming to bed?'

Russ pulled the tartan blanket over his shoulder and closed his eyes, hoping the boy would go. 'I thought I'd sleep down here, I didn't want to disturb anyone.'

'I wasn't asleep. I've been waiting for you to come in. Can I try your jacket on please?' The boy was pointing at the Army tunic that was round the back of a chair.

'If you like,' said Russ apathetically, and gave up his pretence of tiredness to watch the boy. But when Charlie donned the military garment a thought came to his mind and he spoke on it. 'Don't go getting any daft ideas, you have to be eighteen to join the Army.' Charlie simply nodded and buttoned the tunic. Russ was not satisfied and hoisted himself onto one elbow. 'Listen, I don't want to get over to France then hear you've run away to join me. You're to wait right here for Father Guillaume to come and collect you. I want your promise on that.'

Charlie hesitated. How had his father known what was on his mind? Finally he gave his word.

'Right, well take that tunic off now and go to bed, it's late and I have to be away early in the morning.' He laid down again.

Charlie removed the jacket and draped it round the chair-back. 'Will I see you before you go?'

'I don't think so.' With each gap in the dialogue the noise of the pendulum crept back to the foreground. Tick, tock, tick, tock . . . smash the clock, smash the clock. Russ felt ready to scream.

'But you'll be home before Father Guillaume comes?' said Charlie in anxious tone.

'Hardly, it's only a matter of weeks to his coming. I'll be in the middle of a retraining programme.'

The brown eyes were devastated. 'So . . . I won't see you after tonight?'

Russ glanced at him briefly. 'I think it's best, don't you? We're only causing each other pain.'

After a pause, Charlie held out his hand to his father. 'Goodbye then, Father.' Oh, how he wanted the man to grasp his hand and pull him into a rough, paternal embrace.

But the most this filial display received was an insipid handshake and a curt 'Bye.'

Russ slipped away in the early hours, half hoping that one of them might waken and come to kiss him goodbye. No one did.

Not until he had been at the church hall for some time did he realize he had forgotten his promise to Lyn. He snatched a glance at his watch. Even though his home was not far from here it was too late to go back now. She would be searching frantically under her pillow and there would be nothing to find. Oh, God help me! All the while he waited, half-naked, for his medical inspection, he worried about

221

her. Most would have found that laughable – the worries he had, and he was getting steamed up about a tooth fairy! But if his child lost her faith in the tooth fairy where did that leave him?

As soon as the medical was over he dressed and slipped out to purchase paper, envelopes and glue. In the privacy of a lavatory he sat on the seat and used the paper and glue to make a miniature envelope, then set about writing a letter of apology on a piece of paper the size of a matchbox.

Dear Lyn,

I have just seen your father who tells me that you swallowed a tooth. That is all right, you get your money just the same. Sorry it's late but we've had a lot of work to do.

Love from the Tooth Fairy.

Folding the tiny letter he slid it into its envelope along with a threepenny piece, then tucked the lot into a standard envelope which he addressed to Rachel, with a note asking her to put it under Lyn's pillow. Slipping out into the street again he found a boy and asked if he would deliver it for a shilling. 'It's very important war business.' Before he went back inside another thought hit him: he would telephone the NSPCC woman and tell her that Charlie had left for Africa this morning – the priest had arrived earlier than expected. Mrs Ingram accepted the lie – like everyone else she was too involved in the war effort and the boy had obviously not been harmed in any way. Charlie's name was removed from her files.

Russ thanked the vicar whose telephone he had used, paid for the call then went back to the billet.

Rachel wandered downstairs and into the kitchen, pausing to stand and stare. He was gone. For good? She neither knew nor cared. The pig, leaving her with the mess he had created . . . Biddy slouched up behind her, making her jump. 'What time do you call this?' She began to fuss about the kitchen. 'Don't think we're all going to wait for breakfast while you idle in bed.'

Biddy objected. ''Tis only six o' clock, ma'am, the time I normally rise.'

'Well you'll have to start getting up a bit earlier! Have you woken the children?' Biddy said she didn't usually get them up until half past seven. Rachel said, 'All right,' and from then until the children came down chivvied and scolded the maid.

'Where's Rosalyn?' demanded the child's mother when all but this one were at the table.

'She's looking for something,' replied Becky, and before Rachel had time to answer added, 'Mother, you didn't really mean it about wanting to see Father shot, did you?'

Rachel was taken off guard and she stopped tearing about to look at each of her girls. Robina's eyes were filled with tears. 'Of course not,' she answered briskly. 'I was just angry at him for leaving us in this mess.'

'What mess?' asked Beany.

'Oh, Robina, do stop asking silly questions and go fetch your sister or her breakfast will be thrown away!'

Beany went upstairs to relay this message and met her sister halfway, her face was like thunder. 'Haven't you found it?'

Lyn replied with a strident, 'No! There was nothing under the pillow. I even looked under the bed to see if the money had dropped down the back.'

'Maybe he left it under the wrong pillow,' suggested Beany and when Lyn made as if to go and look said, 'But wait till after or Mother'll be mad.'

'He'd better have left it,' said her sister darkly as they went down. 'The little sod.'

After breakfast she searched under everyone else's pillow but found nothing. 'Then it has to be under Bertie's!' She marched into his room and demanded that he search.

When told of the reason, Bertie scoffed, 'You don't still believe in fairies, d'you?'

'Not ordinary fairies.' His sister was scathing. 'But the tooth fairy is different. Father said he would speak with him so he *must* be real.'

'Father's a liar,' replied her brother. 'He lies about everything. There's no such person as the tooth fairy. It's him what takes the tooth from under the pillow and leaves the money there.'

'I don't believe you.' But Lyn's confidence wavered.

Bertie grabbed her arm and dragged her along the landing to what had been their parent's room. On the mantelpiece was a china jar. He lifted the lid and said, 'Look in there!' In the bottom was a sprinkling of milk teeth. 'He sneaks into your bedroom at night, swaps a tooth for threepence then chucks the teeth in there.'

Lyn's lips parted. She did not say anything, just stared at the jar. Bertie slammed the lid back on. 'So it isn't the tooth fairy who forgot your money it's Father, because he doesn't care about any of us.'

'Pig!' Lyn went white and fled from the room.

Despite having wanted to hit back at his sisters for their lack of kinship, Bertie suddenly felt very mean. He remembered his own feelings when a boy had told him that Father Christmas didn't exist – his whole world had caved in. Tramping back to his own room, he heard the closet door slam and knew that his sister had gone there to cry. His own eyes smarted at the spiteful attitude he had shown her. It was his father he had really wanted to punish. Searching a bookshelf, he withdrew a boys' annual and hovered indecisively for a while, then going down he waited in the yard until his sister emerged. 'I'm sorry,' he muttered, head down, and shoved the book at her. Still glaring she took it and offered a sullen thank you. 'I suppose he just forgot, what with going off to war,' said Bertie.

'I'll never believe anything he says again,' she replied strongly.

'Right, I want everyone out of the house until dinner!' At the sound of their mother's voice Lyn and Bertie joined the others. Charlie, knowing that the instruction did not apply to him, plodded up to his attic to wait for Mrs Hazelwood to closet herself in the parlour. Then he would go down and perhaps help Biddy or play with the baby. His half-brother and half-sisters, armed with notepads and pencils, went out of the front door. Once on the pavement, Bertie said he wouldn't be going on the trip to the river with them, he wanted to be on his own. None of the girls tried to change his mind, and he walked on ahead.

They passed a boy in the street but took little notice. The envelope that Russ had taken such pains over was delivered into Rachel's hands. It wasn't even opened. Seeing his handwriting on it she threw it straight on the fire.

As warned, the children stayed out until dinner-time. After being fed, they were packed off again until their next meal. They were quite glad to do this as Mother had been very irritable with them. Alas, she seemed no better for the afternoon's respite.

'Oh, dear God as if I haven't enough to put up with!' Rachel who had just picked up the evening newspaper now threw it down again and looked harassed. Rowena emptied her mouth before asking what the matter was. Her mother snatched angrily at the paper and read aloud in a tart voice, 'Notice is hereby given that the following public elementary schools will not reassemble on Monday August the tenth as the buildings have been requisitioned for use of troops: Scarcroft Road Council School . . .'

'Hurray!' the girls harmonized gleefully. 'How long are we off for?' asked Lyn.

'Oh, they don't bother to tell us an unimportant little thing like that!' replied her mother in hoity-toity manner. She read from the paper again. 'When it is possible for ordinary schoolwork to be resumed an advertisement will appear in the papers.' Bertie asked if his school, Archbishop Holgate's, was mentioned. Rachel consulted the list. 'No – presumably you'll be going on the expected date.'

Bertie made a face as his sisters mocked. '*Anyway*! I'll be going to grammar school, you still go to baby school,' he said disdainfully.

'Can we take a picnic lunch out tomorrow, Mother?' enquired Rowena. 'It might help if we're out for the whole day. We could go across to Fulford on the ferry.'

Rachel said they could.

'Can Charlie come please – oh, please, Mother!' entreated Becky with spaniel's eyes.

'No!' Rachel erected the newspaper to fend off more pleas. Becky fell silent but offered a compassionate look to Charlie.

The doorknocker sounded. Biddy went to answer it. 'It's Mrs Archer come to pay for her hat,' she told Rachel. 'I've put her in the front room.'

Rachel hummed and went off to see to the woman – who was not in the front room but hovering in the passage in the hope of spotting Charlie. Donning her usual smile, Rachel coaxed her into the room. Mrs Archer took her purse out. 'I've just come to pay my bill, Mrs Hazelwood.' Rachel did not encourage first name terms with neighbours, it would lower her to their level. Only Ella was allowed the familiarity, simply because Rachel couldn't prevent it. 'How're you keeping? I saw Councillor Hazelwood in uniform – he's gone then?'

'It looks that way,' said Rachel.

'What about . . . ?' Mrs Archer tilted her hat in exaggerated fashion, obviously referring to Charlie. 'Is he still . . . ?'

'Yes – I've forgotten how much you owe, Mrs Archer.' Rachel hurried over to the sideboard, searching for a bill. 'Oh, here it is.'

Mrs Archer took the bill and extended payment. Rachel stared at the contents of her hand but didn't take it. Mrs Archer waved her money hand with a smile.

After a moment Rachel took hold of the slip of paper. 'What's this?'

The other laughed brightly. 'It's a pound note!'

'I can't take that.' Rachel shoved it back at her.

Mrs Archer turned shirty. 'It's legal tender – don't you read the papers?'

'I don't care about the papers,' said Rachel dismissively. 'I'm not giving you change for that. I'll wait till you have some proper money.'

'That *is* proper money!' objected Mrs Archer.

'Not to me it isn't.'

'Look, it's got a picture of the King on it!' Mrs Archer tapped the white note viciously, thrusting it under Rachel's nose.

'So has my wall,' responded Rachel, 'but that doesn't make it legal tender. I'm sorry, I won't take it.'

'Well all I can say is you must be well off if you can afford to turn your nose up at good money!' Offended, Mrs Archer stuffed the note back in her purse. 'If you insist on gold you'll have to wait for it – some of us are making an effort to end this war!' She stalked off down the passage and on her exit closed the door heavily.

Her next port of call was the shop round the corner. 'I hope you're more patriotic than Mrs Hazelwood!' she told the owner tartly before obtaining her goods. 'I want to pay with this new money.'

'It's all money, isn't it?' answered Mrs Phillips amiably.

'Not to her it isn't!' retorted Mrs Archer. 'I'll have ten eggs please – she looked down her nose at me as if I was trying to pass a forged one! Her of all people! Stuck-up devil – and a pound of butter, Mrs Phillips, please – it was in the bloomin' Press telling us we had to use these pound notes as much as we could – oh, hello, Ella!' She had turned at the jingle of the doorbell. 'By, I've just had a right do with that neighbour o' yours! And a box of candles, Mrs Phillips, please – I sez to her, I've just come to settle up with you, you know, thinking she'd be short of money now her husband's gone off to war . . .'

'Oh, Russ has gone, has he?' Ella leaned on the counter. 'I didn't know.'

'Aye, he's gone – so I sez to her, I've come to settle up and offers her this pound note an' do you know what she sez? She sez, I'm not having that – as if I'm offering her muck! You know that way she looks at you, all snooty like – I sez, eh it's proper money, you know. She sez well I'm not having it, I want gold . . .'

'Don't we all?' said Ella.

'Aye – so I sez . . . oh sorry are you in a rush, Ella? Go on, get served, I'm trying to remember what else I want, she's got me so blinking mad.' While Ella made the purchase of a pack of cigarettes and paid for them, Mrs Archer gabbled on. 'So, I sez to her, if you want gold, madam, you'll have a long wait – *some* of us are making an effort to end this war.'

'And what did she have to say to that?' quizzed Mrs Phillips.

'She couldn't say anything, could she? 'Cause I was right! She never bothers with anything that goes on round here – thinking she's better than us. If I was in her position I wouldn't dare show my face – mindst, she hasn't been doing lately, has she?'

'Still, you have to feel sorry for her,' said Mrs Phillips. 'The way her husband's . . .'

'Oh, I do, I do!' Mrs Archer began to drop the items of shopping into her bag. 'I think it's shocking what he's done – I don't talk to him, you know. Ooh no – do you?' She had turned back to Ella.

'To tell the truth I don't see much of either of 'em, what with being out at work all day,' said Ella, moving to the door. 'Anyway, I'd better go and let our Kim out, he'll be bursting – tara.'

'Bye, love . . .' Mrs Archer watched her go. 'I don't wonder she never sees them, she's too busy with her Suffragette rubbish.'

'Oh no, she's finished with that,' said Mrs Phillips wisely. 'They've called a truce with the Government until the war's over.'

'Well I'm glad to hear somebody apart from me is making a patriotic gesture!' exclaimed Mrs Archer. 'Oh, I've just remembered what I want – give us six pounds of sugar, dear. If this war goes on longer than expected there'll be people hoarding it like gold, selfish devils, I'll get my bit while I can. Here you are.' She put the paper note on the counter. 'If she doesn't want my money I might as well make full use of it.'

After a week of constantly refusing to handle the new pound notes, Rachel was forced to yield or go broke; the new money seemed here to stay. Fortunately she did not have to suffer the children's antics for much longer; that same week news arrived that the occupied schools were being vacated. Things began to calm down – though there was one slight drama when she made the rash announcement to Biddy that the Pope was dead and thereby plunged routine into chaos as the maid insisted on visiting church every single day to pay her respects. Other than this, Rachel's main worry remained the same: how was she going to cope for the next few months without a breadwinner? At least her other worry was almost over: eleven more days to cross off the calendar and Charlie would be gone.

Russ spent a further two weeks in York before receiving orders to entrain for the South. He wondered vaguely, as he and his comrades marched down Holgate Road to the railway sidings, if any member of his family was in the cheering crowd that lined the route. The atmosphere was overwhelming, everyone behaving as though they were at a huge party. There were Union Jacks fluttering from every window and every hand, streamers thrown. Russ stared ahead in military style, but occasionally his peripheral vision caught a pretty woman flourishing a handkerchief and shouting, 'Brave boys! Give it to 'em!'

Brave boys! If only they knew. If only they could sense his misery. He lurched with a grunt as an overzealous spectator launched herself at him and pressed wet lips to his cheek. From somewhere he conjured up a laugh and marched on, wondering why the silly cow had picked on him. But then people behaved like jackasses in war – look at that soft bitch! She was actually waving a pair of knickers. He could never imagine Rachel doing anything so coarse.

The marchers were nearing the sidings where hundreds more soldiers, many still in civvies, were waiting to board the trains. The regiment which he had rejoined was now greatly expanded, a fact which gave him some comfort; it raised the odds against him and Jack being in the same unit. God spare him that constant reminder of his downfall.

There followed a tedious journey which was alleviated from time to time when stops were made to pick up more military. At every station locals shoved oranges and sweets through the blackened carriage windows and flourished Union Jacks. Russ contributed little to the euphoria, though it was impossible to remain depressed with the lewd jokes that were bandied about the carriage and by the time he arrived at the training camp he felt much better. A period of intensive retraining soon altered that. Having previous experience of Army life, his suffering wasn't as pronounced as that of a raw recruit, but it was damned tough for a man who had done little physical exercise in eleven years.

'Come on, Hazelwood, let's get some o' that bloody beef off!' bawled the sergeant instructor, an old regular whose entire body was coated in tattoos. 'How you gonna kill the Hun with a kite like that? You'll never get near him!'

Yet it appeared he had not acquitted himself too badly, for when the course terminated the new, streamlined Russ found himself with the rank of Lance-Sergeant. This increased responsibility gave him less time to dwell on his troubles at home, for he had fresh ones in the mixed bunch of 5 Platoon, D Company. Such was the eagerness of some to be at the enemy that all his time was spent in dousing insubordinate moans over dixie-bashing and playing silly bloody games with wooden rifles and objections that the war would be over before they ever reached the Channel.

Meanwhile, on a different stretch of sea, a ship was heading towards England bearing a letter:
Dear Mr Hazelwood,

By the time this reaches you, you will have no doubt guessed that my trip has had to be postponed. For this I beg your forgiveness and for not informing you sooner, but I have had much to arrange. I feel it is my duty to go to Belgium to tender my help to those unfortunate souls under seige. I know it is your wish for Charlie to return to Africa as soon as possible, but it is my opinion that with the possibility of warships in these waters, this would be most unwise. I therefore request that he remain with you for the duration of the war, which by all accounts looks like being very brief . . .

Now that her father was taking a role in the war, it had become important to Rowena that she follow the latter's progress. For the past month she had been studying the daily reports of the fighting in the local newspaper. The manner of Father's leaving had upset them all, but with Mother's reassurance that she hadn't really meant it about wanting to see him killed – and knowing Mother's bent for making a song and dance about everything – the children had calmed down now. Only Rowena detected the hint of urgency in her mother's manner as August turned to September and the priest still had not arrived. Today, the eldest daughter was reading aloud another extract from yesterday's *Evening Press* which she had sneaked up to the girls' room. Mother wouldn't approve of them seeing the bits about German atrocities on Belgian and Servian peasants. Neither would she have countenanced Lyn's gloating when these were read out. 'Ugh! That's 'orrible – tell us more, Wena!'

'That's the end of it.' Rowena closed the paper to moans of disappointment from the gathering, who were only permitted to be up here because it was raining.

'Father will take revenge on the Germans once he gets there,' vouched Charlie, who was also an avid reader of the reports. 'I wonder when that will be.'

'He must be there already,' answered Rowena. 'If he was still in York he would've called to see us. Maybe we'll get a letter soon – here, listen to this! They're asking for householders to donate knives and forks and plates for the soldiers who're living at the Assembly Rooms. It says they've hardly anything to eat off and they're very cold on a night because of the shortage of blankets.' She presented an earnest face. 'I think we should help. We wouldn't want our father to be cold, would we?'

'Serve him right,' contradicted Lyn, who hadn't forgiven him for lying about the tooth fairy. She was immediately set on by the others and retreated to a corner to sulk. However, guilt over her own malice soon had her edging back into the discussion.

Rowena suggested they form a committee. 'The only thing is, we're at church tomorrow and school on Monday so it'll have to be today . . . and Mother said we weren't to disturb her. She's doing some very intricate work.'

'What's intri . . .' started Beany.

'I think you should ask before you go taking anything,' warned Charlie.

'Wena, what's intricate?'

'It's something very fiddly – but Charlie, if I disturb her she'll be angry and might not let us do it. She's cross enough that your priest hasn't come for you yet.'

'Yes!' Lyn gave her half-brother a poke in the side. 'I thought you were only meant to be here a few weeks. When're you off?'

Charlie hoisted his shoulders.

Becky, sitting on the bed behind him, kneeled up and laced her arms round his chest, pressing her cheek to his temple. 'I don't want you to go, ever. I hope he never comes for you.'

Charlie covered her hands with his.

'Well at least while you're here we don't have Bertie bossing us about,' agreed Lyn. Her brother had spent much of the school holidays in his own company.

This raised a question from Rowena. 'D'you think we should ask Bertie to join our committee?' She was answered straightaway by Lyn who was adamant that it should be strictly for the girls.

Becky asked, 'What about Charlie?'

'He's not allowed out, is he?' responded Lyn. 'An' Bertie's such a miseryguts that he wouldn't want to help if it's anything to do with Father.'

Bertie, on his way down from studying the egg collection, heard this and more.

'A moment ago *you* didn't want to help Father,' retorted Becky.

'Well, I do now! Anyway, Bertie'd only be throwing his weight about. I say we don't tell him.'

Rowena looked at the others. 'It seems a bit mean.'

'I bet there's only you that thinks so,' replied Lyn. 'Let's take a vote on it. Who wants Bertie to come?'

Bertie heard the vote cast against him before slouching to his room. None of them seemed interested in how he had taken to his grammar school. Oh, Mother had asked if he liked it, but when he had said no, she had merely answered that he would soon get used to it. Bertie swore to himself that he would never get used to it. The building was so large he was constantly getting lost on his way to other lessons and some of the boys were like men, making Bertie feel very vulnerable. In its favour, there was no bullying and going here meant he could escape from Charlie for six hours a day . . . but then he had to come home and look at Charlie and see how his sisters fussed over him . . . and witness his father's empty chair. He closed the door and lay on his bed. He was meant to be playing in the school football team, today, but he couldn't raise the interest.

'Right, I'll go and ask Biddy what we can take,' volunteered Rowena. 'She'll know what stuff mother never uses.'

'And we can tell Mother when she's not busy,' said Becky.

After careful thought Rowena answered. 'No . . . I think we should keep quiet about it. You're not supposed to brag about charitable acts.'

She went downstairs.

Biddy was kneeling before the hearth cleaning the oven, her brawny arms streaked with grease. 'What was that, Miss Wena?'

'I said do you know if Mother has any plates and cutlery that she never uses?'

The maid finished her task and closed the oven door, pulling herself to her feet. Without wiping the grease from her arms she began to put her coat on. 'Well, I never yet seen the stuff in that cupboard put to good use.'

'Neither have I,' agreed Rowena. 'So d'you think . . .'

'I haven't time to be conversin' with ye,' said Biddy, now at the back door. 'I've been ordered to go down to the shops for a sack o' spuds.' Rowena said she thought the man delivered them. 'An' so he did until the beloved Army commandeered his horse! As if I don't have enough work, I have to play the bleedin' donkey.' She closed the door on the conversation.

Rowena turned eyes and feet to the dresser, smiling her satisfaction when it revealed just what she needed. Fetching a basket, she began to stack the plates inside and after these the cutlery. When this was done she put a hand to her mouth. Would the soldiers need a tablecloth? She selected one and laid it on top of the basket. By now her sisters' chatter could be heard on the stairs. Soon they had joined her.

'I'm dedicating my hot water bottle too,' said Becky, holding out the earthenware vessel.

Rowena smiled: 'I'm sure they'll be very grateful.'

'And we've taken a blanket off our bed,' said Lyn.

Rowena's' face glowed. 'Is Charlie looking after Mona and Squawk? Good! Get your coats then and we can be back before dinner.'

Rachel hooked a hand over her shoulder to massage the knotted muscles and, after a look at the clock, decided to pack away. On getting up, she tried again to ease the ache in her shoulders by stretching, then went to the kitchen to check on Biddy's progress. 'Did you get those potatoes?'

Biddy continued to stir the pan on the range. 'Sorry, ma'am, but the farmers can't get their deliveries through 'cause the Army's taken all their horses.'

Rachel made a noise of repressed anger, then went over to the dresser to push in the drawer which Rowena had left protruding by half an inch. 'As long as they have their horses they couldn't give a tinker's cuss if we starve – and who's left all these drawers sticking out?'

'Not me, ma'am. I haven't been in there.'

'Well somebody has!' Rachel opened a drawer, took out a tablecloth then rammed it shut. For a moment she continued fussing about . . . then her face took on a glazed expression. Slowly, she reopened the drawer and stared down into it. 'Where's the boy?' she enquired in a tone softer than normal.

'Which one is that, ma'am?'

'The boy, the boy!' Rachel spun on the maid.

'Why, I think he's upstairs, ma'am.'

'He'd better be!'

'Ma'am, what's wrong?' Biddy's eyebrows covered her eyes.

'He's taken my best silver, that's what's wrong! And if he isn't upstairs you are for it, my girl! Go fetch him.' She turned back to scrabble in the other drawers.

Biddy rushed upstairs like a stampeding rhino and burst into the girls' room to be greeted by startled faces. 'Oh, Jesus! Thank God, you're here!' She hurled herself at Charlie, grabbing his arm. 'Herself is thinkin' ye've run off with the silver – ye haven't have ye?'

'No, what silver?' Charlie permitted himself to be dragged to the stairs.

'Her very best silver! 'Twas in that oak cupboard an' somebody swiped it!'

Rowena's heart lurched. She tossed a desperate look at her sisters, before scampering after the maid and Charlie.

''S all right, ma'am!' announced Biddy, trying to catch her breath as she pushed the hapless boy forward. 'I've nabbed him.'

Rachel stalked up to him. 'Where is it?' Charlie could only spread his hands.

'Mother,' came a small voice. 'Which silver is it that's missing?'

Rachel hardly spared a glance for her daughter, all her accusal centred on the boy. 'I only have the one lot of silver! Or should I say *had*, before somebody put their thieving hands on it.'

'Mother . . . I think it was me.'

Rachel paid her more attention now. 'You *think* it was you?'

Rowena turned to the maid. 'Biddy, when I asked you if there was any crockery Mother didn't use which cupboard did you mean?'

'That one,' said Biddy.

'Then . . . it is me, Mother,' admitted Rowena softly. 'I'm sorry, I thought when Biddy said you didn't use it . . .'

But her mother was now engaged in throwing open the cupboard doors. 'My best dinner service! Aagh!' She wheeled. 'What have you done with it?'

Her daughter tried to explain. 'We took it for the poor young soldiers. They haven't enough plates to go round and . . .'

Rachel had entered a state of near dementia, hands clasped to her head. 'The Army's got my best dinner service!'

'We thought you'd be pleased that we were trying to help,' lamented the girl. 'We were thinking of Father.'

Her mother gave a hysterical cackle, then whirled on Biddy. 'Get down there and bring them back!' She flashed a look at her daughter. 'Where did you take them?' On being told, she turned back to Biddy. 'Get down to the Assembly Rooms as fast as you can! And don't come back without them.'

'But the dinner . . .'

Rachel grasped the pan handle and lifted it from the heat, slopping its contents to sizzle on the hob. 'Blast the dinner. Go!'

Biddy grabbed her coat and hared off, reappearing to thrust a letter at her mistress. 'That was on the mat.'

'Go on, go on!' Rachel snatched the letter and shooed her away, then paced out her agitation on the kitchen floor.

'I'm very sorry, Mother,' tendered Rowena yet again.

'And so you should be!' The letter was clamped to her heaving breast.

'I would've asked you but you said we weren't to disturb you and we thought we were taking the stuff you didn't use.'

'And we don't have to look far to find the instigator, do we?' Rachel was glaring at Charlie. 'Not content to drive my husband into the Army he's got to give them my heirlooms too!'

'It wasn't Charlie's idea,' confessed Rowena. 'It was mine.'

'I know who it was!' Rachel's fingers nipped and twisted the letter. Looking down at it, she began to rip it open. However, she had not read more than six lines when her eyes shot up again. 'Rowena, get out of my sight until you're called – not you!'

Charlie, about to leave, turned back. When the room was empty save for the two of them, Rachel flourished the letter in his face. 'Read that!'

He looked at it. 'It's for my father.'

'Yes! And read what it says! See, what your precious father has gone and left me to cope with!' The soulful expression in his eyes provoked her further and she gave loud voice to it. 'The priest isn't coming, I'm stuck with you!' The image of the NSPCC woman leapt into her mind – they were supposed to let her know when Charlie went back to Africa. What could Rachel tell her now?

'I'm sorry.' Charlie folded the letter and handed it back.

She knocked it from his hands. 'I wish you'd stop saying that! It's no good being sorry. Sorry won't set the clock back. Why, oh why did you have to come here?' In all the time he had been here it was the first time she had bothered to ask.

'I wanted to see my father.'

'That's no answer!' she shrilled tearfully. 'I mean, you must've known he didn't want you. No father goes away and leaves his offspring for eleven years without a word.'

'But he sent money,' Charlie pointed out.

'To buy your mother off, you clown! Not because he was concerned about what happened to you. So she wouldn't come looking for him.'

'No . . . my mother always said that Father would come back for us – he told her that.'

'Then your mother was as big a fool as I was if she believed him,' said Rachel bitterly. 'Apart from . . . the other thing.' She pressed a handkerchief to her face, then shoved it back in her pocket.

'What other thing?'

'Never mind! Much as I can't bear the sight of you I wouldn't speak ill of the dead.'

'But you must tell me what's on your mind so I can understand your dislike of me.'

This show of maturity produced another burst of passion. 'You pious little . . .' She strode up to him. 'All right! I'll tell you what your mother was – a harlot! Do you know what a harlot is? Yes, I'm sure you do! In your mother's instance it's a woman who hangs around the soldiers and sells her body for a string of beads or whatever he gave her.'

Charlie didn't understand what she meant by 'sell' but it was obviously something bad. He shook his head. 'She never . . .'

'She stole my husband! He was married to me and she seduced him!'

'But I'm certain she didn't know . . . she never mentioned . . .'

'She knew! The sly – d'you think he would've done that if it hadn't been thrown at him?'

Charlie struggled to equate the two sides of the tale. His mother had always spoken of Hazelwood with affection, had shown implicit faith that he would, one day, come back for his son and had implanted that belief in Charlie. 'My mother never knew he was married to you, I'm sure of it. She truly loved my father.'

'Then it's a good job for her that she died before discovering what he really is!' spat Rachel.

Charlie looked down at his shoes. His mother had been dead for over a year, but he still missed her. He didn't like the things Mrs Hazelwood was saying about her, nevertheless he could understand the woman's hatred. This he told Rachel, adding, 'Though I'm positive it wasn't her intention to hurt you . . . But I didn't ask to be born. I've done you no harm. Why do you . . .'

'*No harm*!' Rachel cut him off with a shrieking laugh. 'You came here, didn't you? You've destroyed us, all of us. My husband was the Sheriff of York, this family was respected and then you turn up and now look at us. There's poor Bertie had to stay off school because of the bullying, there's people whispering every time I pluck up courage to step out of the front door, and what does your hero of a father do? He runs away with his tail between his legs, leaving me to cope with the consequences of his adultery. Tell me something: now that you know what sort of a man he really is, what he thinks about you, why do you stay? You came here by your own steam, you're quite capable of making your own way back to Africa. Why do you stay?'

He deliberated, remembering what Father Guillaume had taught him about being responsible for one's actions. 'I think that as I was the one to drive my father away, I should take his place.' At her frown, he explained, 'I'm the eldest. It's up to me to take care of you.'

'Take care of me? Take care of me! If I need taking care of I have my own son, I don't need you to do it. And if taking care of me constitutes giving away everything of value in this house then the best you can do is get yourself back where you belong, right now!'

Charlie indicated the letter on the floor. 'Father Guillaume says . . .'

'Father Guillaume doesn't have to sit and look at your black face as evidence of his partner's treachery!'

'I'll stay until my father gets back,' said Charlie doggedly. 'It's my duty.'

'You self-important little prig! What makes you think he's coming back?'

'He'll come back.'

His surety made her want to explode. But in the midst of her anger she caught sight of a spider on the cupboard nearby, and recoiled. 'All right! If you want to earn your keep you can dispose of that for me!' She lanced a finger at the creature which was the size of a half-crown. He hung back. 'Well go on! You won't make it go just by looking at it, although you succeeded with your father.' She waited.

'I'm . . . scared of spiders,' came his shamefaced admission.

She gave a nasty laugh, then went to the foot of the stairs to shout for her son. After the spider was dealt with, she and Bertie gave the intruder a look of disdain and left him alone.

In the deafening quiet that followed, Charlie wandered over to the table to pick up the other letter that had arrived in the same envelope.

My dear Charlie,

By now, as I told your father, you will know I have decided to cancel my visit to England. Forgive me, if this seems I have forsaken you, but there are others in far greater need of my presence. You have a roof over your head, are presumably well fed, and judging from your letter, not too unhappy. The people of my homeland are undergoing desperate conditions. I must go and help them, Charlie. I know you will understand this.

239

I was rather disturbed to read that you are denied the comfort of your faith, but hasten to assure you that it is no sin on your part, as long as you pray wherever you are. Since my last correspondence, hastily penned, I have had time to reflect on what I said to you then. Perhaps I was harsh in saying that you alone are responsible for the situation you are in. That was my own inadequacy speaking, I'm afraid. I was angry that I had looked after you all these years just for you to go swanning off after your real father. I say 'real' father, Charlie, because if I am to admit the truth it is to say I had begun to think of myself in that role. No natural father could have loved you more . . .

Charlie was brought up sharp by this admission, and it doubled his guilt. The priest was right; he was churlish to have spurned such obvious paternity in search of something that never was. But it would be, Charlie bolstered himself, one day my father *will* love me. . . . *I feel I am partly to blame for your present turmoil. It was I who perpetuated the myth by leading your mother to believe that Mr Hazelwood had sent messages for her along with the money. On the latter point, of course I forgive you for taking it. It was, after all, intended for your welfare, so your act could not really be construed as stealing. Though I do intend to claim recompense from your posterior for the ruined cashbox and one of my best knives!*

Dearest Charlie, I pray that Mrs Hazelwood and Bertie will be more kindly disposed towards you by now, and that your prolonged stay there will turn out to be happy. If ever you feel like writing to me – and I do hope that this will be often – you will find my proposed address at the foot of this page. God keep you kindly and remember me in your prayers, as you are in mine.

Yours Affectionately,
Father Guillaume.

After the second reading his eyes began to burn. He remained in the kitchen for a long time, his throat heavy with unshed tears, and was not prompted into movement until Biddy's noisy return.

Her red face was partially hidden by a cardboard box. 'Jesus save us, me legs're worn to stumps!'

Charlie gave a little cough to dislodge the emotion from his throat.

The box was unceremoniously dumped on the table, enabling the maid to sprawl her ungainly body into a chair. 'Where's the missus? I thought she'd be here to leap on me the second I got back, her an' her bloody plates.'

'Did you get them?' he enquired anxiously.

'Huh! I did.' She patted the box. 'After virtuously having to scrape the food off them. They'd already been put to good use. An' a right load o' gob I had to take on your account, my lad.'

Charlie didn't bother to defend himself. 'And the silver?'

The creases of discomfort on Biddy's face smoothed into apprehension. 'Well, put it like this, I'm hardly going to receive her thanks when I tell her there's a full bottle o' silver polish goin' to be wasted.' She grimaced and pressed herself from the dining chair to take off her coat. 'It'll be melted down by now if I know the military.'

'It really wasn't my doing, you know.'

'Nor mine neither but 'tis me who'll get the custard pie! Make yourself useful an' lay the plates for dinner – for the love o' Christ, not those!'

'I was only lifting the box off the table.'

'Well, for God's sake be more careful, else we'll both be fed to the Germans.'

Charlie was thoughtful as the maid put the pan back on to reheat. 'Biddy . . . d'you think she'd really like it if my father got killed?'

Biddy glanced at him, saw his worry. 'No, I think for all her fuss she'd be sorry if the master came back dead – pass me that salt now.'

'I'm sorry to get you into more bother, Charlie,' said Rowena later when the two of them were separated from the others. There had been further chastisement over dinner.

'It wasn't just the silver,' he replied. 'It was Father Guillaume's letter. He's gone to Belgium.'

'So you'll be staying a while longer, then?' He gave a melancholic nod. 'I wondered why Mother wanted to speak to you alone. I heard her shouting at you.' At his miserable expression, she said in light manner, 'Becky'll be pleased you're staying,' and smiled to cheer him up.

Nothing else was said until they had taken to the stairs, when Charlie exclaimed, 'Wena, do you know what adultery is?' She shook her head. 'Neither do I. Your mother said it about Father and my mother. I didn't understand.'

'It's obviously something to do with adults,' said Rowena expertly. 'But come on, we'll go and look it up in my dictionary.' It was about time they made proper investigation. 'You go up to the attic and I'll fetch it.'

The dictionary was not very instructive: violation of the marriage bed; illicit sexual intercourse on the part of a married person. They both thought they knew what violation meant, but had to look up sexual intercourse. Finding only the first part, they had to thumb back to the i's for intercourse, which they discovered meant one of several things, none of which made them any clearer on the meaning of adultery.

Rowena put a finger in the air. 'I've just remembered! It's one of the Ten Commandments: Thou Shalt Not Commit Adultery.'

'Oh . . .' Charlie's face was bleak. 'It's a sin, then.' But what was the nature of the sin?

'Becky, what d'you want?' Rowena turned to ask her sister, whose auburn head had appeared round the door.

Becky answered resentfully, 'I can come up and see Charlie if I like – *you're* here.'

'Yes, but we're discussing private business,' said her big sister. 'Please go away.'

'You don't own him, you know!'

'And neither do you!' Rowena changed her tack. 'Look, I'll be gone in a minute and you can have him all to yourself, but this is very important.' Becky made several objections but was eventually persuaded to leave. Though this didn't stop her listening at the door. Rowena turned back to Charlie. 'I still don't get this.' She tapped the book. 'I'm going to ask my Scripture teacher at the next lesson.'

This she did, but the answer was not particularly enlightening. 'It's a sin for a married man to "know" another woman,' said Miss Halford.

'But my father knows lots of ladies besides my mother,' replied the confused child.

And the teacher, not being conversant with the Hazelwoods' 'problem', had laughed simperingly and tried to make herself more clear, but instead made it all the more perplexing. One small fact that did emerge from the conversation was that it was a sin for a child to be born out of wedlock and Rowena, recalling that her father had said he 'wasn't actually married to Charlie's mother', finally began to understand.

'Did you find out?' enquired an impatient Charlie when she arrived home that evening.

'I'll tell you later,' she mouthed quietly.

Becky overheard. 'Tell him what? What have you found out?'

'Don't be so nosey,' answered her sister. 'It's nothing to do with you.' And though pressed, she refused to reveal anything until she and Charlie were up in the attic. 'I'm sorry, I've got some bad news for you, Charlie.' She played with her fingers. 'We were right about the Commandment. My father committed a sin with your mother . . . I'm afraid it makes you a sort of sin too, because you were born out of wedlock.'

'And is that why my mother's a harlot?' The brown face was solemn.

Rowena shrugged. 'Must be.'

'Mary Magdalene was a harlot, wasn't she?' Charlie probed his lip. His companion said she didn't know. 'Yes . . . yes. I think so. And Jesus loved her, didn't he? So it can't be all that bad, can it?'

'I'm sure your mother was very nice,' comforted Rowena. 'And Father must have thought she was, mustn't he?'

They fell silent.

Becky decided she wasn't going to hear any more and crept back down the stairs. But she had heard enough: their father had left them because he was a sinner.

CHAPTER SEVENTEEN

The order had come. On the ship that was to take them to France there was great exhilaration from all but Russ. While those with families to see them off were waving, blowing kisses at the quay and generally making exhibitions of themselves, the Lance-Sergeant was leaning over the starboard rail, looking out across the uninviting grey water. What lay out there for Russ? An autumn wind roared in from the sea, trying to rip the tarpaulins from the lifeboats, shoving itself under the peak of his cap, teasing his ears. Every now and then an extra strong blast would succeed in pushing him from the rail. Russ narrowed his eyes against its force, wondering involuntarily what his own family was doing. Bertie would be at his new school now and Charlie would be gone. '*He'll never be gone!*' he heard his wife cry again. '*Because he'll always be up here, staring out at me, reminding me how little you thought of our marriage!*'

He heard laughing. Not that incessant tide of banter from the other side of the ship, but a nearer, more furtive sound. He turned, but saw nothing and duly brought his face back to the wind and the sea, his thoughts blending with the waves. Shortly, though, the snigger came again. Vexed, Russ pushed himself from the iron rail and went to investigate. At his footfall, there was the sound of hasty scrabbling. 'Well, if it isn't those refined duettists, Wheatley and Dobson!' cried Russ as he rounded upon the culprits. 'And what bit of skulbuggery have we here?'

'Nothing, Sergeant,' replied an angelic-looking private, flustered hands trying to push something back into his pocket.

'Nothing?' Russ stepped behind the shelter of the lifeboat, at once cutting off the blast of wind. He circled the pair. 'Didn't sound like nothing to me, Wheatley.' The two were from his own platoon. During his retraining Russ had singled out the mischiefmakers – to which group these two belonged.

'We were just talking about France, Sergeant,' supplied the other soldier in broad Yorkshire accent. He was a more pugnacious-looking character altogether with dark hair, a broken nose and the beginnings of a moustache on his upper lip.

Russ surveyed them and gave a mental shake of head. They didn't look much older than his own son . . . that brought his troubles seeping back and he was trying to staunch these. 'And France is funny is it, Dobson?'

The green eyes looked up at the sky. 'Well . . . no, Sergeant.'

'*No*, Sergeant? Then I didn't hear you sniggering?'

'We weren't actually laughing about France, Sarg.'

'Oh, I'm sure the bleedin' Frogs will be delighted to hear that, Private. Then what were you actually laughing at?' The angel and the devil swapped guilty looks. 'Come on, out with it. What were you hiding in your pocket when I came round here?'

'Nowt, Sarg, honest!' protested Wheatley.

'Then you won't mind emptying your pockets, will you, Private?' Russ stopped Dobson from reaching into his pocket. 'Not you, lad – him! Come on, I'm a-waiting, Wheatley.'

Lower jaw distorted by resignation, Wheatley dug slowly into his pocket. For the sergeant's inspection he withdrew a handkerchief, his pay book, a box of matches and some playing cards. 'And the rest!' The hand was reluctantly inserted and withdrawn. 'And what might that be, Private?' Wheatley mumbled something and looked out to sea. Russ cupped an ear. 'I can't hear you, Private.'

'A French letter, Sergeant.'

The sergeant's face was clothed with interest. 'Oh? And for what purpose is this French letter, Wheatley?'

'So's he can write home to Mother, Sergeant.' Dobson lost his impudent grin as Hazelwood turned wrathful eyes on him.

'You seem to think this is all very hilarious, Dobson.' Russ started to circle them again; stiff-legged, like a dog before it sinks its teeth in. 'You think this is all gonna be a load o' fun, don't you? Well, stand by for a shock, we're not off to France to plunder the female population, Private, we're off to save them from the bloody Hun.' He cupped his ear. 'What are we going for?'

'To save them from the bloody Hun, Sergeant,' parroted Dobson.

'Correct! So we won't be needing that, will we, Wheatley?'

'No Sergeant.'

'No, Sergeant! I suppose you do know what a French letter is for, Wheatley – no more bloody cracks, Dobson, thank you very much!'

Wheatley offered an embarrassed face and glanced at his partner for support but Dobson was looking at the sky again. 'I think it's what you use when you go with a woman, Sergeant.'

Russ thumbed his chest and bent forward. 'You think it's what *I* use?'

Wheatley shook his head rapidly. 'No, I didn't mean you personally, Sergeant! I meant what anybody can use when they go with a woman.'

'Go where?'

'Well . . . just go,' replied a discomfited Wheatley, his golden eyelashes brushing his cheek.

'Oh, they do, do they? And what particular portion of their anatomy would they be using it on?'

Wheatley glanced at Dobson again. The latter tucked his chin into his chest to hide a smirk.

'Stand up straight, the pair of you!' Both youths shot to attention. 'Worldly little pair, aren't we? Do you have one o' these, Dobson?' The private said he hadn't. 'Intending to borrow your mate's after he's had his go, were you? Just because you've got a bit o' bumfluff on your lip doesn't make you a man, you know. What would your mothers say to all this debauchery? Would she say, oh go ahead, lads, have fun?'

246

'No, Sergeant.'

'No, she wouldn't, Dobson! But you thought that now you were soldiers, now you were away from your mother's care you could do what you liked, didn't you, lad? Well let me tell you that you might have left your mother back in Blighty, but you've found another one here. For the duration of this scrummage I'm your mother, Dobson and I don't want to see no French letters being flashed about, specially by fellows that don't know how to use 'em. Got that clear?'

Both heads tilted backwards. 'Yes, Sergeant!'

'Right! Now put it away before I confiscate it.' Russ held them with steely eyes as he reached into his breast pocket for a cigarette. Once it was lighted he relaxed against a pile of crates. Despite the dressing down he had formed quite a liking for these two lads. In fact there was not a man in his section whom he actually disliked.

'Er, Mother,' began Dobson as innocently as his face would allow. Then at Russ's narrow-eyed glare, said, 'Well, you did say you were our mother, didn't you, Sarg?'

'Dobson,' the name came on an exhalation of smoke, 'you see that load what's being winched aboard that there ship? Pretty heavy, wouldn't you say?' Dobson nodded. 'How heavy – three, four tons? Make a nice mess of your shiny boots if it should happen to fall on you, wouldn't it?' Another nod from Dobson. Russ' chin jutted out. 'Well if you'd like to know just how much of a mess, call me Mother again. I'll be on you ten times heavier than that bloody load!'

'Sar'nt!' Dobson jerked his shoulders back.

Russ relaxed again. 'What did you do before you came in the Army?' It was the first real opportunity he had had to chat with these lads, their time being taken up by hard work. Dobson replied this and that.

'This and that? This and bloody that. Funny sort o' job wasn't it? What firm did you work for?'

'Er well . . . it wasn't really a firm,' evaded Dobson. 'I just sort of had the one master.'

'In service then?'

247

'You could say.'

Russ voiced a theory, taking a thoughtful puff. 'I expect there'll be a hundred lines waiting for you over this little escapade when you get back.' He saw Wheatley bite his freckled lip, and leaned towards Dobson. 'Aye, I'm not so green as I'm cabbage looking, Private!'

'You won't tell, will you, Sarg?' The green eyes were anxious.

'Bit bloody late for that now, isn't it? Anyway,' Russ added grudgingly, 'you won't be the first to lie about your age.' He spat a strand of tobacco from his tongue. 'How old are you, then?'

Dobson replied, 'Fifteen . . . well nearly.' He was still lying. 'It's my birthday soon.'

'Oh well, I'd better telegraph ahead and get the Hun to arrange a party for you.' Russ wondered at the mentality of the recruiting sergeant who had accepted Dobson's word. 'That *was* nineteen, you said, wasn't it Dobson? Just signed on for the duration, have you?'

'No, Sarg.' Dobson's chest swelled. 'I'm a regular.'

'A regular silly sod. What about you, Wheatley, you playing truant an' all?'

The angle of Wheatley's pale eyebrows showed he was offended. 'No, Sarg! I'm nineteen . . . in a couple o' weeks.' He certainly didn't look it.

'Oh, both birthday boys, are we?' The sergeant's expression became derogatory. 'You bloody mugs! What did you want to join the Army for, eh?'

Puzzlement from both boys. 'It's exciting,' said Dobson.

Russ gave a bitter laugh. 'Aye, it should be that all right.'

'What you in the Army for then, Sarg, if it's that bad?' demanded Dobson.

'For some of us, lad,' sighed Russ. 'What's over there,' he nodded out to sea, 'is preferable to what's back there,' a landwards gesture.

Wheatley gave his reason for being here. 'I know the Hun's only in Europe at the moment, but if we don't stop him he'll be over the Channel and doing to our mothers what he's done to the Belgian women. Us British have a duty to put him back in his place.'

'A very noble sentiment, Private,' said Russ. 'Isn't anybody here to wave you patriots off?'

A shake of the head from Dobson. 'Me mam doesn't even know I'm here.'

'You little . . . don't tell me you've run away from home an' all?'

Hastily, Dobson explained. 'I've written her a letter and posted it here. If she'd known where I was before she would've dragged me off home.'

'I should think she bloody-well would! How d'you manage to hide for two months and not be found out?' Dobson said he'd been lucky, making the sergeant laugh out loud. 'So now you think it'll be too late for her to do anything about it, you deign to let her know you haven't been murdered. What about your mam, Wheatley?'

'Oh, she knows I'm here, Sarg. But she didn't want to come and see me off, said she'd only cry.' A grin for his pal.

Russ placed a fatherly hand on Wheatley's shoulder. 'Don't be too quick to mock, lad. Some of us would be very grateful for someone to cry over us.'

Bertie had once watched a blackbird scuffle its wings over an ants' nest, stirring the creatures up in order to have them swarm over it and so rid the bird of its parasites. Mother was like that, he thought now, watching her wring her hands and flap her arms, stirring her family into a frenzy in the hope that they would provide an answer to her problems. 'What will I do? Oh, what will I do!' Rachel flopped onto a chair and leaned her elbows on the table, still wringing her hands. 'I've a dozen people waiting for hats, how am I ever going to finish them with the shop to look after?' She had just received word that Russ' young assistant was also to desert her for the war.

Rowena tried to offer her services. 'I could help you to sew the hats. There's no school today.' It was Saturday. 'I'm very neat.'

'It needs an expert, Rowena,' replied her mother ungraciously and began to pile the breakfast pots. 'Oh, I suppose I shall be up till midnight stitching my fingers to the bone – and all because of your father!'

And that wasn't the only problem Russ had left her. After receiving the priest's letter she had gone to visit the woman from the NSPCC with the intention of confessing that Charlie was still here. Mrs Ingram, snowed under with new cases and not a little impatient at being disturbed, had seemed surprised to see her and before Rachel could speak had announced, 'Mr Hazelwood did tell me that Charlie had returned to Africa earlier than expected.'

Rachel had stammered, 'Oh, did he? Good . . . I wasn't sure if he'd been in touch, what with this war and everything . . . I just thought I'd come and see.' She had apologized for delaying Mrs Ingram's work and left hastily – and thank you, Russell, very much for making a liar of me! It was nice to learn that Charlie had been taken off the files, but there would be hell to pay if Mrs Ingram should learn he was still here. Why hadn't Rachel told the truth? She couldn't keep him hidden forever. It was just one thing on top of another.

Bertie left the others to take the role of the ants and wandered up to his room where he fell on his bed. They probably wouldn't even notice he had gone. The mood of profound desolation he had thought might lessen with the departure of his father had instead grown worse. In moments of inertia it would seize and torment him like a malicious terrier. In a fit of desperation he flung himself from the bed and went to lean on the windowsill. He rubbed a hole in the condensation and peered out at the miserable day. There was nothing to watch, only wet rooves. An idle finger came up to scrawl on the misted pane, 'Fuzzball is a pig.' He sat back on the bed to stare at his handiwork. Almost immediately, rivulets began to trickle from the lower loops of the words . . . like tears. Bertie lurched away and plodded blindly to his sisters' room where the view offered more. There was another battalion of soldiers marching to Knavesmire which was already densely packed with lines of white tents, strings of horses and huge pieces of artillery. The horses, heads lowered against the drizzle, reminded him of his own misery. Once more he spun from the window and tried to ease his pain in movement.

First, he paced the confined area of the girls' room, then moved on to the landing. Biddy's quarters offered scant occupation. He tapped his feet on the lino, fingering the few personal items that were present. Pulling back the covers of the maid's bed, he stared down at the undersheet, then bent and filled his lungs with her smell. A pair of Biddy's knickers were folded over the clothes horse that also held the baby's napkins. Dropping the covers he ambled over to pick the knickers up, holding them open in front of him. There was a hole worn in the crotch. Bertie stuck his finger through and waggled it. He thought of the things his father had done to the black woman. The finger was withdrawn and he went to close the door.

Unbuttoning his trousers, he held the drawers at hip level and inserted his penis through the hole. It made him feel all hot and dirty. The hole suddenly became smaller than it had been; it tightened on him. His skin prickled and he tried to pull himself out but the garment seemed to have grown attached to him. Thinking he heard footsteps he panicked and tugged the knickers free, hurting himself. After a hurried buttoning of trousers he threw the knickers back on the clothes horse and went to put his ear to the door. Then he peeped onto the landing. He had been mistaken. The guilty sweat began to cool and he took the stairs to the attic, rubbing at his crotch.

There was only one put-up bed now. The other had been folded away – a sign of finality. Bertie stared intently at the remaining one, picturing his half-brother's brown face on the pillow. The mood of guilt and despair was overtaken by hatred, hatred for both of them. He bunched his fist and slammed it into the pillow with all his might. He wanted to punish his father for bringing this upon him – but how, when he was no longer here? Bertie's eyes fell on the cabinet that housed the collection of eggs, his father's pride. Moving around the obstacles in the room, he stopped before it and lifted his arms to chest level to pull out a drawer. After an uncertain delay, he picked up one of the eggs and studied it, not really seeing an egg but his father's reaction when he found a lifetime's work destroyed. He saw the egg shatter on the ground though it had not yet left his hand. His fingers closed gently around it, felt its fragility. The merest increase in pressure would begin the destruction. Having crushed one he would be unable to stop. It would be fitting retribution for his father's treachery . . . but then he remembered what his father had said the day that *he* had turned up: 'All these will be yours one day'. Bertie prized the collection as much as his father did, and such mindless vandalism was contrary to his nature.

Replacing the egg tenderly in its hollow, he slid in the drawer. There would have to be some other way to hurt his father . . . and there was only one other thing that his father professed to treasure. All Bertie needed was the method. He slumped over the top of the cabinet. Oh God, he was so bored! Maybe he would find something next door to take his mind off things.

'Hello there, stranger!' Ella Daw showed great surprise at her young visitor. As far as she knew, Rachel's embargo on this house was still in force. 'I'm afraid you've picked the wrong time for your visit, I'm just off to work.' She noticed the sparkles on Bertie's jacket. 'Is it still raining out there?' Bertie said it was and she clicked her tongue. 'I'll have to get me umbrella out and I don't know where the hell it is.' She rummaged about in a cupboard. 'I expect that lad's gone by now, isn't he?'

'He's stopping till the war's over.' A sullen Bertie swung his leg back and forth.

'Oh, why's that – ah, here it is!' She emerged clutching the umbrella.

'The priest he lives with has gone to Belgium instead.'

'Your mother won't be too pleased then. How're them sisters o' yours? I don't see much of 'em these days.'

Bertie said neither did he, and sat down to watch Ella brush her hair. Since switching from making chocolates to munitions she had had it bobbed. Bertie, who loved to watch his mother brush out her waistlength mane, thought the style ugly.

Ella caught his inspection. 'Like it d'you?'

He shrugged. 'It's all right.'

'How gallant you are, Bertie.' She moved away from the mirror, taking quick mincing steps in her hobble skirt, and pulled on a navy blue coat. 'Has your mother heard anything from your dad?'

Bertie fixed his eyes to Ella's shoes with their buttoned gaiters and shook his head. His father hadn't even sent him a card for his birthday – not that Bertie had wanted one, but it just showed how much his father really cared. Some birthday it had been with Fuzzball there.

'I had a postcard from my Jack.' Ella reached onto the mantel and showed the picture postcard to the boy. 'It doesn't sound as if they're having too bad a time of it – your dad should be safe enough.'

Her attempt at reassurance was dismissed as was the card. 'I'm not bothered if he is or not.'

This comment did not seem to surprise Ella who tucked the card back behind the clock. 'Ah well, I'm sorry, Bertie, but I haven't time to listen to grievances. If you want to have a moan come back tonight.' With not seeing much of Rachel now she was out of touch with the Hazelwoods' situation and would like to be brought up to date. 'Don't let your mother cop you though.' She clipped the dog's lead to its collar. 'I'll have to trot. Kim wants his walk before I go to work an' I'm late already.'

'D'you want me to take him?' came the unexpected offer.

'Oh, you are a pal!' She handed him the lead, then took tuppence from her purse. 'Here y'are. Walk him down past the shop and get yourself some sweets, they might help you feel a bit happier. When you've brought him back lock the front door and shove the key through.'

Bertie followed her down the passage. When she reminded him that his mother might see him from her window he replied that she had just set off to look after his father's shop, thereby giving Ella another snip of information. Once on the street, Ella hoisted her umbrella and strode ahead while the boy took his time with the dog.

After walking all of three yards the old dog was none too keen on going further, though being of small stature had no choice but to comply with the boy's insistent hauling. On his return, Bertie shoved his black lace-up under the dog's tail to assist him up the step. Old Kim growled and bared his teeth at such disrespect. Bertie delayed retaliation until he had closed the door, then gave the terrier a sharp kick which launched it, yelping, into a somersault. Then he imprisoned it in the front parlour and began a tour of the house, devouring Kim's personal supply of chocolate drops in the process and conserving his own sweets for later.

Taking the dingy staircase, he examined the upstairs rooms. Only one was in use. He sat on the Daws' marital bed, scooping chocolate drops into his mouth and looking round at the sparse furnishings. When his palm was empty he wiped it down his shorts and went through the contents of each drawer. This done, he looked under the bed to see what kind of chamberpot the Daws employed, then went on to the wardrobe. Aunt Ella's clothes were of a drabber nature than his mother's. Rachel, being her own seamstress as well as milliner, always kept up with the modern styles – though Bertie was grateful she had retained her more feminine hairstyle. His fingers travelled the short row of dresses, then on to Daw's best suit, searching the pockets to see if there was anything of interest. There wasn't.

He pushed the clothes aside to check on the bottom of the wardrobe: one pair of men's shoes, one pair of women's. Behind the shoes lay a bundle. Bertie's prying fingers grappled with it. It was heavier than he had anticipated. He unwound the linen . . . and found a solution to his problem.

'What does she want to see me for?' Charlie was taken aback, not to say overawed, when his half-brother relayed Mrs Daw's request, mainly because Bertie never spoke to him other than to insult. But today he was unusually civil.

Bertie stationed himself on the end of his sisters' bed, showing little interest in the game of tiddlywinks that was being played on the rug. 'She's got a surprise.'

'Bertie, get your big foot out o' me hair,' complained Lyn, seated directly below him. 'Charlie, it's your go.'

Charlie transferred his bemused face to the board and flipped the small disc. 'Are you sure she wants me?' Mrs Daw had never appeared to be very friendly towards him when he saw her in the yard.

'I've said so, haven't I?' urged Bertie. 'Hurry up or she may change her mind.'

Charlie asked the girls if they would object to him slipping next door.

'You know we're not supposed to speak to Aunt Ella now,' cautioned Rowena.

'And you'll be disqualified,' came Lyn's ominous addition.

Charlie craned his head to look up at his half-brother. 'You'd better ask Mrs Daw if it'll wait.'

Bertie responded by kicking Lyn in the back. 'Don't listen to her! Who wants to play stupid tiddlywinks anyway? It's for kids.' He lifted his knees out of Lyn's range as she lashed out.

'I'd just better finish . . .' began Charlie.

Bertie applied his toe to the board, scattering the discs over the room.

'Oh, Bertie, you pig! Now we don't know where everyone is.' Beany thumped the floor in temper, whilst Lyn knelt up to aim several more punches at the culprit before righting the board. 'We'll have to start all over again.'

'Then you won't need Charlie,' parried her brother and ducked as she hurled the board at him. Tugging at Charlie's collar, he made for the door. 'Come on!'

Charlie, encouraged by this sudden fraternization, allowed himself to be led. 'We're not letting you play any more!' yelled Lyn, then to Becky who was following the boys, 'Where d'you think *you're* off?'

When Becky replied that she was going with the boys, her brother pressed a hand to her chest. 'You can't come.' She pushed his hand away and asked why. 'Aunt Ella doesn't want you, she only wants Charlie and me.'

Her chin jutted out. 'I always go where Charlie goes.'

'Look, ' Bertie spread his hands, 'I can't help it if Aunt Ella doesn't want you to come.'

'Then I'm going to tell Mother you disobeyed her,' sulked Becky.

Charlie joined the argument. 'That's mean.'

She swung her shoulders pleadingly. 'Well I want to come with you, Charlie.'

'I don't think you'd better.' Becky was all right to have around when there was no one else, but now that his brother wanted his company . . .

The hurt showed, but still she insisted, 'I want to come!'

'Look, do we need a sledgehammer before you take the hint?' shouted Bertie. 'He doesn't want you. Now stay there!' He took Charlie onto the landing, slamming the door on his sister as emphasis.

Becky waited a few moments, then followed.

Bertie's bonhomie was maintained as they took to the stairs, replying to Charlie's query as to what the surprise was with, 'Ah, wait and see! But it's a good one.'

Charlie could not help an embarrassed laugh. 'Bertie . . . I thought you didn't like me.'

'Course I do!' came the glib response. But Bertie did not meet his eye.

They reached the front door. Charlie decided to test the new relationship by extending a hand. 'We're friends, then?'

Bertie's lips parted. He stared indecisively at the hand, his own on the doorknob. Then, with the briefest possible contact of that hated flesh, said cheerfully, 'Friends!' and swung the door open.

Charlie felt a tidal rush of gladness. Beaming widely, he followed Bertie's example and cocked his leg over the low wall between the houses. Had the journey been longer he would have draped a brotherly arm over Bertie's shoulders – he had always wanted someone to whom he could do this. Often he had gazed from his prison window and watched other boys link fraternal bodies with their pals and had yearned to find some other male with whom to share his affection. The girls were all right, but boys could say things to each other that one could not mention to females. Anticipating this pleasure he moved up to the door behind his brother.

Two women, on their way to the shop, happened to hear the boys' voices and looked over their shoulders. One gave a swift nudge to her friend. 'Eh look, he's there!' Both paused now to stare at the dark-skinned boy who was about to enter the Daws' house.

'After you!' Bertie held the door open and Charlie stepped in.

When he had disappeared the women hurried on. 'Mrs Phillips said he'd gone back to Africa at the end of August,' said one. 'Eh, watch her face when I tell her something she doesn't know!' They both chuckled and made for the shop.

Bertie escorted the other towards the back room, neither boy wiping his feet. The imprisoned dog yapped and snuffled at the door of the front parlour as they moved along the passage. Charlie tapped on the wood before entering, then looked around. 'She's not here.'

'She said for us to come straight in and wait,' explained Bertie, pointing to a chair. 'Sit down, she won't be long.'

Charlie lifted a pair of Ella's stockings from the seat and put them over the back of the chair before sitting. 'Where is she?' He folded his hands on his lap. Bertie told him she was upstairs. 'I can't hear her.' Nothing had altered in his brother's approach, yet Charlie suddenly experienced a flicker of suspicion. 'And I thought she usually went to work until the evening?'

'She's ill,' announced Bertie. 'She's having a lie down. Let's go up and tell her we're here.'

'We can't do that! She might be undressed. Let's shout to her.' Charlie went to the foot of the stairs and called Ella's name. The only reply was renewed barking from the dog.

'You go back in there,' ordered Bertie. 'I'll go up and see what she's doing. She won't mind, she asked us to come, didn't she?'

Whilst Bertie did this, Charlie stepped back into the kitchen where he squeezed his knuckles uneasily and sat on the very edge of the chair as if for a quick getaway. Becky waited too, peering through the back window to see what Aunt Ella's surprise could be. She ducked below the sill as Bertie returned. What he held jerked an amazed Charlie from his seat. 'Where did you get that?'

257

Bertie toted the Mauser with pride. 'Terrific, isn't it? Aunt Ella's just told me we could play with it.' Charlie was sceptical that an adult would allow free access to such a dangerous weapon and said so. Bertie gave a mocking laugh. 'It's not dangerous, you fool! Go up and ask her if you don't believe me.' Seeing that Charlie was going to take him literally he stepped into his path. 'No, better not. She might have gone back to sleep. Here, come and have a closer look.'

On the other side of the window Becky watched spellbound as the two boys took turns to handle the weapon – then suddenly a knot of ill-omen formed in her breast. The rifle was being pointed. Even at her age she knew from her questions to Mr Daw while he was cleaning his gun that one must never point a firearm at anyone.

'Don't worry, it's not loaded,' she heard Bertie's faint words.

There was only time for her to shout, 'Don't!' as the Mauser bucked upwards, emitting a tongue of flame and the boy crumpled on Aunt Ella's carpet.

Frantic, Becky hauled and rattled on the doorknob but it was locked. She scampered out of the back gate and all the way round to the front of the house where she gained entry and ran to the kitchen. Here she fell beside the body and cried out in horror at the blood on his clothes – then turned accusing brown eyes on the perpetrator. 'Oh, Charlie, you've killed our brother!'

CHAPTER EIGHTEEN

'Now don't churn yourself up, Mrs Hazelwood!' The doctor tried to calm Rachel who, fearing the worst, had stayed behind in the kitchen while her son was being examined. 'It's merely a flesh wound. Your boy is in no danger.'

Rachel almost collapsed with relief. She had not been in the shop five minutes when Biddy had come bullocking in and announced that Master Bertie had been 'kilt by the black fella', uncorking a fountain of hysteria from Rachel who had to be given smelling salts by a customer before being able to proceed. When she had arrived home and seen all the blood . . . oh dear God! Luckily Biddy, acting out of character, had had the presence of mind to fetch the doctor and have two neighbours carry Robert to his bed.

'Can I see him?' Rachel begged the doctor now.

'Surely.' The man's face was kind. 'But just let me take a look at you first, you must be shocked.' He proceeded to do so, talking as he did. 'Where is the other boy who was involved?' Rachel didn't care, but looked at Biddy for answer. The maid said she wasn't sure, but told the doctor he hadn't been hurt. 'Well, if he shows signs of delayed shock then send someone for me.' Rachel was needled that everyone seemed to be so concerned about Charlie, but she nodded at the doctor. 'I don't know what your neighbour was thinking about, leaving a loaded weapon lying about the house. I hope she has a satisfactory answer for the police.'

The police! Rachel's blood pressure soared. 'Is there really any need to bring them into it, Doctor?'

'Why yes, a firearm wound . . .'

'But it isn't as if it was a malicious wounding, just a

schoolboys' prank gone wrong.' If this should get into the papers and bring Mrs Ingram back Rachel knew that she would lose her mind altogether.

'I'm surprised you're so benevolent, Mrs Hazelwood.' The doctor closed the jaws of his bag. 'Your son was lucky not to have been killed. I do think your neighbour should be given a lecture at the very least.'

'She's at work,' provided Rachel swiftly. 'But you can be sure I'll have some words for her when she comes in.' She escorted him to the door, making light of the episode. 'I hardly think it's a matter for the police though. They have enough to do with this war.' The doctor asked if she knew whether the gun was licensed and Rachel told him that Mr Daw did not need a licence, being a member of His Majesty's forces.

'He won't be much good on the front without his gun,' said the doctor.

Rachel grew more flustered. 'Well, it isn't the one he uses for his soldiering – oh look, Doctor, I don't want to get anyone into trouble especially when they're serving their country. Can't we just let it rest?'

The doctor took his hat from her. His expression was uncertain. 'Well . . . the police are very busy that's for sure, and far be it from me to impugn those who're fighting for us – but I must be sure that the gun will either be locked up securely or disposed of altogether, or I shall be in serious trouble myself.' After being assured by Rachel that she would report the matter herself should Mrs Daw not comply he departed, saying he would be calling again to see Bertie.

Once he had gone Rachel spun on the maid. 'I hope you realize that I hold you responsible for this!'

Biddy's jaw dropped. 'Me?' She had expected commendation for her speedy action.

'Yes you! The children were left in your charge. How could you be so incompetent as to allow it to happen?'

Pouting lips endorsed the maid's objection. 'Sure, I didn't know he was going to do an eejit thing like that.'

'You're supposed to keep an eye on them!'

'I only have the two eyes ma'am, an' I use them for the babies. Sure, I would've thought Master Bertie could've been trusted to take care o' himself.'

'Master *Robert* could if he didn't have to keep company with savages! Really, Biddy, you know how difficult it is for me to look after the shop, the millinery, the household . . .' Rachel pressed a hand to her brow.

''Tis not my fault the master's run off an' left yese.'

The despairing pose was swapped for one of outrage. 'How dare you! Mr Hazelwood has not run away, he has gone to do his duty. If I hear you saying such things again I shall sack you without reference and then see what fool would employ you. Now get about your business!'

'Yes'm,' was the dull reply.

'And what of the culprit?'

'Nobody's seen him since the accident, ma'am.'

'There's no wonder no one's seen him, it was no accident! My God, he could be running all over the district showing himself to everyone.'

'Maybe he's run back to Africa, ma'am.'

'I've ceased believing in miracles,' retorted her mistress as she dashed away to tend her son. 'He'll come crawling back to give us more pain.'

'Eh, what're you doing in there, my little lad?' Ella, home from the factory, responded to the dog's frantic yelping by opening the door of the front parlour and lifting him up to pet him. 'Aw! Was it that naughty Bertie who shut you in? I'll cut his tail off. He's left my door unlocked as well, the varmint.' She fondled his smelly muzzle. 'Come on, let's go have a cup of . . . oh, who's that come to disrupt us?' The grumbling dog still in her arms, she went to answer the authoritative knock. 'Oh, it's you!' She showed surprise. 'I am hon . . .'

Rachel cut her off. 'This isn't a social visit! I have a very serious complaint.'

Ella stared at her, then riposted smartly, 'You'd best come in then.' She led the way through to the kitchen, then stopped dead. 'Eh, there's blood on my carpet . . .'

'Yes, my son's blood!' snapped Rachel. 'My son who almost died through your stupidity. As if you hadn't done enough to this family already!'

Ella put down her burden who waddled to the fire. 'What the hell are you gassing about?'

'I'm talking about the fact that you keep a loaded gun in the house! I realize of course that someone who has no children wouldn't . . .'

'Loaded gun? Aye, Jack has guns but loaded, no.'

'Then how do you account for that?' Rachel jabbed a finger at the stain on the carpet.

'Rachel,' Ella sighed, 'If I were qualified in cracking codes I'd be working for the Army. Will you just explain in terms we can all understand?' In stiff tone, Rachel told her of the shooting. 'But what were they doing here?' demanded Ella after first enquiring if Bertie was badly hurt. 'They had no right!'

'I believe you asked Robert to lock up for you after he'd taken your animal for a walk,' said Rachel. 'Against my instructions, I may add.'

'Aye I did . . .' Ella slipped her coat off and threw it on a chair. 'But that didn't include checking the lock on my wardrobe door. The gun was in there, so you see it wasn't just lying around, he had to be noseying.'

'Then I admit Robert was in the wrong,' conceded Rachel. 'But to have a loaded gun in the house at all . . .'

'I told you it wasn't loaded! Jack keeps the ammo in a different room from the gun, just in case anyone breaks in.'

'Robert told me he had no idea the gun was loaded!'

Ella sniffed and crossed her arms. 'Well he would, wouldn't he if he'd been up to summat he shouldn't.' Rachel asked what this meant. 'I mean, Rachel, that he must have been having a good old root about upstairs to be able to find the ammunition, let alone the gun. The only instruction I gave him was to drop the key back through the letter box.'

'Nevertheless, I still say . . .'

'You can say what you bloody-well like!' Ella had been on her feet all day and the chemical atmosphere of the factory had given her a headache. 'You're not shoving the blame onto me. That weapon was in perfectly safe condition until your son got his hands on it – and why did he need it loaded, might I ask? Doesn't he know that loaded guns are dangerous? Of course he does! Our Jack's warned him hundreds of times when he's shown an interest. That lad knows as much about guns as anybody. It makes me wonder where Charlie comes into this.' She glared expressively at her neighbour.

'Are you insinuating that Robert intended to . . .?' Rachel wavered, then scoffed, 'That's ridiculous!'

'Is it? It makes sense to me. He hates the sight of that lad.'

'Then how come he gave Charlie the gun?' hurled Rachel triumphantly.

Ella mused over this for a moment, then shrugged and began to fill the kettle with water, placing it on the fire.

For once in her life Rachel had been granted the last word . . . yet she drew no comfort from it, for her own sentence had raised another question. If Robert had known the gun was loaded, why *had* he given it to Charlie?

Though dreading the answer, this was the first thing she asked him on her return.

His prime response was to repeat the earlier lie. 'We were only playing soldiers. I didn't know it was loaded. Honestly, Mother,' he added, seeing she didn't accept this.

Rachel, sitting on the bed, put a hand to his brow and smoothed away a strand of hair. 'Robert, Mrs Daw says she's certain the ammunition was in an entirely different place to the gun. Whatever else Mr Daw might be, he is extremely diligent in the care of firearms. She says . . . she says you must have been searching the cupboards to find the bullets. Is it true?' After a long silence he gave a lachrymose nod. 'But why?' she entreated disbelievingly. 'I mean why did you tell me those silly stories before?'

'I don't know,' he picked at the sheet.

'You do know! You've made me look a fool in front of that woman and you're going to tell me! Robert,' she cupped his face. 'I know you're unhappy about that boy being here, but you wouldn't . . . I mean . . . Robert, you didn't give Charlie the gun hoping he'd shoot himself?'

Straightaway he shook his head.

'You're fibbing! I can tell. Now come on. I won't scold you any more but I must know what happened. The police may get to hear of it and I'll have to explain. I can tell them the gun went off by accident . . . but did it? Robert, I must know.'

Again he shook his head. After a short silence, during which his dark eyelashes rested on his cheeks, he said, 'I told him to pull the trigger.'

Her chocolate-drop eyes were blank at first, then the truth sparked a look of horror. 'You mean . . . you wanted him to shoot *you*?' He nodded. 'But *why*?'

The wound was hurting like mad, transmitting the pain to his eyes. 'No one wants me anymore since he came. Becky used to hang around me all the time, now she hangs around him 'cause he's older and he talks posh. The girls like him better than me.'

Rachel's face was still harrowed. 'Robert, of course they don't!'

'They do!' His sudden movement had jarred him. He covered the bandage with a hand, then went on fervently. 'You never have any time for me either, you're always too busy. I've got nobody . . . I wanted him to shoot me so's you'd all feel sorry for the way you've been treating me.'

'Just to get attention? For heaven's sake, Robert you could've been killed!'

'I don't care,' was his flat answer.

With a moan she hugged him to her breast and petted him. 'My poor dear boy! What has he done to you?' By he, Rachel did not just mean Charlie, but her husband.

Bertie seemed to know this. 'I hate Father,' he wept into her shoulder. 'I hope he gets killed.'

She seized his wet face, distorting his cheeks. 'Robert, he doesn't love Charlie, you know. You must believe that.' Her worried eyes darted over him, only now seeing his real torment. What he must have been suffering for the last five months!

'But Charlie loves him,' sniffed Bertie knowingly. 'I won't share him, Mother. I've always been the only boy. I won't share Father – I'd sooner he was dead.'

She gave another moan and clutched him more tightly. 'Everything's going to be all right. You *are* the only boy. He's nothing . . . nothing.'

'Mother?' came the plaintive whisper from her bosom.

'What love?' She cradled his head in her arms, resting her chin on the shiny brown hair.

'Will you let me have a pair of long trousers now?'

She leaned back to examine his face. 'Oh Robert, you're only twelve . . .' The pleading in his eyes claimed her. 'Oh, very well!' She pressed his head back to her shoulder, rocked and kissed him. 'If they mean so much to you, yes, we'll get some next week. And you shall have a party – you didn't have one for your birthday, did you? We can call it a getting-better party.'

'I suppose *he*'ll have to come?' mumbled Bertie.

'Oh Robert, there's nothing I'd like more than to send him away . . . but where to? We've been deserted on all fronts: your father to his soldiers, the priest to Belgium.'

'You could put him in an orphanage,' said Bertie hopefully.

She could . . . but then there would be people saying, 'That cruel bitch', forgetting what she had been forced to put up with, seeing only this callous act. Besides, Charlie wasn't supposed to be still here. Rachel didn't want to draw attention to him because that would bring the NSPCC back and if they saw Robert's wound they might take him too, saying she wasn't a fit mother. The mere thought of this caused her to hug him closer. 'I'm sorry, dear, he'll have to stay.' She patted his head. 'But don't worry, I'll speak to your sisters and make them aware of how upset they've made you with their behaviour. And *please*,' she lifted his head to look deep in his eyes, 'don't ever do anything like this again. Whatever anybody says or does, *I* love you.'

Downstairs, Charlie was restating his innocence for the third time. 'Becky, I swear, I *swear* I didn't mean to shoot him!' He still couldn't believe that what had happened was real, kept seeing it over and over in his brain but still could not give it credence. After the gun had gone off he had simply stood there looking down at Bertie's unconscious body. Until Becky's accusation had tugged him from his shock. Then he had fallen beside his half-brother, searching frantically for a heartbeat with his ear, while a tearful Becky had sped home to fetch Biddy.

There had been vast relief that Bertie wasn't dead, but still he felt it prudent not to be here when help arrived. He had run off and spent a long time pacing the streets before deciding that he must be a man and face the consequences. One of these consequences was that Becky refused to speak to him when he slunk into the kitchen where everyone seemed to be. The hero worship that had once been his had vanished. In her eyes shone enmity. 'Please believe me!' he told her yet again. 'Bertie told me the gun wasn't loaded.'

Yes he had, Becky frowned and thought to herself, she had heard him. But still she chose to ally herself with her wounded brother and the dumb animosity remained.

'He *told* me to pull the trigger!' Charlie's pink palms beseeched her and the others who had been just as silent and accusing. Then Rachel entered and his expression changed. He didn't know how to approach her, knowing that she would not regard 'sorry' as adequate.

But how strange – the expected attack did not come. He waited apprehensively while she gave Biddy orders to make a pot of tea, watched as she moved tight-lipped about the kitchen, not looking at him.

Don't speak, Rachel felt his eyes following her but issued the mental warning, *if you don't speak I can pretend you're not here. If I keep my hands occupied* . . . This she tried to do by carving a loaf, buttering the slices, rattling the teacups – *but if you say one word* . . .

Charlie looked at each of them, and each looked away.

'May I go see my brother?' Becky's voice cracked the silence.

'Robert's resting,' her mother informed her, putting saucers firmly on a tray. 'But you can go up later – *if* he wants to see you.' There was definite accusation in the comment.

266

Becky was quick to interpret and slumped over the table, cradling her woebegone face in her hands to watch Biddy pour the boiling water into the pot. I wonder what that would feel like if I were to put my hand under it, she thought. Would it hurt as much as being wounded by a gun? Poor Bertie, she felt awful now for the way she had neglected him in favour of Charlie.

Rachel was about to place the bread and butter on the tray, when there came a shrill scream. She spun round, mishandling the plate and littering the floor with bread.

'Jesus, Miss Becky, have you been rollin' in the catnip again? What did ye ever go an' do an eejit thing like that for?' Biddy, kettle still poised over the pot, stared aghast at the girl who clutched her wrist, the hand beyond slowly inflating like a red balloon.

'I just wondered what it would feel like,' she whimpered.

Charlie took a step forward to help. It took another scream from Becky as he tried to tend her arm to bring Rachel out of her stupor. She launched herself at him, grasped both shoulders, spun him round and hurled him away as hard as she could. He stumbled against a dining chair.

For three seconds everyone was silent again, watching his reaction; which was to take another step back, placing him outside the family circle, mouth agape with shock. Then everyone forgot about him, offering only a wall of backs as they attended to the scalded hand. Only a pain-faced Becky noticed his exit. 'Charlie's crying,' she informed them weedily as he slipped away.

Rachel ignored the information. 'Biddy, go pick that bread up and then run along to the doctor's and fetch him back!'

Biddy made a face of disgust as she peeled the bread from the carpet. 'Holy Mother, doesn't it always fall butterside down.'

'It's just like soddin' England,' complained Private Dobson as 5 Platoon, along with thousands of others, disembarked at Boulogne. 'Bloody fish an' chip shops . . .' He ran his

267

fingers through his curly black hair and replaced his cap. The place was awash with khaki.

'I'm sure that'll go down as the patriotic declaration of all time, Dobson – just like soddin' England.' Lance-Sergeant Hazelwood had overheard the grumble as he was issuing his platoon with orders. 'I can arrange for you to have a plate of snails before we leave for the front if you like.'

'We-ell!' The lad screwed his nose up and wrung his hands which were red from the cold. 'I thought it'd be more foreign, like.'

Russ took his elbow and, with his free hand, pointed. 'See them matelots there? Just go up to them and say Joan of Arc, they'll show you how bloody foreign it is. Right! Let's go get summat in our bellies then we can sort out this Hun before tea.'

The repartee among the men helped to keep his mind off his problems, but sometimes it could become testing. Russ, not feeling particularly chatty after the Channel crossing, was glad to reach his billet. Once here, he sought out the lavatory, the only place where one could be completely alone, could sit and ponder for fifteen minutes – or at least until some lout hammered on the door.

He was in for a let-down. The French equivalent was not the oasis of comfort, the reading-room, the place of dreams that he knew from home, but a hole in the ground with a support rail at either side. Russ studied the crude necessity, hand scratching head. It baffled him how anyone could execute a natural function here, let alone read a newspaper. A silly picture formed in his mind of himself performing gymnastic feats on the parallel bars trying to hit the target below. It made him laugh. He unbuttoned his trousers and got on with the job – what did he want to sit and think for anyway?

The next move was to Base camp at Étaples where a period of intensive training began. Intensive torture would have been a more fitting description to the recruits who, up until now, had been merely playing at war. On first arrival the newcomers remained blissfully unaware of what lay in store for them. After receiving certain items of equipment

268

they were allowed to wander around the stalls that had been set up by the locals who came here daily to sell chocolate, fruit and postcards.

The sight of one postcard, embroidered in silk with the words *Happy Birthday*, brought a quick mental calculation of the date, then a feeling of guilt to Sergeant Hazelwood. He had forgotten his son's birthday – Rachel had always been in charge of that sort of thing, he was hopeless at remembering dates. To send one now would only make the omission worse . . . besides, he couldn't recall the dates of his daughters' birthdays either. The thought was abandoned. He turned away from the stall – and was immediately snapped by Private Strawbridge, a keen amateur photographer from his own platoon. Complaints were bypassed. Strawbridge roped in as many as were willing to pose by the stalls alongside the peasants.

Day Two removed any false impression that this was like the places they had stayed at in England. A sweet voice billowed the sides of each tent at five-thirty a.m. 'Right! Let's be havin' you, oh cream of British manhood. Move it! Soldier, what's that bloody thing stickin' up in the middle o' your blanket? Looks like you're sleeping in your own private tent. Get it down! Come on, come on! Rise and shine. Go shave your palms before breakfast. Can't say what that'll be but then most of you won't be able to see what you're eatin' anyway!' At eight, the men were paraded before an officer whom they had not encountered before and whose unfortunate speech impediment caused hilarity especially from Dobson who started to mimic. To his great misfortune he was spotted.

'Sar'nt! We'll have that man out!'

'Get your bloody arse out here now, Dobson,' growled Russ and, marching the private up to the officer, barked Dobson's name, rank and number. Dobson, being a cheeky lad was well accustomed to being hauled in front of the teacher and was not unduly perturbed by this treatment. Taking the officer's emaciated build as a sign of weakness, he stood casually.

The officer's nostrils flared. 'Sar'nt, are you sure you

have this man's name right?' Icy eyes bore into Dobson's. 'Private, might you be related to a fellow called Modo?'

Dobson cocked his head. 'Sorry, sir?'

'As in Quasi – get those bladdy shoulders straight!' Dobson gave a taut jerk. The officer spoke evenly now, hands behind him clasping his baton. 'Dobson, I should like you to see something. Come with me – you too, Sar'nt.'

'Dobson, le-aft turn!' yelped Russ and marched alongside the private. 'Left, right, left, right! I'll have your balls for this, you little bleeder,' he muttered from the side of his mouth.

The officer came to a halt. Russ took five more paces then stamped to attention, shouting commands at Dobson.

'Now tell me, Private,' mouthed the officer. 'What do you see on that tree?'

Dobson frowned and peered at the splintered bark. 'Looks like blood, sir.'

'It doesn't just look like it, Private, it is blood. The man to whom the blood belonged gave this tree a transfusion at dawn this morning. Do you know to what I am referring?'

Dobson faltered, his cockiness dispersed. 'No, sir.'

'He was shot for desertion. Now, though we haven't yet started shooting men for making fun of their officers we could just as easily start a trend. Would you care to be a blood donor, Private?'

Dobson was aghast. 'No, sir!'

'Then you'd better behave yourself, hadn't you? Sar'nt! I trust I can rely on you to keep order among this riff-raff when we get to the front? There's brave men dying out there and I don't intend to replace them with giggling schoolboys. Do I make myself clear?'

'Sir!' Though deeply insulted at the reference to his platoon, Russ performed a rigid salute and marched the private back to the ranks, murmuring, 'Make good use of your bayonet this morning, Dobson. You'll need plenty o' practice for all them spuds you're gonna bash tonight. I'm not having anybody sling mud at this platoon.'

Dobson chanced a question. 'Sarg, did they really shoot one of their own men?'

'Shut your bloody mouth and march!' And Dobson marched on, unaware of just how much the sight of that blood had shaken his sergeant.

There followed a long footslog to a beautiful stretch of coastline where, among the sand dunes, a bayonet fight was arranged. It was all great sport at first, sticking bayonets in sacks and pretending it was Fritz, but after two solid hours of non-stop practice the cutting and thrusting became a mite limp. Slight relief came with a period of rapid loading and firing, but then came a further ninety minutes with the bayonet, and all the time the instructors were on their backs, not allowing a moment's rest, barking, taunting, thumping . . . when it came to marching back to base, D Company could scarcely put one foot in front of the other.

This sort of thing went on for days. They were drilled and driven, ridiculed, derided and marched until their feet bled, then told it was their own faults for not treating their feet correctly. Even Russ in his previous Army life had never met men so callous as those in charge of the camp. Kill, kill, kill, that was what was drummed into them day after day. 'The sooner we get the job done, the sooner we're home.' The brutal routine grew not only monotonous, but very depressing.

'When're we gonna start killing some real Germans, Sarg?' panted Dobson, after disembowelling his millionth sack. 'I'm getting bloody fed up o' this. I mean, when they asked for volunteers I didn't expect I'd be providing work for the sack factories.' He wiped his streaming brow with a sleeve, needing desperately to rest his legs but having learnt better than to give way to the impulse.

'Don't be so bloody eager, Dobson,' grunted Russ. 'These sacks haven't got bayonets, the Germans have.' He urged the boy on, nostrils flaring at the smell of his own sweat that rose in warm puffs from his tunic with each plod. How much longer? His mind echoed Dobson's sentiment. The tedium caused his thoughts to return to his family at home. He wondered how Rachel was coping, what her feelings would be if he really were to get shot. The grimly amusing idea came to him that he might never even reach

271

the front; he could quite easily die here without ever seeing the Hun.

By November, D Company had become used to the brutal regime and had resigned themselves to being here for months. This morning they were greatly surprised when told that there would be no training today. But none of them was likely to question their superiors' newfound compassion. The day was spent footballing, kipping and sifting through Strawbridge's photographs which drew much jocular interest. 'Eh look, Sarg!' shouted Dobson, holding a snapshot aloft as Russ entered the tent. 'Here's one o' you looking really intelligent.'

Russ snatched the photograph and squinted at it, seeking himself in the group. 'Bloody hell, Strawbridge! You've made me look a right prick.' The shutter had clicked just as Russ had decided to blink.

'The camera never lies, Sarg,' defended the private, then objected strongly as Russ applied his fingers to the snap, intending destruction.

'Aw, Sarg, don't rip it up! I've paid good money for that.'

Hazelwood relented, but tucked the offending photo in his breast pocket. 'You can have it back when this war's over, Strawbridge. Until then it's staying out of sight. I'm not having my noble features insulted by this shower. I hope you've not got any more with me on?'

Dobson, who was shuffling through the photographs, shook his head. 'Yours was the last on the film, Sarg. It knackered the camera.'

The sergeant rose to his full height and crooked an intimidating finger. 'Come here!'

Dobson's face fell at the tone. Laying down the snapshots, he scrambled to his feet and came to stand at attention before the sergeant. Russ leaned forward and whipped the hat from the soldier's head. From it he unpinned the regimental badge, then plonked the hat back on skew-whiff. 'And now, Private,' came the growl, 'I'll have your name tag.'

During this display the private's face had adopted a look of horror. 'Sarg, I didn't mean . . .'

272

'Shut up! I've had about enough of your insubordination, Dobson. I'll have your name tag, now!'

With sickened features, Dobson unhooked the tag from his neck, while the others in the tent looked on with grave interest.

'You are incorrigible and worthless, Dobson! What are you?'

'Incorrigible and worthless, Sergeant.'

'Correct! Which is why you're finished here, for good!'

Dobson could scarcely believe that he could be discharged for such a paltry offence – people were always insulting the sergeant. The injustice helped to revive some of his usual grit. 'What for? I've a right to know what I'm being finished for. I'm not off! I've done all this bleeding training. I want to stay here!'

'Oh, he wants to stay here, does he? Lapping it up at Eat-Apples are we, Dobson? Likes being tortured, does he?'

'Yes, Sarg!' Dobson became more persuasive. 'I'm sorry I gave you that cheek. Go on, let me stay . . . I'll clean your boots for a month!'

The sergeant became unexpectedly amiable again. 'Very well, Dobson. I'm not a man without mercy. If you're so attached to this place you can stay as long as you like.'

Disbelief. 'I can?'

'You can . . . mindst, you might be a bit lonely. Here you are then, you might as well have these back if you're not coming with us.' Russ shoved the confiscated articles at Dobson, knocking the breath from him. Then turned away. 'Right, I want the rest of you to trot along like good little soldiers to the quartermaster sergeant who, in exchange for cap badges, shoulder titles and name tags, will give you each a necklace of little pointed things called bullets. At the double . . .'

'Sarg!' Dobson had recovered his breath and his lifted expression showed he was now aware that he had been the target of the sergeant's perverse humour again.

'That's right, Dobson!' Russ spoke cheerfully and took

hold of him by the ear, to a buzz of anticipation from his comrades. 'You've got your wish at last. We're off to the front.'

CHAPTER NINETEEN

Bertie had rather enjoyed his convalescence. For the first few days after the shooting he was kept in bed and his mother had stayed home to take care of him. All he had to do was shout and she would come scurrying to fetch whatever it was he asked for. The girls had been most attentive as well – especially Becky. Once again it was her brother and not Charlie who was the hero to be worshipped. Bertie made the most of this by picking at the scab on his wound to have blood seeping through the dressing when his sisters came in from school, and revelled in the tears that would spring to Beany's eyes when he groaned his agony. The only bad thing about it was having to be in the house all day with his enemy. Of course Charlie wasn't allowed into his bedroom, but there came the day when Bertie was forced to exchange his sickroom for the kitchen sofa. Once he was on his feet his mother returned to her duties at the shop, relying on Biddy to tend him – though before she went out, Rachel would make a great fuss of seeing her son made comfortable. He would be tucked up on the sofa by the fire with a book on his lap and something nice to eat and Charlie would be told to, 'Stay right away from him!'

Charlie had no trouble adhering to this rule. He had given up trying to be friendly. Whether Bertie had wanted to shoot him or had simply wanted to get him into trouble didn't really matter – either way it just showed how much Bertie detested him. You couldn't like someone who hated you so much. Bertie had set everyone against him – even Becky who had always been his friend. Only Rowena was speaking to him, but even this had to be done in private for fear of inviting her siblings' wrath. Little Rhona with whom he had played while the others were at school, now spent her days with Bertie. And though the latter had always scorned the company of females he certainly played on this when his half-brother was around.

Then there had been the party. Charlie had at first been delighted when Mrs Hazelwood had told him one Sunday that he was to be allowed out to evening Mass with Biddy. The maid had been somewhat put out – Biddy always went to morning Mass, her free afternoon was spent visiting her parents; taking Charlie to church would involve trailing right back here then back into town.

'No it won't,' Mrs Hazelwood had said. 'You can take him with you when you go to see your parents.'

'Take him home with me?' cried Biddy. 'Sure I cannot. The mammy'll flay me if I fetch a darkie home!'

'What nonsense!' snapped Rachel. 'The tone of your neighbourhood can hardly be lowered any further than it is. Besides which, it's high time for him to go out or there'll be more vicious rumours circulating about my cruelty.' Rachel didn't see any point in keeping Charlie confined to the house: all her neighbours knew he was still here; they'd probably seen him when he went galloping round the streets after shooting Robert. She had decided that the best way to tackle this was to let the boy be seen, lull everyone into thinking that all was in order and no one could report that she was mistreating him, could they? If Mrs Ingram got to hear of his presence, well, Rachel would meet that when it arose.

And so off Charlie had set with Biddy, drawing many curious glances. People actually called their spouses to the window in order to watch him as he passed. A self-conscious Charlie faced the same scrutiny on arrival at the Kelly home but once the initial moments of suspicion had passed – and the couple had ascertained that Biddy had merely brought the darkie here as a duty – then Charlie enjoyed the chat with Mr and Mrs Kelly. They hadn't been half as despotic as Biddy had made them out to be. Even more enjoyable was the visit to church, then the trek back through town, during which Biddy pointed out all the things in the shop windows that she would buy if only she had the money. Simple pleasures, but after being cooped up in the house for weeks Charlie felt very warm towards Mrs Hazelwood . . . until he got home and discovered that it had all been a ruse to keep him out of the way while Bertie had some schoolfriends to tea.

For Bertie, the most important development was that his legs were now clothed like a man's. His mother had presented him with two pairs of longs. Rachel was relieved to have heard nothing from the police about the shooting and had paid a final visit to Ella Daw, insisting that the gun be kept under stricter guard or she would inform the authorities – though of course this had been a bluff. After this, the two women did not speak again and life just went on as it had done, with no sign that the war would be finished this month either.

'What's that mean?' Dobson asked his friend Wheatley, pointing at a sign on the railway truck into which they were now being loaded: *Hommes 40*, *Chevaux 8*.

Wheatley, who had learnt rudimentary French at school, translated, 'It means men forty, horses eight.' He held up his hands, seeking a hoist and was summarily hauled into the wagon which was fast filling up.

'They'll never fit forty of us in there!' objected Dobson.

'Oh, they will, lad.' Russ came alongside to supervise the entrainment. 'I hope you're fond of horses, by the way?'

'They're not putting . . .' Dobson frowned, then seeing that the sergeant was joking, made a face and clambered into the truck, grunting as Russ threw his kitbag at him.

'Forgetting your handbag, Dobson!'

'I've always wanted to travel first class,' grumbled the private, backing up to allow the last few men on board.

'Better than marching,' commented Wheatley, whose feet were still ulcerated from previous neglect.

'Bloody hell, I think you were right about them horses, Sarg!' Dobson nipped his nostrils. 'What a pong.'

'Oh hang on, I'll just hop off an' buy a pint o' that French scent to alleviate your delicate senses,' said Russ and, after the last man had been crammed on board, perched his buttocks on the edge of the wagon. He had the best of it here; for those inside it was a terrible crush, there being no room to sit down. He looked down as a small boy tugged at his trouser leg. 'Tommee! Jig-a-jig, five francs!'

Russ did not need an interpreter for this remark, 'Bugger off, you little pimp!' and shook him off.

'*J'ai une belle soeur! Très, très belle!* Sister, ver' good jig-a-jig!'

Russ beckoned to the child as if to whisper, then fetched him a stinging blow round the ear. 'That's what happens to little swines what sell their sisters!' As the boy scampered away to solicit another, Russ envisioned his own little girls at home and was about to slip back into his retrospection, when the train gave a sudden lurch and began to groan its way from the sidings. Its wheels growled complaint at the amount of bodies it was forced to pull. Squashed inside the cattle truck, the men waited, cramped and uncomfortable, for it to pick up speed, but it never did.

'Christ, I could walk quicker than this,' said Dobson, and to prove his point squeezed between the outer occupants and jumped from the truck to mince alongside. The others laughed – he had already established himself as the jester – as he fell behind and was forced to run and jump back on. 'Well nearly!' He grinned as his sergeant grasped a handful of tunic to drag him back on board. A lengthy grind followed. When the train finally stopped, Lance-Corporal Haines asked if they were there yet.

To which Russ replied, 'How would I know, since I've no idea where we're supposed to be going.'

'Well, permission to get off an' have a pee, Sarg?'

With permission granted there was a mass exit and putteed legs ran to line up against a hedge. Strawbridge captured this on the film he had loaded before leaving Étaples. The train gave an unexpected jolt and was in motion again. The men, seeing it, began a hurried buttoning and started to run back.

'Sure you haven't left anything behind in your hurry, Dobson?' asked Russ hauling one after the other on board.

'They don't give you much chance do they?' objected an

embarrassed Wheatley on facing raucous laughter at his unbuttoned state.

'The war can't stop for a pee, lad,' chided Russ. 'Oh! and by the way that reminds me. When we get where we're going you'll all be given a piece of string, short arm for the use of. Now I shall expect each man, you as well, Wheatley, to take full responsibility for his piece of string, making sure that it's the same length as when it started. I won't tolerate any frayed ends in my platoon. Of course, some of you will require a longer piece than the next man. Are you with me so far, Wheatley?'

'Yes, Sarg.' Wheatley's angelic face looked concerned. 'Er, what exactly is it for?'

'I thought you said you were with me? I've just told you what it's for! You don't want me to draw a diagram, d'you? You should be conversant with standard Army issue by now.' Russ tutted his exasperation. 'To tie round your short arm, Wheatley – well you don't think the General will allow his men to disappear for a pee halfway through the battle, do you? Be reasonable, lad.'

Wheatley and a number of other young recruits were nonplussed. Dobson laughed mockingly. 'He's having you on!'

'Am I, Private?' asked Russ, mildly.

Dobson, with a sideways look at the others, donned a worried expression. Russ winked at a corporal and lit a cigarette, then leaned his back against the timber and waited to meet the war.

The train stopped for longer next time, enabling the men to light fires and cook a billy-can meal. Before eating, Wheatley took the opportunity to revise on the entry for 'feet' in his small book. Stripping off boots and socks, he soaked his sore feet in the river by which they had stopped, and worked up a lather with his soap.

'Oy, Wheatley!' Private Schofield berated him. 'I don't want a head on me tea, thank you very much. Do you mind getting downstream?'

Wheatley apologized but said he must get this done before the train moved again, he may not get another chance. He was glad he had made this decision, for no sooner had he rubbed the insides of his socks with yellow soap and redonned them, than orders came to retrain. 'I haven't had a cup o' tea yet!' He hurried to relace his boots.

Russ shouted to a particularly overweight man, 'Jamieson, whip out your titty and breastfeed this bairn.'

And then it was back on the train for another interminable stretch of railway. The banter wore down to the occasional acid comment. Some dozed as best they could. Some pencilled notes for their wives. Others, like Russ, sat silently with their thoughts. When the unbelievable happened and the journey ended, the men spilled out of the truck, rubbing aching limbs and surveying the location.

'Where's all the bloody fighting, then?' asked Dobson.

'They've probably heard you're coming to stick it up 'em, Dobson.' Russ narrowed his eyes. There was no sign of the war. He waited for orders.

Orders were to march, which they did for the rest of the day in atrocious conditions. For miles in front and behind him all Russ could see was khaki heads bobbing. The cobbled roads were not conducive to precision marching. Boots slithered and skidded on the patches of ice, calves became knotted, thighs pulled. On top of this, each man carried a pack weighing the equivalent of a well-grown child.

But there was support from the locals who came out of their cottages to cheer and shout, '*Vive les Tommees!*' and press gifts into their hands and make them feel like victors without ever having fired a round – though some of them balked at the kisses from the male population. A girl shouted something at Dobson, who demanded a translation from Wheatley.

'She wants a souvenir.'

'Be generous, Dobs,' japed Corporal Popely. 'Give her your virginity.'

Five hours later they were still marching, desperately tired. It was even more miserable now that the sun had gone down. 'D'you think they've forgotten to tell us to stop, Sarg?' panted Dobson, dragging his feet. 'When're we gonna get to this bloody war?'

'We've reached it, lad,' grunted Russ from parched mouth. Despite his fatigue, Dobson showed alertness and asked where. 'Listen.' The private made proper use of his ears. There was a faint rumbling.

'Guns?'

Russ nodded, not betraying the shudder of apprehension he felt. Dobson formed a grin and looked triumphantly at his friend. 'Well here we are, Wheaters old mate!'

But on receiving orders to stop, he could not help a twinge of disappointment. He had imagined there would be some sort of demarcation line to highlight the fighting, but this didn't look any different from the places they had been before.

'Oh, you were expecting a signpost saying "The Front" were you, Dobson?' scoffed Russ as the weary men of D Company entered the barn that was to be their billet.

'I expected there'd be a bit more action than this,' groused Dobson, unhooking his pack and slinging it down. He made a sudden grab at Wheatley's arm. 'Help! Hold me down, I'm floatin'.'

Wheatley and some of the others also commented on the giddy feeling that the removal of their heavy packs had brought about. 'I feel as if I'm a fairy dancing six inches above the ground.'

Russ gave a tired groan. 'Nay don't say that, Wheatley, these lads'll never dare sleep.'

Young Dobson was still hanging onto his friend, when he gave a cackle and pointed from the open front of the barn. 'Eh, I'm bloody seein' things! It's a number nine bus!'

'Bugger me,' muttered Wheatley in annoyance.

'If that's an invitation, Wheatley, I'd just as soon decline,' said Russ. 'It's an imprisonable offence . . . come to think of it, having to live with you lot night and day is like serving a life sentence.' He peered out into the starry night. Sure enough, a green bus was rocking its way up the road they had just slogged along – and behind it trundled another. 'Bloody typical! You wait hours for a bus then they all come at once.'

*

Dobson didn't know whether to be pleased or disappointed. Morning had just brought the news that this wasn't the front after all. The boring chores continued, the whole day after their arrival being spent digging trenches – which was maddening as there seemed to be no purpose in this, and even more maddening to be within hearing distance of the guns yet be unable to be part of any real soldiering.

After a couple of days they were marched fifteen kilometres to another town. During the march, snow began to fall, making the *pavé* even more treacherous. But their spirits remained high despite the cold: at last, this was 'it' . . . It wasn't. They found themselves in more billets; this time, a girls' school. At first this was viewed as consolation, until they found out that all the mesdemoiselles had been evacuated.

The morning after their arrival, as there didn't seem anything better to do, Russ decided to have a stroll round the town. It gave him an excuse to be on his own, gave him time to think what he was going to do when this was over. It was a nice place, with quaint streets and houses. It could have been some English town, not a war zone. However, his solitude was not allowed to continue for long. As he reached the gates of the girls' school he met up with some of the men from his platoon – Dobson, Wheatley, Jamieson and Strawbridge with his camera – and paused to wait for them, coming out of his meditation as they hailed him. 'Oy-oy! What you lot o' bloody scavengers been up to?'

'Just seeing the sights, Sarg,' replied Dobson cheerfully. 'Eh, it's a dead 'oile is this. I hope we won't be here for long.'

The sound of thumping boots interrupted the dialogue. Instead of entering their billets, they turned their eyes along the road and were met by a strange sight. A band of men trudged wearily towards them. Men? Brigands would have been more apt. None of them had seen a razor for weeks – months, by the look of some. Many sported full beards. Their clothes were covered in mud. Only a handful wore caps. All had greasy hair which curled over the collars of their greatcoats. Their eyes were dulled by overwhelming fatigue . . . but the most shocking thing about them was that under the mud they wore khaki.

'Blimey, they're ours!' breathed Dobson as the men drew nearer. 'Scruffy looking sods.' Rags flapped where puttees should have been. Filthy scarves muffled filthy faces.

As the band of misfits reached the watchers, one of them shouted to his companions, 'We must be in Savile Row – take a gander at these toffs.'

The group, headed by a sergeant-major, came to a halt and viewed the others with derision. 'Must think they're going on parade.'

One noticed the plaque that said this was a girls' school, by which Dobson was poised. 'Christ! they've run out of soldiers, they're sendin' bleedin' schoolgirls now.' To reinforce this opinion, he winked and puckered his lips at Dobson. 'Eh, Mam'selle, voulez-vous givez mois une little kiss?'

Dobson bared his teeth and took a step forward, but Russ gave a low growl of command. The sergeant-major, a Cockney, continued the barracking. 'Are you happy, lads? That's the main thing.'

'Quite happy, Sar'nt-Major,' replied Hazelwood lightly.

'Well we can fucking soon alter that,' quipped the other to much laughter.

The brigands drew round and pressed them for cigarettes which, being outnumbered, Russ and his men had to surrender. With this friendly act the ruffians gave up their sport to ask the others how long they had been in France and how things were at home. It turned out that these were survivors of the original BEF – the Old Contemptibles – and what tales they had to tell when they and the newcomers met up later over several bottles of wine. Russ watched the faces of his young companions as the tales of butchery and disembowelment were bandied back and forth. He should have known better than to let these old sweats frighten him, they were probably making half of it up, but still . . .

Just before the end of November the order came for the battalion to march again. They had been fooled into thinking that this was 'it' so many times, that today there was little air of excitement – except for when Second-Lieutenant Reece in command of 5 Platoon slipped on a patch of ice and someone cried that he'd been shot. It turned out that he had broken his arm, leaving Russ in temporary command of the platoon.

March, march, march. Five, ten, fifteen kilometres, slithering and sliding up the icy paved road. They stopped only once to pick up sandbags, corrugated iron sheets, rolls of barbed wire and digging implements from a Royal Engineers' dump. It was almost dark before they reached their terminus . . . almost, but not quite dark enough to deprive Dobson of his first glimpse of a dead body.

'Eh, look at that!' The bloated carcass of a horse lay at the roadside, still attached to the cart it had pulled in life. It looked like a lead toy lying on its side, all four legs sticking straight out. Wheatley, his freckles conspicuous on a face paler than normal, tapped his friend wordlessly and gestured. Near the upturned cart was another corpse, who viewed their march past with sightless eyes, teeth bared in a rictal grin.

The soldiers' mood changed. Russ sensed this and observed gruffly, 'Don't worry, lads, you'll see plenty more, I don't doubt.'

The nearer they got to their objective the truer these last words became. Scores of dead peasants cluttered the verges, the ruins of their cottages still smoked, flames flickering round scorched timbers. Marching became more hampered by the mounds of rubbish and shellholes that pocked the road. Suddenly, a particularly tall soldier issued a squawk of complaint as something cut into his neck.

The Captain looked back to gauge the cause of the din. 'What's going on back there, Sar'nt-Major?'

Sergeant-Major Copley replied, 'Sorry, sir. One o' the men got tangled in the field telegraph.'

'Well, make sure they take more care,' came the answer. 'It's bad enough these Hun shells destroying our communications without our own men doing it.'

'Sir!' The sergeant-major turned to the culprit. 'Bodley,

keep your head down, you big long streak o' piss. If you want to hang yourself I'll lend you me braces.'

After this the men became more alert and every so often a wave would ripple through the column as men ducked to avoid another wire. Puffs of debris had begun to litter the evening air, air heavy with the smell of graphite. The crump of the big guns grew louder. Wheatley, his former jauntiness supplanted by caution, asked, 'Where are we?' as they were ordered to halt and await instructions.

'The Devil's larder,' said a voice greatly familiar to Russ, who spun around to encounter his old neighbour.

CHAPTER TWENTY

'Sergeant.' Daw delivered the taciturn greeting, shellbursts causing an intermittent gleam in his eye.

Hazelwood's gaze had flickered over the other's Sam Browne, before he replied, 'Sir.'

Daw asked where he would find the Company Commander.

'Captain Capstaff's up there, sir.' Russ pointed up the dark road. Daw left the temporarily dumb sergeant to seek out the captain, after which, the order came to load magazines. There followed the sound of many rifle bolts snapping into place. Russ peered along the road to watch the murky passage of Daw and the captain, wondering how the former had achieved his new rank and imagining how Rachel would sniff disparagingly and offer some acid remark. It was bloody marvellous! All the tens of thousands of men and he had to meet up with the one he didn't want to see.

With his small group joined with the newcomers, Daw set off at the front of the column and led it through a ruined collection of farm buildings, the captain at his side. The night darkened further. Russ plodded on with the others, hoping that Daw was not to be a constant presence. However, he was spared the ordeal of having to speak to the man again, at least for tonight. After walking for a couple of hundred yards the column took a detour through a cabbage field. The ground between the rows of vegetables was extremely muddy and there were continual grunts as men skidded and fell over.

'What's that funny noise?' Dobson asked. It sounded as if there was a beehive nearby.

'Stray bullets,' replied Russ. The familiar whine had

reached his ears long before Dobson's, immediately conjuring images of the veldt . . . and that of course produced
thoughts of Charlie.

'Crikey!' Wheatley ducked.

Russ came out of his dream and glanced at the boy. 'No
good walking like a bloody cretin, Wheatley. If your name's
on it it'll turn corners to get you. Exciting enough for you
now, is it?'

Dobson swore as he slipped for the umpteenth time.
'God, what a stink! These cabbages are bloody rotten.'

'Don't be givin' us that!' shouted Jamieson. 'It's you
who's farted an' you're trying to pin it on the poor bloody
cabbages.'

The stench of the field was quite appalling, inducing
physical sickness in a few. All of a sudden, a brilliant white
light burst upon the sky. Against its glare appeared the
outline of scuttling figures and ruined farm buildings, sharp
silhouettes of war. Then the rocket sank to earth, plunging
everything into blackness more intense than ever.

There followed stifled gasps of surprise as the leading
men, their sight impaired by the magnesium flare, fell
headlong into a dark slit in the earth. This turned out to be
the firing trench. Orders were given for the men to fan out
and inhabit the trench. Wheatley jumped straight in,
incurring the wrath of those nearby for the floor of the
trench held several inches of freezing cold water.

'Christ! Don't they know how to dig trenches round
here?' Dobson, who considered himself to be an expert at
entrenchment, wiped the muddy splashes from his face,
whilst still wrinkling his nose at the smell. 'They could've
picked a sweeter place to dig it.'

Young Captain Capstaff wandered up then. 'I'm sorry
about the conditions, men. We'll see if something can be
done about it tomorrow.' Though he was only nineteen and
fresh out of officer training school, the captain had the
confidence of one much older and a fatherly air towards his
men, which had endeared him to all under his command.
He knew every man's name and treated them with fairness –
even friendship, earning himself the affectionate nickname

of Old Catcrap. After giving orders for sentries to be posted, he told the remainder they could snatch a wink of sleep.

The men of D Company squelched up and down the waterlogged trench looking for somewhere dry to sit, but were resigned to spending the night with their bodies leaning against the wall and their feet embedded in slime. All was comparatively calm but for the periodic bursts of light. The wartime sky was strangely beautiful. Russ swore that he hadn't seen anything so impressive since attending a firework display on Bootham Asylum Fields for Victoria's Diamond Jubilee. A German starshell burst overhead, thrusting out its tentacles of blinding light to grope the inky backdrop. Russ gazed up at the shimmering arachnid until it petered out and was replaced by another, and another. His comrades watched too, held by the beauty, until Schofield let out a squeak. 'Aagh, summat ran over me hand!'

Everyone came to life. Dobson darted a finger at a scuttling shape. 'Eh, it's a rat! Look, there's another!' The animals' eyes shone red in the sudden flare of light, looking incredibly evil. The boy looked round nervously. 'Hell, they're all over!'

'God love us, Dobson.' Russ closed his eyes and tried to assume a more comfortable position. 'What's the Boche going to think of an army what's scared of a few rodents? Now shut your mouth and let us get some sleep.'

The men of D Company shut their eyes . . . but few slept.

When dawn came, Dobson discovered the true source of the stench – not rotting cabbages but rotting men. He gave a wail of alarm as his heavy-lidded eyes came open to find a human hand under his nose. The noise alerted his comrades who jumped into attacking positions, then stared dumbly at the limb which protruded from the wall of the trench, hand cupped as if begging for alms. It was clothed in the blue uniform of a French soldier.

There was united paralysis, until Russ squelched up,

grasped the muddy hand, shook it firmly and said, 'Bong jour! Can vous tell nous the way to Berlin?' and the platoon emerged from its shock.

'Crikey, have I been using that as a pillow?' marvelled Dobson. 'The poor lad.'

'He won't mind, Dobson,' replied the sergeant casually. 'Better that than the other way round. Look, there's dozens of the poor sods up there.' The soft shafts of light fell on more patches of muddy blue. The bodies of the fallen had been used by some enterprising soul to revet the walls of the trench. Might Russ, one day, be used as building material? He understood now, the presence of the rats which still scuttled about completely unafraid . . . which was more than could be said for the men.

But their unease was soon overcome by curiosity: just where abouts was the enemy? Several of the men poked their heads over the parapet. The view was quite pleasant if one ignored the shattered outline of the town which stood on a ridge some couple of hundred yards away. As their eyes travelled back down the grassy slope they fell on a dark line of rucked-up earth that was the German front trench. Dobson felt the hairs on his neck prickle at the thought of his enemy only a short distance away. This was what he had been waiting for. Why then had his limbs become jellified?

A figure appeared in the gap beside Russ. It was Daw. He made instant address of the curious ones. 'Shake your heads!' Puzzled at the odd command, they nevertheless carried it out. 'Still connected to your shoulders, I see.' The second-lieutenant's face was droll. 'You stupid sods! If you keep sticking your heads up like that they bloody soon won't be. Fritz must be havin' his breakfast or he'd've sent a few bullets over. Sergeant! I want to see every man on the firing step, bayonet fixed and ready for him if he comes.'

As the men snapped into action Daw turned to face his neighbour. 'All right, Sergeant? Have a good night?'

Russ replied with a simple, 'Yes, sir.' Daw nodded and was about to move off when Russ added, 'Congratulations, sir.'

His old pal looked back to see if this was genuine, which

it appeared to be. He gave a nod of acknowledgement and an explanation of the new rank. 'Field commission, about a month ago.'

'What company are you with, sir?' Oh Rachel, if you could hear this!

'As of last night I'm with this company – this platoon in fact. I'm replacing Lieutenant Reece.' Jack saw the shadow pass over his neighbour's face and made a caustic addition. 'If that's all right by you of course, Sergeant?' His testiness sprang from the fact that up until last night he had been acting company commander; all the officers in his own outfit had been killed in a recent skirmish, as had a great deal of men. The survivors had been ordered to join up with these new arrivals. Consequently, Daw reverted to his former rank.

'It's fine by me, sir,' replied the lance-sergeant quietly.

'We're not going to experience any difficulty working together, are we, Filbert?' Jack's droopy eyes looked down enquiringly.

'Can't see any, sir.'

'Good.' Daw walked away. He was to return some fifteen minutes later assisting the captain to dole out the rum ration. Just as the group reached Hazelwood's section a sound like thunder came from the sky. The hand tipping the rum jar paused as the roar passed over. Most ignored it, holding out their canteens, until a deafening crash signalled the shell's landing some two hundred yards to the rear. Only then did the novices realize what was going on and some cowered in alarm.

The boy captain resumed his pouring. 'Don't let it put the wind up you chaps. It's the poor devils back there who're getting it.' Even so, they did get the wind up and with little to do after their meagre breakfast but maintain the trenches, their minds began to analyse the situation. It was left to Dobson to put into wry comment. 'I think this is going to be risky you know.'

After digging sumps to drain the water from the trench they tried, throughout the morning, to get a fire going. But it was still far too marshy. Hence, they lunched on bully and cold water. Their legs began to ache due to constant standing, only when darkness came round did they gain relief, jumping out of their pit and running up and down to restore circulation.

Again, sleep was sketchy. By the third night the drinking water had run out and their only means of getting more was to line the sumphole with sandbags and catch the rainwater that trickled down the mud walls. All were thoroughly miserable. Was this what they had been brought here to do? Captain Capstaff saw the despondency in his men and tried to lift it by sharing out some bars of chocolate sent by his parents, telling them, 'We're all in the same boat, you know, chaps.' At which, Dobson picked up two pieces of wood and, with a rowing motion, began to splash along the trench, singing, 'Jolly good boating weather . . .!'

The young Captain laughed and satisfied that he had done his duty and bolstered morale, squelched away.

The men savoured their chocolate squares and nodded. 'He's a grand bloke is the Captain.'

On the fourth night, by now dog-tired, they were relieved and fell back to dugouts. Paradoxically, it brought them within closer range of the German shells which at times seemed to explode on top of them, so there was scant chance of sleep here either. They did, however, manage to light a fire and have a hot meal: Russ dug up a couple of turnips on the march; they made a palatable mash. The next night they left the firing line altogether and marched back to billets where, utterly exhausted, they fell down and slept until very late the next morning.

Their awakening coincided with the delivery of a sack of letters and parcels. There was nothing for Lance-Sergeant Hazelwood, but that came as no shock to him. Though he had written many letters himself none had been answered. Dobson, the only other man not to receive any mail was disappointed and hurt.

'I know she's mad at me for joining, but bloomin' eck, she could've replied to my letter. I mean, doesn't she know what we're up against?' Miserably, he watched the others opening their mail and unwrapping tins of sweets. 'Not even a sherbet bloody sucker.'

'It's your own fault for being a naughty boy,' the sergeant told him.

'What's your excuse then, Sarg?' demanded a resentful Dobson.

'I've been a naughty boy an' all,' was the gruff reply.

After a few days' rest, D Company was sent at night to form a covering party for soldiers from another battalion who were digging a new fire trench. Dobson groaned his frustration until, finding himself out in No Man's Land with no other cover than darkness, the reality of this sank home: here they were, lying on their stomachs in the open with nothing to hide behind but a rifle. Every time a flare shot up to the heavens, so the terror clutched at their throats and they would await the sickening rattle of machine-gun fire, while the working party behind froze into statues until the Very light died away. Added to this, artillery shells from both sides constantly whizzed overhead and stray shrapnel pattered in the grass all around them.

Lying as they were about fifteen paces apart, there was no way that conversation could take their mind off things. This didn't matter so much to Russ who had other things to occupy his mind than the Germans. Dobson, however, found the sense of mortality quite alarming and, inch by inch, shuffled closer to the sergeant until he was almost on top of him. 'Sarg?'

'Dobson, get back where you belong!' The private had made Russ jump.

'Sarg . . . are you scared?'

'Course I am, you clot!'

'Oh . . . good.' Dobson had been most disconcerted to find he wasn't as brave as he thought he was. He made no move to resume his former position.

Russ gave a snort of exasperation as Wheatley's outline appeared next to Dobson's. 'What are you two – Siamese twins? Get back up there, both o' you.'

'I couldn't see anybody,' explained Wheatley nervously. 'I thought you'd gone and left me.'

'Now there's a good idea . . .' Russ turned his head as Daw's voice floated down the line.

'Sergeant, you're supposed to be providing cover for those men back there, not playing Sardines.'

Bloody sarcastic sod, thought Russ, and was still chivvying the two privates back to their posts when another voice piped up, seeking permission to visit the latrine. 'No, you bloody can't, Schofield! Make use of your piece of string.'

Another puff of white breath hit the night air. 'It's not string I need, Sarg, it's a bung.'

Russ sighed. The whizzing bullets did have a loosening effect on the bowels. 'Go on then, but don't make a meal of it.'

'It'd be no worse than the rations we usually get,' grumbled someone.

'Ho, ho, Jamieson – and will you all bloody get back to your posts!' The line of men seemed to have concertinaed. Most did as ordered, but Wheatley lingered. 'Did you hear me, Wheatley?'

The boy was trembling. 'I can't move, Sarg.'

'You'll move quick enough with my cat-stabber up your arse – Wheatley, I have given you an order!'

Just then another Very light flooded the sky, illuminating Schofield as he trotted off to relieve himself. A hail of gunfire crackled out. The terrified men in the working party, instead of standing still, fell flat on their stomachs. So did Schofield, yelping in pain.

Wheatley shouted, 'He's hit! Schofield's hit!'

Hazelwood caught the hysterical tone. 'Keep your napper down, Wheatley, else you'll be hit an' all!' He pressed a hand to the boy's neck, forcing him down, but Wheatley struggled and managed to leap free. Before the light died, his fellows saw him throw down his rifle and scoot off like one possessed.

'Wheatley, come back here!' hissed a frantic Russ. Then, 'Oh, soddit!' he sprang up and raced after the boy.

'Sergeant, get back to your post!' barked Daw over his shoulder.

But Russ ignored him, leaping over the half-dug trench, careering across the muddy field in pursuit of Wheatley. Another flare ignited the sky. Russ heard Wheatley scream,

293

saw him fall. With a groan, he hit the ground himself, using his elbows to pull his body along before darkness enabled him to rise. Finally he reached the shellhole where Wheatley had capsized. He slithered over the top and down to the bottom as the glare came again, reaching Wheatley. There was not a mark on him.

'Wheatley, you little shit!' Coated in mud and furious, Russ grasped the sobbing boy's lapels. 'Do you want your mother to hear you died a coward?' He shook the terrified soldier. 'Hear you were shot by your own side for deserting your comrades? Do you? Do you?'

'No!' screamed Wheatley, then blubbered. 'But I'm frightened, Sarg. Oh! Oh, bloody hell I didn't know it'd be like this!'

Hazelwood slapped him across the face. 'Shut up! Pull yourself together. You're a soldier. You're going back with me.'

The heat of Wheatley's 'No!' hit him full in the face. 'They got Schofield – I can't!'

'You frigging can! They haven't touched Schofield. I've just seen the bugger, he hasn't a scratch.' This was mostly true; the private was in a ditch with a wrenched ankle. 'Wheatley, I won't have own goals in my platoon. If you're gonna get shot it'll be by the bloody Hun – now *moove*!'

With great caution, Russ emerged from the shellhole, dragging the petrified boy after him and, at an awkward crouching run, returned to a severe grilling from Second-Lieutenant Daw.

The next morning when D Company assembled for roll-call, Wheatley had gone.

He was picked up twenty-four hours later, cold, hungry, wide-eyed with fear and returned to his unit. Russ spotted him outside the CO's quarters and instantly went over to him. 'You dozy little devil . . . what did you do it for?' At the lack of answer he took out a flask which held several measures of rum he had saved from his rations and passed it to Wheatley. The boy cupped shaking hands round it and drank with gratitude until it was snatched by his guards.

Wheatley wiped his mouth with his cuff, his eyes amber spheres set in wax. 'What's gonna happen to me, Sarg?' He tucked his blue hands under his armpits and shivered.

Hazelwood repossessed his flask, making light of the offence. 'Ah, probably a bloody good dressing-down. Old Catcrap'll put in a good word for you. I shouldn't worry too much about it.' Yet, haunted by the memory of that blood-stained tree at Étaples, Russ himself felt apprehension over the query. He decided to go and see Daw.

Jack, seated on a crate in his sandbagged lair, was scribbling in a book. 'They've found him then?'

'Yes, sir,' replied Russ. Then, when there was no information about what was to happen to the recalcitrant he added, 'I don't suppose you could forget about Wheatley's bit o' panic the other night?'

'Failure to obey orders, you mean.' Daw kept his eyes on his writings, giving the occasional lick of his pencil.

'He's only a lad, sir, and it was very frightening.' Russ detested having to grovel like this, but he would do so for Wheatley's sake.

'He's a man, Sergeant, and we all get bloody frightened but a fat lot of good we'd be if we all went haring off at the first sign of shooting.'

'Pardon me, sir, but it wasn't as if he was letting anybody down. There were plenty of us left to cover the digging party.'

Daw turned a page and drove his pencil on. 'You've heard the little rhyme about the war being lost for want of a horseshoe nail? We all depend on each other, Sergeant. We can't have men running off willy-nilly while others stay to fight.'

He's enjoying this, thought Russ angrily; enjoying seeing me beg. 'No, I'd agree with that, sir. But Wheatley's got enough on his plate with this spot of AWOL without . . .'

'AWOL?' Daw looked up now. His face was incredulous. 'This is war, Sergeant! In my book the word is desertion.'

'And you always adhere to the sodding book, do you?' hissed Russ, in his concern forgetting the other's rank. 'He could be shot!'

'Quite possibly.' After this laconic statement the lieutenant threw him an interested glance. 'And so could you, Filbert. You heard my command to stay at your post yet you ignored it . . . Anyway,' he went back to scribbling in his book, 'I didn't mention that when I made my report to the captain.'

'Oh, so kind!' said Russ, bitterly insolent.

His attitude irked Daw. The pencil was tossed aside and he laced his fingers over the book. 'Why the great concern, Sergeant? Is he another one of yours?'

Hazelwood's eyes hardened even further at this sarcasm and he took a step forward. 'You . . . that's no more than I'd expect from you! You couldn't give a bugger about any o' these young lads – after all, they're only bloody vermin aren't they, Jack?'

Daw snapped the covers of his notebook together and slammed it down. 'Stand to attention when you're talking to an officer, Sergeant!'

After the briefest opposition, Russ squared his shoulders, but his mouth retained its mutinous angle.

'Now, let me put this to you,' said Second-Lieutenant Daw tightly. 'If you were in a dangerous position and you had a choice to make between me or Wheatley as your back-up, which one would you choose, I wonder?' Russ' eyes answered for him. Jack stared into them for a long time, then said smartly, 'Now go and prepare your men, Sergeant! There's some lads in a corner in a place called Eeprez. We've been ordered to give them support.'

When Russ walked past the commanding officer's quarters again, Wheatley had gone.

'Do they have Christmas where you come from, Charlie?'

The children were grouped around the kitchen table, making decorations out of gummed and crêpe paper. Bertie sat apart, favouring the sofa with his mother who was stitching a hat. Evening was the only time she got to do this now. It was she who responded to the last question.

'Oh Robina, what silly things you say!'

'Why do I?' demanded her daughter with a flourish of her rag-bound hair.

'Don't ask me! Sometimes I wonder if you belong to this family. I can't ever foresee you passing your scholarship.' Rachel turned the hat around in order to accomplish a neat finish. 'All this disruption is going to affect your chances of passing too if it goes on.' She was addressing Rowena now. The disruption to which she referred was the occupation of the schools by the military. Since the ninth of December the juniors of Scarcroft Road School had been transferred to Castlegate School which was quite some distance away. As if this wasn't inconvenient enough the school hours had been reduced. One advantage of this chaos, however, was that no one seemed the slightest concerned about Charlie's education. Rachel had heard nothing from the NSPCC nor any other body.

'But why is it a silly question?' Beany persevered.

'Because Christmas is everywhere,' answered her mother. 'Biddy, pass me the scissors.'

'Why is it?'

'Oh, really!' An exasperated Rachel shook her head. 'Get on with those paperchains or they won't be finished by next Christmas.'

Beany contorted her mouth – Mother always changed the subject if she couldn't answer a thing.

It was then Becky's turn to address Charlie. Now that her brother was mended she felt able to speak to the other boy again, though she was more careful not to show any favouritism. 'What's Christmas like in Africa?'

Charlie shrugged, his tongue travelling the gummed strip. 'The same as here.' His eyes rested momentarily on the child's hand which still bore the scar of the scalding. Though he was participating in a family occupation, in no way did he belong to that family – the scar was there to remind him of that. Oh, they were back on speaking terms with him, but it was in a very conservative manner. One relief was that he was now allowed to go to Mass regularly with Biddy. Mrs Hazelwood didn't seem too bothered who should see him now, although Charlie knew he must never go into the front parlour when she had a caller.

Father Guillaume had written on his arrival in Belgium,

suggesting that Mr Hazelwood arrange some schooling for the boy. But Rachel, who naturally had opened the letter in her husband's absence, had said it was pointless if his stay was only temporary and anyway if she had entered him at school there were bound to be questions over his parentage and she was certainly not going to suffer all that again. She did, however, allow Charlie to get books from the library, so that in between studying and helping Biddy round the house, life was not quite so stale.

'But do you have snow?'

Charlie gave a negative response, hooking the ends of the gummed strip through another. 'It's very hot.' He thought of it then, experiencing a pang of homesickness, and wondered if Father Guillaume was feeling the same way. He longed for another of the priest's letters.

Becky wrinkled her nose. 'I'll bet it's not very Christmasy without snow.'

'It's not snowing here,' Rowena pointed out.

'I know . . . but it's cold isn't it?' The walls of the yard were furred with frost. 'I couldn't imagine Christmas in the sunshine.'

'But when you think of the First Christmas,' said Charlie, 'it wouldn't have been snowing then, would it? I mean, Jesus came from a hot country like me.'

Beany cocked her head. 'Then why wasn't he brown?'

'Put the kettle on, Biddy,' Rachel interrupted. 'We'll have cocoa.'

Charlie seeing that the maid was in the middle of a stack of mending, jumped up. 'I'll do it!'

'Oh, Mona!' Beany turned to her mother in annoyance. 'Mother, she's gone and licked all the sticky stuff off the paper – look!' She displayed a large pile of damp strips.

Rhona delivered her excuse. 'Well, I like the taste.'

'You know what glue's made of,' murmured Bertie, shaping his own decorations from card and tissue paper. 'The skelingtons of dead horses – you've just licked off a whole dead horse.'

Rachel chuckled and broke her thread, holding the finished hat aloft to examine it. Robert had recovered well

298

from the shooting and with plenty of cosseting seemed almost to have returned to his normal self. The absence of his father had probably helped. Though doubtless Russell would upturn everything when he came home. 'Make the most of it, my girl,' she told Rhona. 'It may have to serve for Christmas dinner the way things are going. The price of things . . . I don't know how we'll make ends meet.'

'Maybe Aunt Ella would show us,' said Becky, receiving a quizzical look from her mother. 'How to make hen's meat,' she illuminated.

'How many times have I told you that woman is *not* your aunt!' Rachel remained hostile to her neighbour.

Charlie finished measuring the cocoa powder into each mug and then mixed it to a paste. After pouring on boiling water – Mrs Hazelwood had started to conserve milk lately – he dropped a saccharin tablet into five of them and carried them to the table on a tray. 'Could someone move that pile of paperchains please?' Becky did this, enabling him to put the tray down. 'Where do you want yours, Bertie?'

Bertie answered without looking at him, 'Leave it on the table,' and waited until the other boy had moved away before taking his position with the others.

Charlie sat as far away from Bertie as he could, knowing how any proximity angered his half-brother.

Rowena passed Lyn the end of her chain, 'Stand over there!' whilst she herself ran to the other side of the room to see how far it would stretch. 'Just a few more, I think – oh, Lyn!' Her sister had tried to stretch the chain and it had snapped.

'Well you can leave it until tomorrow to repair and clear away now,' ordered their mother after a consultation of the clock. 'Biddy, put this hat in the front parlour.' She accepted the cocoa from Charlie but gave no thanks as she added a dash of milk from the jug, knowing it was just his attempt to ingratiate himself. God, how much longer would he be here?

Biddy put the pile of mending to one side and went to do as her mistress had asked. When she returned the children were packing the paperchains into a box, after which they concentrated on their cocoa.

'Just over a week to go!' Becky hoisted gleeful shoulders then became ponderous. 'I wonder what sort of Christmas Father will have?'

'Well there's one certainty,' sniped her mother, 'he won't be facing the shortages we are. You can be sure the Army will be well-fed while we at home have to hunt high and low to scrape up a decent meal. We're living like peasants.' This wasn't quite true, but Rachel never missed an opportunity to carp about the Army.

'I wonder if Father'll send a card for my birthday?' said Becky. Three of her sisters had celebrated their birthdays recently, Rowena, Lyn and one year old Regina, and none of them had received a card. 'It takes a letter a long time to get from the war, doesn't it?'

Rachel didn't reply. The children were not to know that she had been throwing their father's mail unopened onto the fire.

'Do you think he'll be home soon, Mother?' asked Rowena. Her mother replied that it was no use asking her. 'Well people keep saying it'll all be over by Christmas.'

'People are like budgerigars,' said Rachel. 'Just repeating what everyone else is saying.'

'Where exactly is he, Mother?' Becky rested the points of her elbows on the table and propped up her chin. Her smallest finger found its way up her right nostril. 'If he isn't going to be home I'd like to send him a present. It must be very lonely for him.'

This seemed to anger her mother for some reason. 'He's got all those men to keep him company, why should he be lonely – and take that finger out of your nose!'

Becky removed the finger to her pink cheek. 'But it's not the same as being at home with your family. We always have such lovely Christmases.'

Yes, they did. Rachel was cast back to the previous Christmas when Russ had been elected Sheriff. They had all piled into the car and taken a trip into the country to pick holly and mistletoe. And Christmas Morning – as every Christmas Morning – the children had tumbled into their parents' room to brandish the contents of their stockings . . . The presents, she turned involuntary eyes on Charlie; what was she going to do about him? After consideration, she addressed them en masse, leaving her seat and pretending to be examining the curtains in case a chink of light might be showing to an enemy aircraft. 'You understand that with your father away there'll be little money spare for gifts this year?'

Little Rhona was confused. 'I thought it was Father Christmas who brought the presents.'

Rachel, seeing her error, turned and said quickly, 'Well yes, of course . . . but with the war on Father Christmas may not be able to get around to making all the toys this year, so I hope you'll be good and just be content with what he brings you?' She came back to her seat and stared into the yellow flames of the fire.

Most of the children said they would. Rachel missed Beany's look of resentment which was soon displaced by a nudge from her eldest sister.

'Will Father Christmas be able to get to France?' asked Becky.

'I suppose so,' said her mother absently.

Charlie asked what Becky intended to send to her father and was told she had been saving for a comb. He was pensive. 'I'd like to send something too.'

'I'm going to bed!' Bertie downed his mug on the table, kissed his mother and left. 'Goodnight.'

'Goodnight, dear.' Rachel's eyes followed him from the room. Guessing that Charlie's words were responsible for his leaving she had the urge to sting. 'I'm sure he won't want anything from you!'

Then she saw that Becky had taken herself to be included in the tart remark and said more kindly to her daughter, 'But I'm sure it was very generous of you, Rebecca. If you really feel you want to spend your money this way then I'll post the gift off when you've bought it.' Straightaway, the others asked if she would also send theirs. She agreed, though not very enthusiastically. Here she was, struggling to continue the ritual of pocket money so that they wouldn't suffer and what did they do? They saved it to buy a gift for the one who'd deserted them!

'So can't I send anything?' asked Charlie quietly.

'I don't know why you're asking me you usually do as you please!' Rachel snapped, and shortly after this packed them all off to bed.

Charlie was the last to go out. He stopped at the door, waiting for the others to go up before saying to Rachel, 'You don't have to buy me anything.'

She looked up impatiently, then realized what he meant. 'Oh . . . well, I wouldn't have left you out, but as it's your own suggestion . . . I am rather short of money with your father deserting me.' She looked away to the fire and said nothing more. The boy left silently.

Alone in the attic, Charlie knelt by his bed and clasped both hands in prayer, a rosary draped between the two thumbs. He knew it was selfish to ask for personal things and for this reason prayed only for his father's deliverance and that this war would soon be over. Yet once in bed he just could not help the plaintive addition: please, please make them like me.

Rachel was at work in the shop the next morning when the dreadful news came via a customer. 'Eh, isn't it atrocious about Scarborough?' The woman was raking amongst the coins in her purse in order to pay for the length of black ribbon.

Rachel continued to wind the purchase around two fingers, then tucked it into a small bag. 'What's happened?'

The woman stared. 'You haven't heard? Eh, it's all over town – they've bombed Scarborough early this morning, and Whitby and Hartlepool. There's trainloads of homeless pouring into York station. Dreadful mess the Germans've made by all accounts.'

Rachel's fingers paused at the corners of the paper bag. 'How terrible! Was there anybody killed?'

'Quite a few, I believe.' The woman took the bag and tendered her money. 'Apparently these big ships bombarded it.'

The coins trickled into the wooden bowls of the till. 'Goodness, are they that close?' Already Rachel could picture hordes of marauding Huns ransacking her home.

'Makes you wonder, doesn't it? I mean, it's all very well when they're in Belgium but when it's your own doorstep . . .'

This conversation was repeated with each subsequent patron. By late morning Rachel felt thoroughly unnerved at the closeness of the enemy.

'Only a week to Christmas,' she twittered to the final customer of the morning. 'It'll be all over by Christmas they keep telling us – they didn't say which Christmas, did they? Oh, goodness! I'll never sleep tonight knowing they're so close. And I suppose this will mean even more shortages. Some Christmas it's going to be.'

The customer pocketed her change and moved away from the counter. 'Well as long as they keep the brave boys at the front strong and healthy, that's what matters, doesn't it?' Rachel opened the door for her, a gust of cold air lifting the woman's scarf as she made her parting remark. 'They're the ones who are fighting the enemy.'

'Yes, I'm sure you're right.' Rachel smiled and closed the door. Her cheerful mien gave way to one of compressed spite. 'Brave boys indeed!'

In a small village somewhere in France, a young man stood with his back to a wall. Around his eyes was a blindfold, neath which only the tip of his freckled nose protruded. His wrists and ankles were bound with rope. He wore a dirt-stained vest and khaki trousers supported by braces. Facing him, a short distance away, a nervous line of British soldiers made ready their weapons. The young man's ears became more alert for the order about to be given, heard the click of rifle bolts. He wanted to call out for his mother . . . but they did not give him time.

CHAPTER TWENTY-ONE

'God rest ye merry, Gentlemen . . .' Russ shivered and flexed his fingers several times to try and restore circulation. It had only just dawned on him that in a few days' time it would be Christmas. Here, the dates ran into one another, the only difference being night and day, hot and cold. A moment ago there had been a distribution of mail and parcels from home and the men were sitting in their waterlogged trenches poring over the contents. Hazelwood watched them enviously for a time then, slipping a piece of paper from the pocket of his greatcoat, cleared his throat and said, 'I wrote home to my missus last week and told her the major had been killed by a Jack Johnson.' This was the nickname for an artillery shell. 'Listen to what she says, "Dear Husband, thank you for your letter. How dreadful to hear about your major being killed by Jack Johnson. What chance do you stand against the Boche if your own men are killing you . . ."'

At the ripple of appreciation he read more purported anecdotes from his wife, then folded the blank sheet into his pocket and reached for his ration tin. In truth Rachel had still not replied to his letters. He had started to invent his own replies when Dobson had become too inquisitive over why the sergeant didn't get any mail. 'Oh I do, lad!' he had exclaimed and patted his pocket where sat the now crumpled sheet, and from then on had given weekly recitations of the bogus reports from home. Becoming so hungry for a letter, any letter, he had considered writing to his sisters to confess his sins. They would be shocked, but at least their reproachful words would give him some link with home. On second thoughts, he had confined his writing to May, to whom he had always been closer than his other

304

sister. He was still waiting for reply. Obviously, he had over-estimated May's understanding nature.

He sought around him and coming up with a flat stone laid it on a section of duckboard that was not submerged. Taking a biscuit from his tin he put this on the stone and, picking up a rock, proceeded to batter the biscuit until it cracked. He then placed the fragments into a metal can and poured a scoopful of rainwater over it. This was left to soak whilst he reached for another can which had been through this process a couple of days ago and had currently been heating over a brazier. Drained of water, the resulting sops were transferred to his billy can and covered with condensed milk. As he consumed it he tried to imagine that he was eating one of Rachel's fruit scones, warm from the oven and thick with butter.

Dobson squelched down the line to where his sergeant was nestled in a funkhole and took up residence in a vacant neighbouring one. His face was coated in a greasy black layer and was thoroughly miserable. 'God, my bloody feet're cold, Sarg.'

'Well I hope you aren't expecting me to unbutton my tunic so's you can warm 'em on my belly – that's the tenth bloody time you've told me that today, Dobson.' Condensed milk trickled from the corners of Russ' mouth. His concentration broken, the warm scone became the mush it was. 'Heard from your mother yet, have you?' Dobson waved a letter. 'Well don't look too happy about it, your face might drop off. What does she say?'

'She says she's gonna give me a good hidin' when I get home,' answered a worried Dobson.

At which Russ guffawed and shook his head. 'What about your dad?' He had never heard Dobson mention him.

'Haven't got one . . . Do you think if I buy her a Christmas present it might help? Trouble is, I don't know what to get her.' Deep in thought, Dobson huddled further into his greatcoat, a hand tucked up each arm, chin resting on knees.

Hazelwood sensed the boy wanted to say something more and guessed what it was: not a word had been uttered about

Wheatley. Days had gone by since they had taken him, yet no one had mentioned it. It was as though none of them could believe it. Personally, Russ thought about the boy a lot, considering that Wheatley could quite easily have been his son. How would he have felt had this been so? It was only thanks to the captain that he and the others had not been selected for the firing squad. Russ knew the young officer had been very upset when orders had come from HQ that Wheatley must be shot as an example to the others. Russ himself had spent the days following the execution boiling with hate for the General who had signed the boy's death warrant.

Dobson's breath came as a white puff in the wintry air as he broke into song. 'Hark the herald angels si-ing! Glory to the newborn King! Peace on earth and mercy mi-ild . . . Sarg, d'you think we'll get leave for Christmas? God and sinners reconciled!'

Russ scraped his fingers into all the corners of the billy, hunting down the last elusive traces of condensed milk. 'Hang on, I'll consult these chicken's entrails.'

'Lah de, dah-dah, dah-dah-dah-dah!' Dobson broke off again. 'I just thought, like – join the triumph of the sky-ys!'

'Thinking's for officers, Dobson, not the rank and file.'

'What with it being the festive season and that, they might let us have a bit o' time off.'

'I shouldn't worry too much about where you are at Christmas.' His meal finished, Russ replaced the can in his pack. 'Fritz'll send you plenty of presents to put in your stocking.' He flinched as a shell exploded nearby and a barrowful of mud cascaded over, adding another layer of filth to their faces. 'I wish they'd start putting some eggs in them shells they keep lobbing at us, I've almost forgotten what they taste like.'

'Do you know what I miss most of all?' said the private, looking upwards. 'A blue sky. This weather's really getting me down.'

'Hah! If that's all you miss go sit next to Fuffin' Fforbes – the air round him is always blue.' Private Fforbes had a very limited vocabulary. Russ began to think of the thing he

306

missed most – felt the haven of his wife's warm moistness lock around him. He gave an inner groan. Oh, get down, boy!

'Do you believe in Heaven, Sarg?'

'Course I do,' said Russ instantly and pointed at Daw. 'Isn't that God down there?' He could not forgive the man for reporting Wheatley's lapse. He was not alone. A ranker officer was never popular, but Daw had other things to his disfavour. Though the men admired his fighting ability they detested his sarcasm and his righteous air.

'Aye . . . but seriously, Sarg.'

Russ glanced at him and shrugged as he reached for his rifle, taking the cleaning implements from its butt. It had already been cleaned today but there was little else to ease bored fingers. 'Seriously? I suppose so.'

Curiosity etched two lines on the bridge of Dobson's nose. 'How d'you see it? I mean, d'you think it's all cloudy and that or will it be a proper place?' Not waiting for answer, the boy gave his own opinion of how Heaven would appear. 'I think it'll be like a lovely big garden – I always wanted a garden, you know. We've only got a yard . . . and there'll be all the people I used to know – least the ones I liked anyroad, and it'll be sunny all the time . . . I just wonder,' his frown deepened, '. . . well, as a kid,' this brought a smile from his sergeant, 'whenever we were going on an outing or summat, I used to get really excited and couldn't wait to get there. Then when we did get there . . . I'd feel sorta let down somehow. I just wonder if it'll be like that when I get to Heaven.'

Russ turned mocking eyes on him. 'And where's the guarantee that you're off in that direction?' On one knee he laid his strip of four by two, on the other his gun oil.

'I wonder if Wheatley's there?'

Russ had somehow known that Dobson would be the one to break the silence. 'And why shouldn't he be?' he asked gruffly, applying the rag.

'Well . . . gettin' shot by his own side, like.'

'It's not just heroes what go to Heaven, Dobson . . . anyway, it's a bit morbid talk for a lad o' your age, isn't it?

You want to be thinking more of what you're going to do when you get home.'

Dobson gave a pensive nod. 'Oh aye, I wasn't reckoning on going today.'

There followed a period of silence, then the youth began in his broad Yorkshire voice, 'Ah say, Sarg . . .'

'Ass hay – that's hoss fodder, isn't it?'

'D'you think there will be any chance o' this being over by Christmas?'

Russ dealt him a cryptic smile which was answer in itself. They had said that about the Boer War, 'Oh, it'll be over in no time!' and look where the ensuing three years had got him.

'Then why does everybody keep saying it will?'

Russ heaved a sigh. 'What, why, where, when, here's that pain in the arse again – don't you ever stop asking questions, Dobson? Why don't you go for a little stroll round Fritz's trenches? See if he wants any human canonballs.'

The chastened private lowered his feet to the quagmire and skulked away. Russ began to think of his family as his four-by-two slid over the gunmetal. If previous years were any indication his girls would be making Christmas decorations now and singing carols round the piano. He wondered how they felt about him. Naturally he had known that Rachel wouldn't write, but had expected more from his girls. Of course, Rachel, feeling the way she did about him, would probably have forbidden it . . . or had she in his absence succeeded in turning them against him too? How was Bertie faring at his new school? Did he still hold his father in such contempt? What manner of Christmas would they be having? Was Rachel managing to do the books or had she left them to Jimmy – or had she simply closed the store down? Home life should be a little easier for her, with Charlie gone. Russ felt a pang of guilt for the way he had behaved towards the boy. After all, it was his fault that Charlie was in existence; the child hadn't created himself. He finished polishing the rifle, replaced the implements in the butt then rested the weapon across his knees and drifted off to sleep.

When darkness fell, Hazelwood and ten others were 'volunteered' for night patrol to sniff out German sniping posts. Visibility was poor. The men had further blackened their faces and all that could be made out was the whites of their eyes which were darted nervously about them as they waited to leave the trench. A gaggle of butterflies churned Dobson's stomach at the thought of going out into that murk. The Hun was bad enough in daylight. He began to feel bullets ripping into his gut and with a shudder fought to overcome his vivid imagination, concentrating on Sergeant Hazelwood who was beside him. The sergeant would never admit to the strong feeling that had developed between them – kicked and drove the private the same as the rest . . . but Dobson knew it was there and felt better at this moment in that knowledge. Nervousness made him talkative and he offered a quip. 'What would you like me to buy you for Christmas, Sarg?'

There was a pause while Russ considered: Christmas and he was still alive. He had come here wanting to die, to find a way out of his shame, but somehow being estranged from home had lessened his suicidal resolve. The thought raised an inward chuckle – what a bloody funny place to come to find out you don't really want to die!

He finally responded to Dobson's query with a growl. 'What I want from you, Private, is not to ask me soft questions like that once we're out there – and how come I always seem to find you next to me, Dobson, when we're preparing for any action?'

'I feel safer next to you, Sarg.' Dobson had long ago given up the idea that this was a big adventure. 'It's sort of like having your dad with you when you're playing near the big lads. Look at all the men we've lost but you're still here. Makes me think you must be lucky.'

Russ had trapped the laugh that had risen to his throat when Dobson had likened him to his father, but now it escaped in a snort. 'Lucky?!'

'Aye, and I reckon what with you being the bravest, I'm safer if I stick by . . .'

309

Hazelwood lopped the soldier's comment, 'What the hell makes you think I'm brave?'

'Well you are! The way you ran after Wheatley to fetch him back . . . you could've been shot.'

Russ turned to him wanting to shout, 'You silly young sod! You think I was being brave? I couldn't have given a bugger if I was hit'. Instead he replied, 'Let me just give you a wee tip, Dobson. If it's a lucky charm you're after, stick to a rabbit's foot or a bit o' clover but for God's sake steer well clear of me. Now shut up – and that goes for all of you! Once we're out there I don't want to hear a peep out of anybody, got it? Any man here speak Boche lingo, by the way?'

'Wheatley did,' said Dobson when no one else accepted credit.

'Right, all hold hands and we'll call for Wheatley's assistance – I'm sure that's very helpful, Dobson!'

The lad gave a smiling shrug. Though the other could be as satirical as Lieutenant Daw his words didn't provoke the same bitterness.

The order came for them to move off. Warning a sentry that this section was going out, Russ began to scale the ladder. Out in open ground he felt naked, his only scrap of cover being the intense darkness between flares. At his instruction the men began a crouched reconnoitre of the area. Dobson tripped and swore out loud as he careened face down into the mud. Hazelwood lashed out to silence him. 'Sorry, Sarg!' Dobson dragged an arm across his mud-clogged nostrils. 'But where are we supposed to be going?'

'Give me bloody strength, Dobson! We're looking for bleedin' Fritz to stick this up him.' Russ jabbed skywards with his bayonet. 'Hang onto my frigging belt if you can't see.' He squelched on.

After another period of stumbling and silent cursing someone rasped, 'He's there!' bringing the entire party to their bellies.

Russ squinted along the shape of the pointing finger. It was impossible to make out what Jamieson had seen in this pitch.

'Machine-gunners,' whispered Jamieson.

Russ was still unable to make out the shape, but could not risk disbelieving the observer and so inched his men forward. Then he saw that the man had been right. There *was* something; a sort of mound with what looked like two machine-guns perched on it. Whispering soft instructions, Russ waved a small party out to each of the enemy's flanks and when they were in situ performed a virtually noiseless charge. Dobson hurled himself forward, preparing to wreak vengeance for the vile conditions Fritz had made him suffer and thrust his bayonet deep into the shadow that was spreadeagled before him, reciting: thrust, twist, withdraw! The feel of metal slicing flesh was different to stabbing a sack. He felt sick. Someone else joined him, their bayonet plunging frenziedly. The Germans made no sound of expiry, other than a long sigh.

'Jesus Christ!' Russ balked at the stench and forgot to whisper. 'Fall back! Fall back!'

Dobson ceased his paranoid thrusting as the putrid smell overpowered him, and with the others began a rapid retreat, slithering and falling over the churned-up ground in his haste to escape.

Then one of the runners gave a panting laugh of relief and pretty soon the whole patrol was guffawing at their foolish action.

'Jamieson,' sighed Russ with exaggerated patience as they thudded to a halt, 'if you can't tell the difference between a machine-gun post and a dead hoss how d'you expect to win this bloody war? And you, Dobson! If you use as many bayonet thrusts as that on each Boche you'll not be around long. Didn't you tumble what it was when you heard the pop and the stink?'

'No, Sarg, I just thought Fritz was on a richer diet than we are.'

Hazelwood quashed the laughter, rasping, 'All right that's enough! What d'you think this is, a bleedin' circus? We're not supposed to let Fritz know where we are.' He ran his fingers over his moustache, relief making him feel light-headed. 'As if your feet don't smell bad enough, Jamieson,

311

you have to get us reeking of dead hoss. Away, I've had enough for one bloody night.' His boots made sucking noises as each was lifted from the mud. 'Still, I suppose it has saved us a job – if there were any Hun in the vicinity that stink'll have driven 'em back to Berlin by now.'

The return to their own trenches was not so easy. In the darkness they stumbled about in circles and became completely lost. Finally, however, they found a landmark, allowing their stomach muscles to relax as they entered their own territory.

'I've just thought what you can get me for Christmas, Dobson,' said Russ, coming out of his crouch and walking upright now. 'A new brain. This one can't be working proper if I allow myself to be landed with a bunch of clots like you. Pff! Bloody dead hosses – now I could've understood it if Fritz'd made that mistake, seen a big lump on the ground and thought it was a member of the British Infantry.' He tucked a boot under Jamieson's wholesome backside.

Jamieson was still grinning when the bullet hit him. Russ didn't cotton on to what had happened at first – thought his playful kick had been heftier than intended – but then he heard a crack and felt something sting his ear. His first confused thought was that he had directed his men into enemy lines. But after flinging himself on the ground he regained his bearings and knew that he was under fire from his own side.

'Stop! You bloody fools, we're British!' he screamed.

The firing petered out. 'What's the password?'

Russ dropped his face to the mud. Christ! What sort of an outfit are they, came the mental scream. Fire first and ask the password later! He racked his brain which, numbed by the unexpected attack, refused to come up with an answer. Instead he lifted his chin and spat an angry expletive.

'Bollocks is not the password,' a voice called back. 'Advance and be recognized.'

Tentatively, Russ scrambled to his feet, showed himself to the trigger-happy sentry, then moved to see how badly hurt Jamieson was. He was dead. Wounded were Privates

312

Dench, Hartley . . . and Dobson. Horrified, the sergeant dropped to his knees by the boy and applied gentle hands to roll him over . . . when Dobson rolled over for himself, completely unscathed. 'You little . . . !' Russ slapped the boy's face, then sat back on his heels and gasped, half in relief, half in fury.

Dobson raised himself on one trembling elbow and listened to the groans of the wounded. 'Told you you were my lucky charm, Sarg.'

Hazelwood threw his despairing face to the heavens. 'I'm beginning to wonder which side we're on.'

A few days before Christmas the battalion was sent to rest billets far behind the line, which promised some kind of celebration after all. Following the customary footslog, Russ and his pals arrived in a picturesque town untouched as yet by German shells. The locals were eager to welcome them, shouting encouragement as the weary soldiers came limping in. 'Boches finis!'

'I wish some bugger would tell Fritz that,' grumbled Russ. His feet were in an atrocious state. All he wanted to do was to get his sodden boots off. A woman stepped out of the crowd and began to hand out small sachets to those on the flanks. Russ acepted one with a 'Merci, mam'selle!' and a grin. Dobson had one as well. Neither of them could decipher the writing, but a quick sniff gave a hint of lavender, producing laughter.

Excitement soared as the word came that they were to march to a brewery. Unfortunately, someone had forgotten to mention that it had been converted to a bath house. But the sight of a tubful of steaming water drove aside any grumbles. Russ was swift to divest himself of the wet puttees and boots, though this was not the ecstasy he had imagined; his feet were even more painful as the circulation began to return; like two throbbing pieces of tripe, chalk-white and pudgy to the touch. The sergeant beside him was already stripped and plunging his hairy body into the hot tub while an RAMC man took charge of his soiled clothing.

Russ did likewise and, taking the sachet that the woman

313

had given him, slipped into the welcoming water. It was the first bath he had had in three months. He groaned in euphoria and submerged his shoulders, then ripping open the sachet rubbed the lavender soapflakes into a glorious lather, inhaling lungfuls of the scent as he massaged his body. Two handfuls of the lather were deposited on his chin. A soapy hand grappled around for the razor he had taken from his pack, then lifted it to shave off his beard.

The luxury lasted five minutes. The 'Poultice Walloper' yelled to him that his uniform was ready and with great reluctance he heaved his dripping person from the water. He found his uniform brushed and pressed. On top was a clean shirt and underwear. His boots were still wet but he could remedy that tonight. Oh! but it was Heaven to be free of the stench of sweat. But the best part of all was to sink onto his straw-filled mattress after weeks of sleeping rough. With beatific smile, Russ was just snuggling down for the night when Dobson poked his face round the door of the NCOs' billet.

'Just thought I'd let you know, Sarg, you're in line for a medal.'

Russ opened one eye. 'Oh God, it's here again! Come on then, Dobson, let's be having it and allow me to get some kip. What have I done to deserve this medal?'

'Provided us with a new secret weapon. They've just stuffed your dirty underpants in a howitzer and sent 'em over to Fritz. He's surrendering in droves.'

Russ picked up a tin mug and threw it at Dobson who disappeared. 'Night, night, mummy!'

Russ slept until eleven the next morning. When he swung his feet from the mattress he was relieved to see they had returned to near normal size, even though they were still very tender. His boots, having benefited from the warmth of the brazier, were dry now. He pulled the paper from their innards and put them on. Then he went to break his fast. While he was eating, a delivery of mail arrived. Names were shouted out and the lucky recipients grabbed their parcels and letters.

'R. C. Hazelwood Sergeant – Arsey Hazelwood, where are you?'

Russ looked up in surprise, then strode over to collect the parcel. It bore his wife's handwriting. With excited fingers he tore it open. Inside were six little parcels; one from each of his children, apart from Regina who was too young to buy a gift. Smiling, he cast a brief but joyful eye at each sender's name – Rhona, Becky, Rowena, Lyn, Beany, Ber . . . no, *not* Bertie. His expectant smile changed to a frown as his eyes read 'Charlie'. The boy was still there! What had happened to the priest? However, he wasted little time in pondering over this. The more pertinent matter was that Bertie was still hostile to him – there was no gift bearing his son's name. All of these six gifts could not compensate for the lack of that one. He could not bear to open them. Laying them to one side he searched around the packing for a letter. There was none. The only concession his wife had made was to address the parcel for the children. The paper was loosed and fluttered to the ground; down to the ground like his spirits. One by one he fingered the small parcels again. Somehow, they made Christmas seem even emptier . . . With a click of his tongue he bundled them back into the wrapping and shoved them out of sight. He was damned if he was going to let this make his leave miserable.

But later he did open them, finding a comb from Becky, one of Rhona's picture books, a homemade bookmark from Beany, an initialled handkerchief from Rowena, a packet of five cigarettes from Charlie and a sticky bag of liquorice comfits from Lyn – 'Bullets to shoot the Germans with'. With a sad chuckle, he decided he must write a letter of thanks. He wrote one to his wife too, but only got as far as 'Dear Rachel', before folding it up. This might be the only break he got for a long time, he was not going to squander it by writing letters that may not be read. He was going to have a damned good time, get drunk and enjoy himself.

His platoon was obviously of the same mind, for when he slipped into the estaminet that same evening Dobson and twelve others were already under the influence of local hospitality. There was only as much space as in Hazel-wood's front parlour and all the drinking was done at one big table in the middle of the room. An oil lamp hung from a beam over their heads, casting the perimeter of the room into shadow. Madame stood behind the bar, which was like the dock in a courtroom.

'Oh Christ,' muttered Private Husthwaite into his glass. 'Don't we get enough o' this bastard?' Nevertheless he made space for Russ on the wooden bench.

Russ snapped his fingers at Madame. 'Witness for the prosecution, please state your evidence.'

'Pardon, monsieur?' Madame came from behind the dock, bearing a large jug and a glass. Her corseted bottom rolled from side to side as if she suffered from some hip displacement.

Russ accepted her offer of beer and passed over half a crown which was examined before he received his change in francs. He sampled the ale, which was no better than it had been in any of the other places they had stopped in. The vinegary taste produced a face of disgust. 'Eh, we usually reserve this stuff for our chips at home.' Madame gave a pronounced shrug and sauntered round the table, refilling glasses.

'Dobson, budge up a bit I can't get you all on!' Strawbridge had his camera trained on the group of drinkers.

Russ groaned, but poised with glass aloft for the photograph. When it was accomplished he took another shuddering gulp then put down the glass. 'Well now . . . and what are our little chums going to be getting up to in the next few days?'

'I'm gonna get a bit of Christmas shopping,' Dobson told him.

Russ laughed. 'Still trying to get round Mother, are we?'

Dobson nodded. 'I've seen one or two things she might like. There's a house down the road that has this real bonny lamp in the porch – red it is. I'm thinking of going over to ask if they want to sell it.'

Russ took this as a jest, but then saw that Dobson was

completely serious. 'Oh, I'm sure that'll go down like the Titanic!' He winked at the others and laughed into his glass, making bubbles in the beer.

Dobson's face fell. 'My dad was killed on the Titanic.'

Russ wiped the splashes from his chin and showed instant contrition. 'Eh, I'm sorry, lad, I didn't mean . . .'

Dobson guffawed and elbowed his sergeant. 'Hah! You should see your face, Sarg! I'm only kidding – me dad got run over by a steamroller.'

'Aye we've heard he made a lasting impression on your street,' Russ beat him to the punchline and cuffed him. He tried his beer again. It didn't go down any better. 'Before you send your mother one o' these red lamps, Dobson, I'd just better tell you what they stand for. I mean, she's going to kick your head in as it is when she catches up with you, I should hate her to really hurt you.' He then explained the significance of the intended gift.

Dobson's jaw dropped. 'You mean there's women what . . . specially for us lads? Well nobody told me!' It was said with chagrin . . . then his face became intent. 'Eh, Sarg . . .'

'No, Dobson!' Russ anticipated the question. 'You stay away from them places.'

'Aw, don't be a killjoy, Sarg,' pressed one of the older men, seizing onto the idea. 'Think what it'd be like to get blown to bits and never had your wick dipped. Let the lad go.'

The others joined the persuasion. 'Aye let him go, Sarg!'

'Well, I'm off!' shouted Husthwaite and stood to emphasize this.

'Listen to the voice of experience, Dobson,' persisted Russ. 'You keep clear o' bloody women – anyway, it'll not be much fun, you know, stood in a queue for hours.' He shook his head.

There was further banter in favour of Dobson visiting the brothel. In the end it was proposed that they all go.

'No we bloody-well won't,' returned Hazelwood. 'I'm staying well away. And if you take my advice you won't take Strawbridge and his camera either, else you'll all be candidates for blackmail.' Dobson wailed his protest.

'I've given my advice,' said Russ airily. 'If you want to waste your brass that's up to you.' He consumed the last of his beer and gave a summoning wave at Madame. 'But if you catch anything nasty, don't come weeping to me.'

With that, everyone except the sergeant rose and, with one man on either side of Dobson to act as moral – or immoral – support, they left the estaminet, laughing obscenities.

Russ glanced at Madame who hovered with her jug. He shook his head and gave one of the phrases he had picked up. 'Vin rouge, s'il vous plaît.' Receiving his bottle of wine he tossed two francs onto the table and filled his glass. 'Ah, that tastes better. Not bad stuff.' He finished it sooner than he had the beer and refilled his glass. In his loneliness, thoughts of home returned and it was not long before he was asking for another bottle. 'Come an' have one wi' me, love,' he slurred at Madame who did not understand. He patted the bench, pointed at her and at the bottle. 'Away, just the two of us – you share with me.'

Grasping his meaning she found herself a glass and allowed him to fill it. This done, he raised his own glass. 'Cheers.'

'A votre santé.'

After both had taken a mouthful, Russ said, 'D'you know why I'm here?' At her gesture of incomprehension he added, 'No, neither do I. What the hell must I have been thinking of . . . I do love her you know.' All the desperation flooded out. Things he could not share with any man he poured out to this foreign woman, who would not give advice, would not condemn because she could not understand him. 'She means the world to me, her and them kids.' He made fists of his hands. 'Bertie . . . I just can't think what to do to get him speaking to me. Have you got any children, love?' He rocked his arms as if holding a baby. 'Compree?'

'Ah oui, j'ai quatre enfants . . . ou plutôt, trois enfants. Mon fils est mort . . . la guerre.' A shrug and a sip of wine.

'I've got seven. Six girls and one boy.' He stared down into his glass. The reflection of the lamp shone up at him.

'No . . . I'm lying. I've got eight. I keep trying to pretend he isn't there . . . but he is.' He gave a snorting laugh. 'He's sent me a Christmas present; a packet of fags. She said I was a coward, leaving her to see to things at home.' His eyes beseeched the listener. 'How can I be a coward? I'm fighting a war, aren't I?' He drank deeply and stared at the dingy wall, then gave an unhappy chuckle. 'No . . . happen she's right. I only came here as a way of escape. Sounds bloody daft, doesn't it? Oh, pardon my French. It's just that I couldn't bear to be in that house any longer with the way they kept looking at me . . . as if they hated me. I kept trying to tell her it meant nothing, that affair. It was just . . . well, you know what it's like when you're away from home. But I can't put it into words, how I feel about her. Sometimes . . . sometimes I could bloody cry . . .' He snatched a drink, almost biting through the glass. 'It's like,' he thrust his fist under his breastbone, 'a lump here that won't go up nor down, like it's eating me away from the inside.' He looked at the woman again. 'You think I'm bloody mad, don't you? Maybe I am.'

He said no more, confining his attentions to the bottle. The others returned half an hour later, still laughing heartily at the revoltingly ugly woman who had answered their knock and had peppered their backs with French curses when Dobson – virgo intacta – had led the hasty retreat. But the sergeant was too far gone to share the joke. He was lying, as he had fallen, with his back on the floor and his knees still hooked over the bench, temporarily dead to the world.

On Christmas Night it was back to the Flanders trenches where, under cover of darkness, the changeover took place. A sergeant from another battalion spoke to Russ before he left. 'Pukka time we've had today, mate.' Hazelwood took this to be facetious and made a rude comment, slopping about in the mud to keep his feet warm.

'No, I mean it! We've been playing football.'

The slopping ceased. 'What!'

'It's bloody right!' said the man on a laugh. 'There's been

319

a truce most of today. Look!' He delved into his pocket and pulled out a photograph. 'This is Freidrich and this . . .'

'Fuck me,' breathed Russ.

The other man's hands fell to his trouser buttons, voice furtive. 'Is there anybody looking?' Then he pointed to the photo again. 'This is his wife and kids. I always thought German women were built like prizefighters but she's a bonny little thing, isn't she?'

'You mean, while we've been getting ourselves poisoned on French beer you've been having a bloody party?' bawled Russ. 'I don't believe it! It's that bloody wine making me hear things.'

The other sergeant filed the picture in his tunic and patted it. 'It's all over now of course.'

'Oh aye, it would be now muggins is back! Eh! Have you buggers heard this?' he called to his men. 'Been having a Christmas party in our absence.'

His informant chuckled and, with his company, departed. With twisted mouth, Russ gave his platoon orders as shells began to fall more copiously and bullets zapped into the sandbagged parapet. 'Any bugger know what time it is?'

'Dead on midnight, Sergeant!' It was Daw who called the answer. 'It's now officially Boxing Day.'

Simultaneously there was a huge explosion in the direction that the other company had just taken. Comparative silence for a moment . . . then dreadful shrieks of wounded men. 'Ah well,' Russ gave an ironic sigh, belying his inner revulsion. 'All over for another year.'

CHAPTER TWENTY-TWO

It was March and the war that was supposed to have been over by Christmas was still on. Yet, there remained an air of optimism on the streets of York. People were still saying, 'We'll soon have them beaten'. Outside the recruiting offices young men still queued to join the Big Adventure. To those at home the war seemed far away and little to do with them. The folk in the Hazelwood residence were no different. Although they often thought of Russ they had grown used to his absence.

Bertie was now fully acclimatized to his new school and though he still showed animosity towards his half-brother it took the form of cold shoulders rather than open warfare. Rachel had recovered from her initial panic and was managing, if a mite haphazardly, to run both shop and household. With all this to occupy her head she had little thought to spare for her errant spouse. Only when his letters arrived did the old anger boil up again . . . as this morning.

She turned from setting the breakfast table as Rowena dashed in with a handful of mail. Normally she made a point of getting to the letterbox first, but somehow today the child had beaten her to it. It just had to be the day when her husband had chosen to write.

'Rhona's got lots of cards!' breathed Rowena excitedly. It was her sister's fourth birthday. 'And look! I think this is a letter from Father – at last!' She pressed it into her mother's hands and waited eagerly.

But instead of opening it, her mother just stood and looked at her, turning the envelope in her hands. Then calmly, she placed it on the fire.

Rowena's expectancy gave way to a cry of alarm as the envelope turned brown.

'It's as well that you know.' Rachel studied the devastated face for a second, then turned back to her task of laying the table.

Rowena couldn't speak. She watched the letter flare and shrivel, then turned a horrified face on Biddy who grimaced and stirred at a pan on the range. 'Have you . . . have you been burning all of Father's letters?' The child's voice was barely audible.

'Yes.' Rachel finished setting the cutlery out and laid the cards at Rhona's place.

'Don't you love him any more?'

'That's rather a silly question, not to mention impertinent! Your father was the one to leave us if you recall.'

Rowena thought about this. Then said, 'If you don't want his letters, would I be allowed to read them? I promise I won't tell the oth . . .'

'You most certainly would not! Any correspondence between your father and me is a private affair and if I choose not to read it then that is a private affair too!'

'Sorry . . .' Rowena traced a pattern on the carpet with her toe. 'Did you burn the birthday cards he sent for us too?'

'I wouldn't dream of it! The fact of the matter is that your father didn't even bother to send any – now go and call the others down to breakfast!'

Rowena tried not to let her sisters see how upset she was and joined in the rendition of 'Happy Birthday to You' for Rhona's sake. After the song, Rhona opened her cards and presents.

'Is there anything from Father?' Lyn knelt on her chair and craned her neck eagerly. Rowena, who had been reading them out to her little sister, murmured a no. 'Good!' said Lyn and sat properly on the chair. 'Well he never sent me one, did he?' she said at Rhona's scowl.

'He never sent *any* of us,' said Rowena. 'You can't expect him to when he's fighting in a war.' She chanced a look at her mother who said nothing.

'When's your birthday, Charlie?' asked Becky.

'February.' He took a piece of toast and spread marmalade on it.

322

'Aw, we've missed it!' Becky touched his hand, but at Bertie's glower removed her fingers. 'I'm ever so sorry. Why didn't you tell us?'

'It would've looked like I was asking for presents,' said Charlie.

'No it wouldn't. You could've had a party, couldn't he, Wena?'

'Never mind,' answered her sister. 'We know now. We'll give him one next year.'

Rachel saw the look on her son's face and said sharply, 'He'll be gone by then,' clattering their empty bowls together. 'Now hurry up, it's nearly time for school.'

After the episode of the burnt letter, Rowena made sure she was about whenever the postman called, not merely to see if her mother destroyed any letters, but to try and intercept one for herself. It was almost a month before another arrived. Being Easter, there was no school but Rowena still rose early and as she came downstairs a delivery of mail dropped onto the mat. She flew up the passage to pounce on it. A green envelope stood out among the others. She saw to her delight that it was from Russ and stuffed it into the pocket of her pinafore just as her mother came down the passage. Luckily her back was to Rachel which hid her action, and when she turned the dimness of the passage camouflaged her blush as she handed the rest of the mail to her mother.

Rachel flicked through the envelopes and, finding nothing to offend, set them aside to read later. All through breakfast Rowena hardly dared move for fear that her mother would hear the letter crackling in her pocket. She sped through the meal, finishing well before the others and asked if she might be excused. Fortunately, Mother didn't detect the red cheeks and she scurried up to her room to open the precious envelope.

'My dear Rachel,

   I hope this letter finds you and the children in good health. As ever, I cannot tell you where I am but you know my heart is with you . . .'

How romantic, thought the child and nibbled her finger-nail.

'. . . I suppose it's silly of me to keep writing when my letters are obviously unwelcome, but I do so in the hope that my genuine plea for your forgiveness will one day be answered. I still care very deeply for you and our children. I treasure the gifts they sent me at Christmas. Did you give them the note I sent with my last letter to you? I keep hoping they will write back to me. In between action the boredom really gets to you and a letter, however short, would be a Godsend. It gets very lonely here too. It sounds funny, doesn't it? Saying I'm lonely amid thousands of men, but I'm lonely for you, Rachel. I wish most desperately that I was there with you and Bertie and our darling girls. I know it's a bit late for such a declaration but I do beg you to believe the sincerity of it. I hope, too, that Bertie is settled into his big school and that Charlie is no longer there to remind you of the hurt I caused you. Why didn't the priest come for him when he was supposed to? I do wish you would write and tell me. I worry about you so much and if there's anything I can do please let me know. I long for the day when this is all over and I can be with you to tell you in person how very sorry I am for everything I've done to you. I really didn't love her, you know . . .'

Rowena read the closing words, then folded the letter solemnly. Poor Father, one of the girls should write to him – it could only be her. But alas! when she looked on the envelope for her father's service number there was a great smudge of mud making it indecipherable. She would have to wait until another one came – but what was she to do with this one now? She couldn't bear to destroy it. Looking round for a hiding place, she plumped for one of the pictures on the wall. Finding some brown sticky tape in her drawer she used it to fix the letter to the back of the frame, then replaced it on the wall. She wouldn't tell the others that Mother had been burning the letters. Oh, if only Mother would read one, she would see the way Father felt for her. This sparked further thought: if Rowena were to intercept the next letter she could open it and place it between the pages of the newspaper so that her mother could not help but read it – what a splendid idea!

They had been at this place called Eeprez, or Wipers as
most of the men had started to call it, for over four months,
being shuttled from sector to sector but used mainly as
reinforcements for the front line which was in very poor
shape. The trenches here were extremely shallow and had
to be built up with sandbags. Tonight, the men of 5 Platoon
were returning from rest billets where they had enjoyed a
tepid shower, but as Dobson pointed out this seemed, 'A
total waste of time! I'm still carrying two tons of lice.' He
tried to reach the spot between his shoulderblades.

Russ answered in polite tone, 'Yes, but at least they're
clean lice, Dobson,' then bawled for his platoon to take up
positions.

'I wonder what sort o' lice Fritz has.' Dobson placed one
foot on the firestep and leaned casually on his knee.

'Eh God, the thoughts you have – same as us 'cept they
itch with a German accent.'

Hours passed. Morning was sounded by the clank of the
dixies bringing gunfire tea. Russ pulled a cigarette from his
pocket and lit it. Beside him, Dobson offered, 'Fancy a
sandwich with your gunfire, Sarg?'

'Where'd you get a bloody sandwi . . .' Russ turned,
then swung out at Dobson who was holding out a dead rat
sandwiched between two biscuits. 'You soft little bugger!'

Dobson cackled and hurled the 'sandwich' up in the air,
whence it was pierced by a sniper's bullet. After this brief
display of crack shooting came the normal barrage of
morning hate, and later a period of calm. Russ made use of a
periscope and surveyed the outside world. Things were just
starting to grow. Indeed, it was a typical spring outlook:
blue sky, sunshine, an exhilarating edge to the air. He saw
himself strolling by the River Ouse, pushing the pram
containing Rosalyn and Becky – the three youngest not yet
born – and at his side walked Rachel holding the eldest girl's
hand, her face glowing from the nippy temperature. And
there was Robert, running on ahead, full of excitement, for
this was his Breeching Day and he had in his pocket a bright

new sixpence donated by his father . . . his proud father. The day progressed as usual – well, perhaps not quite as usual for around five o'clock the German guns fell silent.

Russ cocked his ear. 'How very considerate, they've clocked off for tea – get brewing, Dobbo.'

The guns remained speechless for the ten minutes it took to drink their tea. It was very odd but no one complained. 'Eh, wouldn't it be nice if they'd run out of crumps?' said Dobson thoughtfully.

'Huh! I can't see German efficiency allowing that,' opined Russ, tipping the dregs from his mug and throwing it at the private. 'Right then, my lovely lads, off your arses! Jump to it, Dobson – at least try and make Fritz think there's summat human over here.'

'Permission to use the latrine, Sergeant?' At Hazelwood's growl the private responded brightly, 'Well I *am* only human, Sarg,' laughed and made off down a communication trench.

He had been gone maybe five minutes when it happened. There was no warning given, for nothing of this sort had happened before. Russ thought he detected a faint hiss. Frowning, he employed his periscope again. A cloud blocked its view. Not one of the wispy shapes that pompommed the sky, but a strange greeny-yellow . . . Russ took his rifle down and examined the tiny mirror that was fixed to its bayonet – then looked up as a layer of mist rolled over the parapet. He took one sniff and started to cough. It grew worse – he couldn't get his breath. There were others in the same plight, staggering blindly along the trench, trying to escape. He felt as if his brain was about to burst out of his skull, his eye sockets, his nose. He found the communication trench, stumbled down it . . . someone pressed a cloth over his mouth, suffocating him. He fought them, retching vile foam . . . pain, pain and more pain. *I'm going* . . .

April was coming to a close and there was no sign of another letter from Father. Rowena thought, he's grown sick of not getting a reply. Let down on yet another morning, she did a last furtive shuffle of the mail before carrying it to the kitchen and eating breakfast. It was as she was participating in this meal that a knock came and Biddy went off to answer it. When she came back she hesitated at the mistress's chair, then extended her arm.

Rachel stared at the thick wrist. A napkin came up to dab at her mouth and nervous eyes gripped the telegram. Then the napkin was deposited on the table and an arm was raised, slowly, so as to delay the opening for she feared what was in it. Then with a sudden move it was snatched from Biddy's hand, torn open and read.

The children, ignorant over the substance of the piece of paper, continued to eat. Only when their mother gave a small exclamation did they view her with concern. When she failed to make further utterance Rowena looked at Biddy who stood gormlessly by, then directed her eyes back to her mother and put a hand over the one holding the telegram. Rachel could not escape her mental paralysis, but handed over the message. Rowena gave a cry too. 'Father's missing!'

Charlie's stomach contracted in shock and he gasped with the others. He asked what had happened and his half-sister showed him the telegram which stated that Sergeant Hazelwood was missing, not how this had come about. Fear tickled his insides – what if his father had been killed? All this time Charlie had put up with the insults from Mrs Hazelwood and Bertie purely for his father's sake . . . He looked at Bertie whose face was impassive, and all at once hated him for having that which he had never known – his father's love . . . and now he might never know.

Rowena's doe-like eyes flew to her mother. 'What can we do?'

'Do?' said Rachel stupidly. *I don't believe this!*

'We have to help find him!' cut in an anxious Becky, chewing a strand of red hair.

Rachel took the telegram back and folded it with dull resignation. 'That's hardly practicable, Rebecca. He's somewhere in the middle of Europe.'

'But aren't you worried?' Beany's muddy eyes welled her

own concern. 'He might be . . . could have been . . .' She could not bring herself to say killed and pulled at a flap of tablecloth, screwing it in her fists.

Rachel seemed to come to her senses, then cottoned onto what they were all thinking. 'No, no! If anything serious had happened they'd have told us straightaway. He's probably . . .' She broke off – she'd been going to say he was probably in a prison camp but that would hardly comfort them. The silly fool, getting himself captured! She looked at Bertie who had volunteered nothing. Bertie tried not to let the shock reach his face but inside his heart pounded. 'You mustn't think the worst. Your father'll turn up, I'm positive.' Leaving the table she tucked the telegram behind an ornament on the mantel. 'Now, eat up it's nearly time for school.'

'But . . . we can't go to school today!' gasped Rowena. For one moment she had taken the expression on her mother's face to be concern, but it wasn't there now.

'And what's wrong with today?'

'But Father's missing!' It was obvious now to Rowena why there had been no more letters.

'And being absent from school is going to find him is it?' That was harsher than she had intended. It was natural that they should be worried about him even if she wasn't. She sought to comfort. 'If you like I'll go down to the War Office later and make enquiries, but I'm sure he won't have been hurt or they'd have said. It wouldn't do any good for you to stay off school now, would it – your education's suffered enough this term. Biddy, clear away please.'

And the children were forced to go to school. But they continued to worry all day. Lyn questioned people in her class, 'Have you ever had a telegram about your father being missing?' Most of them said no they hadn't. One said he'd had a telegram when his father was killed. Finally someone said more helpfully, 'Yes, we had one saying he was missing then we found out he'd been taken prisoner.'

Lyn related this to the others at home time. 'I hope Father hasn't been captured – it's worse than being killed.'

'Don't be stupid,' said Rowena. 'Nothing's worse than being killed.'

'Yes it is!' argued Lyn. 'Surrendering to the enemy is . . . a fate worse than death! Eh, here's Aunt Ella, shall I ask her if she's got any Easter eggs?' They hadn't seen Ella over the holiday period. In days gone by she had brought Easter eggs home, which they would devour in the secrecy of her house – not that Mother minded them having Easter eggs for she provided this treat herself, but she would have grumbled if she'd known Ella had supplied them. Now of course with the restrictions on confectionery and Ella working in munitions, there was scant hope of her bringing eggs home – but they could ask.

'Lyn, don't you know there's a war on?' Rowena caught her sister's arm and held her back as Ella approached, saying under her breath, 'Besides, you know very well we're not even allowed to talk to her now.'

'We weren't supposed to before but we did,' objected Lyn.

'And Mr Daw might know where Father is,' suggested Becky.

'Becky, remember what trouble you caused last time by telling Aunt Ella about Mother's private business! Just say hello and walk on.'

This they did. Ella smiled as she passed and returned their hellos but said nothing more. If she asked an innocent question like, 'How is your father?' it would get back to Rachel who'd think she was spying, the clot.

The moment the girls were indoors they started to pester their mother for news. Rachel lied and told them she had been down to the War Office where she had been informed that steps were being taken to find their father. 'So, are you happy now?' The girls said yes, but she could see this wasn't wholly true. I shouldn't have said anything about the telegram, she told herself, looking at their faces. I should have waited until I had some definite news . . . The arrival of another telegram some weeks later removed any uncertainty.

Madam,

It is my painful duty to inform you that, no further news having being received relative to no. 25632 Lance-Sergeant

Russell Charles Hazelwood, Reg. King's Own Yorkshire North Riding, who has been missing since 22–4–15 . . . regretfully constrained to conclude that he is dead and that his death took place on . . . I am to express to you the sympathy of Lord Kitchener . . .

Seized by shock, Rachel's hands pressed the telegram over her gaping mouth as if about to eat it. *It can't be!* She had expected him to turn up, had truly anticipated this telegram to say he had been taken prisoner . . . In a daze, she lowered the piece of paper and read it again. It read the same. Tears misted the words. *Russell was dead!* Despite all he had done to her she had once loved this man. Again she heard his cheery voice, his children's laughter, the warmth and hardness of his body . . . then the shocking image of bullets piercing that same body, blood gushing, the fear on his pleasant face – then in the same breath she cursed him: damn you to hell, Russell! How am I ever going to cope? I've got the shop, seven child – no! eight children. Oh, dear God, what am I ever going to do?

She broke down and sobbed. Thank heaven she had been alone to receive this news. The children hadn't arrived home for dinner yet. There were only the two littlest ones at home – and *him*. Oh, the dear children! How was she ever going to break the news? Already she could hear their grief. She couldn't bear that on top of her own. But where was the need to tell them straightaway? Maybe . . . maybe in a few days she would feel strong enough to break it to them.

She blew her nose, gave a long shuddering sniff and wiped her eyes. For a time she paced aimlessly about the front parlour, remembering the good chapters in her life, seeing her husband so vividly it didn't seem as though he was dead. There would be all his clothes and belongings to dispose of. But she couldn't do that before telling the children . . . and she couldn't tell the children. She gnawed on a corner of the handkerchief. Then, with a sigh, she inspected her blotchy face in a mirror and went to the kitchen.

On ascertaining that Rhona and her sister were upstairs, she spoke to the maid. 'Biddy, I don't want you to say anything to the children about this telegram that just came. Not a word.'

Biddy was wiping her hands. 'Yes'm.' Then she noticed the bloodshot eyes and asked concernedly, 'Is it about himself – is he safe?'

'Never mind what it's about! I shall relay the content when I deem it fitting.' Rachel turned and headed back to the parlour. As she did so she heard Rhona laughing merrily. The tears came again.

Mrs Phillips picked up a tin of mustard from the shelf and ticked it off the list she was holding, at the same time chatting to Ella Daw. Their topic was Rachel. 'Ruby Parker said she'd had a telegram the other day.'

Ella's face turned serious and she fingered a button on her coat. 'Oh hell . . . I hope Russ is all right.'

'Oh, I thought she might've said something to you.' Mrs Phillips sounded disappointed.

'She hasn't spoken to me since . . . oh ages ago.' Since Bertie's shooting, but Ella wasn't going to raise that here.

'Nor me neither,' sniffed Mrs Phillips. 'She must be getting her shopping somewhere else, I haven't seen her in weeks – she'll be quick enough to come here when she runs out of summat though.' She wandered around the shelves of stock, collecting boxes and tucking them under her arms. 'I've asked one or two folk if they've heard anything about Councillor Hazelwood but nobody seems to know owt. If he has been killed he'll be the first one in your street, won't he?'

Ella nodded thoughtfully. 'Aye, we've done well up to now. He can't be dead though – I saw the kids larking this morning, they were bright as buttons. I'll have to write and ask my Jack.' She removed her basket from the counter to make way for Mrs Phillips' armful of goods. 'He never tells me anything, you know.' She smiled fondly. Mrs Phillips asked how Jack was keeping. 'Oh fine, thanks – he's an officer now, you know.'

Mrs Phillips loosed her burden on the counter and acted surprised, 'Ee, I say!' although she had heard this long ago. Then she spotted a telegram boy in Queen Victoria Street.

At her diversion, Ella turned to watch anxiously until the boy found the right address. 'Aw no, it's poor Mrs Skilbeck again – by doesn't she have some bad luck.' She bit her lip and stared at the woman's haggard face as she received the telegram, imagining herself in that position. 'It must be her Ronnie; he's the only one left. Did you know her other lads got ki . . . aye, course you would. Poor old lass.'

She and Mrs Phillips watched until the woman's door closed then Ella turned back to the counter. 'Aye well, it's no good me stood standing here. I'll see you later.' She made for the door.

'Er, let me know if you hear anything about your neighbour!' called Mrs Phillips.

'I wonder if they'll find Father tomorrow?' A small voice – Becky's – wavered through the darkness, drawing complaint from her bed companions.

'I was just going off then!' Lyn turned onto her left side, facing the wall and dragging the covers with her.

This disturbed Beany who slept on the other side of Rebecca and she hauled the covers back with a loud objection of her own.

'Go to sleep, Becky,' murmured Rowena from the other bed which she shared with Rhona.

'I can't,' the voice quavered. 'I keep thinking Father's been shot.'

This thought had been keeping Rowena awake too, but she told her sister not to be so silly. 'Father's probably just been moved to a different camp. There are millions of soldiers, the army must get mixed-up as to where they all are.'

'But it's been weeks,' argued Becky, eyes shining over the green eiderdown.

It had been a month since the telegram had arrived but Rowena was wise enough not to correct her.

'If he has been killed . . .' began Becky.

'He hasn't!' Rowena cut her off as Beany started to cry. 'The telegram said he was only missing – anyway, if anything had happened Mother would've told us, wouldn't she?'

This seemed to calm Becky, but Rowena's heart fluttered at the recollection of the burnt letters – Mother hadn't told them about those, had she? Oh please, God, don't let Father be dead. And while the others fell asleep she herself lay fretting almost until the dawn.

She had barely lost consciousness when angry voices were rousing her. 'Becky, you filthy pig, I'm sopping!' Rowena parted sticky eyelids. Two figures stood, arms outstretched, between the beds. The pink outline of their bodies shone clearly through the drenched nightgowns where it clung at thigh and buttock. Another pathetic figure sat amid a puddle of wet bed linen, tendrils of damp hair clinging round her neck.

'I'm sorry,' whimpered Becky as Rowena stumbled from her bed to attend the crisis. 'I didn't know I was doing it.'

'Why didn't you go before you went to bed?' demanded Lyn, beginning to shiver as the morning air cooled her dripping garment.

Becky protested that she had done, but her sisters continued to harangue until their noise drew Rachel into the affray. 'For pity's sake it's like a monkeys' teaparty in here!' She glared at the now naked figures. 'It's five o'clock in the morning!'

'Becky's wet the bed,' supplied Beany, clinging her arms around her nymphlike body and chattering her teeth.

Rachel went wild, dragged Becky from the bed, tearing at the saturated linen. 'As if I haven't enough to do!' She went to bang on the nursery door. 'Biddy, get up and put these sheets in to soak! Rebecca Hazelwood, you are a naughty child! How old are you supposed to be? Only babies wet the bed. Look at this mattress – oh, give me strength! If this happens again you are for it!'

This threat only served to worsen Becky's incontinence, for the next morning the mattress which had taken all day to dry was once again awash . . . and the next, and the next.

Charlie lay in his bed waiting for the yelps of complaint that had become his regular alarm call. 'Ugh, Wena, she's done it again!' And then in would storm Mrs Hazelwood and a sharp crack would follow which, Charlie knew, was

Becky receiving her punishment, and then would come the sound of sobs and Biddy stamping along the landing with the bundle of wet sheets and nightgowns.

The cracks seemed to get louder each time. Charlie could envision the red handprint on poor Becky's rear. On top of the worry over his father, it all grew too much for the boy, who was very fond of his red-haired sister. Consequently, he spent the hour before breakfast devising a plan to help her with her predicament. In the evening after the children were put to bed he crept down to their room, tapped on the door and, on admittance, told of his plan.

'Becky can come and sleep in my bed. And in the morning she can sneak back down and be dressed before your mother gets up.'

'She'll probably just soak your bed, Charlie,' said Rowena.

'I know, but I can keep that secret. Your mother never comes up to my room. I can dry the stuff when she goes out to work.'

Both Lyn and Beany agreed that this was a marvellous idea and were swift in pushing their sister from the bed to go with Charlie. It was rather a tight squeeze for two in the put-up bed, but Charlie dared not take any sheets to put on the spare one. However cramped, Rebecca much appreciated the kindness and told him so.

'Ssh, you'd better not talk in case your mother hears you,' warned Charlie.

'Oh yes, I forgot!' She kissed him and snuggled up. 'Goodnight, Charlie.'

In the morning, having no need of an alarm for the drenching served to wake him, Charlie hid his eyes while the child struggled with her clothes. Then, still in his own wet night attire, he stripped the bed and put the bottom sheet in the bowl he normally used for washing his face. The mattress was a fraction harder to deal with but, as he had forecast, he was able to dry this in front of the fire once Mrs Hazelwood had gone out . . . though after a week the stench of it was almost unbearable to sleep with.

'I'm sorry to keep doing it, Charlie,' Becky lamented on

yet another morning. 'I try and wake up in time but it's always too late. You can look now.'

Now that she was dressed, Charlie unveiled his eyes and rolled out of bed. 'It doesn't matter.' He picked up her wet nightgown between thumb and forefinger and carried it to the bowl.

Becky struggled to pull her stockings onto damp legs. 'I wonder if there'll be any news of Father today.'

'Maybe.' He used a pencil to press the garment under the water. Bits of it kept ballooning out.

Without warning she started to cry. Charlie turned from the bowl, not quite knowing what to say. 'He'll be all right, Beck.'

'But you don't know that!' It came as a sob. 'Three people in my class have had their fathers killed. Why doesn't Mother do more to find him?' This question was repeated later when the children, with no school to attend on this rainswept weekend, congregated in the girls' bedroom. 'Why doesn't she do something, Wena?' A tearful Becky pleaded with her sister who dared not speak her thoughts. 'She just sits there as if she doesn't care.'

'That's because she doesn't,' supplied Bertie, sitting on the bed, back propped up by the wall, an open book on his knees.

'Oh, what a rotten thing to say!' Becky jumped up from the rug to glare at him.

'It's true,' said Bertie. 'And I don't care either. I hope he has been killed.'

'You're a bloody bugger!' shouted Lyn and her sisters chorused their disapproval, Charlie too.

He came to sit on the bed beside his half-brother, about to give his opinion until Bertie snapped the book shut and said, 'That reminds me! I've got to clean some dogmuck off my shoes,' and made for the door. Before leaving, though, he gave a scathing addition. 'And if he has been killed it's your fault, you drove him away.'

Charlie looked into the girls' faces and saw that they held this belief too. 'I didn't want him to go away,' came his unhappy murmur. 'He's my father as well, you know.'

His half-sisters looked at each other. Somehow he still didn't feel like their brother. Even though they liked him, for he was a good-natured boy and was always doing things for them, he still didn't feel like part of them. Bertie did. Bertie, for all he lorded it over them and boasted, and was not so pleasant as this boy, *was* their brother.

Becky tried to lighten the negative mood. 'Well, I say we've waited long enough. We should do something about finding him.'

'Like pee the bed?' enquired Lyn. Becky went pink.

'There was no call to say that,' reprimanded Charlie. 'I took her in with me so she'd be spared your moaning. She can't help it, you know.' He put a supportive arm round Becky.

Lyn was contrite. 'Sorry . . . I agree with you, Beck, we should do something to find Father – but what?'

Beany had an idea. 'There's lots of soldiers on the Knavesmire we could ask some of them if they've seen Father.'

Charlie explained the futility of this. 'They haven't been to France yet, they've just joined up.' He looked at the collection of blank faces and said optimistically, 'Don't worry, something'll turn up.'

It did. The children found out from the newspaper that there was to be a military parade the next Sunday. 'If we can get mother to take us,' Rowena told the others excitedly, 'we might be able to talk to someone who can tell us where Father might be. There'll be thousands at the Minster. There's bound to be one among them who knows him.'

Sadly, before the children could make this suggestion, Rachel informed them that she would be out on Sunday morning. Not being very adept at business she had allowed one or two of her customers to run up large arrears. Sunday was the only day she was free to collect these. Though it was a job she did not relish.

'We hoped there might be somebody who's seen Father,' pressed Rowena. 'Couldn't you take us after church?'

Rachel felt the usual sickening jolt at the mention of her husband. Every time one of the children brought him into the conversation she was afraid their next question would be, 'Is he dead?', to which she would have to reply honestly. She had maintained the deception very well up to now, saving any tears for the privacy of the night. This ability may have been aided by the fact that she still couldn't believe it herself, felt numbed by it all. Each time she opened a drawer or a cupboard there were his belongings to bring him back to life. She looked at them all now and steeled herself to say it. They had a right to know – for goodness' sake it had been over a month! What if they learnt it from someone else? It was a wonder they hadn't already. Rachel had told no one outside of course – with being out at work all day she rarely had words for her neighbours. She wouldn't have told them anyway, it was none of their business and would only provide them with more to gossip about. But they may get to know of Russell's death from the casualty lists in the paper. As yet his name hadn't appeared – Rachel had checked thoroughly, for it would be dreadful if the children learnt of their father's death from an outsider. She must, she must tell them.

But even now cowardice prevailed. As on previous occasions she deflected the subject. 'I'm sure I'd much rather not have to be collecting debts but I have to put our livelihood first. I'll be going out very early and won't be back until dinner.' A dispirited Rowena asked, what about church? Rachel said that Biddy would take them. Biddy protested that she had her own church to go to. Rachel snapped that she would have to go to an earlier service in that case, and the argument was over.

'Sure, I don't see why I should have to get up at the crack o' dawn on a Sunday,' sulked Biddy in her mistress's absence. ''Tis the only bit o' rest I get.' A thoughtful Lyn asked where Biddy's church was situated and was told. 'A leg-ache from yours.'

'Yes, but where? Is it anywhere near the Minster?' Biddy told Lyn that it was, but asked why. 'Because I've an idea how you can get your sleep-in and get to church an' all.'

Sunday came. Biddy had told her mistress on the Saturday night that she had decided not to go to Mass so she wouldn't have to disturb Rachel by getting up early. After breakfast Rachel went about her debt-collecting. A short time later, Biddy set off with the children. When they got up to the main road they caught a tram, using their pocket money to do so. Rowena paid for Biddy's ticket. Bertie demanded that she pay his fare too. Although he didn't mind missing church he was adamant that this venture was a waste of time – he didn't even want to find his father and he definitely wasn't going to forfeit his pocket money in doing it.

'You won't tell Mother, Bertie, will you?' asked Rowena uncertainly.

'I might do,' he said airily.

Lyn rose up at the pomposity of his remark. 'You big turd.'

Blows were exchanged. 'Lyn, stop it,' ordered Rowena, and to Bertie in pleading manner, 'I'll buy you some invalid toffee. Please don't tell Mother. She'll be angry with Biddy for not taking us to church.'

'Why do they call it invalid toffee if anyone can eat it?' asked Beany.

Lyn bared her teeth. Her shoulder hurt where he had thumped her but she wouldn't rub it. 'I hope it makes him into an invalid! I hope his legs rot and his teeth drop out.'

'Lyn, please!' Rowena was becoming frantic in her efforts to win her brother over. 'Bertie, I'll buy you a full quarter if you don't tell.' It appeared that the pocket money she had saved was all going to be spent on him. He made a non-committal gesture and Rowena had to be satisfied with that.

Reaching Duncombe Place where vast crowds lined the route of the march, they said goodbye to Charlie and the Irish girl who warned them before slipping into her own church, 'Now be sure not to move from this here path till I come out.' She paused to study their innocent faces. The poor wee spalpeens, thinking they were going to find their daddy here . . . 'I'll light a candle for the master,' she said kindly before taking the last step into church.

'What does Father want a candle for?' frowned Lyn.

Rowena didn't know and turned to face the road. 'We'll never be able to see from here.'

Someone in the crowd heard this and made space for the children to squeeze to the front. Lyn smiled sweetly. 'Thank you so much.'

'What a polite child,' commented the woman to her neighbour.

Bertie decided with an exaggerated yawn that he wasn't going to wait around here all day. 'Give me the money and I'll go an' get me own toffee.' Rowena reminded him of Biddy's order. 'D'you think I'm off to take any notice of what that dummy says? If you don't give me the money I *will* tell Mother and old Biddy Buggery will get the chop.'

Rowena nudged him for the swearword in public, but was compelled to fund the purchase. 'But please, Bertie, don't get lost. Take a note of the landmarks.'

He sighed and gestured at the Minster. 'I can hardly miss that, can I? Anyway, I'm not coming back I'm off straight home.' With this he disappeared into the crowd.

Rowena looked extremely worried and showed annoyance at Lyn who said, 'I wish it was Bertie who'd gone missing and not Father.'

'Oh, they're here!' Becky shouted as two columns of men appeared and began to march along the final stretch of route to the Cathedral.

'Where's the band then?' Lyn grabbed a handful of her eldest sister's bodice and swung her head out to get a better view. Normally the first indication of the parade would be the distant sound of a band which would gradually become louder and louder and then burst upon the spectators in chromatic brilliance: trumpets, trombones, bassoons sparkling in the sunshine, and of course the blood-stirring thump of the bass drum . . . There was none of this today. The only rhythm was the clip of boots. Instead of colourful dress uniforms everyone wore standard khaki. The only splash of red to be seen was at the throats of the boy scouts who marched with the parade.

'What're they doing?' asked Beany as a fleet of VAD ambulances crawled into view.

'They're bringing the wounded heroes to attend the service, dear,' the woman nearby informed her.

Beany cast a worried glance at her eldest sister. But Rowena shook her head positively. 'Father won't be in one of those, he's only missing.'

Then Becky leapt into the air and stabbed a finger. 'He's there! Oh, Wena, look he's there . . . oh.' Her face collapsed as the man drew near enough for her to see that it was not her father after all. 'It isn't him.' The finger fell back to entwine its blighted hopes in a strand of red hair.

'Clod-pate!' Lyn was equally disappointed.

Rowena, seeing the downcast face, placed a comforting hand on Becky's shoulder. 'We didn't really expect to find Father here you know, Beck. He's probably somewhere in France.' Oh I do hope so, came the desperate thought.

The pathetic countenance was lifted to hers. 'Then why did we come?'

'To ask any of these soldiers if they've seen him.' The men continued to file past and Rowena leaned forward. 'Excuse me!' Her politeness went unnoticed. 'Oh heck – excuse me!' she shouted a little louder. One soldier appeared to look at her. 'Do you know my father, Mr Hazelwood? He . . . oh, he won't stop!' The eyes had left her as the soldier continued past. Lyn suggested that she run alongside. 'But Biddy said we had to stay here . . . oh, all right!' Rowena dashed into the road and tried to keep march with the nearest soldier. 'I'm sorry to trouble you but do you know my father Mr Hazelwood? We had a telegram to say he was missing and we're trying to find someone who might know where he is.'

'Sorry, pet,' muttered the soldier. 'Don't know him.'

Rowena fell back to ask the man behind, only to get the same response.

'What regiment is he with?' asked a more sympathetic listener. Rowena's black stockinged legs moved like pistons to keep up with him, lifting her pinafore. 'I'm not sure, but I think he's a captain – or a sergeant.'

'Captain Hazelwood?' The officer shook his head. 'I'm sorry, my dear. There are so many regiments, you see.'

'Please could you find out for us?' begged Rowena earnestly. 'Anything at all, we'd be so grateful.'

'I'll see what I can do,' promised the officer and at her smile of gratitude marched on, leaving her to find her way back to the others.

Infected by her enthusiasm, the younger girls asked, 'Have you found someone who knows him?'

'No, but someone's promised to help,' she panted through a relieved smile. 'Oh, I feel much better!'

Her relief was somewhat diffused when she had to explain to Biddy where her brother was. 'Oh, glorious Son o' Heaven! That boy will get me hung. If he should arrive home on his own an' the missus is there . . . Come on! We'd best get our skates on.'

'Biddy Kelly, can I never trust you?' shouted Rachel when her arrival on the doorstep coincided with theirs and the maid was forced to admit that Master Robert had wanted to come on his own.

'Sure, 'tis only a few yards from the church, ma'am,' said Biddy, praying fervently that Bertie would be inside to greet them.

Her faith was rewarded when they entered to the sound of Bertie's footsteps creaking the bedroom floorboards. 'It's just as well for you!' Rachel pointed a rigid finger. 'If anything had happened to that boy – go get the vegetables ready for dinner!' She herself opened the door to the front parlour, the children followed her in. 'Was it a good service?'

'Oh . . . er.' Luckily for Rowena her mother, as usual, didn't wait for an answer. 'Needless to say all my footwork was for nothing. Not one penny! Not one penny have I collected. Pretended they weren't in – gone to church, one neighbour said. Imagine it! I don't know how they can sit before their Maker with consciences like they must have.'

'So won't you get your money, Mother?' asked Beany, quick to move the topic from the church.

'Oh, I'll get it all right!' Rachel wore her Sunday best – a lilac skirt, a jacket to match with flounced cuffs and a trickle of lace at her breast, amethyst earrings, white shoes and gloves. She tugged these off and laid them neatly on the sideboard. 'I'm sick of being taken advantage of. They won't expect me to call again on the same day but I shall. I'll go after dark so they can't see who's at the door without answering it, then let them pretend they aren't in! Right, I think I'll just go and soak my feet before dinner.' Jabber, jabber, jabber, she rebuked herself. It's no good, you'll have to tell them. I'll tell them after dinner. No you won't, coward. Yes, I will! She started across the room. 'And you children had better wash your hands and faces too!'

Dashing up the stairs she opened the bedroom door . . . and came face to face with a ghost.

CHAPTER TWENTY-THREE

'There must've been some mix-up,' said a waxen-faced Russ as the joyful girls danced around him, pulling his head down to smother it in kisses – 'Oh Father, Father, you're safe!' They had heard Rachel scream and immediately poured up the stairs. Charlie hadn't caught the commotion, being enthroned on the outside lavatory at the time. 'I've been in hospital. I thought you'd been officially informed.'

The girls' happiness turned to vociferous concern. 'Hospital?'

'No, I'm all right now,' he reassured them, smiling. 'It was only a whiff of gas that put me out of action.' Only a whiff of gas . . . he suppressed a shudder as he relived that moment of incomprehension, then the terrible scouring of his nostrils, his throat, his lungs; the weeks of pain, sickness and diarrhoea – and apparently this made him one of the lucky ones! On release from hospital he had been sent to a training camp where the instructors had set about repairing his lack of stamina by driving him round and round the parade ground, 'Get those knees up, you bloody waster!' while his lungs had screamed and his legs had buckled . . . and Rachel had known none of this.

After her first expostulation, 'I thought you were dead!' his wife had made no other offering, too faint for speech. But now the fury surged through her at the Army's incompetence. 'Come along now, children, you can see your father later,' she said in a voice that advertised its anger. 'He must be tired and I want to speak to him privately.' She shoved the happy girls from the room, then spun to glare at him. 'Would you like to tell me how on earth the Army could say you were dead when you were in one of their own hospitals?'

'I wish I knew! Bloody staff. I can only think . . .' Russ sought for explanation. 'Well, after a battle men aren't always in one piece.' His voice had softened and he glanced at her. 'Some of them literally disappear off the face of the earth.'

'But you didn't! You're here!'

He sighed. 'I know, I know . . . but there's hundreds of thousands of men over there, Rachel. There might be two or three or even half a dozen with the same name and rank . . .'

'But you all have different numbers!'

'For Christ's sake I'm just trying to think of an explanation! It could be something as daft as a staff wallah picking the wrong form up!' He controlled his temper and said firmly, 'I'm sorry, if I'd known what was going on I would've let you know I was safe, but I expected they'd have told you where I was. I thought when you didn't bother to come and visit me at the hospital that you didn't care . . . There didn't seem much point in writing when you hadn't replied to any of my other letters.'

'I burnt them – but that's no excuse for the Army's laxity! They told me you were dead!'

He stared at her for two seconds, then turned away to rest his weary body on the bed they had once shared. 'I'm sorry, it must be very disappointing for you to have me turn up like this. I'll try to oblige when I go back.'

'Oh, you *are* going back then?' She stood, arms akimbo, watching him.

'Try not to sound too upset about it, Rachel.' He gave her a humourless smile. 'Now that they got me back in A1 condition they've given me seven days' leave before sticking me back in the jam.' He moved his head emphatically. 'Oh , if I could get out of it I would, believe me. I must've been mad to go in the first place.'

Her response was brusque. 'It was your own decision, wasn't it? No one drove you to it.'

'No . . . they didn't. Were the children very upset when they thought . . . ?'

'Thankfully I hadn't got round to telling them! They only knew that you were missing.'

'Well, that's something I suppose.' Russ leaned on his knees and stared at the floor.

She studied his slumped posture. 'I can't nurse you, you know.'

'I don't expect you to,' was his subdued answer. 'Anyway, I've told you I'm fit and well.'

He certainly didn't look it – looked old and worn out, his skin pasty. She would have had to look twice to recognize him on the street. 'Yes, well . . . as long as you understand that I have the shop to see to . . . can't be running up and down for invalids.'

He looked up. 'Jimmy's gone to the war, then?'

'Oh yes, I forgot, you wouldn't know about that.' She crossed her arms. 'In fact there's a lot of things you don't know – the main one being that the boy is still here.'

Surprise ejected him from the bed. 'Still . . . ? I knew he was here at Christmas, but . . .' He tried to make sense of this. 'Well why hasn't the priest come?'

She told him of Father Guillaume's decision to go to Belgium and at his gasp cried, 'Yes! He's another one who's more concerned with helping a bunch of foreigners than seeing to his duties here.'

'Oh, Christ . . .' He fell back on the bed, hands pushed under cheekbones. 'I'm truly, truly sorry for putting you through this, Rachel. I'd never have gone and left you with it if I'd thought the boy would be staying this long . . . How long does the priest intend to leave him here, did he say?'

'For the duration of the war,' said Rachel evenly. 'But that will be over by Christmas, won't it?' She turned her haughty face away, then noticed his kitbag and bridled. 'I hope you aren't expecting to sleep in here?'

His blue eyes toured her face for long moments. The spark had gone from them. Then wordlessly he pressed himself from the bed and went to pick up his kit.

A stab of conscience urged her to say, 'You don't have to do that now . . . Biddy will set up the other bed later. I expect you'll want something to eat?' At his grateful nod she opened the door. 'Come down to the kitchen then.'

Whilst she had been upstairs, Bertie had arrived. His

345

mother gave little rebuke other than to say he should stay with the others in future. There was no mention of the military parade. Charlie, having been told the good news by the girls, was waiting to greet his father, face beaming. But Russell's eyes went straight to his other son. 'My, Bertie – long trousers! You've grown into a real man.' There was a sudden flush on Bertie's face which Russ deciphered as pleasure. But when the boy spun and left the room he knew it for fancy and sagged into a chair.

The girls hounded him for tales of the war which he tried to deflect as best he could. Strange that it was the girls who asked questions and not Charlie, who used to be so eager to learn about his father's career. Russ chanced a look at the boy's face. At once the crooked smile was there . . . but the unguarded expression that had preceded it had been studious with just a hint of compassion – not a normal boy's expression at all. But then what was a normal boy, Russ asked himself as he turned away, thinking of the youngsters in the trenches. He had been much relieved to find that Dobson had not suffered in the gas attack, having received a letter from the lad while he was in hospital. He still did not know who had saved his life though.

Their questions wearied him. After lunch – in which Bertie refused to participate – he asked his wife if she would mind him having a lie down. 'I was up early this morning. I'm feeling pretty worn-out.'

To the children's chagrin he slept all afternoon. There was discussion as to what they could do to amuse themselves. Sometimes, Mother would take them for a walk but today she had boarded herself in the front parlour. Biddy was absent too, visiting her parents. Rowena wished she could get away as well; she just wanted to sit in a quiet corner and think of a way to heal her parents' marriage; instead, being the eldest girl, she was forced to look after these rowdies. She suggested they go and see the Army horses tethered on the greenbelt, which met with approval.

Becky said that she was just going to the lavatory and they should go on ahead. However, after they had gone she made no move to leave the kitchen, consumed with thoughts of her father. What must it feel like to be gassed? A girl she knew had had gas at the dentist but she hadn't needed to go to hospital after it. Was it anything to do with her father being a sinner? Had it been punishment? Poor Father, he looked so ill . . .

In the parlour Rachel's thoughts were with him too, though they were much angrier thoughts. Then she sniffed. That smells like . . . another sniff . . . gas! Jumping up she opened the door. The smell grew stronger. 'That stupid Biddy Kelly . . .' She marched into the kitchen – and there was Rebecca with her nose to the gaspoint!

Oh no, not another one! She ran over, dragged the suicidal girl away and turned the gastap off, then threw open all the doors and windows, finally catching hold of Becky and pushing her out into the yard, ordering her to 'Breathe deeply!'

Becky, who had only taken a few sniffs of the gas, recovered very quickly. Seeing she was all right, Rachel sighed her relief and helped her back inside to sit on a chair. 'Oh, my God!' She clutched her head, cursing her husband. 'Is he trying to smash this entire family – Rebecca love, why didn't you say you were upset instead of trying to kill yourself?'

Becky looked perplexed. 'Can gas kill you?'

'Of course it can!' Then Rachel frowned. 'Isn't that what you were trying to do?'

'Oh no,' replied Becky. 'I just wanted to know what Father felt like.'

Rachel's emotion changed to anger. 'For heaven's sake you could have blown the house to smithereens and us with it! You stupid girl!' With another oath, she grabbed the door handle and underwent a rapid opening and shutting process, trying to help the gas on its way. Becky hung her head. This attitude irked Rachel and reaching for her daughter she thrust her into the yard. 'Off you go – out! Until you can behave sensibly!' She continued her attempts to waft the gas from the house for a while longer. Then, out of spite for her husband who lay sleeping upstairs, she slammed the door loudly – see how you like that! Coming back here, putting stupid ideas into the children's heads – and stormed back to the parlour where she fumed for a good while longer. The token was wasted; Russ, used to sleeping through much worse, never heard the door bang, but slumbered on until teatime when Charlie was sent to fetch him.

The boy opened the attic door then, seeing that his father still slept, lightened his footstep and approached the bed. Forgetting that he had been sent to rouse Russ, he just stood there looking down at him. Sleep was the one time when his father didn't look upon him with resentment – Charlie didn't want to spoil the moment. Yet even in repose there was something in his father's expression that saddened him – a crease to the brow, spelling a torment that even sleep could not erase . . . Russ' eyelids flickered, lifted slightly, then came wide awake at the sight of the brown face that smiled down at him. Once his mind became adjusted he relaxed, 'Oh, it's you,' yawned and stretched. There it had been again – that look he had seen downstairs. Charlie was balanced on the edge of his bed. With the latter pushed against the wall Russ was unable to roll off it without asking Charlie to move. He lay there for a spell, hands tucked beneath head, and fixed bleary eyes on the boy who had caused so much destruction. 'Looks like you're going to be here for a while, then.'

'Just while the war's on,' answered Charlie.

'That could be years. Years and years . . .'

'Oh no, the papers say we're winning,' said Charlie with certainty. 'I've been following all the battles and I know all the French names. I've got this chart, well it's like a map and you stick flags into it to mark our progress and . . .

Russ interrupted. 'Apart from that, what else have you been doing with yourself? Does Mrs Hazelwood let you go out now?'

'Oh yes, I go to church and I sometimes walk with the girls to school then take a stroll on the Knavesmire. Then I come back and help Biddy.'

'In the kitchen? That won't help your education much.'

'Mrs Hazelwood allows me to get books from the library.'

Russ shook his head. 'You need a proper education. I wonder if we could get in touch with Father Guillaume. He'd tell us the best place to send you.'

Charlie felt pleased that his father cared enough to want to send him to the best school. 'Will it be in York?'

'Shouldn't think so.' Russ started to raise himself, forcing Charlie to get off the bed. 'Anyway come on, we'll go down and have some tea, then I'll take a look at that letter he sent, see if it's got an address.'

'It has,' Charlie told him as they went down. 'I've written to him myself.'

Bertie heard the two chatting as they passed from the landing to the stairs. He had been shocked at the sight of his father, who looked skinny and old. And with that one sighting all the pain and the unrest had come rushing back. Bertie didn't know what to do. So he stayed where he was.

Russ didn't need to ask why his son was not at the tea table, but said to his wife, 'I'll take mine in the other room if it'll make things easier. I wouldn't want Bertie to feel ostracized.'

'What's that mean?' asked Beany.

Rachel seated herself, ignoring the child's question. 'He won't come down, locked himself in his bedroom. I don't know where he found the key. It's been missing for ages. I'll take him something later. It's no use forcing him to sit with us if he doesn't want to.'

'Mother, what's ostracized?'

'I was just saying to Charlie that he should be at school,' said Russ, waiting to be offered food like a guest. 'It could be ages before the priest comes for him. He's been without education for a year. I don't suppose Father Guillaume was expecting it to last this long – the war I mean.'

'Father, what's . . .'

'Robina, do be quiet!' snapped Rachel, frowning her annoyance both at her daughter and Russ' statement. 'I won't have him going to Robert's school and causing more trouble for him!'

Bitch! thought Charlie, what do I want to go to his school for? He felt a reassuring hand on his knee and smiled at Becky.

'I was thinking along the lines of a Catholic establishment,' said Russ. 'That's what he's always been used to. Anyway, Father Guillaume can help us with that one.' He asked Rachel if he might see the letter the priest had sent.

'I don't see why not, it was addressed to you. I'll get it after tea.' She saw that he was not eating and added, 'Well, you'd better help yourself.'

Later he read the letter, and said that as the priest was now in Belgium he might as well wait and give his reply to the Red Cross when he got back there himself. Here, the children expressed acute dismay. He assured them that it wasn't so bad and promised to come and see them again as soon as he could. 'And I'll tie a label round my neck this time so I don't get lost again.'

'Might you bring the doll next time you come?'

He looked down at Beany. 'I will indeed – I would have brought it this time if I hadn't come home on a stretcher. I have brought one or two souvenirs, though I don't know if they'll interest you lasses. They're only German badges and whatnot. I brought you something,' he told his wife, and went off to fetch it.

On being offered the silver mug, Rachel merely sniffed. 'Looted, I suppose.'

'The house had been shelled. It seemed a waste, leaving all that good stuff lying around. If I hadn't picked it up someone else would've.'

'Oh, I'm quite sure they would! Have none of you soldiers any scruples?'

'No, they give us lime juice to prevent that.' Russ lectured himself – you should know better than to waste a joke on her.

A small hand felt its way into his. He smiled down at Becky. 'Can I whisper?' came her request.

'It's not very polite to . . .' began Russ. Then bent down and put his ear at her disposal. 'Oh, go on then!'

She shielded her words from the others with a hand, 'I don't mind you being a sinner, Father,' and drew back to smile encouragingly.

'Oh . . . well, thank you, me love.' Discountenanced, he

kissed her hand and straightened his spine. What on earth had their mother been telling them?

'That tooth fairy didn't come,' said Lyn, testing him.

'Didn't he?' Russ arched his eyebrows. 'The varmint! I'll have to have another word with him.'

He had failed the test. Lyn looked him in the eye. 'Bertie says there isn't a tooth fairy. He says it's you who takes our teeth.' She saw his face flinch. 'He says you tell lies.'

Her sisters flexed their shoulders, anticipating an outburst from their mother, but the voice was merely cool. 'If you've finished eating you can go out and play until supper.' Rachel wasn't going to defend him – he *was* a liar.

Russ watched them trail from the room. When they had gone he turned to his wife and said quietly, 'I sent her a little note . . . you must've burnt it?'

'If it was in an envelope addressed to me I will have done!' Rachel opened the door of the scullery and told Biddy to take a tray up to Master Robert.

After Biddy had passed through on her way to the stairs, Russ murmured, 'That's what she thinks of her father . . . that I'm a liar . . . because you burnt the letter.'

'Don't blame me for your inadequacies as a father!' Rachel whirled as Biddy came back down to say the boy wouldn't answer. 'Really, Biddy! I don't know what I pay you for!' She grabbed the tray and made for the stairs.

However, she too failed to receive an answer and after several harsh raps – 'Robert, I demand that you open this door!' – was forced to return to the kitchen. 'That boy is so infuriating at times!' She slammed the scullery door on Biddy who had gone back in to wash up.

'I hoped he might be over it by now,' replied her husband sadly.

'And so he was until you showed your face!' Rachel started to walk away, then stopped and clapped a hand to her brow. 'Oh my God, I haven't told you that, have I?' Ordering him to sit down she gave a résumé of the shooting incident.

He interspersed her monologue with groans. When she had finished he gave a prolonged sigh and tilted his skull over the back of the dining chair, facing the ceiling. 'I knew he'd taken it badly but my God . . . well that's made my mind up about sending Charlie to school.'

'It's going to cost money you know. The uniform and everything.'

'I'm quite prepared . . .'

'*You're* quite prepared? Who's slaving to earn that money, might I ask? You don't imagine that ten of us can exist on the pittance we get from the Army?' He asked if she had not received the money for the car. 'I've no intention of breaking into that! This war might last for ages.'

'We're not that hard up, Rachel – and you do want to be rid of him, don't you?'

'I certainly do! But completely, I don't want him coming back here every evening.'

'I'm talking about a boarding school, you'd only have to see him in the holidays – and not even then if you didn't want to. Let me arrange it for you before I go back.'

'Make penance for your guilt, you mean.'

'Whatever you like,' he replied tiredly. After a gap he had a sudden thought. 'Have you had any more trouble from that NSPCC woman?'

'No – and it's no thanks to you I might add! Why did you have to go and tell her he'd gone back? I would've looked a proper fool if she'd allowed me to get my words out. After she said what you'd told her I had to go along with the pretence.'

'I thought I was doing you a favour.'

'God protect me from your favours! It's only because this war's still on that I haven't heard from her and if the schools weren't all to pot you can be sure we'd have some busybody banging on the door enquiring about your precious Charlie's education – but are they bothered about *my* children's schooling? Oh no!' The children had only just been allowed back into their normal school buildings.

Russ lost patience. 'Well if we get Charlie into boarding school we won't have to worry about that, will we?'

Instead of snapping, she mulled this over. 'I agree it would be worth the money. It would help Robert too, having him out of the way.'

'I made the suggestion as much for Robert as for you. I can't bear the way he looks at me . . . d'you think if I took that tray up he might let me in? I'd like to have the chance to talk to him before I go . . . just in case.'

She gave him a scornful look. 'I think you should leave well alone.'

'But he *isn't* well, is he?'

'Just leave my son to me! I know best what his needs are.'

'Rachel, I'm . . . I'm frightened I'm going to die before I can make it up to him. I was nearly a goner this time . . . I couldn't have him spending the rest of his life hating me.'

'That's all you're concerned about, isn't it?' Her eyes were vicious slits. 'That you've slipped in his estimation. You don't really care what Robert's going through, you just want his forgiveness. If you genuinely cared for him as much as you make out then you'd see what your presence here has done to him – he was just beginning to settle down . . . Probing his wound isn't going to heal it. Just leave him alone!'

He sat looking at her for a while, then enquired tiredly, 'Would I be upsetting anybody if I went to bed?'

Her theatrical look at the clock forced him to explain, 'I know it's early, but we don't get very much sleep on the front. We have to make the most of it while we can.' He rose, shoving back the chair with his calves. 'I'll nip out and say goodnight to the girls.'

His daughters thought it was a huge joke that Father was going to bed before they were. 'Aren't you even going to tell us a story?' asked Lyn as he turned to go in.

He looked back at her. The little face was aggressive. He came back and put a hand on the knobbly shoulder. 'I did send the money for your tooth, you know, but it must have got lost in the post.' He wouldn't tell her that her mother had destroyed the letter.

'Why did you always pretend that it came from a fairy?' she demanded.

He sat on the garden wall, hands rubbing knees. 'It's nice to believe in magic, isn't it?'

She took a while to decide that it was. 'But it's not nice to lie.'

353

He moved his head in agreement. 'Sometimes though, Lyn, it's kinder to tell a lie, just a white one so people don't get hurt.' He dug into his pocket for a sixpence. 'There you are, that's for your tooth – with interest.' Two more of the girls said that they had lost teeth while he had been away. Russ laughed and delved back in his pocket. 'I suppose you'd all better have one.' A handful of change was withdrawn and the coins selected.

'Don't forget Charlie,' Becky told him.

How the hell could I forget him? thought Russ and handed each child sixpence. 'That can take the place of a story tonight. I'm a bit tired. But I'm going to be here for a full week so we'll have plenty of time for stories.'

'And football matches?' suggested Lyn.

'Aye, good idea,' nodded Russ, then kissed them good-night. Charlie stood twiddling his sixpence, watching enviously.

Before her father had reached the door Rowena chased after him to say in a low voice, 'I would've replied to your note Father, if Mother had given it to us.'

Russ looked stern. 'How did you know about that – I hope you haven't been reading your mother's letters?'

Realizing what she had done, Rowena blushed. 'I didn't mean to . . . I was just worried that we hadn't heard from you . . . do you know that mother's been burning your letters?' He nodded. 'I only took one – and I didn't read it properly, I just wanted to know you were safe. I was going to write to you but I didn't know where to send it. Could you tell me so I can write when you go back?'

He touched her face. 'It's a very kind thought, lass and I'd love to hear from you . . . but I think it might get you into trouble with your mother . . .'

'It could be a secret . . .'

'No, that's not fair. Your mother's done a lot for you, it wouldn't be right to go behind her back. I won't be lonely if I know you're thinking about me.' He kissed her once more and went inside.

When Rowena joined the others Becky exclaimed, 'Oh Charlie, I won't be able to sleep with you, will I? Father'll be there.'

Lyn groaned at the thought of a drenching. 'I wish he hadn't bothered to come now.'

Charlie rebuked her. 'Well I'm glad to see him.'

'Huh, I don't see why, he only wants to get rid of you.' She was asked what made her think that. 'I heard him and mother arranging for you to go away to boarding school.'

'That's because he cares about my education!' corrected Charlie and stalked off to the other side of the road to lean on the railings.

'You've upset him now, meanie,' scolded her red-haired sister.

'Well I'm sick of him!' spat Lyn. 'It's him that's made Father and Mother maungy. Everything's gone wrong since he came – and now we have to put up wi' you peeing our bed again!'

Rowena tried to end the argument. 'Becky can come in with me and you can have Rhona.'

'We don't want her! She's always trumping.'

Russ could hear them quarrelling as he plodded up the staircase. Bloody women, came the weary thought. As soon as they're born they're moaning. On the landing he paused to look at his son's door, then defied his wife by tapping on it. 'Bertie? It's Father . . . your mother's worried about you, lad. I know my coming back has upset you, but don't take it out on her. You've got to eat . . . I'm going to bed now so if you want to go down I shan't be there to annoy you.' He turned the knob. 'Bertie?' At the silence, he turned to the attic stairs, then revolved to add softly, 'When I go back you can have the birds' egg collection. I'd like you to have it now, just in case anything happens to me.' Still no answer. 'Anyway . . . goodnight, son.' He finally retired.

Russ was woken by banging in what he assumed to be the middle of the night but was in fact only nine o'clock. The rude awakening produced a wave of nausea and he rolled over in discomfort. The banging grew more frantic. He opened his eyes to a shady presence.

'It's Mrs Hazelwood.' Charlie, clad in pyjamas, was quick to explain that it hadn't been him who had woken his father. 'Bertie still won't come out.'

With a grunt, Russ swallowed the bile that had leapt to his throat and rolled to his other side. Soon though, the din compelled him to rise and stagger down to the landing.

'He won't come out!' announced Rachel. 'Won't answer at all.' She noticed that the girls had come to see what was amiss. 'Get back into bed!' They jumped and disappeared. Rachel's eyes conveyed her fears to her husband. 'What if he's harmed himself?'

Even after hearing about the gun incident the thought hadn't occurred to Russ, but it now had the effect of piercing his befuddlement. 'Move out of the way!' With one more unanswered shout to his son, Russ rammed his shoulder at the door several times. It would not yield and he rushed downstairs to fetch a screwdriver, with which he eventually removed the lock.

Rachel stood back as he prepared to open the door, picturing Bertie swinging by his neck from the light fitting. The door was opened – the curtains billowed at the sudden draught, continuing to ripple over the open window. There was no dangling body. The room was empty. Rachel went into hysterics and hurled every possible abuse at her husband. 'It's all your fault! You've driven him from his home!'

There followed a feverish search for a note, but none was found. Russ combed his fingers through his hair and stated his intention. 'I'll go for the police.'

Russ searched throughout the night – searched not just the endless rows of buildings but his mind too, trying to think of what to say to Bertie when he found him. Sorry, was no good. It hadn't worked before and it wouldn't work now. This wasn't an ordinary upset; Bertie really hated him, must do, to feel incapable of being in the same house even for a few days. The only comfort he could give his son was to say he wouldn't come home again. That would mean he would be parted from his little girls . . . but it was the price he must pay, he couldn't have his son driven into exile.

There was no need to make this promise. By morning he had patrolled every street, every back lane on South Bank, he had toured the riverside, had gone right into town, but he had not found his son. Leaden-hearted, he made his way home in the hope that the police had had more luck.

They hadn't – Rachel's face told him that the moment he was through the door. 'Did you search the woods?' she hectored as he coaxed Lyn out of her chair and sat in her place.

'There wasn't much point till it got light.' He hunched over the table.

'Well it's light now!'

'Yes,' he answered tautly. 'I just thought I might have a cup of tea before I set about that job. I have been on my feet all night.'

Rowena brought her father a cup of tea. She had been up for hours, not just out of concern for Bertie but because of the wet sheets. She had enlisted Biddy's help with these. They were hanging out on the line. Mother was too preoccupied to notice and so Becky had escaped punishment.

Unsmiling, Rachel ordered the maid to fetch her master some breakfast.

'No, tea'll do, Biddy,' insisted Russ quietly. 'I couldn't face anything more.'

Rachel looked at the clock and said, 'Schooltime.'

Some of the girls showed reluctance to go while Bertie was missing.

'Couldn't we just wait till he gets home?' asked Becky.

'The last thing I want is you under my feet, Rebecca. Now go along.'

After they had left, Russ asked his wife if he should call on the neighbours to find out if they'd seen Robert. She replied that she had already done this last night and again this morning while he had been out searching. 'Nobody's seen him.'

He pulled his lips from the cup sharply; the tea was red hot; he blew on it. 'You asked everybody?'

'Yes, of co . . . course I have!' Her impatience hid the fact that she had excluded Ella Daw from her enquiries – she wasn't going to lower herself by knocking on that door, and anyway Ella wouldn't have been very helpful.

'Do you want me to carry on searching then?' Russ tried his tea again. 'Or shall I give you some help at the shop?'

'You don't think I'm opening the shop today!' she almost yelled. 'What sort of mother do you think I am? I must be here in case he comes home.'

Tiredly, he acquiesced and, after succeeding in drinking his tea, hauled his tortured body back onto the street to look for his son. The search of Knavesmire Wood where he had been found after his last abscondment turned up nothing. Two days later Bertie was still missing. Rachel was almost demented with worry. Her husband tried to persuade her that it might take her mind off things if she opened the shop and for this reason only she agreed to do so. 'I might as well be there! He isn't likely to come home while you're about.'

She wants me to say I'll go back to my unit now, perceived Russ. But I won't – I can't. It would be hell enough going back when his leave was up, he couldn't bring the day of reckoning forward. Instead, he volunteered, 'Would you like me to come and help?'

'No I would not! You'd be better employed looking for your son – your legitimate son, I mean.' She held her feathered hat with one hand and rammed a pin into place with the other.

'Rachel, I have searched every blasted inch of town, there's nowhere else to look!'

'Go down to the police station and see if they've got any news! I don't want to be cooped up all day in that shop with you, I want to be on my own!' She marched down the passage, struggling into her light jacket.

Russ put his cap on, gave an angry tug at the peak and followed, waving aside her impatient glare with, 'Don't worry! You won't have to be seen with me, I'll walk six paces behind.' He dreaded to think what she'd do to him if she knew that this uniform had not long ago been infested with lice. Had it not been fumigated while he was in hospital he would no doubt have brought her a few little strangers home.

The front door was opened and sunlight streamed down the passage. Rachel stepped out, leaving the door for her husband to close. Ella happened to be leaving too. Rachel did not speak to her. Russ, forgetting the antipathy between the two, raised his cap. 'Morning, Ella.'

She acknowledged him with a curt nod. 'Honoured to be on leave, aren't you? I haven't seen my Jack since he went.'

'I got gassed.' He didn't know why she should make him feel guilty. 'I've been in hospital.'

So, that's what the telegram had been about. Ella's attitude changed. 'I'm sorry to hear that, Russ. I haven't had a letter from my Jack in ages.' She moved through the gate. 'He's in charge of you again, so he said in his last letter.' She threw a gloating look at Rachel who turned her nose up – he hadn't mentioned *that* to her. 'Yes, he's done very well for himself has Jack – Second-Lieutenant.' She latched the gate. 'Still a corporal are you, Russ?' You shouldn't tease, she chided herself as Rachel began to prance away, he's got enough folk round here on his back. She added more conversationally to Russ, 'See your Bertie's following in Father's footsteps.'

Rachel stiffened and turned slowly. 'What did you say?'

Ella directed her face from the man's to the woman's. 'Saw him marching along to the railway with another batch the other day.' She noticed their startled faces. 'Don't tell me you didn't know?'

Russ wheeled on his wife. 'I thought you said you'd asked everybody!'

But she ignored him to shriek at Ella, mincing right up to her. 'He isn't thirteen years old! Do you think we'd sit and let him join the Army? Why didn't you tell us before?'

Ella was shirty again. 'Rachel, you made it quite plain that your family is none of my concern.'

'But this is an emergency! He's been missing for two days!'

'And I'm supposed to know that, am I, when you've never spoken to me in months?'

Russ cut the argument short. 'What day did you see him, Ella?' He was told Monday.

'You watched him march away to his death and didn't say a word!' cried Rachel.

359

Ella drew in her jaw, creating three chins. 'Well I thought you'd know all about it since you're always keen to impress upon me how close you and your children are!' With this she stalked off down the street.

Once the wave of disbelief had ebbed, Rachel spun on her husband. 'You've got to go and fetch him back! Don't wait for your leave to be up – go now! He's my son and he's going to be killed!'

She swept back into the house, barging into the kitchen where a surprised maid and Charlie surveyed her from the sink. She levelled a trembling finger under the boy's nose. 'If anything happens to him . . .' Suffused with emotion, she could say no more, her finger like a deranged metronome.

Russ tried to put a comforting arm round her but she hurled it off. 'What are you still doing here? Get your bags and go!'

Charlie dared to ask his father what had happened. 'Bertie's joined up,' replied the man coldly. Then to his wife, 'I'll go now.' He looked at the three of them, then went upstairs to collect his kitbag and a photograph of his son.

CHAPTER TWENTY-FOUR

On leaving, he went directly to the War Office and informed them of the situation. A promise was made that everything humanly possible would be done to find his son. In the meantime, Russ visited both the railway sidings and the station to interrogate ticket collectors, guards and the stationmaster about a contingent of recruits for the King's Own Yorkshire North Riding regiment who had left York two days ago. All were very sympathetic when he explained his reason for asking. Several lists were consulted, but eventually he was informed that there had been no contingent of KOYNeRs in that period. Could his son have joined the York and Lancs or the KOYLIs? Russ nodded and said it was possible, though it subdued him to think that his son had even scorned his father's regiment.

Whatever regiment Bertie had chosen, he was still no nearer to being found. It was a very worried man who boarded the southbound train some time later. When he reached Southampton he made more enquiries but was again thwarted. There were so many troopships leaving for the front every day full of underage boys, who would notice another one? There was some refuge to be found in the fact that Bertie would have to undergo training before being sent over to France. Maybe the Army would run him to ground before he faced the guns. This reassuring sentence was included in the letter he wrote to his wife. She would not burn this envelope; it might contain news of her son. Russ also dashed off a letter to Father Guillaume, telling him that Mrs Hazelwood could not stand any more of Charlie and that the priest must make arrangements for the boy to attend boarding school at Russ' expense. Even as he wrote he could hear the faint booming of the guns on the other side of the Channel. It induced a churning in his bowels. That was what he was going back to. He dropped the pencil and buried his head in his hands, squashing nose and mouth. Oh Christ! Will they get me this time?

On the boat over to France he was surrounded by new recruits, laughing and joking, smart uniforms, neat haircuts. Because of the urgent need for reinforcements he did not have to pass through the dreaded Bullring with them, but went directly to his unit in Belgium.

Ironic, that he should have to come to the middle of a war to find someone who was glad to see him. Dobson and the rest of his comrades greeted his return with an effusive bout of swearing. 'Oh, friggin' hell we thought we'd seen the last of this old bastard! Who said they'd paid Fritz to turn the gastap on? Tell him you want your money back.'

Shrouded by darkness, Russ and the rest of the company wound their way along the zig-zag of trench to take up their positions. 'And who was it risked the wrath of the platoon by saving my neck?'

'I did!' Dobson thumped his chest proudly. 'Carried you on me back for three miles.'

Russ cocked a dubious face over his shoulder. 'You'll be getting a medal then?'

'No, he was shot at dawn yesterday,' supplied Lance-Corporal Beech. 'He's a lying sod, Sarg. It was the Lieutenant who saved you.'

'Daw?' Hazelwood's voice rose in amazement.

'Mr Daw, if you don't mind.' Russ spun round to find his old neighbour had sneaked up behind him. 'All right now are we, Lance-Sergeant Hazelwood?'

'Yes, sir . . . I believe I have you to thank?' Arriving at his destination, Russ took position.

'Don't mention it.' Daw lit a short stub of cigarette as the others drifted about their business, leaving the pair to themselves. Russ asked, how come Jack hadn't suffered from the gas attack. 'It was only bad luck that any of us got it,' said Jack. 'It was well dispersed when it got to us, you just happened to take the worst of it. I grabbed you as you came running up the communication trench. It wasn't meant for us – you ought to have seen what it did to them poor darkies down the road. Christ, what a bloody mess. Anyway, we've been issued with these masks now, so we'll be ready for the next lot.'

Russ made a face, then offered genuine thanks, asking if any more of the platoon had suffered. He was told three others were still absent. After a further period of dialogue on the state of the war, Daw asked, 'How's things at home, Filbert?'

The lack of formality invited similar treatment from the lance-sergeant who had also lighted a tab. He drew long on it, its red glow secreted in the cup of his palm. 'About as peaceful as they are here.'

'Them two women of ours still giving each other the evil eye?' When Russ nodded grimly, Jack made a sound of amusement. 'Funny buggers women, aren't they?'

'Oh aye . . . as funny as bleeding piles. Did your Ella mention anything about Bertie getting shot when she last wrote?'

By the surprise on the Lieutenant's face she hadn't. 'I thought this was where people came to get shot. How did he manage it in Blighty?'

Russ told him, and had the perverse satisfaction of earning Jack's apology before saying equably, 'Ah, it wasn't your fault, Jack. He loaded it himself. The lad's disturbed, very disturbed . . . if that's anybody's fault it's mine. And now . . .' he turned sickened eyes to the other, 'the silly little sod's run away and joined up.' Daw closed his own eyes and uttered an oath. 'If there's anything you can do to find him, I'd be grateful.'

The Lieutenant nodded and said he would see what he could do. 'Is he with our lot?' At Russ' shake of head he straightened and ground the butt of his cigarette with his heel. 'Ah well, I don't suppose it makes much difference, he'll still be a bugger to find – by the way, the captain wants to see you.' He walked away, leaving Russ apprehensive.

However, all the captain wanted was to tell him that he was now on sergeant's pay. The promotion had apparently come on the day of the gas attack. 'Good to see you back,

Sergeant.' Russ thanked him. 'Here, have a piece of this. It's champion, as you might say.' Captain Capstaff handed over a slice of fruitcake sent by his mother. Russ took it, balancing it on his palm until the young man said with a smile, 'I did intend for you to eat it, Sergeant.' Russ took a polite nibble, then issued suitable compliment, for the cake was delicious. 'Makes you think of home, doesn't it?' said Captain Capstaff.

For a second, Russ stopped chewing, looking deep into the wistful young face. Then he nodded, gave a weak smile and took another bite of the cake.

The countryside was preparing for autumn but there was still no sign of Bertie. Russ was growing more worried by the day. His son may have finished his training by now and could be in the front line. He had made dozens of enquiries of his Commanding Officer and others, but though they appeared genuinely concerned they could only tell him that everything was being done to find the boy. Each newcomer whom Russ met faced an inquisition and was shown Bertie's photograph, but the only response it drew was, 'Sorry, chum.'

The move to a new sector brought a fresh batch of contacts, but none of them any use. Perhaps, came Russ' wild thought, perhaps they've found him and sent him home and Rachel hasn't bothered to tell me. Would she be so cruel? Oh, yes . . . yes. He had scribbled innumerable letters but got no reply. Surely, *surely* she couldn't still be burning them? Not when they might have contained news of her son. Whichever way, there was no answer. Whilst he was in action his worry was put aside, but sometimes when they were stuck in some uneventful place for days his fears became magnified. The mining village they were in now had been one such place, until the Jocks had started moving in.

Russ, on two days' rest, stood and watched the kilted battalion march down the street to the skirl of pipes. Even with the khaki aprons over their tartan they were a magnificent sight, though he would never have admitted it to one of them. As the tail of the column neared his standing place, who should he see prancing jauntily behind but Private Dobson who, in between giving a nasal wail, sang rude verses about the Scotsmen's lack of trousers. Three others from Hazelwood's platoon were egging him on. Russ collared them as they were about to pass him and warned them to desist. Dobson carried on marching.

'Eh, Jock! There's always summat I wanted to know!'

The man at the rear anticipated the question and growled, 'How would ye like your nose bitten off, sonny?'

Dobson merely laughed and, acquiring a stick, performed the ultimate insult: lifted the edge of the tartan kilt and began to hoist it higher. At this point Russ decided he had better save Dobson from himself.

'Dobson, you've got a Blighty leave coming up in three days, don't you want to live to enjoy it?'

'Aren't you interested to know what's under there, Sarg?' laughed Dobson as Russ lunged for him.

'I'm more interested in hanging onto my own small blessings thank you very much – Private, I said leave it!'

With a final flourish of his stick, Dobson fell back to join his sergeant. 'Where's Strawberry and the others got to?' he looked round.

'I've no idea, but they've more bloody sense than you. Now bugger off, don't be incriminating me.'

But it was too late. The order for the Highlanders to halt was barked out and with an abrupt stamp of boots they came to a standstill. Even as Russ was attempting to divest himself of Dobson's companionship the Scots were falling out. Within seconds they were thundering full cry up the street towards him. Russ took the only sensible action – he ran.

Dobson's mouth fell open as the horde of yelling warriors streamed at him, then he too sped. The Scotsmen teemed down the street after him, wielding clubs and bayonets which all served to increase Dobson's speed. In and out of the winding streets he pelted following his sergeant's route, but no amount of evasive action could shake off his aggressors. Russ kept screaming for him to go away, but

Dobson stuck with him. Side by side they thudded breathlessly round a corner – and suddenly found the way ahead blocked by a wall of khaki. Dobson threw one horrified look at his sergeant, another over his shoulder. Russ saw an opening, grasped a fistful of the boy's tunic and swung him into the narrow passageway seconds before the tartan mob swept around the corner. There was a door at the end of the passage. Russ took it, and found that their sanctuary was someone's kitchen.

The woman looked startled as they burst in through her door. Then seeing that they wore khaki acted as if she had been expecting them. 'Ah, mes amis! Asseyez-vous!' and hustled them into her best room to give them bread and wine.

Struggling for breath, Russ gave a tight grimace at Dobson and tugged his uniform into place, face like a beetroot. 'Just you bloody wait . . .' For answer, Dobson grinned, nudged him and nodded at the window through which could be heard ghastly yells as the Scots clashed with the English. Cap in hand, Russ smoothed his hair. 'By Christ, Dobbo, you don't know how lucky you are.' He offered his thanks to Madame and took advantage of her hospitality. He also questioned her presence – the village was supposed to have been evacuated. Had Madame understood, she would have told him she had lived here for thirty years and it would take more than the Boches to evict her. Dobson settled himself on the chair to watch the fun outside, smiling gaily. Madame winced at the sound of the blows being exchanged and shook her head, muttering something about savages. The private tut-tutted with her, drawing a reluctant laugh from his sergeant who muttered. 'God help the poor bloody Boches.'

Dobson sprinkled his tunic with crumbs as he tore off a mouthful of bread, munching appreciatively. Then he noticed the sergeant's preoccupation. 'Any news of your lad yet, Sarg?'

Russ had been staring at his plate. Dobson's voice brought him to life and he sank his teeth into the bread, giving a slight, negative movement with his eyes.

Another shower of crumbs settled into the folds at Dobson's groin. 'I think they've discovered he's underage by now an' sent him home.'

'That's what Thought thinks, is it? They didn't seem too bothered about you, Dobson, why should they care about my lad?'

'Well, looking at his photo he's a bit more obvious than I am,' said the private. 'He's only a bairn – I'd say his ba . . .' remembering the woman's presence he cleaned up his words, 'His voice hasn't even broken yet.'

'Considering that you're right and he has been sent home, why haven't I been informed?' asked Russ.

Dobson pulled the corners of his mouth down. 'Don't ask me – look at the cock-up when you were gassed. Your wife thought you were dead, didn't she?'

Russ nodded and was silent. Outside, the sounds of battle had moved further down the street.

Dobson used his tongue to dislodge the bread from his gums, then guzzled his red wine. 'What was it you did to her that was so bad?'

Russ eyed him sharply. 'Who says I did anything?'

'Well . . . she never writes to you, does she?' When Russ tugged the piece of paper from his breast pocket Dobson waved dismissively. 'That's a load of cobblers – you made it up. Come on, I won't tell anybody. It must've been summat pretty bad.'

Russ tucked the paper away and leaned forward, signalling for Dobson to do the same. The private downed his wine and moved onto the edge of his chair, putting his head close to the sergeant's.

Russ' voice was confidential. 'Well you see it was like this . . .' With a swift action he grabbed the boy's nose and gave it a vicious twist, lifting Dobson right out of the chair. The private screamed. The woman cried out, 'Ah, non!'

Russ waved her back into her seat, dragging the boy to the door by his nose. 'It's all right, love, I'm just helping him with his adenoid problem – merci for the wine!'

They were back in the trenches, waiting . . . waiting . . .

Veee-bang! An enemy shell exploded to their rear displacing tons of earth and thrusting it high into the air as if some huge mole were at work. The terrain was a contrast to their last picturesque venue – a deserted coalfield, inhabited only by slagheaps which towered above them like huge black boils. Dobson put his eyes to the periscope fixed to the sandbags. There was little reflected in it at the moment. After a while, though, something moved. The horizon began to undulate. Dobson squinted, trying to make out the phenomenon. 'Sarg, there's summat . . .' Russ pushed him out of the way and took a quick look in the periscope . . . as the gyrating skyline evolved into a thousand bobbing pickelhaubes.

'Jerry!' breathed Dobson.

'You don't say?' Russ brought his rifle into position as the Captain shouted orders. 'And here's me thinking it's the Brighouse and Rastrick Band come to entertain the troops.'

D Company tensed as the line of field grey advanced. This was to be their first real experience of hand to hand warfare, having previously seen Jerry as a distant target – which had been hairy enough. Dobson trained his eye down the barrel of his rifle. 'I'll never hit 'em,' he jabbered. 'They're too small.'

'Give 'em time, they'll grow,' muttered Russ, flexing his fingers around his weapon. *This time they're going to get me. I know they are.*

Still there was the ponk of shells leaving the howitzers, the whistle and the bang and the churning up of the ground. Dobson swallowed and tried to wet his lips but his mouth had gone dry. His chin had become glued to his rifle. 'Blimey, there's millions of 'em, where do I start?'

'Pick one out,' instructed Russ calmly. *Why am I calm?* he asked himself. *I don't want to die, I don't. Bertie, where the hell are you?* 'Train your sights on him and when you get the order bring him down. Remember target practice, don't just fire for the sake of it.' This brought inward ridicule – here you are telling Dobson what to do and you've never shot a man yourself!

The advancing grey wall grew faces, determined and

368

hard. Daw gave the order to open fire. There was a deafening volley and when the smoke cleared the line of field grey had disintegrated.

'I got him!' shouted an excited Dobson.

'Then get another bugger!' bawled Russ. Thoughts of Bertie were gone. Even thoughts of his own death. All his mind saw were the targets to be hit – not men, targets.

Volley upon volley ripped through the attackers, bringing down hundreds until the remainder took cover in order to regroup. In the lull, Dobson laughed to the pal on his left. 'Eh it's easy, Schofe! I thought I'd feel sick when I shot a bloke but there's that many you can't be sure whether it was your bullet what got him or somebody else's. It isn't that bad.'

'Keep bouncing up and down like that, Dobson, and you'll find out how bad it can be.' Russell's arm began to tremble with delayed shock and he focused his attention on the ground before him waiting.

Dobson chanced a look over the parapet at the litter of German helmets. 'I wouldn't half mind one o' them. Can I get one, Sarg?'

'Are you totally without reck, Dobson? They haven't finished yet – eh up, they're here again!'

Dobson crouched over his rifle and prepared to fire . . . and then there was a funny *thwack*! and his neighbour went down. He looked agog at the gaping hole in Schofield's brow where the bullet had emerged. There were glistening splinters of bone and blood on his own sleeve. Another man went down.

'Christ! How did they get round our flank?' yelled Russ and immediately altered his rifle to the parados, unleashing rapid fire. Dobson had fallen to his kness and was gawping at his pal. 'Dobson! Leave him and get shooting!'

The normally garrulous private was rendered dumb as yet another of his comrades was gunned down by a sniper. Russ turned from his firing position, grabbed the boy, slapped him and barked, 'Dobson, if you don't move now I'll have you court martialled!' and the private instantly broke into action.

In the next bay, something toppled into the trench beside a young soldier. He pressed his back to the wall and, idiotically, covered his eyes. The stick bomb went off, peppering the men of D Company with mud and bits of flesh. Daw had scrambled into the position beside Russ. 'The captain and Lieutenant Roy have had it. Looks like we'll have to fall back . . . if we can get out.' There was firing to three sides of them now. Stuffing his empty revolver back into its holster he grabbed a rifle – which he much preferred – off a dead man.

Russell's weapon had become so red-hot that it attracted slivers of mud which blocked its working parts. With a curse he thumped the butt then rammed it at the ground several times. Trembling fingers sought for his pull-through while he shouted to Daw, 'How long d'you reckon we can hold them, sir?'

The Lieutenant himself was reloading. He gave a competent flick of the bolt, slipping the round into the breach and threw himself into action again, bullets spurting from his rifle. 'As long as we have to!' But he too was becoming worried. For the last hour the Captain had been anticipating the order to withdraw, but none had come – a shell had brought down the field telegraph. So a runner had been sent. He had not returned yet. Now the Captain and the only other lieutenant with the company were dead and the decision was Daw's.

Russ succeeded in dislodging the blockage from his rifle and once again put it to good use.

'How many men have we got left?' Daw shouted, knowing it was futile to ask how many lost; the evidence was everywhere.

'Put it this way, I won't need an abacus.' Russ chanced a quick look to right and left. The sight and sound was pitiful. Dead comrades – and bits of them – littered the section of trench that was visible. Even as he observed, a German shell exploded further along the line sending arms and legs flying through the air. Those nearby who remained unscathed were assailed with human debris. The sergeant scurried off down the line to count the living, having to stand upon the bodies of the fallen when their number blocked his way. He returned with the news that there were about thirty.

'We'll have to get that bastard sniper if we're to have any hope of . . .' Daw did not have time to say any more – the Germans charged. No amount of fire would keep them from storming the trench. As both Lewis guns were put out of action, Daw was forced to give the order to fall back, knowing that his men were going to be cut down by snipers as they left the trench.

But then came a cry that curled Dobson's blood. A screaming band of Scotsmen teemed from behind a slag-heap, hurling bombs at the sniping posts and halting the German charge. A cheer arose from D Company who abetted with lusty fire while the grimy-faced Jocks put the Germans to rout, winkling any stragglers out of shellholes with the same ease as they might enjoy a seafood delicacy.

A breathless runner appeared at Daw's shoulder. 'Major Frazer says to retire, sir!'

'Retreating?' piped up Dobson when his sergeant passed on the order.

'Not retreating, just advancing backwards. Come on, jump to it!'

And the exhausted remnants of D Company fell back, dragging with them the red-stained bodies of the wounded . . .

It started to rain. An age later, they reached safe ground and slumped down at the roadside while stretcher bearers took command of their wounded. The dead had been left at their killing ground. Drenched as Russ was, it seemed pointless to unroll his groundsheet, but he did so, wrapping it around him. 'Feeling all right, now, Dobbo?' he asked from his position of collapse.

A weary Dobson did not answer yes or no, but breathed, 'I can't believe they're all . . . I mean, one minute there's Schofield laughing an' joking, and the next . . .'

'Aye well, that's the way of it,' said Russ and informed him gravely, 'They got Old Catcrap an' all . . . poor little sod.' Now that the imminent danger was past he had chance to dwell on the gallant young captain.

'Oh shit,' Dobson said with feeling, and capsized onto his back. So did everyone else and all fell instantly asleep, uncaring of the downpour.

When Russ opened his eyes it was morning. He sat, rubbing at his shoulder which was still sore from the constant recoil of his rifle. The rain had stippled the black powder marks on his face. He resembled a collier, eyes standing out like blue glass. He yawned, inhaling the taste of gunpowder and looked along the road. A band of prisoners was being herded in. Russ slapped Dobson's thigh. The boy woke, shouting his alarm. 'Want to see one up close, Dobbo?' He tossed a casual gesture at the bedraggled looking specimens being shoved and pushed by a platoon of Highlanders.

Dobson's interest was stirred. He screwed his fist around a pink eye. 'That the lot what nearly had us yesterday, Sarg? Sorry looking crew aren't they?'

Russ clambered to his feet as the party neared and called to one of the Highlanders. 'You the lads who got us out of that jam on the Redoubt?'

'Aye, what's left of us,' growled the kilted soldier, shoving a captive in the back. Russ then asked if they had taken many casualties. 'Go see fer yersel'' came the suggestion.

Later, Russ and Dobson were able to meet this. Nestled in a shellhole they peered out over the result of the Highlanders' heroic charge. It appeared that the German retreat had merely been a ploy to lure the Jocks into a square of machine-gun fire. Hundreds of corpses were strewn about the coalfield in all the inelegance of death; bloodied tartan flung carelessly aside to reveal the Scotsmen's secret. That which seemed so interesting to Dobson only the other day was now cruel to look upon.

Russ turned to his young companion and said softly, 'How d'you like the war now, Dobson?'

The youngster faced him. His eyes had the stunned look of a pole-axed beast, and he knew that the sergeant didn't really expect an answer.

CHAPTER TWENTY-FIVE

1st October 1915
My dear Charlie,

I hope this letter finds you in good health as it leaves me. I was truly distressed to hear from Mr Hazelwood that you have not been receiving education. That is most unsatisfactory, but is about to be remedied forthwith. I intend to write a letter to a colleague of mine in the north of England who will give you the education befitting your intelligence. It may seem a long way from home to you, but I have my reasons for selecting this place, not the least of them being that you will be very happy there. With the war showing no signs of being over I cannot say when I shall be able to come for you, but I trust it will be soon. I am so glad to hear that you are now permitted to go to church, and I hope that your brother Bertie is more kindly disposed towards you now . . . Do write soon with all your news. I pray for this war to be finished and for us to be together – though you may be so settled by now that you may not wish to rejoin the company of a doddering old priest!

> *My warmest regards,*
> *Father Guillaume.*

Dear Father,

Your letter was most welcome but only a poor substitute for your company. I do not have much news at the moment. I don't know if my father wrote you, but Bertie has run away to the war. I hope they find him before he gets killed or Mrs Hazelwood will blame me. She blames me for everything. She shouts at me more and more, but I suppose that's because she's worried about Bertie. At Sunday Mass I lit a candle for him, also one for you and Father. I will go to the college if that is what you want . . .

> *Love from Charlie.*

Each time a letter dropped through the door Rachel sped down the passage hoping for news of Bertie. Even her husband's letters were opened, though as soon as she found they contained nothing of interest they were flung on the fire in disgust.

There had been few enquiries as to Robert's disappearance – Rachel did not encourage callers – but one of those who did pay a visit was the boy's schoolmaster. Rachel had been quite rude at first, assuming his presence to be because of some lack of liaison at the school. 'I did write and inform the headmaster!' she told the man before he could state the intention of his call.

The teacher was accustomed to dealing with awkward pupils and replied kindly that yes, he knew that Robert had run away to join up. 'I didn't come because I fear for his education. I just wondered if you'd had any news. Robert's a nice boy, this is just the sort of patriotic thing he would do. A lot of Archie's boys have gone to be officers – naturally they are a little older than your son.'

Rachel did not disillusion the man about her son's reasons for joining up, but merely nodded.

'I'm going too,' the master revealed with a bashful smile. 'I can't sit there marking papers while our fellows go off to fight. That's one of the reasons why I came to see you, to let you know that I'll do everything I possibly can to find Robert and get him sent home.'

'That's extremely kind of you.' It seemed to the master that his gesture had taken her aback, and so it had. 'Sometimes, I feel that nobody cares,' said Rachel.

'Oh, I'm sure they do, Mrs Hazelwood.'

'The Army doesn't, that's for sure! They've done absolutely nothing to find him.' Months, he had been gone. What the devil was the Army playing at? It wasn't as if Robert looked older than he was. All they had to do was open their eyes and they would see that one of their soldiers was only a baby.

She had been back and forth to all the Army depots she could think of, had even wandered around Knavesmire in the pouring rain, searching every face – until one soldier had made a very vulgar proposition and she had sped home in distress to cry over the birthday presents that lay on her son's bed, unopened. All she could do was to carry on as normal and wait . . . and wait . . . and wait.

Another Christmas was spent in the trenches. This time, by order, there were no games of football nor exchange of photographs. Each side kept behind its own barbed-wire. By the spring of 1916 little ground had been won by either faction, each performing a kind of military square dance – two steps forward, two steps back, dig those trenches, tote that pack!

For Rachel, the waiting became unbearable, though her concern seemed not to be shared by anyone else in the household. 'Father went missing once and came home safe and sound, didn't he?' comforted Rowena. 'So why shouldn't Bertie?' Two inches of snow in the early days of March eradicated all thoughts of Bertie and of the war. The white plain of Knavesmire grew stripes and whorls of green where the girls and Charlie had rolled giant balls of snow to make a snowman.

But during the night the war returned. Intermingled with the peaceful, drifting flakes came a deadlier shower of Zeppelin bombs to wreak misery on Yorkshire and seven other counties. As yet, York itself remained unscathed . . . but the enemy was striking more and more inland targets at each raid. After that night, whenever the gas pressure lowered – the sign of an impending Zeppelin raid – Rachel feared that her home and family would appear in the newspaper's list of strikes. With the dual worry, sleep became a luxury. Fatigue compelled her to rely on reflex to get her through the day. She rose, dressed, breakfasted, went to the shop, came home, went to bed . . . and lay awake fretting half the night.

Easter brought a deluge and complaints over the price of fish. Buds began to sprout on the trees on Knavesmire. In the front garden Rachel's roses showed tiny red shoots. The children were sprouting too; Rhona had just been enrolled at the new Knavesmire School which was much nearer to home. With the Army and other authorities still jiggling

375

with the older elementary schools, Rachel had decided to put her here; there was less chance of occupation by the forces. The air turned warmer and the sky blue. April Fool turned to May Gosling . . . and still Bertie was missing.

This Tuesday evening, Rachel was in the kitchen, thinking about her son as she usually did when sitting idle. It was ten-thirty. The children were in their beds and the maid was tidying up before going off to hers. Rachel was watching the lumpish figure uninterestedly, lost in thought, when the lights dimmed.

'Ah, Jesus!' Biddy pawed her chest in alarm. ''Tis a raid! 'Tis a raid!'

'Stop being so stupid! They haven't bothered to visit us before, have they?' Nevertheless, Rachel's eyes were touched by fear as she leapt up and began a nervous pacing, waiting for the lights to return to full power. She would not go to bed until they did so.

A rumble of what sounded like thunder brought Biddy to her knees and she crossed herself rapidly. 'Hail Mary, Mother o' God, pray for us sinners . . .'

'Shut up!' Rachel hared around the room twisting all the gaslamp switches off, then feeling her way along the darkened passage, she opened the door to the street. The rumble was louder out here, but her hopeful examination of the sky betold no lightning. It was a raid all right. Where there were gas lamps, young boys were shinning up the standards to snuff the flames; the electric ones had been shut off at the main supply. She moved out into the street and was joined by others, Ella among them. Rachel chose not to look at her but clutched the edges of her knitted jacket and pulled it round her, pressing her knuckles into her ribs. 'Are they near?' It was said to the man on her left.

'About ten or fifteen miles, I'd say,' murmured the elderly Mr Parker, looking up at the sky. 'Oy, don't do that!' He pointed at a boy who had struck a match. 'You silly little devil the Zepp'll see it – get it blown out now!' Looking along the street he shouted to a woman that he could see a light through her doorway. The door was closed rapidly. The grey-haired Mrs Parker finished buttoning her coat and moved out of her doorway to stand on the path behind her husband, placing her blue-veined hands on his shoulders, one thumb unconsciously working her wedding ring round and round and round. All heads were lifted to the sky.

'Oh!' Rachel cried out and grabbed for support as the ground beneath her feet tremored and the thunderclaps rolled closer. She asked fearfully of Mrs Parker, 'D'you think I ought to get the children up?'

The older woman nodded. 'It might be a good idea, love.'

Rachel rushed back into the darkened house. 'Biddy, get the girls' coats!'

Soon, the girls and Charlie, still confused by sleep, wandered out onto the pavement, nightgowns showing neath the hems of their coats. Beany yawned and screwed a knuckle into her red puffy eyes before looking round at all the people. The thunderclaps had ceased. All was silent now. 'Mrs Mountain's got her nightie on,' she observed.

'Ssh!' said Mr Parker. 'The Germans might hear you.' He rubbed an apprehensive hand over his upper arm.

All was completely calm. The streetful of onlookers wriggled their toes in their slippers and waited, faces turned upwards. It was a beautiful clear night, the sky bedecked with stars. A sky for lovers. A young soldier home on leave from the front slipped an arm round his wife of three months, pulling her into the doorway to bury his face in the warm curve of her neck. She tilted her head back, the clinging touch of his lips painting ecstasy on her face. They forgot about the other people in the street, carried away by the joy of their belated honeymoon and the beauty of the night. The soldier's lips grew more passionate, his hands ran wild . . . then his face emerged from his wife's shoulder to look at the sky. The romantic setting was ruptured by the low growl of a Zeppelin.

Amongst the thirty faces peering upwards, Rowena thought: it's rather like standing on the platform of a station and hearing the approach of an express train – the growl became a roar and the express would burst through the station, flashing past, rackety-rack! rackety-rack! fluttering skirts, swooshing hair over faces and in a flash was gone. But there was one difference here; the growl magnified to a roar, the whole night shivered with it . . . yet they could not see their enemy. He hovered somewhere above them, waiting to excrete his deadly eggs, but they knew not where. Rowena fumbled for Beany's hand and grasped it tightly. Charlie's hands gripped Rebecca's shoulders, his wide eyes glued to the sky.

Then unexpectedly the roar ceased – as abruptly as turning off a light. The silence which followed was even more nerve-racking. What had happened? Where was he? Had he gone? Becky was the one to ask this.

'He's shut his engines off for some reason,' whispered Mr Parker, eyes scanning the heavens. 'Probably taking his bearings. Ssh, don't talk else he'll know where we are.'

The silence seemed interminable. Their necks became cricked and their eyes kept blurring out of focus with staring at the sky for so long. Thirty pairs of ears strained for a sound. It was all so very eerie . . . With a roar, the engines whirred back to life. 'Look, there he is!' Mr Parker forgot to whisper and jabbed a finger skywards. A great 'Oh!' arose from the spectators as all caught sight of the long, cigar-shaped airship which nosed its way across the sky over Knavesmire with amazing ease for such a bulky craft. They were all admiring its dexterity when there came a flash of blue light. 'Take cover!' someone shouted and everyone fell automatically into a squat.

The impact of the bomb was even worse than they had anticipated. Though it had fallen several hundred yards away the shock waves bowled some of them off their feet and set their ears ringing. Children cried out. Mothers made them lie down and protected the young bodies with their own. Rachel ordered Biddy to get her big body across the girls, but poor Biddy was too numbed to do anything except wail and pray. Charlie followed Rachel's example and shielded two of the youngest, though he wished someone would protect him, he was very, very frightened.

'It's coming towards us!' screamed a woman who had chanced a look. Another explosion occurred. This one was totally different – less of an explosion, more of a huge sizzle, like a basket of chips being placed into fat, only much louder. When the cowering people glanced up, flames were lighting the sky. The blaze seemed very close but no one had the chance to speculate as to where it was for the Zeppelin gave birth to another litter of bombs. Six explosions came in rapid succession. The air stank with the afterbirth.

As abruptly as it had started, the bombing stopped. Rachel crouched over her children behind the low garden wall, heart racing, listening to the roar of people's homes being destroyed, waiting for the Zeppelin to return. After a brief interlude the Zeppelin performed a deafening encore – *one! two! three! four! five!* Rachel bit her lip and pressed her face into a child's warm back. It seemed endless.

The pilot of the airship turned his motors off, looked down with satisfaction at the blossoming flames and smiled. Let them stew for a while.

Hours seemed to pass after the last explosion. 'Has he gone, d'you think?' Rowena lifted a frightened face above the garden wall and looked up. Barely had the words emerged than the pilot – as if hearing them and acting out of mischief – dropped the remainder of his load with thunderous accuracy, before sallying off towards the North Sea, leaving a trail of black smoke like a snail's thread to mark his passing.

After a long period of uncertainty the all clear sounded and everyone got to their feet, rubbing at knees, shushing frightened children. 'Great, wasn't it?' said Lyn unconvincingly. In the next street a woman was screaming hysterically. Rachel, sick with fright, brushed at the soil which clung to the girls' nightgowns.

'What happened to our anti-aircraft guns? That's what I'd like to know! I could do better with a peashooter!' She hustled the children and the maid back into the house and slammed the door.

'Yes, we are all safe and well, Rachel, thank you for asking,' said Ella, at which Mr Parker laughed shakily whilst tending his wife.

379

'Has she heard anything of their Bertie yet?' Ella asked the couple, trying to sound calm.

'I don't think so. She doesn't have much to say to me,' said Mrs Parker, clutching her handkerchief.

'Me neither.' Ella surveyed the sky. A rubicund glow marked the area of stricken houses. 'I mean, how was I to know he'd run away if she didn't tell me? Eh, he wants a good braying does that'n – he's overspoilt. Anyway . . . I'd better go in. 'Struth, I couldn't do with this lot every night, could you – eh, look at them two!' She elbowed Mrs Parker and they both found a smile for the young soldier and his wife who were engaged in a clinch. 'I'll bet they were at it all through the attack! It'd take more than a German balloon to separate them.' Ella drew in a wistful breath and let it out again. 'Phew! I still feel a bit shaky. Does anybody fancy a cup o' tea? Away then, I'll get kettle on. I can't see me sleeping after this lot.' And a number of folk piled into Ella's house where they calmed their nerves with her brew and tried to guess just how many homes had been destroyed.

The combined mumble of their voices penetrated the walls of Rachel's bedroom. She flung herself onto her side, wrapped her arm across her chest and used a finger of it to plug her ear, blaming her inability to sleep on her inconsiderate neighbours, when in truth it was the fear that the Zeppelin would return which kept her awake. The children were frightened too, but at least they had someone to cuddle up to. She had no one. No one. She pushed her face into the pillow and cried.

Wednesday's paper was full of the Zeppelin raid – apparently the biggest so far, with bombs being dropped all along the east coast from Norfolk to Aberdeenshire. Censorship forbade naming York in the accounts but when Rachel read that 'in a certain place in Yorkshire' a night of devastation had taken place, she knew well enough where that was. Nine people had been killed and three times as many injured, houses completely destroyed. When the funerals of the victims took place, hundreds of people lined the route to the cemetery.

So obsessed did Rachel become with the fear of another Zepp raid that lesser events went completely unrecorded. Another Monday dawned – which Monday, Rachel did not know nor care, she felt absolutely worn out from lack of sleep. Dragging her sluggish limbs out of bed she performed the usual, automatic routine, allowed Biddy to set the children off for school and went to work. Something was different today, but she was too estranged from reality to unravel it. In fact she got through an entire working day without realizing that she had forgotten to observe the new Daylight Saving Scheme by putting her clocks forward at the weekend. Only when she arrived home did she learn of her error.

'We all got into trouble today!' The girls clamoured round her the moment she got in. At her blank face, Lyn said, 'You forgot to put the clock forward and we were an hour late for school!'

'And then Biddy wasn't in when we got home for dinner so we had to go back to school without none!' cried Beany.

'Sure, how was I to know about the daft clocks?' objected the maid.

Rachel gave a shout of frustration and threw down her bag. 'Will you all please shut up! Biddy, is the clock right now?' The maid shook her head. 'Then do it – and alter the others while you're about it. Oh, God! As if they haven't plunged the country into enough regulations without messing up the time as well! But ask them to do a simple thing like finding a little boy and can they? Oh, no!'

Rowena, sorry for joining in with the others' complaint, sat by her mother. 'I'm sure they'll find Bertie soon . . .'

'Will everybody stop saying that!' Rachel covered her ears. Then seeing she had upset the girl said, 'I'm sorry to shout . . . but all everyone seems to do is talk – none of them are doing anything! I'm so worried . . .'

Russ was worried too. However, before the summer rose there came exciting talk that brought with it a touch of relief: there was to be a big push that would finish this stalemate once and for all. This meant that the war would be

381

over and Bertie would be safe. A year had gone by and still he had heard nothing of his son, though his efforts to find him remained undaunted. He could only pray that Bertie was still alive.

At the end of June they received written verification of the battle – as if they needed it; for the past week their artillery had been lobbing everything it had at Jerry, pulverizing his lines. The sound that came as a mere rumble on English shores assumed myriad decibels here. The effect was physically sickening. Russ became disorientated by the ceaseless roar in his brain. The gunfire seemed to speak to him, reverberating the names of past battles – *Ver-dun-dun-dun! Looosss!* All that kept him from going mad was the thought that Jerry was on the worst end of it.

On the eve of battle there was a church parade then a concert on the village green. The British Artillery still pounded non-stop, yet there seemed to be little answering fire, allowing the men to devote their attention to the band. Russ sat quietly, listening, wondering if Bertie had been found yet and if Rachel had received word from the priest about Charlie's education. For the moment he considered writing a letter as others were doing, but abandoned this as pointless and simply sat and enjoyed the music. It seemed an anomalous situation, the band playing on the village green in the middle of a war.

After a time he pressed himself from the ground and wandered off, if not to be alone at least to gain short respite from Dobson's prattling. Soon he became aware that someone was walking beside him, not having to look to know it was Jack, for the corner of his eye had shown someone very tall.

They strode without speech for a while, then Daw said, 'I don't suppose you've got any pliers on you, Filb?'

Russ glanced up then; saw the pain-racked face. 'Oh Christ, it's not that same bloody tooth that was bothering you back home, is it?' With Daw's sheepish admittance he asked, 'Why the hell didn't you have it seen to?'

'I can't!' Pain heightened the tone of Jack's reply.

'What – not even by the dentist here? Well don't expect

me to do it. Tell you what, I know where there's a Jerry sniper. Stick your head up and he'll put a nice little plug o' lead in it . . . mindst I can't guarantee he'll leave your head behind.'

'Some bloody friend you are,' muttered Daw.

'I can't understand you, Jack – what's the difference between me pulling it out and a dentist? I mean surely it'd be less painful if he did it, him having all the right stuff.'

Daw found difficulty in explaining it himself. 'I just have a sort of . . . thing against 'em.'

'You'll end up having to go.'

'Thank you for your help, Sergeant. If I'm still around tomorrow I might think about it.' Jack strode away.

Later, using the darkness as a screen against the German observation balloons, they moved to forward trenches, stopping at an RE dump to draw extra equipment. Due to all movement having to be done undercover of night, the roads to and from the trenches were thronged with traffic of every description, creating a scene similar to that when the chocolate-bashers at home broke up for the evening. But all normality dispersed when they passed Basin Wood. Here a pioneer battalion had dug a vast communal grave in preparation for the morrow. The sight produced as big a hollow in Russ' stomach.

By the early hours of the morning they were in position. Now as he sat and waited for the dawn, Sergeant Russ Hazelwood surrendered to his earlier decision to write a letter. Even in the confidence that this was to be a decisive battle, in realistic terms there would be men who died today. Russ could be one of them. His indelible pencil scrawled a note in similar vein to all the others he had sent her, begging her forgiveness, telling her how much he loved her and the children. When it was done he tucked it into his Army paybook. If he were still alive this evening he could rip it up. If not . . . then someone else would send it.

Dawn broke to the most beautiful clear blue sky. Russ must have been napping, for he seemed to remember that a moment ago it had been dark. His insensible eyes told him, at first, that he was lying on his back in the middle of

Knavesmire . . . then his sense of smell brought him fully awake to the reality and, stretching, he heaved himself upright. The gunners were still in good form with a ponk, a scream and a bang! Yet, amidst all this there rose the sound of birdsong. Russ identified a lark. Looking up he could see it hovering above the battlefield trilling its heart out. The silliest thoughts came when one was preparing to lock with the enemy: would the lark still be alive by eventide? Would the nightingale get to speak? And how many hundreds of tiny mammals would have been annihilated on these green acres when the battle was won?

In the hour before the attack the new company commander gave last minute orders and the rum ration was doled out. Then the men sat back, lit cigarettes and chatted.

'D'you think Fritz might've gone, Sarg?'

'Why, if it isn't Private Dobson!' exclaimed Russ on finding the boy next to him. 'What a fine young fellow you are – just stand there while I rip the hairs out of your nostrils. Dobson, do you seriously imagine I'd be stood here if Fritz had buggered off?'

'Well he doesn't seem to be chucking much at us, Sarg.'

'It's just as bloody well isn't it? Get that tin helmet on! What d'you think they gave it you for – to piss in?'

'It's uncomfy, Sarg,' grumbled the lad.

'As uncomfy as a hole in the head? Get it on!'

Dobson did as he was told, then scanned No Man's Land, the more distant part of it veiled in gunsmoke. 'Can't see anything moving out there.'

'There's going to be something moving very shortly, Private.' Daw had strolled up unnoticed. He now consulted his watch. 'In ten minutes' time, to be precise. We're going to push that Hun all the way back into his mother's womb.' Russ saw that there was no pain on the lieutenant's face this morning – the tooth had obviously had a liberal dousing of rum.

Dobson waited until Daw had gone past, then said, 'D'you know what they've nicknamed the lieutenant, Sarg? The Ice Man. Nowt seems to scare him, does it?'

Russ laughed inwardly at the thought of Jack's dental

problems. 'They've got a nickname for you an' all so I heard, Dobbo – The Rapist.' He ran a derogatory eye up and down the other. 'Mindst . . . it's only an honorary title.' Poor Dobson had tried his utmost to lose his virginity but none of the women he met would take him seriously.

Shortly the barrage from their artillery lifted, signalling that the first wave of infantry was about to go over. Sergeant Hazelwood's battalion was to be in the second wave, its objective to make for any gaps that the gunners had blown in the German wire and press on for the enemy's second line. After receiving such a pounding it was doubtful that Jerry would offer much resistance. There was great confidence all alone the line.

Somewhere a whistle was blown and the first wave poured from their trenches whilst Russ and his fellows waited for their turn to come. The delay produced the usual nerves. Though each man tried his best to hide it, the fear emanated from him in a peculiar smell. Not so much fear of dying, but that he would make a fool of himself in front of his comrades. Their anxiety was transmitted to their eyes. While their mouths laughed and joked, their eyes belied their true feelings. The only one who did not need to make false banter was Daw. Russ glanced at him and wondered what the other was thinking. Jack seemed totally unaffected by what lay ahead, cool as ever. Daw, cigarette halfway to mouth, caught his neighbour's inspection, and winked through the tobacco smoke. Russ gave a half smile and turned his eyes back to the parapet – then flinched as the grass growing there was meticulously scythed away in a rattle of machine-gun bullets. As usual to staunch his nerves he leant on humour. 'Dobbo, you're always cracking on you need a shave, just stick your chin on that ledge.'

The sun rose higher. Russ gave his platoon orders, 'Any man who isn't into position in two seconds flat will be severely shot.' D Company cowered in their slit of earth, trying not to listen to the cacophony of battle and wondering how it was progressing. There were, too, thoughts of their families at home. And then Lieutenant Daw had a whistle poised at his lips. His other hand cradled a watch. In one swift second the timepiece was returned to his pocket and the whistle shrilled in perfect unison with others along the line. 'At 'em, lads!' Daw withdrew his revolver and began to scale the ladder, as did Captains Dench and Reed, Lieutenants Pugh, Slater and Carr – those who were second in command had been left behind to rebuild the battalion should any of these others fall. Their men followed under the weights of full packs, some falling back dead the moment their heads poked over the rim.

And what a diabolical sight was to greet them – far from bridging the enemy's first line their predecessors had never reached the German wire. Hundreds of them carpeted No Man's Land, their blood and brains soaking into the ravaged earth. This stark reality gave the men of D Company the impulse to fall, play dead, but the instinct not to let the side down overpowered their fear. The entire battalion set off at a walk, towards the trench that their first wave had vacated. The distance seemed vast.

Already, only yards from their own burrow, men were beginning to keel over, but Daw led his section onwards through the yellow bursts of shrapnel, his revolver ever-flaming. The staff-planners, supremely confident that the German lines would be breached easily, had ordered each platoon to carry rolls of barbed wire, shovels and picks and mallets on top of normal packs for strengthening their new positions. Before the front line trench was reached, however, these were already being discarded as their bearers were hit.

Russ stepped over a wounded Lewis gunner, knowing that to stop and help would bring punishment. He shouted to two men to pick up the gun and strode on, rifle at the port. All around him men pitched forward and were still. Some, wounded but still able to walk, staggered back towards him grinning ruefully, fingers clutching blood-sodden tunics. Down went the captain of A Company, followed by Lieutenants Pugh and Carr. The ground kept erupting beneath their feet, hurling them high into the air on black geysers of earth – and then suddenly, row upon row were toppling like skittles as the German machine-guns broke into fresh voice. Momentarily distracted by the carnage, Daw faltered and instantly fell wounded, slithering down into a shellhole which was already the grave of several men. But the small rent in his arm was not enough to incapacitate him and he dragged himself forward, yelling to his men who, seeing him drop, had come to a standstill.

Russ shouted too, weaving his way in and out of the dead. The ground was now an obstacle course of debris: gas masks, water bottles, rifles, boots . . . with the legs still in them, rolls of wire, tin hats. They were in reach of their own front trench now. Daw ordered his section into it to regroup and found it crammed with hundreds of fearful faces who, their officers gone, looked at him for instruction. Gasping for breath, Russ surveyed their predicament. Literally piles of their fellows lay before the German wire, some draped over it like crows hung up by the gamekeeper to scare away other vermin, cut down as they had tried to find the supposed gaps made by their artillery pals. Shells burst around their position, rendering them deaf and light-headed. Russ waited for Daw to say they should pull back as other sections were doing. Amazingly, Daw ordered them over the top and forward. Dobson couldn't believe such a foolhardly action. 'Christ, he's a bloody sadist!'

Russ shoved him out of the trench. 'I don't care what religion he is, if he says fight we fight!'

A dash of thirty yards and their own barbed-wire defences were breached. The men had abandoned their leisurely pace now, scampering from crater to crater which pocked the devastated landscape. By inches, they made their way towards the enemy barbed wire, their number growing fewer by the second. The man to Hazelwood's left went down. He was wearing a yellow armband to show he carried wirecutters. Russ squatted to his haunches and took possession of the cutters, then ran on. His lungs were beginning to ache; a sequel of the gas.

Quite by chance, Daw found a section of enemy wire that was almost undefended. Russ attacked the spiked coils with the cutters and dragged the strands apart – though this was by no means easy as the belt of wire was extremely dense.

All the while he was hacking and snipping the wire, Russ expected to see his own blood spurting from his breast. But safer here than the gaps prepared by the artillery, for in front of these lay hundreds of dead. Daw kept his eye on the German machine-gunners who were concentrating on these gaps, bringing down the Allies who were like sitting ducks. 'Christ,' he muttered to Russ. 'Bring on the orange sauce.'

The final wire was snipped. Once through, Lieutenant Daw charged for the trenches as if at the head of a thousand men. A German machine-gunner spotted the small group's infiltration and began to enfilade. Simultaneously, there was an explosion. When the huge fountain of earth finally came to rest Daw fell with it. Russ, finding himself in charge, had no option but to proceed with the attack. Miraculously, Dobson was still at his side cheering – despite the order not to do so – but his voice was highly pitched. There came another vicious burst of staccato. Dobson grunted and doubled over, tipping forward on his chin with his bottom sticking in the air. Russ heard his cry, knew he should go on, but instead went back and dragged the wounded boy down into a shellhole. With no one to drive them on, the rest took cover.

Dobson was whimpering, a look of puzzlement on his face. His intestines, like unravelled wool, were looped around his bloodied fingers which scrabbled to return them to their rightful place. He kept gathering them together and stuffing them in, but they kept popping out again, glistening red and grey in the sunshine. At first, shock acted as anaesthesia, but now the pain came in one savage rush. The boy's scream was a mixture of disbelief and affrontery. 'Mam!'

Hazelwood was rummaging madly in Dobson's pack, looking for his field dressing. 'All right, lad! Mother'll look after you.' When his frenzied hands found the dressing and presented it to the wound he saw it was pathetically inadequate. Dobson shrieked incessantly. A panicked Russ shouted, 'Chin up, Dobson! Knit one, purl one . . .' Dobson died.

For the moment the roar of battle disappeared – then was

eclipsed by Hazelwood's own cry of rage as he charged from the shellhole, bayonet levelled at the enemy, screeching his intention. The rest of the attackers streaked after him.

He withdrew a bomb, hurled it, fell flat as the ground blew up, then ran on. Then somehow, he was upon the machine-gun post, despatching the concussed and wounded with a meaningful jab of his blade. As the rest of D Company thudded up behind him he was already swinging the machine-gun round to face the Germans. In another second he began to strafe. Someone appeared at his elbow but he was too crazed to notice who, he just wanted to kill.

'Well done, Filbert lad!' Daw seemed indestructible. The fall he had taken was not as a result of a bullet but the explosion which had knocked him over. Here he was, stunned and sleeve dripping blood but still in command. Once more he led the men on the enemy, hurling bombs and everything available.

They reached the pulverized section of trench and jumped in to confront the terrified survivors. 'Kamerad!' A weapon was dropped and hands raised. Daw pretended to have trouble with his vision. 'Here, hold this gun, Sergeant. I've got something in my eye.' Russ emptied the last of Daw's bullets into the dismayed young German. Daw recovered his sight. He veered round a bend, came across a dugout and tossed in his final bomb, pressing himself against the breastworks. There was a dull thump and smoke poured from the dugout. The men ran on.

Russ, still wild for vengeance, lunged with his bayonet at all he encountered. Daw, his gun empty, pulled a nail-studded club from his pack and used it for crushing skulls. Those who had been about to surrender saw that they were to be granted no mercy. They made for a communication trench, the British in pursuit. A shell burst nearby, wiping out yet more of Daw's small army. The rest chased the fleeing enemy until the Germans began a counter attack and forced them back from whence they came. Valiantly, Russ and the others fought to hang onto the ground they had captured but with no more bombs were compelled to stumble backwards and leap for No Man's Land. With enemy fire to all sides, they made for a huge crater and dived into it.

From here, Daw panted for someone to volunteer as a runner. A young lance-corporal was selected and, with all the chance of a grouse on the Glorious Twelfth, set out for his own lines. The ten remaining were forced to lie sick, wounded and paralysed with terror for twelve hours until – aware that there was to be no assistance – they could use the darkness to make the return to their own lines. All day they lay in the hot sun, battered, bruised, half-crazed with the sights they had seen and made crazier by the constant bombardment from their own side. When finally darkness came, Lieutenant Daw gave the order to move off. This was enacted with temerity, the men dragging themselves on their bellies for the greater part of the way. It was not easy; they found that every yard of ground was covered by a body.

Rowena spread the evening newspaper on the floor, back page uppermost, and read out loud the headlines, summary to her daily report of the war. '*Great British Offensive Begins. Attack Opened This Morning. 16 Miles Of Trenches Stormed By Our Troops. Many Prisoners In Our Hands.*' She looked up, brown eyes sparkling. 'It must be nearly over now. We're really giving Fritz a pounding.' Though it wasn't just the battle which made her so radiant; she had just heard that she had passed her scholarship exam and would start the new term at the Municipal Secondary School for Girls. Her mother had been overjoyed, for she had anticipated failure after so much school disruption, and she was now busy cutting out new dresses to mark Rowena's achievement. It was nice to see Mother smiling for once. The tips of Rowena's long hair caressed the page as she knelt over it to read the rest, her narrative punctuated with 'Valour, victory, progress, Germans punished, massive advances . . .'

The others clapped and cheered as their sister related tales of derring do. 'I wonder if Bertie's taking part?' said Becky after the final paragraph had been read.

Lyn uttered a groan. 'Oh God, I hope not! He'll be strutting around and boasting for all he's worth when he comes home.'

'Give him his due,' reproved Charlie. 'It must be very scarey to be shot at – he's got guts.'

'That's what I say!' Becky leapt up. 'And I'm going to make him a medal, Father as well. Has anybody got any silver paper?'

Charlie said he would find a bit from somewhere. 'Wena, does it say how many Boches were killed?'

She consulted the paper again. 'Can't see anything . . . hey!' She touched a speculative finger to her lips. 'I wonder what they'll do with all those dead Germans?'

'Make them into sausages,' riposted Lyn, and they all broke into giggles.

Only in the morning was the true carnage apparent. Flags of truce were raised in order for both sides to sweep up their ghastly litter. Russ was one of the survivors who waded out into the morass of No Man's Land to bring back the dead and wounded. The sight which loomed through the pall of gunsmoke was like nothing he had seen before. Yesterday's trees stood raped and mutilated, every leaf gone, branches splintered. Hardly a blade of grass was to be found. The earth looked as if it had been at the mercy of some drunken ploughman, violated by shellholes so numerous that in many places they ran into each other, some so deep they gave the impression of going right down to Hell.

Barbed wire entanglements had been uprooted and tossed aside – like a fey woman discards a necklace – half buried under a layer of bone and tissue and the tons of equipment left by those who had been blown to bits. Human debris, men cut in half by machine-gun fire, armless torsoes, bright-pink gaping holes, ragged limbs. The horror produced vomiting. Many wept as they came across the bodies of dead pals. In Russ' dazed estimation there must be six or seven thousand dead within his sight. It seemed, too, as if this destruction had been repeated all along the line, for as he laboured throughout the day, tales of a shambles percolated from other battalions. Though most of the men were ignorant of the true magnitude – sixty thousand of their chums had fallen yesterday, some twenty thousand would not rise. Such butchery would have been unbelievable, even to the handful who had seen it through from Mons, but Hazelwood, gazing out over the endless carnage, had the reality imprinted on his mind forever.

He turned as the sergeant working with him muttered an opinion, 'Now I know why they brought us here in cattle trucks.'

Russ moved his head. 'No . . . I've seen cattle treated with more compassion than this.' And the grisly task proceeded.

During that day he helped to bury hundreds of his fellows, drifting from corpse to corpse, collecting pay books, sometimes glancing at the pencilled wills in the back of them – 'To my chum Fred I leave my penknife . . .' – before answering the shout, 'There's another live one 'ere!' Piling the dead into shell craters and ruined trenches where the flies sucked their fill and the stench of hot blood drew the bile to his throat.

He never traced Dobson's body, though he did stumble on the chewed-up remains of Lance-Corporal Heath, Privates Husthwaite and Strawbridge of D Company. Russ gazed down at the latter's cadaver. A Brownie camera was nearby, spilled from the machine-gun ravaged satchel. The instrument was shattered, its film exposed in untidy coils. It reminded him of Dobson's intestines and he staggered away.

Of D Company, Russ was one of only eight unwounded. In all, the battalion had permanently lost sixteen officers and four hundred and fifty men, almost three-quarters of its attacking force.

At midday, Russ ferried yet another screaming victim to the dressing station, at which point exhaustion prompted him to take a rest. With the stretcher disposed of, he lit a cigarette, tried to unclamp the jaws that were welded together by tension and closed his eyes. He took fierce drags, his mind seeing young Dobson's body, but transposing it with the face of his own son. When he opened his eyes and glanced to his right a ragged collection of German prisoners was trickling in. Oddly, he felt no desire to kill them now, felt only self-disgust for his mad spell of bestiality. The day before yesterday he would not have believed himself capable of such evil. His only thought now was poor buggers, they're getting it as much as we are.

The prisoners were deposited nearby. After a moment's perusal the sergeant wandered over the blood-caked ground to sit beside one of them, proffering a cigarette. The enemy's acceptance was warily grateful. His black-nailed fingers quivered as they placed the Woodbine between his lips, awaiting the Englishman's match. A long exhalation, then an appreciative nod. The enemy surveyed the shambles with eyes that were dead and, gesturing with the cigarette, said something in German. His meaning was clear. Russ took a long drag himself and nodded disgustedly, 'Bloody crackers,' while the cries of the wounded blended together into one inhuman howl that lent him a glimpse of hell.

While the battle continued around him, Russ spent the next two days ferrying the badly wounded from Basin Wood to Euston Dump where they were collected by ambulance. On the fourth day of July there was a tremendous downpour which flooded the trenches and almost drowned the numerous stretcher cases that lay in them, as yet unattended. It was with real gratitude that the sergeant and what was left of D Company marched to their rest area that night . . . though they took part of that dreadful place with them; along with the clarts of mud on their boots, clung tiny fragments of their comrades.

Alas! there was to be little comfort here either. Russ had just sufficient time to write to Dobson's mother and underline a printed sentence, 'I am well and unwounded' on a field postcard for his wife – she wouldn't care, but he thought it best to tell her after the last cock-up – before the company was ordered to stand to in expectation of a German attack. Consequently, the men who arrived at their new sector were far from rejuvenated, and the mounds of unburied bodies that lay putrefying in the summer sun sparked off murmurs of insurrection over, 'That bloody butcher, Haig' who had sent them into this abattoir.

The fact that so many regiments had been almost wiped out meant a period of reshuffling. Hazelwood, those officers who had been left out of battle and the remainder of the battalion were linked with survivors from different regiments and also a batch of conscripts. In other words, thought Russ bitterly, a set of mongrels. It followed, then, that the men under his charge could no longer be enthused by regimental pride. Add this to the huge slaughter most of them had witnessed and any motivation they might have had was reduced to nil. Hazelwood's new platoon was not alone in these feelings and Field Punishment, instead of being isolated, became the order of the day. Far from subduing the mutinous mood it served to intensify the men's anger. Russ had a devil of a time keeping them in line. Gone was the camaraderie experienced before the Somme. The sergeant felt unable to rely on any of these men who were, in effect, strangers and owed him no loyalty. Even harder to enthuse were the conscripts who didn't want to be here at all. And oh God . . . he did miss little Dobson.

There had been few decorations handed out for that first day of July, mainly because there were few officers left to witness acts of gallantry. Somehow, though, Lieutenant Daw had been among those honoured. His shallow wound was healed now. Today in some muddy field he was receiving a medal for his infiltration of enemy lines with only a handful of men at his disposal. He had also been granted a captaincy and appointed command of Hazelwood's company. Thank God he wasn't receiving his medal at Buckingham Palace, thought Russ. Rachel would have a seizure. The handful of men who had helped to earn Daw his medal had got recognition too, but as far as Russ was concerned they could stuff their medals. All the sergeant yearned for was sleep. After the savagery of that first day on the Somme the normal pattern of four days in the front trenches was no longer operable and they had been in this same position for weeks on end. Russ was nearing exhaustion. Thus, his temper was constantly being tested, as it was today.

'Where's that bloody Piltdown Man?' he bellowed of his lance-corporal, a veteran like himself which gave them some sort of affinity. The private in demand, Jewitt, was nicknamed for his habit of vanishing underground at every opportunity.

Lance-Corporal Holmes peered to right and left, then gave a snort of annoyance. 'I've just this minute dug him out o' the bloody pit, Sarg. No sooner you turn your back than the little sod's back in there. I'll go an' . . .'

'As you were!' interrupted Russ impatiently. 'I'll go. I've had enough o' that little skiver.' Jewitt was one of the more recent conscripts. He had been appointed company pioneer whose job it was to empty the biscuit tins that served as latrines. Far from turning his nose up at this, Jewitt deemed it a cushy number, a licence to keep him away from the firing line. Russ was forever having to reprimand him for his vanishing acts. 'Talk about the bloody Missing Link.'

Jewitt, however, was not in the latrine area. The sergeant stormed back up the trench that had been dubbed Windy Passage, ducking his angry face into every cubbyhole as he patrolled the network of trenches. 'I'll bleeding kill the little scrimshank! Lonsborough, have you seen Piltdown?'

Though Lonsborough denied knowing Jewitt's whereabouts, the sergeant knew at once that he did. 'Come on out with it, Private!'

There was an awkward silence, then, 'I think he's gone to see his pal, Sarg.'

'Aw, that's nice,' said Russ casually. 'Where does this pal live – bleeding Scarborough?' He asked the name of Jewitt's pal.

'Private Hopwood. He's in the Cat and Cabbage,' divulged Lonsborough, referring to the York and Lancaster Regiment. 'On field punishment.'

Russ spun on his heel. 'Jewitt'll be joining him if he deserts his post again – and so will them that cover up for him!'

Instead of sending someone to fetch the boy, Russ went personally. The prisoner on Field Punishment Number 1 was a pitiable sight. The youngster had been lashed to a howitzer by his wrists and ankles. His position among a group of trees afforded no solace, for the heat of the sun bore through the leafless branches. There was a constant buzz of flies around his head. Unable to lift a hand to brush them away he could only loll his head from side to side and shudder as the insects crawled into his ears and up his nostrils. The sweat trickled between his shoulderblades and sparkled on his brow, his damp hair sticking to it.

Private Jewitt uncorked his water bottle and, with a quick look about him, applied it to the dry lips. His friend had been standing here for one and a half hours. With his legs spread and lashed to the hot metal it was agony. 'Here you are, chum.' Jewitt tipped the water bottle gingerly, allowing a drop of water into the parched mouth whilst keeping an eye open for the guard. His stance was one of furtiveness – not simply because he was out of bounds, but because this was Jewitt's natural pose. His shoulders had a permanent stoop that even an RSM could not unbend. Maybe it was an attempt to make himself less conspicuous for he was very tall and thin. If so, then it was unsuccessful – made him look even more conspicuous than ever; when this crouch was twinned with Jewitt's foxy eyes it epitomized slyness. And this of course made him a target for every NCO.

'Jewitt!' Russ came striding into the clearing, the effect of his voice bringing the water bottle away from the prisoner's face and splashing the front of his vest. A guilty Jewitt prepared for the roasting . . . but the sergeant's eyes were for the prisoner. 'Bertie!' He rushed forward and cupped filthy hands to his son's face. 'Oh Christ, Bertie! You daft little . . . Here let's get you untied! Oh, lad . . .' Impatient fingers picked at the knots in the rope and all the while he struggled to release his son he talked to Bertie, asking what he had done to warrant this.

Freed, Bertie put his feet together and rubbed his wrists. 'I shot the Captain.' At his father's look of astonishment he added bitterly, 'Oh, don't worry – only in the foot.'

'Thank Christ for that,' breathed Russ, envisioning Wheatley's body being dominoed by bullets. He looked more carefully at the boy – no, not a boy, thought Russ. Those eyes had seen the realities of war, his body drilled to that of a man's and his mother's pudding basin haircut sheared into regulation style . . . 'How did it happen?'

Bertie looked away, massaging the ache in his shoulders. 'We were off over the top the day before yesterday. I got the wind up and let me gun off, put a hole in the Captain's foot.' He wanted to laugh at the memory of the officer dancing about but he wouldn't whilst in his father's presence. 'I thought he was going to shoot me.'

'What the fuck's going on here?' The guard sergeant appeared from nowhere. 'Who's untied that man?'

'Man? Man!' Russell's temper came to the boil. 'Has no bugger got eyes in their head round here? This lad is thirteen years old . . .'

'*Fourteen!*' yelled Bertie. 'I'm bloody fourteen! You don't even know!'

'I asked who fuckin' untied him!' bawled the guard sergeant.

'I fucking have!' Russ yelled back. 'He's my son! He shouldn't even be in the Army let alone trussed up like this!'

The other swore again. 'And I'm expected to know how bloody old he is, am I? Come on, you!' He grabbed Bertie. 'We'd best have this out with your CO.'

'Hang on!' Russ put a hand out, then removed it at the look it produced on the guard sergeant's face. 'Just let me have a word with him, will you? Please,' he added more politely. With the other's consent he tried to clamp reassuring hands on the boy's shoulders. 'Don't worry, son. We'll get this sorted out with your CO and you'll be off home.'

Bertie shrugged the hands off. 'I don't want to go home!' Oh, he did, he did, away from the blood and the noise . . . All he wanted was to sink into his warm bed and have his mother tuck him in and smooth his brow . . . but Charlie would be there.

A frustrated Russ thumped his son's arm. 'Well you're bloody-well going! Your mother must be grey with worry.'

'I don't see too many grey hairs on your head, Father!'

Russ took control of his voice. 'Listen, it's me that's been trying to find you, showing everybody your photograph. See!' He fumbled for the snapshot to illustrate how much his son meant to him. 'I've been carrying it around with me since you ran away, hoping somebody might recognize you, hoping to God I'd find you before you got hurt.'

Bertie delivered a nasty laugh. 'Hoping the picture would remind you what your son looks like. Do you carry *his* picture round too?'

In a fury, Russ tore the photograph to shreds and scattered the pieces. 'Sod the picture! I don't need that to tell me who my son is!' His tone became earnest. 'Bertie, you know how much I think about you, always have. I understand what a shock it must have been to find out about Charlie, but I don't look upon him as my son – you're my son . . . I love you, Bertie.' He snatched an embarrassed glance at Jewitt who ran a hand over his neck in the same manner and distanced himself from the pair. The guard sergeant was not so compassionate and made a point of listening to every word.

But Bertie didn't care who was listening, he didn't want to listen himself. Turning to the guard sergeant he said, 'I'm ready to go.'

Russ exhaled, all his spirit emerging with that breath. 'I'll see you before you go home then, Bertie.'

'I don't have a home now,' replied his son. 'You destroyed it.'

Completely deflated, Russ watched the boy limp away beside the man, then turned on Jewitt. 'I'll overlook your skiving this time, Private, seeing as how you were helping my lad . . . You won't say anything about this, now?'

Jewitt promised he wouldn't. He had been rather surprised to discover that his sergeant possessed human emotions. 'I'm sorry, I hadn't a clue he was your lad or I would've let you know before. He told me they called him Hopwood.'

Russ grimaced. 'As you may have gathered, Private, me and my son don't get on too well. How come you know him, anyway?'

398

'I don't really,' admitted Jewitt. 'We just came over on the same boat. I felt sorry for him 'cause he told me . . .' he broke off, as it clicked that the man Hopwood had spoken about in such derogatory terms was the sergeant.

Russ guessed. 'He told you all about his troubles at home. About Charlie as well?' When Jewitt asked if this was the coloured boy, Russ gave a tight smile. 'I trust you won't repeat any of what he told you, Jewitt, otherwise . . .' He didn't finish. Jewitt, acting hurt, said that the sergeant didn't need to use threats, he had never broken Hopwood's confidence.

'I never saw him again till we were sent to this place and were billeted near to each other. He seemed a quiet lad, didn't have much to do with anyone else.'

Russ fingered the redundant pieces of rope. 'And what about this?'

'I only learnt about it by accident. Overheard two blokes talking when . . .'

'When you were skiving in the bog.' Hazelwood nodded and, after poking at the discarded pieces of photograph with his boot, began to walk away. 'How many times have I told you it's the most dangerous place to be? There's nowt Jerry likes better than a sitting target. One o' these days . . .' With a heartfelt sigh he told Jewitt he was going to ask Captain Daw to have a word with Bertie's CO. 'You get back to your section – and keep out of that bleeding lat!'

Bertie did not complete the rest of his punishment. After his CO had been acquainted with his true age he was given a ticking off, officially discharged and ordered to return to Blighty. Before his son left, Russ went to visit him. The atmosphere between them was still that of a brick wall.

'You promise to go straight home and not re-enlist?' pressed Russell.

'Why should I do that?' Bertie's experience of war had terrified him, but he managed to hide it very well. 'I only joined because I thought you were home for good.'

'Oh Bertie . . .' Russ gave a helpless gesture. 'It's tearing your mother apart, all this bad feeling.'

'And who's responsible for it, Father?' shouted Bertie.

'I am . . . I know that . . .'

'Oh, good!'

Russ saw that he would never have his son's forgiveness, could only be grateful that he had found him and he was now going to safety. 'Ah well . . . goodbye, Bertie. Give my love to your mother and the girls. I'd be grateful if you'd do that much for me. It won't cost you anything and I might not live to give them it myself.' He had hoped that the thought of his father's death might sting the boy to repentance. But Bertie's expression never even wavered. 'Maybe Charlie will be out of your hair by the time you get home. I wrote to the priest last year and asked him to arrange for the boy to go to boarding school, I can't say what's come of it because your mother never writes to me. But I think we can assume that he'll have gone by now. So you see you won't have to get on with him at all. Take care of your mother. She needs a man to support her. Tell her not to worry, if I should happen to get any Blighty leave I'll spend it with Aunt May down in Gloucester, I shan't bother her again.'

Bertie nodded, tight-lipped, then simply walked away. It was only when Sergeant Hazelwood received a later summons from his Commanding Officer that he learnt that the troopship carrying his son to safety had been shelled by a German gunboat under the guise of a merchantman. There were no survivors.

CHAPTER TWENTY-SIX

'A year!' Rachel was complaining to Charlie. 'A blessed year since that priest of yours promised to get you into college and never a word since. He's as irresponsible as my husband. I'll give him another couple of weeks and then I think you can start looking for a job.' She saw Charlie's look of surprise. 'Well you are fourteen! Old enough to be contributing to your upkeep. Other boys have to – those that haven't been stolen by the Army!'

Yet another family dinner was being eaten without Bertie. Rachel had stopped laying an extra place in the hope that he would suddenly walk in and sit down. Her worry had long since reached its crescendo and was now on its way back down – one couldn't remain at such a fever pitch; life just had to carry on. But still she damned the Army for its incompetent and long-winded handling of the situation. Upstairs there were now two sets of birthday presents waiting to be opened by her son. 'Robert'll be twenty-one before they manage to find him. Men! They're all the . . .' She broke off as Biddy brought a telegram in. 'Oh, not another!' She sighed impatiently and inserted a portion of sausage in her mouth before snatching the envelope. 'I wonder what they've done with your father this time.' Sure in the belief that it pertained to her husband, she opened the telegram.

'Is Father missing again?' asked Rhona as her mother's face changed. The hand holding the telegram started to shake, slightly at first, then more violently as though Rachel were caught up in an earthquake. Before anyone had the chance to ask what was wrong she screamed, 'Robert!' and broke into racking sobs.

The girls being too shocked, Charlie made the unforgiveable error of trying to comfort the hysterical woman. She launched herself at him, slapping him about the head and shoulders, anywhere she could reach, so that he backed away in alarm.

'Why was it Robert? Why isn't it you who's lying dead at the bottom of the sea?' Her arms windmilled at him. 'What did he ever do to anyone? While you cause grief and pain to all you meet – get out of my sight!' She landed one more blow as he fled upstairs to shut himself, weeping, in the attic, while she broke down, thinking only of her own bereavement and nothing of her daughters' who had to turn to Biddy for comfort.

Even Lyn cried freely – there was no one who would laugh at her, for all were equally stricken – but she couldn't understand why she *was* crying, for she had always fought with Bertie. Becky buried her head in the maid's lap and sobbed her heart out, for she had loved her brother, as had Rowena who had to cuddle the little ones. Even if Robina had felt nothing for Bertie she would have cried in sympathy with her sisters, and the younger ones cried because they were frightened by the wailing. Biddy was the only one free of tears, trying her best to console in her clumsy Irish brogue. And none of them gave a thought to Charlie who had to bear this alone.

The younger ones recovered after having a good cry, but Rowena continued to burst into tears every half hour, when of course Beany joined her. Rachel, after her long spell of hysteria, was flattened, wandering ghost-like about the house as if in search of her dead son. It's a mix-up, she kept telling herself. In a couple of weeks there'll be another telegram to say he isn't dead. He *isn't* dead.

That same evening Ella Daw, having heard the news from Biddy over the yard wall, decided to put aside her differences to go and offer commiserations. Rachel was sitting, glassy-eyed, at the kitchen table, screwing and unscrewing a damp ball of handkerchief. The children – but not Charlie who still dared not leave his attic – were with her, all sporting red eyes. Lyn noted with interest that Aunt Ella was wearing trousers. Rowena put an arm round her mother who did not appear to be aware of Ella's presence. 'Mrs Daw's here, Mother.'

'I've just heard, Rachel,' began Ella in grave tone as the woman lifted bereft eyes to her. She sat down opposite and reached over to clasp Rachel's hand which was cold. 'I'm ever so sorry. Eh . . . it's just tragic.'

'I can't believe it,' murmured Rachel frowning. 'It only seems like yesterday I was nursing him . . .'

'Aye . . . I know how you feel.' Ella bolstered herself with a deep breath and revealed, 'I've just lost my little Kim. Thirteen years we had him – he was nearly the same age as Bertie. I just can't believe he's gone.'

Only now did Rachel appear to be fully aware of her neighbour's presence. She looked at her in wonderment. There were tears in Ella's eyes. Her answer emerged on a breath of disbelief. 'You're comparing my Robert to a dog?' She came up slowly from her seat. 'How dare you? How *dare* you say you understand my loss! He was my *son!*'

Ella was mortified that her intended comfort was being rebuffed. She rose, intending to leave forthwith, but Rachel hadn't finished.

'And you can number yourself responsible!' she yelled, brown eyes wild. 'You're the one who started all this!'

Ella didn't understand for the moment. When she did she looked Rachel calmly in the eye and said quietly, 'If you're harking back to that letter business, Rachel . . . I never wrote it.'

On the woman's silent departure Rachel pressed her knuckles into the table and swayed in anguish.

Then it was Biddy's turn to say the wrong thing. 'I don't think she intended it as an insult, ma'am. She loved that wee dog o' hers. She was only tryin' to make ye feel better.'

Rachel's eyes fixed her with such venom that she shrank. 'And well you might talk about making people feel better with your countrymen taking up arms against us! Isn't it enough that our boys have to fight the Germans without being attacked from across the Irish Sea?'

''Twas only a bit o' trouble in Dublin, ma'am,' offered Biddy in hurt voice.

'And how d'you imagine this war started? I'll bet someone said, "Oh, 'tis only a bit o' trouble in Belgium!" And that traitor Casement . . . we're being attacked from all sides – you might even be in with them for all I know.'

'Me?' spat Biddy at this neurotic conjecture.

'Yes you! Goodness knows you spend most of your time sneaking about the house, I can never find you when there's work to be done . . .'

'What?' cried an astounded Biddy.

'Lazy! You are a lazy Irish slob! Look at these pots, they're not even cleared away.'

'But we've only just eaten . . .'

'The coalscuttle's half empty . . .'

''Cause you won't pay the coalman!'

'He's profiteering like the rest of them! The sink's filthy . . . you're nothing but an idle baggage!'

'Right, that's it!' Biddy ripped off her apron and threw it down. 'I've put up with all kinds of insults from you over the years but bedamned if I'm being told I'm idle. My God! I'm two inches shorter than when I started what with all the running about ye've had me do, it's worn me legs away. I'm sorry to leave yese when ye've just had this dastardly shock but I can't stand any more – I *won't* stand any more!' She pounded upstairs to fetch her belongings while Rachel continued to rant at the foot of the stairs. A slam marked her departure. The children watched a crazed Rachel charge down the passage after her, fling open the door and shout down the street – a thing their mother would never have done in her right state of mind, 'Good riddance, you idle baggage! You ought to be executed like that other traitor!'

Then she stormed back in, rushed up the stairs and invaded Charlie's room. He looked up, startled, as she seized a large brass candlestick and descended on him.

The girls heard his cry of protest. When they rushed up to see what was happening they saw him holding up his arms as protection as the weapon came down again and again.

'Mother, stop!' Rowena tried to catch her mother's arm. 'Please! It's not Charlie's fault!' Becky and Robina were sobbing.

'It's *all* his fault!' raged their mother. 'You devil!'

Charlie gave a howl of agony as the heavy candlestick made contact with his arm for the fifth time. Rachel fell back, panting and staring wildly. Then, with the sound of sobbing, she seemed to come out of her fit and gazed upon him with horror as he supported his fractured arm with another that was cut and bruised. With a shriek, she flung the candlestick aside and fell beside him, hands clasped over mouth in abhorrence of what she had done. 'Oh, God! Oh, God!'

'It's all right,' he gasped through distorted lips.

'It's not all right!' She made one final howl of despair, then broke down, swaying and moaning like an animal.

Russ had been granted a precious green envelope – precious, not only because a man might have to wait a month to get one, but because missives of this colour were not subject to regimental censorship; the sender could be as intimate as he liked without fear of local derision. He could tell her anything – tell her how he had wanted to cry when they had given him the news about Bertie, but how he had not been able to; tell her of his last meeting with his son; tell her how sorry . . . oh God, that word, Russ closed his eyes, that ineffectual little word he had used as a shield so many times . . .

He pictured Rachel in her grief. She came crashing into his mind, her bonny face distorted by anguish, fingers clawing and scratching at him, ripping his flesh, screaming at him, *'Murderer! You did it! You killed him! I hate you! Don't you ever come back!'* Then she took hold of him and banged his head against the wall again and again, slapping, kicking, ripping his hair out, gouging his eyes and with every blow he shouted, *'Yes, more! Again! Hit me again!'* Rage and self-hate boiled through his veins trying to volcano from the top of his head . . . but like the tears he could not shed he suppressed it, kept it bottled tightly inside, savoured it, kept it simmering . . .

After staring at the blank page for half an hour, he

crumpled it in his fist and tossed it into the mud. Die, he said, *die*.

'How's she taking it?' Mrs Phillips asked Ella after the latter had told her that yes, she had heard right, Bertie was dead.

'I don't know how she is and I don't care.' Ella slapped her money onto the counter. 'I'm damned if I'm going cap in hand to find out after the way she spoke to me – you'd think it was me who'd killed him!' She tucked her chin into her neck, snapping her purse shut. 'Anyway, she's never once asked about my Jack. Not once in two years.'

'Is that Mrs Hazelwood you're talking about?' enquired another woman who had entered halfway through the conversation.

'Aye, we're just on about their Bertie,' muttered Ella.

'Aw I know, it's terrible.' The woman's face creased in sympathy. 'He was only thirteen or fourteen, wasn't he?'

'Well sorry as I am, I shan't be going out of my way to offer help,' said Mrs Phillips firmly. 'She must've heard about our Fred being wounded but she was the only one round here who never popped in to ask how he was – walked right past the door, she did. It's them little lasses I feel most sorry for. I'll bet she's got them running around after her now she's sacked Biddy – oh, didn't you hear about that? I'd've thought you could've heard her a mile away, screeching down the street she was – "Good riddance, you idle baggage!"' She chortled, then looked serious again. 'That poor lass, the eldest, what's her name? Rowena, she looks like a little old woman. Have you seen her? She came in here to do the shopping. I tried to find out what sort of state they're in, but she plays her cards pretty close to her chest does that one.'

'Here's another who'll be keeping well out of it an' all,' stated Ella. 'I feel sorry for the kids, but I've had my nose bloodied enough. If she wants to keep herself to herself she's welcome.'

What made it so unreal was the lack of a body. Rachel stitched mechanically, her glazed eyes fixed to the hat on her lap but not really seeing it. The days had bled into weeks and still her only vision was that of her son floundering in the water, his face going under, the salt water filling his lungs. She could taste the salt on her own lips . . . and yet she still kept telling herself it wasn't so, Robert wasn't dead. Despite the condolences and the letter from his commanding officer it was a mistake.

She had left the house only once. What an ordeal that had been. People had come up to her, heads cocked to one side as if they were deformed and with earnest faces would enquire how she was feeling. *How did they think she was feeling?* But she did not scream at them, had replied politely that she was quite well considering, thank you, and then slipped away. Worse than these were the people who had seen her coming and had deliberately crossed the road to avoid having to talk to her, as though losing her son had made her a leper. After this she had left the shopping to Rowena and had stayed inside.

But even here she wasn't completely safe, for people would call asking her to make them a hat – 'If you're sure you feel up to it of course'. She didn't feel up to anything, but she took their orders, for with the shop closed she had no income other than the separation allowance from the Army. Besides, as the well-meaning visitors would say, 'You want to keep occupied – take your mind off things'. Which was all very well . . . but she sewed with her fingers, not her mind.

The spate of madness was over, but to Rowena the mood she was in now was just as frightening as the rages. Normally, Mother rushed about the home like a whirlwind, now she just seemed to sit there in a trance, and when she did move it was as though someone were holding her ankles. She had never listened to anything the children said of course, but now it was more than that. She didn't appear to know they were even there. Rowena wanted to ask her questions about Bertie, but daren't for fear of invoking another tempest. There was no one else she felt able to talk to about her brother. Biddy was gone, and she couldn't go and see Aunt Ella. The others were too young to understand, and she was rather frightened of the form teacher at her new school. Oh, how she wished her father was here. She battled to fix her eyes to the book she was working on . . . but she just kept thinking of her brother.

With Biddy's departure and the girls' return to school, Rachel had been forced to stay at home to take care of the youngest child who was nearly three, and prepare the meals for when the rest came home. Though quite often they were greeted by a neglected child, an empty table and a vacant expression, leaving Rowena to take command. Somehow, Rachel had gathered sufficient wits to place an advertisement in the press for a general maid, but even though it was in for three nights not one person applied. Probably they were all working at the munitions factories. Rachel had never been on her own before. For the nineteen years of her married life she had always had someone to help her cope. For the first time in her occupation of this house a layer of dust was allowed to settle. This in itself showed how ill she was, plus the fact that they were now all sitting in the best parlour instead of the kitchen with books and bits of material strewn all over the place.

After a time she finished stitching the hat and, taking her scissors, cut the thread. Putting scissors and needle aside, she lifted the hat. There followed a moment of ponderance . . . then Lyn started to laugh. Mother had sewn the hat to her skirt.

'Stop it.' Rowena saw the look of confusion on her mother's face. 'Lyn, I said stop laughing! It's not funny.' She sprang up and took hold of the scissors, carefully unpicking the stitches while her mother just sat there like a mute. Lyn bit her lip. Then, after a look at Beany, exploded into giggles again.

Dealing her a warning glare, Rowena put the hat on the table and asked Rachel, 'Should I make the drinks, Mother?'

There was a long silence, during which Rachel stared from one face to another. Then she nodded wanly.

'I'll help.' Charlie, arm in a sling, rose and made for the door.

408

Rowena stopped him. 'You can't do it one-handed. Lyn can come and help.'

Subdued, Charlie reseated himself and stared at his feet. Why, when things were just beginning to settle down, did Bertie have to go and die? And then there was the worry about Father Guillaume. Charlie didn't think as Rachel did that it was mere irresponsibility which stopped the priest from writing. He had the dreadful feeling that something had happened to his friend, for he knew that the Germans were no respecters of the priesthood.

In the kitchen, the normally placid Rowena unleashed her frustration on her younger sister, rebuking her for laughing at their mother's mistake.

'Well it was funny,' objected Lyn, kneeling on a chair to arrange the mugs. Her hair was a mass of snarls. With no Biddy to drive her, Lyn couldn't see the need to brush it or to get washed – her fingernails were ridged with dirt.

'No it wasn't! Mother's ill, she doesn't need you to make her feel worse!'

'You would've laughed normally!' came the objection.

'Normally, yes! But things aren't normal, are they? Our brother's dead.' Rowena's face screwed up in pain. 'Don't you care?'

'Of course I do!' The wide mouth took on the appearance of a frog's.

'I don't think you do, otherwise you'd know how Mother's feeling and not be so cruel!'

Lyn's eyes threatened tears. Before they showed she ran from the kitchen and into the lavatory. Rowena grasped the back of a chair, wanting to cry herself. It was all so horrible. She wished there was an adult there to tell her what to do. The page in her mathematics book was still blank. She had tried to do it as soon as she had come in from school but then she had to get the tea ready, throughout which Beany and Lyn had fought and Mona had whinged and refused to eat the prepared meal, and then Regina had been sick: all whilst Mother had been closeted away in the front parlour. And then there had been the washing up to do. She had attempted to tackle the maths straight after this, but her

409

mind wouldn't seem to function. This was partly because she hadn't been listening properly when Miss Greenwood demonstrated on the blackboard. Her mind kept straying to Bertie and Father. Even if she had been capable of doing them, there would be no chance of this in the morning before school, for she would doubtless have breakfast to see to and the sheets and nightgowns to wash, for Becky was still wetting the bed. Charlie had offered to do these, but how could he with his arm in plaster? Then at lunchbreak she would have to slip out of school to do the shopping. Being at secondary school made it all the harder to keep a check on her sisters. The responsibility made her feel as if she were carrying all the members of her family on her narrow shoulders.

A blast of steam brought her round and she lifted the kettle from the heat. With the bedtime drinks made, she took them through to the parlour. Lyn sidled in some minutes later but she didn't speak or even look at her. After the cocoa was finished she ordered the girls to bed. There was more fighting which she tried, in vain, to quell while her mother sat like a zombie. In the end she covered her ears against the caterwauling and cried at the top of her voice. 'Stop!'

Silence. Everyone looked towards Mother who had not batted an eyelash. 'Now get to bed!' commanded Rowena sternly.

'Rowena Hazelwood, I don't seem to be in possession of your homework book. Can you tell me why?'

For the two hours since entering school Rowena had been dreading this question from Miss Greenwood. The waiting had not helped to provide an excuse. 'I'm afraid I didn't have time to do my homework.'

Unforgiving eyes peered at her over the spectacles. 'And why not?'

'I had to help Mother about the house.'

'I'm sure that is commendable, but so do most of the girls in your class. Having a little housework to do is no excuse for neglecting your education.'

Rowena did not contradict and bent her head. 'No, Miss.'

'Hold out your hand.' Rowena did so, to receive a stroke of the ruler across her knuckles. 'Now tonight you will do the exercises which you failed to do yesterday and will also complete this further exercise on page fifty-three.'

Pleading brown eyes were lifted to the teacher. 'Miss Greenwood . . . I don't know how to do them.'

'Rowena Hazelwood, I spent ninety minutes yesterday giving examples on the blackboard! Are you telling me I wasted my time?' Rowena whispered that she had not understood. 'Everyone else seems to have understood! Might it be that you weren't paying attention?' The teacher snatched a textbook and proceeded to give an example on a scrap of paper. 'There! Do you understand now?'

Rowena didn't, but was too ashamed and afraid to say no, and nodded.

'So I shall expect your homework book on my desk tomorrow with the two exercises completed!'

Needless to say, Rowena was unable to carry out this order. If she didn't know how to do them last night she was hardly going to fare any better this evening. And again, when she arrived home she found her mother in a state of catalepsy and numerous chores to see to. It was not unexpected when she received another six strokes of the ruler the morning after.

Rowena, being a child who could not share her worry, told no one and so her persecution went undetected for yet another week. Her mother, boarded up in her own grief, did not notice the face drawn by lack of sleep. Nor did any of her sisters appear to think it necessary to enquire. Charlie, however, did . . . only to be told that it was none of his business.

Two more weeks passed and still they were without help of any kind, with Rowena taking responsibility for the running of the house and the shopping. The situation at school grew worse – unbearable . . . but this evening was to see an end to it, one way or another. Rowena sat with her family in the front parlour, listening for the creak of the gate

411

and the knock at the door. All through tea she had been waiting, listening. With every external noise her heart would leap . . . then silence would reign to extend her torture.

When the knock did come, she almost jumped out of her skin. Her mother lifted dull eyes and said, 'Answer that, one of you.'

Rowena pulled at her hair, looking at the others. Charlie jumped up and went down the passage. Rowena listened. The sound of a woman's voice brought a sudden prickling to her armpits and a flush to her face.

Charlie reappeared. 'It's Rowena's form teacher to see you, Mrs Hazelwood.'

Rowena stood as her teacher was shown in, rubbing at her thumbs. Her mother was asking Miss Bannon to sit down. Rachel wore a polite, if manufactured smile. 'What can we do for you, Miss Bannon?'

The woman looked around, her eyes resting a while longer on Charlie. 'I'd prefer to speak to you in private, if you wouldn't mind.'

Rachel frowned, then dismissed the children. Rowena paused at the exit then, when her teacher turned to look at her, she flushed and closed the door.

'What're you doing?' whispered Becky as her sister bent her head to the wood. Rowena motioned for her to go away, but when this wasn't complied with had to go into the kitchen with the others, and so missed what was said.

Rachel gave the offer of tea which was declined. The woman sought to enquire after Rowena's father before embarking on her intended theme which was not going to be pleasant. 'I trust Mr Hazelwood is continuing to keep out of harm's way on the front?' She knew from the girl's school writings that Hazelwood had joined up. She was not, however, prepared for Rachel's answer.

'The Germans killed my son.' There was no emotion.

Shocked, Miss Bannon donned a sympathetic expression. 'Mrs Hazelwood, I'm so terribly sorry . . . I had no idea. Rowena never mentioned it. He must have been very young.'

'He spent his fourteenth birthday on the front,' answered Rachel gravely. Then explained, 'Robert ran away to join the Army, we've had people searching for him for the past year.'

The teacher nodded and sighed. 'These young boys, they see their brave fathers marching off to war and seek to emulate them. He must have been very proud of Mr Hazelwood – as you yourself must be.'

'Proud?' Rachel frowned her incomprehension, then let out a peal of unpleasant sounding laughter. 'Oh, I'm sorry, Miss Bannon! But if you knew how funny that was . . .' She calmed herself and without further word resumed her stitching which the teacher's entry had interrupted.

'Well . . . I'm sure we're all greatly indebted to boys like your son, Mrs Hazelwood,' murmured the teacher, un-settled by this odd display. 'Laying down their young lives . . . Oh, this is going to make what I have to say awfully difficult . . . Mrs Hazelwood, I'll delay no further. I'm here because Rowena has been caught stealing.' She waited for the words to make impact which they did immediately. When a horrified Rachel asked from whom, she said, 'Several people, I'm afraid. A member of staff among them.'

Rachel let her sewing drop and whispered, 'I don't believe it.'

'I'm sorry, but your daughter was caught red-handed.' Miss Bannon frowned here, recalling the look on the girl's face when she was caught – it was almost one of relief, as if she had wanted to be caught. 'Pupils' belongings have been disappearing for several days now. Only when Rowena grew bolder and decided to plunder the staff-room was she exposed as the culprit.'

At Rachel's dumb shake of head she added, 'I know it's terribly hard to credit. I would never have believed it myself had she not been caught in the act. I feel rather cruel at having to break it to you at such a dreadful time, if I'd known I might have waited . . . but you had to know of course, especially since Rowena is to be suspended.'

Stupefied, Rachel echoed the last word.

'She could, by rights, have been expelled. But in view of her past excellent record the headmistress opted for clemency. Obviously something must have greatly disturbed Rowena to force her into such action . . . Anyway,' she rose and made to leave, 'I won't intrude further, Mrs Hazelwood, but will leave it in your hands. We shall expect Rowena back at school in a fortnight.' She saw that Rachel didn't intend to rise with her, and so let herself out.

Rachel sat there, staring into the fire for a long time. She could not believe this was all happening to her. One thing on top of another. Where were all the righteous busybodies now? When she needed someone to tell her what to do. Her breast felt like a kettle about to boil. There were screams inside her skull, crashing back and forth like waves against a sea wall: help, help, help! Only when the door flew open and the children stood there with looks of fright on their faces did she realize that the scream had escaped.

Rowena flung herself at the overwrought woman, sobbing, 'Oh, Mother, I didn't mean to do it! I didn't! Everything seems so mixed up, I couldn't do my maths and the teacher kept punishing me and she couldn't show me how to do it and she just kept getting angrier and angrier and I had all the housework to do and . . .' She buried her face in her mother's lap, each outdrowning the other's cries, while the rest of the family stood helplessly by, not understanding what had caused this.

Charlie came forward and, with a nervous look in his eye as if fearing another assault, clasped Rowena's shoulder with his undamaged hand. 'I can help you with your maths, Wena.'

Sniffing, she held up a tear-sodden face. 'They're too hard for you. Anyway it's not just that. You don't know . . .' Oh, the shame of being caught! Yet perhaps it was worth it to feel Mother's arms around her. Though it was a different Mother: there was a staleness to her embrace that Rowena had never smelt before.

Charlie let his hand drop as Rachel collected her daughter to her breast. 'How can you possibly help?' she hissed. 'If Rowena can't do the work there's little hope that you can.'

Charlie insisted that he should have a look at the work. Rowena told him that her book was upstairs. 'I'll fetch it!' He left them temporarily. When he returned he was smiling. 'They're easy! I'll soon have these done.'

Rachel was annoyed that he vouched success so glibly. 'Are you making out that Rowena is stupid?'

His smile was dampened. 'No . . . I'm just saying she needn't worry any more. I know how to do these.'

'But it's not you who has to do them, it's me!' wept Rowena.

'Then I'll teach you! Come on, Wena, let's go in the kitchen and I'll show you before bedtime.'

Rowena wanted her mother to say, 'Not now, I want to talk to my daughter'. But alas, Mother only sighed and returning to her apathy allowed Charlie to take charge.

He herded them from the room, telling the younger ones that it was their bedtime while Rowena went directly to the kitchen with her book. Lyn shrugged the boy's hand from her elbow as he piloted her at the stairs. 'Just 'cause you got our brother killed you needn't think you're the boss, 'cause you're not!'

Shocked, Charlie hung back and opened his mouth to protest. But by then Lyn and her sisters were at the top of the stairs. Head down he went into the kitchen, but managed to brighten a little as Rowena opened her book for assistance. 'We'll soon have these done.'

She spread her arms over the book and laid her head upon them. 'It's not just the maths, Charlie.'

'I did say I'd let Becky sleep with me again, and see to the sheets.'

She moved her head. 'It's not that either. It's everything.'

He waited for her to go on. In time she looked up at him and admitted shamedly, 'I've been stealing.'

In place of the condemnation she had expected he asked simply, 'Who from?'

'Lots of people . . . I'm so ashamed.'

'I did it once,' he said, almost as if he were boasting. At her look of interest he elaborated, 'I wanted this statue of

Our Lady. It belonged to Father Guillaume. I used to look at it every day and think how it would be to own it. Then one night I stopped looking and took it, hid it in my room. But when I'd got it I didn't feel like I thought I'd feel, if you see what I mean. It still didn't belong to me . . . so I ended up putting it back. I stole some money too, so's I could come here and see my father. What I'm saying is, a lot of people do it, Wena. It isn't that bad.'

She gave a negative response. 'It was different with me. I didn't want the things I stole, didn't even like them. It just seemed the only way to make Mother notice me. I had it all worked out. She'd say, Rowena! how could you do such a dreadful thing? And I'd say because I'm so unhappy and then she'd say . . . but she didn't, did she? She doesn't even seem bothered in my reasons.'

'Perhaps she is, but she doesn't know how to help you. You can talk to me if you like.'

She couldn't explain to him how much she needed her mother. 'It's not the same.'

He was hurt, but concealed it well. 'I know. But often you can tell your troubles to someone who isn't so close to you, someone who isn't important.' After a pause, he prompted, 'You blame me for Bertie being killed, don't you?'

She spoke into the table. 'Not really.'

'You do. You all do. If I hadn't come then he'd still be alive.'

She offered no contradiction for she knew it to be true.

'I'm upset too, you know. Even though he didn't like me he was my brother.'

'Only your half-brother. You haven't known him all your life, you can't miss him as much as we do – and you didn't even like each other. Besides, it's not just Bertie. Ever since he was killed Mother's been treating me like I'm a grown-up, asking me what to do, leaving me to get the meals, see to the others. I'm not a grown-up, Charlie. I don't want to be one, it's too much . . . and then there's poor Father.' She started to weep again. 'I'm so tired! I just want to go to sleep.'

Gently, Charlie prized her wet face from the page. 'Careful, you'll make all the ink run. We don't have to do this tonight. You go to bed, and tomorrow I'll get the breakfast and see to the others.'

'And there's no clean pants and socks . . .'

'I'll deal with that as well, I've nothing else to do all day.' He hugged her. 'Don't worry, lass, I'll take care of you now.'

'Oh, Charlie,' she accomplished a wet little laugh. 'You sounded just like Father.'

It was true: living for so long among them, the Yorkshire accent had rubbed off on him. He took this as a great compliment and, returning her fond expression, escorted her up to the girls' room. The others were not asleep. He ignored their glares to accompany her right up to her bed. Pulling her nightgown from under her pillow he laid it on her lap. 'Becky, will you squeeze in the other bed so your sister can have a decent night's sleep?' There were immediate objections from the others but he stilled them and waited to see Becky tucked in before leaving.

When he had washed several pairs of socks and pants and hung them to dry, he decided to tackle some of Rowena's homework so she wouldn't have so much to do. Igniting an oil lamp he placed it beside the book, then sat down and waded into the mathematical problems.

He must have dozed, for the shock of the deafening bang nearly sent him up to the ceiling. Someone was at the back door hammering for all they were worth. Stumbling to open it, Charlie whispered forcibly, 'All right, I'm coming!' It was some seconds before his left hand managed to turn the key. All the while the person on the other side continued to rap.

'Did you think I was knocking for my own good?' demanded the man as Charlie opened the door.

'No, I just thought it was a funny time of day for a woodpecker to be at work,' retorted Charlie.

'Oy! Now watch it, you cheeky monkey!'

'I'm sorry,' said Charlie impatiently. 'But your knocking has probably woken everyone up. What do you want?'

'What do I want? What do I bloody want! I want that light out, that's what I want! Don't you know it's an offence to have an unshielded light?'

Charlie, still muzzy from his nap, looked at the kitchen window. 'Oh heck! I'm sorry, I'll draw the curtains right this minute.'

'A bit late for that now!' The man tapped Charlie's breast. 'You've earned yourself a ten shilling fine.'

Charlie came fully awake. 'I haven't got ten shillings!'

'Then you'll have to go to prison, won't you?' sneered the special constable. 'Aye, sorry you cheeked me now, aren't you?'

'Please,' began a nervous Charlie, cupping his injured arm in hope of drawing sympathy. 'I'm really sorry. I promise never to do it again.'

'That's not good enough! I'm here to uphold the law and . . .'

'Fred Wilson, what the hell is all this racket?' Ella's head appeared over the wall of the yard.

'Get that bloody light out!'

Ella hurried to slam her kitchen door. 'There! Now how would you like your lights putting out – permanently!'

The man said there was no need to take that attitude, he was just enforcing his authority. To which Ella replied, did he have to make so much noise about it. 'Some of us have to get up for work in the morning.'

'Listen,' Wilson directed a finger at Charlie. 'This lad has contravened Government instructions on the use of artificial illumination . . .'

'Charlie, go in and draw your curtains,' Ella interrupted smartly and the boy hurried to comply. 'There! That's settled. Now can we all sleep?' At the man's insistence that this must be reported she gave a groan. 'This family who you're intent on persecuting have just had their only son killed in action!'

'Aye . . . well, I didn't know that – but I have my job to do! We can't have people flashing lights all over the place, you know, else there'll be more folks getting killed.'

'And that's why you're waving that torch about, is it?'

said Ella. 'I think I'll have to get on to the authorities myself and tell them there's this man what keeps signalling to enemy aircraft.' She stalled his objection. 'And I bet they'd find it very strange that a man who's supposed to be a member of the defence forces gives his house a German name.'

'It was already called that when I moved in!'

'But you didn't change it, did you?' said Ella craftily. 'That's plain daft!'

'Aye, it bloody is! Just as it's daft to bully this lad. Now get on with you, you soft old sod. Charlie, get off to bed and don't worry, if there's any fines to be paid then I'll be paying 'em.' She turned back to Wilson as Charlie closed the door. 'But it won't be for failure to shield a light, it'll be for actual bodily harm. 'Cause if you don't stop your gobbing and get out o' that yard I'm gonna take that torch and shove it somewhere painful!'

Charlie sighed with relief as the man's grievances moved to someone else's yard. Going to the table he looked at the maths book. All the exercises were completed; he must have done them before nodding off. Stacking the book and pencil on the dresser he turned off the lamp and went to bed. A slit of light shone from under the parlour door. Mrs Hazelwood was still up. He wondered for a moment whether to go in and tell her about Rowena's worry, but then thought better of it and went up to his attic.

But his earlier catnap prevented him from sleeping. He rolled from his left side to his right, back to belly – even tried lying with his head at the foot of the bed and his feet on the pillow. Counting sheep did not work either. He made a tent of the covers, using himself as the pole, and sat cross-legged inside the dark cocoon wondering if he stayed under here for long enough would he suffocate? *Just because you got our brother killed you needn't think you're the boss*, came Lyn's voice. That was what kept him awake. It's not true. I wasn't responsible for getting him killed. Another voice came: *no, but you're glad he's dead, aren't you?* I'm not! He tried to shut his mind to the voice, but it persisted. *Yes, you are. You have no reason to feel sorry, he meant nothing to you.*

419

He was my brother! *No, not really, he didn't even like you. Look at all the names he called you, the way he treated you, the way he tried to come between you and Father.* I still didn't want him to die! *Yes you did, admit it. You're glad he's gone. Because now you're the only son, aren't you?* I just want Father to love me! *Yes, and when he comes back now he'll have to love you, because you're his only son.*

Charlie shot from the bed, trying to escape the voice. He caught sight of a shady, anguished face in the standing mirror and, after slight hesitation, went right up to it, staring at the reflection. Fresh voices came. Afrikaans voices from his childhood. *Git your black arse out of my way, Bantu!* Was this why his father didn't want him? His brown skin. Then Bertie's voice chanted *Fuzzball, Fuzzball, Fuzz . . .*

Yes, I am glad you're dead! shrieked his mind. *I am, I am!* Spinning from the mirror he went to the cabinet that housed the birds' eggs and began to pull out the drawers one after the other. Look, Bertie! I'm touching the eggs. See! he put a finger to each egg, you can't stop me, I can do this as often as I please because you're dead and now I'm the only son. The only son, and that gives me the right to Father's love.

Leaving the drawers as they were, he fell to his knees by the bed and clasped his hands in fervent prayer, eyes shut tightly. But he couldn't bring himself to pray for forgiveness . . . for he had meant every word.

CHAPTER TWENTY-SEVEN

'Rowena won't get up,' announced a tousled Beany coming into the kitchen the next morning.

'There's no need for her to,' muttered Charlie, wishing she wouldn't shout; he had a splitting headache that extended right into his eye sockets. 'She hasn't got any school today.' He had taken his arm out of the sling and was coping in an awkward fashion. This afternoon should see an improvement; he was going to get the plaster cut off – that was if Mrs Hazelwood remembered. He placed a pot of tea on the table. Beany asked why her sister didn't have to go to school. 'She's been suspended.'

'What's suspended?' But Beany didn't hear the answer. She had noticed the table and now stood gawping, as did the others who followed her. The table was neatly laid with racks of toast and a bowl of cereal at each setting, a jug of milk . . . indeed, how it had always been before Mother went funny. Lyn, climbing onto a chair, demanded to know who had done it. 'I have,' said Charlie. 'Your sister needs a rest so I've taken over.'

Lyn set her mouth. 'I told you last night! Don't think . . .'

'Would you care to prepare breakfast tomorrow?' offered Charlie. 'And dinner and tea?' He received a sullen no. 'Then sit down, shut up moaning and eat your food. I've got to see to Squawk.'

'Becky's peed the bed again,' Lyn informed him spitefully before he reached the door. 'That's four wet nightgowns instead of two. They're on the floor, sopping.' Charlie said, hadn't it occurred to her to bring them down? To which she replied, 'Wena always sees to that.'

'Well she won't be seeing to it this morning!'

Beany asked again what suspended meant and was told by Lyn that it meant hung. At her look of alarm Charlie said testily, 'It means she doesn't have to go to school that's all.' When Beany asked why, he sighed heavily. 'She's just taken something that didn't belong to her.'

'You mean stolen something?'

'Not real stealing! And you're not to say anything to her about it.' He turned back to Lyn. 'Go fetch those wet things down.'

'*I'm* not touching them!' Lyn jabbed a thumb at Becky. 'It's her what's done it.'

'Whoever's fault it is that's no reason to leave everything to Wena!'

Rhona giggled. 'Ooh, Charlie, your voice went all funny!'

Charlie gave an annoyed cough. His voice had been playing all kinds of tricks on him lately, sounding all right one minute and the next it would give a sort of hiccup. 'Becky, you'd better come back in with me tonight. I'll have had the plaster off then.'

'Thank God,' muttered Lyn as he dashed off to the nursery.

Charlie accosted the crying child, wiped her face with a flannel, sat her on the chamberpot then brought her down for some breakfast, by which time his efforts had been well demolished by the others. There was a request from Becky for more toast. Charlie looked at the empty rack whilst pandering to Regina's tastes. 'Who's eaten it all?'

'Don't look at *me*,' said Lyn crossly and left the table to fetch her books.

'Haven't you forgotten something?' shouted Charlie. She turned back to him. 'You didn't ask my permission to leave the table.'

She was enraged. 'I don't need your permission, bugger!'

'You do if you're going to eat any dinner – and stop swearing.'

She didn't know if the threat was genuine or not, but thought it wise not to test him. Slouching back to her seat she plonked herself on it and said pettishly, 'Please may I leave the table?' This was as bad as Bertie being here.

'You may.' Charlie grinned at Becky as her sister flounced out. 'Oh heck, you want some more toast, don't you.' Finishing with the youngest he glanced at the clock. 'I think I'll just have time to do some, but make sure you're ready for school while I'm doing it.'

'Biddy always did plenty of toast the first time,' taunted Beany, who had also demanded more.

'Well Biddy's not here,' replied Charlie. 'And if you throw that at me again you'll be another one who isn't going to get any dinner. You've all got to start behaving yourselves. It's all this disagreement that's made your sister ill.'

'It's nowt to do with me!' Beany's eyes turned misty.

'Yes it is! And if I'm going to look after you I'm going to expect some gratitude and a bit more help.'

'You big show-off, you won't get it from me!' Eyes brimming over, Beany charged out.

Charlie sighed, then concentrated on the toasting fork.

'I wish Father would come home,' said little Rhona. 'Nothing funny's happened in ages.' She grinned in reminiscence and shuffled round to talk to Becky. 'D'you remember how he used to dress up as a lady and peep through the window? Ooh, he was funny!'

'Yes, well I don't suppose Father's having much fun now,' murmured Charlie, handing out a piece of toast to each of them.

'Is this all we're getting?' Rhona held it up derisively. Now that she had started school she had an air of self-importance which she paraded quite regularly. Charlie tried to snatch the toast back. In avoiding him she dropped it on the floor. Covered in bits it was uneatable. 'That was your fault!' She too, stormed from the room. Charlie flopped into a chair as Regina started to grizzle. This was no good at all. Somehow he was going to have to get round them.

Shortly after midday the children returned to find a strange woman in the kitchen. Mother must have hired a new maid at last. By the appetising smell coming from the range it seemed she was a good cook too. Her back was to them as they entered. Rowena was sitting on the sofa and obviously feeling much better after her prolonged sleep. She smiled at their entry, then hid her face as the maid spoke in a queerly-pitched Irish accent. 'Away now an' wash yer hands before I set yese dinners out! Ye'll have me thinkin' I'm entertainin' a load o' coal-miners. An' I want it all eatin' up else I'm going to take one o' yese to clout the rest.'

The puzzled girls did as they were told, trooping meekly past the maid and into the scullery to wash their hands. Rhona, the last in line, glanced inquisitively at the newcomer as she passed. The maid tossed her a look over her shoulder. Rhona turned away – then looked back quickly and burst into peals of laughter. 'Oh, Charlie, you rott'ner!' and, bounding up to the grinning 'maid', delivered a punch before doubling over in a fit of giggles.

Charlie, dressed in the mobcap and dress that Biddy had left behind, kept up the pretence, mincing up to the range and bringing the steaming container of soup to the table. Beany and Lyn had obviously not forgiven him yet for this morning; they did not laugh as much as the others – though it was hard trying to keep a straight face with Charlie looking such a fool.

The noise of long-forgotten merriment served to lure Rachel from her parlour tomb. She took one look at Charlie, tutted, 'Stupid clown,' and turned to go.

'Mother.' Rowena, guilty at having disturbed her mother's bereavement with her laughter, jumped up and entreated her, 'Won't you have some of Charlie's soup?'

Rachel looked back. 'He made it?'

'Yes!' He grinned from beneath the frilled mobcap. 'I got it from one of your cookery books. Shall I dish you some out?'

She turned away, murmuring, 'No thank you, I'm not hungry.'

Charlie tried not to let this worry him and moved around the table ladling out soup. When he came to Rhona, she smiled up at him and with a look of fondness said, 'I like you, Charlie. You're funny.'

He grinned back. 'I like you too, Mo . . . Rhona.' He glanced at Beany and Lyn to see if they had softened at all, but they were having a private conversation.

'If Father is killed, I wonder who'll get the eggs now Bertie's dead.'

'Oh, Lyn!' Rowena put her spoon down. 'What a thing to say!' Her eyes glistened and she buried her head in her hands before slipping from the table.

'What's up with her?' demanded Lyn. 'I mean, everyone knows Bertie's dead. I don't see why we shouldn't talk about him.'

'There's ways and ways of talking about people!' Charlie's voice had a sharp edge to it. 'You wouldn't have said that in front of your mother, I'll bet. And it was very callous to anticipate Father's death.'

A shamefaced Lyn turned on him. 'Well you needn't think you're getting the eggs! By rights they belong to the next in line and as Wena isn't interested that means me.'

'I'd be entitled to them if I wanted them,' argued Charlie. 'After all, I was older than Bertie.'

'I don't see what that's got to do with anything! You're not one of us are you? The eggs are a family heirloom.'

Deeply hurt, he told her scathingly that he didn't even want the eggs. 'I could start a collection of my own if I wanted. That's the whole point of having a collection, accumulating them yourself.'

'Yes, well if you do start a collection don't you dare take the ones in the Elephant Tree!' Charlie told Lyn there was no such thing. 'The tree on the other side of the Knavesmire, stupid! I call it that 'cause its branches are like elephant's legs.'

Beany pushed her and said through clenched teeth. 'I thought we were going to keep that a secret?' The nest was high up and well-hidden in the branches.

Lyn's face blackened further at her own slip, but Charlie scoffed, 'Don't worry I won't go pinching your daft eggs. Just get on with your dinner. I have to go to the hospital this afternoon to get the plaster off.'

*

Rachel had forgotten, as he had expected she might. She looked at him blankly when he pointed at the clock and said, 'We'd better set off shortly.' Only when he touched the pot on his arm did she stir.

'Oh . . . oh, yes.' She began to rise lethargically.

'I could go on my own, if you like,' offered the boy, though not really wanting to; he was afraid of what the doctors might do to his arm.

She stopped rising, 'All right, I feel awfully tired,' and fell back in her seat to stare at the fireplace.

'Would you like me to go with you?' asked Rowena.

Rachel suddenly became more decisive. 'No, you'd better stay at home. It wouldn't look good, you wandering the town whilst suspended from school. I'm sure the boy can manage to find the hospital; can't you?'

Charlie confirmed this and left, returning three hours later with his arm back down the sleeve of his jacket. 'Did it hurt?' Rowena examined the proffered arm which looked rather emaciated and a lighter colour than its partner with bits of skin peeling from it.

He smiled and shook his head, raking his fingers along it. 'No, it just feels a bit funny, as if it doesn't belong to me. Ooh, it's lovely to be able to have a good scratch!' He pulled his sleeve down, then noticed the time. 'I'd better start thinking about making the tea, the others'll be in any minute. Oh, Lord, there's the sheets to bring in! I hope they've dried. Then the little 'un to see to! A woman's work is never done.'

A chuckling Rowena stopped him from leaving his chair. 'The sheets're back on the bed and I'll see to Squawk. She's probably still enjoying her nap. You sit here and have a cup of tea. There's one freshly made.' Charlie asked if he should take one to her mother. 'No, she's got one.'

'Has she said anything to you, about school and things?' Rowena shook her head sadly.

'Never mind . . . and never mind Squawk either! Wait till you hear her crying before trailing up there. Sit and have a cup of tea and talk to me.'

She sat down and accepted the cup he brought her.

Charlie settled back and crossed his legs. 'Nice this, isn't it? Just you and me before the brats come in,' he said like an old married man.

Rachel joined them for tea but as usual ate little. Besides not having much appetite she just couldn't seem to swallow. Her hand was raised and lowered automatically from plate to mouth but she had no idea what she was eating. She simply stared at the cloth and chewed until she could stomach no more, then left them for the quietude of the front parlour.

Rowena went to wash up, leaving the others at the table. Rhona showed considerable interest in the state of Charlie's arm as he scratched furiously, producing a puff of dry skin. 'Eh, Charlie . . . I wonder if you keep scratching skin off will you be white underneath?'

This made him thoughtful. 'Would you like me better if I was?'

She examined his arm for signs of whiteness. 'No, you're best when you're brown. You wouldn't be half so nice if you were the same as us.'

'I'd still be the same person if I was white.'

Becky gave her opinion on this. 'That's daft! Course you wouldn't. Anyway, you're special. No one else round here has anybody brown in their house.'

'But brothers and sisters are usually the same colour, aren't they?' he pressed, thinking of what Lyn had said earlier – you're not one of us. 'Maybe you'd feel I was more like a brother if I was white.'

'We've had a white brother,' said Rhona.

'D'you think . . . well, is it my fault that Bertie was killed?'

Rhona was obviously too young to understand, but her ten year old sister looked pensive. What Becky should have replied was, no, it's my fault, he went away because he thought I didn't care about him any more. But then, if Charlie hadn't come here in the first place she would still have been treating Bertie the same, wouldn't she? So really it *was* Charlie's fault for making her love him. Hence she said bluntly, 'Yes.' Then, as his eyelids lowered, added, 'But I don't blame you, Charlie. I still love you.'

'So do I,' agreed Rhona. 'When're you going home?'

He gave a worried smile and shrugged. Two years, he had been here now. Never in those early months had he envisaged the barriers lasting this long. One by one, though, he reassured himself, you're breaking them down. You've got these two on your side, and Rowena. Pulling his sleeve down he gave a final rub, then said to Lyn and Beany, 'Come on then, show me this Elephant Tree of yours.'

Lyn took the chewed pencil from her mouth. 'Huh! So you can swipe our eggs.'

'How can they be your eggs while they're still in the tree?'

She spat out a soggy piece of wood. 'They would be if we could reach them.' When Charlie said he could reach them, the chewed end of the pencil was levelled at him. 'You dare!'

He adopted nonchalance. 'All right, suit yourself. If you don't want them . . .'

The girls swapped disbelieving expressions. 'You mean you'd get them for us?'

'Well what time do I have to start a collection with you lot to look after? Come on, while it's still light.'

No sooner had the offer been made than Charlie was being dragged across Knavesmire. Fifteen minutes later they stood looking up at the tree. Charlie squinted. 'Can't see it.'

'You see that branch that's shaped like a letter F?' said Beany.

'Oh, I see it now!' Charlie rolled his sleeves up and hauled himself onto the first large branch, dragging his body higher and higher up the tree.

'It's like the Indian Ropetrick,' giggled Beany as Charlie vanished among the branches. There was a golden edge forming around each leaf. Some fluttered down as he rustled his way through them. Twenty feet up, encased in a welter of twigs, Charlie searched for another foothold, found one and strode onto a large branch where he paused to look for the nest. Just a bit further.

How bloody stupid, was his thought as he reached the nest and inserted his fingers to clutch at emptiness. How stupid to take their word that there'd be eggs in at this time of year. He shouted down, 'It's empty!' and muttered to himself, 'Closet-brains.'

Wails of disappointment filtered up through the leaves. 'Are you certain?'

'Come up and check if you like!' the acid reply descended. He started to come down. 'Wasting my blasted time . . .'

Unfortunately, he came down a little faster than he had planned. The breath was knocked out of him with a noisy grunt as his body hit the ground. Before he blacked out he felt an excruciating pain in his arm . . .

'You can consider yourself very lucky!' Rachel glared down at the pathetic figure in the hospital bed, with his bandaged head and arm, his face grazed and cut by the branches. 'If Robina or her sister had been standing directly beneath you I dread to think what would have happened. What sort of trick was that to be teaching them? Stupid boy!'

'I'm so . . .' At her intensified glare he bit off the word. 'They wanted to start an egg collection like . . . Mr Hazelwood.' He used the title Father sparingly now, knowing how it irritated from his lips. 'They told me about this nest . . .'

'Oh, so it's their fault, is it?' she replied loudly, then compressed her mouth as the other patients in the ward and their visitors all turned to look at her. If Charlie's action had served any purpose it was to bring her out of her trance – even if it were just to pour more anger upon him.

'No, of course it isn't. It was no one's fault. I just slipped.'

'But what an idiotic thing to attempt the same day as you had your plaster off!' Then Rachel remembered with a twinge that she had been responsible for the plaster in the first instance and said huffily, 'Anyway, there are dozens of eggs cluttering the attic that they could have had . . .'

'Would you like to sit down?' With stiff movement,

Charlie indicated a hard chair. Apart from breaking his arm again he had dislocated his shoulder and it was doubly painful. Apparently, a woman who lived nearby had sent for the ambulance. Rachel must have arrived while he was having his arm set in plaster.

'I'm not stopping that long. I only came because I knew there'd be forms to fill in . . . oh, very well then. But just for a second.' She scraped the chair to the bedside. Apprehension had almost prevented her from coming here. Would the doctors be suspicious about Charlie's repeated injuries? But no, they had just seemed to think it was the result of usual boyish behaviour.

An uncomfortable silence followed.

'Is there anything you need apart from flannel and pyjamas?' Her query was not made from affection, she was merely showing him the courtesy she would have shown anyone in his predicament.

But Charlie misinterpreted it. 'That's very kind. I wouldn't mind something to read if I'm to be here long – do you know how long, by the way?'

She gave a negative flick of her head that wiped out any misunderstanding; she hadn't even bothered to ask the doctor. 'Rowena will bring your library books.'

'Oh, they're due back tomorrow!' He covered his mouth.

Rachel said in that case her daughter would return them. 'I dare say she can bring you some more.'

'Thanks . . . I'll be pleased to see her. Tell her to bring her school books and I'll go over the sums with her.' He studied her face at length before deciding whether to go further. 'Mrs Hazelwood . . . I think you ought to talk to Wena.' She beheld him sharply. 'About her stealing . . .'

Rachel looked round to see if anyone had heard this, then whispered, 'That is none of your business!'

'I know, it's yours . . . but you don't seem as if . . .'

'How dare you . . .'

'She's so unhappy!' He could see she wasn't going to permit him to speak unless he blurted it out all at once. 'It's because you don't talk to her, I mean really talk! She's done ever so much since you've been ill . . .'

'Ill, ill? What're you talking about, ill?'

'. . . and you never say thank you, even. Never bothered to ask her why she was stealing. It's because of Bertie . . .'

She pushed her chair back and shot upwards. 'You despicable wretch! Trying to lay the blame on my son . . .'

'I'm not!' He leaned forward in the bed. 'Honestly! I'm just trying to explain why Wena was taking things, it's because she wanted to make you talk to her – about Bertie . . .'

'*Shut up!*' Her face contorted with her detestation of him. Then Rachel turned her back and tore from the ward.

All the way home from the hospital her mind seethed. How dare he? The impudence! Implying that she was responsible for her daughter's dishonesty. Through her mind rebounded all the vile words she could think of, which only served to keep her anger at boiling point. Even the brisk march down the road to her home could not reduce it. Rowena's innocent offer of tea on her arrival home was met by a stream of accusations.

'Why did you see fit to tell that boy the reasons for your thievery and not your mother?'

Rowena was so knocked off balance by the outburst that all she could do was to stand with her mouth open. Her sisters who were drinking their suppertime cocoa looked alarmed too. 'Well! Are you just going to stand there gaping like a fish? You accused me of not talking to you! Well now I'm here, come on, out with it! You miserable girl, how could you do such a wicked thing?'

Rowena found her voice, though it was weak and threatened tears. 'Mother, what have I done?'

'You've laid the blame for your own wickedness on your poor dead brother!'

'Oh, no . . .' Rowena began to shake her head.

'That black fiend told me so!'

'But I never blamed Bertie! I only wanted to talk about him!'

'Yes! Malicious, spiteful talk!'

'No, I loved him!' Rowena burst into tears.

Rachel stood like a cat about to strike, glaring at the

431

pitiful figure for another ten seconds . . . then her own face crumpled and she gathered the distressed child in her arms and wept with her.

'Oh, Mother, I didn't mean to !' Rowena shivered and wept as the two of them sank onto the kitchen sofa, blind to their audience. 'I just wanted to talk about him, but . . .'

'But I wasn't here.' Rachel clasped her, rocked her to and fro. 'I know, I know.' One arm still wrapped tightly around her daughter, she mopped her eyes and sniffled. 'It's me who should be sorry, love.' She disengaged herself in order to clear her nose of mucus, then cuddled up again. 'I didn't realize what you were going through. It was selfish of me even to think that others couldn't feel his loss too. It's just that . . . I couldn't talk about him. I suppose I must have thought that if I didn't talk about it, it wasn't true. But it is true . . . Robert's dead!'

They both fell to sobbing again. Robina and Becky joined the miserable group and a long time was given to shedding tears. When it was over, Rowena said tentatively, 'Mother . . . D'you think he felt any pain? I worry about it so much that I can't get to sleep.'

Rachel felt the ice-cold water seep into her mouth, her throat, her lungs, expanding them until they burst. 'No . . . I shouldn't think so.'

There was a long period of silence. Rowena snuggled close to her mother, revelling in the show of affection. Though there had never been any lack of it before it had been given as if to a possession, a prize dog or cat, not as one person to another. Rachel felt a difference too. She had never really seen her children as separate individuals, as people who hurt and grieved as she did, just as little bodies to be kept neat and clean and brought out to display whenever there was company. But where were those neat little bodies now? For the first time in weeks Rachel looked properly at her daughters – saw how neglected they had become.

'Charlie's been so good, hasn't he? So helpful.'

Rachel stiffened. How could you? How could you voice his name in the same breath as your brother's?

'He's been organizing everybody and getting them off to school, did my housework, the cooking.' For Becky's sake Rowena didn't mention the wet sheets.

Resentment forced Rachel from her seat, breaking the bond between them. 'Well he won't be here to do it tomorrow, will he? So it looks like I'll have to do it.' Her anger was experienced twofold: as if it wasn't enough to praise him, her daughter was making out that she had been shirking her duties as a mother.

Rowena sensed that she had said something wrong and tried to make amends. 'We'll do it together.'

For a second there was still that detached coldness . . . then Rachel assumed a forgiving smile and nodded. 'You'd all better get ready for bed now, it's late. Come here, Rosalyn and let me brush your hair.'

It took several minutes to do this. Rowena watched her sisters kiss their mother and make for the stairs, while she herself held back.

'Mother?' There were still dozens of questions to be asked. 'Do you . . . d'you think you'll ever forgive Father?'

Rachel, taken unawares, said, 'You're too young to understand what he did to me, Rowena.'

'No I'm not. I know . . . at least I think I know he committed a sin by being Charlie's father.'

Her mother inhaled deeply, tasting salty mucus. 'Oh, you don't know the half of it, love.'

'I'll try to understand if you tell me.'

'I can't.' Rachel gripped her arms about herself. 'I can't even bear to think of it, let alone speak . . . God trust that you'll never have first hand experience, never know how it feels to be betrayed, see everything you've worked for destroyed.' And your son killed, she thought but didn't say it aloud.

Rowena plaited her hair. 'What about when the war's over? Will Father be coming back?'

Rachel examined the worried face. 'I expect so.'

'I'm positive he never loved Charlie's mother as much as he loves you. I can't bear the thought of you being unhappy.' Emotion made her nose run. 'Can't you try to forgive him?'

Rachel appeared to revert to her trance. 'Once . . . when I was a little girl, my mother bought me a lovely coat. I was so proud of it that I refused to keep it for best – kicked up such a fuss that Mother had to allow me to wear it for school. One day, I went to the cloakroom and found another girl trying it on. She was the dirtiest girl in the school . . . I never felt the same about that coat again.'

For some reason this parable conveyed much more to Rowena than any rational explanation. She never raised the subject again . . . though she clung to the desperate hope that one day Mother would change her mind.

CHAPTER TWENTY-EIGHT

Charlie was only detained in hospital for a couple of nights. An ambulance brought him home on Saturday, though Rachel was instructed to keep the boy in bed for another few days due to him having taken a nasty bump on the head. This did not suit her and she made strident objection at the thought of having to run up and downstairs with his meals. Charlie assured her there was no need to do this; he would come down.

'Oh yes! And have everyone blame me if you fall down the stairs because you got up too quickly!' she replied caustically as she settled him into the attic room. 'You'll stay where you're put.'

'Has there been any news from Father Guillaume while I've been away?' he asked.

'Huh! I gave up on him long ago. I suppose you want something to eat now, then?' She left him and went downstairs.

Rowena was his first visitor, bringing with her a pile of library books. 'I hope you haven't read them. I didn't know what to get.' She placed them on his blanketed lap. 'I did ask Mother if you could borrow some of Bertie's books, but she wouldn't hear of it I'm afraid.'

This wasn't the only thing to be refused. Rowena's suggestion that perhaps Charlie might be more comfortable in Bertie's room had been met by a look that bespoke treachery. However, Mother had condescended to let Charlie have Biddy's bed in the nursery where it was warmer. Before Rowena could tell him this the other girls arrived, encircling his bed. Becky welcomed him home, telling him how glad she was that he hadn't been killed.

She handed him the comic which she had bought with

her pocket money. 'I just had a little peep at it first, but I knew you wouldn't mind.' At his thanks she turned to her other sisters, saying tightly, 'Beany and Lyn have got something to say to you.'

'Sorry about your desolated arm, Charlie,' mumbled Beany. 'It wasn't a trick, you know. We really did think there were eggs in that nest.'

'We wouldn't want you to think we sent you up on purpose so you'd fall,' added Lyn.

This nasty thought had never occurred to him and he said as much. 'When I get this pot off I'll try and find a nest that does have some old eggs in – only we'll pick one that's a bit lower this time!'

Then Lyn pulled a grubby bundle from the pocket of her pinafore and handed it to him. Her face was to the floor, where her unlaced boots scraped the wood. 'Sorry, it's all clagged together,' she muttered as he took charge of the bag of toffee. 'But it's been in me pocket since yesterday.' It had been murder, knowing it was there but saving it for him. It wasn't often they were able to afford toffee these days.

He was touched. 'That's all right, the paper will come off after I've sucked it awhile. Tell you what, we'll share it out now.'

Lyn, who had been hoping he would say this, brightened considerably and edged closer in order to have first pick. Everyone got a piece of the paper-clad toffee and, as they sat on his bed, chattering away about the Zeppelin raid that had taken place while he was in hospital, little balls of damp paper were picked from their tongues and lined up on a nearby trunk.

They stayed with him until they heard their mother's voice summoning them to eat. At their departure, Charlie caught Rowena's arm to remark on how well she was looking now. She smiled and perched on his bed a moment longer. 'It's thanks to you. Mother and me had a long chat about . . . oh, Bertie and everything. I feel heaps better.'

'I'm glad.' He gripped her hand. 'And before you go back to school we'll have you doing that maths standing on your head.'

The tone of her answer implied that she wasn't looking forward to going back. But she showed gratitude for his help and on impulse kissed his face – just as her mother opened the door. Rowena felt her face redden with guilt and shot from the bed. 'Sorry, Mother, I was just coming . . . see you later, Charlie!' She rushed out.

Charlie, too overtaken with pleasure at Rowena's loving gesture to notice Rachel's shock, smiled his au revoir and settled back to accept the meal she had brought.

A stony-faced Rachel came forward and put the tray on his lap. 'My daughter had the idea that you'd be rather uncomfortable in this room so you're to have the bed in the nursery when it's been made up. I suppose she told you.'

'No, she didn't.' He smiled. 'But thank you. Rowena looks a lot better, doesn't she? Thank you for that too.'

'Why thank me?' she asked coolly.

'Well, you know . . . I realize I upset you the other day, saying you should talk to her more. But you do see that it was the right thing, don't you?'

Rachel arched her back. 'If I choose to speak to my daughter then I shall do so, I don't need anyone to instruct me – least of all you!'

Charlie's smile evaporated as she slammed the door on him.

The war rolled on. Perhaps it would be over by this Christmas, for the press reports which Rowena read out to the others were very favourable – though she did not read out every item; the lists of casualties had become alarmingly long. However heroic the deaths might be, she felt that the younger ones should be spared this as they would only worry about their father . . . as she was constantly doing. Privately, she always paid great study to the photographs of the dead soldiers to make certain that her father was not among them. But to the others she would read out the less personal articles: 'Listen here! There's three people got bubonic plague in Bristol – they say it's the work of an enemy agent who's been releasing infected rats.' And no mention was made of the trains full of stretcher cases brought to York's military hospitals.

It was as well that she did read the newspaper so closely, for in doing so she was able to prevent the fiasco that had taken place earlier in the year when her mother had forgotten to alter the clocks. This time all arrived at school at the correct hour – though Rowena secretly longed for some excuse to bring another suspension from the dreaded place. Oh, with Charlie's help the maths was no longer a problem – he was a much better teacher than Miss Greenwood – but the whispers and pointing fingers were. People just wouldn't let her forget, would make great play of taking their belongings with them when they left the room and more than one person had openly called her a thief. She had no friends there, but she must suffer it for her mother's sake. Mother had enough to bear and at least Rowena had a friend at home in Charlie. She wondered if this Christmas would be any less austere than the last two, but then that was hardly to be expected. More importance was given to creating a Christmas atmosphere for the men on the Western Front. Rowena felt that this was as it should be and she herself had been knitting a balaclava from odd bits of wool she had collected; it was very brightly-coloured. Father would like it.

November saw another Zeppelin raid. In December Lloyd George formed a War Cabinet. Rachel, still affected by her only son's death, continued to act the recluse, the blinds on the Micklegate store pulled down. The old Rachel who constantly dusted and cleaned was gone. In her place was a much slower moving creature – though there were spells of nervous activity when one of the girls failed to arrive home from school at the correct time, when she would chew her fingers and plait the tassels on the tablecloth nervously until they came in. But mainly, the only time her children saw any life in her eyes was when she was ticking Charlie off – which, for him, seemed to be his every waking moment. He could not do a thing right. Since regaining the use of his arm he did all sorts for her – filled the coalscuttle, cleaned the grate, lit the fire, helped the girls get ready for school, washed the dishes, cleaned the carpet, even cooked some of the meals – but she gave no thanks.

Even when she wasn't in the same room he could feel her hate, feel her thoughts: *why was it Robert and not you?* It was as though the very walls had soaked up all her bad feelings and released them on Charlie. Inevitably, her depression infected him. But what could he do? Before Bertie had died she had said that Charlie would have to get a job if they didn't hear from Father Guillaume soon. She appeared to have forgotten all about this. Charlie could have reminded her – it would get him away from the house – but then who would look after the place and see to the meals? Certainly not Mrs Hazelwood in her state of mind. The only remedy, he decided, was to get her out of the house and back to the shop. Risking more displeasure, he made this suggestion.

'And who is to look after the house while I'm out all day?'

He did not remind her that he had been the main contributor to this for months now. 'I've plenty of time.'

'And you're qualified to run a household, are you?' He told her that he could try. She became meditative, her thoughts a jumble. How long had it been, this nightmare? Almost four months, a long time for the shop to be closed. But then why should she worry? Earlier in the year a scheme had been set up to give financial assistance to the wives of serving soldiers who were left with a business to run. Rachel had applied for it, so there was no more concern about the mortgage and rates; the shop could stay closed . . . but then she did have a family to keep. A sovereign was worth only three-quarters of its pre-war value, all the essentials had rocketed – coal, milk, bread, potatoes – they might soon be unaffordable if she didn't make some effort. Oh, but she had the money from the Army and from her millinery work, she would get by somehow. Why should she put herself to the trouble of running his blessed shop?

And then she glanced at Charlie and was given a reason: if she were out of the house all day she wouldn't have to see him, would she? Not that she saw much of him now, but he was there all the same, she could feel him creeping about the place trying to avoid her. And Robert . . . she was going to have to put her mind to something else if she wasn't going to go completely insane.

439

'I'll reopen tomorrow,' she decided suddenly to his great relief. 'And we'll see how you frame. You can manage Regina, I presume?'

As Charlie had been sharing a room with this child for the last couple of months he felt confident enough to say, 'She's no bother. You know, she doesn't seem to need anybody to play with, she amuses herself quite well.'

'You don't have to tell me that, I'm her mother.'

Again he had said something to annoy her. He had become used to these tight-lipped displays to know that.

But she took heed of his idea and the next morning saw her preparing to reopen the shop. Before the girls had left for school she was on her way, leaving barely an instruction for Charlie, apart from to say that they would have their main meal in the evening as she wouldn't be coming home at midday, and if anybody called wanting a new hat he must tell them that Mrs Hazelwood was fully booked at the moment.

After all had departed, Charlie lifted Regina from her chair. 'Are you going to help me with the washing-up, Squawk?'

'Ooh, yes!' She reached her arms onto the table to transfer the dirty crockery to the sink but Charlie rushed forward as her incompetent hands knocked a cup over, saying he would put them in the sink and she could wash them. He lifted her onto a chair at the sink and instructed her to make sure she washed all the marmalade off the plates. Each plate she pulled from the water was handed to him with the question, 'Have I got all the marmalarmalade off?' He laughed – Regina often added an extra syllable to the words her tongue could not cope with.

This task deducted a good half hour off the morning. When the blobs of 'marmalarmalade' had been sponged from the tablecloth and the drips wiped off the hob, Charlie prepared to go to the shops. 'No sheets today,' he said cheerfully.

'Becky's a good girl now, isn't she?' ventured Regina.

'Very good – come here, let me wipe your mouth and do your hair.' She squealed and wriggled as he pressed a cloth to her face. 'Sorry, am I too rough?'

440

'Yes and that cloth smells!' She screwed up her eyes, one of which was brown, the other blue.

Charlie put it to his nose. 'You're right.' He searched the kitchen and finding a bottle of likely-looking stuff he sprinkled it neatly onto the cloth, sniffing, 'That's better,' and dabbed at her face.

There were more screams as he tried to drag a brush through her long fine hair. Finally he gave up and simply encased the mess in a bonnet. With her coat on, Regina was put into her folding car and trundled down to the shops.

His first purchase was bread which had, long ago, ceased to be a home-baked commodity. Seeing Charlie was going to leave her outside, Regina squawked and so he had to take her into Mrs Phillips' shop where she immediately ran around pointing and touching, 'What's that? What's this?'

'Mrs Hazelwood's got you doing the shopping now, has she?' said Mrs Phillips, hands planted on counter, round face congenial.

'I don't mind – could I have one of those loaves, please?' Charlie pointed and Mrs Phillips reached for it. Normally, in this shop there was an unidentifiable smell; a combination of everything in stock; a sort of oaty, peppery, bready smell. But today, that was obscured by the onions frying in the back room.

'How is she these days?'

'All right.' Charlie tried to take the loaf but she held onto it.

'I haven't seen her for a long time – till this morning, that is.'

Charlie said, 'Oh . . . can I have the bread please?' and held out his hand.

Before handing it over, Mrs Phillips said, 'Somebody told me she'd closed the shop.'

The boy took hold of the bread and stuffed it into his bag. 'She's reopened it this morning.'

'Has she? Who's looking after you lot, then?'

'I am,' said Charlie and turned to go.

'Eh, Charlie Chaplin, haven't you forgotten summat?' Mrs Phillips laughed at his face. 'The money!'

'Oh sorry!' He came back hastily and gave her half a crown.

She took her time in scraping his change together, trying to squeeze more information from him. 'Will she be getting herself another maid then, now Biddy's gone?'

'I don't know – can I have my change please? I've got a lot of things to see to.'

'I'll bet he has,' murmured Mrs Phillips to a customer when the boy and his small charge had left. 'No wonder she doesn't need a maid when she's got herself a genuine slave.'

'Ow! Watch where you're going, Charlie.' Ella lifted her foot off the ground and puckered her mouth. In his hasty exit he had jumped off the step onto her toe as she came around the corner. He showed compunction, and tucked his hands under Regina's armpits, swinging her into the pushchair. 'I hope you haven't emptied the shelves in there, I want something special for Mr Daw's tea – he's home on leave.'

'Oh, I didn't know.' Charlie paused to smile. 'That's nice for you.'

'It is, love. A pity it's not more than seven days, but you can't crib when some folks'll never be seeing their husbands again.'

She was about to move into the shop when Charlie said, 'Er! Did Mr Daw say how my father is?'

Ella looked back at his anxious face. Jack had spoken briefly about their neighbour, saying that Russ was very badly affected by his son's death. 'He didn't say much, Charlie, but he did mention that Russ was still going strong when he left him.'

'Was he . . . was he very upset about Bertie?'

'I should say that's only natural, love, wouldn't you?'

Charlie nodded. Ella wondered what was going through his mind. Then he lifted his head abruptly and said, 'Right, thank you!' left her with a tight smile and pushed the pram on to the butcher's.

With the purchase of all his requirements he told Regina that they had time to visit the swing before the others came home for dinner. This took them down by the river, the sight of which had a relaxing effect on Regina's bladder. No sooner had she been sat upon the swing than she said, 'I want to pee-wee.'

'Oh, you little pest! Why didn't you ask to go at home?' He lifted her down. She stood there and he asked what she was waiting for. She replied that she needed him to help her. 'I'm not doing it!' It was all right at home but somebody might see him here! She crossed her legs and said she couldn't go on her own. He tutted and said they had better go behind those bushes. After a brisk walk he helped her to do the necessary, her dress getting rather damp in the process. He was on his way back to the swing, grumbling over her inefficiency, when he stopped and said, 'Where's the pushchair?'

'Maybe it's fallen in the river,' she said helpfully.

'It can't have done, the brake was on!' Idiotically, he rushed back behind the bushes to search. 'God, it's been stolen! And it had all the shopping in it. Oh, no!' He made another futile search, then turned to stare at the child. 'Oh, no!' Flopping onto the swing that hung from the tree he pressed his hands to his cheeks in despair. Mrs Hazelwood would kill him!

'I haven't had my go yet.' He frowned at Regina as she repeated her claim, 'It's not your turn.'

'Oh . . . bugger the swing!' Leaping up he grabbed her. 'We'll have to find whoever took it. They can't have got far.'

She made wailing complaint as he set off and demanded to be carried. With a sound of exasperation he hefted her onto the crook of his arm and proceeded in an ungainly jog. It was hopeless of course. The culprit had long gone. Hampered by his burden, Charlie had no chance of catching up. All that remained was for him to go home. Regina's weight made the journey seem twice as long.

At midday the girls – all except Rowena, whose school was on the other side of the city – came in for lunch. They beheld their plates in astonishment. 'Is that all we're getting?' was Lyn's demand.

'It's all there is,' Charlie told her. 'There's some cheese and . . .'

443

'There's not enough to bait a mousetrap!' cut in Beany. 'I thought you were meant to be looking after us.'

'Somebody stole my pram,' announced Regina.

Lyn asked what relevance this had. Charlie told her. 'The shopping was in it.' She asked couldn't he buy any more. 'Lyn, I've no more money! Even if I did they wouldn't sell me any.' The shopkeepers had begun their own form of rationing.

'Well we can't exist on this!'

'Oh, leave him alone,' said Becky. 'It's not Charlie's fault.'

'Yes it is! He didn't take care of the shopping so it's his fault we're starving.' Lyn sat down and ripped off a mouthful of bread. The others joined her, all save Becky showing animosity. Then Lyn grasped the full horror of the situation and laid down her bread. 'I hope we're getting more than this tonight?'

Looking sick, Charlie shook his head. There were cries of protest. 'Well you're getting more than I am!' he retorted. 'I've gone without my share.'

'I should think you bloody-well have after you've been so careless with our food,' shot Lyn.

'Stop being so mean and stop swearing!' defended Becky.

'It's nowt to what Mother'll say!'

This was just what Charlie had been thinking: Oh, God! What would she say?

After their paltry lunch the girls returned to school. 'Shall I wash the pots?' asked Regina, bringing a sigh to Charlie's lips.

'That won't take much doing, will it?'

'Are you angry at me?'

He looked at her solemn face, then raised a smile and swung her onto the chair. 'No . . . come on, let's get cracking.' He had just put the plates into the sink when a breathless Becky entered. Her face was pink with exertion and pleasure as she dropped her burden onto the table. 'There you are! No need to worry now – except about the pram.'

Wiping his hands, Charlie came up to gape at the

cabbage, carrots and potatoes that had rolled out of the newspaper parcel. 'Where did you get those?'

'Mr Payne's allotment. I didn't pinch them. I saw him working as I passed so I asked if he could spare a cabbage to stop you getting into bother. He gave me all this. Isn't he kind?'

Charlie was grinning now. What a relief! Even without the meat he could have some sort of meal ready for Mrs Hazelwood's homecoming. 'Becky, you're a cracker!'

She smiled her pleasure and dashed off to school.

This wasn't her only accomplishment that day. On her return from school she carried another parcel which turned out to be a loaf of bread. 'It's yesterday's but it's not stale or anything. Mrs Phillips gave it to me.' At Charlie's surprise she added sheepishly, 'Well, I did happen to mention that we were rather famished. She likes me does Mrs Phillips.' The poor child was not to realize that the bread had been given as an inducement to gossip about her family affairs. When Rachel entered shortly after six o'clock, looking worn out, Charlie was lifting tureens onto the table. 'Right, now your mother's here we'll have the plates out, Beck.'

Rachel lowered exasperated eyelids at the shortened name, but did not feel up to remonstrating. She had just turned into the street to see Ella Daw's rear view – and strolling beside her in his officer's uniform was her husband, their arms curled round each other like a couple of sweethearts . . . it made Rachel sick. She had purpose-fully stepped back around the corner and waited so that she would not have to follow the spectacle all the way to her front door. But the sight remained with her. How did he manage to stay alive, while her son . . .

She accepted the warmed plate that Becky handed to her. 'So . . . what have you been doing at school today?' She tried to sound as if she cared.

'Makin' sandbags,' said Lyn.

'And digging an allotment,' Becky reminded her sister.

'Huh!' said Rachel disdainfully, then glared at the youngest who was tapping on the table with her spoon. The tapping stopped. Her attention drawn to the child, Rachel noticed a red rash on Regina's chin and in an alarmed fashion leapt up to feel her brow for signs of temperature – it could be measles! But when Charlie assured her that Regina had been perfectly well all day, she sat down again.

'Doesn't it smell good, Mother?' Rowena viewed the meal eagerly.

Rachel offered half-hearted accord and took the lid off each tureen in turn. 'Where's the meat?'

Charlie tried not to look at Becky's guilty face. 'I'm sorry, there isn't any.'

Rachel frowned. 'I wasn't aware that there was any shortage.'

'Well, there isn't but . . .'

'There wouldn't be any of anything,' revealed Beany, 'if it wasn't for Becky.'

Charlie froze, while Becky fired a look of hatred at her sister. Mrs Hazelwood was waiting for enlightenment. 'I'm afraid the shopping got stolen.' When she demanded to know how, Charlie muttered out the facts.

'So in effect it's not just the shopping which was stolen but the pushchair too!'

'I'm sorry.' Charlie didn't bother offering the excuse that Regina had been partly responsible. Blaming the baby now, she'd say.

'So where did you get the extra money to buy all this?' Rachel indicated the food.

Before Charlie could speak, Beany explained, 'Becky got it from Mr Payne's allotment.'

'You stole it?' Rachel's face was clothed in horror.

'No! I'm not a . . .' Becky snatched an abashed look at Rowena, then went on, 'I told Mr Payne what had happened and he very kindly donated these. Mrs Phillips gave us the bread. She said she wouldn't see us starve.'

Rachel was outraged. 'You've been begging!'

'Not rea . . .'

'My own children scavenging the streets for food! That woman will be telling all and sundry, saying I'm not fit to look after my family . . . and all because of your stupidity!' Her finger was directed at Charlie. 'You said you could manage! I'd never have entrusted you if I'd known you were so lackadaisical. You wretched, wretched boy! Well we can't eat this. I refuse to allow you to lower us to charity!' She bounced from the chair and began to scrape the food into the waste bin.

Charlie felt his eyes burn. He watched her destroy the meal that had taken him ages to prepare, watched the horrified and hungry faces of the others turn slowly to him in condemnation. Then something went pop! He leapt from his seat, face on fire and hurled at her, 'I'll bet you even blame me for the bloody war, don't you!' and rushed from the back door.

The unexpectedness of this was sufficient to prevent Rachel from destroying the entire meal. She looked at the half-empty bowl of potatoes in her hand. Then, after a long pause, she returned it to the table, voicing sullenly to Rowena, 'You'd better share these out. I wouldn't have you going hungry because of him – but don't you ever, *ever* beg for charity again!' With this dire warning she sailed off to the front parlour.

Rowena turned to a wet-eyed Becky who asked softly, 'Should we go after him?'

Her eldest sister said that it was best not to. 'He probably wants to be by himself.'

'Just as well he's gone,' grumbled Beany, eyeing the depleted table. Becky's hackles rose as Rowena dipped the spoon in the bowl. 'Don't bother giving me any – give mine to the pig!'

Charlie was still running. He had burst from the yard, out of the lane and into the street. By order, since the first air raid, no gas lamps had been lighted. Only at the busiest road junction was an odd electric bulb allowed to burn. Charlie did not care; he was already blind with pain and anger. He did not know where the path was taking him, he just had to run. His feet hurtled him down the long, sloping terrace. The cold air abrased his windpipe but he fought the discomfort. Only when the pavement began to incline did he slacken his pace and finally slowed to a walk, puffing and wheezing. He was through with trying to be nice to them – apart from Wena and Becky none of them were worth the effort – especially *her!*

He walked on, crossed the road, made a couple of turns then eventually came to wander by the Ouse that sparkled in the moonlight. He walked for quite a while, stooping to gather a handful of stones which he tossed pettishly at the water. In time he came upon the murky figure of a boy who, as he drew close enough to see, looked about the same age as himself. He was sitting on the bank, head bent, fingers playing with a twig. As Charlie neared the boy looked up, but just as quickly reverted his eyes to the river. Charlie stopped nearby and looked at the water too, scuffing his shoes around a patch of gravel.

'What are you doing?' he asked finally.

The boy granted him a cursory glance, 'Nowt,' and swapped the twig for a handful of pebbles.

Another period of silence, then, 'Do you ever get sick of women?'

'I get sick of everybody,' answered the boy, plopping pebbles into the river.

'So do I,' agreed Charlie, and came to sit beside the boy, huddling up against the cold.

'Specially at school,' added the boy. 'What school d'you go to?' Charlie said he didn't go. The boy's eyes quizzed him, then saw that he was probably too old for school. 'Lucky bugger. I've got two years yet.'

'I wish I could go,' said Charlie. When the boy told him he was mad he explained, 'You'd get bored if you were stuck at home all day.'

'You're joking!' After a laugh, the boy looked confused. 'How come you're at home all day? How old are you?' When Charlie said he was nearly fifteen the boy asked, 'Can't you get a job, then?'

'I've never tried. *She* says I might have to get one soon though. She's always moaning about having no money.' When the other enquired who she was, he answered, 'Mrs Hazelwood, the woman who looks after me.'

'Haven't you got any parents, then?'

'I've got a father. He's married to Mrs Hazelwood. My mother's dead. Is your father in the Army?'

The boy's expression altered and he looked away. 'No, he's got an important job here, on the railway.'

'Soon as I'm old enough,' vouched Charlie, 'I'm going to join the Army and fight for my country.'

The boy didn't appear to like Charlie's intimation that his father must be a coward if he wasn't fighting. ''Tisn't your country though, is it?'

'Yes it is. My father is British, that makes me British.'

'You can't be, you're black. Anyway, I'm glad my father hasn't gone,' said the boy firmly. 'I don't want him to be killed.'

'I don't want mine to be killed either . . .' Charlie leaned on his knees, looking miserable. 'I wish he'd come back. I wonder how much longer it'll go on?'

The boy shrugged, then said, 'You don't like this Mrs Hazelwood?'

'It's more a case of her not liking me . . .' Then Charlie admitted, 'No, I don't like her, but I've no choice. I have to stay with her until Father Guillaume comes for me.'

The latter comment required an explanation. Charlie found himself telling this boy almost everything: the humiliation, the prejudice, the sadness . . . at his misty-eyed conclusion he found a comforting hand on his arm.

'I know how you feel,' said the boy gently.

Inexplicably, Charlie's anger surged at the meek, sympathetic face. 'How could you know?' He flicked his elbow so that the hand fell away.

The boy hesitated. Then he divulged, 'My father's not really on the railway . . . he's in a detention camp. He's German.'

Charlie turned to him and, before the boy looked away, saw the result of two and a half years of persecution in the blue eyes . . . almost the same amount of time that Charlie himself had suffered. The boy was about to go further, to open his soul as Charlie had done, knowing that here he would find understanding and friendship.

He was wrong. 'You're a bloody Hun!' Charlie leapt for

him, fingers grasping the boy's neck, pushing him back-wards in order to straddle him. 'I've been sitting here talking to the enemy!'

'No, I'm English!' The boy screwed up his eyes in pain as the fingers encased his throat.

Charlie lifted one of the hands and began to slap the boy round the face. Slaps grew to punches. He wanted to hurt. His victim struggled and bucked, trying desperately to escape his persecutor – just one of many. 'Bloody Fritz! Filthy German!' All Charlie's pain was used to form that fist, to smash into that hated face.

'Oy!' A figure loomed out of the darkness.

The exclamation stayed Charlie's hand. His eyes flicked up to take in the special constable who was hurrying down the path. His victim took this opportunity to thrust him aside and scrambled upwards, clutching his face. Charlie stared at him. When the boy took his hand away there was a dark wetness smeared under his nose and on the palm he presented in evidence. He was sobbing.

Charlie felt a wave of revulsion for what he had done. It took him to his feet, sent him off and away down the tow-path, running as though his life were the issue, not knowing where, just running to escape that terrible deed. His throat screamed as he pounded along one street and then another. It had grown even darker, for which he was glad. It hid his shame. He took a swift turn, and found himself in a back lane where there were no inquisitive eyes to invade his agony. He slammed himself against a wall to shed copious tears.

How could he have done such a despicable thing? He knew the boy had seen in him a friend, someone on whom he could unload his pain – and what had Charlie done but given him more. Why? Here was the first person who could have really understood Charlie's problem . . . and Charlie had driven him away. The teary, blood-smeared face haunted him. Still weeping, he banged his fist at the wall, trying to drive the image from his mind. But all this achieved was to produce another image: that of a shocked Father Guillaume, 'Charlie, how could you be so cruel?'.

Well you don't bloody care what happens to me either! came the mental yell. Otherwise you wouldn't have gone off and left me here. Giving the wall a final thump he ran on, dashing away the tears that blinded his passage.

Somehow, without planning it, he ended up in the street where he least wanted to be. By now he had lapsed into a walk, his tears dried for the time being, though the evidence of their passing still marked his face. Inside the gate, he paused, then lashed out at Mrs Hazelwood's rose bushes, scattering the last precious bloom of the year. Then with purpose in his step he went into the house and deliberately sought out Rachel who, it happened, was alone in the kitchen. The children had gone to bed. He had lost track of the time. It must be quite late. The look on Rachel's face verified this. She was about to rebuke him for being out so long. He leapt in first. 'I want to go home!'

She forgot her previous objection to counter, 'Don't be stupid, there's a war on.'

'Stupid, stupid!' His voiced cracked. 'You're always telling me I'm stupid! Everything I do is wrong. I hate it here! I want to go home.'

Her reply was barbed. 'Much as I would love to see you go it's hardly possible until the priest decides to put pen to paper! You'll just have to put up with your grievances like the rest of us.'

He was about to press the matter, but felt the tears sting again, and he wouldn't cry in front of her. As he thundered past the girls' room Becky scrambled out of bed to poke her head round the door. 'Charlie, are you all . . .' The click of his door nipped her solicitations. Hearing her mother's foot on the stair, she closed the door hurriedly. Rachel wound her lethargic passage up the staircase. Outside her bedroom she faltered. There was the sound of weeping from along the landing. Damning herself, she leaned her brow against the jamb, pressing it into the wood. She must stop, she really must . . . he was only a child.

The sobs still in her ears, she was about to let herself into her room when she realized the sounds did not emanate solely from the boy. Turning to the girls' door, her hand lingered some seconds before tightening on the knob and twisting it. She wandered in and held the lamp over each bed, searching for the one who grieved. Becky's wet face glistened in the beam of light. Without speaking, Rachel came forth and placed the lamp at the child's bedside. Rebecca was positioned on the outside of her eldest sister who appeared to be fast asleep, as were the three girls in the other bed. Still mute, their mother bent and kissed Becky's cheek, then smoothed away the trickles with a thumb. This tender gesture promoted more tears.

'Ssh,' murmured Rachel softly.

'Oh, Mother, I'm sorry!' sobbed Becky. 'I didn't know it was begging.'

'You'll wake the others,' whispered Rachel, putting a finger to the child's lips. 'We'll talk about it tomorrow.'

'But will you forgive me?'

'Yes.' A kindly smile before the hand left Becky's cheek.

'And Charlie?'

Rachel picked up the lamp, about to go. She closed her eyes tiredly at the mention of him, then opened them to look down on the anxious face, and yielded with a sigh. 'Yes . . . and Charlie.'

Rowena, who had been feigning unconsciousness, felt as if someone had lifted the heavy blanket that had been stifling her for months. As Rachel slipped from the room, she gave in to the feeling of release which her mother's comment had induced, snuggling up to Becky, and promptly fell asleep.

CHAPTER TWENTY-NINE

Slowly, her eyes came open. She blinked confusedly for a moment . . . then experienced an acute and unexpected ripple of good-feeling. It was daylight. For the first time in four months she had not woken to pitch blackness in a state of terror. The curtains that she had taken to leaving open in order to temper this condition, now admitted a beam of winter sunlight. Thankfulness closed her eyes for a brief span, then she opened them to stare at the ceiling whilst collecting her thoughts.

There were things to be done today, things to be said . . . Robert came to her suddenly then and she wept, but it was done silently, gazing through the blur of tears at her boy as he had been when alive, not the ghastly vision which had been torturing her every night . . . just a young boy with sun-tinted hair and a rather boastful manner. The sense of release overwhelmed her, the tears dripping quietly down each side of her face and into the hollows of her ears. The pain was still there – she knew it always would be – but it was no longer destructive. He would come to her every day of her life, but in this form she could face him. Oh, Robert . . . With the vision still present in her mind she rose and pulled on a dressing gown. After washing she selected a dress from her wardrobe, donned it then sat before the mirror to brush out her hair. Her reflection pulled her up. The features in the mirror had been further sharpened by pain. This was how others must have seen her – a little ferret of a woman. Experimentally, she tightened the muscles around her mouth, curling it into a smile. It didn't work – looked false. But then who would be expecting her to go around with a smile on her face when her only son was dead?

Thoughtfully, she began to brush her hair, remembering her daughter's tears of last night. How many more had been shed that she had failed to notice? Then her mind floated along the landing to the boy and once more she stopped brushing. How would you feel if you were that boy's mother, watching him being victimized for something he couldn't help? Angry with herself, she dragged the brush through her hair several times then wound it up and fastened it. With one last imposing stare at her reflection she went down to the kitchen.

Before she had reached the bottom step the sound of ashes being raked alerted her to his presence. She stopped at the kitchen door and stared in at him. He was trying to do it quietly, coaxing the ashes through the bars to drop onto the tray. The task was almost done. He placed the scraper on a cloth and gripping the tray pulled it towards him. Holding it delicately he was about to take it into the yard when he turned and saw her. Alarm flashed across his face.

'I didn't mean to make you jump.' She moved into the room.

'I . . .' He looked at the tray of ashes.

She went to the back door and opened it for him. He thanked her and hurried past to dispose of the ashes. When he came back she was brushing the hearth.

'Sorry if I made a mess.'

'You can hardly clean a grate without making a mess.' Sorry, sorry, that was all he ever seemed to say. She replaced the brush and shovel on the brass stand, then nodded at the tray he was still holding. 'Put that back then.' He did so, then looked at her. 'You might as well carry on, seeing as you've started.' He set to laying the fire, placing homemade briquettes of coal-dust and clay among yesterday's cinders, feeling incompetent and clumsy under her stare. When it was lit she told him to go wash his hands whilst she wiped the hearth with a damp cloth. On rising to her feet she found him watching her.

He felt he should speak. 'Will you be going to the shop today?'

'Yes, but I shall come home early. We don't do very

much business after five. So you don't have to worry about cooking anything.' He took this as an advertisement of her distrust, which showed in his expression.

'Don't think I'm still blaming you for yesterday,' she told him. 'But it's my job to be here to see to my family. I've been very neglectful lately.' For Heaven's sake don't say anything understanding or I'll scream, she begged silently.

But he was too startled by her admission to answer, at least for a while. When he recovered he chose his words carefully. 'I'd still like to help if I can. I know I'm not much use, but . . .'

'Yes, you can help,' she said briskly as she set about filling the kettle at the sink. 'We'll forget about you finding a job for the time being. As I'm home early I shan't have a lot of time to cash up and do the books.' She did not admit that these latter were in a very bad state due to her ineptitude. 'If I bring everything home with me, perhaps you could do it? You seem to be good at everything else.' You just can't stop, can you? she admonished herself. Can't stop these petty barbs.

He smiled tentatively. 'I'll help all I can.'

'Good.' Her response came in a pleasanter vein. 'Now go fetch me the – oh!' She had lifted the enamel washing up bowl from the sink, disturbing a big black spider which now scuttled round and round in panic. After dithering for a moment with the kettle in one hand, the bowl in the other, she put both down and clasped her hands trying to think of a way to get it out. She looked at Charlie, who stared back but did not offer any advice. For God's sake, you're forty-one years old! Isn't it about time you stopped relying on others and grappled with your own problems? Looking around, she took a glass tumbler from the draining board and placed it adroitly over the creature. Tearing a piece from a cardboard packet she began to slip it under the edge of the glass, so that by pressing the card to the bottom of the glass the spider would be imprisoned, enabling her to lift it from the sink. She did so delicately, holding her mouth askew as she moved to the door. 'Open it, Charlie!' Her palm felt the spider's panicked feet drumming through the card. It made her squirm, but she didn't drop it. She remained sensible, moved through the door and shook the prisoner on to the floor of the yard.

And with the spider's liberation she felt as if she, too, was emerging from a prison. You've done that, she told herself staunchly – you can do anything!

He wished there was more fighting, for whilst he was active he wasn't thinking about Bertie . . . like now. His eyes were staring at a photograph, the one he had confiscated from Strawbridge, the one of himself and the others and Dobson . . . but he was seeing Bertie too. He saw him lashed to the gun, he saw the pieces of his photograph fall to the mud, he saw the look of contempt as his son said goodbye, he saw a gaping mouth fill with seawater, a young face disappear beneath the waves . . .

A loud recitation from Private Jewitt interrupted his thoughts. 'He was known as Mad Carew, by the girls that he'd been . . . around with. Has it dropped off yet, Lons?' Jewitt positioned himself beside the private whom he had addressed and lit a tab.

Russ took his eyes off the photo to study the pair. The young men had only been here six months but already they had adopted the mannerisms and sayings of the veterans. For a long time the sergeant had tried not to like them. He had made that mistake with others – Dobson and Wheatley in particular – and he wasn't going to suffer that pain again. From now on they were just soldiers . . . It hadn't worked. Somehow, in spite of being idle, crafty and a sneak-thief, Jewitt had made the sergeant like him.

'Back to billets again tonight, old chum,' said Jewitt. 'I wonder if the mam'selles will be there.'

Russ watched Lonsborough's face light up – no, he corrected himself, behind that lustful spark there was something moribund; the look of one who lives in a graveyard.

'Bound to be if they know I'm comin',' Lonsborough replied.

'Gerraway! It's my beautiful body they can't get enough of.'

Snatching at every carnal opportunity as if it might be their last . . . which it might. All those fine young boys he had seen disintegrate into bloody lumps of flesh. They shouldn't be here, thought Russ. They should be scrumming in the mud of the rugby field, groping in the back row of the picture house, but not *here* . . . There was a sudden explosion. Russ watched the effect. The war had produced a strange malady he had dubbed 'Retractable neck'. The men were like tortoises; at each bang they would draw their necks deep into their shoulders. Then, when the smoke had cleared, out would pop their heads to peer balefully about them.

'He's going nuts you know,' remarked Lonsborough gravely. He shoved a cigarette in his mouth, brought his dirty face close to Jewitt's to draw a light from the other's tab. Behind his cupped hands it appeared to Russ as if the two were kissing.

'Who, old Filbert?' The soldiers had once heard Daw use this nickname and had instantly adopted it . . . though now it had taken a different connotation.

Lonsdale finished sucking the fire into his cigarette, but their heads remained close together. 'He keeps looking at that photograph, have you noticed? As soon as there's a lull he gets it out and stares at it.'

'Sounds a bit like you,' joked Jewitt.

'Soft sod . . . You watch, next full moon an' we'll be having to tie him down. I've seen it often enough to know the signs.'

Jewitt, who liked the sergeant, grew sombre. 'He keeps talking to me about his lad. I don't know what to say.'

Lonsborough shrugged. Death was so frequent a visitor that his thoughts were more on who would die today than who had bought it six months ago.

'He hardly ever gets any mail, you know. I asked . . .'

'Jewitt! Are you gonna sit there kallin' all day?' Russ shoved the creased photograph into his pocket – he had guessed by their lowered voices they were discussing him. He got to his feet. 'All I can hear is pss-pss-pss. I'm beginning to think I'm in the bleedin' reptile house. Look!

There's a section just about to cave in up there. Take hold of this here sandbag – oh sorry, Lonsborough!' He made much of brushing the soldier's tunic where his hand had distorted its fit. 'I didn't realize it was human, what with it being stood there motionless for so long. Shift your arses, the pair of you!'

The two grasped sandbags and were about to carry out the order when Captain Daw, just returned from his Blighty leave, stumbled down the narrow trench. They moved aside to allow him passage. When he was past, Jewitt's startled eyes followed him. 'God, there must be a big one coming up – did you see his face? It was white as chalk.'

Lonsborough returned an apprehensive nod. 'D'you know anything about it, Sarg?'

'What's that?' Russ had slipped back into his vacant stare.

'The Captain, he's lookin' awful windy. Jewitt here says there must be a right big one comin' up.' The men didn't like Daw, but his fearlessness always impressed them. If he was looking afraid then God knew what lay ahead.

Russ came back to the world, and said in a grim tone, 'It is a big one, Lonsborough. It'll be known as the Battle of Le Molar.'

Jewitt had never heard of the place and set his head at a slant. 'Is that around here, Sarg?'

'Quite near. It's just below these two densely thicketed areas called Les Nostrils in a barren plain known as Le Gob.' He grunted as he turned away. 'He's off to have a tooth pulled.'

Jewitt and Lonsborough roared their appreciation – the valiant Captain scared of the dentist! Russ strode off, wondering how he could joke whilst hurting so badly inside. *Oh, Jesus, it hurts, it hurts . . .* Poor Jack, he shouldn't have divulged his secret fear in front of the men. But what did it matter? What did anything matter? Mud. Mud everywhere. He sloshed along the waterlogged trench inspecting the breastwork as he went. The men had been repairing all night but the slime continually gave way to gravity. Each step was accompanied by a slurping sound as the mud hugged his feet. They had been issued with rubber waders now, but scant use they were in some places with the sludge up to one's thighs.

He had once seen a horse drown in this mud. It had been one of a pair hauling a gun carriage. All of a sudden the pair were floundering in the quagmire. In seconds they were up to their knees, the weight of the carriage preventing their escape. Men had swarmed over the animals like termites, cutting harness and fixing ropes about the lathered necks. They had succeeded in pulling one of the horses free, but the other's struggles had forced it deeper until only its neck and head was showing. Someone ran to fetch the assistance of an officer's revolver to put it out of its misery. When they came back the horse was gone. Russ remembered the terror in those rolling eyes, but slowly that look had dissolved into resignation as it was finally sucked under. Wounded men had died this way too . . .

The sweat sprang to his armpits though it was bitterly cold. He felt his own mouth fill with mud; it squirted from his nostrils and out of his ears . . . *stop! stop!* he charged his mind, and started to sing in order to provide another focus for his brain. But the visions stayed with him, pressing their way through the words. Oh Christ, it was coming again! He sought out a dark place where he could battle with his terror in private. The cubbyhole was occupied. 'Get out!' barked Russ to the three mud-caked privates, who slunk like weasels into the daylight, leaving behind their stench. He presented his hands to the fire, hands that were chapped and raw beneath the dirt. They began to quiver. He tucked them under his armpits and squeezed. Go away! But the tremor began to spread. It crept oh, so stealthily through his body, chattering his teeth, juddering his bones.

He doubled over and began to rock. 'It's the wrong way to tickle Mary. It's the wrong way to go! – *concentrate*! It's the wrong way to . . .'

'Tea, Sarg.'

Hazelwood yelled his shock out loud. His manic eyes glared at Jewitt who stood at the entrance to the dugout. The private pretended he had seen nothing, though the laugh he gave was awkward. 'Sorry, Sarg! Did I make you jump?'

Russ fought with his swirling thoughts, eyes fixed to Jewitt's young face. So many young boys . . . Slowly, the panic subsided. He took a deep breath and sat up. 'What was that, Jewitt?'

The private came inside and parked his rear on a crate by the fire. 'I brought you some tea, Sarg. Where's your mug?'

Russ, still not fully sensible, groped around his pack then held the tin mug out to Jewitt who filled it with muddy looking tea. Nodding his thanks to the private, he wrapped his hands around the warm metal, staring down into it. Jewitt put aside the can and began to delve into his own pack, selecting a tin which he duly opened.

'Might I be so impolite as to ask what you're doing, Jewitt?'

Jewitt studied him evenly, then grinned. 'Havin' me snap, Sarg.'

Hazelwood regarded the tattered muddy uniform. Jewitt was wearing a woman's hat that he had found on the road, fingerless gloves and a sheepskin coat that he had probably stolen from someone. 'What a bloody state . . . Around these parts, Jewitt, I'll have you know we dress for dinner.'

'Right, Sarg!' Jewitt began to unbutton his trousers. 'Any preference as to which side I dress to?' Grinning more widely, he dug into his tin of pork and beans, then made a face. 'Christ, I'd like to know what they put in here – it certainly isn't pork.'

Russ stared into the fire, pictures in his mind.

Jewitt, despite his complaint, ate the contents of the tin then brought out some biscuits and a tin of Tickler's plum and apple jam. 'Want some, Sarg?'

'You must be joking. Your plums'd taste sweeter than that.'

'Now we've got to keep our strength up,' quipped the private, spreading a dollop of jam on a biscuit.

'Eating for two, are we, Jewitt?'

'I did offer you some.'

'Ah . . . I can't stomach that muck any more.' Russ

shook his head and took a sip of tea which tasted of onions. 'You get past eating.' There might be hot food coming tonight with the ration party but that was no more appetizing. Even the thoughts of home-baking could not stir him now.

'Sarg . . . I heard that the Captain's servant copped it this mornin', is that right?'

'Thinking of having a change from latrine duty, are we? I wouldn't fancy the Captain's chances if those mitts were dishing up his grub.'

'Would you put in a good word for me, Sarg?'

Russ gave a tight laugh. 'The word I'd put in, Jewitt, is shirker.'

'It'd benefit you an' all, Sarg,' Jewitt proposed earnestly. 'I might be able to smuggle a few leftovers in your direction.'

Russ was still smiling, his pain subdued for the minute. 'I'm not sure I want anything you've handled, knowing the places you frequent. Oh, all right, Jewitt! I'll see what I can do.' He underwent a furious period of scratching then, with a sharp sound of annoyance, pulled off both his greatcoat and tunic. Striking a match, he ran it down the seams of the filthy garment, enjoying the intermittent puff as a louse was incinerated.

Jewitt gave up trying to eat the hard biscuit, 'It's like chewin' a lump o' donkey stone,' and tossed it into a corner. There was a scuffle as the missile disturbed a rat. 'I'll do that, Sarg.'

'You wouldn't be trying to suck up to me, Private?' Nevertheless, Russ let the youth continue the delousing process whilst listening vaguely to Jewitt's babble. The pile of dead matches at his feet grew as one after the other was run along the seams of the tunic. 'I'll bet you're not as useful as this at home – only if you want something from your poor mother.' Jewitt smiled as he worked. 'Got any brothers and sisters, have you?'

'No sisters, I had six brothers but I'm the only one left now.'

A fresh wave of horror rippled Hazelwood's breast. It

461

always amazed him when it happened. After the things he had heard and seen one would not expect him to be surprised any more, but he often was. 'Your parents have lost *six sons*?'

A nod. 'Two were regulars, went down at Mons. Another joined up 'cause he couldn't stand being a coward. Me, I got more white feathers than Sitting Bull before I let them rope me in. The others were conscripts an' all. Didn't even get past their first day in the trenches.' A small laugh that muffled his true feelings. 'Never mind, they won't get me. Seventh son of a seventh son. I was born lucky. There we are, Sarg!' He handed back the jacket which was in a very poor state due to this regular treatment. 'Think I've got all the little bastards – given 'em chilblains anyway. They won't be so eager to dance about so much.'

Russ offered gruff thanks, whilst inside the dread was once more rumbling. *Jewitt's parents had lost six sons.* This boy was their only remaining child . . . and he was in Hazelwood's hands. The enormity of this responsibility unleashed a fresh tide of panic. 'You can get back on duty now, Private!'

Jewitt came out of his squat. 'You'll speak to the Captain, Sarg?'

'I'll do what I bloody-well see fit! Now move, soldier!'

And as the nonplussed Jewitt made for the daylight, Russ fought to stem the blood that poured from every crevasse of his mind.

It was freezing cold in the church. Charlie tucked his hands between his legs and shivered. He had come here for Mass, but the thought that worried his brain caused his eyes to keep flickering towards the confessional. He should go in. He should go and confess the way he felt about Bertie. All through Mass he thought about it. If he begged forgiveness, would it be genuine? Or was it that he hoped this act might exorcize the ghost which had haunted him for months? The church had almost emptied by the time he decided to join the pew of confessants. Being the last in line gave him a chance to compose himself. But after the initial, 'Bless me,

462

Father,' he couldn't think of what to say. In the end, he confessed some paltry digression, sat for a moment praying mentally for help, then made for the outside as quickly as he could.

'One moment, young fellow!'

Charlie revolved swiftly to see that the priest was following him.

The man gave a beckoning smile. 'Hold on a moment, will you?'

'I'll be late for my dinner.' Charlie kept his distance.

'I won't keep you that long.' Father Duncan came down the short flight of steps to stand on the pavement, barring Charlie's way. 'I just want to ask you something. Come on, it's cold here, there's a fire in my study.'

Still Charlie tarried. 'My mother will be worried if I'm late.'

'Your mother doesn't practise her faith?' The priest had never seen the woman with her son.

'She's ill.'

Father Duncan cocked his head in knowing fashion. 'Is she ill every Sunday? You always come with Biddy Kelly as I remember.' At Charlie's miserly reply, he said, 'You seem disturbed. I'm not going to beat the living daylights out of you. It's Biddy Kelly I'm after knowing about.'

'Oh, I haven't seen her in . . .'

'Tell me in my study!' The priest captured Charlie's arm. 'It won't take five minutes but in that time we could both be dead of cold.'

The warmth of the priest's fire caused Charlie's nose to run. He perched on the edge of the chair looking out of place. 'Now then!' Father Duncan took the chair opposite. 'As we've never been introduced, let's start with names. You always seem to slope away quietly after Mass.'

Charlie performed a huge sniff and gave his first name.

'Charlie what?'

The boy gave his father's surname.

'So, Charlie Hazelwood, can you tell me why Biddy Kelly doesn't come to Mass any more?' Charlie said maybe the priest should ask her family. 'They're as wise as you are! You were saying you hadn't seen Biddy for . . .?'

'About four months or so. Mrs Hazelwood gave her the sack.'

'That an odd way to refer to your mother, isn't it – Mrs Hazelwood?'

Charlie stared at the kind face, then lowered his eyes. 'She's not really . . . not really ill and not really my mother. My mother's dead.' Hesitantly, he embarked on the complicated story, telling the priest about Father Guillaume, his own longing for his father's affection and finally Bertie's death.

Father Duncan thanked the instinct that had made him follow the boy from the confessional. There was a great deal of pain here. At the end of Charlie's monologue the priest raised his eyebrows and sighed. 'Well, I never anticipated my enquiry about Biddy Kelly would spark off such a lengthy story – no, no!' he waved aside Charlie's apology. 'It's thoroughly intriguing, and it's me who should be saying sorry. To think that one of my flock was undergoing such torment and me not even bothering to ask his name . . . Well!' He slapped his cassocked knees. 'I'd better make a start at redeeming myself.' Rising, he went to a bureau. 'What was the last address you had for Father Guillaume?'

'I don't think it'll do any good to write,' said Charlie. 'We've written dozens of times and it's over a year since we've heard from him.' He nibbled at a piece of skin on his lip with his teeth. 'Something's happened to him, I'm sure.'

'Give me the address anyway, and the one in South Africa too. I'll make enquiries.'

Charlie provided both, then looked at the clock; he had been here half an hour. 'I really must go, Father.'

'Oh, yes! You run along. I'm going to write a couple of letters right this minute. One way or another, Charlie, we'll get you some education. It's not right for you to have to do the work of a housemaid.'

'I don't mind. Anyway, I'm a bit old for school now.'

'Rot! And wait till I catch that Biddy Kelly, walking out on you like that.' Charlie told him not to blame Biddy, Mrs Hazelwood had said some awful things to her. 'Oh now, don't you be sticking up for her! I know that girl. She can be an idle so and so, too idle to get her body up for Mass, by the look of it. Off you go, Charlie. I'll see what I can find out. Whatever way, we'll meet here next Sunday . . . I don't suppose you'll be coming to Midnight Mass? No, no, one can't expect a young lad like you to be on the streets alone at midnight. Never mind, I'm sure you'll say your prayers at home.'

Charlie said he would and left. He would have to run now or he'd be late getting back to help with Sunday dinner. But getting this off his chest had helped enormously. Next time he went to church he felt sure he would be able to fulfil his confession.

Christmas Eve. Rachel fought her way home through the last minute shoppers, feeling none of the festive bubble. After a hard day at the shop she was not looking forward to all the preparations that lay ahead for the morrow. Even in these frugal times there had to be some sort of special meal for Christmas Day and the house made presentable in case of visitors. Though she doubted there would be anyone coming. However, when she stepped from the cold evening into her kitchen, she found that her list of preparations had been whittled down. A blast of warm air carried the scent of baking to her nose. The children, instead of creating a mess, had tidied all the waste from their decorations – which now adorned the walls – and had dusted and swept the room. The cushions were plumped and sat to attention on the sofa, the hearth was polished, the grate leaded. Bidding her to be seated, Rowena divested her of the basket and handed her a cup of tea. Charlie grinned from his position at the range and said the meal wouldn't be long. An afternoon's carolling round the piano had made him feel very Christmasy. They had done their caterwauling while Rachel was out so as not to upset her.

Rachel sat there looking from one shining face to the next, smelling the branches of pine that they had collected from the pavement outside the florist's. There was a crib on the floor beside the hearth, made up of a cardboard box, a handful of straw and several cut-out figures. The atmosphere was overwhelmingly Christmas. Unbearably so. She wanted to escape, but forced herself to smile and commend them for their hard work. She managed to endure it until she had eaten the meal which Charlie and Rowena had concocted. Congratulating them on their excellent fayre, she said that she must go upstairs to change, for the day's exertion had made her feel grimy.

She went not to her own room, but to that of her dead son. Closing the door she leaned on it for a while, gazing at Bertie's things, before moving to the bed. She smoothed the coverlet. She pictured him on previous yuletides, opening his gifts. Saw him at different stages of his life: a blond-haired baby . . . an apple-cheeked soldier. Tears blinded her. She must find something to do, to get her over Christmas.

Hurrying from his room she went to her own and began to pull at the drawers of the dressing table. Tidying them would take an hour or so off the ordeal. As her fingers ripped the contents from the drawers, they came upon a framed picture of her husband which she had shoved from her sight the night he had left her. She picked up the brass frame, presenting it to her face. The photograph showed a man of twenty-three in dress uniform. Such a smart, handsome chap . . . with a scrabbling movement she took the back off the frame and removed the picture, tossing it onto the floor with all the other unwanted articles, then proceeded with her task.

But later, when it came to bagging up the rubbish, she looked at the photograph again and, instead of screwing it up, laid it to one side.

Midnight. For lots of reasons, Charlie could not sleep. After tossing about for a spell, he left his bed to steal downstairs. Once in the kitchen, he used the glow of the fire to light his path and went to kneel by the crib – not praying, just letting the feel of Christmas wash over him. He wondered what his father was doing now. Wondered about many things. Shortly, he did offer a brief prayer, then went up to bed.

His journey was interrupted by a startlingly white figure, which caused him to draw in his breath and cross himself, thinking it was Bertie come to haunt him.

Rachel, too, bit back a scream and, hand to breast, heaved a sigh of relief. She finished closing the door of the girls' room, put a finger across her lips and disappeared into her own bedroom. Charlie looked at the closed door for a second, smiled, then went to bed . . . where he found an apple, some nuts . . . and a photograph of his father.

Morning brought the usual excitement as the children found their small gifts. Rachel was at the range when they tumbled into the kitchen and instead of rebuking them for their noisy entry she smiled and said she hoped next Christmas would see the end of the war and a return to prosperity. Charlie asked if she wanted any help.

'Maybe with the dinner,' she told him, and continued making breakfast.

'Thank you for the picture,' he ventured shyly.

'Well, I thought you may as well have it,' she approached the table with a fistful of spoons and a tin of corn syrup. 'It was no use to me.'

For once there was no intention to wound, but her thoughtless remark had the effect of tarnishing the gift and the boy was rather quiet for the rest of the morning.

After Christmas dinner had been made, consumed and thoroughly enjoyed and the pots washed, Rachel sprang her surprise. They were all to go to a pantomime film at the Electric Cinema. Beany, ever the excitable one, gave a scream of delight. 'I do hope you'll control your inclination to do that in the cinema,' reproved her mother. When asked the subject of the film she replied, 'Robinson Crusoe, and apparently there are a lot of other films on with it, so let's not delay. Go get your coats – and quietly!'

There was a gleeful exodus. All save Charlie tore off to put on outdoor wear. He did not rise, but proceeded to gather up the mess of sweetpapers and nutshells they had left. Becky remembering past events, broke her dash to linger at the foot of the stairs where she could still see into the kitchen.

'Leave that, Charlie,' said Rachel. 'Or we may miss the start. Go get your coat on.' She watched his expression as he tore off to join a gladdened Becky. It made her feel utterly wretched.

It was the first film performance Charlie had ever seen and he enjoyed it tremendously. When they emerged from the cinema in Fossgate it was as a gibbering, laughing mass. They made the brisk walk through the cold fog to the nearest tram stop. Rachel listened to their laughter and wondered if any of them was aware how much she still grieved inside . . .

'Why hello, Mrs Hazelwood!' A young woman was smiling into her face.

Rachel focused her eyes to see that it was her ex-maid. 'Biddy . . . how are you?'

'Oh, I'm fine!' A large hand primped the Marcel Wave which had dropped from the moist air. 'And yourself? Is Mr Hazelwood still on this side?'

'What?' Rachel was staring at Biddy's attire – a fur wrap.

'I said is all well with himself?' Biddy noticed that Rachel was mesmerized by the fur and performed a clumsy twirl. 'D'ye like it?'

'I'm sure it's very nice,' mumbled Rachel as Biddy called, 'Oh, there's Michael! That's my gentleman friend, he's waiting for me.'

'He must be very well-off,' opined Rachel, feeling prominently shabby in her three-year-old coat.

'Oh, he didn't buy this!' laughed Biddy and stroked the fur. 'Real squirrel, ye know. No, I'm on good money meself, at the munitions – two quid a week.' She conversed with the children, asking them if they'd like to stroke her coat, then made a face when Charlie told her that Father Duncan wanted to see her. 'He'll be lucky! Ah well, I'd best not keep Michael waiting. Happy New Year to one and all!' She lumbered away.

'Two pounds a week,' muttered Rachel to no one in particular. 'As much as a man. Small wonder I can't get help if the factories are paying those sort of ridiculous wages.'

'Never mind, Mother.' It was Rowena. 'We don't really need a maid now, do we? We're quite capable of looking after each other.'

Rachel stared at her, produced a sudden smile and said, almost cheerfully, 'Yes dear, we are!'

The others absorbed this mood. 'I'll bet it wasn't real squirrel,' scoffed Lyn.

'No, it looked too stripey to me,' agreed Beany. 'I'll bet it was off a stray tom.'

Everyone laughed, then cheered as the tram arrived and all piled on board. Charlie led the way to the front and with Regina on his knee chatted happily all the way home. He noticed from time to time that the woman sitting nearby kept staring at him, but then he had grown used to that kind of look.

Rachel hadn't. The woman's smug expression annoyed her. The eyes moved over Charlie's exuberant brown face and his kinky hair that twinkled with diamonds of fog; then took in Rachel, looking her up and down. She's thinking he's mine, came Rachel's angry thought, and she turned her face to the window. But all she could see in the darkened glass was the woman's smirking reflection. She was glad when the tram reached The Mount. Beckoning to the children she rose and waited for them to stumble to the exit. As Charlie lifted Regina from his lap, the woman who had been staring took something from her bag and thrust it at him. He accepted the white feather dumbly.

Rachel paled with fury. As the tram lurched to a standstill she stepped forward and dealt the woman a hard slap round the face. 'He's not even fifteen, for God's sake!'

A stunned Charlie looked back, until Rachel gave him a dig in the ribs, 'Get along!' and followed him off the tram, while the red-faced woman sat looking out of the far window, trying to pretend it hadn't happened.

All the way home, Charlie damned the woman on the tram for causing the resurgence of Mrs Hazelwood's temper. The poor boy was not to realize he had just been given the most precious Christmas gift he could have wished for – Rachel's acceptance.

CHAPTER THIRTY

There was no such festive spirit in France. 'I knew damn well you wouldn't last five minutes!' Sergeant Hazelwood informed Jewitt as the company limp-marched to new billets that night. Jewitt had kept his post as servant to the Captain for three hours, which was the time it took for Daw to discover the private's vocation for skiving. He had been put back on the biscuit tins without ever having gained one of the perks. 'I suppose I'll be in the shit for recommending you. Don't you dare ask me for anything again.'

'I won't Sarg, I promise.' Jewitt placed one weary foot in front of the other. 'Er . . . just lend me your back to take the weight off me feet.'

The sergeant gave a growl and cuffed him, then marched on into the cold needles of rain.

What should have been a relaxing time was marred by the obvious change in mood of the French hosts from the last time the company was here. The meals the soldiers were given were not much better than they received on the line and whilst before they had been included in the family conversations – even if neither could understand the other – now, Russ noticed a definite lack of friendship. Hence his reply to Jewitt when they met up again and the private asked what his billet had been like: 'I was made to feel right at home.'

The march to their new sector was marked by a snowfall, adding inches to the waterline. There was little activity on the fighting side, though the constant need to mend trenches helped to ward off boredom. A few days after he had arrived here a belated Christmas parcel turned up. Even before Russ had opened it the package itself brought comfort. When nothing had arrived at Christmas he had feared his girls blamed him for killing their brother. First out of the paper was the helmet upon which Rowena had laboured for three months. He smiled at the colours and attempted to don it, but the tight row of cast-on stitches cut into his brow and would go no further. Giving up the fight, he replaced it with his own lice-infested headgear, smiled over it for a second, then read the letter which Rowena had slipped inside it. This gave all the news from home, plus the information that Charlie had not yet left for college. Russ cursed as he fingered Charlie's gift – a pamphlet about wild birds – what the hell was the priest messing at? He must write to him again if he still had the address.

The other gifts earned a smile. Then he put them all into his pockets, using the brown wrapping to shove inside his tunic as a chest-warmer. When the hand came out of his tunic it automatically bore the group photograph – so creased now that it was in danger of tearing. He handled it with reverence.

Private Jewitt paused some five yards away to watch the sergeant. He didn't know why he should feel sorry for him, Hazelwood was always bawling at him and they were all in this together. But the death of his son had really knocked him flat. Oh, he still sometimes joked and swore . . . but then so did Jewitt, and he knew how depressed he himself felt sometimes at being here – even while cracking a joke. So what the sergeant must be feeling like after two years in the trenches . . . He put on a cheerful face and continued his approach. 'Got something for you, Sarg!'

Hazelwood's bleak eyes came up from the photograph to settle on the huge bulge in Jewitt's pocket. 'I didn't know you were that fond of me, Private.'

Jewitt's throat cracked a laugh. He delved in his pocket and withdrew a large half-sausage and from his other pocket a silver knife.

'There's no bloody wonder we've outstayed our welcome with the Frogs,' breathed Russ after a loud exclamation. 'How many more things have you lifted this week?' He put aside the photograph to rub some Zam-buk into his knuckles which were cracked and bleeding, then reached

471

over to smear a little on Jewitt's whose were in the same state.

Jewitt began to slice the sausage, offering the first cut to his sergeant. 'I think if we're being shot at defending their country the least they can do is show appreciation.'

'And so they were, until light-fingered soldiers started pilfering their valuables.' Russ flicked the skin aside and devoured the meat. 'Haven't you got any bread to go with this?' The sausage tasted of Zam-buk.

'Eh, we are on rations, Sergeant,' chastized Jewitt. Then gave a smirk and, from his tunic, produced a loaf.

Russ coughed out a guffaw and waited expectantly. 'Butter?'

'Aw, come on, Sarg! Even I'm not that sneaky . . . I might just have a bit o' cheese though.' The production of the lump of unwrapped cheese incurred more amusement.

'Jewitt, you are a bloody case.' Russ accepted the piece of cheese, picking off bits of fluff that came from Jewitt's tunic.

The private called his friends over then to share in the booty and for a time they simply chewed and stared out of their shallow trench at the white blanket of No Man's Land. To one unfamiliar with this place it might have been a scene from a Christmas card, but Russell's mind told him what was hidden beneath that soft and innocuous blanket . . . and came the ever-recurring nightmare to cram his mind with awfulness. Red and gaping wounds, the glint of bone, a slaughterhouse stench, demonic screams, rotting men . . . Patches of red started to ooze through the virgin layer and the sergeant began to tremble.

On New Year's Eve there were more celebrations in the Hazelwood residence. It was best, Rachel decided, to make the most of these rare occasions. For the rest of the year they had to live with this damned war, at least let the children enjoy themselves for tonight. The New Year had always been a time of celebration for Rachel and her husband, but with the onset of the trouble the woman had dispensed with it. As at Christmas, she did not altogether feel like merrymaking, but she had matured enough to consider the feelings of others in the house. Besides, when one tried to give pleasure to others one often discovered that the enjoyment became mutual. That was why, as the hands of the clock moved towards the first chime of the year, her children were not yet in their nightclothes – though some of them were on the brink of sleep.

Rachel sat among her brood thinking of things past. Her eyes fell on the pile of lumber by the back door, causing her to feel that there were many significant things happening tonight. The lumber was part of tradition. One would place it in a pile by the back door along with a sweeping of dust, then when the hour of midnight struck the whole lot would be tossed out into the yard so that New Year would begin with a clean sweep. In normal years the pile would merely be a token, for the houseproud Rachel allowed neither junk nor dust to accumulate. This year, however, there was a great deal of both, not just the tangible sort, but also in her mind. There must be a clean sweep all round.

As the time grew closer the woman sought to give her children a further treat and wet their glasses with the remainder of the sherry that had been purchased three years ago. She, Rowena, Becky, Lyn and Charlie – for the others had fallen asleep – stood waiting for the hour to strike, when the eldest girl broached the subject of first-footing. Rachel acquiesced. If there were to be celebrations they may as well be done correctly. 'We need a dark man and a fair lady.'

Becky grabbed her half-brother's arm. 'We've got our dark man. Lyn, you'll have to be the fair lady.'

The tomboy made ape-like grimaces. 'I'm not a lady.'

'You certainly aren't,' laughed her mother. 'But you're the fairest of us so we'll have to make do. Oh, stop complaining! Be quick before it strikes.'

The two concerned were hustled out into the yard and the door slammed on them. Lyn hugged her arms around her body. 'Blimey, I hope they don't keep us shivering out here for long!'

'I'll warm you up.' Charlie put his arm round her, knowing how she detested such displays and laughed gleefully when she thumped him.

'You bloody bugger!'

'You've just got time to make a New Year's resolution, Lyn.' He danced away from her attack. 'I resolve to be a proper little lady for the rest of the . . .' He broke off with a laugh as she swore and hit him again. 'Ssh, listen!' He warded off her assault. 'It's chiming.'

Lyn held her ear alert to catch the muffled sound of their chiming clock. In a second, she and Charlie burst upon the others, shouting, 'Happy New Year!'

'Happy New Year, Mother!'

And there were hugs and kisses between the girls and Rachel. Charlie stood back watching and smiling reticently, until Becky grabbed hold of him and hauling his head down kissed it. 'Happy New Year, Charlie!'

He glanced awkwardly at Rachel, expecting her displeasure, but all she said was, 'Happy New Year, Charlie,' and though she didn't go so far as to kiss him he felt as though she just had.

'Mother, could we go wish Happy New Year to Aunt Ella?' It was Rowena.

Her mother's face lost its smile for a moment. Then with her nod it returned. If she were to start the New Year clean then this too must be sorted out.

From the yard there were shouts of complaint. 'Her yard door's locked!'

This didn't deter Lyn. 'Come on, Charlie, we'll climb over!' And with that she was hoisting herself over the wall, an enthusiastic Charlie in pursuit. Both hammered on the door.

Now, up and down the row of houses there were sounds of jubilation. Due to war conditions there were no church bells ringing, but that didn't seem to spoil people's fun. Rachel could hear them laughing as they enacted their customs. She wrung her hands and shuddered as she waited for Ella to respond to the children's knock. 'Maybe she's in the front and can't hear you – knock a bit louder.'

Lyn did not need any encouragement and all but battered the door down. Suddenly in an upstairs room a lamp was ignited. This registered with Charlie who noticed now that

474

the entire street seemed to be flouting the regulations; if Jerry flew over now he would have a field day.

Rachel put a hand over her mouth as a figure thrust aside the curtain and hoisted the sash.

'What the bloody hell . . . ?' Ella glared down at the perpetrators of this nuisance.

'Happy New Year, Aunt Ella!' called the children.

'I'll give you Happy New – you've just dragged me from my bed! Some of us have to be up for work, you know!' With this she hauled down the window and was gone.

They all looked at each other guiltily, Rachel's hand still clamped over her mouth. Then the skin around her eyes creased and she let out a snort of mirth which in a split second had the children giggling too as Charlie and his half-sister scrambled back over the wall. Once in the house the whole tribe roared out loud at the memory of the enraged Ella Daw without her false teeth and her hair in curlers.

The laughter petered out as a familiar shout echoed in the street. 'Get that bloody light out!' Rachel, still smiling, went to check her own curtains, then turned around to behold the host of shining faces and was attacked by guilt, guilt at being happy. 'I think it's time we were all in bed.'

'Oh, but I haven't had my sherry yet!' objected Beany who, along with the other slumberers had only woken up with the noise of her siblings' merriment.

'Oh, Mother!' Becky remembered. 'We haven't sung Auld Lang Syne.'

'I could have my sherry while we're singing,' said Beany as the others prepared to give voice.

But Rachel said no to both motions. 'Robina, it's far too late for sherry now and I think we've upset Mrs Daw enough for one night without singing. Come on now, everybody up to their beds. I'm very tired myself.'

After a chorus of moans the girls kissed her and did as instructed, Charlie following.

Rachel paused, her hand set to douse the gaslight, checking on everything before going up to the loneliness of her bed. She didn't know why she had bothered to deny them their request, for with the closing of her eyes the words of Auld Lang Syne came creeping into her mind to bring the tears that she had not wanted to shed in their presence.

In tune with Rachel's sentiment, Charlie decided to begin the New Year in proper fashion too. For him this meant going to church to confess the way he felt about his dead half-brother. It was not easy, admitting to God that he had been glad when Bertie was killed – but then God knew that already, didn't he? Telling it to someone else had helped, even if it did bring penance and the request that he perform an act of contrition. To Charlie, the past three years had been one long act of contrition – for the sin of being his father's son. Still, he paid his dues to God and felt the better for it.

Yet there was still the worry over Father Guillaume's silence. It was February before Father Duncan had any definite news for him. Charlie sat in the priest's study, knowing by the Father's reluctance to begin that the news was bad.

'As I told you, Charlie,' started the priest, 'I wrote two letters. The one I sent to the address in Belgium has produced nothing . . . however,' he held up an envelope, 'I did get a reply from Sister Bernadette in South Africa.' There was another long hiatus. 'I'm afraid I have some very bad news for you, Charlie.'

Something leapt in Charlie's breast, producing the image of his friend being dragged away by Germans. With thickened tongue he put voice to his fear. 'He's been injured.'

The priest looked down at the carpet, then into the boy's eyes again. 'I'm afraid it's much worse than that . . . Charlie, Father Guillaume is dead.'

Even though he had been prepared, the shock was so savage that it robbed him of an answer.

His informant's voice was soft. 'Sister Bernadette apologizes for keeping you in ignorance for so long, but she herself has only recently learnt of Father Guillaume's sad demise . . . It appears he was thrown into prison by the Germans and his physical health suffered – so much so, that by the time Sister Bernadette discovered his whereabouts he was already beyond help. I'm truly sorry, Charlie.'

Charlie nodded . . . then bent his head and began to cry.

Father Duncan stood silently, turning the fateful letter in his fingers. 'Unfortunately, it doesn't appear that Father Guillaume had time to make arrangements for your education before he was captured. Sister Bernadette has given me leave to attend to this and I shall take immediate steps to send you to the college which Father Guillaume had selected – if that meets with your agreement?'

Charlie gave a huge, shuddering sniff, reached into his pocket for his handkerchief and nodded.

'Perhaps I should come and speak to Mrs Hazelwood about it?'

Charlie cleared his nose and wiped his eyes before saying, 'There's no need. She'll be satisfied to hear she's going to see the back of me.'

Father Duncan sensed the fullness of the boy's pain and sent out an aura of sympathy. 'I think we'll get Mrs Plumb to make us a cup of tea – and I believe she has just baked so we may be treated to a slice of her fruit-loaf. I can tell you it's absolutely mouthwatering.'

'Your dinner's in the oven!' snapped Rachel without looking up from her plate. Her annoyance stemmed not only from the fact that he was late, but that he had not been here to help with the preparation of the meal.

Charlie hung in the doorway, watching the family at their lunch, listening to the busy scraping of knives on plates. 'I'm sorry I'm late. Father Duncan wanted to speak to me.'

'Then you'll have him to blame and not me if your meal is dried up,' answered Rachel, still not caring to look at him.

'I'm not hungry.' Charlie turned to go.

Her eyes came up then to spear his retreating back. 'Oh! So I've wasted my time and food, have I?'

He didn't look back. 'Father Guillaume is dead.'

Rachel's mouth stopped working on her vegetables and

she stared at the spot where he had been. The stairs creaked as his foot took the tread. She turned to look at her children, who stared back concernedly, then abruptly reapplied her cutlery to her meal.

Rowena studied her mother for a moment, then asked, 'Please may I leave the table?'

'You haven't finished yet,' said Rachel quietly. 'And I think the boy would prefer to be alone for the time being. You can go up later.'

The meal was resumed, though more subdued than it had been before Charlie's announcement. Later the girls crept up to his room and tapped on the door.

'Oh, leave him,' said Lyn after the taps went unheeded. 'Let's go out and play.'

'You let go if you want to,' returned her elder sister with soft annoyance, and tapped again. 'Charlie, may we come in?'

Charlie lay on his side, staring at the wall. His grief was compounded by feelings of guilt. He felt deeply ashamed that his last act towards the man who had brought him up had been one of callousness: transferring his love to one who hardly knew him and didn't even care.

Lyn gave a snort. 'Well I'm off out! Who's coming?'

Only Rowena and Becky refused, exchanging looks of disapproval as their sisters scampered off to get their coats. Becky tested the efficacy of her own knuckles. 'Please, Charlie, open the door. There's only me and Wena now.'

There was another period of silence, then a muffled voice said, 'It's not locked.'

They went in to sit on the bed, one on either side of him. 'We're very sorry about your friend, Charlie.' When he gave no acknowledgement Rowena asked, 'Was he killed by the Germans?'

'They put him in prison. He died there.'

'What did they put him in prison for?'

He moved his shoulders apathetically. 'Because he was helping people, I imagine.'

'I hate the Germans,' said Becky with vehemence.

I hate myself, thought Charlie.

'Mother's just said she'll take us for a trip on The River King this afternoon,' said Rowena, trying to cheer him. 'As a sort of early birthday treat for you.' Charlie would be fifteen this week. 'It leaves at two-thirty – are you coming with us?' Charlie said he wasn't in the mood.

'It might take your mind off things,' advised Becky.

He didn't respond. The girls looked at each other over his recumbent form. 'Well, we'll come up a bit later,' Rowena told him. Charlie had helped her in so many ways and now that he needed her she didn't know what to say. Quietly she left, Becky too.

Charlie cried again.

A while had passed since the girls had been to visit. Charlie, head throbbing from shedding so many tears, lay as they had left him. The weight of his grief turned his body to lead. His mind hovered between conscious and semi-conscious, brimming with self-hate. His lethargy was just driving him to the brink of sleep when the door opened. Involuntarily he brought his head up. Rachel looked into the desolate eyes before the head fell back on its pillow.

'I came to see if you're going on this trip with us. If you are we'd better go now or we'll miss the boat.'

'I'll only spoil it for you.'

She hesitated, then told him, 'The girls understand you've suffered a loss, they won't pester you.'

'I meant my presence will spoil it for *you*,' he rejoined hostilely.

Taken aback, she was lost for any reply for a second. Then she said quietly, 'I'm sorry about your priest.'

'Well you won't have to put up with me for much longer because Father Duncan's going to get me into the college – if that was your concern over Father Guillaume's death!'

'That *wasn't* my concern at all!' She was offended and took five crisp steps up to his bed. 'I came to offer my condolences.'

Charlie couldn't bring himself to believe that this was genuine. All she cared about was that she wasn't going to be rid of him. She didn't care about Father Guillaume's pain, she didn't understand how much Charlie had cared for him. How badly he wished his mother was there, to put her arms round him, rest his head on her softness. How long it had been since someone had hugged him, really hugged him. The thought of his mother brought fresh sobs to rack his body.

Rachel clasped her hands in front of her, grinding their palms together like millstones. Of course he wouldn't believe her – why should he? She had shown him nothing but disdain and petty cruelty. Yet she did feel sorry and she wanted to show it by putting her arms around him, comforting him, not just for his loss but for the way she had blamed him for her husband's crime.

But he wouldn't want the ministrations of this skinny stick of a woman.

'I know how upset you must be,' she said with dignity. 'And if you want to stay at home this afternoon then I won't press you . . . but I would like you to come if you feel able.' With this she performed a silent exit and went along the landing to her dead son's room, where she wept profusely.

The snow had gone. Once again there was deep and stinking mud. This part of the trench was only twenty-five yards from the German lines and some men from his platoon were enjoying a jocular exchange with the enemy. A coalscuttle helmet was hoisted on a bayonet, and immediately converted to a colander by the British. 'Here's one for Mr Lloyd George!' The Teutonic accent was closely followed by the whistle of a shell which exploded far off target, bringing a derisive retort from the British. Russ put away his photograph and thrust himself from his hunkers to wander aimlessly along the bays and bends of the firing line and into a communication trench.

From his dugout, Jack Daw watched his old friend's erratic passage. He looked like a tramp with his lousy beard and long hair, coat stained with mud. For a long time Daw had known that Russ was on the verge of a mental breakdown, but could do little to help him. The medical officer here refused to recognize any ailment other than amputation or death. If Daw were to send the sergeant how would the doctor react? 'Nerves? Nerves, Sergeant? We've all got bloody nerves! I've got nerves. Men know when they've touched on mine, I give 'em a kick up the arse for coming to see me with imaginary bloody ailments like nerves! Get back on that line and test Jerry's nerves instead of my patience!'

Daw himself felt completely exhausted. His company had been up here for six weeks without rest. All they and the Germans were doing was throwing shells at each other and sniping the occasional unwary target. He, who revelled in hand to hand fighting, was sick as hell. Russ stumbled on, muttering instructions to those whom he passed. His head came up at the Captain's shout and he sloshed his way back to where Daw was standing.

'I've just received word that all men under the age of nineteen are to be withdrawn from the line. Seems the public've been giving the War Office some stick over it.'

'That'll mean half our battalion.' Russ looked around at the young faces.

Daw nodded grimly. 'I don't know how they expect us to win this bloody war if they take half our fighting force. Anyway, they're to go to Eat-Apples for instructional duties.' He gave a wry laugh. 'An' the public'll think they've done the poor sods a favour!'

Russ left the Captain to inform those to whom the rule applied. As bad as this place was, he was glad that Jewitt wasn't among those going to Étaples. Jewitt, for whose life he had made himself responsible; Jewitt, whose deliverance from this catacomb had become an obsession with the sergeant. Thoughts of the lad produced another: he hadn't seen Jewitt for fifteen minutes, and he always liked to be sure of the private's whereabouts.

'Jewitt! Anybody here seen Jewitt?'

Someone sang, to the tune of *Has Anybody Here Seen Kelly*, 'Has anybody here seen Jewitt? S-k-i-v-er!'

Russ narrowed his eyes, his mind settling on a spot some distance away at the far end of the trench. As his right foot struck out in pursuance, a Minenwerfer was launched from

481

the enemy's line. He heard the pop and, as he walked, performed the customary upwards glance to gauge its landing place. Its wobbling arc stopped him in his tracks for a split second – it was going to come down on the latrine! The shell began to descend. Russ came out of his paralysis, screamed Jewitt's name and drove himself forward. Men called out a warning, but he ignored them, pushing his way through the knot of soldiers who were running in the opposite direction. 'Jewitt, get out o' there!'

Everyone in the vicinity threw themselves sideways as the shell made contact, one of them catching the sergeant and embedding his full length in the slime as the world erupted.

Russ was up before the smoke cleared, taking five staggering paces before he saw the futility in proceeding – the entire latrine area was completely blown away. His body drooped in chronic despair. His jaw sagged . . . when out from the cover trench came a soldier painted from head to toe in the contents of the latrine that had been flung for yards. Lonsborough started to roar with laughter. 'Good job you're wearin' khaki, Jujube!'

'Well you're the bloody same – look at you!' yelled Jewitt as the rest of his pals broke into loud laughter, and tried to wipe his face with his sleeve, only succeeding in making matters more comical.

The sergeant was laughing too. Daw heard the sound as he came out of his dugout to supervise a roll-call. He had almost reached the group of laughing men when the one who laughed the loudest of all began to run back towards the firing trench. There, he was over the top in four quick movements and before anyone could stop him had launched himself, still laughing, across No Man's Land towards the enemy's line.

Jack let out an expletive. Striding up to the nearest man he grabbed his rifle. In a trice he was on the firestep and levelling his weapon in the direction of the crazed figure. There was sharp objection from Jewitt as the Captain took aim. There were also jeers and catcalls from the German trench as the laughing madman danced towards them. Soon there would be the sound of their rifles . . .

Daw squeezed the trigger. Jewitt's hand flew to his mouth. There was a crack and the figure disappeared. Giving him no time to get up, Daw was over the top himself and closing the gap between them at a crouching run. Jerry still cheered, his bullets whizzing past Daw's ears, as did those of his own covering fire. When the Captain reached Hazelwood he was lying face upwards, eyes open and unblinking. For one dreadful moment Jack thought the accuracy of his firing was open to question. He threw himself flat and put a hand to Russ' temple whilst running his eyes over the rest of his body for wounds. There it was, exactly as he had intended it, in Hazelwood's thigh. Private Jewitt came splashing up and hurled himself beside the pair. Whilst their comrades provided rapid covering fire the two of them dragged the wounded man through the morass to safety, rolling him over the parapet, whence he toppled into the trench with an agonized groan.

Jack knelt by him, calling for stretcher bearers and helping to cover Russ with a blanket. 'You'll be all right now, Filbert,' he whispered close to his friend's ear. 'I've dealt you a nice little Blighty. It might make you limp . . . but then Rachel will appreciate that.'

Jewitt was astounded at the show of tenderness from this hard man. Only on reappraisal did he understand that he had misconstrued the Captain's action – he had thought Daw had intended to kill Sergeant Hazelwood but had missed.

Daw glanced at Jewitt as a moaning Russ was carted away. The tenderness was gone. 'Looks as though we're going to need a new latrine trench, Private. See to it!'

Charlie was recovering quite well from his own emotional wound. How strange that it had been Mrs Hazelwood who had helped it to heal, rather than the girls; she who did not even like him. Life was very odd. She had actually smiled at him when, red-eyed, he had caught them just as they were leaving for their outing and told them he had changed his mind. It was that smile and the matter-of-fact acceptance of the girls that had set about this change. He suddenly felt

483

. . . ordinary. Not special because he was black or a bastard or a bloody nuisance, but ordinary, an ordinary member of an ordinary family. It was a good feeling. Now, when Rachel dispraised him, it was not in a vindictive manner, but just the way she was with her daughters. It could even be sort of pleasant, making him feel he mattered. There were, of course, times when the guilt of his behaviour towards Father Guillaume would bring private tears. But that was not today. Today he felt quite cheerful as he unloaded his purchases on the kitchen table. She would be pleased when she came home and saw the lovely piece of meat he had bought – and for not much more than he would have paid for a scraggy bit of offal at the butcher's.

He had been waiting at the back of the queue when a soldier had stopped to chat to the woman in front. What Charlie had overheard had made him and half a dozen others follow the soldier into a back lane. Here, the soldier handed out parcels of meat while his companion collected the money, telling the buyers that they would be here next week, but, 'Don't go shouting it about the streets,' one of them whispered to Charlie. 'We don't want too many coming. It'll put the butcher out of business.' Charlie had sworn to keep it secret and had hidden the parcel under his jacket until he got home.

He was the first to arrive back. Earlier in the year he had seemed to spend hours waiting in queues and would often get to the last shop on his list to find there was nothing left. But lately he had devised a Saturday roster, whereby each child who was old enough to be given the responsibility would take a different queue and so manage to get all the family's requirements with the minimum of waiting. One by one the girls returned with their purchases, the younger ones travelling with Rowena.

'It's no good, I'll have to have a baby,' puffed a red-faced Beany, slamming her parcel of fruit onto the table. Charlie smiled at Rowena and asked why. 'Because then I could go to the front of the queue!' She flopped down, a wet cloth draped over her face. 'It's not fair! Three ladies pushed right to the front without having to wait at all – and I'm certain that one of them wasn't having a baby, least she didn't look like it to me.'

The doorknocker sounded and Lyn groaned from her spreadeagled position on the mat. 'Oh, bug . . .'

'That's your resolution broken!' Charlie stabbed at her with a finger. 'You owe me threepence.' He had bet her this amount that she couldn't stick to the New Year's proposal. So far she had managed to keep her mouth sweet.

'I wasn't going to say it! If you'd let me finish I was going to say oh, Bugthorpe!'

'You're a lying little toad.' Charlie went to answer the door himself.

This could be the arrival of the letter he had been waiting for. Father Duncan had finally made arrangements for him to go to college. Charlie would have a lot of catching up to do on his studies, even though he had done an immense amount of reading over the past three years. He was looking forward to going in some ways, though now that Mrs Hazelwood was being decent to him it wasn't so pressing that he should leave. He opened the door, parted his lips with surprise and took the telegram from the man with the patch over his eye. He was about to close the door, then saw that the man was waiting and said, 'Thank you,' again.

The man curled his lip and hobbled away, empty-handed. Charlie took the telegram in to show to the others. Rowena was afraid; one only received a telegram when it was bad news.

'Well we won't know until your mother comes home.' Charlie felt a niggle of annoyance at the telegram for overshadowing his clever purchase of the joint. Yet there was anxiety too: what if something had happened to his father? He laid the envelope on the table for all to stare at.

Rachel stared at it too. She had begun unloading a basketful of stockings – the children always got new stockings at Easter – when Charlie said, 'This came,' and held it out to her, making her blood coagulate. Everything around her spelt cosiness – the table set neatly for tea, a singing kettle, a tableful of well-behaved and rosy-cheeked girls . . . why then, did her skin crawl?

Ever so slowly she took it from him – then thrust it straight back. 'You read it!'

He looked at her and she jerked her head impatiently. Trying to imagine what he might find, Charlie unfolded the telegram, was silent for a spell, then said gravely, 'Father's been wounded, they're sending him home.'

There were cries of mixed emotion from the girls. Rachel allowed the trapped breath to slip out. Charlie could not tell if it meant relief or disgust. She took the telegram to read it for herself, then went to file it on the mantel.

Rowena waited for more information, but her mother had started to brew the tea. 'Is he badly hurt, Mother?'

'It doesn't say – Charlie, did you get that special priced margarine?' Charlie told her that Robina had acquired it. 'Good.' Then she sniffed. 'What's that smell?'

He remembered the meat in the oven and told her about it. 'I didn't know what time to put it in, I hope it's done.'

Rachel opened the oven door. There was disbelief on her face . . . but not the kind he had hoped to produce with his special bargain. She tutted loudly. 'This is what the Army get while we at home have to make do with stuff I wouldn't normally feed to a dog!'

His face fell. 'I'm sorry . . . I won't get any more next week.'

'You will!' She rounded from the oven, carrying the roast and looked for a dish to put it on.

'But I thought you were angry at me.' He could never fathom her constant change of mood.

'Not at you, you've done very well, it's beautifully cooked. It's the Army that sickens me. It's bad enough knowing they're getting all the good food, but when you think there are soldiers lining their own pockets from the food that was meant for those who are fighting . . .'

He said carefully, 'So you want me to get some more next week?'

'Yes, but don't get caught – Regina, do sit still or you're going to spill your drink!' The child had begun to rock and chant with the others, 'Father's coming home! Father's coming home!'

Becky laughed and covered the small hand. 'You don't even remember him!'

'Do be quiet, all of you,' scolded Rachel. 'You'll get indigestion. Rowena, bring me the carving knife, if you can remember what it looks like; it's been so long since we've needed it.'

'When's he coming, Mother?' enquired Beany as the meat was dished out.

'Soon – now could we leave the questions until after our meal? I've had some devilishly awkward customers today and I can't do to listen to you mithering as well.' They chorused apology and got on with their meal which all agreed was splendid, despite the absence of potatoes which were in short supply.

But for Rachel, the succulence of the meat was tainted by her nauseous state of mind. She kept asking herself the same questions that the children wanted to know: how badly was he wounded? What was the nature of the wound? when was he coming? And one more what would he expect of her?

Some of these questions were answered when a letter arrived from Jack Daw a few days later. In actual fact it came by way of the man's wife. Jack had deliberately enclosed the letter with one to Ella saying, 'Get yourself round there, stop being bloody stupid and sort things out between the two of you. There's enough idiocy out here without having to put up with it when I get home.' So before she had gone to work, Ella had brought the letter round, tapping on the back door and waiting to be admitted. Since the New Year's Eve incident she had taken to saying hello again to Rachel if she should meet her, but until now had not ventured across her threshold.

Despite this fact, Rachel hadn't seemed surprised to see her, had taken the letter from her, invited her to sit down and 'Would you like a cup of tea?' as though nothing nasty had ever passed between them. Ella refused the tea, but sat down to watch her read the letter. Three years of war and bereavement had certainly transformed Rachel. Certainly not for the better as far as looks were concerned . . . yet

487

there was some quality that had not been there before; a kind of dignity.

'Shell-shock,' muttered Rachel, folding the letter.

Ella nodded. 'I don't suppose our Jack would mention it to you, but I will: you nearly didn't get Russ back. He'd lost his reasoning, went running off towards the German guns. Jack put a bullet in his leg – just enough to bring him down and send him home.'

'If you're expecting me to thank your husband . . .'

Ella slapped the arms of the chair and rose before she became involved in an argument. 'Aye well! I've done what I came to do . . .'

Rachel's expression folded into one of regret. 'Wait . . . I didn't mean it how it sounded.' She searched for words. 'I'm sure Jack's motives were well meant . . . it's just that I'm not sure I want him back, Ella. I was just beginning to get used to coping alone. I don't know that I want his interference or even his presence.'

There was a strained pause, then Ella said, 'I think from what Jack says that you'll still be copin' alone. Have you ever seen anybody with shell-shock, Rachel?' The other shook her head; it was just a newfangled term that had appeared in the language of late. 'Well, Russ may not be that bad physically . . . but I shouldn't expect him to be his old cheerful self.'

'Huh! That's the last thing I want, his old cheerful self.' Her voice softened then. 'Anyway . . . none of us is our old cheerful self.'

Ella agreed, and said presently, 'You've not had a very good war, have you, Rache?'

Rachel thought what an odd observation this was, but merely shook her head.

'I really was sorry about Bertie, you know . . . are you over it now?'

The old Rachel would have flared at this stupid query – as if one ever got over the death of a son. But this Rachel said, 'It's hard, but I get by.' Then she made the consideration of asking after Ella's husband.

'Oh, he's managing to stay upright,' replied Ella. 'I do

worry about him though . . . Look at all these poor lads bobbling around on one leg.' She shivered, then put her fears to one side. 'Anyway, he says you and me are to make things right between us, so what d'you say?'

'I say that's a sensible idea,' replied the other evenly.

That was another thing about her, thought Ella, there isn't that aimless chatter that there used to be. 'Aye, so do I! So if there's anything you need, anything doing, just give me a shout.'

'You'll be busy enough with your own job,' said Rachel.

Ella divulged that she wasn't at the munitions now. 'It was giving me too many headaches so I thought I'd get a job with a bit more fresh air. There was hell on when I said I was leaving. The overlooker said, "You can't go without a leaving certificate." I sez, "I'm bloody well off and you know what you can do with your leaving certificate." I'm working on the land now – out at Bishopthorpe. Anyway, I'm never too busy to help a neighbour, so think on what I said.'

Rachel opened her mouth to say that was very magnanimous of Ella, considering the waspish comments that had been thrown at her, but Ella cut her off. 'Ah-ah! Say nowt, just shout.' So saying, she rose and left.

After she had gone, Rachel sat there for a long time thinking about what this would mean. She was still thinking about it when Charlie and Regina came in from their walk – the rest were at school. She started and so did Charlie, he had expected the house to be empty.

'Goodness, is it that time?' She ran to collect her coat and hat. 'I'd better get down to the shop. Custom is bad enough without having complaints about late-opening hours.'

But the sudden sight of him had answered one of her questions. When she returned in the evening she would make her decision known.

The younger ones had bounced off outside to play, leaving Charlie and Rowena in charge of the washing up. Rachel sat on a dining chair and eyed their activities at the sink, rehearsing in her mind what she was going to say. She had been rehearsing it all day but it didn't make it any easier. She would just be about to broach the subject, when one of them would say something to the other and the words would slide back down her throat. Go on, she primed herself, say it now.

'Your father may have to remain in bed for a time when he comes home.'

Rowena turned from the sink. 'We supposed he might. Charlie and me . . . Charlie and *I* were talking about it last night . . . where will he be sleeping, Mother?' Before the latter part of the sentence was uttered she had reverted her eyes to the sink.

Rachel caught the implication. 'If you're saying he should go in Robert's room . . .'

Rowena spun back quickly. 'No, no . . . but don't you think it might be rather uncomfortable in the attic? For somebody who's wounded, I mean. You see,' once again she concealed her eyes, 'Charlie thinks it'd be better if he were to go back to the attic and Father were to have the nursery.'

'And Regina?' asked Rachel, icily patient.

'Me and Becky could fit her in our bed so she wouldn't disturb Father.'

'You appear to have everything nicely organized,' sniped her mother.

'Don't blame Rowena, Mrs Hazelwood,' said Charlie, on seeing the girl flush. 'It was my idea entirely. I just thought it might be helpful, save you having to run up and down an extra flight of stairs to see to Father.' He still used the last word sparingly, though she did not seem to mind so much now . . . at least she hadn't until the news had come of her errant spouse's homecoming.

'And what makes you think that I'll be the one running up and down after him?' Her query unanswered, Rachel launched straight into her proposal. 'I'll put it plainly: there's no way I can run the shop and look after an invalid – because that's what your father's going to be, for a while anyway. It's his leg. I had a letter from Mr Daw this morning. It's not serious,' she added hastily at Rowena's

490

open-mouthed concern, 'but he will probably have to stay in bed. Apparently he's in hospital at the moment but they have to make room for the more seriously wounded, that's why he's coming home. So . . . I'm afraid you're going to have to add nursing to your endless capabilities.' She was looking at Charlie. 'At least until we hear from the college.'

For the moment he was speechless, blinking from Rachel to her daughter. Then he said, 'If you like, I could look after the shop so you . . .'

Rachel held up her palm to stay his suggestion. 'I may as well be frank. I don't feel that I could nurse a man who's hurt and humilated me as much as your father has.'

Rowena hid her face. The sink became blurred. Charlie, too, felt a pang of dismay. It was going to start all over again – just when he had won her. But as he silently continued washing the crockery he began to see that here was the opportunity he had been wanting since he had arrived: the chance to earn his father's love. 'I'll do my best,' he told her.

CHAPTER THIRTY-ONE

There didn't seem to be much wrong with him, apart from the limp. Rachel pursed her lips in irritation as two men helped him from the ambulance and towards the house, all three laughing and joking.

'Hello, Rache!' he called as they eased him between the gateposts. 'Has Biddy got the kettle on?'

'Biddy isn't with us anymore; I've sacked her.' She stepped aside for them to enter. There was no one else there to greet him. The children were at school and Charlie, unaware that his father was coming in the morning – for Rachel's information had stated the afternoon – had taken Regina for a walk.

'Where shall we put him, missus?'

Rachel directed them to the former nursery and stood meekly by as they put him to bed. There had been some weeks between her receiving the telegram and him actually coming home. Weeks of uncertainty. How would she feel when he did come? What would she say when he mentioned Robert? She didn't really want to talk about her son to anyone – least of all him.

'There you are, chum.' One of his helpers tugged the blankets up to his waist. 'Get a nice cup o' tea down you, you'll be right as rain.' He looked expectantly at Rachel, but when no offer of tea was forthcoming he and the other man left.

Rachel stood and looked at him, playing with her fingers.

'I hope I'm not keeping you from anything,' tendered her husband, though in friendly vein.

'I was about to go and open the shop. I didn't know you'd be here this early.'

'Neither did I. They packed me off before breakfast.'

492

'Do you want . . . ?' Her fingers wavered towards the stairs.

'No . . . no, don't go to any trouble.' Russ waited for her to say, it's no trouble, but she didn't, forcing him to add, 'I wouldn't mind a cup of tea, though, if you can spare the time.'

She gave an abbreviated nod and went down to make it, carrying one cup back to his room and again standing to watch him while he sipped it. He asked, wasn't she having one? 'I'm afraid I'm going to have to leave you to your own company. I promised a customer I'd have some cream braid for her this morning. She's coming at eleven . . . I wasn't to know you were coming this morning.'

Unease fluttered within his breast, yet he said cheerfully, 'Oh, don't worry about me! I'll just lie here and enjoy the luxury . . . what time will you be back?'

'Dinnertime,' she replied on her way out. 'But Charlie will be here before then. I'll leave a note for him. He'll no doubt keep you company.' With nothing further to add she left. Not a word, she thought. Not a word about his son.

The door had no sooner closed than he started to sweat. He wanted to shout, please don't leave me alone! but the words merely screamed around his head while he struggled for breath. The hot tea slopped over the brim of the cup, marking the sheets. Palsied fingers rattled it back onto its saucer and transferred it to the bedside table. He wrapped his arms tightly about himself and shook, and shook . . .

'Take your coat up to your room like a good girl,' ordered Charlie when he and Regina returned. 'I'll just go and unload the shopping.' While he disappeared into the kitchen the little girl clambered up the stairs. It wasn't until she was passing her old room for the second time that she heard the creak. Without hesitation she reached up for the knob and opened the door – and saw a strange man in Charlie's bed.

Russ' attack of panic had subsided now. The face which stared back at the little girl was quite normal. 'Why, hello, Rhona!' He smiled and leaned forward, arms open. 'Aren't you coming to say hello to me?'

493

Something about the man frightened Regina and she let out a scream, 'Charlie! Charlie, there's a man!'

'No, don't . . .' Russ put out a hand in an attempt to quell the scream. It didn't work. He started to get out of bed. The child screamed even louder and backed away. 'Please, Rhona!' The screams reminded him of the time he had come home when Bertie was a baby; he had cried too. Russ covered his ears and swayed.

At the first noise, Charlie had bounded up the stairs and now stood in the doorway gaping at the man on the bed. 'Father . . . Squawk, it's all right, it's Father!' He bobbed down and put an arm round the child to show her it was safe, tried to lure her to the bed, but she shrieked all the louder.

'Take her out!' begged Russ, hands glued to the sides of his head. 'Get her away!' He fell back against the pillows as Charlie hurried the child from the room, curling up into a foetal ball and moaning like one deranged.

Regina had stopped screaming but her breath still came in little wet sobs. Charlie dried her eyes and picked her up to cuddle her. 'He won't hurt you, Squawk. He's your father. I thought you were looking forward to seeing him?'

'If he's Father why doesn't he know my name?' She sniffed into Charlie's shoulder.

'He does – and stop wiping your nose on my jacket.'

'He doesn't! He called me Rhona.'

'Did he? Well he has been away a long time. He won't realize how Rhona has grown – and you do look like how she used to look.'

'He's scarey, I don't like him!'

'Don't say that, you'll make him sad,' replied Charlie.

'Why isn't your face pink like ours, Charlie?' said the tear-stained child out of the blue.

'I was left too long in the oven,' came his pat response. 'Look, I've got to go in and see Father. You frightened him with your screaming.' She said she hadn't meant to. 'I know.' He touched her reassuringly. 'Now, d'you think you can stand quietly without doing anything naughty while I go in? Unless you want to come in too and see him?'

She refused this, but peeped inquisitively around the door as Charlie opened it. The man had his head under the pillows.

'Father?' Charlie placed a gentle hand on his shoulder. The trembling had almost stopped. Slowly, Russ' head emerged. 'I'm sorry Regina screamed,' supplied the boy. 'She didn't know who you were.'

'Regina?' A frown, then he remembered the baby he had left behind. 'I thought she was Rhona.' He pulled himself into a more comfortable position.

Charlie grinned. 'She said . . . Rhona's at school now.'

'I can see you're still here though.'

Charlie's smile levelled at the brittle tone. 'Father Guillaume died before he could make any arrangements.' He paused for Russ to insert his condolences, but none came. 'Father Duncan's arranged a place for me at college. I should be going shortly.'

'Good.'

That word hurt ten times more than any cruelty Rachel had inflicted on him. Charlie covered his feelings by picking up the cup and saucer. 'Would you like me to get you another cup of tea, Father?'

'No . . . but I would like you to stop calling me Father.'

Revolving slowly, Charlie went to the door, closing it after him and telling Regina to come down to the kitchen.

'Will he be staying?' asked the small girl as they went down.

'Of course he will, he's your father,' said Charlie, and hoped she wouldn't hear the catch in his voice.

Rachel came in at lunchtime, going straight to the sink to wash her hands. 'You saw the note, I presume?'

Charlie looked at her dumbly. He was still bruised from his father's words.

'I left a note on the table to say your father is home.'

Charlie ducked under the table, then gave voice to his discovery. 'The draught must've blown it off. We got a bit of a shock when we came in and found him. Regina screamed the place down.'

She threw up her eyes and tutted. 'I must say, there doesn't appear to be much the matter with him. I hope he didn't keep you talking all morning instead of doing what you're supposed to be doing?'

'He didn't want to talk to me.'

Rachel caught the hurt tone. 'Oh . . . so what's he been doing with himself, then?'

Charlie said he didn't know, making no mention of the man's strange behaviour with Regina. Before anything else could be discussed the rest of the girls came in and when told that their father was home pelted straight upstairs to greet him, Becky carrying the silver medal she had made to pin on his jacket.

However, they were to reappear in less than two minutes looking dejected. They said nothing at first, but when Rachel commented upon Robina's quivering lip, Lyn burst out, 'He told us to go because we were too noisy – and we were only welcoming him home, weren't we?' Her indignant face made consultation of the others.

Rachel bristled, but continued to dish out the lunch. As soon as it was served, though, she told the children to get on with it while she went up with a tray.

His smile, which had formed at her entry, evaporated as she placed the tray on his lap and said acidly, 'It's your business how you mistreat the boy, but if you think I've allowed you back into this house simply to upset my daughters, then you can think again! They've suffered enough at your hands. If you can't be civil to them you'd better go somewhere else.'

Russ stared at the icy face. 'I didn't mean to hurt them . . . they just made me feel suffocated.'

Her expression told him that she did not understand. She was about to turn away, when he said, 'Would you like to see my photograph?' Reaching for the tattered picture on the bedside table he held it out to her. 'These are the boys who fought with me.' She did not take it and he held it to his own face, smiling fondly. 'Good lads, they were.'

'Yes, well you're at home now so I expect no rough soldiers' behaviour.'

He didn't appear to hear her and began tapping the figures in the photograph. 'That's Dobson, that cheeky-looking one there. And that's Schofield, Wheatley, Jamieson . . .'

'Do you really think I'm interested in who they are? Just remember what I told you!' With this she flounced out.

Russ didn't hear her go, his eyes still on the photograph, whilst his lunch grew steadily cold.

The stench of the dead followed him home. He lay there in the dark, listening, listening . . . The pulse behind his ear began to thud. A voice said, 'Sarg . . . are you scared?' He pressed his hands over his ears, but the voice came again, 'Sarg . . . Sarg . . .' A globule of fear bubbled to his throat. He struggled to subdue it . . . and then his brain became a whirlpool of blood. The heat seeped over the top of his skull, down into his neck, into his shoulders . . . He fought it, but the terror rolled on, enveloped his belly, his bowels, his thighs.

He bucked his tormented body from the mattress and put his feet to the lino. Ignoring the pain in his leg he lifted his weight from the bed and reached for the walking stick that had travelled with him in the ambulance. He began to stump about aimlessly. His fevered brain told him to run – but where to? Seeking escape, he threw open the door of his room and stepped onto the landing. Left hand holding the stick, right hand on the balustrade, he made his painful way down. Dark, everywhere dark. He felt his way along the wall to the gaslamp and used the last match in his box to light it. With the coming of the soft yellow light his panic began to subside. It only ever lasted seconds, but to Russ it was a lifetime. Breathing heavily, he limped further into the kitchen and folded onto the sofa, staring for ages at the fireplace until he felt relatively calm.

Acid began to nibble at the lining of his stomach, a legacy of the terror. He hauled himself up and visited the breadbin, carving four thick slices. Finding no butter, he dug his knife into a lump of margarine, plastered it on. The meal was supplemented by a glass of milk. He returned to

497

the sofa to consume the results of his sortie. With the eventual easing of his torment he decided to go back to bed. Reluctant to move from lightness into dark, he sought the aid of a paraffin lamp. There were no tapers in the brass cup by the fireplace, but he found a box of matches on the mantel and struck one. The sulphur crumbled. Muttering a curse he tossed it on the hearth. The same happened with the next half dozen. It appeared the matches were damp. Throwing the box aside he looked round for a newspaper, found one and tore off a strip to use as a taper. The lamp was ignited. He took it to bed.

In the morning, Rachel was presented with the remains of his midnight feast. The state of the kitchen blocked her entry. There was a breadboard on the table covered in crumbs. Her eyes moved to the hearth which bore a plate and a glass coated in dried milk, and several spent matchsticks. She moved into the room, then turned quickly as Charlie came in behind her. 'Did you come down last night?' He shook his head and looked at the breadboard. Her expression was grim, she hurried over to the breadbin and lifted the lid. What had been a whole loaf yesterday was now reduced to a three inch wedge. She slammed the lid back down. 'The greedy . . . !' Charlie asked what was the matter. She wheeled on him. 'Your father has just deprived us of our daily bread and not content with that he's guzzled all the milk!' Furious though she was, she did not confront him at that moment, but buzzed around the kitchen conjuring up eight meagre breakfasts from somewhere, then set the children off for school.

Following routine, Charlie helped her with these tasks then took Regina out for the usual walk. Instead of going to open the shop, Rachel sat down and waited. By eight-fifty she thought that she might have to abandon her pose in order to go and open up but, when the following seconds brought the tap of his walking stick on the floor above, she set her mouth and waited for him.

Shock flickered across his features when he came through the doorway and saw her sitting there. Then he smiled lopsidedly. 'It didn't sound as if anyone was in. I thought you'd gone to work and . . .'

'And forgotten your breakfast,' she finished for him.

'No, no, I . . .'

'Well, I'm afraid there won't be any breakfast!' She rose and strutted up to him. 'Because some thief came in the night and stole two days' bread allowance.'

His face creased in guilt. 'Oh, hell . . . it was me. I'm sorry, I didn't give it a thought.'

'Oh no, you wouldn't, would you? You've been fed by the Army, you wouldn't have to worry about a little thing like shortages. That presumably is why you also drank the milk reserved for the children's breakfasts and ruined the best part of a box of matches. I suppose they're in plentiful supply over in France. I shouldn't think the "brave boys" have to pay tuppence for a box of matches!'

'I couldn't help it,' he stuttered. 'They were damp.'

'If you had enough brains to see that why didn't you leave them alone! They were on the mantelpiece to dry out. Anyway, I can't stand here listening to excuses, I have a business to run. As you deprived us of bread you'll have to make do with a cup of black tea until dinnertime – and please be kind enough to wash the pot and cup after you've used them! We don't have a servant any more.' She waltzed out.

Russ stood for a moment, then limped back to bed, picked up his photograph and stared at it.

It was still in his hands when Charlie came up to see if he needed anything. 'I'm not allowed to have anything,' murmured Russ. 'It seems I've eaten more than my share already.'

'I don't suppose you'd know being away for so long.' Charlie's tone was forgiving.

'That's what she said: I don't suppose you'd know, having been living it up in France.'

'Would you like me to make you a cup of tea?'

'I've had one. I wouldn't like to steal anybody else's.'

Charlie craned his neck to get a glimpse of the photograph in the man's hands. 'Can I see it?'

'If you like.' Russ didn't hand it over, but allowed the boy to take it.

Charlie ran his eyes over the group. 'Are these your men?'

'They were – they're dead.'

Slight shock. 'What, all of them?'

'Except the one that looks like a half-wit.' At least I don't think I am, thought Russ. Or am I? Who can tell the difference? The boy was asking their names. 'Next to me is Dobson,' said Russ, having no need to refer to the picture. 'On his right is Lance-Corporal Heath, the one on the end is Private Jamieson. Front row, left to right, Wheatley, Schofield, Corporal Popely . . .'

After the men had been named, Charlie handed the photograph back, 'When your leg's better will you be going back to the war?'

'I've been discharged, unfit for duty. When my leg's healed I'll be going back behind the counter.' If it had only been the leg he would doubtless have been going back, but as a quivering jelly of cowardice he was no more use to the Army – though his discharge was subject to reappraisal by the Army Medical Board.

'If the war goes on for another three years, I'll be old enough to go myself.'

'Still want to be a soldier, d'you?'

Charlie nodded. 'We've got to beat them, haven't we?'

'Why?'

Charlie's furry eyebrows met. 'For what they did to Bertie.'

Bertie. This was the first time he had heard the name spoken in this house. He had not dared mention it himself for fear that he would have to tell his wife the whole story. 'It wasn't the Germans who killed Bertie.'

Assuming the blame, Charlie dropped his gaze. A moment passed, then he offered, 'Do you want me to bring you anything, then?'

'If I want anything I can just as easily come and get it. I'm not a cripple.'

'Right . . . I'll go, then.' Charlie left quietly.

Russ picked up his photograph.

★

Uncanny, how letters addressed to one Hazelwood or the other had the habit of arriving at the most inopportune times. Russ had only been home forty-eight hours when the one for which his wife had been begging for three years finally arrived: Charlie was to go away to college.

'Of all the times he has to choose!' declared a chagrined Rachel to the boy after reading it. 'Who's going to be here to look after Regina? Not to mention him.'

'I won't go,' decided Charlie. 'It'd probably take me too long to catch up anyway.'

'I thought you wanted to go?'

'I do, but . . .'

'Then you'll have to go.' Her manner was decisive. 'I don't see why you should have to run about after him anyway. He was fit enough to come downstairs and pinch our bread, I'm sure he could manage to keep an eye on Regina and do a bit of tidying up while I earn our living. Yes, you must go.' She looked at the letter again. 'Go as soon as you like, it says. So!' She folded the letter back into its envelope. 'We'd better get you some new clothes – you can't go with your pants full of holes. You'll want a haircut too.' An involuntary hand went to the boy's head. 'Here!' Finding her purse, she handed him some money. 'You can go to the barber's this morning.' Charlie's was not the kind of hair one could cut round a pudding basin. 'Leave Regina with her father.'

The barber, having cut the boy's hair on several occasions, welcomed him with a smile. 'Morning, Charlie! Sit down while I go and fetch my scythe.'

Charlie made a rueful face into the mirror and plucked at a clump of hair. It had grown to resemble sphagnum moss. 'It is a big long, isn't it? But I have to wait till she gives me the money to get it cut.' He sat down.

'You want to try getting yourself a job.' The barber flung a cloth round Charlie's neck and tied it behind. The boy said he was going away to college tomorrow. 'Oh, that's why you have to look smart, eh? We'll have to make a special effort today, then.' The scissors and comb began to move over Charlie's head. He stared into the glass watching

501

the clumps collect on the bib. 'I hear your dad's home.' Arthur, the barber, knew all about Charlie. What gossip he hadn't picked up from other customers Charlie had volunteered himself. 'Got wounded didn't he?' Charlie's reflection nodded. ''Spect he's pleased to be out of it. Way things're going I could be getting called up meself.' Arthur was in his late fifties. 'Bet them lasses're glad he's safe aren't they?' Another slight nod from Charlie. 'What about you?'

'Mm?'

'Well, you must be pleased to see him home?'

'I don't suppose I'll be seeing much of him after today.' Charlie was asked where the college was situated. 'Up north somewhere. I can't remember the name of the place.' The barber asked if he was looking forward to it. Charlie did not answer directly, but gave a little laugh. 'I'm a bit nervous really.' There would be another load of strangers to conquer.

'All boys, is it?' Arthur received a yes. 'Shame.' He grinned into the mirror. 'What're you worried about then?'

Charlie held back, listening to the chatter of the scissors as they worked around his ear. 'I think I may have something wrong with me.'

'Nothing catching, I trust?' The scissors were moved to a different angle. At the lack of response Arthur glanced into the mirror. 'Well?'

'It's embarrassing.' Charlie's face burned.

'There's only me and thee here,' said Arthur, contorting his arm this way and that. 'And I shan't laugh at you. Not till you've gone, anyroad.' Charlie liked the barber, but it was difficult to begin. At his reticence Arthur guessed. 'Ah, one o' them sort o' problems, is it? Well, your father's home now, can't you talk to him?'

Charlie muttered a no. His father thought little enough of him as it was, if he should discover that Charlie was abnormal too . . . He had been worrying over it for quite a time. Living as he did in a houseful of women he had no one in whom he could confide, and he certainly couldn't tell Father Duncan.

'Away then, bend my lug, that's what I'm here for.'

Charlie looked at Arthur's reflection. 'Well . . . you're an expert on hair aren't you?'

'Only on heads and faces, lad. If you're expecting me to trim around John Thomas I'll have to charge double.' He grinned at Charlie's expression. 'How did I know? I have been a lad meself, Charlie. Stop worrying.'

Charlie's face brightened. 'It's normal then?' With the affirmative answer he was emboldened to mention about his pyjamas being damp on a morning. 'I'm sure I haven't peed myself . . . it's not that kind of wetness, anyway.'

'Happens to all of us, lad. There's nowt wrong with you.' Vastly relieved, Charlie asked the barber what it was. 'It's the stuff babies are made of – shows you're a man. But don't you go showing off now and planting it in any young lasses.' Seeing the renewed puzzlement, Arthur sighed, 'Ah dear! Well, it's like this son,' and proceeded to give Charlie a rough outline of the masculine role.

Charlie was so relieved and pleased to be told he was normal that he wanted to go straight out and tell someone, but the only people he saw were females and it wouldn't have been fitting to tell them. They wouldn't have understood anyway. When he reached home, the first person he encountered was another female; Regina was pushing her doll's pram up and down the pavement outside her house. She saw Charlie and came to meet him as far as she was allowed, which was three doors away from her own where she stopped and waited for him. 'The barbara's cut all your hair off.' She turned the pram clumsily and trotted home with him.

'Yes.' He walked with the striding gait of one who has discovered his masculinity.

'Looks nice. I'd like mine like that.' She turned the pram through the gateway.

'Girls don't wear their hair short like this. This style's for men. What's Father doing?'

'He's hiding under the bed. I frightened him.' It was announced with pride.

Dismayed, Charlie went straight upstairs, but found his father on top of the bed and looking relatively composed. 'Are you all right?'

Russ looked at him. 'Why shouldn't I be?'

'Regina's just told me she frightened you.'

Russ sneered. 'Me, frightened of a three year old! What d'you think I am, lad? I've been through a war. She just got on my nerves with her screeching, that's all. I sent her out to play.'

Charlie saw the fluff in his father's hair, recognized the lie, but said nothing further on the subject. He had much more important things to tell his father.

But before he could, Russ spoke again. 'Now you're back I might just have a stroll to the end of the street, give this damned leg some exercise.'

Charlie stepped back to give his father room. 'I'll come with you.'

'No, I'd prefer to go on my own.' Russ stood up gingerly. 'You stop here and look after the little un.'

'All right . . . I'll help you down the stairs, though.' Charlie tried to take hold of his father's arm.

'I don't need helping! For Christ's sake go find something else to do with yourself.' Russ hobbled past the boy and went downstairs.

He lingered in the front doorway for long seconds, then took the first positive step into the outside world. Still within his own boundary, he looked up the street to his left. Suddenly, it seemed very long, though there were only eleven houses in this part of it. He hesitated, weighing his surroundings and noticed for the first time that Rachel's rose bed had gone. In its place was a neat row of cabbages. It was this that gave the true realization of how she had changed – though not towards him; she still held him in the same contempt.

Steeling himself, he took another five steps and was on the pavement. Devoid of cover, he found himself checking every tree and every window where a sniper might be lurking, then set his sights on the end of the street and began to walk. He would stroll down this side and walk back on the other. Halfway to his target, he was accosted by a neighbour, an old man of seventy-eight, who emerged from his gate to shuffle alongside him.

504

'Home again, Russ?'

'Again? This is only the second time in three years.'

'Nay, is it? Doesn't seem like five minutes since I were last talking to you. When're you going back then?'

Silly stupid old fart, thought Russ, but managed congenially, 'Oh, they've finished with me, Mr Powell.'

'What?' The rheumy eyes looked him up and down. 'You must have had it cushy. There doesn't look much amiss. I'll bet you get a damned sight more pension than I do an' all.'

Russ clamped his lips over the retort and said, as they reached the corner. 'I'll see you. I'm only going this far,' and left the old man, crossing the road where he leaned against the iron railings for a time. Ignorant old bastard. He gritted his teeth against his anger and in time it receded.

Knavesmire was still dotted with white tents. He could hear the voices of the training officers ringing out as they assembled the new recruits. There was a mock battle going on. Russ could see groups of men lying on their bellies, waiting to go over the 'top'. A whistle blew. The men rose as one and began to advance on the 'enemy' over the green belt . . . and then Knavesmire became the Somme. The visions leapt at him. His fingers gripped the iron rails as he watched the carnage taking place. He could not let go – dare not let go. The queasiness overpowered him. Men were falling, being blown to bits . . .

Ella Daw turned into the street and saw him there. Faltering, she came across the road to stand at his elbow, only now seeing the terror on his face. All of Jack's letters could not have conveyed the reality more succinctly. Suddenly, she understood that which had hitherto remained between the lines.

Russ did not feel the hand on his arm. Only when she spoke did he flinch and look at her. 'Walking my way, soldier?' The voice was cheery. 'Here, you can carry my shoppin'.' Prising his grip from the fence, she hooked the handle of the bag over his fingers, then steered him firmly in the right direction. 'How's your leg?'

He took a deep breath and began to return to normality. 'Oh . . . it's healing nicely.'

'Must be odd coming back to this quiet after what you've been used to?' She received a nod in reply. 'Aye, I noticed when our Jack came home last time he couldn't seem to settle, cleaning his gun umpteen times . . .' She broke off. Maybe that had been the wrong thing to say. She glanced at Russ, wondering whether to raise the subject of Bertie, then decided not to. 'I think he'd like to hear from you if you get time to write.' They had reached her gate.

He gave a laugh. For a moment he appeared as his old self, but his eyes spoke differently. 'I think I might be able to find a few minutes.'

'Coming in for a cup of tea?' She took her bag from him.

Russ hesitated, looked at his own door, then said, 'Aye, why not?' and followed her inside.

That night, Charlie heard his father cry. He was lying awake worrying about how he was going to fit into the college and about the train journey, when the sound of his father's unhappiness percolated his own concern. He lay there for a spell, listening. The weeping persisted. Rising, he crept down the stairs to the landing. Here he hung back, uncertain, then opened the door of his father's room. Submerged in grief as he was, Russ did not hear him. The first sign of another's presence was when he felt his hand being taken in someone else's and squeezed gently. He looked up to see his comforter's identity, but on seeing who it was, said nothing and let his head fall back to the pillow.

Charlie said nothing either, just sat on the bed, gripping his father's hand until the crying was over.

Russ gave a shuddering sigh, slipped his hand from the boy's grasp and muttered thickly, 'I'm all right now. Go back to bed.'

The next morning Charlie, all togged up in his new suit, took his leave of them; Rachel first, as she was the person he met on rising. She surprised him by saying she would be accompanying him to the station. 'I might as well. It's not far out of my way, is it?'

'How will you go on about the books?' Charlie was still helping with the accounts.

'Oh, he can do them, make himself useful for a change. Here, put this in your bag. It's a long way up to Durham.'

He took the tin, prised the lid off and looked inside. There was a packet of sandwiches and an orange. His face lit up. Oranges had become a rare treat; the last one he had had was at Christmas. 'Ooh, that's very generous.'

'Yes, I thought so too. Think on, when you're eating that you'll be eating fourpence.' But Rachel said it with a smile.

He pushed the tin into his bag. 'Mrs Hazelwood . . . oh, it doesn't matter.'

She knew him well enough by now to know what this entrée meant. 'Oh, come on, out with it! What pearl of advice are you going to leave me?'

'Not advice . . . I just wondered if you heard Mr Hazelwood last night?'

'Heard him? Doing what?' Yes, she had heard him. It had shocked her.

But at this point Rowena entered and Charlie, not wanting to upset her, said, 'Oh, I think he was dreaming or something.' He greeted Rowena with a smile and began to help with breakfast. Shortly, the others came down and during the meal the conversation was all about Charlie's new school.

During the fifteen minute interval between breakfast and schooltime, Becky told Charlie how much she would miss him. 'Like mad,' she said, endorsing this with a hug and a kiss. Rowena, brushing her hair, waited until her sisters had gone up to say goodbye to her father, and her mother was out in the yard before issuing her own sentiments. Clasping the handle of the brush she turned from the mirror and gripped her bottom lip between her teeth. 'It'll be ever so funny not having you here, Charlie.' With a querulous smile she held out the brush. 'Will you brush my hair for me?'

After a moment's surprise he took the brush. Rowena stood with her back to him looking into the mirror, through which she could only see from her eyes upwards. Charlie began to stroke gently at her hair. At once her scalp prickled in ecstasy. 'Ooh, that's lovely,' she murmured. 'It makes me feel all tickly inside.' His eyes smiled at her through the glass. After a dozen more strokes, Rowena said quietly, 'Did you hear Father last night?'

Charlie ceased brushing for a second. The eyes in the mirror were anxious. His arm began to move again and he nodded with a tight smile.

'I wonder what's wrong with him . . . he's so strange since he came home.' She put a hand up to clasp the one holding the brush.

Charlie felt the fear and put his other arm around her. 'He'll get better, Wena.'

The sound of the others on the stairs broke their intimacy. After wishing him much luck, Rowena went off to school and a little later so did her sisters, leaving Charlie to make ready for his journey. With Rachel still in the yard hanging out the washing, he offered instructions to the youngest child who was gazing into a hand mirror. She had just discovered that her eyes were two different colours and was now winking them alternately – blue, brown, blue, brown. 'Now you must promise not to frighten your father while I'm away, Squawk. He'll be the one who's looking after you and you're not to upset him.'

'Will he play with me like you do?' she asked, distorting her face.

'I shouldn't think so, his leg's still poorly. You'll have to make your own games.'

'I don't like him,' sulked the child.

'That's naughty. You're only thinking of yourself. Father's been fighting in the war, he doesn't feel like playing games. If you promise to be good and not upset him then I'll play with you when I get home.' Regina asked when that would be. 'Not long – the summer holidays aren't far away.' He squatted and made a face into the mirror over her shoulder, luring the sulk away.

She nodded unenthusiatically and said she would be good. Charlie patted her, then went to give his parting regards to his father and to see if he was ready for the tray that Rachel had prepared.

'I just came to say goodbye.' Charlie put the tray on his father's lap.

'Goodbye?' Russ looked up at him quizzically.

'I'm going to college. I did tell you yesterday.'

'Oh aye.' Russ examined the contents of the tray.

'Regina's promised to be good.' His father looked at him, then looked away. 'Goodbye, then.'

'Goodbye.'

Charlie turned to the door.

Russ frowned at the retreating back and added sparingly, 'Good luck.'

CHAPTER THIRTY-TWO

The Victorian station echoed with the announcement of train times, the *psssh!* of steam and the rumble of wheels. People converged on the train, clutching their coats about them. Whatever the season, the cold always bounced up from the stone platform. Charlie, one of the last to board, paused at the carriage door, unsure how to take his final leave.

Rachel tugged his tie straight and gave him a push. 'Right, go on then, or the train will go without you.'

'Goodbye.' He accorded her a nervous smile, then stepped up into the carriage as the guard came down the platform slamming doors. There was a vacant seat on the near side. Barely had he taken it than the whistle sounded and the train gave a bump into motion. It jerked and jolted, then began to pull away more smoothly, taking him out of York. He did not look back. She had turned to walk away the instant he had embarked and he didn't want to look back at an empty platform.

Yet, as the engine sallied round the elegant curve of rail, he could not help a wistful rearwards glance.

Rachel lifted her hand, saw the look of surprise and pleasure that her simple act had produced. Then, sighing, she went to open the shop.

The journey was not quite as monotonous as Charlie had feared from its first stages. There was a family in his carriage and the children kept him entertained. After a while he began to peel the orange, not because he was hungry, merely for something to do with his hands. He had dissected it reverently when he noticed he had a captive audience. A skein was half-raised to his mouth, then, with a smile he handed it over to the little girl, treating her two brothers likewise. Appreciating his kindness, the adults chatted with him amicably, though most of their conversation centred on the war. On leaving the train, Charlie found a cab to take him to the college where, after introducing himself, he was put in the charge of a likeable boy named Adrian who showed him first to the dormitory and then around the rest of the college.

'You'll probably get a nickname,' the fair-haired Adrian told him as they strolled the grounds. 'No one's called by his real name here.' Charlie asked what Adrian's was. 'Blossom.' Adrian laughed. 'I'm interested in botany. What's your hobby?'

Charlie elevated his eyebrows. He hadn't had time for hobbies. 'I haven't really got one.' When Adrian asked what he had done in his spare time he answered, 'I played with my younger sisters.'

'Poor devil! Well, you'll get plenty of time for a hobby here. What do you fancy?' At Charlie's shrug he said, 'What lessons did you like best at your other school?'

'I haven't been to school for three years,' Charlie divulged.

Adrian stopped dead. 'Good grief!' But when Charlie explained the situation the boy was sympathetic. 'It must've been rotten for you. Will you ever go back to Africa?'

'I've nobody there,' said Charlie. 'Father Guillaume's dead. That's why I've been so long in getting here. He arranged for me to come but then . . . well, what with the war and things . . .'

'Oh well,' Adrian smiled. 'If you want help with cramming – which you certainly will – I'll be glad to oblige.'

'Thanks.' Charlie warmed to his new companion.

'And we'll have to find you a hobby,' added the other.

'My father collects birds' eggs,' said Charlie. 'But I wouldn't know one from another.'

'Oh, Peg does that, you could ask him for advice. He's called Peg because of his queer teeth, by the way.' Adrian looked to his right as another boy ran past shouting, 'Hello,

Blossom! Hello, Darkie!' and was gone. 'Oh, that's it then,' said Adrian as they looked back at the fleeing figure. 'Darkie Hazelwood.'

And this was how Charlie was introduced to his classmates later. They seemed a nice bunch, asked him all about himself and appeared to be genuinely interested in his answers. By nightfall he was relieved and happy to have settled in so quickly and a sneaky glance at the unclothed bodies as the boys changed for bed showed him that Arthur had been correct about him being normal. When all were attired in nightclothes there were cups of cocoa and further conversation. The atmosphere was not one of a school but of a large family. Charlie turned to Adrian. 'I'm going to like it here. I don't know why I was so nervous of coming.'

'You'll know when we have a maths lesson,' Adrian replied, making the others laugh. 'No, I'm only joking. Old Rattyarse is a bit of a stickler but his heart's in the right place.'

'In his wallet,' said Peg and laughingly explained to Charlie that the maths teacher gave an end of term prize of ten shillings to the person who made the most improvement or put in the best effort. 'You could have a chance of winning it, Darkie. You don't have to be brainy, just work hard.'

Charlie grinned his approval then turned back to Adrian. 'What're you going to be when you leave here, Ade?'

The wideness of Adrian's smile showed he thought this a funny question. 'Same as everyone else.' Seeing Charlie's bemusement he added, 'A priest of course'.

The cup was lowered from Charlie's lips, revealing a look of stupefaction.

'Didn't you know it's a junior seminary?' asked Adrian.

Charlie reared in alarm. 'I'm not going to be a bloody priest!'

Adrian regarded him with calm interest, as did the others. 'There's no law says you have to be. Honk over there is going into science, and Peg hasn't decided yet, have you?'

Charlie was definite. 'I'm going to join my father's regiment.'

512

'Then what did you come here for?' asked Adrian, mood altering. 'Soldiers don't need an education, they're totally stupid, going round killing one another.'

'My father isn't stupid!' Charlie jumped to his feet.

Adrian did not rise, but looked up grimly for a time at the angry figure. Then he brought himself to his feet, his face affable once more. 'I apologize.' His hand came out. Charlie glared at it a moment, then took it. 'It's just that my father was wounded and two of my brothers were killed in France,' explained Adrian.

'My brother was killed too,' said Charlie. 'And my father wounded. Sorry.'

'And you still want to be a soldier?' Adrian was amazed. 'If you could see what this stupid war's done to my parents . . . anyway, let's not argue over it, especially at bedtime.' He kneeled to perform a prayer.

Charlie followed suit, then climbed into bed. He had harboured this ambition to be like his father for so long. 'Actually,' he confessed as Adrian got into his own bed, 'I'm not that keen to become a soldier. I just want to make him proud of me.' It came as a whisper.

'Don't you think he'd rather have you alive?' asked Adrian.

'I'm not really sure.' Charlie rolled his head to look at his friend. Then the lights went out.

As he had expected after the educational laxity of the past three years, Charlie found his new regime tremendously exacting to begin with. While the others had the weekends to themselves, Charlie would be crouched over a text book or being given extra tuition from a sympathetic master. The only time this swotting was eased was at prayer. These oases of tranquillity were such a blessing – as was Adrian who coaxed and supported and listened. They had only known each other a short time but Adrian was the sort who formed instant friendships. He had the ability of making the person he was with at that moment feel as though they were his one and only friend.

Charlie turned his head now to look at the sleeping

occupant of the neighbouring bed and smiled. Only the blond hair was visible, sprouting like marron grass above the blanket. Everyone else was asleep except Charlie who always woke very early. He raised his head a fraction, eyes roaming the dormitory, then dropped it back to the pillow feeling an immense wave of happiness. How long he had yearned for male company, and here he was with an abundance of it. Stretching, he allowed his foot to slip over the edge of the mattress and swing in childlike content. When it began to cool he drew it back under the covers, then with impish glee he inserted it under Adrian's blankets and pressed it to the warm flesh.

There was a sharp inhalation, then a grumble of complaint. Adrian pulled his knees away from the cold intrusion and rolled onto his back to peer over the blankets. 'Darkie, you rotten old bugger. I was having a lovely dream.' Charlie grinned and asked if it included him. 'No, it didn't or it would've been a nightmare.' Adrian stretched and, reliving his dream, gave an ecstatic groan.

Charlie probed. 'I'll bet it was about a girl.'

'No it wasn't, then! If you must be so nosey I was down in Cornwall wallowing in the blue green sea until some lout woke me up.'

After a grinning pause, Charlie said, 'Ade?' His friend groaned and pulled the covers over his head. 'Do you ever dream of them?'

The bleary head emerged. 'What?'

'Girls.'

A hesitation, then Adrian's glazed eyes became thoughtful. 'Sometimes.'

'Do you think you'll miss being married?'

Adrian pulled himself up and punched his pillow. 'Why do you always leave it until the crack of dawn or the middle of the night to make these searching questions?'

This was answered with another question. 'When did you decide to become a priest?'

'When I was eight.' Adrian saw his friend's look of astonishment. 'Oh, I've had lots of second thoughts since then, but I'm as sure now as I'll ever be.' He rubbed the sleep from his hazel eyes.

'I never know what to make of God,' confessed Charlie. 'One minute everything's sailing along fine, then – bump – down you go!'

'That's not God, that's people.'

Charlie nodded. 'I suppose so. You never answered my question: will you miss being married?'

'Do you actually mean married,' asked Adrian, 'or do you mean will I miss not ever having "done it"?'

Charlie laughed at the sly look on his friend's face. 'Both.'

'I think,' said Adrian, arching his body to scratch his rear, 'that to me, serving God is more important than either of those things. It's the most important thing in my life.'

Charlie admired his friend's single-mindedness. 'I couldn't say what the most important thing is in mine.'

'I could,' said the other. 'It's your father.' Charlie was always talking about the man.

Charlie looked startled, then gave a woeful nod. 'It's stupid of me, isn't it? He's never shown me the least affection. If I'm to be rational Father Guillaume was much more of a father to me . . . and I deserted him. I feel really bad about that, wish I could make it up to him.'

'What d'you think Father Guillaume would have had you do with your life?'

'Be a priest, I supp . . .' Charlie gave a laugh. Adrian had a great knack of getting to the truth of the matter. 'Maybe I owe it to him.'

'Darkie, being a priest is a commitment to God. It shouldn't be viewed as an obligation to others. Is it partly because you'd miss not having a family that you're reluctant to join the priesthood?'

' 'Struth no . . . I've had enough of families. I don't know that I even want to get married. All I've ever seen of matrimony is unhappiness.'

'But you've not exactly been in a normal situation, have you? Do you think Mr and Mrs Hazelwood will ever be reconciled?'

'I can't see it,' came Charlie's pessimistic reply. 'Neither of them is making the least effort . . .'

The day that Charlie had gone, Rachel put it to her husband that it was time he got back into the running of the shop. 'I really don't see why I should slave away when you're here doing nothing.'

Russ looked uneasy. 'I'm not sure my leg would stand up to it yet.'

'You don't need legs to do bookwork. Good heavens it isn't much to ask.'

'Oh, I can do the books,' he supplied hurriedly. 'If you don't mind fetching them home.'

'Right, well here you are then!' Rachel presented him with a couple of ledgers and a thick wad of dockets. She saw his expression as he flicked through the pages, and flared. 'Oh, I'm so sorry the figures aren't as neat as you'd do them!'

He was swift to praise. 'Oh no, no! You've done a splendid job.'

'Yes well . . . Charlie helped me.' Crossing her arms, she came to look over his shoulder at the figures. 'When you went away, I didn't know how to do the ordering or anything, I just had the old invoices to go by. One or two people I couldn't find, there was a Mr . . . what's his name?' She reached over and rippled the pages. Russ caught a whiff of her scent. 'There! Mr Cranley. There was no address or anything for him, I had to buy off one of the other suppliers. I hope his nose won't have been put out of joint. If it is it's too bad.'

'No need to bother about him,' said Russ, with mordant smile. 'He was a damned nuisance anyway.'

He spent the evening balancing the books, as indeed he did every evening after this. His wife became more tolerant to his presence. Russ wished he could be more tolerant of himself. There wasn't a day went by without him thinking of the carnage. With every night returned the blood and pus of the trenches and the ones who had died.

There were reminders, too, from the live ones. This morning, Becky ran into the kitchen and pressed a letter into his hand. 'Ah, thank you, me love!' he responded with a smile as she dashed out again, then examined the envelope, making no move to open it.

Today was Empire Day. 'National Food Saving Day,' as Rachel pointed out acerbically while conserving the crumbs from the breadboard for some future use. 'What the devil do they imagine we've been having for the last three years, banquets?' The children would be taking the afternoon off school and many places of work were closed, but Rachel would have gone mad if she had had to stop in the house all day so was going to open the shop. It didn't matter that there would be little custom, only that she was out of his company. He was unchanged in spirit, though his flesh was healing well. She hoped it wouldn't be long before he could return to the shop and allow her to resume her millinery work. 'Aren't you going to open it?' She was not too busy to notice the way he fingered the letter.

'Aye . . . I suppose I'd better if somebody's taken the trouble to write it.'

She wondered whether that was a dig at her for burning all the letters he had sent, but hadn't time to dwell on it. Finishing the clearance of the table she took the pots on a tray to the scullery. The letter was opened.

Dear Sarg, just thought I'd pencil a few lines in between emptying the old biscuit tins – don't worry, I only used the paper once. Russ smiled and projected his voice towards the scullery. 'It's from Jewitt.' Hoping the boy's words might amuse her, he read it out loud. *'How is your leg? Healed up nicely, I hope. I know you will be sorry to hear that old Lonsborough bought it last week. He cut his finger on a bully tin and didn't report it, got lockjaw . . .'*

'Oh hell.' The tone of Russ' voice became grave.

'Not a very heroic end, was it? We have got a load of new chaps up here now and they are no good to anyone, always getting wind up. Still, things are going quite well and I hope to be on my way to Blighty tomorrow on a seven day leave – look out girls!'

Rachel came in to collect the tablecloth and sniffed. 'Typical soldier.'

Russ flared, dropping the letter to his knee. 'And just

517

what is a typical soldier? I'd be obliged if you could put me straight on that. I've seen kids who're barely out of the cradle fight like demons, I've seen big tough sergeant-majors cry like babies, I've seen weedy little men who are born killers – there's no such thing as a typical soldier!' After glaring at her, he picked up the letter again and, ironing his tone, read, '*I might just call and see you as well when I have unloaded my DCM on my mum . . .*'

'Oh, he's got a medal then?' Rachel gathered the four corners of the cloth and shook it in the yard.

'No, he means Decent Covering of Muck.' Russ continued with the letter. '*You will know about Captain Daw, what with you two being neighbours. We will miss his . . .*' Russ didn't consider 'spunk' a fitting word to read out to his wife so interchanged it with '. . . *courage, but can't say we'll miss his sarkiness. The new Captain is a bit of a greenhorn. He won't last long. Who knows, I might get his job. Well, Sarg, cheerio for now and if I don't see you on this leave I'll definitely call on you at the end of the war. Love and kisses, Piltdown.*'

Rachel had stopped folding the cloth to stare at him. 'Has something happened to Jack?'

Russ looked uncertain. 'It sounds as though . . . surely Ella would've told us?'

His wife shoved the tablecloth in a drawer. 'I'd better go round.' Russ said, wouldn't she be at work? 'I won't know if I don't go.' He asked if he should come. 'No, let me find out what's happened first.' She left by the back door.

Ella had taken Empire Day off. She beckoned Rachel into the scullery and answered the tentative question, 'Aye it's right – he's been wounded.'

'Oh dear.' Rachel touched her breast. 'Badly?'

Ella nodded and leaned on the sink. 'His leg's had to come off at the knee.'

Rachel inhaled sharply. 'Oh Ella, I am sorry! But why didn't you come round?'

'I had no idea you were a surgeon Rachel, or I might've done.' She flapped her hand. 'Oh, take no notice of me. I'm just that mad . . . I didn't tell you 'cause I reckoned you had enough troubles of your own. I suppose I should be grateful I'm getting threequarters of him back . . . but you just can't help feeling bitter, can you?'

'No.' Rachel's thoughts meandered to her son. Absent-mindedly, she picked up a dishcloth and began to wipe up the spills of tea from Ella's worktop.

Ella made no objection, but watched her. 'D'you know, I can't think of a family round here who hasn't lost somebody or had them maimed. And what is it all for? I'm blowed if I can say. I mean, has it brought us any more freedom, prosperity? Has it buggery.'

'I suppose getting the vote doesn't seem as important now,' ventured Rachel.

'My God, Rachel, it's more pressing than ever that we get it! Who's been running the country while our men have been getting blown to pieces – us women! Just let them reject the bill this year, there'll be hell on. No . . . we need that vote and we need women in Parliament so that this never happens again – I mean can you ever imagine a woman Prime Minister getting us into this lot?' At Rachel's negation, she sighed. 'Eh, I don't know what I'm going to do about looking after Jack, what with having to go out to work. He'll be in hospital a fair while o' course but he'll have to come home some time.'

'Well don't worry about that,' answered Rachel, suddenly noticing she had the cloth in her hand and putting it down. 'I can look in on him and cook his dinner.'

'Oh, that would be a help – do you mind?'

'I wouldn't have offered if I minded. I have to cook a dinner for that useless article of mine, one more won't make much difference.'

'Oh champion! Eh, I'll give you the money o' course and you can take what you like out of the garden.'

'I wouldn't dream of taking money. If we can't all help each other it's a bad thing. Though I will dib into your garden. I notice your cabbages are further on than mine.'

'Ah well, I have access to some nice cowpats where I work.' Ella smiled and asked, 'So, how is Russ coping now?'

'Well, if you can call doing a bit of bookwork coping,

519

then he's coping. D'you know Ella, he hardly shifts from that sofa. I've told him he should be back at the shop now his leg's mended but he says he isn't ready.'

'Well, I don't want to stick my nose in . . . but I've seen him trying to turn the corner at the end of the street. It's as if there's a string pulling him back. He just turns round and comes home. Don't force the lad.'

Instead of resenting this interference as she once might have done, Rachel took heed of it. 'I didn't know . . . when he says he's been for a walk I never bother to ask where. What d'you think's the matter with him?'

'I don't know what's in his head, love,' sighed Ella.

'Has he . . . has he ever said anything to you about Robert?'

'No, our conversations don't get that deep. Why, do you think that's what his problem is?'

'I wouldn't know. He's never once mentioned his son.' Rachel's face softened. 'But then, neither have I . . . I can't.'

'Would you like me to talk to him about it?'

'No.' Rachel turned to put a hand on the doorknob. 'I'm not really that concerned about what's troubling him.'

'Still as bad as ever, is it?'

Rachel postponed her exit to ruminate. 'Well . . . we just sort of tolerate each other.'

'How's Charlie doing at that college, then?'

'Oh, he seems to like it.' Rachel opened the door. 'We had a letter from him last week saying he's catching up – slowly of course, but the main thing is he's happy there.'

Ella considered this a strange remark from one who had previously contributed towards the boy's unhappiness. She stepped into the yard to watch Rachel go. 'Thanks for coming, Rache. I appreciate your offer of help.'

At lunchtime Rachel closed the shop. When she reached home she went straight upstairs. It was Robina's birthday soon and having purchased some material to make her a dress Rachel wanted to keep it a secret until the day. The best hiding place would be Robert's room. No one ever went in there. She reached his door and opened it. A figure spun guiltily from the mirror. Rachel gasped, thinking for a fleeting moment that it was Robert. Then, 'Rosalyn!' she shrieked. 'What *do* you think you're doing?'

Red-faced, Lyn took the cap from her head, allowing the trapped hair to tumble to her shoulders. Her legs were encased in long trousers – Robert's trousers.

Rachel flew at her, gave her a hearty slap on the arm and commanded her to take them off immediately. 'You have no right even to be in here! Let alone wearing Robert's clothes.'

Lyn tried not to cry, though the blow had hurt. 'I asked Father. He said it would be all right.'

'Well it's not all right!' Rachel pushed the child backwards onto the bed and tugged the trousers over her heels. 'This is Robert's room! These are Robert's clothes!'

Divested of the trousers, Lyn righted herself and pulled the pinafore over her head. 'Well, I only wanted to be important!' she hurled, before running away down the stairs and locking herself in the lavatory.

Rachel hugged the trousers to her chest and stared after her for a second, dwelling on the words. Then she marched down the stairs to the kitchen.

He was sitting on the sofa. Just sitting there, staring at that blessed photo. The room was a shambles and the girls were shrieking outside in the yard, and there he was just sitting there like a dummy. She flew at him, still clutching the trousers. 'What were you doing, telling Rosalyn she could wear these?'

His eyes came up slowly from the photograph. 'What?'

'You needn't think I'm going to drive myself into the ground while you idle here all day! I had enough of that while you were in France. Look! Look at the state of this room! Couldn't you even wash a few cups?'

'Rowena said she'd do it before . . .'

'And what's wrong with you might I ask? She's had more than her fair share to do, just as I have. You needn't think you're treating my house like the sergeants' mess. I'm sick of coming in and finding you just sat there staring at that blessed photo. That's all you ever seem to do, as though you and those soldiers of yours were the only ones to suffer in this war. There were others, you know! Your own son, for one. But could you care about that? No! You let his clothes be used as playthings.'

At the mention of his son he turned away. 'I didn't suppose Bertie would mind.'

'And how would you know? You didn't have to cope with his unhappiness when you were away in France!'

'You think I don't care what happened to our son?' he breathed incredulously, the photograph resting in his lap.

'And where were you when he needed you?' she flung at him. 'Playing at blasted soldiers in France!'

'And what d'you think I've been bloody doing there?' he yelled back at her. 'Gaily striking matches one after t'other? Making meself doorsteps with half a pound of butter on each slice? Do you? *Do you?*'

The madness in his eyes stopped her outburst. In a flash of discovery it came to her – *he had been killing people!* They stood facing each other, he half-crazed, she wholly terrified. Then she began to back away from him. He saw the fear and showed instant remorse. 'Rachel . . .' His hand came out to her.

But she rushed from the kitchen and up to her dead son's room where she shut herself in, breast heaving with fear and revelation.

Having heard the argument, the girls had quelled their noise and made themselves scarce. A short while later, Lyn crept back, first checking that her mother was not in the kitchen. Rowena was in the scullery, washing the cups. The door to the other room was closed. 'Don't go in,' her eldest sister warned her softly. 'Father's upset. He wants to be on his own.'

Lyn ignored this as was usual when anyone gave her an order. Closing the door behind her she went to stand by the sofa. After hovering a moment she said, 'I'm sorry to get you shouted at, Father.'

He pretended to be blowing his nose. 'I can't see why you

wanted to wear trousers anyway, a pretty little thing like you.'

She balked. 'I don't want to be pretty. I want to be a boy.'

Russ shoved his handkerchief away. 'Nay, that's daft.'

'No it isn't. Boys are more important.' Her hands twisted two portions of her hair into an even worse mess than it had been.

He tried to smile. 'Don't let your mother hear you say that.'

'She thinks so too.' Her father said he was sure she didn't. 'Then why is no one allowed to go in Bertie's room or touch his things?' she demanded with jutting lip. 'And why did he have a room all to himself while all of us have to share?'

'That was only because, well, it's not the done thing to have boys and girls sharing a room and Bertie had no other boy to share with.' When Lyn reminded him of Charlie he said, 'That's different – look, girls are just as important, you know. They grow up to be mothers. A funny old world it'd be if it were populated by boys, wouldn't it?' He took the gangly child on his knee. 'Eh, poor old Spindleshanks. It's my fault you got into bother. I didn't think.' He gave her a crushing hug. 'Never believe you're not important. You're important to me and I know you're important to your mother. She's just . . . well she's angry at me and she took it out on you. That happens sometimes. I'll bet you've done it yourself, haven't you?'

After a short gap, she nodded. 'I took it out on Charlie when Mother told him to take charge of us. It wasn't really his fault, was it?'

Russ did not answer, but gave her knee a final brisk rub and told her to go out to play. As she got off his knee she said, 'If I ask you something will you promise not to be mad?' He smiled and gave his guarantee. 'Well . . . the next time you look at your birds' eggs would you let me do it with you?'

'Oh . . . I don't think I'll have time to bother much with them now.' Apart from not having the slightest interest in them anymore, he couldn't bear to look at them. They reminded him too much of Bertie. Seeing her downcast face he said kindly, 'Now you're twelve I reckon you're quite capable of handling them, don't you?'

Her face lit up. 'Aw, can I look at 'em now?' At his smile of consent she pelted off to the attic. Russ stared after her for a moment, then wandered up the stairs.

His wife was still in their dead son's room. When he opened the door she recoiled from him, apprehension on her face.

'I just came to apologize,' he murmured. 'It was thoughtless of me.' With that he closed the door.

Rachel gazed at the wood, then turned her eyes back to her son's possessions. By leaving his room as it was, turning it into a shrine, she was only prolonging the torment. Robert wasn't coming back – a lot of boys wouldn't be coming back . . . a lot of fathers too. There would be orphans needing clothes.

Smoothing her skirts with her palms, she got up off the bed and after the briefest indecision began to take his clothes out of the tallboy. Jumpers, vests, shirts, trousers, all were transferred lovingly to the bed in neat piles alongside the unopened birthday presents. Socks, scarves . . . occasionally she would pause to rub some garment over her cheek or to slip her hand into a glove, flex the fingers, trying to feel that she was holding Robert's hand . . . but one after the other his belongings joined the pile.

The drawers were empty. She looked round. There were pennants on the wall. Her fingers unpinned them, then moved on to the pieces of military bric-a-brac scattered about the place. So much did she blame the Army for his death that she could scarcely bring herself to touch the badges and relics. Every item with which she made contact increased her anger and sense of loss. She picked up the school satchel and flung the wretched things into it then covered them with the flap and squeezed the whole lot with such savagery that the buckles punctured her hands. Then she looked at the pile of clothes on the bed . . . and put every single item back into the drawers. The only thing to leave Robert's room with her was the satchel containing the military junk, which she cast into the dustbin.

CHAPTER THIRTY-THREE

It turned out that Jewitt did not call to see him. However, Russ' concern that the lad had 'bought it' before his leave had come, was assuaged with the coming of another letter from the private apologizing for not having had the time to visit. Although worried over Jewitt's welfare, Russ was somewhat relieved that the private hadn't come. His presence and conversation would only restir nightmares.

His other recurring nightmare came home in the summer. Charlie arrived to a house almost as unsettled as the one he had left. No one was at the station to meet him, but then he had not expected this. After spending half an hour trying to get a cab he gave up and deposited his case at the left-luggage hall, then walked home.

They had just eaten lunch when he got there. All looked up from the table as a brown face peered round the door. 'Charlie!' Rebecca flung herself at him to be greeted in avuncular fashion. He seemed to have matured even more since being at college.

'Blimey, aren't you tall!' observed Lyn and received a similar remark in exchange.

Rachel was looking down at the trousers which had become too short. 'Tut! I should've bought the bigger size – never mind, I'll try and lengthen them before you go back. Sit down, Charlie. Rowena, fetch his plate from the pantry. It's a salad,' she informed the youth.

He thanked her and, disentangling himself from the girls, he sat at the table. 'Hello, F . . .' He clamped his lips over the rest of the word and fingered the cutlery, abashed. Russ nodded, then left the table to sit on the sofa behind Charlie. The latter picked up a knife and fork as Rowena put the salad before him. She had altered greatly too –

almost a woman. 'Most of that's from Mrs Daw's garden,' she told him. 'Except the dandelion leaves; we picked those.'

'Do you like tomamotatoes?' asked Regina. Charlie laughed and said he did. 'So do I.' She looked at his plate so enviously that he was forced to spear a piece of tomato and pop it in her mouth.

'No more!' Rachel warned her, and to Charlie. 'You eat that up.'

Rhona was whining, 'Mother-r, mother-r.'

'Shut up,' said Beany.

'Mother-r, tell Beany to stop saying shut up. Mother-r . . .'

Rachel had been concentrating on Charlie's manly appearance. As another, 'Mother-r!' irritated her ears she snapped, 'Oh, Mona, do shut up!'

Lyn covered her mouth and sniggered. Rachel looked at her in annoyance – then realized she was guilty of using the adulterated name and was forced to splutter a laugh. Everyone else laughed too, except Russ who had been too busy thinking to hear the joke. Even after their hot exchange he still found it impossible to speak about Bertie to his wife – but that didn't mean he wasn't thinking about him. Sometimes he looked at Rachel, trying to guess if she were thinking of their son too, but didn't dare to ask her, for fear that she would want to know more . . . and then he would have to tell her he had killed her son.

Lyn suddenly noticed something about her elder sister. 'Eh . . .' She prodded at Rowena's chest. 'You're getting doodahs.'

'Get off!' Rowena lashed out, blushing crimson.

'Rosalyn, please leave the room at once!' commanded her mother.

'But . . .'

'I will not have such talk in this house! Up to your room until you have learned more polite conversation.'

Lyn obeyed, leaving behind a period of embarrassment. Charlie drove his teeth into his meal so that he wouldn't laugh – he had noticed them too. After a while the questions

526

resumed. Rachel and her daughters assailed him for information about the college. Only his father showed no interest. On exhausting his own news, Charlie asked for theirs.

'Mr Daw's been wounded,' provided Becky. 'He's had his leg off.'

'Oh yes, I've just seen him.' Charlie pressed a last strip of bread into his mouth and brushed his hands. 'I forgot to say.'

'Here?' Rachel pointed at the floor.

'Yes, some men were helping him indoors as I came in.'

Rachel turned to her husband. 'Oh there you are, you'll have something to do this afternoon.'

'I'll let him get settled in before I go . . . Maybe later on. I don't expect he'll want crowding.'

'Will you take us for a walk, then?' asked Beany.

'Aye, maybe.' Russ lit a cigarette and listened to his children make plans with Charlie for the afternoon.

'Oh Lord!' Rachel remembered. 'Ella won't be in yet. I wonder if I should take him any dinner? She never mentioned anything about him coming home today, I wonder if she knows? We can't leave him sitting helpless with nothing to eat.' Disappearing into the scullery she set about remedying this, and in ten more minutes took the resulting meal round.

'I'm sorry I can't give you anything hot,' she told Jack and made to put the plate on his lap then, rethinking, placed it on the arm of the chair. 'We didn't know you were coming. Ella will be surprised, won't she?'

He nodded and thanked her. She tried to keep her eyes fixed to his so that she would not appear to be staring at his infirmity. Then, without asking if he wanted one, she set about making a pot of tea. Both said little until the tea was poured. Rachel clasped her hands uncertainly.

'Right, is there anything else I can get you before I go?' At his shake of the head she told him that Ella shouldn't be long now. 'I'll go then . . . Russ said he'll be popping round later, when you're settled in . . . 'bye, then.'

Jack said a taut goodbye. When she closed the door he

put the edge of his hand under the plate and sent it spinning across the room, contents and all.

'I thought you'd still be nattering next door,' said Rachel to her husband when she got home that evening. She smiled at the girls who, being off school, had prepared tea. 'How did you find him?'

'I didn't.' Russ felt her enquiring glance but did not return it. 'I haven't been.' He took a seat at the table.

She paused in tying her apron strings. 'You mean to tell me you've been sat here with nothing to do all afternoon and couldn't drag your idle body ten yards to see how your friend is?'

Charlie slunk into the scullery; there was going to be a row.

Russ waved a dismissive hand. 'He wouldn't want to see me.'

'How do you know if you never go and ask?'

He turned on her. 'Because I don't want to bloody see him! I don't want to sit looking at him with his leg blown off!'

Her face creased into disblief. 'What? Fancy saying a thing like that about a man! You make me sick. If I can put aside my grievances to help him I'm sure you can!' She hauled a chair out and sat at the table. The children looked down at their plates. 'The poor man's been sat there all on his own . . .'

'I've been on me own as well.'

'Then you should know how he feels! He was the one who saved your life when you lost your marbles!'

'Don't tell me what he did – I *know* what he did!'

Beany's mouth trembled. Under the table Rowena felt for her hand and gripped it.

'And this is how you repay him? Letting him sit all alone because you can't bear the sight of his leg?'

Russ shot from his chair and thrust his face at her. 'Because he reminds me, you silly cow! I'm trying to forget it, to put it all behind me but how can I when he's sat there with his leg ripped off!' He had shocked her into silence with his language. 'And him!' He jabbed a vicious finger at Charlie. 'How can I forget when he keeps turning up?'

Rachel found her voice. 'Don't you bring Charlie into this! He's been here doing his bit like the rest of us. He's done more in this war than you ever have. You, who swanned off without a thought, leaving us to live in penury!'

'Are we moving house?' Beany's tremulous lips enquired of her sister, who squeezed her hand and shushed her.

'And don't change the subject,' continued Rachel. 'We were talking about . . .'

'My friend! Yes, I know! You were always quick to remind me he was *my* friend and not yours, so just mind your own business!'

'A funny way to treat your friends!'

'I'll bet he feels the same as me!' raged her husband. 'Go on, go ask him! He won't want to sit looking at me and remember the blood and the shit and the stench!' As she reeled from the table in disgust he shouted, 'Aye! You'd frigging swear if you'd seen little lads with their guts hanging round their ankles!' He was almost screaming. 'Rats picking the meat off your best pal's skull!'

Rachel slapped her hands over her ears. 'Stop it! Stop!'

He was breathing heavily, gripping the back of a dining chair and leaning the upper half of his body over it, about to shower her with more filth . . . when he heard Robina sob, and gazed at his children in horror. 'Oh, Christ!' He unclamped his hands from the chair and raised them to his mouth. The eyes that stared over them were bloodshot and full of self-recrimination. But he could say nothing and stumbled up to his room.

Rowena leaned over to curl her arm round her mother who sat pale and speechless. Charlie pulled out his handkerchief and dried Regina's tears.

'I hate me father,' said Lyn vehemently.

The next time Russ spoke to his wife it was to tell her he was going to make the effort and get back into the running of the shop. Rachel wondered whether it was her words or

Charlie's presence that had finally driven him back but, needless to say, did not argue.

It was strange being at home all day again. On the first morning when Russ had gone and the children were out playing, she paced about wondering what to do first. Then the thought came to her that in three years there had not been a spring clean, not a proper one, so armed with dusters, soap and water she began in the attic and worked her way down. It was when she was in the girls' room that she came across it. All the pictures were unhooked from the walls and the cobwebs wiped from the backs of them. One of them concealed something more than cobwebs. Rachel frowned and her fingers picked at the brown sticky tape that secured a letter to the frame. Tearing it free, she put the picture down and took the letter from its envelope.

My dearest Rachel . . .

Something lurched inside her, making her flop onto the bed. But she read on . . .

I hope that my genuine plea for your forgiveness will one day be answered. I still care deeply for you and our children . . .

No you don't! Rachel's eyes swam. She blinked furiously.

I wish most desperately I was with you and Bertie . . .

She screwed the letter into her fist and thumped her knees, lips pressed tight to contain the tears. Then she straightened the letter and forced herself to read to the end.

I truly didn't love her, you know . . .

Rachel took her eyes from the words and stared into thin air. I wonder what she was like? It was a long time since she had entertained this thought. She didn't want it now. Coming to life, she screwed the letter up, shoved it into her apron pocket and went about her cleaning, rubbing more strenuously than ever.

When she came to Bertie's room she sat for a while, thinking of the orphans, then took all his clothes from the drawers and piled them on the bed. The tallboy was manoeuvred from the wall, dust swept away, skirting-board washed, the tallboy replaced, all the drawers were given new liners . . . and back went the clothes yet again.

Exhaustion claimed her at lunchtime, compelling her to

530

ask for volunteers to prepare the meal. As usual Charlie and Rowena were the ones who helped. The former could feel Mrs Hazelwood's eyes on him as he moved about the kitchen; it made him uncomfortable.

What was she like? Rachel wanted to ask the boy . . but she couldn't.

Charlie found the rest of the school holiday very tense and was almost glad when it was time to go back to the college. Though he had quite enjoyed the days spent picnicking with his sisters they could not compete with Adrian's partnership. To tell the truth, he grew rather bored of them and of the incessant bickering of his father and Mrs Hazelwood. Funnily enough, the latter was much more kindly disposed towards Charlie than her husband.

Russ noticed this too and longed for the school holiday to be over as much as Charlie did. There seemed to be even more bad feeling from his wife when the boy was around. At least now that he had gone back to the shop there could be fewer battles, and he was quite pleased with the way he was coping with the business; his attacks of panic were growing less frequent. In late summer Charlie left for college, the girls went back to school. Life was as near normal as it would ever be – peaceful, one might almost say. Too peaceful sometimes. Today, Sunday, Rachel had taken the children to church. In the deathly silence he could hear Jack moving about next door, the thump of his crutches. The man had been fitted with an artifical leg, but it rubbed and chafed so he rarely wore it. Russ only knew this from second-hand sources; he had still made no move to visit his neighbour. He knew also, from Rachel, that Jack was chronically depressed, yet still he did not go, answering his wife's prompting with, 'Jack could have called to see me if he wanted, couldn't he? I've told you he feels like I do, wants to be left alone.'

Ella had confirmed this to Rachel but neither could understand the view. How could two people who had depended on each other for their lives be so indifferent now?

Thump, thump, thump. Today the sound was driving

531

Russ mad. He lit a cigarette and drew on it savagely. 'Shut up!' he yelled irritably. 'Bloody shut up!'

There was silence for a while . . . then thump, thump, thump. Russ sprang up and began to fidget about the room, picking stuff up, putting it down, making himself a cup of tea. Silence again. He sat down. There was a louder thud. He tensed. The noise stopped. His cigarette grew shorter – suddenly there was an almighty bang from next door. *God, he's shot himself!* Russ careered into the yard, on into the lane and through his neighbour's kitchen door.

Jack looked up as he burst in.

'Jesus Christ! What you been doing?' Heart still palpitating, Russ stared at the hole in the ceiling and the mess of plaster on the floor.

'Bloody fly,' muttered Jack. 'Buzzing round, driving me mad. I couldn't reach it with the newspaper . . . fell over. So I shot the fucker.'

Russ collapsed into a chair. ' 'Struth, I thought you'd shot yourself, you mad bugger! Ella said you were depressed . . . Oh, God, let me get me wits together.' He breathed deeply for a time. Then a laugh slipped from his mouth and he looked at the other. 'She's gonna rip your other leg off when she gets in – where is she anyway?'

'No idea.' Jack ejected the spent cartridge. Then a fresh buzzing caused him to swear and level the gun at the ceiling.

Russ flinched as another round massacred the plaster. A sweat broke out on his body. 'Eh steady on, Jack . . . here, give us that paper. I'll get the sod for you.'

But Jack continued to fire until the buzzing stopped and the ceiling was a mass of holes. Finally he said, 'Do you know where I went last night?' Russ who had been cringing from the noise now began to uncurl and shook his head. 'A concert at the Mansion House for the wounded heroes. Going to entertain us with a dance troup to take our minds off our problems, they said – an audience of a hundred with not forty legs between them an' they entertain us with bloody dancers! They have no idea, no bloody idea what it's like out there. They read all this crap in the papers about the jolly old war and "cheerful despite the wounds" – what am I going to do now, tell me that? Who's going to employ me? I'll end up on the streets selling matches.'

'I think you're aiming a bit high there, Jack.' Russ used his sleeve to wipe his brow. Beneath his arms the sweat prickled.

'You count yourself bloody lucky.' Jack directed a finger at him. 'You had your business to come back to.' He put the gun aside.

Russ pinioned him with steely eyes. 'And you think that makes it easier? You think having two legs and two arms makes it any easier to get used to? I'll never get used to it, never! I can't settle, I feel . . . itchy all the time, can't relax. God knows how much I hated it over there but – it sounds bleedin' stupid – it's as if I miss it. People like you an' me, we're like foreigners, nobody here understands. Oh some of them say they do and nod sympathetically, but they don't really know.' And the guilt, he agonized privately. The bloody guilt at being left alive when all your mates are dead.

Jack echoed him. 'Aye, they keep telling us how proud they are of what we've done an' what do they do for us? Sweet F.A. They fix us up with a leg that looks like it's been modelled out of bean tins, entertain us with a load o' silly bastards and leave us to get on with it. You go outside what do you get? A load of shit. I could punch their stupid faces . . . I feel so bloody frustrated sat here like Little Boy Blue.'

Russ became thoughtful. 'Why don't you go back on the Council?' At the look of scepticism he added. 'There's nothing to stop you putting yourself up again at the next elections. Should go down well, wounded war hero.' He gave an ironic smile.

Jack was pensive. 'Are you thinking of . . . ?'

'Oh not me, pal!' cut in Russ. 'I'm allergic to limelight.'

'Aye, how is that lad of yours? Rachel says he's at college.'

Russ nodded and looked at the carpet, thinking not of Charlie but of Bertie. 'Doing quite well by all accounts.'

'Not that you're concerned, eh?' cognized Daw.

Russ gave a brief presentation of palms. 'I just can't see him as mine, part of me.'

'Rachel appears to've got used to him.'

'Aye, she can say his name without spitting now. That's cause all her spleen's reserved for me.' He looked at the clock. 'She'll be back soon. I suppose I better shift . . . shall I come and see you this afternoon?'

'If you like.'

Russ made his way slowly to the door. As he reached it he paused but didn't look back. He knew he should say thank you to Daw for getting him sent home, but was not sure the thanks would be genuine. He turned his head.

'Thanks for coming,' said Jack without looking at him.

Russ simply opened the door and left.

'Where've you been?' Rachel was already home when he got back. 'I was going to send out a search party.' He told her he had been to see Jack. 'Oh, and what bribery did he have to use to lure you from the sofa?' She covered her Sunday best with a pinafore.

He sat down. 'I heard the gun go off and I thought he'd shot himself.'

'Goodness!'

'He hadn't. Seems he just found a rifle more effective than flypaper.' He told her about the mess Jack had made.

'The lunatic! I should have made sure Ella got rid of that blessed gun years ago. What did she have to say to his madness?' On being told that Ella was not at home she grabbed a broom. 'I'd better go and clear up the damage before she gets in, then.'

Russ stopped her. 'He isn't helpless, you know. He made the mess, he can sweep it up.'

'But . . .'

'Leave him a bit of self-respect, for Heaven's sake!'

'Like *you've* got, you mean.' She put the broom aside. 'Well, I'd better start on the dinner.'

'The rice is on, I've poured the carlins into that pan. I don't know if I've mixed the Yorkshire Pudding powder right, but it's done anyway.'

She wheeled in surprise. 'Oh . . . thank you.'

534

He nodded, then rustled the newspaper in front of his face.

Despite his initial move, Russ was to see little of Jack. Following his friend's suggestion, Daw channelled his anger into local politics, resuming his membership of the Labour Party and standing up for the rights of amputees. He found work too. Discovering that the NER had held jobs open for employees who had joined up for the war, he decided to ask if their charity extended to the disabled. Rewarded with a desk job, he settled down to being a civilian for the rest of his life.

The fight raged on. The streets of York were full of old men, limbless boys and children, the factories and trams run by women. By this fourth winter of the war everyone, including Russ now, had grown used to making food and other commodities spin out. Yet there came new hardship with the shortage of coal.

'I can't think why they don't just abolish Christmas altogether,' said Rachel to her husband as this yuletide season approached. 'Every year there's some new shortage . . . oh, there's the postwoman. Go get it, Rowena, will you.' She continued serving breakfast.

The girl came back with two envelopes, both addressed to Mr and Mrs Hazelwood. She paused with them in her hand until Rachel motioned for her to hand one to her father and took the other herself. She found it was a card and a letter from her sister in America, and smiled as she read it. After she had done so, she told Russ, 'Elsie says it looks like the Americans will be reaching the front soon.'

''Bout bloody time,' muttered Russ and folded his own letter, looking annoyed.

'Well?' Rachel was waiting to hear who the other letter was from.

'It's from the boy.' Russ shoved it back into the envelope and started his meal. 'Asks if we'll mind if he doesn't come home this Christmas. Seems he's been invited to stay at his posh friend's house.'

There were 'Aws!' of disappointment from the girls,

especially Becky, but these were drowned by Rachel's reaction. 'Of all the . . . !' She snatched the letter to read it for herself. 'He puts us through all sorts of turmoil, lets us spend hard-earned cash on his education and now we're not good enough for him! And he doesn't give us much notice to say we do object, does he?' Greatly offended, she disposed of the letter and sat down to eat. 'I shouldn't wonder if he writes and tells us he's spending his Easter holidays there too!'

This is exactly what Charlie did, inviting more comments on his ingratitude. There was plenty more to complain about in the new year too, for ration cards were introduced. But for Ella this was over-ridden by some splendid news.

'Whee-hee!' She leapt into the Hazelwoods' kitchen like some pantomime dame, scaring the wits out of Rachel who happened to be alone at the time. 'Have you heard, Rache – we've got the vote!'

'Oh, Ella you frightened the bloomin' life out of me!' But after she had recovered, Rachel smiled broadly. 'Well, at least that's something good to come out of the blessed war. I'm really pleased for you, Ella.' She began to search round for the needle she had dropped in her fright.

'Eh, it's not just me, you soft clown.' Ella closed the door and came right in, sallow face alight. 'It's for all of us. Least, them of us over thirty. Victory!' She clenched her fist in triumph.

Rachel found the needle and got out of her crouch, arching her back. 'We won't see you campaigning anymore, then.'

'You what? I shall have more than ever to do now! I hope they don't hold the General Election yet. I need a good few months to get the Socialist message across. I don't want these women wasting their votes after all we've fought for 'em. I don't suppose you'll be supporting Labour?'

Rachel put her hand on her hip. 'Do you know, I really couldn't give a damn who gets into power. They're all as bad as each other.' She sat down, sucking the end of her thread and poked it at the needle's eye.

'Nay be damned! You haven't seen what a Labour

536

Government'll do yet. Give 'em chance. Eh!' She bent over and nudged Rachel, foiling her attempts to thread the needle. 'You never know, our Jack might be the first Labour Prime Minister!' She laughed and dashed out to broadcast the news.

'If he is I'm emigrating,' muttered Rachel and, finally succeeding in threading the needle, drove its point home.

A month after this, spirits were doused by a massive German offensive which robbed the Allies of any ground they might have captured and continued to press them further and further back towards Paris. So bad was the situation that the Government was discussing conscription for men up to sixty. Those who had been discharged as medically unfit were re-examined.

Russ, whose attacks of panic had lately begun to dwindle, now experienced an acuteness of terror as great as he had ever known, at the thought that he might be called upon to rejoin the fighting. When the summons came for him to attend the medical he had worked himself up to the threshold of insanity. Little was needed to push him over the edge.

'I think this is a waste of time,' he laughed nervously to the orderly who ignored the remark and told him to, 'Wait there!'

It was always the waiting that was worst. Russ stood there for half an hour, breathing jerkily and feeling nauseous, until the orderly returned and instructed him to strip to his waist, line up with the other men and, 'Wait over there!'

The far end of the queue disappeared around a corner. Russ took his position, staring forward at the regiment of naked shoulders. To calm himself, he began to count the pimples on the white back of the man in front, some bright pink, others topped with little beads of pus . . . fourteen, fifteen . . . The queue shuffled forward and he lost count, beginning again. How can they say you're fit, he tried to bolster himself. You'll be all right. You'll be fine. One, two, three . . . the queue shuffled, taking him nearer his fate. Soon he would reach the corner. What lay ahead? Abandoning the pimples he fixed his frightened blue eyes on the

537

paint that was flaking off the walls. It looked like skin. Unconsciously, he began to pull at the bits of skin around his thumb, ripping at them until they bled, then shoved the thumb in his mouth, sucking at it. Why did blood have such a metallic taste?

The man in front had reached the corner. Russ would be next. His lungs felt as if they were stuffed with cotton wool. A deep breath, another shuffle and he was around the corner. There were still twenty men ahead of him, prolonging the agony. The foremost soldier stepped behind a curtain and the line moved up. With each man who disappeared around the curtain the panic grew worse. He felt the desperate need to go to the lavatory, but after seven trips this morning he knew that his bowels had been drained and it was the terror that set them straining. Run, he told himself. *Run!*

'Next!'

His turn had arrived. The man behind him shuffled up, preventing escape. He could only go forward – behind that curtain. And there he was, with the MO dabbing a stethoscope about his chest. 'Breathe in . . . breathe out!' After a brief listen to his lungs, the doctor straightened. 'And what's been the trouble, Sergeant?'

Russ was still taking deep breaths. 'I was gassed and shot in the leg as well, sir . . . and I've been discharged with shell-shock.'

'Mmm, well you don't seem too bad now – drop your trousers!'

After a cursory look at Russ' scar, the medical officer lifted his head. 'Splendid. A1 – next!'

'Wait! You can't send me back, I'm not fit!' Russ' trousers were still round his ankles.

'Nonsense! You're in perfect shape. Pull your pants up, Sergeant!'

'I'm not!' Russ grabbed the doctor's arm. 'Please! I beg you, don't send me back . . . oh, please.' Naked and vulnerable, he tucked his chin into his chest and started to blubber, body racked with sobs.

'My God,' muttered the doctor and shook his arm free.

'Pull yourself together, soldier!' He snatched Russ' file and flicked over a few pages, studying it more closely than he had before. After a scornful word with his assistant about Hazelwood being, 'No bloody good to anybody,' he told an orderly to employ the rejection stamp for this file and shoved Russ from his sight. 'Next!'

Still sniffing and sobbing, Russ stooped to catch at his waistband and hauled his trousers up before stepping out from behind the curtain. Everybody was looking at him. He pulled out a handkerchief, using it to cover his humiliation and to hide the looks of derision and pity from his own eyes, eyes that never wavered from the floor until their owner was out of the building. Even in the street he felt that people knew how he had behaved in there. Never had he felt so emasculated . . . but at least it had saved him.

This being a Wednesday afternoon and half day closing, he went straight home. Rachel, seeing him pass the window where she sat working at her sewing machine, expected him to come straight into the parlour with his news, good or bad. But when his footsteps faded and a call brought only silence, she left her sewing and tripped along to the kitchen.

Russ' stance forbade any impulsive rebuke she might have made. His back was to her and his head bent; it must be bad news. Her stomach flipped. 'They're sending you back.' He shook his head, but did not lift it. 'Then . . . ?' Rachel took a stride nearer, and noticed he was looking at something in his hand. Her frown was etched deeper when she saw what it was. 'I didn't know you'd won a medal . . .'

He turned it over and over in his fingers, face lifeless. 'Lots o' men got one,' he said gruffly. 'It means nowt . . . nothing at all.' And to her even greater surprise, he tossed it onto the fire.

It took a good many weeks for him to regain the state he had achieved before the upset, and even by early summer there were incidents when his fear made a laughing stock of him. One Saturday in June, he took the girls to watch the school hockey championships, while Rachel very kindly took his place at the shop. At first everything was fine, he enjoyed a

539

cheer with his daughters when Beany's school earned a goal. But in a trice, the players on the green field became soldiers and the loud chants of 'Scar-croft! Scar-croft!' became battle cries . . .

'Have you got earache, Father?' Beany stopped jumping up and down and stared at him. One by one his other daughters stopped too. Their father had his hands pressed tightly over his ears, eyes screwed shut. The crowd was still cheering. Russ ground his palms into the sides of his head, trying to repel the screams of the wounded, the boom of the guns . . .

Rowena grasped his arm, then drew her fingers back quickly as if burnt. He was trembling.

'What's up with him?' whispered Becky fearfully.

'I don't know.' Rowena felt that they were all looking to her to take action. She was unsure what to do. Oh please, she begged, don't let Father have one of his screaming turns here.

He was shivering visibly now. The people nearby had noticed and were observing him strangely. Lyn, who was uttering the same silent prayer as her sister, kneaded her hands and watched in horror as a tear emerged from his squeezed-up eye. Oh don't, please don't, Father. There's people I know . . .

'Eh, look at Nutty's dad – he's crying!' The boy who had voiced the amazed remark to his friends received a black glower from Lyn, both for the observation and the nickname.

'Shut your mouth, Smelly.'

But the boy and his gang of friends came to have a closer look. 'What's up wi' him?'

'It's because of the war,' said Rowena, trying to steer her father away from prying eyes. 'He doesn't like noise.'

The boys hovered. Their leader nudged a friend, then shouted, 'Bang!'

Russ jumped and pressed his hands more tightly over his ears. The culprit roared with laughter.

'Smelly Shelley! Smelly Shelley!' retorted a furious Lyn. 'Go on, get back to your pig 'oile!'

'Bang! Bang!' The boys laughed with glee and danced around Russ – until Lyn flew at them, hands bunched, mouth biting, feet kicking, and they ran to a safer distance where they continued to sing, 'Nutty's dad's a coward! Nutty's dad's a coward!' as the Hazelwood girls hurried their father away, leading him home like an infant. Unluckily for the tormentors, the half-time whistle had just blown and the teacher, witnessing their prank, came over to bang all their heads together, and informed them that Sergeant Hazelwood had risked his life for the likes of them – they should be deeply ashamed of themselves. It was sad that the Hazelwoods were no longer around to see this retribution.

Away from the din of the sportsfield, Russ began to recover, seeing now his daughters' miserable faces. He filled his lungs and let the breath out heavily, several times, then murmured, 'I'm sorry . . . it was the noise.'

'Did it give you earache?' asked Beany, slipping her hand into his. He gripped it and nodded. 'Oh, it's terrible, earache, isn't it? You'll have to take something for it.'

Russ gave a pained smile, then looked at his eldest girl. Rowena knew that he was not suffering from earache, but didn't know what to say. Her face showed this. Russ put his arm round her shoulder and touched his greying head to hers briefly before encompassing the rest in his gaze. 'We're one short, aren't we?'

Becky jabbed a thumb over her shoulder and Russ turned to see Lyn dawdling ten yards behind. The sight of that skinny young figure – shoulders sagging in disgrace, eyes to the pavement – bit into his heart and conscience. He tore his eyes from her and looked up at the sky. Oh God, how he must have shamed them back there. Are you just going to let it go on and on he asked himself, prove to the doctors that they were right about you being no bloody good to anybody? Or are you going to fight? I'm sick of bloody fighting, came a weary inner voice. For God's sake, man! These are your children – see the way they pity you. A father should be somebody they can look up to – *fight it*! Somewhere deep inside his brain a tiny light was kindled.

Russ cupped imaginary hands around it, refusing to let it be extinguished by the breath from that other voice which said, it's no use, why bother?

Gradually, the flame took a hold, grew stronger. Yes, there were times of relapse when he quaked and sobbed like a lunatic, but the flame remained bright, was fanned by the love of his children, and slowly the upsets became fewer.

As July came upon them, Russ found that he was actually looking forward to the rounds of garden parties and fêtes that the school holiday month would bring. His biggest hope, however, was that Charlie would once again be spending his break with his friend and not coming here to disrupt things.

This selfish thought made him sit back and look at the contrasts between home and the Western Front: over there the men were as one against a mutual enemy, at home the war seemed to have made little impression on people's natural selfishness. Oh, they formed their committees to roll bandages and dug up their lawns to provide vegetables, but behind the camaraderie there remained that age-old attitude of fuck you, Jack, I'm all right – you only had to look at the example of the munitions workers whose current strike was depriving their Army of the means to win this war. People pushed and shoved and moaned in grocery queues, argy-bargying because the woman in front had got an eighth of an ounce more sugar than they had. There was none of the tenderness of war . . . *the tenderness of war*. Russ pondered on the phrase. The conchies would laugh their little cobblers off at that, but it was very true – oh yes, he would not deny that there were moans and grumbles in the trenches, the odd selfish bastard who'd snaffle another man's rations and those who robbed corpses; but a dead man would not miss a silver watch, and most soldiers of his acquaintance would share what little they had, would sit and nurse a wounded pal – or even a complete stranger – for hours under continuous fire . . . But all that was lost to him. Now he had slipped back into his old selfish ways. And he prayed that Charlie would not come home.

But Charlie did come home in the summer – although he

informed them straightaway that the last fortnight of his holiday would be spent at Adrian's home.

Rachel sniffed and looked him up and down. 'You seem to be quite well-in with this Adrian.' They were alone at the moment.

He sensed the bitterness. 'I'm sorry . . . I didn't think you'd mind if I wasn't here. I thought it might make things better for you and Mr Hazelwood.'

'I notice you don't call him Father now.'

Charlie picked at a cuticle. 'He doesn't like it.'

Rachel felt sorry for him and her expression lost its hardness. 'Ah well, you must go where you feel most comfortable.' She started to busy herself. 'Is Adrian's father in the Army?'

'No he was wounded like my . . . Mr Hazelwood. He's got a hook on his arm.' Charlie grinned. 'I was really frightened of him at first, but he makes us laugh with the things he does with it.' He went on to tell her all that had happened at Christmas. She watched his face closely. It was obvious he was a lot happier.

She picked up the kettle and went to the scullery. 'What was your mother like?'

He assumed he had misheard and said, 'Ade's mother? Well, she's . . .'

'No . . . *your* mother.' At his silence Rachel turned from the sink and looked at him. 'I've often wondered.'

Charlie's look of startlement faded into one of reverie. He propped his chin with both hands, elbows on table. 'She was . . .' he screwed his face up, in search of a description. 'Just my mother.'

'Was she pretty?' Rachel's face had turned back to the sink. The kettle filled, she brought it back to the range.

'No . . . not really.' He shuffled his feet under the table.

'You don't have to feel embarrassed at saying yes,' said Rachel quietly. 'She must have had something about her, otherwise he wouldn't have . . . I just keep trying to understand.'

Charlie did not want to regurgitate old hatred. Luckily, he was saved from further discomfort with the arrival of the girls, with whom he spent the remainder of the time before tea.

His father, of course, was not very pleased to see him here when he came in that evening, but managed to treat him civilly for once. Charlie asked how Mr Daw was. Russ said he didn't see much of him now they were both at work.

'It looks as if he's going to be re-elected for the Council,' Rachel told Charlie. 'I don't know – there are others who can't even get a job. He always falls on his feet does that one.'

'Foot.'

She looked at Russ.

'Foot – you mean foot, don't you?'

Rachel gave a soft laugh of understanding. The children smiled too. After tea, Charlie asked if he could read the newspaper. 'We're not allowed to see them at college.'

Russ tossed him today's copy and he caught it. On reading several lines he said brightly. 'The war's going well, isn't it? Our tanks have punched a hole in the Hindenberg Line. Looks like it might be over soon.'

Russ dismissed this observation. 'I shouldn't get too optimistic. According to the paper the Hindenberg Line gets breeched every week – and these tanks aren't all they're cracked up to be either.' He envisioned the broken down tanks on the Somme, tangled up in barbed wire, running into each other, one climbing up the other's back . . . like copulating dinosaurs.

Charlie said no more. In fact, during the rest of the holiday his conversation with his father was extremely sketchy – not that he was made to feel left out, for he was included in all the family's activities from the attendance of a garden fête at Middlethorpe Lodge to a trip to see Mary Pickford on film at the Victoria Hall. Oh no, he was included in everything . . . everything except his father's affection. However, by the time he was ready to go to Adrian's there was one spark of light; for all his father's opinions that the newspapers were full of propaganda it looked as if they were correct when they spoke of great victories and an imminent end to the war. Two months later

544

Charlie and the rest of the British public knew that their suffering was finally coming to an end.

Russ was at the shop when Armistice came. He was sipping a late morning cup of tea when, hearing churchbells for the first time in years, he wandered out into the street.

'It's over!' A passer-by grabbed his hand, shook it vigorously and ran on to tell the next person. Joyful voices echoed up and down Micklegate. 'It's over! The war's over!'

Russ had often wondered, whilst sitting up to his hips in mud, what his feelings would be at this announcement. Nothing. He felt absolutely nothing . . . for the war was still going on inside him. Not just this war, but the one he had created for himself at home. Slouching back inside, he sat down and resumed his cup of tea, his mind turning anticlockwise, returning him to conversations with the boys who would not be coming back.

Rachel was no more enthusiastic. Neither she nor Ella were among the crowd that gathered in St Helen's Square, kissing and hugging perfect strangers, congratulating each other on their war effort. What was there to celebrate? One had lost a son, the other had a maimed husband.

The children heard the news at their respective schools and were granted the rest of the day off, filling the streets with the sound of their innocent patriotism. Two old ladies smiled fondly as the Hazelwood brood marched past and turned the corner. 'Aren't they enjoying themselves, the poor little mites.' And a hearty voice filtered round the corner, 'Oh, we don't give a fuck for old Von Cluck . . .'

The rest chortled as Rowena gagged Lyn. 'Mother's going to be mad enough having us under her feet without hearing that!'

Mother wasn't mad – she was crying. She tried to wipe the evidence from her eyes at their unexpected entry, but they saw at once. They also saw the sack of clothes in the corner. 'Have you been given the day off? That's nice. I'm sorry I wasn't expecting you, I'm just going out.' She blew her nose, making herself look busy. 'I won't be long, I'm just going into town to take these clothes for the orphans. Don't touch anything in the pantry.' She left.

'Did you see what was in that bag?' a sulky Lyn asked the others. 'Those were Bertie's things – she might have let me have the trousers.'

Rachel stood opposite the building that served as a collection point for the charity. She stood for a long time, unable to hand over the sack, feeling that once the clothes were gone, Robert was gone too . . . but Robert was gone already. Squaring her shoulders, she set off across the road and walked straight into the building. 'I've brought these.' She held out the sack to a woman. 'I thought they might be useful for the orphans.'

'Oh right, put them over there, will you?'

Just that. No 'thank you', no 'that's very kind of you'. These are my son's clothes, she wanted to say. My dead son – can't you imagine what I've been through before I could bear to part with them? But the woman had gone back to issuing orders to her underlings. Rachel looked down at the sack in her hand . . . then went to put it on the pile of other sacks.

She came out of the building and looked up and down the street. It was packed with revellers – probably most of them drunk, thought Rachel. In the sky above, aeroplanes performed stunts over the jubilant city. From every window hung a Union Jack. As Rachel lowered her eyes they fell upon a young woman whose face was uplifted to the sky. It took a moment before she identified Biddy who looked dreadful, her face a sickly yellow. This wasn't helped by the unfortunate combination of a green hat. Rachel watched her for a couple of seconds. The girl seemed to be alone and not particularly enjoying the celebrations. Poor Biddy . . . Rachel went up to her then and asked how she was.

The yellow face stopped watching the aeroplanes. 'Oh hello, Mrs Hazelwood! I'm fine – how are you?'

Rachel said she was better now that this war was over, to which Biddy heartily agreed. 'I wondered,' went on Rachel, 'now that it is over, there won't be much need for all these munitions factories, will there? Would you like to come back and work for me?'

'Ye must be joking!' laughed Biddy. Then more politely, 'Ah no, they'll be needin' munitions for a good while yet. Anyway, I couldn't afford the drop in wages.'

'I would've thought your health is more important than money,' said Rachel, though not angrily. 'The munitions has bought you a fur coat but have you seen what it's done to your skin?'

Biddy said that there was nothing wrong with her skin, thank ye very much. 'An' ye'll never get anyone to work for three bob a week nowadays.'

'I could go to five,' offered Rachel. She didn't really need a maid any more, but felt so sorry for Biddy.

Biddy just laughed again. 'The days of slavery are over, Mrs Hazelwood – but I wish ye good luck in findin' somebody. 'Bye now!' She lumbered off.

'Good luck,' murmured Rachel, then made her way home.

Her route took her up Micklegate and on a whim she decided to call in on her husband. How might he be celebrating Armistice? She hesitated outside the shop and peered through the window, between the articles on display. Russ was serving a woman. His mouth worked smilingly as he measured out the red, white and blue ribbons, but the moment the woman was served and turned her back the smile faded. Even after the customer emerged, Rachel continued to watch him.

Russ sighed and leaned back against a display cabinet, closing his eyes. When he opened them again he was looking at Rachel.

'I wondered if you'd be closing up for the day, everybody else is.'

'Er . . .' He shook his head to remove the confusion, then smiled. 'Sorry, I just wasn't expecting to see you here.'

She approached the counter. 'I've been to take Robert's clothes to the charity place.'

'Oh.' He dipped his eyes and began to wind a tape measure round his fingers.

'You'd think they'd be grateful, wouldn't you?' she asked softly. 'I mean, I didn't expect them to salaam all over

547

the place but I might've found a thank you rather nice, considering they were our son's clothes.'

Our son. She normally said *my* son. 'Oh well . . . I suppose there's been that many killed . . . people forget, don't they?'

She nodded, mouth turned down at the corners. 'They must do.'

They looked at each other for a long time – then a car backfired and suddenly Russ had vanished. Rachel leaned over the counter and stared down at him. He was lying prone, hands over his head, trembling. Swiftly, she moved around the counter and squatted by him. 'Russ? Are you all right?' She placed a hand on his shoulder, feeling the tremors.

He remained as he was for some seconds. Then, slowly, he ascended to a kneeling position. 'The guns . . .'

'It was only a car.' She scrutinized the white face. 'Making that silly noise that they do – they should be banned!' She helped him to his feet and brushed the dust from his waistcoat. 'This floor wants sweeping.'

He looked into her face. 'I am sorry, you know.'

Her expression tightened, not with anger but with pain. After a tortured spell, she said, 'I know . . .' then gave him a final brush and moved briskly to the door. 'Come on! I'm sure there's no call for us to stand here this afternoon, there won't be much custom with everyone drunk.'

He reached for his overcoat. 'A lot of folk are wanting ribbons.'

'Then they can buy them somewhere else today!' And she actually smiled at him.

CHAPTER THIRTY-FOUR

There wasn't a time when either of them thought, this is it –
it's all over, or experienced a flash of lightning. They just
sort of grew back together. Neither acknowledged this, but
they both knew that the barrier which Charlie had put
between them was slowly being dismantled. Only when the
time neared for Charlie to come home was it reconstructed –
not by Rachel, but by the boy's father. Russ could not and
would not recognize Charlie as his son. Even though he
cried over young Dobson, even though he celebrated when
he heard that Jewitt was home safe and sound, even though
he agonized over Bertie's loss . . . the only way he saw
Charlie was as the obstacle that prevented him and Rachel
from getting back together. When, in December, a letter
came from the boy, Russ hoped it was to say that Charlie
was spending yuletide with his friend. He was disappointed; Charlie was coming home; there would be no Christmas
reconciliation. One way or the other he had to get rid of the
boy.

A trough of anti-climax had followed the Armistice. At
first, there had been street parties and Union Jacks strung
from door to door to welcome home their heroes . . . but
those same heroes were now queueing outside the soup
kitchens. Even those who had known the personal bereavement of war were just beginning to grasp the enormity of
the aftermath: the blood and bones of almost an entire
generation had been left behind to enrich the fields of
Europe. And those who possessed only the tiniest amount
of sensitivity saw that their world had changed; nothing
would ever be the same again.

One of those for whom this realization was most acute
was Russ' sister May, whose husband had been killed an

hour before the ceasefire. Since Russ' confession she had never corresponded with him nor his wife, but once her tears dried she picked up her pen and scribbled a few poignant lines, *I do not even know if you are still alive, but I pray that you will be reading this with Rachel . . .* ' Naturally, she had no idea about Bertie, for Russ had been too crazed to inform her; the mention of his son in her letter, as though he were still alive, brought tears to his eyes. At the foot of the letter the sentiment was expressed that, '. . . *We have to hang on to our loved ones who are left*', and she added that as soon as the hardships of war began to fade then he and his family must come for a holiday again, '. . . *and if the boy is still with you then he must come too.*' Everyone, it seemed, was willing to accept Charlie. Everyone but Russ.

The General Election had been and gone. All that brouhaha about getting us the vote, Rachel had declared, and what happens – they return that rascal Lloyd George! But better this than the Labour crew. Naturally after all her hard work, Ella had been bitterly disappointed at the result, but she swore that she and Jack would continue to fight on behalf of the Labour Party – and there had been consolation in the Council elections. Jack was to be next year's Sheriff. On first hearing the news, Rachel had been stunned, but then she smiled and said convincingly, 'Congratulations, Ella. It's high time you had a bit of luck.'

'Aye, you're right there,' Ella agreed. 'But, you know, in spite of us losing the General Election, we're off in the right direction, Rache. Mark my words, next time it'll be Labour.'

Rachel merely smiled. 'We might even see you in Parliament, Ella.' A Bill had just been passed allowing females this distinction.

Ella wagged a playful finger. 'Now, now! Many a true word, Rache . . .'

Rachel herself had voted Tory, for the simple reason that this was whom Russ backed. It was more a token of support for him, rather than a political gesture.

She paused in her knitting to arch her spine, caught his eye and smiled. 'Ooh, I shall have to stop, my back's killing me, and my eyes. Navy wool is bad enough to knit with in daylight but in this dinge it's hopeless.' The gas pressure was very low at the moment. 'And you should stop as well, else you'll be needing glasses.' Russ had been straining his eyes over the evening newspaper. 'Is there anything of interest in it?'

Welcoming the chance to share words, Russ folded the press. 'Just more of the usual. You know, I've been thinking of investing in some of these War Bonds; it'd bring twice as much interest as we're getting from the bank.'

Rachel said she had been entertaining the same idea and both decided that they should not delay further. 'Rowena, put the kettle on, love, we'll have cocoa.'

Rowena inserted her needle into the hankerchief she was embroidering and left her seat at the table. 'Could we have a piece of toast for supper, Mother?'

'You can have two slices between you,' answered Rachel.

The smallest girl tapped at her father's arm. 'Give me a tickle with your 'tache, Father.' This was one of the tricks he had used to gain her friendship; she had grown quite fond of him now. Russ bent his head and nuzzled her with his moustache. She screamed her delight and ran off.

'Regina, watch the milk!' She had almost knocked the jug over. With only two pints a day between eight of them this would have been a smacking offence. At her mother's sharp cry she shrank into a squat.

Rachel tut tutted, then continued to chat to her husband. Rowena knelt in front of the miserly fire and put a slice of bread on the toasting fork, watching and listening to her parents. Since the war had ended the atmosphere in the house had grown steadily better. If Father hadn't quite been forgiven, then it was Rowena's opinion that he very soon would be. He still sometimes cried on a night, but in the daytime he was very much like the father they used to have – or near enough. Rowena watched the smiles on her parents' faces. The sight brought a smile to her own mouth, though she was too deep in concentration to know it. She continued to sit and watch, bursting with hope and happiness.

'Keep the home fires bur-ning!'

Her father's hearty rendition made her jump and she looked at the toasting fork to see flames licking the bread. In her daydream she had not noticed how close it was to the fire. With a cry, she blew on it, then looked woefully at her mother. 'Sorry . . .' It was uneatable.

Rachel had to laugh. 'I wouldn't've thought it possible to burn anything on that scratty fire, my feet are blue with cold. Oh, throw it away and get another slice! I'll close my eyes.'

Rowena threw the burnt toast on the fire. It fell out onto the hearth.

'Even the fire doesn't want it,' said Russ, and when Becky giggled he dug a finger in her ribs. 'Eh, who gave you permission to laugh?' At his tickling she laughed the louder. 'Oh, she's going to lay an egg! Eh, keep her laughing everybody and we'll have eggs on toast for supper.' He kept tickling her. 'Come on, get them laid! Oh, there's another one – we can sell a few on the black market at this rate, four bob for half a dozen!'

After the laughter died down and the toast and cocoa were consumed it was the children's bedtime, all except Rowena who was allowed to stay up later. 'Right, 'flu inspection!' said Rachel and ordered them to line up in front of her. Terrified of the deadly influenza that was sweeping the country, she made close examination of her brood night and morning, making them drink mineral water to flush out the impurities. Each forehead was tested for signs of fever, eyes for brightness. In the medicine cabinet an assortment of bottles stood in preparation, on which Rachel had, 'Spent a fortune'!

'I hope you realize,' said Russ to his girls as they came to kiss him goodnight, 'that if none of you get this 'flu there'll be a fine imposed for money-wasting.'

Rachel smiled with the rest, but when she and Russ were alone she confessed, 'I do worry about them . . . it only takes one in a class to spread it round the entire school.'

'Rowena won't be there much longer, will she?'

Rachel shook her head as though disbelieving that she

was the mother of a young woman – in fact all of them were growing up; Becky and Lyn were at Grammar School and Regina would be starting school soon . . . the house would be empty. Russ asked if she knew of her daughter's intentions, career-wise. 'She says she wants to be a typewriter. I'd prefer she stayed on at school but she doesn't want to – says she hates it. I doubt she'd pass her matriculations anyway, so there's little point.'

'Well there's one thing,' sighed Russ. 'She won't have the trouble finding a job that some of these poor lads do . . . I had young Jimmy in today asking for his post back.'

'Oh, he got through the war unscathed then?'

'Not entirely, he's had a hand blown off . . . but at least I won't be worrying about him putting his fingers in the till.' Russ smiled.

'Can you afford to employ him?'

'It's not a question of affording. I have a duty to employ him.'

Rachel said, 'I know what you mean. I saw Biddy on Armistice Day. She looked awful. I felt I just had to offer her a healthier job . . . she laughed at me.' Rachel laughed too and stood up to draw the curtains. Sick of the regulations imposed on them in the war, many people, herself included, had taken to drawing the curtains later than normal or leaving them open altogether.

Russ watched her. She was wearing a new shorter length skirt that exhibited her nice legs. From the thigh the skirt was pleated, but above this it fitted snugly round her hips. He couldn't take his eyes off them.

Rachel felt his stare – not for the first time; he had been watching her like this for weeks. Just because I smiled at you, she told him mentally, don't think there'll be any return to 'that', because there won't. It unnerved her, knowing what he was thinking about. What if . . . well, he had been without sex for four years, hadn't he? What if he forced her? After all, he was a different person, she hardly knew him. If he could kill people then it would be easy for him to . . . She imagined her own response to his rape – biting, scratching, struggling. Experiencing difficulty in breathing she tried to force the vision aside as she held out her hand for his cup. Russ noticed how it trembled. Was it because she was afraid, or because she wanted him? He wished he knew, wished she would come right out and tell him where he stood. He dared not make the move himself, scared it would set him back four years. Draining the last cold drop he parted with his cup and watched her take it to wash.

What the devil are you talking about! Rachel asked herself, saying he's been without sex for four years – how do you know that? He never went without it before, did he? Not like you, lying alone in your bed, aching to be held and touched . . .

The time for bed came around. The coals were doused with a cupful of water. Each wished the other goodnight. Russ went to his bed, Rachel to hers. She shut her door . . . but she couldn't shut her mind.

In spite of the continuing shortages, it promised to be a brighter Christmas. If only Charlie wasn't coming to interrupt the normal pattern of things, Russ felt sure that the magic season would bring him and Rachel even closer. Fortunately, Charlie's college did not permit the boys to come home until Boxing Day, so at least the main days of Christmas would be spent enjoyably.

Oh, it was a joy! To sing carols around the piano, to sit round the table like they used to do, with a cheerful fire, cards on the mantelpiece, homemade crackers at each setting. Look at their faces! Everyone was happy, content, there were no grumbles about the Army, no carping because someone hadn't been pulling their weight, all were smiling and chatting and treating him like the father and husband he used to be . . . well almost.

Ella came in to wish them Happy Christmas. She was asked if she would like a sherry. 'No, I can't stop, love. We're off to the Mansion House to meet the Mayor and his wife. We're having five hundred children for tea. Imagine that, Rache! Anyway, I'll have to dash. Just thought you might like to hear how things're going – bye!' Once outside, Ella gave a devilish grin.

'Like to hear.' Rachel formed a wry smile as the door closed on Ella. 'Show off, she means. Five hundred children for tea – why can't she have bacon sandwiches like we have to make do with?'

For a second no one got it, then someone giggled – Mother had made a joke!

'Well!' She laughed with them. 'It was the way she said it.' She adopted a haughty voice, 'We're having five hundred children for tea! And after all she said about the Mansion House . . . ah dear, poor Ella, still having to poach other people's children. But, I suppose she's lucky in a way, never knowing the heartache of losing a son.'

Russ feared the mention of Bertie was going to ruin things, but then his wife smiled sadly. 'We'll have to do something about Robert's room. It seems silly crowding the girls into that tiny space when that's lying empty.

'Ooh, can I have it, Mother?' Lyn was the first to ask.

'Yes, you and Robina can . . .'

'Aw, can't I have it to myself?' begged Lyn. 'Bertie did.'

'I told you that was because boys and girls don't sleep in the same room,' Russ reminded his daughter.

Rachel was looking at the disheartened face, hearing again the voice cry, *I only wanted to be important!* The children had suffered badly in this war. It was time they were made to know that each of them was important, if only for a night. 'I've got an idea. Before we start to use Robert's room properly each of you can spend one night in it all to yourselves. You can have your turn tonight, Rosalyn.' There were cries of glee. Lyn came to squeeze her mother's neck. Rachel returned the hug, then went to stir the fire. 'It's a bit silly, me sleeping in that big room on my own as well.'

Russ became alert. His heart beat faster.

'I should let you girls have it and move my things into your room so there'll be more space when Charlie comes home.'

Oh, the crushing disappointment! Russ turned away so that she would not see the destruction on his face.

'On second thoughts, I'll leave it until summer, there's enough to do at Christmas without making more.'

'If me father went back in your bed,' suggested Becky, 'there'd only need to be two of us in each room.'

Russ cringed. Oh God, what's going to be her reaction to that? But Rachel pretended not to have heard.

Later that Christmas Eve, the family were gathered in the kitchen, employed in their usual festive activities. Rachel was bent over the oven checking on her baking. Russ, as had become his wont, was watching her every move, running his eyes over her hips. The girls were grouped round the table making yet more decorations, when the door opened and Jack Daw limped in.

He took off his cap and gave it a flick to remove the droplets. 'Merry Christmas to one an' all.'

Both Russ and Rachel showed surprise, but returned the wish. Rachel pulled a chair from under the table and planted it nearer the fire.

'Come and sit down, Jack. Did you enjoy your meal at the Mansion House?'

Jack muttered that it had been, 'Not bad.'

As he stumped over, Beany finished making her cut-out dolls and said, 'Watch this, Mr Daw!' before opening the folded newspaper. Her visage turned to one of rage when, instead of joined-up dolls, emerged ten separate little cut-outs. 'Aw!'

Jack said bluntly, 'You've folded it the wrong way,' and sat down.

In a fury, the child ripped the cut-outs to shreds, bringing instant rebuke, for waste paper was worth money these days.

'Oh give us another piece!' her father gestured. 'I'll fold it for you. Now then, what can we do for our new Sheriff?'

'Our new Sheriff is doing well enough for himself, thank you very much.' Jack gave his twisted smile and rubbed at his leg where it joined the artificial one. 'Happen you were right about the wounded hero bit, eh? No, I just came round to see if you fancied joining me in a pint of Wincarnis. Ella's gone off to do some charity work or other. I thought, I'm not stopping in on me own on Christmas Eve. How about it?'

Russ was about to refuse when his wife surprised him by saying, 'Go on, you may as well go for half an hour or so. I'll be busy until bedtime with these preparations. Take one of the spare front door keys in case I've gone to bed.'

He raised a speculative eyebrow, said, 'Oh . . . oh, all right I think I will,' and getting his coat followed Jack into the yard.

Later, when the children were abed and her work was over, Rachel sat by the fire nursing a cup of tea and going over all her thoughts. A look at the clock told her she would probably be on her own for another hour. She decided to use the interval to take a bath. Locking the doors, she left a note for Russ should he arrive earlier than anticipated: 'I'm in the bath.' Then closeting herself in the scullery she lifted the worktop over the bath and turned the taps on. Whilst waiting for it to fill she collected a towel and took the soap from the sink. After a thoughtful sniff of the latter's unexciting perfume she gave way to impulse and raced up to her room. From a drawer she took a tablet of scented soap that had been a Christmas gift from a previous year but which had until now only been used to perfume her clothes. Lifting it to her nose, she inhaled deeply – then re-membered the taps were still running and bounded down-stairs to arrest them.

There was more water in the bath than was proper in these austere times, but Rachel thrust aside the guilt and, stripping, stepped into the bath. After washing herself she lay back, the water lapping at her chin and the scent of ottar of roses filling her lungs.

Russ halted outside the front door to exchange last minute words with Jack. The latter used the wall to take the weight from his stump. Retaining the habit of the trenches he shielded the glow of his cigarette in his palm whilst taking a long drag. 'Well, Russ . . . I hope things come all right for you.' During the walk home the conversation had worked its way round to the state of Russell's marriage.

Russ' lips hauled on his own cigarette. 'Aye, thanks, Jack, so do I. Sorry to drag you home early but I want to keep on the right side of her over Christmas, if only for the kids' sake.'

Jack said for him not to worry. 'I wasn't reckoning to stay till closing time meself. I get fed up after an hour or so.' He winced as he got to his feet. 'I'll have to get Ella to sandpaper me leg. See you.'

Russ wished him good night and inserted his key in the lock, entering quietly so as not to disturb anyone. The kitchen was empty; Rachel had gone to bed. No, she wouldn't have left the light on – oh, there was a note. He leaned on the table. *I'm in the bath.*

He took off his coat and hung it up then went to warm his hands by the fire, rubbing them against each other. The clock ticked. He looked about for something to occupy him until she came out. Tonight's newspaper lay on the sofa. He sat down and read the passages that he had overlooked earlier. The sound of splashing drew his eyes to the door of the scullery. He stared at the varnished wood. *I'm in the bath.* Was it an order to stay out . . . or an invitation? He touched his tongue to the corner of his mouth, wondering. His nostrils began to twitch and his breathing became deeper. Rattling the paper into reading position he commanded his eyes to take in the words . . . but soon they were straying to that door again.

Folding the paper, he stood. His hands smoothed his hair back several times as if trying to drive the thought away. A palm ran itself around the back of his neck, kneading. A movement in the mirror caused him to look at himself – a nervous, shifty-looking wretch. Altering his expression, he leaned closer to the glass. You look quite presentable, chin cleanly shaven, moustache trimmed, clean shirt, clean all over. He heard the splash of water again. His chest rose and fell. Wheeling from the mirror he clutched his arms around himself and hugged tightly. *I'm in the bath.* His body felt like a bag of water. He ran his hands up and down it, into his groin. With a silent curse, he strode to the passage to retrieve his pack of cigarettes from his coat. Sticking one between his lips he struck a match . . . but before he lit the cigarette his eyes, once again, became glued to that door.

The water was growing cool. Rachel lifted the top half of her body and reached for a towel, wrapping it round her as she lifted one dripping foot out of the bath, then the other. Russell should be home soon. She paused to cock her head, listening for the sound of him. All was quiet. She continued to dry herself, humming softly.

The door to the kitchen opened. With a small gasp she clutched the towel to her breast. 'I left you a note – didn't you see it?' Her eyes were round.

Russ stood there gazing at her. Her honey-brown hair was tied up, but frizzy little wisps of it clung round her face. The latter glowed pink and radiant . . . like the rest of her body. The towel hid most of it, but even the sight of her shoulders and upper chest excited him. He wanted to press his mouth to them.

With the lack of an answer she became frightened, her brown eyes dilated. 'Russell . . .'

Suddenly, he became alive to the effect he was having on her and he took a step forward. 'I thought . . . well, we've been getting on better lately, I hoped we might . . .'

She stepped back. 'Get away!'

He kept coming. 'Rachel, love.'

She stumbled backwards, hauled on a drawer, scrabbled inside it. Her hand emerged clutching a vegetable knife which she held in front of her. 'Stay away from me or I'll kill you!'

This stopped him. The longing died – horror spread across his face. Then even this faded. Not a word did he speak as he turned away and limped from the scullery, closing the door after him.

She kept her defensive position for some seconds, the knife trembling, her whole body trembling . . . but with what? Fear or longing?

After a time, she felt composed enough to remove the towel, and slipped into her nightclothes. Tying the sash of her dressing gown she emptied the bath, cleaned it and replaced the board. When all was straight she set her feet at the door. A nervous peep round it told her that Russell was no longer here. She released the breath she had been holding and stepped into the room. Loosing her hair, she ran a brush through it, smoothing back all the damp wisps from her temples. The face that looked back at her was strange, made her stop and examine it. If this was the woman he had seen then no wonder he had got the wrong idea – she looked positively wanton, her eyes not brown, but almost black with the dilated pupils, cheeks flushed, lips pumped up with blood. Rebuking herself, she finished brushing her hair, turned off the light and crept up the stairs.

Russ sat on his bed, staring at the photograph. With the creak of the stairs he lifted his face . . . but at the soft click of her door his eyes dropped back to the picture.

Rachel was woken by a shout. It had happened quite regularly over the past year. Groaning, she turned over, waiting for the muffled sobs that always pursued it. They came on cue. Rachel knew from past experience that she would not sleep until they were over. But tonight for some reason they went on and on. *He's going to wake the children if he goes on much longer.* This thought finally persuaded her to get up and check to see if her daughters had been disturbed.

Remembering that Rosalyn was now in Robert's room she went here first. There was no sound, but something urged her to go right up to the bed. It was empty! Panic swamped her. Hand over mouth she spun and ran to the girls' room. There, in bed with two of her sisters, she found Lyn. Relief buckled her legs. Fighting back the urge to exclaim, she left them asleep and crept back to the landing. Here, she leaned against the wall to recover. He was still crying. It took many more minutes before she summoned the will to go in.

He did not check at her entry, but kept on sobbing. She approached the bed with caution. 'Russell . . .' Even now he did not look up. She adopted a tentative perch on the bed and put a hand to his racked shoulder. At once, one of his hands flew up to clutch it, like that of a drowning man. She fought the terrified reflex and left it there. She sat thus for a long spell, indeed, until he had finished crying. With the silence, she slipped her hand from under his, rose and made as if to leave.

His head came off the pillow. 'Don't go!'

She turned back to look at him, lips parting.

'Please.' He reached out to her. 'I promise I won't touch you. Just stay with me.'

She took hold of his hand and when he pulled aside the covers slipped into bed beside him. He made no move to put his arms round her, just kept gripping her hand. But in the small bed it was hard not to make contact with his body. She felt its heat burning into her side. Nothing was said. She stayed until he fell asleep.

In the morning he woke to find himself alone and assumed it had all been a dream. The fact that his wife made no mention of it when he came down reinforced this belief. She had plenty of opportunity to comment; they were alone for fifteen minutes before the girls came down, but all she spoke about as she prepared breakfast was the weather.

'And what happened to you last night?' she finally said as the children came down, all giggling and excited over their Christmas gifts. He looked at her, but she was addressing one of the girls. 'All that fuss you made about wanting a room to yourself! You gave me the shock of my life when I looked in during the night and found the bed empty.'

Lyn stopped chattering and bowed her head. 'I was lonely.'

Her mother gave a soft chuckle and proceeded with breakfast. But her statement had made Russ think: she *had* been there last night, he hadn't dreamt it.

When the girls had gone to play on a slide down the street, he said, 'You must think I'm not much of a man, crying and carrying on like that.'

She froze for a second, then carried on with her mixing. 'Of course I don't . . . half the trouble is that blessed photograph you keep looking at. The war's finished, you should tear it up, it's no good dwelling on the dead, it isn't going to bring them back.'

'You think tearing up a bit o' paper is going to make it all disappear?' he asked cynically.

'I'm not saying you'll forget, but sitting looking at it all the time . . . it's only tormenting yourself. Goodness knows I've done enough of that myself.' She whipped furiously at the mixture in the bowl.

'I saw him.'

She stopped mixing again. 'What?'

'Bertie . . . I saw him in France. I was the one who had him sent home . . . got him killed.'

She abandoned the bowl to flop down at the table. 'Tell me.'

'I shouldn't have brought it up.'

'Tell me!'

After a sigh he began, leaving out the bit about finding Bertie on Field Punishment, knowing how it would hurt her. 'I met up with him on the Somme. He'd enlisted under a false name. I tried to make it up with him, but he was still as hostile as ever . . . hated me.'

'How . . . how was he?' Rachel plucked at the chenille tablecloth.

He lied. 'Quite well . . . I can't help thinking, Rachel, what if I hadn't met him? Would he still be alive?'

She jumped from the chair, tucked the bowl under her arm and began to lash at the batter. 'He'd probably still be dead. Been shot or . . .' Her face crumpled in grief.

He moved over to her, 'Oh, Rache,' prized the bowl from her hands and put it on the table, then took her in his arms, squeezing her. 'Please don't.' She cried noisily into his shoulder, while he hugged her so tightly he almost cracked her ribs, begging her to stop. Finally it ended. She pulled away, searched her apron for a handkerchief and mopped her face.

'I shall have to get on with dinner.'

'Don't leave it like this,' he entreated softly.

She whirled on him. 'Well what do you want me to say? Don't think I don't know why you've told me this. You want me to forgive you. That's why you've always clammed up at the mention of his name, that's what half of these nightmares have been about, haven't they? Guilt, guilt about killing our son!' On the heels of accusal came regret. 'I didn't mean that . . .'

'Yes, you're right.' Russ sat down with a bump, eyes glassy.

'No!' She came up to stand in front of him. 'We have to stop blaming each other, ourselves. It's been said a hundred times – it isn't going to bring him back!'

All of a sudden his arms shot out and imprisoned her, pulling her almost off balance. He pressed his cheek into her belly, whispering, 'I'm sorry, I'm sorry!'

At first she tried to worm away, pressing her hands against his head as a lever. But slowly she gave in and instead used her hands to cradle his face, holding it to her abdomen and kissing the top of it . . . and then she felt his hands cup her buttocks, moving round and round. His face was now turned right into her belly, kissing her, rubbing. At once she recoiled. But the look in his eyes drew her back. She stood there and let him run his hands over her, their pace growing frantic.

'The children might come in!' But her eyes said she wanted him.

He checked, breath coming rapidly, waiting for her permission. When she made no further objection he stood, without releasing her, kissing her neck, her face, murmuring her name over and over again. And then she was kissing him back, letting him do things to her, feeling the heat of his palms, pressing her hands to his temples and dragging his lips down.

'Come on,' he said, voice urgent, and led her to the stairs. All the while he looked back at her, terrified she would change her mind. When they reached the landing he swept her into what had once been their room and closed the door. Here, she moved away from him, and stood by the bed, fingers playing with the brooch at her throat, waiting . . .

His eyes swept her, the longing burgeoned . . . yet something held him back. Like a starved man faced with a banquet, wanting to gorge but knowing he would be sick. Come on, *come on*, he urged himself. He swallowed and closed the gap between them. His rough fingers fumbled over the brooch. Tender of face, she stopped him and unpinned it herself. She had unbuttoned the top two buttons of her blouse when he asked gruffly, 'Can I do it?'

Dropping her hands to her sides, she allowed him to disrobe the top half of her body. Stepping back, he trailed the backs of gentle fingers over her breast . . . it was agony. Feeling himself about to burst he ripped off his own clothes whilst she stepped out of her skirts. When both were naked they came together. At the slightest contact Russ let out an ecstatic moan and gathered her into bed.

And then came panic, blind, irrational panic. In his haste he treated her more roughly than he had intended, pushing himself right up into her, ignoring her little gasp of discomfort, clawing her buttocks to wrap her flesh all around him. Inside she felt him spurt. 'Oh hell . . .' He slumped on top of her, face buried in her hair. After a period of silence, but for their breathing, came a muffled, 'I'm out of practice.'

Her body rippled with soft laughter. He revealed his face and let out a chuckle of his own. 'I've said the right thing for once. Oh . . . !' He scooped his hands between her and the mattress and squeezed her tightly. 'Rachel, Rachel . . . I do love you so! Can I stay like this?'

She moved her head in agreement, allowing him to lay there in the fork of her legs, bearing the full weight of his body, each nuzzling the other's face, murmuring tenderly. In time, he started to move. Less violently than before. It lasted longer too, building up to a climax so intense and overwhelming that it robbed them of speech for a long time. Eventually, he rolled off her with a huge sigh of something that sounded like triumph . . . yet the mattress began to tremor as his body convulsed. Alarmed, she turned her face on the pillow. His own head was turned away. When she extended concerned fingertips to his shoulder he faced her and she saw tears . . . but tears of laughter. It brought a chuckle to her own lips. 'What's so funny?'

His face was puckish as he gestured at the picture on the wall. 'I don't know if you noticed . . . but your mother's been watching us all the time.'

The hand that had touched his shoulder covered her mouth, but she laughed behind it. Still grinning, Russ shuffled round to press the front of his body into her side, hooking a leg over hers. Thus they lay until Rachel spoke again. 'I want to get married.'

This had the effect of making him laugh again. But, 'I'm serious,' she murmured, cradling his face. 'I meant it, what I said to you when Charlie came, about not feeling as if I was ever married to you.' At his groan of concern she added, 'No, no, don't think I'm stirring it all up again. It's just that . . . if we're to share a bed again, I want to feel that I'm properly married.'

A little of his fear was eroded. 'So . . . you'll have me back?'

She showed surprise. 'That's rather a funny question considering the compromising position we're in.' Both laughed and stroked each other. 'But I mean it, Russell, I want us to retake our marriage vows.'

He teased a piece of hair from her neck and said quietly, 'I'll keep them this time.'

She gave a thoughtful nod, then both embraced passionately until Rachel caught sight of the clock over his shoulder and exclaimed, 'Oh, my goodness that chicken will be burnt – and the injuries I suffered in getting it!' Christmas fowl were in short supply. She leapt out of bed and began to dress, urging him to do the same. When she had got as far as pulling on her skirt she saw that he had not moved but was laying with his hands raised to grip the head board, a wide grin on his face. 'Russell, I said get dressed! And what's so amusing?'

He rolled leisurely from the bed to pull on his pants. 'I'm just wondering – what do we say when the vicar gives us a talk about begetting children? Say, oh it's all right, Reverend, we've got six already?'

'Oh, Russell!' She aimed a swipe at his head which he evaded to grab her again.

'Well there's one thing, lass . . . we'll have plenty of bridesmaids.'

Still smiling, she put her hands round her back to unhook his embrace. 'I think that would be taking things a bit too far – and we haven't got six we've got seven.' She finished dressing, saying at his look of dismay, 'It's no good trying to forget him.'

The beautiful morning was dulled. Russ hauled his braces over his shoulders. 'I don't look upon him as mine.'

'Well he is yours!' She pushed him off the bed in order to make it. Then her face softened and she tapped his arm in passing. 'Oh, don't let's start that again . . . but look, I've come to terms with him being yours, why can't you?'

Russ lowered his head and shook it. 'I just can't . . . I keep seeing Bertie.'

'And so do I . . . but you might at least try to be a bit less sullen when he comes home this time. Let's keep it a happy Christmas.'

He smiled at her. 'I'll be happy if I'm back in here with you.'

She took her hand away. 'No . . . not yet – at least, not until Charlie goes back.' An awkward laugh. 'I seem to have my mental block too. I don't think I could be in here with you, knowing Charlie was above us. It wouldn't seem right.' At Russ' collapse she touched him again. 'It won't be for long . . . come on, we'd better go down. I can hear the girls.' And before he could respond she had flown down the stairs.

'Don't you dare say anything to spoil it!' Rowena was whispering to Beany as they came through the back door, faces rosy – not merely with cold, but with excitement; Lyn, having run home to go to the lavatory, had seen her parents kissing and had run back quickly to tell her sisters. Now, all were eager to see the results.

'Why are you only telling me?' demanded Beany. 'Why not Squawk?'

'Because you're the one who always asks questions, wanting to know everything!' said Rowena. 'This is private between Mother and Father. If you start getting nosey it might make Mother . . .' she clammed up as a bright-eyed Rachel suddenly bounced into the room, looking somewhat abashed.

'Hello! Had a good slide?' She went straight to the oven to check on the bird.

The girls said they had. Then their father entered. Rowena looked at him – and knew that Lyn had not invented that kiss. Mother had forgiven him. She shared a conspiratorial look with her sisters.

Becky bit her lip and grinned into her coat front.

Russ shoved his hands into his pockets. 'Well, what a fine collection of faces. They look as if they've been up to mischief to me, Mother.' This drew a giggle from all and Rowena's cheeks grew pinker as she imagined her parents in an embrace.

'*We* haven't been up to mischief,' chanted Lyn.

'Oh, there you are, you see!' objected Beany to her eldest sister. 'It wasn't me who spoilt Mother and Father's fun.' She was dealt a hefty nudge.

Russ stared hard at them all, then shared a startled look with his wife . . . then both began to laugh. And the house was filled with Christmas joy.

CHAPTER THIRTY-FIVE

When Charlie came home on Boxing Day he sensed that something had changed – felt that chill of alienation he had experienced on coming here four and a half years ago. Not immediately, for to his delight Rachel and three of her daughters were waiting at the station to meet him. Having not expected anyone he had stepped off the train and was making directly for the ticket barrier when, hearing his name called, he spun to see a red flare bobbing its way through the crowd and beneath it Becky's smiling face. Dropping his case to the platform he caught her in a hug as she burst upon him.

'All this time and we nearly missed you!' Rachel, having decided to carry Regina, had caught up with the group. 'We've been waiting down that end of the platform – Merry Christmas, Charlie! How are you?' With a grin and a Merry Christmas of his own he assured her he was feeling great, then greeted Rhona who had come too. He asked about her sisters.

'Lyn and Beany have gone for a walk with Father,' she told him. 'Wena didn't want to come.'

This hurt him – he had always considered the eldest girl as one of the closest to him – but he said, 'Then they can wait for their presents. When we get home you three get yours first.'

And so they did. When their sisters arrived with Russ the small gifts were brandished with glee. But Charlie's mind had left the presents. The moment his father and the rest of the family were together he knew that something was different. It wasn't the way they behaved towards him, but how they behaved towards each other. During the meal that followed, there were certain looks that passed between them, especially between Mrs Hazelwood and his father. Looks that made Charlie feel an outsider again. Then there was Rowena. At their meeting, she had been hard pressed to form a simple hello, had shunned his attentions and greeted everything he said with bad humour. Even as he smiled at her now she turned her head away.

'Won't you be going to Adrian's at all these holidays?'

It was Rachel who spoke. Charlie stopped trying to work out what had happened here and looked at her. 'No, he's off to his grandparents. Maybe in the summer . . .'

Rachel poured herself another cup of tea. 'We thought perhaps you might like to invite him here in the summer. I'm sure we could put him up, for a day or two at least.'

Before Charlie had the chance to offer gratitude his father said, 'Maybe he'd rather be at his friend's home.'

Rachel spotted the boy's expression and said, 'Well, it's a long time until the summer – have some more bread if you like, Charlie.'

When the meal was over, Charlie handed out the remainder of the gifts. Everyone tore at the paper . . . everyone except his father.

'I'll open mine later.' Russ placed the gift on the dresser and began to read a magazine.

Oh, Russell, thought his wife despairingly, then enlisted her daughters to clear the pots. Charlie offered to help but was told to sit where he was and enjoy himself.

Enjoy myself! thought Charlie with a glance at his father's face. Rachel looked into the kitchen. Why doesn't he say something to the poor boy? she thought impatiently. He can't spend the rest of Christmas making out he isn't there. 'I hope you didn't spend too much on these Christmas presents?' she called to Charlie, wanting to make him feel part of things. 'Have you got yourself a little job or something?'

He smiled. 'No, I won the end of term prize for having made the most progress during term. Ten shillings.'

'And you went and spent it all on us? I think that's extraordinarily kind of him, don't you, Russ?' She received a grunt from her husband. 'Well done, Charlie, that's a splendid achievement.' *Russell will you stop reading that magazine and talk to the poor boy? Be nice to him.*

But Russell was not reading the print, he was in fact priming himself to speak to the boy. He had decided upon his words, all he had to do was say them. But he couldn't do that with an audience. The magazine was discarded for a pack of cigarettes. He stuck one in his mouth. Charlie did not bother to jump up and light it, his mind had left the room and was now with Adrian. He and Ade had talked about it a lot. Charlie had almost made up his mind to be a priest. Almost, but not quite. He still did not feel the conviction that his friend had. It wasn't that he felt unable to serve God, it wasn't the thought of not having a family, nor even the question of celibacy. It was his father. To become a priest would be admitting failure.

'Come in the front, lad, I want to talk to you.'

Startled, Charlie looked at his father. Russell was heading for the front parlour. Charlie snatched a look at Rachel who smiled and nodded at him over the heads of her daughters. Boosted by this, he got up and followed his father.

Russ was standing at the window gazing out, though there was little to see except the distant glimmer of lamps. 'Close the door.'

Charlie did so and at his father's command, sat down. Russ came to sit down too, on a chair by the fireplace. He flicked the ash from his cigarette into the cold grate. Economy forbade a fire in here as well as in the back room. 'Me and Mrs Hazelwood have come to an arrangement. We're back together.'

Charlie's face lit up and he came to attention. 'Oh, that's . . .'

'Before you applaud, I ought to tell you how this is going to affect you.' Russ narrowed his eyes as the smoke from his cigarette partially blinded him. 'I know Mrs Hazelwood said you could invite your friend in the summer, but with only three rooms and the attic it makes it a bit of a squash.

'Oh well, it doesn't matter,' said Charlie amicably. 'Ade won't . . .'

'What I'm trying to say is, it'd be better if you could arrange to spend your holidays at his house.'

Charlie noticed that his father had said holidays and not holiday. 'You mean . . . all of them?'

'Yes.' Russ took a last pull at the cigarette and thumbed it into the grate. Then he looked straight at Charlie. 'When I said Rachel and me are back together again, I meant we would be back together if it wasn't for you. How old are you now?' Charlie heard his voice say that he was almost seventeen. 'Good, then you're old enough to understand my meaning. While you're in the house, she won't . . . she doesn't feel able to sleep with me. I can't say I'm comfortable about it either. You act as a reminder. So, if you didn't come it'd give us a chance to put our marriage back together. You understand that? I mean, you're nearly a man, you'd be leaving here of your own accord soon anyway, wouldn't you?' Charlie was speechless. 'Will you be going on to another seminary when you leave that place?'

'That depends on whether I decide to be a priest,' muttered Charlie, mind whirling.

'Well, you've obviously given up the idea of being a soldier. You seemed really keen on that a few years ago.'

'Adrian says soldiers are stupid.' Charlie used it to hurt, but it was a poor sword against his father's weapon.

Russ gave a cold snort. 'Happen your Adrian's right.' He heard Becky's voice calling for Charlie. 'Anyway, that's all I wanted to say. Sounds as if those lasses want you.' He strolled back to the window and stared into its dark pane, watching Charlie's reflection leave the room.

A dazed Charlie entered the kitchen, whereupon Becky pounced on him. 'We're playing Happy Families!' She shoved him towards the table where he sat down, watching the cards being shuffled. He felt dead inside.

'Charlie, are you listening?' It was Beany. He said sorry and asked her to repeat herself. 'Have you got Master Bun the baker's son?'

Charlie studied his cards and gave a no. When it came to his turn he had to be prompted yet again. Lyn threw the card he had asked for. It overreached the table and fell to the floor. Bending for it, he accidently caught his head on Rowena's skirts and lifted them above her knee.

She let out a shriek. 'You stupid idiot! Why did you have to come here for Christmas? Everything was all right till you came!' and fled from the room.

Charlie looked at his other half-sisters, none of whom seemed the least bit concerned. Pushing back his chair he went to the understairs cupboard and took out his holdall. Rachel stopped what she was doing to watch.

'Charlie, where are you off?' called Becky as he reached the door. He didn't answer – just went straight down the passage and out of the front door. Becky turned to Rachel in alarm. 'Mother, I think he was crying!'

Rachel leapt into action, running to the front parlour. 'Russell, what on earth have you said to that boy?' Her husband turned. 'He's just walked out with his case! Rebecca said she thought he was crying!'

Rowena, sitting at the top of the stairs, bit her lip. Oh God, it was she who was responsible! But oh, she was so mixed up these days. One minute she felt like hugging Charlie, the next she felt like punching him. She didn't know what was the matter with her.

Russ stiffened – odd, he thought, how fear always strikes you in the arse. He felt the muscles here turn spastic, remembering the night that Bertie had run away . . . and he hadn't come back. The spectres came: Bertie, Dobson, Wheatley, all of them pulling and tugging at his gut. *Go after him! He's your lad!* He fought them – no, my lad's dead. *Yes! and you're going to kill this one too*.

Rachel was pulling at his sleeve. 'You've got to bring him back – Russ, are you listening to me?' She shook him. 'What's wrong with you?'

The spectres vanished, but the fear did not. Pressing her aside he made his way down the passage . . . only it was not the passage; he was back in the trenches, running towards the latrine, trying to warn Jewitt to get out before it was too late. He opened the door and dashed through it, but he was still in the trench. He started calling, 'Charlie! Charlie!' and ran down the dark street. He heard the guns exploding but ran on, turned into a communication trench. The Captain shouted to him but he ran on . . .

Jack Daw turned to watch his friend teeter at the crossroads. 'Straight on if you're looking for Charlie!' He had just passed the boy who had been running too.

Russ slipped on something in the road, righted himself and ran on down the terrace. He was forgetting his age. At the foot of the slope breathlessness forced him to stop. He doubled over, hands on knees, to catch his wind. With every inhalation the cold air sliced his lungs. Got to find him! Got to find him!

Restored, he uncurved his spine and cast a desperate look about him. 'Charlie!' He continued in the same direction, though confining his pace to a trot. Reaching the main road he strained his eyes for the boy. There were plenty of folk about, but none of them was Charlie. Crossing the road and some waste ground he came to the river. No, the boy would have no need to come here. He would be heading back to the station. Russ was about to strike back for the main road, when the sound of boyish laughter lured him to the river. He stumbled down the path and came across two boys who hurled stones at something in the water. Not something – *someone!* 'Charlie!' He broke into a run. Charlie's head was bobbing in the water, he was being pelted by stones! His face kept going under. Russ felt the water closing over his own face. Reaching the boys he lashed out and gave each a hefty swipe round the head, 'You little sods! What d'you think you're playing at?' Then he left them to turn to their victim. The boys ran away. Russ stumbled to the river's edge, knelt down and reached out his hand to . . . a balloon. Charlie's head turned into a dark balloon that floated away on the current.

Russ sagged and fell on all fours, head lolling to the ground. He was going bloody mad again! He uttered a laughing sob. Then something drew his head up to look to his left.

Charlie was standing there, suitcase in hand, looking at him. Under his father's glare, the youth explained. 'I heard somebody shouting Charlie. I thought they meant me.'

'You dozy little sod!' Russ bounded to his feet and strode up to Charlie. 'It was me shouting. What did you go off like that for and scare us half to death?'

Charlie's voice was flat. 'You told me to go.'

'But not like that! Didn't you realize . . .'

'You told me to go!'

'Oh God! What's the point in talking, you don't understand . . .'

'No, I bloody don't! I don't understand why you hate me so much.'

Russ held his son with haunted eyes, then seemed to wilt. Charlie turned to go. 'Wait . . .' Russ put up a staying hand. 'I can't have you going and thinking that.'

Charlie stopped with his back to the man. 'No, I was wrong. You don't hate me – you're indifferent to me.' He presented his face. 'Which is a bloody sight worse. Well, you've got your wish to see the back of me. I'm sorry that I can't wipe out the time I've spent here. Believe me, I would if I could.'

'D'you think I came running after you, nearly giving myself a seizure because I was indifferent to you?' shouted Russ. His voice was carried away on the cold night air. No one eavesdropped; they were alone on the river bank.

'I don't *know* why you came after me!' yelled Charlie, his face distraught.

Russ pleaded with his vivisector. 'Look . . . Mrs Hazelwood said I have to bring you back . . . and I want you to come as well.'

'Why?'

'Does it bloody matter why? Can't it be enough that I've asked you?'

'Of course it matters! It's like me saying I'm going to be a priest, is it because it's what's expected of me or because I want it?'

'And do you?'

Charlie slung his case to the ground and sat down, leaning on his knees. 'I still don't bloody know.'

Russ came and sat beside him. Only now that his blood had stopped pulsing through his body did he feel how cold it was. He turned the collar of his jacket up, then pulled out a pack of cigarettes and nudged the boy. 'Here, have a coffin nail.' Charlie accepted one and held it between his fingers until his father struck a match. Russ cupped the flame against the night breeze and put it to the other's cigarette. His son's face was illuminated in the match flare, then dimmed as he drew the light away to his own cigarette.

'It wasn't just because of what you said that I decided to go,' Charlie confessed. 'I don't know what I've done to Rowena but she's been detestable all afternoon.'

His father underwent a period of thought, then said, 'Ah . . . well, I can tell you it's nothing you've done. Since you were here last our Rowena's discovered she's a young woman. You know, these monthly things they have.' Seeing Charlie did not comprehend he was forced to explain. 'I thought the same as you, that I'd upset her. One minute she's nice as pie, next she wanted nothing to do with me, couldn't understand it. I was forgetting that she's fifteen.' He sighed. ' 'Sfunny, you go away to war leaving children and when you come back you find women . . . Anyway, that's what it is. And if her mother's anything to go by we can expect to get our heads bitten off every month.' He allowed himself a humorous thought. 'Can you imagine what it's going to be like when they're all grown up? Seven of the buggers for us to deal with.'

'You're talking as if I'll be coming back,' said Charlie.

Russ trod his thoughts for a while, then said, 'I liked that bird book you sent me whilst I was in France.'

'That's just as well,' Charlie told him through a cloud of smoke and misty breath, 'you've got another one this year.'

Russ nodded. 'I'll open it when I get back . . . you shouldn't've wasted your money on me.' Charlie said nothing. 'I must say, if it's patience that makes a priest you'll make a damned good one, Charlie, putting up with a swine like me for a father.' He inserted the cigarette between his lips and scooped up a handful of stones which he aimed one by one at the inky river. Charlie was reminded of the time he had sat here with the boy whose father was a German. His father seemed on the verge of a confession too.

Could Charlie give him Absolution, or would he receive the same treatment as Fritz?

'I'm glad you've given up your idea to be a soldier. I've seen hundreds of young lads die in war, I wouldn't want to see you go like that . . .'

Charlie's response was guarded. 'I thought that's just what you did want.'

Russ turned to stare at him. 'My God . . . I'd never wish that on anybody.'

'Not even me? I was the one who got Bertie killed, wasn't I?'

'I never blamed you for that, did I?'

'Not outright, but then you rarely said anything outright, did you?' Charlie had had enough of the cigarette and tossed it at the river.

Russ stared at him for a moment longer, then took another chestful of tobacco smoke and shook his head. 'No, that's me, always the snidey bugger. I never did blame you for Bertie's death. I always knew who was responsible for that – me; like I've been responsible for all this family's troubles. It was just more convenient to blame you.' He puffed on the cigarette which was little more than half an inch long, nipping it expertly between his thumb and third fingernail. 'But I hope you're not waiting to hear a moving confession of how I really loved your mother, Charlie, or how I loved you all along, because I've finished with lies. She was just there when I needed her. It was totally selfish. You? You just happened. When you came here it wasn't a child I saw, but my own guilt, my own inadequacies. You were . . . an embodiment of my treachery.' He smiled half-heartedly. 'There's eloquence for you. Wasn't it obvious that I'd blame you? Not justifiable, but obvious?'

Charlie was forced to acknowledge this trait of human nature, then made a dangerous admission of his own. 'Just like it was obvious I'd be glad when Bertie died.' He paid no regard to his father's look of horror. 'Obvious that now I was your only son and you'd have to love me.'

Russ used the minute stub of the cigarette to light another. His chest throbbed with pain, for both himself and the boy. Emotion clogged his throat. He cleared it and spoke. 'I can't tell you what you want . . .'

'No, you don't have to,' said the youth quickly. 'I know . . .'

'We just have to make do with each other, Charlie. You as my son, me as your father . . . not much of one, I know, but . . .' He shrugged. 'I do admire you for the way you've come through this and I know Mrs Hazelwood respects you, and the girls are very fond of you as well . . . I can only try.'

Charlie nodded. At least he had his father's recognition. It was a start.

'That priest was more of a father to you than I ever was. You'll not go far wrong to follow his vocation rather than mine.' He started plopping stones into the river again. 'Though I can't say I have much belief in God after the things I've seen. Mind you, one of the bravest men I ever met was an Army chaplain, a left-footer like yourself. I once saw him carry a wounded man for a hundred yards on his back. There were shells going off all round him and bullets rattling like crazy but he never wavered, he carried that bloke right back to our lines then blow me if he didn't go over the top again and carry another in the same way – and they weren't even Catholics! Marvellous he was, bloody marvellous.'

Charlie's lips parted. 'That's it,' he breathed. 'That's what I'm going to be.'

Russ expelled a stream of smoke. 'A padre?' And then he caught the inference. 'Oh, I see. Half soldier, half priest.'

Oh the joy of being certain of something for once in his life! Charlie's breast swirled.

Russ saw the ecstasy on his son's face and mistook it for childish ambition. He responded accordingly. 'Just give it a bit more thought before you go jumping in. God forbid that there should be another war like this one, but if there is . . . well, people, especially the flag-wavers, seem to have this jolly idea that war's just a case of going bang! and the enemy falls down with a neat hole in his chest. It's not like that,

577

Charlie. It's messy and cruel. You haven't seen what happens to a man when he's machine-gunned through the bowel, what happens to all his body waste . . .' He gulped and shuddered. 'I'm not deliberately trying to frighten you, or belittle your plans . . . I just want you to understand. You have to live with it to know . . .'

'I have lived with it,' replied a more mature-looking Charlie. 'I've seen what it's done to you.'

His father nodded dispiritedly. 'Aye, if ever there was a testament to the destructiveness of war, it's me.'

'As you say, God forbid that there'll ever be another war,' murmured his son. 'But if there is . . . well, I'd like to be able to help those poor men in some way.'

'But this is what I'm trying to say, Charlie,' protested his father. 'It's not just the men. Bombs don't discriminate. Chaplains get killed too.'

'And you don't think I'm brave enough to face that if it should happen?'

Russ looked deep into his son's face. 'Oh, I'm damned sure you're brave enough . . . it's just that I wouldn't want to see it happen.'

Charlie smiled then. 'It'll be quite a few years till I'm old enough. But it's definitely something I want to do.'

Russ succumbed with a nod. 'And what Charlie wants to do . . .' He returned the boy's smile. 'I wish you well in it, Charlie. Sincerely. And . . . forget what I said about spending your holidays at your mate's. I'd like you to come home.'

After an awkward silence, he began to rise, saying, 'If we sit here any longer we'll be getting piles. Away, Cha . . .' He broke off with a laugh. 'I suppose as you're going to be a priest I should be calling you Father now.'

Charlie scrambled up and mirrored his crooked grin, made the sign of the Cross and said, 'Bless you, my son.'

And, sharing a soft chuckle, the two men walked home along the tow path.

A Selection of Arrow Bestsellers

☐ The Lilac Bus	Maeve Binchy	£2.50
☐ 500 Mile Walkies	Mark Wallington	£2.50
☐ Staying Off the Beaten Track	Elizabeth Gundrey	£5.95
☐ A Better World Than This	Marie Joseph	£2.95
☐ No Enemy But Time	Evelyn Anthony	£2.95
☐ Rates of Exchange	Malcolm Bradbury	£3.50
☐ Colours Aloft	Alexander Kent	£2.95
☐ Speaker for the Dead	Orson Scott Card	£2.95
☐ Eon	Greg Bear	£4.95
☐ Talking to Strange Men	Ruth Rendell	£5.95
☐ Heartstones	Ruth Rendell	£2.50
☐ Rosemary Conley's Hip and Thigh Diet	Rosemary Conley	£2.50
☐ Communion	Whitley Strieber	£3.50
☐ The Ladies of Missalonghi	Colleen McCullough	£2.50
☐ Erin's Child	Sheelagh Kelly	£3.99
☐ Sarum	Edward Rutherfurd	£4.50

Prices and other details are liable to change

ARROW BOOKS, BOOKSERVICE BY POST, PO BOX 29, DOUGLAS, ISLE
OF MAN, BRITISH ISLES

NAME..

ADDRESS..

....

....

Please enclose a cheque or postal order made out to Arrow Books Ltd. for the amount
due and allow the following for postage and packing.

U.K. CUSTOMERS: Please allow 22p per book to a maximum of £3.00.

B.F.P.O. & EIRE: Please allow 22p per book to a maximum of £3.00

OVERSEAS CUSTOMERS: Please allow 22p per book.

Whilst every effort is made to keep prices low it is sometimes necessary to increase cover
prices at short notice. Arrow Books reserve the right to show new retail prices on covers
which may differ from those previously advertised in the text or elsewhere.

Bestselling Fiction

☐ Hiroshmia Joe	Martin Booth	£2.95
☐ The Pianoplayers	Anthony Burgess	£2.50
☐ Queen's Play	Dorothy Dunnett	£3.95
☐ Colours Aloft	Alexander Kent	£2.95
☐ Contact	Carl Sagan	£3.50
☐ Talking to Strange Men	Ruth Rendell	£5.95
☐ Heartstones	Ruth Rendell	£2.50
☐ The Ladies of Missalonghi	Colleen McCullough	£2.50
☐ No Enemy But Time	Evelyn Anthony	£2.95
☐ The Heart of the Country	Fay Weldon	£2.50
☐ The Stationmaster's Daughter	Pamela Oldfield	£2.95
☐ Erin's Child	Sheelagh Kelly	£3.99
☐ The Lilac Bus	Maeve Binchy	£2.50

Prices and other details are liable to change

ARROW BOOKS, BOOKSERVICE BY POST, PO BOX 29, DOUGLAS, ISLE OF MAN, BRITISH ISLES

NAME...

ADDRESS..

....

....

Please enclose a cheque or postal order made out to Arrow Books Ltd. for the amount due and allow the following for postage and packing.

U.K. CUSTOMERS: Please allow 22p per book to a maximum of £3.00.

B.F.P.O. & EIRE: Please allow 22p per book to a maximum of £3.00

OVERSEAS CUSTOMERS: Please allow 22p per book.

Whilst every effort is made to keep prices low it is sometimes necessary to increase cover prices at short notice. Arrow Books reserve the right to show new retail prices on covers which may differ from those previously advertised in the text or elsewhere.

Bestselling Women's Fiction

☐ A Better World Than This	Marie Joseph	£2.95
☐ The Stationmaster's Daughter	Pamela Oldfield	£2.95
☐ The Lilac Bus	Maeve Binchy	£2.50
☐ The Golden Urchin	Madeleine Brent	£2.95
☐ The Temptress	Jude Deveraux	£2.95
☐ The Sisters	Pat Booth	£3.50
☐ Erin's Child	Sheelagh Kelly	£3.99
☐ The Ladies of Missalonghi	Colleen McCullough	£2.50
☐ Seven Dials	Claire Rayner	£2.50
☐ The Indiscretion	Diana Stainforth	£3.50
☐ Satisfaction	Rae Lawrence	£3.50

Prices and other details are liable to change

ARROW BOOKS, BOOKSERVICE BY POST, PO BOX 29, DOUGLAS, ISLE OF MAN, BRITISH ISLES

NAME. . . . .

ADDRESS. . . . .

. . . .

. . . .

Please enclose a cheque or postal order made out to Arrow Books Ltd. for the amount due and allow the following for postage and packing.

U.K. CUSTOMERS: Please allow 22p per book to a maximum of £3.00.

B.F.P.O. & EIRE: Please allow 22p per book to a maximum of £3.00

OVERSEAS CUSTOMERS: Please allow 22p per book.

Whilst every effort is made to keep prices low it is sometimes necessary to increase cover prices at short notice. Arrow Books reserve the right to show new retail prices on covers which may differ from those previously advertised in the text or elsewhere.